KING BLOOD

Also by Simon Clark

Nailed By the Heart
Blood Crazy
Darker

KING BLOOD

Simon Clark

Hodder & Stoughton

British Library Cataloguing in Publication Data

Clark, Simon
King Blood
1. English fiction – 20th century
I. Title
823.9′14 [F]

ISBN 0 340 66061 9

Typeset by Hewer Text Composition Services, Edinburgh
Printed and bound in Great Britain by
Mackays of Chatham PLC, Chatham, Kent.

Hodder and Stoughton
A Division of Hodder Headline PLC
338 Euston Road
London NW1 3BH

This is a big book, so this time I'm going to dedicate it to a whole bunch of big-hearted people:

ROY BULLOCK, ANDREW DARLINGTON, BEV EVANS, BRIAN GOULTHORP, MARTIN KELLY, DES LEWIS, ANDY ROBSON, MARK SAMUELS, STEVE SNEYD

ANDREW MURRAY (1958–1996)

KARL EDWARD WAGNER (1945–1994)

AND FOR KAREN SHARP, MY SISTER, WHO INTRODUCED ME TO HORROR FICTION

AND ESPECIALLY TO MY WIFE, JANET, FOR HER SUPERHUMAN PATIENCE AND FORBEARANCE WHILE I FINISHED THIS MONSTER

THIS IS THE END

ALL RIGHT. PICTURE THIS:

Before you is desert.

A desert that is black, forbidding, evil-looking.

There are ruined buildings, burned-out cars, stark dead trees. And, swamping everything, a black ash that streams out of the sky like Hell-blown snow.

Picture a fiery sky. Cloud streaked yellow and orange. Lightning prowls the horizon.

Picture a river. The water that flows there is the colour of blood – a brilliant, luscious red.

Picture a dam formed by the skulls, the ribcages, the bones of a hundred thousand dead. Picture a crow standing on a skull. The bird dips its beak into the socket to feed on the remains of an eye.

Now imagine that those waters tumble over the bones in a bloody waterfall, with enough force to send out a full-blooded roar that thunders across this nightmare land.

Imagine people are running through the wasteland. Dozens of them, their eyes gleaming bright from blackened faces. They are dressed in the tattered remnants of business suits, jeans, summer dresses. Some are in uniform – nurses, police, army.

And running just ahead of this pack is a young man. He's stripped to the waist. His bare chest is soot-smeared. A bright sheen of sweat covers his face.

Just for a moment you wonder if he is leading the group.

Or then again. Is he being pursued by them?

And, if he is, what will happen when they catch him?

As he runs along the banks of the bloody river something extraordinary happens.

Floating gently down from the sky come hundreds of sheets of paper. Some fall into the river to be swept away.

Others drift down to the ground. There they lie, pristine white against the coal-black ash.

1

The handwriting that covers every page is explosive. As if whoever furiously scribbled down the words had something vitally important to say.

Only they knew they didn't have time to write it all down before . . .

Before what?

One by one, the sheets settle on the blackened earth like huge oblong snowflakes. Sentences stand out:-

NEW YORK: *I heard it coming. Like a train roaring down its track. Then with a godawful thump the tidal wave hit the city; it tore through the apartment blocks, smashing them to shit, spilling screaming men out of their beds and into the water.*

Ours is one of the few blocks to remain standing. I see the ocean lapping at second-floor windows . . .

FLORIDA: *This morning half the world blew to Kingdom Come. At least it felt that way. As I stood on the balcony I watched Disneyland and make one almighty leap toward Heaven. Epcot Centre, Magic Kingdom, Thunder Mountain. Everything just lifted. Then came the flames, reaching halfway to the sky in a curtain of fire.*

JOHANNESBURG: *Thousands of corpses, most in nightclothes, are woven into a deathly mat that covers many roads – Commissioner Street, Klein Street, Twist Street. In some places they lie four or five deep, arms and legs stretched stiffly out. Hundreds had sought sanctuary in the Anglican Cathedral on Bree Street. Corpses form gruesome clots of rotting flesh in the cathedral doorways . . .*

MADRID: *Explosions have left dozens of craters. Now Oeste Park resembles the surface of the Moon. Against an evening sky, the Royal Palace burns brightly. Vivid red flames burst through windows to writhe like fiery demons across the face of the building.*

SYDNEY: *The opera house looked as if a pissed giant had stomped on it, caving in the once beautiful roofscape. Everywhere 'there are bodies . . .*

LONDON: *A Zodiac inflatable dinghy nosing through debris on a lake. The camera zooms in: the debris are floating corpses. A girl in* *a white wedding dress drifts by. Smoothly the camera pans upward. There are gasps from the people in the room.*

We are looking at the Houses of Parliament. The huge building is like a strange stone ship anchored in the middle of a lake. The clock in the tower of Big Ben is forever frozen at ten to two.

More shots: Nelson's Column, now a shattered stump, rising out of the waters that cover Trafalgar Square. A silent journey along Charing Cross Road. The wake from the boat bobs drowned heads in the water before splashing against shop signs – Murder One, Pizza Hut, Foyles, Waterstones, Boots . . .

WELLINGTON: *Fires rage across the city. But it isn't the buildings that are burning. The flames vent from great gashes in the earth itself. As if a row of rocket motors had been upended into the ground, then ignited, sending jets of blue flame a hundred metres into the air with a screeching sound that overwhelms the TV crew's microphone . . .*

SKK-REEEE-CH!
I curled into a ball. That godawful sound battered my skull so hard I thought it would burst like a smashed egg. Twenty paces away a ball of flame ripped out of the ground. The heat-flash singed the hairs on my arms to ash. Seconds later, falling all around me, came a cascade of skulls, thigh bones, knuckles, pelvic bones, smouldering spines, chunks of rotted meat, lungs, skin and a flaming heart.

A face landed flat on my leg. It had been torn from the skull in one piece . . .

Jesus, what had happened to these people?

THERE IS NO RULE THAT GEOLOGICAL CHANGE MUST BE GRADUAL. GEOLOGICAL CHANGES DON'T NECESSARILY TAKE PLACE OVER CENTURIES OR MILLENNIA. CATACLYSMIC MOVEMENTS IN THE EARTH'S CRUST CAN WREAK PROFOUND CHANGES IN DAYS, HOURS, EVEN MINUTES. IN THE MEDITERRANEAN ALONE THERE ARE NOW OVER TWO HUNDRED CITIES SUBMERGED BENEATH THE SEA.

TWO HUNDRED AND FIFTY MILLION YEARS AGO, AT THE BOUNDARY OF THE PERMIAN AND TRIASSIC PERIODS, HUGE VOLCANIC ERUPTIONS RESULTED IN THE EXTINCTION OF NINETY PER CENT OF MARINE SPECIES,

WHILE SEVENTY PER CENT OF TERRESTRIAL VERTE-BRATES WERE WIPED FROM THE FACE OF THE PLANET.

Her eyes glistening in the evening light were so trusting. I found myself looking down at her breasts with their pink nipples. I couldn't help but notice the bruises stood out so vividly they looked as if they'd been daubed there in black ink . . .

She lifted my T-shirt so she could press her breasts against the bare skin of my stomach, and she whispered, 'You can do anything you want to me. Anything at all. You know that, don't you?'

I bunched her hair in my fist as a wave of desire came roaring through me . . .

Seconds later we were rolling over and over on the grass, peeling off our clothes, kissing, biting, caressing, panting out our sheer naked lust for each other. I kissed her full on her warm lips. Then, panting hard, I gripped both her hips in my hands . . .

Today that meadow was a genuine slice of hell.

Still chanting, the madmen carried the woman into the field. Trying desperately to break free, she writhed, twisted, back arching, hips lifting.

In the centre of the field was a wooden pole set upright in the earth. The top of the pole would have reached my shoulder.

It was pointed.

That's when I knew what they were going to do to her. I think that's when the woman realized, too. Because she began to scream. A bitter mechanical scream that went on and on . . .

I've promised myself to tell everything how it happened. And not to censor any of it. Not one word.

But I wouldn't blame you now if now if you skipped the next few paragraphs. It is dirty, it is disgusting, it is degrading; what I witnessed is burned into my memory for life.

All I can do is warn you. If you can take it, keep reading.

THIS IS WHAT THEY DID TO THE SCREAMING WOMAN:-

The mob carried the woman towards the pole. As they did so, men and women began tearing away the woman's clothes . . .

Her heavy breasts bounced as they lifted her, twisting and screaming, above the sharpened point . . .

* * *

JESUS, SWEET JESUS . . . WHERE DO I START ALL THIS?
Did it start with the arrival of the whole damn city on your doorstep?
Or was it when the river turned to blood?
Or perhaps when the stones beneath your feet became hot?
Maybe it was the coming of the Grey Man?

Now, picture once more the black desert. The burned cars. The city in ruins. The running men and women.

At last, the question of whether the bare-chested man leads the pack, or whether the pack pursue him, is answered.

At that moment he stumbles.

Instantly the mob falls on him. Gripped in their hands are kitchen knives, or razor-sharp slivers of glass from broken TV screens, or beer cans that have been beaten into crude yet lethal blades.

The bare-chested man struggles to his feet. A knife wound parts the flesh of his forehead into a pair of jagged lips.

Fists swinging, he hammers himself free of the people. Again he runs.

There's a chance he will escape. He's young; he's fast.

He runs towards the banks of the river, long legs kicking out. Bare feet splash through black dust. The slipstream flutters sheets of paper.

Just when it looks as if he'll make it, a woman hurls a housebrick. It strikes the man's head. Clutching the back of his head with both hands, he falls forward, mouth wide open in agony.

The mob pounces, stabbing with their knives. He is instantly buried beneath the bodies of his attackers.

Suddenly, his fist breaks through the confusion of flailing limbs. The man holds his clenched fist high.

As he does so, the hand unfurls. The fingers stretch out, spasming, quivering, as if he is trying desperately to reach something unseen in the sky. Something wonderful.

Furiously the mob stab.

Picture the sheets of paper covering the black ground.

Picture spots of crimson now flecking those once pristine white pages.

Imagine the crimson spots running, streaking the paper red. A bright, living red. A red that glistens in the fiery light.

What is this place?

You may well wonder.

5

This is where there is no rule by a government of elected representatives. There is no prime minister. No president.

Because this is your future:-

This is the country where **BLOOD** is **KING**.

CHAPTER 1

JESUS, SWEET JESUS . . . WHERE DO I START ALL THIS? Did it start with the arrival of the whole damn city on your doorstep?

Or was it when the river turned to blood?

Or perhaps when the stones beneath your feet became hot?

Maybe it was the coming of the Grey Man?

No. I'm going further back than that. You know, I think all this really began the night of Ben Cavellero's party. That was the night I planned to grit my teeth at last and do something about Kate Robinson. And it seemed the perfect night to do it.

Looking back now, I can almost imagine that night slipped from a magic dream.

It was July; deliciously warm; a million distant points of light filled the sky; shooting stars drew trails of silver down from heaven. Ben Cavellero's garden was filled with young people who were laughing with sheer happiness and optimism and hope, for they all knew that this was the summer they were stepping across that great dividing line, from adolescence to becoming adult men and women.

Right then, they had every reason to laugh, joke, drink Ben Cavellero's wine, eat his food, and fall in love beneath his cherry trees. At that moment they had the world at their feet. They had the opportunity to go out and *DO* anything and *BE* anything they wanted. They were young; all the girls were beautiful.

And of them all, the most beautiful was Kate Robinson. In a moment I'd ask Kate to walk down to the orchard with me, alone.

As I strolled through that garden I felt I belonged to a football team that was on a winning streak so strong, so damned, so incredibly, wonderfully strong, that nothing on Earth could beat it.

It should have been one of the best nights of my life.

But that was the night Satan finally lost his rag. He took his shoulder to that almighty underground gate. And he didn't stop battering until he'd busted it to shit.

Because that was the night all Hell came thundering through.

7

CHAPTER 2

My name is Rick Kennedy. And it was the night of Ben Cavellero's party. I was nineteen years old.

It was, as I've said, that fine evening in July. The time nudged toward nine. The sun dropped down behind the hills in this amazing splash of red that covered half the sky.

The garden heaved with people. Three-quarters of them had just left school, eager to do nothing more than laze out the summer before heading off to university or college.

After a long slog I'd got the band together, the tour dates booked; record company scouts, tongues out, hungrily drooling, were already sniffing at our heels. My plans were working out so well I could have believed my fairy godmother had gone wand over tip and given them all a liberal sprinkling of pixie dust.

Music thumped from speakers hung in trees. Everyone was on this incredible high; the air buzzed with excited talk. You could have just reached out, grabbed all that happiness and wrapped it around yourself like it was a big, warm bath towel.

I'd positioned myself next to the barbecue so I could get a clear view of Kate Robinson where she laughed and chatted with her friends. The first time I saw her, in a café in Leeds, I felt what I could only describe as dismay. Something happened inside of me that I just could not control. My heart started pounding, I felt as short of breath as if I'd just sat on the bottom of the swimming pool for a full ninety seconds. We'd been introduced by Howard Sparkman. I exchanged all of a dozen words with her ('Nice to meet you . . . nice summer we're having . . . the cappuccino's not bad here. Goodbye.') But Kate Robinson moved into my dreams. I didn't want her to. I didn't need distractions. The band would demand everything I'd got. But human nature didn't give two hoots about my plans.

Kate Robinson, whether I liked it or not, was lodged tightly in my head. And for the last six weeks that's where she'd stayed.

I shifted my position a step or two to keep her in sight through a pale blue veil of barbecue smoke that was now rising from a rack of sizzling chickens.

She was taller than every girl there. And I noticed there was something about her that made men look at her twice. Almost as though they'd seen something that had surprised them but they didn't know what; it was enough to jerk their heads round to grab a second gander. I looked for it too as I drank an ice-cold beer. I still don't know what quality she had but it struck you so hard it stole your breath.

She was extremely attractive, but it was more than that. More than the way her blonde hair fell down over one shoulder and onto her chest. Perhaps it was her eyes. Nearer to green than blue, they had an almond shape that was almost oriental. It wasn't difficult to imagine that the blood flowing in her veins was the same as that of Genghis Kahn's warrior princes who'd swept from the far east to the very gates of Europe, slicing off the heads of Christian and Moslem alike without prejudice or favour to either faith. Then again. Maybe it was the eyebrows that were so striking. As black as crow feathers, they were a marked contrast to her fair hair. To complete the portrait: her long back had a breathtaking curve to it as she stood there, wine glass in her long sensitive fingers, lightly touching her front teeth with the nail of her first finger, smiling as someone told her an amusing story. And I couldn't tear myself away from those green eyes as—

'Penny for them.' Howard Sparkman put one hand on my shoulder from behind as he leaned forward to spear a sausage with a plastic fork. I was too moonstruck to reply. He playfully cuffed my ear with his free hand. 'Penny for them, I said.'

'Huh. Pardon?' I focused on his heavy round face grinning up at me.

'By heaven, we're really away with the fairies tonight, aren't we, sunshine?'

'Oh, I was just thinking about something.'

'Something? Some*one*, more like. Am I right or am I right?'

I grinned. 'Make yourself useful – pass me another beer.'

'I'll trade you. You grab a plateful of chicken, bread, coleslaw, potato salad, oh, some of those shrimps, celery, that pink stuff in the big bowl – I don't know what it is, but it's so blinking gorgeous I could marry it. And you might as well pack on a fistful of sausages.'

'You're still sticking to the diet, then?'

'Oh, don't you start.' He laughed. 'I've got Ruth on my back all the time.'

'I wouldn't complain. Just look at the dress she's wearing!'

'Rick, dear boy, she's my cousin.'

9

'Then it's legal?'

'But not possible . . . oh, that's a long story. Come on. You grab the food, I'll grab the beer, then tell me about the band.'

With two huge platefuls of food and a mess of beer cans clustering round our feet like a whole litter of devoted puppies we sat on Ben Cavellero's patio bench and talked. It was that kind of night. Everyone was talking about the future. Everyone had plans. Everyone was so high on champagne that nothing seemed impossible.

I'd met Howard Sparkman when I first moved to Fairburn. He'd have been eleven, I was nine. He'd been sitting in a tree that overhung our garden. 'Hey . . . hey, kid,' he'd shouted down, 'Got any snap?'

'Snap?'

'Yeah, snap. Y' know . . . chocolate, apples, cake . . . food?'

'No.'

'Aw shit, I'm starving. Oh well, you might as well climb up here with me then.'

'Is it safe?'

'As safe as a house . . . that's full of dynamite, with shitty wiring and a truck full of matches parked outside.'

As far as I knew Howard had stopped climbing trees. Now he wore gold-rimmed glasses; his face was as round as a full moon and he worked for a bank in Leeds. But he still ate like a hungry hippo. The man loved, just *loved*, eating and drinking. But to buck the stereotyped image of a beer-guzzling, fast-food chomping slob, over the last year he'd put his heart and soul into getting his pilot's licence. If, on a fine Sunday afternoon, a light aircraft glided over Fairburn, gunning its engine in a series of throaty burps, you could bet your bottom dollar it would be none other than Howard 'Sparky' Sparkman enjoying another of his forays into the wide blue yonder.

As we sat there, him licking the barbecued-chicken juice from his fingers, he talked about opening a restaurant one day. I believed he would.

'Quick, Rick,' he said, happily, 'grab that bowl of garlic dip. On the table behind you.'

'What's the restaurant going to be called?'

'*The Trough.*'

'And on the menu?'

'We're having none of these poncey little dishes with a leaf of that and drip of this. If you come to *The Trough* you'll eat like a Viking.' He held out his meaty hands. 'Huge platters of beef . . . whole fish

10

. . . mountains of potato . . . gravy lakes. You'll need a shovel, not a spoon.'

'When we play that record-breaking gig in Leeds I'll bring the band.'

'Bring the audience, too.'

I grinned. 'It's a promise, Howard.'

He took a swig of beer. 'I was talking to Stenno down at the garage. He's just come back from Tenerife.'

'Ah, honeymoon boy. Did he look tired?'

'Tired? He looked knackered.'

'Knowing Sue, she won't have let him get out of bed the whole fortnight.'

'Anyway, the volcano, Mount Teide, erupted while they were there. It began half-way through the honeymoon. Sue had just gone to bed. He was in the bath when the whole building started shaking; there was this huge banging sound on the walls.'

'What did he do?'

'He shouted to Sue, "What the hell was that?" She replied, "I think it was an earthquake." And he shouted back, "Thank God for that, I thought you'd started making love without me."'

We both laughed, feeling warm and relaxed. Overhead the sky turned a deeper blue. People moved about the lawn chatting, sipping wine from fluted glasses. Kate Robinson was biting into a breadstick. Even from where Howard and I stood, I could see the perfect white of her teeth.

There was no warning of what happened next. He could have fallen from that dark blue sky. One minute there was laughter and music. Then there was the man lying on the grass.

He was screaming, kicking his legs. At first I thought he was wearing some kind of mask.

It *was* a mask. Of sorts.

His face was covered in blood.

CHAPTER 3

'What the hell happened to him?'

'Someone's used his head for a football.'

11

'Careful!'

'You'll need something to mop his face . . . Christ, have you seen that cut over his eye?'

'A towel . . . Ben, we need a towel. Is it OK if—'

'Sure, sure, grab one from the bathroom. I'll get the first aid box.'

'It looks like a casualty job. It'll need stitching.'

'As far as I can see it's just the one cut. I don't think – hey, hey, take it easy. It's OK, we're trying to help. Just try and relax, we'll . . . *stay down* . . . it's OK, we're trying to help you . . . calm—'

If a man, his head drenched with blood, falls into the middle of a garden party you'd try and help. Right? You'd do your best, even if it was just to call an ambulance. But this guy would have none of it. He writhed on the grass, crying out in this weird voice, 'Leave me alone . . . don't touch me, don't touch me . . . no, don't do that. *No, let go of me.*' His eyes were screwed shut; he wore the same kind of expression on his face you'd see if a sadist had scrubbed his bare flesh with sandpaper.

In the end people moved back a couple of steps to leave him to squirm there on the lawn. Anyone trying to touch him or soothe him would trigger that weird sobbing voice, 'Leave me, leave me alone . . . don't touch me. Not again, not again, not again . . .' Where he squirmed his head left bloody smears on the grass.

I glanced round at the concerned faces looking down at the guy. We all must have felt the same kind of helplessness. It's one thing to take care of someone with a gashed head. But someone behaving as weirdly . . . well, let's not beat about the bush . . . as downright *crazily* as this, threw you completely. Was it drugs? Was he schizo? Would he suddenly jump up and attack *us*?

At last, Kate Robinson was the only one to do something positive.

Kneeling down beside the man, she made the gentle soothing sounds you'd make to a baby; then, taking the towel, softly, softly she began to dab his face.

Instantly his eyes snapped open. Christ, the shock of seeing his eyes made us all catch our breaths. Like white plastic discs, they blazed out of the face. The pupils and irises shrank down to black dots in the centre of those pale circles. Everyone held their breath, seeing sheer blinding terror shooting from the man's eyes.

I moved forward, ready to pull Kate back if he started lashing out at her with his fists.

He looked totally terrified, as if he'd rather blow out his brains than endure another minute.

'There . . . it's OK. OK. Everything's going to be all right . . . there . . . take it easy . . . everything's fine . . .' That was Kate's voice, a low soothing whisper.

Then came the transformation.

It was like someone had found the 'Off' switch. The man stopped writhing. He sighed and closed his eyes; you could sense those quivering muscles relaxing and softening beneath his skin all of a sudden. All that moved now was his Adam's apple in his throat, bobbing slowly as he swallowed.

'Crisis over,' someone said behind me.

'It must have been the shock,' came another voice, sounding relieved that we no longer seemed to have a bloody lunatic on our hands.

People moved forward again, wanting to help. Kate still dabbed the blood from his face.

'Jesus Christ. I don't believe it.' Howard Sparkman looked down at the injured man in amazement. 'Jesus. I didn't recognize him. Not with all that blood. Rick, have you seen who it is?'

I looked again at the man's face. 'Stenno? Hell's bells, it is as well.' Stenno, the mechanic from Fullwood's garage. We'd been talking about him earlier that evening.

Howard looked as if a bad taste had pumped up into his mouth. 'Stenno said he was coming to the party. Look what some bastard did to him. Jesus wept. Look at his eye.'

A nightmare thought hit me. 'Where's his wife? Shouldn't she be with him?'

Kate looked up at me in alarm. She was thinking the same as me. If Stenno and Sue had set off for the party together, then just what the Hell was happening to Sue right now?

A swirl of concerned murmurs ran round the party-goers as their faces turned white. I looked round the garden, still brightly lit by the setting sun, half-expecting Sue to come limping in through the gate, her face soared red from a dozen scratches, her clothes ripped.

Howard Sparkman slapped his forehead. 'Think, Howard, think. What did Stenno say to you last week? Party . . . Sue. Sue . . . *got it*.' His eyes lit up behind the glasses. 'Sue's on nights this week at the hospital. He said she wouldn't be able to come.'

'Thank Christ for that.'

'The bastards can't get away with this,' I heard Howard say to a gang of our old school friends who started pitching in with their own thoughts.

'Dean's all for calling the police.'

'The police? What good will they do?'

'Andy's right. Whoever's done this'll be long gone by now.'

'It might be the Beeston gang again.'

'Could be. One of them is a kid with red hair tied in a pony tail. Barry Fripp caught him ripping the radio out of his car.'

'Same one that pulled a screwdriver on Dean?'

'That's the one.'

'Bastards probably jumped Stenno as he cut down through the wood from his place.'

'Well, people, what the Hell are we waiting for?'

'What do you mean?'

'The police'll do nothing if they catch them.'

'What're you suggesting?'

'That we find them and beat the living crap out of them, that's what I'm suggesting.'

'I'm with Andy. If we give them a pasting they'll never forget they'll think twice about coming up here again.'

There. That's how it all started.

What we'd got ourselves worked up about wasn't particularly fresh. We were a close-knit group in that little village high on its hill outside Leeds. We'd been having rumbles with gangs from the city ever since we'd hit our teens. No doubt our fathers in their time had done the same.

But it was going to be different that night. For me, anyway. Because that's where all this really started for me. And I was never going to be the same again.

CHAPTER 4

Pumped up on Ben Cavellero's booze and our own righteous anger we poured out of the garden. We left Ben Cavellero and the party guests doing what they could to help Stenno. Although this was

14

something of a private battle with the Beeston gang, there were some out-of-towners there at the party who wanted to do their bit. They were as outraged as we were, and the simplest way to get rid of that outrage was to quench it nicely with a satisfying helping of sweet, sweet revenge.

Ben Cavellero's house stood a good kilometre from Fairburn village. By car you'd reach it via Oak Lane which does this eccentric winding route down from the village as far as the River Tawn then back up to Ben's house. The quick way is the path through the wood.

That, we decided, was the route Stenno had taken. That's where he'd been attacked by the Beeston beasts. And that's where we'd find them and where we'd slam their butts all the way to Shit City and back.

If I close my eyes now I can see it all as clearly as if it happened yesterday. There must have been fifteen of us walking in that purposeful way that told anyone we were on a mission to kick ass. Dean Skilton, his long brown hair tied back in a pony tail, was talking the loudest. He gestured with those hands that always looked too big for his body. His freckled face was flushed from alcohol as well as anger. The sun was resting on the hill. In the distance the city of Leeds was in shadow now and already its lights had begun to twinkle. Overhead, winging through the deep blue, was a tourist jet on its way to Leeds-Bradford airport. Behind us you could still see the line of poplars that marked the edge of Ben Cavellero's garden and the red tiles of his house's roof glowing warm in the dying light of the sun.

I noticed three girls were following. One was Kate Robinson. It was tempting to hang back and let her catch up but that could have been interpreted by the others as me turning chicken so I pushed on hard, slightly ahead of the gang.

'Ssh . . .' Howard Sparkman held up a finger. 'Hear anything?'

We stopped and listened. There was bird song; the faint sigh of the jet as the pilot throttled back. A dog barked in the distance.

I shook my head. 'Nothing out of the ordinary.'

'You think it was that gang from Beeston?' Dean frowned. 'We don't know for sure that—'

'We know for sure that someone bopped Stenno,' Andy cut in. 'He didn't nick himself shaving, did he?'

'Well, I don't hear anything.'

Howard rubbed his jaw. 'It's a Hell of a big wood between

15

here and the village. There's half a dozen paths I can see from right here.'

'Then we split up. Search until we find the twats.' Andy detested the idea of letting the thugs get away with it. 'As soon as one of us finds them, give a shout and we all come running. Right?'

I shot a look back as we fanned out along the woodland paths. Kate and her two friends weren't far behind. I thought they'd maybe wait there as we searched the wood but they showed no sign of slowing.

I felt uneasy about that. They weren't local. They certainly wouldn't know their way around the wood. What would happen if they came face to face with the Beeston gang? Assuming, that is, it *was* the Beeston gang that had beaten up Stenno. For all we knew he might have simply tripped over his shoe laces and cracked his face on a rock. Then again, what if some vicious lunatic were on the loose? Now, rather than thinking what I'd do if I got my hands on the bastards, I was beginning to wonder if the girls would be safe. Maybe I should double back and at least keep them in sight, I thought.

The paths radiated away through the wood. Before I knew it I was alone beneath that dense canopy of branches. Somewhere far away I heard a voice. I cocked my head to one side, holding my breath, so I could pick up more of the sound.

No mistaking it, it was Howard Sparkman grumbling aloud to himself. He'd probably trod in some dog crap or something, knowing him.

Smiling, shaking my head, I pushed deeper into the wood where the leaf cover was thick enough to bury everything in shadow. I even began to bump into tree trunks, it became so dark. I thought about Kate Robinson again, imagining how her blonde hair and green eyes would look almost luminous in this near-darkness. Her lean body that looked as taut as a bowstring. How she . . .

Thump.

A branch clipped the top of my head. It was now so damned dark I could hardly have seen my hand if I'd dangled it in front of my eyes. How I was going to see anyone else in there God alone knew.

Even so, I pushed on. I wanted to take a crack at those thugs, too. They were becoming a frigging disease lately. They'd already been barred from Fairburn's two pubs. But they still plagued the place. And when they were seen in the evening, inevitably someone would be reporting a stolen car or a burgled garden shed in the morning.

16

Hell, it was dark in there. I couldn't see the path now. And the way my feet sank into the soft earth told me I must have actually lost the damned thing several minutes ago. I checked the luminous dial of my watch. 9:30. I walked on with unseen branches pulling at my shirt sleeves like ghost fingers.

At this rate I might just walk straight into the gang; they'd beat me senseless before I could open my mouth to shout to the others.

And what would happen if Kate and the other girls came across the gang?

Mental images began to flicker up inside my head of Kate being grabbed by the thugs. *'Look what we've got here,' says an ugly kid. He's wearing a cruddy T-shirt, his stinking sweat forming dark stains beneath his pits; it's emblazoned with the slogan* BEASTING THE VIRGIN. *He's gripping a fistful of Kate's hair in his fist, then he swings her so hard against a tree her head jolts back to clunk painfully against the trunk. She stands there panting, her eyes darting left and right in terror as he runs his stumpy fingers down her bare shoulder. He pulls that evil grin again. 'OK, boys, let's get the story straight. She consented to this. Right? She said she'd always wanted to be screwed by—'* I shook my head, but the images wouldn't be dislodged. Now every ten steps I paused to listen, half-imagining I could hear panicky cries for help. My heart began to beat so hard I could hear the thud transmitted up through my body into my neck and ears.

Again I shook my head and walked on. I'd heard nothing. It was only imagination playing tricks. After all, we all must have been affected by the way Stenno plunged into the garden like that, his face covered in blood. Then there were his eyes. The way they had stared out from that mask of blood. How white and round they were, like discs of white plastic. And why had the pupils and irises shrunk to tiny black dots? Why, you couldn't even see any colour at all. And that look of terror had hit you like a punch. Just what the hell had he encountered in this wood?

Leaves rustled. I looked round quickly, my mouth dry; my heartbeat cranked up a notch.

Thud-thud. Thud-thud—

Christ . . . there really *was* someone there. I froze. My eyes were wide, as with sheer will-power alone I tried to punch my vision through the gloom.

I could see nothing.

Maybe I should shout? But if there was nothing there when the others came running I'd be a laughing stock. I wasn't ready for that humiliation. Rick Kennedy. The man who was afraid of the dark.

I headed for where I judged the noise was coming from. I stretched out my hands, going by touch alone now.

Fingers touched my palm.

Hell!

I grabbed.

And grabbed a sapling.

Idiot.

My mouth was dry now. My heart beating faster; breath coming in shallow pulls. Someone was there. I was sure of it. The sense of . . . of *presence* was just so strong. Palpable. Yeah, that was the word. Palpable. You could reach out and touch that sense of presence hanging in the air.

Every five paces I stopped, held my breath, listened hard.

But my heartbeat was like a bass-drum now. I could hear nothing but that lump of muscle in my chest going:

Thud-thud-thud-thud . . .

'Come out, come out, wherever you are,' I whispered.

I stepped sideways now, so strongly did I anticipate someone aiming a blow at my face or my bollocks.

My skin crawled as though insects with pointed feet were marching over it.

This dark . . . this fucking darkness. I could see nothing. But I knew, by Christ, I *knew* there was someone there. They moved just ahead of me, teasing me. I knew it. I had this absolute, total, utter conviction they knew perfectly well where I was all the time, and that they were just playing a game with me.

Any moment now they might double back . . . maybe I'd see a glint of a knife blade, too late, as it sliced the air down to my face, cutting my—

'*Hell.*'

I felt it in my face. I swung my fist. It hit me again. This time I grabbed with both hands.

A branch. A stupid branch.

I patted it with a sense of relief. But I knew it was idiotic to carry on like this. It was too dark to see anything at all now. For all I knew I might be heading for the old quarry. All I needed was to step over the edge of *that* and I'd find myself Glory bound, complete with wings and harp.

18

It was as I started back – or at least what I thought was the way back – when I smelt that odour.

I sniffed. It came up at me so strongly it took me by surprise. It struck me then that it was the same kind of smell you get on a hot summer's day when there's a thunderstorm and the rain hits the sunbaked soil. But this soil smell was just so strong it seemed to force its way up my nostrils to penetrate right into my brain.

Shaking my head, I walked on.

Then with a burst of surprise, even a level of gratitude that was so high it was almost bizarre, I found myself in a small clearing where a big tree had toppled in a winter storm. Above I could see a ragged hole in the canopy of branches; stars pricked the deepening blue.

Here the smell grew even stronger. I remember looking round at my feet, puzzled, wondering what on Earth caused it.

For Christsakes, I reasoned, *it's just some stupid smell. Probably badger wizz or weasel spoor or something.* But it was so strong and so out of place I found myself looking down at my feet.

Then I saw the weirdest thing.

All around me the soil was moving. It moved in a slow undulating motion. I shook my head. It was just so impossibly weird. That, and this warm soil smell.

I crouched down trying to see what was happening. Then my eyes adjusted to the gloom. And I saw it wasn't the soil that was moving: it was what was coming *out of* the soil.

There they were. Thousands of them. For all the world it looked as though men by the hundred had been buried alive, and now they were just slowly, slowly, slowly easing their fingers up through the soil; up . . . up until they broke through the surface. Then they slowly flexed their fingers, enjoying the warm evening air against their skin after years of confinement, locked inside a cold, damp grave.

I crouched there. Stared in amazement at the pink sticks standing proud of the ground.

My eyes were wide enough by then to admit any available light. At last the penny dropped.

'Worms.'

Thousands of damned worms. All sliding out of the ground at once. But for some reason they had all, down to the last one, decided to stand on their tails and hold their bodies erect so that they stood out from the ground like some loony-tune crop of fingers. The guys should take a look at this, they really should. Even better, I told myself, grinning, bring the camcorder. This would make one of those great tail-end stories on the news. You know the sort: cute dog goes windsurfing, amusing cat drives golf buggy – that kind of thing. The money it earned might buy a set of new microphones for the band.

I could, I decided, get home and be back with a camcorder inside half an hour. I checked the time. 9:47. Yeah, could do it easy. Then video the little buggers doing their strange night-time dance.

I stood up.

The first thing I saw was the face. In the gloom it seemed to hang suspended in midair. No body. Only a face.

A face with two eyes that seemed to stare right through to the back of my skull.

I opened my mouth to shout for the others. But no sound even got past my lips. For some reason I locked up tight as a statue.

The next thing I knew I was flat down on the ground with all those dancing worms.

Immediately I tried to get up. But I couldn't move. I couldn't breathe. I was only conscious of being held face down by a hand pressing between my shoulder blades while another hand forced my face against the soil. Now I could see the worms in close-up as they stretched toward the sky. The worms' bodies – pink, wet, segmented.

That's when I knew I wanted to scream.

Because I knew what it was that Stenno had encountered. It had been that face in the darkness.

And as I felt myself being held there I felt this great wave of terror. It came from somewhere in the depths of my guts. It swelled up and up and up. A brutal terror. A ruthless, overpowering terror that stabbed at my heart; a sheer terror that swamped every other thought and sensation.

No sound came from my mouth; but, as those strong hands forced me down against the ground, inside my head I screamed and I screamed and I screamed.

CHAPTER 5

It was dark now, the party in full swing. People danced on the lawn or on the patio to a string of old rock-'n'-roll standards.

Howard Sparkman grinned as I walked in through the garden gate. 'What kept you, Rick Kennedy, old son?' The grin widened. 'Or should I say *who* kept you?'

'No one kept me anywhere. I've been looking for whoever attacked Stenno. How is he, by the way?'

'Someone's taken him to the hospital to have the eye looked at but it doesn't seem life-threatening. He managed a couple of beers and even laughed at one of Dean's filthy jokes. Now . . .' His eyes beamed through the gold-rimmed spectacles. 'Aren't you going to tell your old buddy Howard who you've been pressing up against a tree?'

'Chance'd be a fine thing . . . oh, pass me a beer, my mouth tastes like you've slept in it.'

'Charming.' Howard winked. 'So you're playing the gentleman, then? You're not going to kiss and tell?'

For a joke it was wearing a bit thin. 'You've lost me, Howard. What do you think I've been up to?'

'You must have done *something*, the time you've been gone.'

'Time I've been gone? That must be all of five minutes longer than the rest of you. We looked round the woods for the Beeston gang. I found sweet FA and I take it you found nothing, either. Then we all came back.'

'But we've been back ages, dear boy.'

'Ages? We've been all of twenty minutes.'

'Rick . . .' Howard tapped his watch. 'Everyone bar you came back here an hour ago.'

'An hour? Pull the other one, Howard.'

'OK, OK, I'll mind my own business; too nosy for my own good. Here . . . have one of these chops. They are absolutely freaking amazing.'

I took a swallow of beer. It felt like liquid ice in my throat. Why was I so thirsty? I felt as if I'd just hiked across the burning sands of the Sahara. And what was all this leg-pulling about me disappearing? I'd looked at my watch not more than five minutes ago and the time had been 9:47. I checked my watch.

'Rick. Rick old buddy? Are you OK?'

'Fine . . . yeah, fine.'

'Well, you don't look fine. You got a piece of bone stuck in your throat?'

'No . . . really, Howard. I'm fine. If you could pass me another beer?'

'Sure. You sit down. No, Rick, on the wall just there, you don't look too steady.'

'Steady?'

'You look as if you're going to keel over.'

'I'm fine.'

'Rick. Sit.'

'Hell, Sparky, you sound like my mother.'

'Yeah, I'm two years older than you so it's my prerogative to be your mother, father and your dear old Aunt Nellie rolled into one. Sit there, I'll get you a drink.'

I watched Howard bustle away to get the beers. And just for a moment it seemed I was peering at him from the bottom of a deep, deep pit. I could even see the dark sides going way up into the distance, with a blob of light at the end containing Howard hurrying to the drinks table.

And I knew why I felt the way I did. It wasn't the booze. It was because I'd just gone and looked at my watch. In my heart of hearts I knew it should have shown it was coming up to ten o'clock. But I'd just looked at the thing and it read 11:01.

But just minutes ago I'd looked at the watch in the wood; the time had been 9:47.

OK, I've a reputation for being a little careless sometimes. I'll lose the change out of my pocket, forget my jacket in a restaurant or mislay a friend's telephone number. But I'd never lost a whole hour before.

I went over what I'd been doing in the wood. We'd been hunting for the Beeston gang. We'd split up. I'd ended up blundering through the darkest part of the wood. Then there was the clearing created by the fallen tree. Oh, yeah . . . I remembered now. There was something about the soil; something . . . comical? Yeah, comical; it'd been funny the way . . . the way . . .

The way *what* happened? Damnation, Rick, why can't you remember?

Funny smell?

Yeah, I remembered, that all right. Like rain on sunbaked earth.

'But what was so funny about that face?' I bit my lip. The words came out of my mouth but it didn't seem as if I'd spoken them.

Then, all of a sudden, a splash of memories erupted inside my head. *The worms. The face.* Then suddenly . . . what? Just what in Sweet Fanny Christ's name had happened?

22

My mouth turned dry. My heart began to beat hard again. I remembered seeing the face, the staring eyes. Then I was flat on my face. I was being held down. I couldn't move. The sense of sheer strength had been enormous. But what then?

I remembered feeling afraid. But it all seemed so muted now, as if it had happened years ago. I took a swallow of beer and shook my head. I was unharmed. My clothes weren't even crumpled. Sure, there was a flake or two of dried leaf here and there on the front of my shirt, but they brushed off without leaving a mark. So why did I feel so weird when I pictured that face staring at me, how it hung there in the darkness like there was no body attached?

I drained the can thirstily. Maybe I'd been working too hard with the band the last few weeks. With most of them having day jobs we had to practise in the evenings in Pete's garage. Sometimes the rehearsal sessions could go on into the small hours. More than once I'd still be hitting the guitar strings at two in the morning, knowing full well I'd have to be up at seven to reach the supermarket by eight.

I yawned and pinched a chop from where Howard had left his plate on the wall beside me. *That's it, Rick, old buddy. You've just been flogging away too hard. So relax, enjoy the party.*

The air was warm. Above the stars were shining in all their heavenly glory; the Milky Way left its creamy smudge down the centre of the sky. The music sounded good. Twenty lanterns hanging in trees filled the garden with this soft amber light.

The sense of near-panic I'd had a moment or two ago at losing an hour vanished as quickly as it came. I felt part of the human race again. The world was normal once more. *I* was normal.

Now where the Hell was Howard Sparkman with that beer? He'd probably been lured away by a bowl of potato salad or a particularly wicked blue-cheese dip. People stopped by to chat.

Ben Cavellero stood by a table, pulling corks from wine bottles. He looked up and gave me a cheerful wave. At thirty-nine Ben should have been someone's favourite school teacher. You know the sort, they'll begin the lesson, 'Today we're going to have a rigorous appraisal of the work of Edgar Allan Poe.' Then, five minutes later, he's telling some hilarious story about a neighbour's cat raiding his kitchen or the day lightning smote his chimney pot. He had greying curly hair and eyes that crinkled when he gave one of his characteristically friendly smiles. He never seemed to hurry anywhere, never had to raise his voice and young people gravitated to him for friendly and always wise advice end encouragement. Some parents wondered if there was something seedy going on, all these teenagers hanging round with an older man? But in all honesty there were never even any rumours. In his way he just seemed completely non-sexual. He appeared to be simply loyally wed to his twin hobbies of landscape painting and travel.

For any wannabe musician, writer or artist Ben Cavellero was an inspiration. In his twenties he wrote serious plays about serious social issues, peopled with serious characters. They made no money whatsoever. He lived in a bedsit in Leeds, scratching a poor living writing reviews for the local papers. Then, when he was thirty, he wrote a light-hearted whodunit mystery for a local theatre group. The play had been picked up as a vehicle for some old TV detective. A year later he banked his first million. Ben was hounded by impresarios to write more plays. But then he realized that was not what he wanted. He'd made enough money to keep him comfortable for life. So he decided to devote his time exploring the world through travel, and himself through his paintings. And he was the happiest man I knew. To see him standing behind his easel in a field down by the river, the brush in his hand, taking infinite care and a hell of a lot of pride in painting a tree, you could see the man had found Heaven on Earth.

'Sorry I was so long.' Howard handed me a beer. 'Ruth has been calorie-counting again. She reckons I've eaten enough to keep a family of four going for a fortnight.'

'No worries, have a chop.'

'Cheers.'

What Howard had seen I don't know but he shot me a strange, almost knowing look. Then I saw him catch Ben Cavellero's eye. Some understanding passed between them. Howard said hastily, 'Damn, I meant to tell Ruth about next Thursday's bash at the Lotus.'

He backed away from me, shooting me those strange knowing looks. I stood up and started to scan the party-goers for Kate. But that's when I noticed everyone had turned to look at me. The music stopped in mid-flow, leaving the kind of silence that makes your ears ring.

Everyone had stopped talking now. And I was the focus of their attention.

They all shared Howard's knowing expression. And for some reason I felt acutely embarrassed. As if they'd all somehow seen me do something shameful – something I wasn't even aware of myself.

The dryness came back to my mouth. Jesus. That lost hour. Perhaps something had happened in the wood. Everyone at the party knew about it. Everyone, that was, but me. My palms began to sweat, my face burned, my breathing turned into those shallow tugs of air that made my head begin to spin.

It could have only lasted a second or two. But it was one of those occasions that seemed to last for minutes. I was the focus of attention. I felt like the suspect under the anglepoise lamp.

And, by Christ, I found myself sweating. I was ready to crack and burst out, 'Yes! I admit it. I was in the wood. And I went and—'

Then it became bizarre – no, scrub that. It became surreal: they clapped me. They actually stood there and applauded. I stared in utter bewilderment.

Ben Cavellero stepped forward and in that gentle voice of his said, 'Rick, perhaps we shouldn't have sprung this on you. But we've another guest.'

Ben stepped back. Again I had the strangest feeling that my world had been knocked out of kilter that night and a string of bizarre events were parading themselves before my eyes.

The new party guest stepped forward into the light. Immediately the sensation that gripped me was that the face of the new guest was uncannily familiar. Then I knew why. It was the face I saw in the mirror every morning.

Or, at least, an extremely fine copy.

The first time I tried to speak it was a croak. The second time my voice box worked, or just about. 'Stephen?'

'Long time no see, Kid Kennedy.'

I'd forgotten the nickname my older brother had given me way back when, before I could even walk. Now Stephen Kennedy, the brother I'd not clapped eyes on in five years, had just appeared with all the suddenness of the Ghost of Christmas Past.

CHAPTER 6

And that's how my brother, Stephen John Kennedy, came back into my life after five whole years. Simple as that. One moment he was no more than a heap of hazy memories and a photo on the dining room wall. (It was one of those glossy showbiz pics: blow-dried hair, a yard of dazzling teeth, twinkling eyes. With a huge scribbled signature in red felt-tip that somehow turned the looping 'y' in Kennedy into a happy-smiley face; the TV station must have pumped them out to fans by the hundred.) The next minute he was there in Ben Cavellero's garden.

I know I must have gawped. Seeing him in the flesh after so long was nearer to shock than surprise. He was long and lean and incredibly handsome. He walked with such a lithe, springing step you'd swear he had bedsprings tied to his five-hundred-dollar trainers. And, Christ, yes, he turned heads. You couldn't miss the way the girls at the party actually stretched their necks (I swear, no kidding) to twice their natural length.

My big brother. Five years older. And, no doubt about it, larger than life. He wore this orange silk shirt, speckled green in a kind of spattered-paint effect. The jeans seemed to have grown over his long legs like a newly evolved epidermis. And the teeth, the hair, the smile and the eyes looked as if they'd been taken to the jewellers where they'd been carefully polished until they outshone the garden lanterns.

Ohhh baby . . . one glance at him and you knew that here was a man who was handsome, athletic, witty, charming, articulate, who radiated confidence, was wealthy, successful and owned an adoring public. He could have been someone you could easily hate; but instead of coming across as ultra-smooth and arrogant there was an air of ruggedness about him and a modest twinkle in the eye that said, 'Hey, buddy, don't take all this showbiz good looks too seriously; *really*, I'm just one of the guys.'

'Hey, long time no see, kid brother.' Stephen actually hugged me. Not a traditional way for Yorkshire men to greet one another, no matter how long they'd been separated. I blushed. Howard Sparkman laughed, slapped me on the back.

For a moment we were the centre of a crowd of people asking Stephen what life was like in the States, which TV station he worked for – that kind of thing. Then they drifted back into their own groups. It was the polite thing to do. They left us alone to get reacquainted. Immediately there was a rapport; we laughed as we talked and Stephen would keep patting my arm or throwing a gentle play-punch at my shoulder. I realized he was as moved by all this as I was and just wanted the physical reassurance I was really there.

26

'It was Ben's idea to spring this on you,' Stephen said with a grin.

'I take it everyone else was in on the conspiracy?'

'Sure. Here, grab a beer. I'd been telephoning Howard all week to make sure you were still going to the party.'

'So the reason for the party was—'

'Was a big reunion bash. I didn't want to phone you and say I was coming because in all honesty I didn't have a clue I could definitely make it. All last week the station had been threatening to fly me out to LA to cover some music awards ceremony. I told them no. The awards weren't particularly prestigious. They said yes. I said no freaking way . . . to cut a long, long ball-breaking story short I swapped assignments with Jeff Koerner who hosts the late shift. He owes me for bailing him out of some deep shit he'd got into with an Apache girl who claims she's having his baby. Uh, Apache's a dance troupe, I should clarify, not part of our Red Indian Nation. Trouble is, I'll probably end up covering some pop fest in Bolivia or somewhere. Christ, what am I talking about me for? I'm here, that's what matters. How's the Kid, then?'

'Well, in the last five years I grew up.'

'Hell, you did. Look at that . . . you must be nearly as tall as me!'

'Taller.'

Stephen laughed and playfully punched my arm again. 'No, *I'm* the big brother. Even if you grow another foot you've always got to pretend I'm taller than you. Pity my poor ego, man.'

'You've not gone and got yourself married, then?'

'No way. Anyway, I'd have to bring any girl home first for Mom's approval. By the way, how is she?'

'Last I heard, fine. You knew she's been bought in by an agricultural college in Italy to lecture?'

'Yeah, she wrote me just last week.'

'How's Dad?'

The smile died a little. 'He got married. Again.'

'To that student in New York?'

'Mandy? That was her name, wasn't it?'

'Maggie, I thought.'

'Maggie, Mandy, Wendy, it doesn't really matter. No, he hitched up with a lawyer from North Carolina.'

'Young?'

'Twenty-six.'

'Christ.'

'That's Dad for you. There's some life in the old dog yet.'

We'd tried to keep the talk about Dad as light-hearted banter but something cold and grey was slipping into the conversation so Stephen punched me lightly on the jaw, took a swig of his beer, grinned broadly again and said, 'What's all this Howard's been telling me? That you've quit the day job and started a band?'

'The man's not wrong. I'm working my week's notice, then we're hitting the road.'

'That's amazing. Congratulations.' Stephen was genuinely enthusiastic. 'Come on, tell big brother everything. Every detail. What are you calling yourselves?'

We didn't even notice what was happening anywhere else; we were head-to-head, talking as thick as thieves who were planning the heist of the century.

You'll gather Dad wasn't flavour of the month. In his way he had done his best to give us everything we needed, financially, morally and sometimes parentally, but he never seemed a fully paid-up member of Family Kennedy.

When I was born Stephen was six and Family Kennedy were living in a timber house on the outskirts of Edmonton in Canada. We lived there until I was three. The only thing I remember about it was the fact that the house seemed as big as an aircraft hangar. It was painted white and there was a moose head hung on the study wall. I'd spend hours searching the house for the rest of the body. Dad was a troubleshooter for a big agricultural resources company. He'd be sent all over the world to advise farmers. His speciality was teasing productive crops out of crappy soil. We moved around a lot. So, three years in Canada, two in the United States. Then brief stays in Italy, Spain, Morocco, Malta, Kenya, then finally back to Britain where we moved to Fairburn just a few miles outside Leeds in West Yorkshire.

For years Dad would have phone calls from different women. Stephen told me these were his girlfriends. I though it was just some kind of joke told by older brothers. But when I was nine Mum and Dad split. We were given a choice. Either we could live with Mum or live with Dad who opted for a teaching post in the States. The simple outcome was that Stephen, then fifteen, left with Dad; I stayed with Mum.

Ben ambled up, smiling, blue eyes twinkling with a quiet mischief. 'Gentlemen. Everything is ready for you now, if you'll kindly step this way.' He gave a gentlemanly bow.

I groaned and turned to Stephen. 'Oh no, they've got something planned for us, haven't they?'

'Got it in one. Come on. Time to face the music.'

'What music?' I shook my head, grinning.

'Don't worry, you're not expected to play an impromptu concerto for electric guitar. Nothing like that.'

The other party-goers had gathered on the patio; they had filled their glasses and sat on chairs as if they were going to watch a show. Then I realized that's just what it was going to be.

Someone had set up a camcorder on a tripod facing two straight-backed dining room chairs.

'Uh-oh,' I said under my breath to Stephen, 'I've got a bad feeling about this.'

'If you're going to be a professional performer this comes with the territory,' he whispered back. 'Wherever you go, even social occasions like this, you'll be expected to perform; it can get boring, and it can get embarrassing if you're at a friend's funeral. I kid you not, sunbeam, it's happened to me.'

We were shown to seats in front of the camcorder and while Dean Skilton fiddled with the machine's battery pack Stephen leaned sideways to whisper, 'It's OK, I helped set this up. It'll get the bit where we have to sing for our supper out of everyone's system. Besides . . .' He gently punched my shoulder. 'I want to take a memento back to the States with me.'

'But what the Hell are they going to do?' As I whispered I caught Howard's eye; he grinned and gave a thumbs-up.

Stephen smiled. 'OK, Rick, I'll apologize in advance. This'll suck. But do your big brother a favour: humour me, OK?'

I nodded good-naturedly as he leaned forward to squeeze my forearm in his big hand. I didn't mind anything that night. The whole world and everyone in it was beautiful and everyone was my friend. Already, I'd pushed to the back of my mind what had happened earlier that evening. Losing an hour? Big deal. I had just been overworking, that was all. And the big grey face floating there in the darkness? Trick of the light; or a patch of fungus on a tree. Yeah, that'd be it. I could go back in the morning, I decided, and find a dirty great toadstool growing out of some tree trunk. Something

29

yours truly misinterpreted in the gloom. Then yours truly had tripped over a bramble or something and knocked what little sense he had out of his tired old brain.

Sorted. The whole experience was well and truly sorted and forgotten.

CHAPTER 7

Stephen darted away to the booze table on those spring-assisted feet and bounced back with a couple of glasses.

'Rick . . . drink this. It's tequila.'

'I don't usually—'

'Come on, trust me, bro, call this a taste of show business. Drink it down in one . . . wait for it, wait for it . . . when I tell you. Then in about five minutes you'll get the tequila rush; you'll feel on top of the world and that's when you put the audience where they belong. At your feet.'

Dean had stopped fiddling with the camcorder. He gave a frantic wave to Ben who, with a broad smile, approached us.

'OK, Rick. Drink up.'

We both downed the tequila in one. Stephen smiled. I nearly gagged as the spirit blazed a trail down my throat, hit my stomach, then threatened to roar all the way back mouthwards again to burst out through my teeth like seawater through a whale's blowhole.

I gritted my teeth, swallowed, coughed. It stayed down. Through watering eyes I saw Ben approach with this amused kind of bobbing walk as if he was going to throw a bucket of water over us. Then he stopped.

'Ladies and gentlemen. Your attention, please.'

All went quiet. All eyes fixed on us. I caught sight of Kate in the audience. She was smiling.

Ben continued. 'Stephen Kennedy. Rick Kennedy. *These are your lives.*'

Someone – somewhere – hit a button: music played on cue.

Normally anything like that would have embarrassed the hell out of me. But that night it was OK. Oddly, I felt as if a part of me had been missing for a major part of my life. Now it had come back. I felt whole

30

again. Stephen was enjoying every moment, laughing good-naturedly when Howard brought out huge blow-ups of photographs of Stephen and I as children. Even the obligatory bare-arsed shots of us on a Canadian bear rug.

In his quiet voice Ben Cavellero said, 'Why don't you introduce yourself, Stephen? You'll do a far better job than I ever could.'

Stephen bounced effortlessly to his feet. I watched in something like awe as he switched on the professional persona and talked to camera like he was reading from an autocue. 'Good evening. My name is Stephen Kennedy. Just three weeks ago I had my birthday. I am now a full one-quarter of a century old. I host a music show on KSTV which is a new-ish terrestrial TV station based in Seattle. Video jock is how my role is best described. And this ugly mush is inflicted on Seattle's young and innocent Tuesday to Friday every week from six till eight. Hobbies . . . hobbies, let's see . . . ah, painting the town red, driving way too fast, dating girls, dating more girls . . . and, you know, for some reason . . . I just can't stop playing pool. Why? I don't know. It's such a dumb-assed game, but it's become an addiction with me. Stupid, stupid, stupid but I'm in love with the game. So, please, please, if there's any known cure for pool, tell me, please . . . I'll be your friend for life.'

It was typical DJ chatter but I could see he had the ability to project this warmth, so that the audience fell for him lock, stock and barrel.

Now Stephen was playing the audience like an expert angler landing a trout. 'People tell me I must be dumb if all I do for a living is stand in front of a camera saying, 'That was a video by REM; this is a video from Oasis; after that a new video from Armana. No. I do have genuinely intellectual pursuits. Last year I wrote a serious medical book.' He scanned the audience. He had them in his hand. 'A very, very serious medical text book. It's a self-help guide about premature ejaculation. I've got a few copies with me tonight but they're in short supply so I'm afraid it's a case of first come, first served.'

The laughter came freely. I looked at the faces of my friends and I saw a bunch of people totally relaxed and enjoying themselves. Occasionally Ben would drop in the odd question to me to ease the evening back from becoming completely a one-man show.

'Rick. What's your earliest memory?'

'Being shot.'

'Shot?'

'Yeah, being shot.'

'Where?'

'In a wood in Italy.'

'No, Rick, I mean in which part of the body were you shot?'

'In the back of the head.'

'Good God. Any serious damage?'

'No,' I laughed. 'No serious damage. It was a BB gun.'

'Now, Stephen.' Ben turned to Stephen. 'What's one of your strongest memories?'

'Uhm . . .' He thought soberly for a moment, looking up at the stars. 'That would have to be . . . shooting someone.'

'Who?'

'Him.' Stephen, grinning, aimed an imaginary pistol at my head, pulled an imaginary trigger.

Ben turned back to me. 'You've forgiven him by now for using you for target practice?'

I grinned. 'Just about. But I remember it hurt like hell, and nearly gave my mother a heart attack when she found me in the kitchen. Do you remember?'

'Hell, can I forget? You wore this Scooby Do T-shirt. It was white. At least, it should have been white. All the back of it was drenched red with blood. I thought, 'That's it, I've murdered my brother. I'll get life.' And ten minutes later you were sat watching a video with this huge bowl of ice cream on your knee smothered in strawberry candy strands.'

'And as punishment you had to sweep leaves in the yard?'

'Right. And the yard was so big you could have parked a dozen trucks in there.'

'Rick,' Ben said, 'give us an idea of what makes you tick. What are your hobbies?'

'Mainly, it's music. If I've any free time it's either practising the guitar at home, practising with the band in Leeds, or fixing up gigs.'

'Anyone special in your life?'

I tried not to do it but I couldn't help myself. I glanced at Kate Robinson. She was looking back at me with that direct, green-eyed gaze of hers; I tried to look cool but I heard myself stammer. 'Sasha . . . if anyone doesn't know by now that's my guitar. It's a Fender Stratocaster.'

'Why Sasha?'

'I bought it from this old lady in Huddersfield. It belonged to her son.' I shrugged. 'He'd just died and she told me he called the guitar Sasha. And that's the way it stayed.'

I saw Stephen give me a wink of approval.

'And now you've formed a band?'

'Yeah, Thunder Bud.'

'But you're no stranger to composing songs?'

I put my hands over my face in mock shame. 'Oh no, Ben. You can't do this to me. Tell me you won't?'

'Sorry, the Cavelleros have forefathers who were in the Inquisition. Play the song, Mr Sparkman.'

Somewhere Howard hit a button. Instantly a mushy disco beat pumped from the speakers in the trees.

'Yes, Rick Kennedy. It's that famous song, *Kiss Crimson*. As recorded by . . . where's my list? Ah, here we are: Beat Girl, Jilly and Joe . . .'

Someone shouted good-naturedly, 'Never heard of them.'

'Neither have I,' I replied. 'And I wish I hadn't heard their version of the song.'

'Wait.' Ben held up the sheet of paper. 'There's more. Claude Couer, Paris cabaret singer. A group called Blochet . . . another group called Cyber Funk Tha'ang, Spanish, wasn't it?'

'Nope, Greek. Castro Nostro were the Spanish punk band. This is the Cyber Funk Tha'ang's version. Played in every beach disco from Corfu to Crete but not one place outside Greece's territorial waters . . . so how the heck did you get this?'

Ben returned to the list. 'Also versions by Mr Zee, Sarah Lee Suemann and the famous version by that Norwegian TV cop who's name no one can pronounce. Mr . . .?'

'Mr Thing, I call him. I can't pronounce it either.'

Stephen slapped me on the leg. Playfully I slapped him back. The tequila was getting a grip and we both started giggling like a duo of fools.

'Come on, Rick,' Stephen said wiping away the tears. 'What's the history of *Kiss Crimson*?'

'Oh . . . pleeeeeeze . . . you don't want to know.'

'I get girls calling me up from Montana, Idaho, Chicago, Washington DC. Stephen, they say, tell us the history of *Kiss Crimson*. We want to know.'

'All right, all right . . .' I fought down the giggles. 'Sixteen years old, right?'

'You were sixteen?'

'Right . . . I said that, didn't I?'

'Sort of.'

The audience laughed with us, feeling that fine old tequila burn by proxy.

'Anyway. I was fifteen?'

'Sixteen, Rick, sixteen.'

'Yeah, whatever. Anyway. I wrote this song.'

'*Kiss Crimson*?'

'Right. I played it in that old high school band I had back then, Terror Firmer. There was this girl at school . . . Tracy Turner . . .'

Wolf whistles from the audience.

'That's the one.' I grinned back at them. 'Tasty Turner as she was better known. Anyway . . . where the Hell was I? Oh, yeah. Tasty – I mean – Tracy Turner asked me if she could include the song on a demo tape she was recording in Manchester. Sure, I said, then forgot all about it. Then out of the blue, months later, I get a call from Tracy – only now she's called Cher Gaynor and she'd been packaged into a group called Beat Girl. *Kiss Crimson* went onto their first album which made it to, let's see, number fifty-three in the charts.'

'But it made money, Kid,' Stephen said, lounging back in the chair.

'It made money,' I agreed. 'And it's still making it. The PRS cheques keep rolling. And the music publisher pays a royalty every Christmas and Midsummer's day. But for godsakes . . .' Grinning, I covered my ears. 'Can't anyone put me out of my misery and turn that racket off? They didn't use the whole song, only the chorus and the guitar riff. The rest is a computer-driven drum beat. It's murder.'

Everyone laughed but Stephen leaned forward and held up his beer bottle in toast. And, quite seriously, he said, 'I'm proud of you, Rick. I wish I'd pulled something like that off when I was sixteen.'

The audience were getting drunker. The time was way past two. If we'd have been in a town the police would have been called long ago to close the party down, but there were only the badgers and the bats to hear us out there on the hillside at Ben Cavellero's house. So we drank, barbecued more sausages, and, by starshine, all the girls fell in love with my brother Stephen Kennedy. Tirelessly, he still performed to camera, even though by this time Dean had switched it off.

34

'Food. Now believe it or not, boys and girls, I can actually cook,' he was declaiming to the lens, bottle of wine in his fist. 'I'm not a great cook, but I'm not a bad cook. Now this is my favourite recipe . . . if you're at home, grab a pencil and paper. If you're in bed, ladies, grab your lipstick and write it down on your old man's back. If you've got no lipstick borrow your old man's lipstick and still write it on his back . . . you want a drink of my wine, you have a drink of my wine . . .' Ruth had claimed him; both her arms were tightly round his waist. I glanced at Howard Sparkman; he just smiled and nodded in approval. He didn't mind.

'Right . . .' Stephen was slurring happily. '*All rii-iight*! This is what you do to make tomato jam, although now I guess I should call it tomato jelly. Take one pound of sugar; one pound of tomatoes and boil together in a pan. Then how do you know when it's ready? Take a little, little bit out on a spoon, put it on a little, little plate. Then leave it to cool. Once it forms a skin it's ready for the jar. And it tastes absolutely freaking *gorg-eous*.'

Next thing he and Ruth were sharing a single chair; they were eating one another's tongues; her long curly black hair hung down over the back of the chair, sweeping the ground as she turned her head from side to side.

I'd intended doing what I'd promised myself I'd do. Finally make a move on Kate Robinson. But she'd left with her friends.

But I was on too much of a high to worry that much. I knew where I could get hold of her phone number. Maybe I'd ring her Sunday.

I lounged back in one of the canvas chairs and looked at my friends. Some I'd known since I was nine. Right then it felt just so amazingly, wonderfully, incredibly good to be alive and to be there, and to be part of it all. There was Howard Sparkman munching something black and burnt from the end of a stick. The delighted expression on his face sang clear and loud that he loved every mouthful. I scanned the faces of other old and trusted friends: I saw Dean Skilton, propping up a tree; he was half-asleep, a champagne bottle hanging from one hand. That's right, Dean; even if you can't stay awake don't let go of your booze. The rest were there, too: Sophie Edwards, Barry Fripp, Andrew Lewis, Joe Field, Craig Hartnel.

I felt this deep, deep contentment and kinship. I can close my eyes and see them now. Laughing, talking, finding lost jackets and shoes, ready for the night-time stroll back home.

35

You see, I remember it so well because that was the last time I would see them all together in one place. And for some, it was the last time I would see them alive.

CHAPTER 8

The following day, Saturday, old man Robyns, the manager of the small supermarket in West Garforth where I'd been working through the summer, noticed that my eyes had bags bigger than the sacks of carrots I was shifting in the warehouse. He owed me a few hours in lieu so good-naturedly he urged me to grab them while I could, and maybe catch up on some sleep.

So I was back in Fairburn by 2:30 on that glorious July day with the sun shining and children blasting each other with hose pipes in gardens; everywhere there were girls and yet more girls in shorts and halter tops showing acres of golden, golden skin.

Humming the melody line of a song I was composing, I cut from Boycott Drive to Trueman Way and headed for the house with ivy rising in a green blush across the brickwork. That house had been home for the last ten years. It stood in line with a dozen other houses: all similar but different enough to be comfortably distinctive. There was a BMW or two parked in garden drives. I gave a cheerful, ''Allo, Roger!' to a middle-aged man in RayBans waxing his Porsche. He was the anchorman on the local TV news programme.

Trueman Way had been colonized by partners of law firms, senior policemen and successful sportsmen. It certainly wasn't the worst place I could have spent my teenage years. At school I pretended I hated it, but secretly I loved the broad street lined with cherry trees that, when they were in blossom, looked like they were heaped with strawberry ice cream. I was proud of the neighbourliness. I could walk down the street, hearing a barrage of friendly greetings: 'Good morning, Rick . . . How's life treating you . . . Grand weather we're having . . .'

The view from the back of the house was down over fields to the flat valley bottom that rolled away to the city of Leeds in the hazy distance. The front windows looked out on a meadow known as King Elmet's Mile. Just why it was so named was vigorously

debated at parish council meetings, because King Elmet's Mile was
a two-hundred-metre-wide band of grass stretching the length of
Trueman Way. Which was far less than even one half of a mile.

'*All right! Kid Kennedy!*' Stephen's full-blooded shout came from
the lounge as I heeled the back door shut behind me. 'I didn't expect
you till six.'

'I'd got some time owing to me. They've given me the afternoon
off.'

'Why didn't you phone? I could have fixed you some hash.'

'No probs. I've eaten. Are you decent in there?' I called cheerfully
through the door. 'I mean, are you alone or did Ruth call?'

'Yes, I'm decent and, yes, she phoned this morning.' Stephen
sauntered into the kitchen sipping from a two-litre Coke bottle. He
wore cut-offs, a loose white cotton shirt and squash shoes.

'And?'

'And I'm meeting her tomorrow evening.'

'Nice one.'

'And Carol phoned. She's driving me to York on Monday for a
day of culture round your fine museums.'

I shook my head, grinning. 'You'll have to take that dick of yours
in for a retread by the time you fly back home.'

He winked. 'No rest for the wicked.'

I pulled a carton of orange juice from the fridge and took a long
hard pull. 'Christ, it's hot.'

'Sue Rothwell, you know her?'

'Yeah, heiress to the Rothwell family fortune. They own the biggest
house in Fairburn. Why?'

'She dropped by earlier. Asked if we fancied going up to use
her pool.'

'You're putting me on?'

'Nope.'

'Hell, she's never even spoken to me before, never mind getting
an invite to wallow in the pool. Have you seen the size of it? You
could float an aircraft carrier in there.'

'You hang onto my shirt tails, kid, I'll take you places you've
never been before.'

'What time?'

'She says get there about seven. She's got some more friends
dropping by.'

'They'll be snooty.'

'So . . . we'll lower the tone. They'll love it.' Stephen thumbed the button on the TV mounted on brackets over the freezer. 'I just wanted to catch the end of this.'

'You're not developing a taste for cricket, are you?'

'Cricket? No, it's years since I saw a match. Can't stand the game these days.' He nodded up at the TV. 'Have a gander at that. Mount St Helens popped her top again in Washington State.'

'But that's miles from where you live in Seattle, right?'

'Yeah, but pretty awesome, eh? I once toured out that way with Dad about seven or eight years ago. The last vacation we had together before he went completely pussy-holic. Wow, look at that lava stream. You'd need asbestos stockings to surf *that* momma.'

For a moment we stood and watched the spumes of fire and the orange gobs of lava spurting into the sky. Then came shots of cars and houses being engulfed by volcanic ash. The reporter told of six deaths caused by the eruption. Four of those were sightseers who hadn't heard about what fates befall curious cats.

The news report went on to recap about the spectacular increase in volcanic activity over the last eighteen months. Scientists were already linking some losses of transatlantic shipping to volcanic activity on the ocean floor. There were the usual computer animations to help us poor saps out in TV Land to understand it all. Off the east coast of America there was something picturesquely known as the Blake Ridge-Carolina Rise where vast pockets of methane gas were locked up beneath layers of ocean sediment. In the last three months four of these gas reservoirs had erupted without warning, killing millions of fish and tearing apart a couple of merchant ships.

An expert was wheeled in to link these methane eruptions and volcanic activity with some other less spectacular geological comings and goings, along with a rash of quakes along the world's fault lines.

This was a cue for library footage of the quakes that had torn Los Angeles in two again and killed half the population of Tampico in Mexico.

'You must remember,' the professor of something or other was saying through this amazing handlebar moustache that looked as if it had been nailed to his upper lip. 'You must remember that the Earth is basically a ball of molten rock and iron enclosed by a comparatively thin skin of cooler solidified rock. Occasionally she can flex her muscles and that's when the Earth will literally move for all of us.'

Cut away to pretty lady reporter smiling nervously at the slightly mucky joke.

Prof continued, 'Two hundred and fifty million years ago huge volcanic eruption on a global scale resulted in massive extinctions at the boundary of the Permian and Triassic periods. Do you realize that this dramatic period of volcanic holocaust resulted in ninety per cent of marine species and seventy per cent of terrestrial vertebrates being wiped out?'

'Knows his stuff, doesn't he, Kid?' Stephen gazed dreamily at the TV that now showed shots of a lava flow crumbling into the sea in clouds of steam.

Prof was getting into his stride now and really buzzing the lecture through that handlebar moustache, 'For a million years the volcanoes expelled between two and three million cubic kilometres of lava. Abrupt global cooling would have resulted due to sulphates being projected into the atmosphere by these devastating eruptions. Ice caps expanded, sea levels dropped and whole species were wiped off the face of the planet.'

There came another report about hydrothermal vents that spewed out boiling water in an area known as Broken Spur in the mid-Atlantic and how these were spreading out across the ocean floor. As always the reporter rounded off the piece with an 'And now a nearer-home story' about some mud springs in Wiltshire. There were shots of a hydro-geologist lowering a probe that looked something like an old baked-beans can on the end of a line into the mud and announcing that over the last ten months the temperature of the mud had increased by three degrees Celsius.

'My God, Carruthers!' Stephen aped an upper-crust English accent. 'Three degrees. Could this really mark the end of civilization as we know it? Saddle up my filly, boy, we'll head for the hills.'

'We're already there. This is the highest point for miles around.'

'Well, we'll saddle up some pretty filly anyway and ride her around the garden until she drops.'

'In this heat, I'd drop first,' I said, grinning, and took a hefty swig of orange juice.

'Young lad like you?' Stephen laughed. 'You should have loads of energy. Hey—' He stood up, struck by an idea. 'Race you down to the bridge again on Oak Lane.'

'You've got to be kidding.'

'I kid you not, kiddo.'

'I need to phone round the others in the band about rehearsals tomorrow.'

'It can wait.'

He looked at me, the grin still in place, but I saw the challenge writ large in those blue eyes.

'What kind of start do I get?'

'*None!*'

With that he ran across the kitchen, swung open the door and tore across the back lawn.

I couldn't stop the grin on my own face as I followed.

Already he'd reached the wall that separated the garden from the dirt track that ran down through the fields at the back. I dodged round the loungers on the grass, then long-jumped the ornamental pond and followed hard.

I was laughing under my breath. Suddenly the years had rolled back to when I was nine and he was fifteen. This used to be a regular Sunday afternoon event. 'Race you down to the bridge' he'd say. In those days no way could I even half-compete with a fifteen-year-old so he'd give me a head start. Sometimes still nonchalantly lounging on his bed, munching an apple as he thumbed through *Playboy*, he'd tell me to get running and he'd catch me up. And then beat me to the bridge.

He always did, of course. I'd run as fast as I could, little pvc trainers slapping down on the cinder track, my Robocop mask jiggling round the back of my neck, held there by shearing elastic. Then I'd hear the muscular thump of his feet hitting the ground. Then it always happened to me. The strength, for some reason, would go right out of my body when I heard those pounding feet. I could almost believe he had vampire powers and had the ability to drain the strength out of me and into him. I'd feel as if I was running in slow motion even though the bushes at the side of the track were just a green blur.

Sometimes he'd nearly let me reach the bridge. Then I'd hear a cry. I'd turn and see him hobbling along; he'd point at his foot, his face a picture of agony. I'd see him mouth the word 'ankle.' Panting, I'd stand there, waiting for him to hobble up.

Then, suddenly, the grimace would snap to a grin and he'd bound by me shouting, 'Sucker!' And, naturally, he'd always reach the bridge first to bounce up and down triumphantly, his fists punching high into the air.

Now I had him in my sights. He was about twenty paces ahead of me, his hair blowing out in the slipstream, arms pumping, long legs eating the track. The sheer speed caused the white shirt to inflate, making it appear as if he had an impossibly huge torso and arms.

I'd run races at school but I wasn't that much of an athlete. It was more a lack of competitive spirit than lack of leg muscle and stamina. But when I saw my brother sprinting down that track, cinders coming up in splashes of black as his feet struck the ground, something clicked inside me. This heat ignited in my stomach until it felt as if I'd swallowed a burning log. That heat streamed out into my arms and legs. I locked everything into that run; I felt as if something inside me had shifted up a gear and, believe me, I felt as if I actually flew along that track. I'd never felt so determined or run so fast.

I'd heard Stephen shouting comments, 'Come on, rubber legs . . . I've seen faster tortoises . . .' But as I drew level with him he clammed up and I saw a look of concentration come into his eyes that bordered on the ferocious.

He'd not anticipated this. That the little brother could grow up and run as fast as he could.

No, scratch that . . . replace with *run FASTER than he could.*

Arms windmilling, panting like race horses, we cannoned down the grass slope that separated the track from Oak Lane. Now we slammed onto hard tarmac, feet sounding like gunshots. Now the river was on our right, the meadow on our left. The bridge was up ahead about two hundred metres away, spanning the river like a timber finishing tape.

This sheer rush of energy kicked through me. And, Christ, it felt so good . . . so amazingly, fucking good. I was faster than him; I heard him panting some way behind me. Already I saw myself jumping up and down on that bridge, fisting the air like I'd seen him do, shouting those same taunts he'd used on me when I was that little nine-year-old, puffing and panting along the lane like a knackered old steam engine that was on its last lumbering run to the scrap heap.

Now I was the winner. I wondered what effect that would have on Stephen. I'd never beaten him at anything before – ever.

Revenge.

Christ, that's the feeling that was spilling through me from burning head to beating sole. Revenge . . . sweet, sweet, sweet revenge.

'Rick . . . Rick! Christ . . . will you . . . will you take a look at that?'

I thought it was the old sprained ankle trick. But there was some inflection in the voice – astonishment coloured with something near to disgust. I slowed and looked down into the river.

The sight of it stopped me dead.

Stephen came up panting. Even though he was holding his side where the stitch stabbed deep he, too, was staring in wonder at the river.

'Christ, what the hell's happened there?' he panted, looking down the steep banking. 'Where did all that blood come from?'

I wiped the sweat from my eyes. He was right. It was as if someone had drained off all the water then opened some huge sluice in a slaughter house. Now blood – or something that looked like blood – came gushing through the channel in a foaming, swirling wash of crimson.

I shook my head. 'Strange. During the summer it's usually half the level it is now. And we've had no rain in days.'

Hypnotized, we watched the blood-red water rush downhill in the direction of the footbridge. A log slid by, rolling over in the flood of bloody red, the grue dripping thickly from what remained of its branches.

'Hell,' Stephen said in a low voice. 'You know what caused it, don't you?'

'No. What?'

He nodded at something at the bottom of the banking. 'Take a look for yourself.'

I stepped onto the grassy bank that separated road from river and looked down. An unpleasant taste was rising up through my throat as I saw that lying there, half in and half out of the water, was a . . .

I looked closer. 'It's an old car tyre. That – *uph*.'

I felt the flat of his hand thump me between the shoulder blades. I went forwards. The only way I could stop myself pitching skull first into that crimson grue was to turn, fall flat on my stomach and grab at the long grass.

'Sucker!'

I looked up to see the huge grin on his face. Then he was gone.

Damn! Fell for it again. Just like that gullible little brat with freckles and plazzy Robocop mask dangling around my neck.

Swearing meatily, I scrambled up the bank to the track and ran like Lucifer himself had got a taste for my ass.

I ran hard, air blasting into my face, but it was all shitstew by that time. When Stephen was almost at the bridge he stopped, shot me that wicked grin, then moved like he'd been filmed in slow-motion. One distinct step at a time, arms pumping mechanically in that same stop-go-stop way, he completed the last five taunting steps onto the bridge. Then he jumped on those feet that I swear to this day were spring-assisted; he punched the air and shouted, 'Sucker! Where were you, Kid Kennedy? Where were you?'

'Cheat.'

'What, me?' The blue eyes were wide with sweet innocence. 'Me, baby brother? No way. Look, next time I'll give you a sixty-second start.'

'I don't need a sixty-second start.'

'Absolutely. You need a new set of pegs to replace those chalk sticks you've got sticking out the bottom of your fanny.'

'You mean backside.'

'I know what I mean. And I ain't talking Yankee.'

'You fucking—'

'*Right!* I'm a fucking go-getting cheat, a fucking winner, I'm a fucking success . . . I'm like fucking you – a fucking Kennedy!' He jumped down from the bridge and swung his arm, getting me in a neck lock. For a second I really thought this was it. Brother versus brother. *We'll punch each other out.* But he gave a kind of Cherokee Brave whoop and ruffled my hair with his free hand.

It was sheer exuberance on his part. And that flash of anger that had seared across me a moment ago was gone. We were both laughing, Stephen ruffled my hair again. 'We're the Kennedys. We've got balls of steel. And when we see something we want no one – nothing, *nothing on this fucking planet, gets in our way*. And don't look at me like that. I know you're ambitious as hell. You'll get *exactly* what you want from life. Because whatever Dad might or might not have done for us, he gave us that need to win. You feel it, don't you? It burns in your guts.' He rubbed my stomach. 'It burns there. And it'll burn and burn until you get that thing you want. You know I'm right. Come on, kiddo, I'll buy you a beer.'

We headed back up the hill, slapping each other on the back and roaring with laughter. Anyone passing by would have wondered what kind of exotic powders we'd been inhaling up our nostrils. But it was sheer high spirits. The Kennedy brothers were a team again. Everything in the garden was rosy.

And all the time that river of red flowed remorselessly by. It would

43

have taken spit-all effort to imagine that the Earth was one almighty animal; that someone had hacked through an artery worming beneath its dirt skin. Now its life blood was spurting into that channel that had once held the River Tawn. And a million gallons of blood were haemorrhaging away to the distant, distant sea.

CHAPTER 9

'Rick. Who are all those people?'

I opened my eyes. Stephen had come into my bedroom and was standing at the window, one hand pulling the curtain aside, the other hand on top of his head as if he'd seen something he didn't understand.

I rubbed my face. 'Uh . . . what time is it?'

He looked at me without answering. The blue eyes were calm but there was a message contained in the look he gave me that rolled a massive ball of ice clear through my stomach. I shivered and my skin goose-fleshed.

'What people?' I was out of bed and on my feet.

He looked back out of the window. '*Those* people.'

I didn't like the tone in his voice; I didn't like the way his blue eyes stared unblinking out of the window as if he'd just seen the cherry trees fruit human eyes.

What people? *Those* people . . . I don't know what people . . . was nothing to do with me . . . I didn't do nothing . . . Just for a split second panic had me in its quivering fist. For the first time since Friday night I remembered that face in the wood. How it seemed to float above the ground. And how the next moment I'd been flat on my face, feeling a hand effortlessly hold me down.

Now there were mysterious people out there. Would they all have grey faces? Would they . . .

'Jesus Christ Almighty.'

All thoughts of that bodyless face vanished. I stood beside Stephen and stared out at King Elmet's Mile.

Or, I should say, I stared at where King Elmet's Mile should have been.

'What on Earth are they doing here?' Stephen whispered in awe.

I looked out there with him. I saw a clear blue morning sky bisected by a single white jet trail. I saw the front garden. The red block driveway leading to twin wrought-iron gates. I saw the front lawn, with the diamond-shaped flowerbed cut out of its centre filled with wallflowers; Mum would hoe that diamond with such dedication that the soil was as loose as bread crumbs. I saw the privet hedge and Trueman Way beyond. Then I saw what was clearly impossible.

I saw people.

Not a dozen people. Not two dozen. Not fifty. Not a hundred. Not five hundred, not one thousand.

I saw *thousands.*

Thousands and thousands. It was just a living sea of heads stretching across the road, across the meadow and up to and, as far as I could tell, into the woods. Looking left, I saw the road packed with more people. Beyond that Boycott Drive was choked with a log jam of more human beings.

I turned and looked at my clock radio to fix the time in my head. It was Sunday morning. The time, 7:11. At that moment it seemed important I should remember the fact. I had the feeling that someday I would have to stand up at a public tribunal and give evidence about what I saw that day.

And what the Hell did I see? I saw Fairburn submerged under a tidal wave of human beings – men, women, children. Trails of blue smoke from fifty campfires stood in spindly columns in the still morning air.

And Stephen and I stood there and we watched. We didn't move. I don't think we even breathed. There was just this incredible fascination for what was laid out there before our eyes. Even though all the public places were packed tight with people, all the private gardens were just as they always had been. Civilization still held sway there, and the garden boundaries were respected even though drive gates might have been left open.

All I could compare it to was on open air rock concert. The same massed crowds making themselves as comfortable as they could with nothing more than grass to sit on.

'Some of those people are in their night clothes,' I heard Stephen say in a hushed voice. 'Pyjamas and dressing gowns. Look at the baby wrapped in a blanket.'

Stephen was looking at individuals in the crowd – not just a mass of heads. I zoomed in, too. There were middle-aged women in nightdresses with duvets round their shoulders like mediaeval cloaks. Most people were sitting on the grass or half lying. Mothers and fathers sat with children and babies on their laps. Grown men stood in pyjamas or day clothes, or a bizarre mixture of the two. On their faces were the expressions I'd seen on kids who'd just started a new school. A kind of lost and lonely expression, with just a dash of expectancy as if they thought someone would come along in a minute or so and tell them which classroom they should be in.

At 7:17 the telephone rang. I learned later that everyone's telephone had rung at exactly the same time. When I answered it, I heard a kind of long-drawn sigh; slowly it faded to an echo that shimmered eerily for ten seconds or so before dying away into silence. Oddly, it reminded me of the sigh our dog Amber had made as she had lain on the blanket in the garden. It had been my fifteenth birthday. And after a long, healthy life Amber was now dying of old age. And as she finally slipped away, the spark fading from her eyes, I heard her make that long, long-drawn-out sigh that seemed to come not from her lungs but from somewhere even deeper inside of her. Perhaps from the part where her soul was anchored. Now it was letting go.

We buried her in that diamond of soil there in the middle of the garden.

And now I'd just heard that same sigh as something beautiful died. Of course, it must have been just some silicon chip the size of your little fingernail going on the fritz at the telephone exchange in Leeds. But that's the sound it made. And in twenty thousand homes all the telephones had rung like a twentieth-century death knell.

I looked out at that living carpet of humanity, their shoulders hunched, faces stamped hard with exhaustion. That morning I'd planned to drive into Leeds for the rehearsal, and by devious means I'd arranged we'd go out in the evening to the Pizza Express where I knew Kate Robinson and her friends would be eating – where I could oh-so-coincidentally bump into her, casually chat, then move in and ask her for a date.

That wasn't going to happen.

I knew that as clearly as I saw ten thousand refugees squatting out there on the field with no food, no shelter, no water. The world had changed. The future was going to be different.

We were going to be different. We were going to *have* to be different. Or we would die.

46

I shook my head, feeling cold and dazed. 'Stephen . . . what do you think happened?'

He looked at me. 'There's only one way to find out.' He walked quickly from the room.

CHAPTER 10

That's the Brits for you. They'd rather die in the gutter than ask for help.

All that Sunday not one of those thousands asked for anything.

On Monday people started coming to the door. Not a mad rush, mind you: just the odd one, maybe a young mother in a muddy nightie with a toddler hanging onto her fist; or an old guy in PJs and a raincoat that'd seen sunnier days; or a father in a tracksuit and shiny brogues.

'I'm sorry to trouble you, but my children are hungry. Could you spare them a slice of bread?'

Or:

'I've managed to get hold of some tinned stew but I haven't any matches to light a fire. Could you spare me a box . . . not a full one, mind, just a few matches.'

Or:

'I'm sorry to give you any grief, sir, I really am. But I think my daughter's picked up some bug. She's three years old. I just wondered if I could . . . no, I'm sorry . . . it's rude of me to ask. Goodbye.'

Or:

'Ah, my wife's not feeling too well, young man; do you have any aspirin?'

Or:

'My baby's feeling cold. I must have a blanket.'

Getting that bit more desperate, that bit more demanding with every hour that passed. I did what I could for the people who did knock on the door, we all did. But I realized that for every one who came and asked for food or matches, or a pair of old shoes, there were hundreds who suffered in silence, either too proud or too shy to ask. Which only confirmed what I'd realized years ago: those who shout loud enough get what they want; those who politely keep quiet and wait in turn get sweet Fanny Adams. Such is life.

So, it was clear enough to me then that when people started to beg from complete strangers it meant just one thing:

Civilization was turning belly up.

Within an hour of Stephen and I staring out at what looked like a re-enactment of a refugee camp on the edge of some African war-zone, we'd heard enough to get a pretty clear picture of what was going down.

Sometime Friday night the people of Leeds had woken with sore throats. Their eyes watered. They started coughing. Within an hour everyone in the city was choking. Eyes were streaming, throats felt on fire, folk couldn't breathe; their lungs hurt so much they felt full of broken glass. Thousands must have thought they were having an asthma attack or a coronary. But it was soon clear it was more than that. Families, neighbours, the cops in the police station, the staff at 24-hour filling stations – the city's entire population were gasping for breath.

The instinct for self-preservation kicked in. Those that could drive, drove. Those that could walk, walked. The entire population of Leeds just upped and went.

That same instinct drove them uphill as they guessed the cause of their problem was a toxic gas. If they headed for the high ground, they realized, they could reach good, sweet air.

A few hours later they did. And one of those pieces of high ground was Fairburn.

Now we had forty thousand souls camped out in a village of seven hundred. As I said, many were in their nightclothes. They had no food, no shelter.

They depended on the mercy of the good folk of Fairburn. As you'd expect, its residents rolled up their sleeves and did what they could.

There had been an emergency meeting of the parish council, which luckily included a good few of the movers and shakers of Fairburn. Later that day Ben Cavellero called.

I offered him a beer but he declined in favour of a mineral water. Stephen and I sat on the breakfast-bar stools in the kitchen as he leaned back against the worktop and said, 'The shit's hit the fan. We're expected to feed the forty thousand and we've no food.'

Stephen opened a beer. 'We can pool what food we've got; that'll keep them ticking over until the emergency services get their act together to provide proper feeding stations.'

Ben looked at each of us in turn. 'As I said, *the shit has hit the fan.*'

'This can only be temporary. Whatever gas it is down there in Leeds'll dissipate in an hour or two, then everyone can go home.'

'I hope you're right, but something . . . peculiar has happened.'

'Peculiar? It's some kind of toxic spill, right? Or some factory's caught fire like . . . where was that place in India?'

'Bopal,' I supplied.

'Yeah, Bopal,' Stephen took a deep swallow of beer. 'Yeah, there was a discharge of toxic gas there that killed thousands. Luckily, from what I've heard, there's been no fatalities in Leeds, but—'

'Stephen. Rick.' I'd not seen Ben like this before. He was edgy. He glanced back at the door as if afraid of being overheard. 'Don't get me wrong, I'm not scaremongering. But something's just not right. I don't think Leeds is the only place to be affected.'

Stephen and I glanced at each other and said the same thing. 'Terrorists?'

Stephen added, 'They think there's been some kind of gas attack? Has London—'

'London's a different matter again. Early this morning one of the parish councillors had a call from his brother who lives in Chelsea. The brother said, I quote: 'Shit . . . shit. The house is surrounded by water. I'm on the landing. Shit, you can actually see it coming up the stairs.' That's when the phone went dead.'

We shook our heads. None of this made much sense. We'd just got our heads round the fact that the population of Leeds had been gassed from its beds. Now London? Hit by flood?

'But we've heard nothing on the news.'

'Precisely. But not all the London-based stations are on air. And those that are broadcasting are using different presenters and DJs.'

'Then the government are covering all this up?'

Ben shrugged. 'It's too early to claim any conspiracy. The radio station in Bradford is covering the story about Leeds, but it's all pretty vague. No one really knows what's happening.'

'So I suppose we sit tight.' Stephen managed a smile. 'Bang goes our pizza in town tonight.'

49

Then it hit me. Kate Robinson lived slam in the centre of Leeds. What had happened to her?

Twenty of us sat on the back lawn at Pat Murray's house in the village. It had been a slog just getting there. The four-minute walk had taken twenty minutes because we literally had to step over people who lay or sat elbow to arse in the road. It was now mid-afternoon on that first Sunday. Most people had recovered from their long hike from Leeds up to Fairburn and were telling each other their experiences and also telling each other what they thought of the tinpot shit-for-brains government for not organizing emergency food deliveries. It got worse at the centre of the village where they clustered a hundred deep round the village pond for water.

Howard Sparkman caught my eye. 'The place is going to be hit by one almighty diarrhoea-flood if they keep drinking that pond water.'

Dean chipped in, 'When we were kids we all used to stand on the wall and pee in there on the way home from school.'

'You still do, Dean, you still do.'

'Ah . . . if I can just have a word with you ladies and gentlemen.' Pat Murray was a fit-looking seventy-year-old with a friendly twinkle in his eye. He'd held a senior position in the local fire service before retirement and there was something solid and reassuring about him. If he'd said 'Ladies and gentlemen, a nuclear attack has just been launched, but no harm will come to you if you put a brown paper bag over your head,' well, I think most of us would have believed him. Another of life's truths. If you want someone to trust you, it's not what you say, it's the way that you say it that counts.

'As you all know, there's been an emission of toxic gas in Leeds that has resulted in a mass exodus. I'm sure you all agree that somehow we've managed to get more than our fair share of refugees in Fairburn.' Quiet laughter from the audience sitting cross-legged on the grass. 'So we all need to lend a hand to make sure our fellow Yorkshiremen are looked after until they can return home.'

'Does anyone know how long that will be?' asked a girl in her twenties.

'Not yet, unfortunately. We need to know the exact nature of the gas leak before we can allow people back to their homes. But privately we're saying the buses should start rolling up tomorrow evening to ferry everyone back.'

50

'Surely they can manage until then?'

Pat raised a grey eyebrow as the girl continued. 'Sorry if I sounded callous. But it seems a waste of time to go to the trouble of setting up . . . setting up what amounts to a refugee camp for just twenty-four hours or so?'

'I'd agree, if they were all healthy young lads and lasses like you. But we have a fair number of both very young and elderly people living rough out there. They are absolutely dependent on us providing for them. Do you think we'd have a clear conscience if we sat back and let them fend for themselves?'

The girl flushed red on hearing this and kept her mouth shut for the rest of the meeting.

Dean poked a finger in the air like he was still at school. 'What's this about London?'

'About London? I don't know anything about London.'

'Big place with Big Ben sticking out of it, somewhere in southern England,' chipped in Howard. Everyone laughed again, including Pat Murray. There was still this general feeling that what had happened that morning was just a blip on the steady line of normality. In a few hours, everyone was sure, the population of Leeds would be back in its homes and everything would be hunky-dory. In the meantime we'd all play at International Rescue. Then we'd look back and laugh about the day Leeds came to Fairburn.

Pat was adamant he'd heard nothing about London. There was no news on the radio, although that means of communication was now suffering from interference. You'd switch on the radio and you'd swear the DJ was frying eggs for a hundred at the other end of the microphone. The power had been cut so we didn't have a functional TV among us. Pat's wife had gone to hunt for a battery-powered mini-TV but hadn't returned yet.

Pat moved briskly on: 'Although we have a good number of skilled professionals in the village who are good on logistics – experienced at moving people and materials about and who can formulate complex plans of action – the truth of the matter is we're very short of food, tents, blankets, clothes, medicines, that sort of thing. So we're relying on people – volunteers like yourselves – to go out and forage for us. This means, I'm afraid, a little looting – albeit lawfully-sanctioned looting. You will be S Group. I'd be grateful if you would fix that in your minds: S Group. What we're desperately short of now is baby food.'

'Baby food?'

'That's right, Dean.' Pat gave a friendly smile. 'To you young single men, that is food for babies. Those funny little animals that appear nine months after you've forgotten to put your overcoat on.' More laughter. 'We need you to bring back as much powdered baby food as you can find. Don't worry about bottles, teats and the rest of the gubbins, we've got plenty of those. Now, if I can hand out these photocopied maps it will show you where to concentrate your endeavours.'

Again that mood danced in the air. We were breezy, even cheerful. We'd do our bit to help; then in a day or two everyone would be back home. Normality would return to that chunk of Yorkshire. Trains and buses would run on time again. Salad sandwiches and ice cream for tea. Cricket on the village green. *Star Trek* on TV. Someone in church saying, 'God is good.'

And as I sat there on the lawn, thoughtfully chewing a stalk of grass and watching Pat Murray briskly hand out the maps, I remembered what they always say at the start of a long and bitter war that drags on for years: 'It'll all be over by Christmas.'

CHAPTER 11

Monday night. Day two of the refugee camp on our doorstep. At midnight I took a leak before heading to bed. Stephen was already zedding away in his room. From the open bathroom window I could catch the faint smell of wood smoke from camp fires. I sniffed again. It had been dry all day but I could smell the soil in the garden.

It was exactly as I'd smelt it on the night of Ben Cavellero's party. Like warm summer rain had drawn the aroma from moist soil.

I flushed the toilet and went to swill my hands under the tap (thankfully, water still flowed sweet and clear). I reached for the towel.

The next thing I knew I stood in the kitchen. It was dark. I fumbled round the worktop for the torch and switched it on. The battery-powered clock on the wall told me it was 1:30.

I looked down at my bare knees. I was wearing nothing but the shorts I normally wore for bed. Strands of dried grass still stuck to my knees. The bathroom towel still hung from my left hand.

My mouth felt so weirdly dry I had to gulp down half a carton of orange juice to knock the edge off my thirst.

What had happened to me? Where had I been?

I rubbed my stomach. The muscles felt twitchy as if I'd just had the shock of my life, but for the world I didn't know what the hell it was.

All I did know was that it had gone and happened again. I'd lost an hour of my life and I didn't have a clue what I'd done in that time. The image of that grey face came back. Had I seen it again tonight? I turned to look at the door that led into the back garden. I had the torch. I could go and look. But for some reason the very idea terrified me. If I opened that door I knew what I'd see just outside.

There would be that grey face; there would be those eyes that had the power to stare right through to the back of my head. Jesus, Jesus, I didn't want to experience that again. Fear shook my hands so much that it made the torch beam send a circle of light wobbling across the kitchen wall. No. I didn't want to see that face again. Just the recollection of it appalled me. But why, for godsakes? I began to rationalize it away again. *That Friday night. What did you see, Rick? Surely it was just fungus, or a . . . or a piece of raw wood where a branch had been wrenched from the trunk in a gale.*

So, what is it you saw, Rick?

I saw an awful thing. Grey-faced. Eyes that stabbed you in the heart . . . terrible eyes . . . it wants me . . . it has plans for me . . .

My heart thumped, my mouth turned paper-dry. I didn't know . . . Christ, I couldn't say why, but I was so frightened sweat pricked out through every square centimetre of my skin. I turned my back on the door and headed quickly for the stairs. No way in Hell would I open that door tonight. No way would I see what lurked in the garden. I wouldn't allow it to take me again. No way would I permit those filthy great hands to seize me . . .

But what did *happen to you, Rick? Why can't you remember?*

Six steps up I stopped.

And I told myself, 'You're not going to let this thing beat you, Rick.' That's when I did something stupid.

I turned round, walked right back down those steps, crossed the kitchen floor, opened the door . . . and walked outside.

* * *

Tuesday. We still had our refugees. Tents appeared on the village green, football field and sundry bits of grassland. Life became more organized and here and there you'd see orderly queues of people standing in line for breakfast. We – S Group, that is – were still hunting down supplies of baby food. The little tykes were devouring it as soon as we could get our hands on it.

It was decided that we should now see if it was safe to take the hunt for baby food toward the suburbs of Leeds, where we could crack open the big supermarkets – but we were warned not to go into Leeds itself because the gas might not yet have dispersed.

Stephen and I walked down to Fullwood's Garage. We chatted in a fairly light-hearted kind of way. Every so often I'd think about the hour I'd lost the night before. I wondered if I should tell Stephen, but in the warm light of that July morning it seemed too absurd to even give jaw time to. Now the memory of me coming to in the kitchen with the bath towel in my hand seemed no more real than a bad dream. Even my late-night hunt round the garden dressed only in shorts, nervously flashing the torch into hedge bottoms, jumping when I disturbed a neighbour's cat, was nothing less than laughable. At least, it seemed like that now. But last night, alone in the dark, my heart pounding like it desperately wanted to escape through my chest wall . . . Hell, I admit it, I was scared.

Also we had more important things to occupy our minds. Motorbikes were being organized for us because the word coming back from people who'd scouted the fringes of city was that most of the roads were blocked by abandoned vehicles. We couldn't carry much baby food on a bike but at least the bikes would get us through.

The sun burned through the early-morning mist. In the fields the acres of humanity were slowly coming to life after another night beneath the stars.

'Lucky this didn't happen in winter,' Stephen said. 'They'd have been dropping like flies from the cold.'

'At this rate they'll still be here come winter.'

'Pessimist.'

'Nope, realist. No one's heard a dicky-bird from London yet.'

'Well, your Prime Minister's still at Number 10.'

'So they're telling us.'

'Come on, you cynic, you, S Group are waiting for us. All right, campers!' Stephen cheerfully shouted as he walked into the garage. I saw he brought a big smile to their faces. He had a knack of cheering people up just by walking into a room; now he walked amongst the twenty or so people there, dishing out hifives, slaps on backs and light-hearted comments. 'Hey, dig the boots, Dean, so wellingtons are *de rigueur* this summer . . . Wow, old Sparky.' Howard Sparkman grinned like a school kid singled out for an affectionate ribbing by a favourite teacher. 'Sparky, my man. Where did you get that shirt? I mean where did you *get it*? Don't tell me, don't tell me. You bought it from *Stripy Shirts 'R Us*.' But instantly he could morph that high-octane DJ voice into one that was sensitive, concerned. 'All right, Stenno. How's the eye, buddy?'

Stenno, sitting on a pile of used tyres, pulled a weak smile. One eye was nearly puffed shut. The hospital dressing covered the eyebrow. 'OK, Stephen. Thanks.' Then he looked back down at the oil-blackened concrete floor as if he was working out some elaborate piece of mental arithmetic.

I decided to grab the opportunity before Pat Murray arrived to ask Stenno what exactly had happened on Friday night. I remembered what I'd seen . . . what I *thought* I'd seen when we went into the woods. Now I had this urgent need to compare notes with him. Had he seen who had attacked him? What had frightened him so much?

Skirting the inspection pit, I headed toward him.

'Boys and girls. Can I have one moment of your time, please?'

Too late. We were being called to attention. Howard caught my eye, stood up straight, arms by his side military style, and smiled. I shrugged. I'd grab a minute with Stenno before we left.

I saw today that Pat Murray's place was taken by Bill Fullwood, the owner of the garage. Even though way past seventy he still dressed like a grease monkey in a baggy boiler suit and boots with steel toe-caps. There wasn't much in the way of hair on his head, but what there was (you know what old men's hair is like: baby-fine, white) floated in the air and made you think of the way a swimmer's hair floats when they're under water. He was one of those people who seemed such an ancient fixture of the village you'd swear he'd been there as long as the village church. He shopped at the supermarket where I worked and as far as I could tell the old man lived on nothing but tinned tuna fish. Still, he looked all right on it, if he was still wrestling gearboxes out of cars at his age.

The garage was an Aladdin's cave of ancient bicycles, motor bikes – there was even a dusty Jag parked in one corner whose tyres hadn't kissed road tar in twenty years. It seemed to be contentedly waiting for the day it would be lovingly carried away to some motor museum.

'Gather round, boys and girls.' The voice was kind but tired-sounding. 'I don't want to strain these old vocal cords more than need be.'

We all moved closer, with the exception of Stenno who stayed on the tyres as if his butt had been bolted there. He stared at the floor. There in body; not in mind.

'Boys and girls, we have a splendid treat for you today. We have scoured this fair land for motorcycles. Mr Stenton and I then burned the midnight oil affixing panniers and servicing the engines so they will take you to your destinations, then return you safely home. Those of you who haven't ridden these wonderful two-wheeled stallions before will receive proper instructions how to do so. The rest will proceed to said machines and go forth to their appointed destinations. Which I have written down here on ... now, now where did I put it?' Slowly he searched through his pockets, then reached inside his boiler suit sleeve. 'Ah, here we are ... maps and pencils at the ready, boys and girls. Mr Dean Skilton, and Mr Howard Sparkman. You are to make haste to Scarcroft. Miss Melody Gisburn and Mr Tony—'

'WHAT HAVE *YOU* COME BACK FOR!'

You couldn't have swivelled heads faster unless you'd fired a gun into the garage roof. Everyone spun round to look at Stenno. His face had bleached white. But his ears flushed an absurdly brilliant red. He'd come off his stack of tyres and was slowly advancing towards the group.

'Why did you pick on me! Clear off ... go on. *Clear off!*'

He walked towards us. But he moved in a strange way. For all the world it looked as if someone had put a ring through his nose, threaded that with a line, then handed me the line to reel in. Arms down by his side, he walked bent forward at the waist, his face jutting out towards us as if pulled by that invisible line. The eyes blazed in an unblinking stare, the lips of his mouth peeled back to show his tongue clenched between his teeth.

It was one of those moments when there seemed to be nothing you could actually do. Other than just wait and see what happened next.

What did happen next was a mixture of the absurd and the frightening.

His eyes locked on me; he pointed his finger at me. Then he ranted.

'What you come back for! Why did you pick on me!' He repeated the words over and over in a throat-stripping shout. 'Why me! Why me! Why don't you leave me alone! You fucking well touch me again . . . don't you fucking dare! Don't you fucking dare!'

His eyes were like I saw them on Friday night when he lay on the lawn, face covered in blood. Iris and pupil shrunk to a black spot. And they were locked on my face. And I mean face, not eyes. I'd been in plenty of fights before. Then it was all eye contact, closer and closer until your noses were almost touching. But you never broke eye contact.

Then Stenno barely made it. Those black dots in the middle of their whites flicked around my face as if he was seeing boils the size of yogurt cartons erupting from the skin. And all the time he was yelling. 'Go away. Leave me alone. Touch me again, touch me again and I swear I'll kill you. *I'LL KILL YOU!*'

He still advanced. One step at a time. Face jutting forward. Eyes still blazing. But they were blazing as much with fear as anger. For some reason he was terrified of me. People moved aside as he approached. They were obviously puzzled and shocked by what was happening. But ready to leave the two of us to sort it out between ourselves.

'Bastard . . . bastard!' he screeched at me in a spray of spit. 'Bastard!'

Stephen moved smoothly forward, holding out a calming hand. 'Easy there, buddy. There's no problem.'

Stenno still aimed his rage and terror at me. 'Bastard . . . out that fucking door . . . fucking bastard!'

'Easy, Stenno.' Stephen said gently. 'Let's just talk about this.'

'Do you know what that fucker did to me?' Out came the spit scream again. 'Fucker hurt me. Fucking well hurt me. Go away. Go a-fucking-way. D'ya hear me?'

Now the eyes of the others were flicking from Stenno to me. Rising through their shock and their fear there would be a fight was curiosity too. What had I done to make Stenno as angry, as crazily angry as this?

Stephen made calming noises. Bill Fullwood, as Stenno's employer, had a go at exerting some authority. 'I don't know what's happened between you two. But this isn't the place or the time.' He shot me a glance. 'You'd better take a walk until laddo here calms down.'

But Stenno's fury was volcanic. He still approached in that single-step way, his face thrust forward as if I was slowly pulling him toward me, hand over hand, with that invisible line.

'*Basss – tarddd . . .*'

'Easy, Stenno—' began Stephen.

Bill pointed a trembling old-man finger at me, then at Stenno. 'I don't want to know the ins and outs of this argument. Rick, you wait down by the Swan; someone'll call you later. We'll get—'

'Friday night . . .' The voice came cracking from Stenno's throat like he was on fire. 'Friday night . . . do you know what that *thing* did to me?'

Everyone stared at me. On top of the shock of seeing Stenno flip his skull another emotion came charging in. Guilt. I actually felt guilty. I found myself searching my memory for something I might have done to him. It must have been pretty foul for him to react like this. White-faced, red-eared, spit spraying out from his mouth at every screeched word. That weird single-step walk, steel-capped boots clumping down onto the concrete floor as he approached me, his menace and his terror fusing into one emotion that was as dangerous as it was shocking.

Stephen touched my arm and said softly, 'Rick. Walk away from this. Do as the old man says.'

Easier said then done. One second Stenno was taking one halting step at a time toward me. The next he'd reached across to a shelf, picked up a piece of iron the size of a baseball bat and had positioned himself between me and the garage doors.

Shit. Showdown time. Believe me, I'd no argument with Stenno. But if he took a swipe at me with that thing I'd have to try and tackle him. Either that, or stand there calmly and wait for my skull to be crushed. Neither option appealed. But I knew what I'd have to go for.

He was working himself into a roaring fury. I knew the attack would be just seconds away.

Stephen saw it, too. Somewhere on the edge of my vision I saw Stephen making eye contact with Howard and Dean as if to say, 'Help me grab Stenno and calm him down.'

I don't know what their reaction was, I was too busy concentrating on Stenno. He was all meat. Once he started moving I couldn't block the blow, I'd have to dodge. Dodge fast or I'd be coffin fodder.

He held the iron bar high in both hands like he was taking a swing in a baseball game. My head would be the ball.

He shook the iron bar. He was winding himself up for the first swing.

I backed off. The others looked at each other helplessly, knowing the man intended to murder me.

Still he screeched at me, spit flying from his mouth, 'Friday night! Do you know what the bastard did to me. Do you? Do you know what it did? I – I'll fucking crush him!'

He swung. The bar was heavy and took time to pick up speed. It wasn't difficult to back-step to avoid the scything blow coming from left to right.

He swung again.

Again I back-stepped easily.

The obvious thing for me to do now was bide my time, then, when the opportunity presented itself, simply run for the open garage door.

Slash. The club swung again.

And again I back-stepped. To my left and a little behind me the sunlight blazed in through the doors, illuminating a vast swathe of oil-stained concrete floor. The next time he swung the iron bar I'd turn and run before he got chance to lift the bar for another swipe.

He raised the club for a downward hit, like he going to hammer a tent peg. This time I'd run.

But this time, I stepped back on a slick of wet oil. My foot slipped out from under me. I fell back. I'd have gone all the way supine, but my butt slammed into the radiator grille of that old Jag. My balance was shot I couldn't move back any further; the next blow would crack my skull.

I looked up at that white face. Those black-dot eyes still blazed down at me. Hating me. Wanting nothing more than to shatter my skull; to splatter my brains, my blood, my ruptured eyes all over the bonnet of the car.

Then he paused. The expression, locking his mouth wide open, was nothing but all-out, mind-blowing terror.

He looked down at my face as if I'd undergone some even more terrible transformation.

'NO! DON'T DO THAT TO ME AGAIN, DON'T DO IT AGAIN!'

From all directions Stephen, Dean, Howard, even the old man rushed in, to stop him slamming that iron bar down onto my head.

I threw my arms up to protect my face; held my breath, gritted my teeth, as—

Shit.

He moved with a crazed speed.

The club blurred through the air. But he no longer held it. He'd thrown it wildly at me. It buzzed above my head; I felt its slipstream tug my air and—

BANG!

It crashed down hard behind me.

Now Stenno backed off, shaking his head, panting. The eyes still locked on me in that pure, nerve-rending terror.

He screamed. Then ran.

His workman boots hit the concrete like hammers. And he was gone. Dean ran to the door, looked out, then turned and shook his head, arms out, which I read to mean Stenno wasn't coming back.

A sense of relief went through everyone like a wave. I took a deep breath, pulled myself to my feet.

I stood there looking at the faces that looked back at me. I felt like a condemned man. The silence seemed to go on and on. And like that Friday night I felt as if people were expecting me to confess some terrible, terrible sin.

At last the old man ruefully rubbed his jaw and nodded at the Jag behind me. 'Well, that saves me at least one dusting job.'

I looked back at the car. The iron bar, meant for my face, had gone clean through the windscreen.

CHAPTER 12

We'd been riding the motorbikes less than five minutes when Stephen signalled for me to stop. We'd been asked to try our luck at a supermarket in Headingley. Supplies of baby food were still needed but there was a growing mood of confidence in the village. Rumours were flying that the crisis had all but passed. Soon the army would roll in with fleets of buses and trucks to take the refugees back home.

Stephen sat astride the bike, feet on the floor, the motor ticking over. He pulled off his helmet, scratching his head where it had rubbed. He was wearing shades and I felt nothing but pride that I was the brother of this guy with the cool LA rock star good looks.

'Hey, Kid K, you all right?'

'I'm fine.' I twisted the throttle lightly and the bike gave a satisfying snarl.

Stephen looked me in the eye. 'Is what that guy did still bugging you?'

'Stenno? It was the way he looked at me. *Just me.* As if I'd shafted his wife or something.'

'He must have taken a hell of a knock on the head on Friday night, you know.' He looked at me sympathetically. 'If you ask me that guy's still a little out to lunch. You follow?'

'I suppose you're right. Weird way to act, though.'

'Sure you're OK?'

'No worries.'

He nodded, started to put the helmet back on over his head. Then he looked at it as if the thing smelt too cheesy for words. With a grin at me, he lobbed the helmet into the ditch. 'We're on a mission of mercy.' He laughed. 'No one's going to book us for not wearing a shitty helmet.'

I shook my head, smiling.

'*All right*. Rick, you know *C'mon Everybody* by the late great Mr Eddie Cochran?'

'Know it? The band plays it every gig.'

'C'mon on, then. Let's rock and roll.' He twisted the throttle and rocketed away. Above the roar of his bike I could hear him singing at the top of his voice.

With a cowboy yodel I slung my helmet into the bushes and followed. Soon we were riding side by side, wind zithering our hair, singing in harmony and shooting these massive grins at each other.

The road was empty. The sun shone. A couple of horses were playing chase-me, chase-me in a nearby field. We passed the occasional abandoned pram or bike or duvet that had been spalled off from the exodus of city folk on the way up to Fairburn. But it didn't seem particularly horrific. All this would be cleared up in next to no time, or so we told ourselves. Then there would be TV post mortems and public enquiries aplenty until we were bored to death with it all.

That's what we were telling ourselves right then. But the truth was going to be a whole different ball game. The truth was going to be nothing less than evil. And the future was going to be Hell.

So, naively, we rode along the country roads, hitting shadow beneath trees then bursting into brilliant sunlight again.

As soon as we joined the main Leeds road we saw human life

again. There was an army checkpoint consisting of a green truck and half a dozen soldiers sitting in the shade of a tree.

A squaddie stripped down to nothing but camouflage trousers, a bush hat and a *Land Of Hope And Glory* tattoo scrolling across his chest flagged us down. 'No, you don't, lads. You'll have to turn back the way you came.'

I told him, 'We're looking for supplies. We've got some hungry mouths to feed.'

He looked down at the bikes we were riding. 'Where did you get these from?'

'They were loaned to us.'

'Stolen? Right?'

'No.'

Stephen began to explain, 'We volunteered to help find food for—'

'You're American?'

'Yeah, I'm American. Look, we'd be very grateful if you'd let us through to—'

'You dropped lucky, then. You here on holiday?'

I saw Stephen shake his head, puzzled. 'What does it matter? I'm staying with my brother here until—'

'Until the twelfth of never. America's fucked.'

'America's what?' Stephen cast me a glance and I guessed he was wondering if this tattooed squaddie had been standing out in the sun too long.

'America,' the squaddie said cheerfully. 'It's fucked.'

The sun felt like a chunk of hot iron pressing against the back of my neck. This I didn't need. A surreal argument with a sun-addled squaddie.

Stephen tried to talk his way, patiently, diplomatically, through the log jam in the man's brain.

'Look. Here's a letter from a Dr Abraham Hanson of the Woodside surgery in Fairburn.'

'Fair-what? Never heard of the fucker.'

'It's a village about five kilometres back that way.'

'Best go back that way, then. You're not coming through.'

'Look,' Stephen struggled to keep cool. 'We need to go through. We're looking for baby food.'

'Baby food?'

Yes, it's the stuff you feed to babies, you fucking arsehole. I thought it, but didn't say it. Though I was mightily tempted.

'There are about forty thousand people camped out at Fairburn,' Stephen explained in a voice that was all reason and light. 'There's a lot of babies up there that need feeding. If we can't get—'

The sullen no-go, no-way look in the man's eyes suddenly changed. He'd obviously suddenly got a mental picture of hungry babies crying for their feed.

'Corp! Hey, corp!' he shouted. 'Moment of your time . . . *please*.' The squaddie managed to make the 'please' sound like a profanity.

Corp ambled up with a two-kilo plastic bag of rice in his hands that he was trying to tear open.

'What's up, Spud?' He looked us up and down before returning to the bag.

'These two lads want to go through to Leeds.'

'You don't want to go there, lads. Place isn't safe.'

'We don't want to go into Leeds itself. We're picking up supplies of baby food from supermarkets on the edge of town.'

'You're wasting your time. All the shops are shut.'

'We know. We're breaking in.'

'Breaking in? Sure you've got authority?'

'We've got this letter.'

Corp read it, bored, before returning to the problem of the tough plastic that was for the moment keeping the dried rice from its appointment with a pan of boiling water. 'It's risky, boys. A: we don't know if the gas has dispersed. B: you'll have to be quick on the draw with that piece of paper of yours – our lot'll be shooting looters, you know?'

'We'll be careful.'

'You're American?' asked Corp, now taking his teeth to the plastic.

'Yes, I'm American.' I heard the sigh in Stephen's voice that clearly meant, *Oh Christ, here we go again.*

'I told him, Corp,' the squaddie said with near-brutal satisfaction. 'America's fucked.'

'Oh, shit.' Corp's teeth had ripped a hole in the bag; rice trickled out over his fists. 'Shitting stupid packaging.'

'What shall I do with these two, Corp?'

Corp was more interested in getting the rice into his pan. 'Uh? Oh, let 'em through. Just say we can't guarantee their safety.'

The squaddie turned back to relay the message to us. Stephen smiled politely. 'It's OK, we heard.'

'Like the man said, be quick with the quack's letter or you might end up with a shell between your ears.'

'We will, thanks.' Stephen gave an artificial smile. 'And have a nice day.'

'And make sure you stay out of Leeds. It's all—' The sound of our bikes' engines drowned him out.

As we headed into the suburbs we slowed to little more than walking speed. I pulled level with Stephen and said, 'What do you think that squaddie meant by "America's fucked?"'

'Search me. At first I thought he'd been out in the sun too long but the other guy was going to say the same thing.'

'There's been nothing on the news?'

'There has been *nothing* on the news,' Stephen agreed. 'That's just it. A big fat heap of nothing. Nothing specific, anyway. There's only been general news reports. And have you noticed the national stations don't even mention what's happened in Leeds anymore? As far as the rest of the United Kingdom is concerned everything is just hunky-dory here.'

We rode through a deserted housing estate. The streets were littered with blankets, pyjamas, socks, bedroom slippers, suitcases stuffed any old how with clothes, carrier bags with more clothes. And, resting on a garden wall, a bird cage with a budgie lying dead in the bottom.

We paused to look round at the cluttered streets. We were smiling at each other; not because there was anything amusing or comic about the litter of personal effects dropped by people in their hurry to escape. The scene was simply too surreal to comprehend. Smiling was a way of dealing with the emotion it evoked.

Because I realized then there was something frightening about the emptiness of the housing estate. All those semi-detached houses. All stripped stark bollock naked of human life. Just three days ago everyone who lived here had woken up choking for breath. That invisible gas had simply driven them out with what belongings they could snatch up as they stumbled from their houses. Clearly, many had realized as they'd hurried coughing and spluttering through those night-time streets that they'd tried to bring too much and they'd just dumped a suitcase here, a duvet there.

So there we were, with the sun burning down, slowly weaving in and out of all those dumped holdalls, carrier bags, boxes, stiletto shoes, overcoats, broken prams.

I felt my chest tighten. Was it the gas still lingering there? Or was it just because I found myself imagining only too clearly the panic that must have gripped that community when they woke up in the middle of the night knowing that for the first time in their lives the very air had turned poisonous?

And at that time it was still a mystery where the gas had come from. Most guessed it was some kind of toxic spill from a chemical plant. On top of that, there were rumours circulating about a freak flood hitting London. Hard on the heels of that one were more stories about a major fire burning out the heart of Coventry and some kind of earthquake hitting Edinburgh. Not that those were taken seriously. At the time.

'Rick . . . Rick.' Stephen pointed at a mini-mart at the end of the road. 'We'll load up there.'

It took a good twenty minutes of hammering to smash in the front door. Normally the store's alarm system would have been shrieking distress all over the neighbourhood but with no electricity it stayed mute.

We soon had the bike's panniers full of the drums of powdered baby food. We filled backpacks, too. Stephen suggested that we get back to Fairburn as quickly as we could, then return with cars or even a truck. Although the roads were cluttered they weren't impassable.

I was more than ready to kick off the bikes and head back to Fairburn. To tell you the truth that silent hundred acres of middle-class suburban housing was preying on my nerves. A ghost town? No. I wouldn't even have called it a ghost town. Ghosts would have given the place a sense of occupancy. Here there was no one, and nothing but an oppressive sense of emptiness.

'Hang on, Rick. I'm going to help myself to a soda. Want one?'

'Yeah, sure, my throat's as dry as sandpaper.' In truth, I wanted us on those bikes and tearing out of town, but my throat had a dried-out burning feel to it. I could down a can of coke or whatever in ten seconds flat – then we could fire up the bikes and fuck off fast.

The mini-mart, with the shutters locked down and the electricity killed, was a gloomy, shadowed place. I began to realize that if the townspeople didn't return soon looters would move in to pick the shelves clean as a whistle. Even I was wondering whether to find space in my backpack full of baby-milk powder for a bottle of scotch or two.

'Stephen? Where are you?'

'In the back. Through the door between the chill cabinets. Hold your breath as you come through, the dairy products are just a teeny-weeny bit past their sell-by date.'

'Jesus Christ, you're not kidding.' The fresh foods were rotting on their shelves. I tried to keep exhaling all the way through into the back room, which served as a warehouse-cum-rest room complete with kitchen sink, kettle, carton of rancid milk and two easy chairs.

'What are you looking for?' I asked.

'I just wanted to rinse my face in the sink. It must be the dust but my eyes are stinging like crazy.'

I remembered my dry throat. 'Stephen. I think it must the gas; my throat feels as if I've swallowed sandpaper.'

He turned on the cold water tap. It ran fast and clear. 'I don't think we need to worry too much. As far as the general viewpoint goes it was more an irritant than anything truly life-threatening. I'll just sluice my face and we'll hit the—'

'What the Hell's that noise?'

Stephen smiled. 'Sounds like your quaint British plumbing. Just listen to those pipes sing.'

'Hardly sing it sounds more like a jet taking off.'

'Well, as long as it's cold and wet.' He began to splash water on his face. 'Shit . . . they've got their hot and cold faucets mixed up. The water's warm.'

'Stephen . . .' I noticed the pressure increase behind the water, driving it so forcefully from the tap it slammed against the sink bottom before splashing out onto the floor. 'Stephen. There's something wrong about all this.'

'Just give me a minute to get some water into my eyes . . . feels like I've slept in contacts.' The plumbing now thumped and clanged as though legions of demon drummers were beating the pipes with iron bars.

Stephen cupped water to his face. 'All right. You don't know how good that feels. Maybe we should—'

Brrrrrr . . .

It sounded like a speedboat powering through the pipes from the mains. I could almost track the motor-like sound as it entered the mini-mart beneath the wall behind me and passed under my feet, making the concrete floor vibrate.

Instinct. That's all it was. I jumped forward and pushed Stephen away from the sink so hard he fell flat on his face on the floor.

'Rick! What the hell are you playing at, you—'

The rest of what he shouted was drowned by a head-battering roar. One second water streamed from the tap. Then, with a burst of spray, it turned to steam.

I moved back, but not before I took some scalding drops of water on my arm. Stephen was on his feet in a second. He watched in disbelief as clouds of steam came out of the tap with a terrific *scree—eeech*.

He shouted something. I couldn't hear a word above the god-awful noise. Soon the room was full of steam so thick you could hardly see beyond the tip of your nose. Blindly we made it through the door, through the gauntlet stink of rotting food. Then we were out in sunlight.

Stephen shook his head. 'Of all the kitchen sinks I could have chosen I had to pick the one plumbed in by son of Basil Fawlty. I mean, did you see that mother? You could have cleaned truck engines with a steam jet like that.'

'Are you OK?'

He grinned. 'I'm fine. Probably cleaner than I've been for a day or two . . . but fine.' As I climbed onto my bike he slapped my arm. 'Say, quick thinking, Kid K. If you hadn't shoved me that steam spray would have taken my face clean off.'

The thing had shaken me, but I forced a smile. 'That's what brothers are for. Come on, let's go home.'

With the backpacks on our shoulders clunking with cans of baby food we eased the bikes forward, down that road of spilled clothes and discarded baby buggies.

'I know a short cut,' I shouted to Stephen. 'Take the next left.'

It was short cut all right. But not to Fairburn. It was a short cut straight to the shit-stinking heart of Hell itself.

CHAPTER 13

Hell is a street in Leeds.

How do you know you've just ridden a motorbike straight to Hell? This is how:

SIMON CLARK

ONE: THE SMELL
The stench rolling down that tree-lined residential street suggested the sewers had backed up to overflowing. Now the summer sun was baking up a rich stew of what, a few days ago, four hundred thousand people had been flushing away down their lavatories.

TWO: DEAD BIRDS
Sparrows, pigeons, starlings, blackbirds; they littered the streets in little balls of fluff and feathers. We tried to avoid them, but occasionally one would go *pop* beneath our tyres.

THREE: THE DEAD MAN
Stephen signalled me to stop. 'Rick. Did you see that back there?'

'No. What?'

'Well, you'd best not look, then.'

I saw a reflection of my puzzled face in his sunglasses. 'What're you talking about?'

'Back there.' He jerked a thumb over his shoulder. 'There's a guy lying dead under a blanket at the side of the road.'

'You sure?'

'I saw his legs poking out from under the blanket.'

'I mean, are you sure he's dead?'

'Good point.' Stephen wiped his mouth with the back of his hand. 'Wait here. I'll check.'

I climbed off the bike, pulled it back on to its stand, ready to follow.

'Hey, whoa, whoa. Where do you think you're going, Rick?'

'I'll come with you.'

'No, sunshine. You stay put here.'

'You can't pull the big brother trick on me, Stephen. I'm nineteen, in case it's slipped your mind.'

He took a couple of steps towards me, putting his body between me and whatever lay under the red blanket about thirty metres along the street. 'Rick ...' He took off the shades and fixed me with the blue eyes. 'Have you ever seen a corpse that's been lying out in the sun for three days?'

'Have you?'

'No ... but last year I called on an old pool-hall buddy of mine who'd decided that life on Earth wasn't for him. I walked into his apartment just ten minutes after he'd taken his head off with a shotgun. So, Rick, if you are really, really itching to look a dead man in the face, walk this way. Only I do not recommend

68

the experience. OK, you coming?' Grim-faced, he held out an arm as if he was going to lead me there by the hand.

I gave a shake of my head and turned my back on the thing beneath the blanket.

Sure. Believe me. I was curious to see what a dead person looked like. I'd never seen one before. In fact, people go through their whole lives without ever seeing a single corpse. In the cold flesh, that is; we've all seen them on TV. Society buries its dead. But what you don't really realize is that society buries its dead at the moment of death. Hey presto! They disappear behind hospital screens, or are zipped from sight in body bags, or are hidden in mortuaries and chapels of rest until they're nailed down into coffins ready for the funeral.

I glanced back over my shoulder at Stephen crouching down ten paces from the body to give it the once-over. And I found myself resenting the way he'd treated me like some oh-so-sensitive little child who'd sob over a squashed butterfly.

An airliner passed overhead, no doubt waiting for air traffic control to give it the green light to land. There was a surge of noise from the jet engines as it rode through the dazzling blue sky, then out of sight once more over the rooftops.

I shrugged my shoulders to reposition the straps of the backpack to make it more comfortable.

Then I saw one of those weird things that always seem to pop up to juxtapose grim tragedy (in this case, the guy being left to chill beneath his blanket) with the bizarre.

I'm looking up a driveway, right? To a three-storey building with ceiling-to-floor windows on the ground floor. A sign says: *SOVEREIGN PLACE. RETIREMENT HOME.* And there, slap in the middle of that driveway, was a glass fish tank. The size of a portable TV, it was still full of water. Needing something to take my attention from what Stephen would soon be examining down the street, I sauntered across to it.

I wrinkled my nose. The smell was worse. Though I couldn't pin all the blame onto that fish tank even though the water had turned green and two goldfish lay belly-up in all that slime.

I looked back to where Stephen crouched, one hand clamping a handkerchief to his nostrils, the other holding a stick which he used to lift the blanket.

Thankfully, from this distance, I couldn't see what lay beneath the blanket.

I turned away, glad to look at the old folks' home that still wore a look of near normality with—

'*Uhhh . . . Chrr—rist . . .*'

I locked my eyes onto the old folks' home. That's just it. The place shouldn't have looked as normal as that. Not with white-haired old ladies behind the day-room windows, snoozing the morning away in their Shackleton high chairs until lunch.

It was completely involuntary. If I'd stopped right then, counted to ten, I wouldn't have done it. But I ran straight up to the windows. And took a long hard look inside.

'Stephen!'

There, sitting in the chairs, were ten or more old women. One old man in pyjamas lay on the settee.

If they'd looked as if they were asleep it wouldn't have been as bad as that brutal sight that hit me straight in the eye.

Most still wore their day clothes. All were dead.

But it was the look of sheer bloody agony on their faces. They hadn't died peacefully in their sleep. Their mouths yawned so wide I'd swear some of the jaws had dislocated. Eyes stared wide open. Their faces still blasted out a picture of sheer dismay, sheer agony, sheer terror. They had died slowly, knowing full well they could not breathe that lung-scalding gas that had filled their home.

Now, in the stifling heat behind those greenhouse-like windows, the agonized faces were inflating with liquid as internal organs rotted and melted, turning faces black.

I backed away, a bad taste rising. I swallowed it down. Then turned, intending to walk back to tell Stephen what I'd found.

Then I saw what had been hidden by the hedge.

I tried to walk steadily by it. I tried to shut out of my mind what I saw. I tried to turn my head so I couldn't see them.

I tried. And failed.

CHAPTER 14

Grotesque. There's no other description for it: grotesque, grotesque, **GROTESQUE**. I remember feeling anger as well as horror. Perhaps, like we all do, we pretend old people die calmly, with dignity. These, through no fault of their own, had not.

I walked down the drive toward the bike, the backpack full of baby food swinging against my back. 'Stephen.'

The more mobile of the old men and women from the home had tried to escape the gas. Maybe some had made it.

These had not.

They had tried to reach the cars parked at the side of the home. One car – and it was so perverse some little splinter of gallows humour inside of me wanted to laugh out loud – well, listen to this, one car was actually a hearse. Big, black and sleek, it stood there with all the doors open, including the big coffin hatch-door at the back.

A fat old boy sat on the ground, his back to one of its tyres. Frozen to his face, that look of terror as he'd suffocated. He wore what must have been the first item of clothing he could put his hands on in the panic – a woman's pink dressing gown trimmed with white lace at the hem and sleeves. It had rucked up around his waist to show his shitty underpants.

Half in and half out of the back of the hearse, where the undertakers slide the coffin, was a naked woman. All of ninety years of age, she lay face down in the back with her bare arse hanging out in the not-so-fresh air. A couple more old dears lay near-naked or stark naked on the grass, mouths and eyes wide open, their bellies nine months pregnant-looking from the gas brewing in their guts.

'Stephen.'

Some of the corpses had shat. One or two bled from their mouths, leaving heads haloed by a pool as black and as sticky as tar. The meat flies buzzed. One old woman, dressed in a daffodil-yellow frock, lay on the grass. Fanned out in her fingers, like she was holding a hand of playing cards, were photographs. They showed her sitting happily beside her grandson at his birthday party as she helped him blow out the candles.

The expression on her face now made you imagine she'd been forced to dance barefoot on broken glass. Her dentures had slipped out of her mouth with the rush of puke that, now dried, glued her hair to the lawn.

For no real reason I heard a voice in my head whisper:

> *God is great,*
> *God is good.*

I walked toward the entrance gates. My eyesight had gone to shit. I couldn't breathe. I nearly tripped over the corpse of a naked woman. That's when I felt a hand grab my shoulder.

'Christ, the bastards . . .' It was Stephen's voice, filled with disgust. 'The bastards. When the gas came they left the poor devils to die.' He looked down at the naked woman laid flat out by our feet. 'Something's started feeding on them. Rats or foxes. Uh . . . just look at the mess they've made of her fanny.'

'Fanny!' I remember shouting. 'Fanny? What're you talking? Yankee or English?'

I ran. Was I laughing? Yanked to the brink of madness. Or was I crying? Shit knows. All I did know was that there was a strange sound working up through my belly to stutter out through my lips.

I made it as far as the bushes at the far side of the road. A branch snagged the backpack; it stopped me from running any further.

There I puked my breakfast up. No, I didn't, I puked my whole bagful of guts up – and probably a fair chunk of my heart, too.

At last I stopped. Dazed, I looked down where I'd vomited.

And I saw I'd vomited onto the bare legs of two little children who lay dead on the grass beneath the bushes, their arms tightly around one another in one last post mortem cuddle.

I turned away. And although there was nothing left in my stomach, I vomited again.

'You sure you're OK now?' I opened my eyes. Stephen was tipping Perrier over my head and rubbing the back of my neck. Concern filled his blue eyes.

'Fine.'

'Can you stand?'

'Shit. I thought I *was* standing.'

'Rick. I don't want to hang around here. There's no sign of life – birds, cats dogs, anything. I think the gas must have settled here. The place is in a dip between two hills. We should get – hey, hey, kid. Take it easy. Don't spark out on me again, OK?'

'Give me a drink. I'll be fine.'

'You're not fine. We'll take this nice and easy, OK?'

I made it back to the motorbike, legs switching between jelly and elastic. After a couple more minutes of managing both to shiver and sweat buckets at the same time I nodded to Stephen and started the engine. Overhead the jetliner, cutting a note of normality through the sky, made another pass.

Stephen anxiously scanned my face, trying to gauge how fit I was to ride. 'Rick. You've had a hell of a shock. Why don't we grab a car and I'll drive you back home?'

'No.' Call it pride but I was determined to ride the bike back. 'Believe me, Stephen. I'm all right.'

All right as long as you can forget the old woman lying bare arsed and rotting in the hearse; all right if you can forget the two little children dead in the grass. All right if you forget everything, full damn stop.

I rocked the bike forward off its stand. Stephen slipped the sunglasses back onto his face, nodded grimly and slowly accelerated away.

We soon saw signs of recent activity – human activity, that is.

We slowed the bikes as we passed a parade of shops. 'Looters,' said Stephen matter-of-factly.

Some of the shop windows had been smashed. Booze and tobacco had been stripped from supermarket shelves. Computer and video stores were picked clean.

As we cruised on, the slipstream tumbled banknotes along in the gutter. Perhaps people already realized that money was worthless now.

Stephen slowed to a crawl, feet out at either side of the bike, almost walking it along. He glanced at me and nodded at a car that had run up onto the pavement and into someone's garden wall the force of the impact scattering bricks across the lawn. The car was stuffed with computers and TVs. Two men sat in the front seats, heads tilted savagely backward, their mouths and eyes wide open.

My first thought was that this pair of looters had been shot as they tried to escape with their haul, but the bodies appeared to be unmarked. I shivered. The gas had got them, too.

'Rick,' Stephen called back over his shoulder to me. 'Whatever this gas is, it keeps coming back. We best get away from Leeds pronto. OK?'

'Suits me. I've got no reason to hang round here.'

'We best warn the others as well.' He jerked his head back at the gassed looters. 'It's obviously still taking some people by surprise.'

We upped the speed now, weaving round abandoned cars, gassed cats and dogs, a guy with jailbird tattoos kneeling in the road, his head resting on a stolen TV like he was grabbing forty winks. But one look at the blood that oozed through his lips from his gas-scorched lungs told us he'd be sleeping until dear old Gabriel blew his horn.

We pushed the bikes faster, the tick of the engines becoming a full-blooded roar. We were both eager to reach the high ground where, we hoped, the gas wouldn't reach us even if it did ooze back into the low-lying areas.

At the top of the hill we paused to look back. We'd left the houses behind now. Fairburn was a ten-minute ride away along a pleasant rural road.

'It looks almost normal now, doesn't it?' Stephen nodded at the rooftops of houses with their satellite dishes, TV aerials all gleaming in the summer sun. In the distance the office blocks shone like slabs of crystal. If we hadn't seen what was down there . . . even so, it didn't look much different from the place I'd known for the last ten years.

Overhead the jetliner made its pass, the engines moaning as the pilot slowed the big plane ready for another circuit of the city. We watched it glide by, probably two thousand metres above our heads. Then, high over the city, it seemed to hover, unmoving, looking like a silver crucifix against the blue.

In the plane the passengers might have been reading a book or listening to Streisand on a Walkman, unaware of the tragedy that had hit Leeds. Those bothering to look out of the windows would only see Toytown-sized houses and factories and the occasional flash of sunlight reflected from windows far below.

As I watched, that was when the note of the engine changed. The airliner seemed to rotate slowly in the air and hang there, still looking like a silver crucifix nailed to the clear blue sky.

Then it dropped.

Nose first, the plane came down in a vertical dive.

It fell a good three kilometres away from where we sat on the bikes. A ball of white smoke mushroomed into the air. I found myself waiting for the flames. I saw none. And the sound of the impact seemed to take forever to arrive.

At last it did, a low thundering roar that rolled up the hillside.

I looked at Stephen. For a moment he seemed to be hunting through his vocabulary for the right words to say. Then he shrugged. There was nothing he could say. Same with me. All I could manage was a shake of the head.

In just seventy-two hours the city of Leeds had become a Hell on Earth. Fairburn lay a few minutes' ride away. Although it surely was no Heaven it should have been better than those corpse-strewn roads we'd left behind us. It wasn't.

It was worse.

CHAPTER 15

The instant I saw the woman sitting on the wall in Trueman Way I knew what she was going to do. I'd never seen her before, nor the teenage girl sitting beside her, but I knew as sure as night follows day that she was going to speak to me.

And I knew I wasn't going to be comfortable with what she'd say.

She locked her eyes on mine in a way that suggested she was determined to follow through with some plan she'd made come Hell or high water.

'You live in a house on Trueman Way.'

I shook my head. I didn't stop walking.

'You do.' She smiled warmly, but her brown eyes were as hard as flint. 'You live at number nine; the one with the white door.'

I shook my head puzzled. 'Why do you—'

'You do, don't you?' She didn't give me a chance to reply but surged on. 'My name's Caroline, Caroline Lucas; this is my daughter, Portia. She's sixteen.'

I noticed the girl shoot her mother a surprised look, as if mummy dear had just claimed her daughter was a two-hundred-pound Eskimo chieftain. Mum then shook hands with me, talking all the time. She and daughter Portia were clearly part of the exodus from Leeds. Although their clothes and faces were clean, their shoulder-length hair neatly brushed, they wore the now distinctive refugee look. That look was stamped into their body posture and the way that, although they might look you in the eye at first, their eyes would always drop away as if they'd done something they were ashamed of. I wished they wouldn't do that. I really wished they wouldn't. But we'd split into two races. Those with homes and those without. And you could tell the two apart as clearly as if you'd marked the refugees across the forehead with green aerosol paint.

The woman, in her late thirties, attractive and athletic from no doubt lengthy work-outs in some exclusive fitness suite, introduced me to her daughter again, prompting the girl to shake hands with me. The daughter looked out of her depth and repeatedly looked to her mother for prompts.

'It's a wicked mess, isn't it?' the woman said with an inappropriately broad smile. 'I've heard that some people tried returning to their homes yesterday but the gas came back in the middle of the night and drove them back out. Have you heard where the gas came from?'

I said I hadn't.

'Nor me. But I think it's more serious than they make out.'

I tried to sound reassuring in a woolly kind of way, saying that they'd soon be home.

'That would be wonderful. To sleep in a bed again. With clean sheets. And a real bath. Not a cold-water shower in a canvas cubicle.'

I sympathized.

'You're lucky to still have your house. It looks huge.' She caught my arm as I started to walk. 'You live alone there, don't you?'

'But why—'

'You do, don't you?'

'No, with my brother.'

'Is he home?'

'No, he's in the village. We've just come back from picking up food for the camp.'

'You know, you really have astonishing eyes. I've never seen a shade of blue like that. Portia was just telling me that – *wait.*'

I'd really made up my mind to walk away from the pair.

'Wait.' The woman, smiling prettily, had caught me by the forearm, but then she slid her fingers down lightly over my bare skin to hold my hand. I should have gritted my teeth, walked on without an *au revoir* or anything. But her eyes looked so trusting; her voice sounded so small. She could have been a helpless child standing there.

'You've no idea what it's like to sleep in that field. We've one blanket between us.'

I softened. 'OK. If you follow me I've a couple of spare blankets you can have . . .' She looked up at me, the smile so hopeful that I found myself tagging more items onto the list. 'I might be able to find some spare clothes.' Christ, I sounded so high-and-mighty that I despised what was coming out of my mouth. Like I was some knight in shining armour dishing out a few crumbs to the hungry peasants. 'I'll make you something to eat . . . you can have a hot bath.'

'Look.' Smiling tenderly, she squeezed my hand. 'I'm not going to beat about the bush. You've got a big house. Allow us to stay. We'll cook and clean for you.'

'But—'

'No buts, please. Let us move in. Just for a couple of days.' She smiled, kissed the back of my hand and held it to her cheek, her eyes shining brightly. 'Look, I really want to go to bed with you. I'll be in your hands entirely. You can do what you want; I'll do—'

'There's no need for this.' I looked up and down the street. There were clumps of people sitting on the grass verges but they paid us no attention. 'You'll be home in a few days, then—'

'Hush. Please hush.' She spoke in a low, husky voice. 'This is what I really want. I want to go to bed with you.'

I noticed her wedding ring. 'But your husband won't—'

'I'm not married.'

The daughter looked sharply at her mother again. The look of astonishment in her wide eyes could have been funny. But after what I'd seen that morning there wasn't a laugh inside me. Anywhere.

'Portia will sleep with you, too. She's talked about nothing else.'

Portia looked bewildered and frightened, but she still nodded as if someone jerked her head up and down for her.

'Only you must use a condom with Portia. I don't mind either way.'

'No.' I tried to pull away.

'I'm extremely accommodating. Either way. I don't mind.'

'I'm not interested.'

'Please. I'll—'

I tugged my hand from her grasp and walked away. I heard her shout behind me: 'All right, then. You don't need to wear a condom for Portia. She'll have sex without one, won't you, Portia? Portia, tell him you'll let him do it without a condom. Tell him, Portia, *tell him*!

I heard the daughter's frightened voice. 'Yes. You can do it without one. *Please! You can do it without one!*'

All I could think of were those two children lying dead beneath the bushes. The poor dead children. I'd puked on them before I even realized what they were. Then we'd left them there under the bushes, their bird-pecked eyes oozing blood like terrible tear drops down their cheeks. My brain felt overloaded; it couldn't process any more. I just cut and ran, leaving the two behind on the path calling after me.

CHAPTER 16

It was a shit day. Every ten seconds or so the mental video in my head would replay what I'd seen that morning: the old folk lying dead and bloated in their Shackleton high chairs; the bare-arsed woman lying half in and half out of the hearse; the dead children; the jetliner falling out of the sky. Then we'd returned with the supplies of baby food. One of S Group breaking into a shop in Pudsey had been mistaken for a looter and been shot dead by the army. I didn't know the dead guy's name. And I was already too overloaded with the sights and odours of death for it to have much impact on me at that moment.

Stenno had been in the garage. He was changing the tyre on an ambulance. He looked like a toy robot whose batteries were almost flat. He still worked, but in a peculiar slow-motion kind of way. When he looked at me his eyes were deadened. He didn't show any sign he'd even recognized me.

I doubled back along the field behind the houses, in the hope that mother and daughter wouldn't follow me. All I wanted was a drink and a hot bath. As far as I knew Stephen wouldn't be far behind me.

I used the gate that led through into the back garden, then walked up along the lawn by the garden loungers and ornamental pond.

The first thing I noticed was an empty orange juice carton outside the back door. Then I saw the back door itself was open by a hand's breadth. I pushed it open.

I stood and stared, not believing my eyes.

The kitchen was heaving with people. All strangers. All refugees. They were almost climbing over each other to pull open cupboard doors and drawers, or to yank boxes from the pantry.

A middle-aged man in silver-rimmed spectacles looked back over his shoulder at me; before Friday night he could have been an accountant with a comfortable house, a comfortable life-style, in a comfortable suburb of Leeds. 'Sod off,' he shouted at me. 'We were here first.'

'No, you weren't,' I yelled, feeling a fury erupt inside me. '*I* was here first. *I live here.*'

'No one's stopping you living here, mate,' another man said as he stuffed apples into a bin liner. 'But you're not keeping all this stuff for yourself.'

'Jesus Christ!' I screamed. 'Do you know where I've just been? And do you know what I saw? Of course you fucking don't. There's dead children down there; they've— hey, put that fucking back. You! Yes, I'm talking to you – put that back.' Someone had picked up a glass jar where my mother kept the dried spaghetti. I'd bought it for her that first Christmas after Dad and Stephen had left home. She'd opened it as she sat by the Christmas tree. Then she'd put her head in her hands and cried silently for ten minutes solid. I'd sat there in a wounded silence, not knowing what the Hell I could do about it. Now some bastard was dumping the thing into his swag bag; all it meant to him was the handful of spaghetti inside.

'Give me that,' I shouted.

The man looked up at me. He had dyed black hair which at one time I imagined was combed into an Elvis quiff. Now it hung like rats' tails over his eyes. 'Go on, then. Take it from me, why don't ya?'

I had to force my way through the pack of men looting the house. I'd had enough. I was yelling at the man, shaking my fist in his face. If I'd a gun, so help me, I would have slammed a whole magazine full of slugs into that greasy rat-tail hair.

'Give it back to me,' I snarled.

Ratman just jeered. 'You're nowt but a little boy . . . nowt but a little boy. Go find your mother.'

I lunged at him. I'd picked on the wrong man. He must have had muscles in his piss. He picked me up easily and threw me back toward the door.

'Try that again,' he said, pointing a stubby finger at me, 'and I'll take yer fucken head off.'

'Go easy on him,' said one of the men uneasily.

'You're not the one he's having a go at, is it?'

'He's only a kid.'

'He's going to end up with a thrashing if he tries that trick again.'

It wasn't a case of me showing no fear; I was showing no common sense. What I'd seen that morning had made me so angry that I was determined to take it out on someone.

I pushed by the guy with the silver spectacles and swung my fist at Ratman's head. My aim was lousy but sheer anger pumped some force into it.

The blow connected with his forehead. It did no damage worth mentioning but the man glared murderously up through the rat tails of hair. 'I warned you, you stupid idiot. After I've got through with you, don't you ever say I didn't warn you.'

'Well, what you fucking waiting for? *Shit sucker!*'

I made little 'Come on' motions with my fingers. There was no room for a fight. That kitchen was crammed with men filling sacks and boxes, but all I saw was red. Red-hot fury. It didn't matter that Ratman would beat my face to the colour and texture of strawberry jam. All I wanted was to expel the rage that filled my gut to bursting: the sheer rage at seeing the poor dead bastards in Leeds; the rage at the mother wanting to give me her daughter (who couldn't have been a day over fourteen whatever mummy dear said); and the sheer raging fury at seeing my home being ransacked in front of me and knowing I could do damn-all about it.

The man pushed the others aside; his chest was puffing in and out like that of a boxer ready to go into overdrive. 'You asked for this!' he roared.

One second he was coming at me, the next his expression had changed and he was swinging sideways to crash against the freezer door.

'Hey, take it easy.'

I looked to see Stephen at my side; obviously he'd come through the door, sussed the situation, and swung the man into the freezer as he launched himself at me.

'So there's two of you, is there?' the man snarled. 'I don't mind, I'll take the pair of you apart.'

'Listen, hey listen, bud. I've no intention of fighting you. Me and my brother are going outside now. We won't interfere again, all right?'

Ratman was having none of it. 'So you can shove me around and get away with it? No one shoves me around, OK?'

'OK,' Stephen held up his hands soothingly. 'OK, I'm sorry. I'm just looking out for my brother, OK? I don't want to see him get hurt.'

'Sorry isn't enough. The pair of you are going to pay.'

I was ready to wade in. Only Stephen held me back by a fistful of my T-shirt.

'Look, I'm sorry: what more can I say?'

'Sorry isn't enough, I said. I'm going to teach you pair of faggots that—'

'Oh, for goodness sake, Les.' The man with silver spectacles spoke quietly but with enough authority to catch Ratman's attention. 'Leave it, will you? We came here to get food for our families, not pick a fight.'

'But they—'

'He's apologized, hasn't he?'

'They'll get the end of my boot before I leave here.'

The man in spectacles was loosing his patience. 'Go on, then, go fight them. But if you do, you'll lose your share of the food, and you're out of our team. Do you really want that?'

I thought Ratman would argue the toss about this. But being part of the team, whatever that was, must have been of importance to him because he shrugged, contented himself with giving the pair of us a dirty look, then returned to filling his sack from one of the food cupboards.

'Stephen. He's got the spaghetti jar. I'm taking that back.'

'No, you're not, Rick.' Stephen caught me off balance and pulled me. 'You're coming outside to cool off.'

'No, I'm—'

'It's not worth fighting over.'

Half guiding, half pulling, he managed to get me outside into the back garden where he sat me on one of the loungers.

'Rick. Don't ever try pulling a stunt like that again. OK?'

'They're ransacking the house!'

'Right. And you can take on ten grown men, I suppose?'

'I'd have—'

'You'd have got yourself pasted.'

Grinding my fist into my palm, I stood up, then paced the lawn beneath that hot afternoon sun. I hated the idea of letting the bastards get away with just walking into my home and taking what they wanted. For all I knew they might be upstairs pissing all over the carpets.

'Talk about biting the hand that feeds you . . .'

'Let it go, Rick,' Stephen said calmly.

'But we helped these people! We risked being gassed by going into

81

Leeds. That guy from our team got a bullet in the head because he was mistaken for a looter. All the poor bastard was doing was finding baby food for their bloody children. Is that fair?'

'I know. But these people are grateful. You're saving their babies' lives. You went—'

'And this is the thanks we get?'

Stephen kept his voice calm and low. 'There are forty thousand people camped out there. Did you see forty thousand people in your kitchen? No. You saw ten men who are so frightened at losing their homes – and their dignity – that they're trying to claw something back. Even if it's just going back to their wives and children with a few chocolate cookies and a can of ham. Rick, it's human nature. They need to show they can still provide for their families. That they haven't been reduced to the status of beggars.'

'Only thieves.'

'Sure. But they feel as if they can do something positive to put food in their children's bellies.'

'The feeding stations are—'

'The feeding stations are providing two meals a day. One of those is porridge. The other's a small bowl of stew.'

My brother was right. Basically I was so angry with the whole human race right then I just wanted a whipping boy on whom I could piss my rage. I realized there and then that this whole situation was turning me into nothing more than a ranting fascist.

Sighing, I nodded and managed a smile. 'Message received and understood.'

'So I can trust you not to rush round beating up any more refugees?'

'You can.'

He gave a grin. 'Once they've finished in there we'll clear up and I'll cook you one of my famous pasta and pesto sauce feasts.'

'You might have a struggle to find the ingredients.'

With his forefinger he touched the side of the nose and smiled. 'Your wily old brother's learned a trick or two. I stashed some food in the attic yesterday.'

As we talked I let my gaze wander towards Leeds, shimmering in the heat haze in the distance. The smoke from the crashed airliner still rose into the air. With no fire service on hand the flames were probably spreading unchecked.

Stephen's powers of persuasion bordered on the hypnotic. Within

82

twenty minutes he had me believing that today would be nothing more than an unpleasant blip in what would be a thrilling and rewarding life. He started talking about the band, and the songs I'd written. And did I have an acoustic guitar so I could play them to him? It didn't even seem so bad when the looters left. Most of them walked out with their heads down, ashamed of what they'd done. One carried a bottle of red wine.

Stephen quipped, 'You'll find that goes best with a red meat dish or cheese. Oh, and be sure to open it an hour before dinner and serve at room temperature.' The man blushed with embarrassment and hurried out of the garden.

I knew with absolute conviction that Stephen Kennedy, Seattle video jock, was a tower of strength.

What I didn't know was that soon lives would depend on it.

CHAPTER 17

A week to the day after the mysterious gas drifted into Leeds I left the house and walked down towards the woods. It was dusk. The sky formed a deep blue ceiling above my head; Venus twinkled above the horizon; before me the path led downhill through the meadow.

With no food in the house I was eating at Ben Cavellero's now. Dinner was in an hour.

You see, I'd recently got into the habit of this evening walk. It was an oasis of peace and solitude away from the refugee camp, which lately crackled with hundreds of arguments as those forty thousand people became fed up to the back teeth of living within an arm's length of their neighbours.

A rabbit scampered away in front of me. I wondered how long it could keep a couple of steps away from those ever-simmering cooking pots. No animal was safe from the hungry stomachs back on King Elmet's Mile.

I moved in a slow, reflective stride. Thoughts moved by as though on a conveyor belt in front of my mind's eye. Sometimes it was images of the old folk lying dead in the retirement home; or the mother and daughter offering to become my sex-slaves; or newer ones of a middle-aged couple stoning a black

Labrador to death, a greedy gleam in their eye: they'd eat well tonight.

But the truth of the matter was I wasn't sleeping well at night. When I did manage to sleep I was plagued by a recurring dream. I dreamed I was being visited each night by . . . by what?

I didn't know what. I hadn't a clue. Mostly I saw nothing. But I'd wake, choking with terror, my head lathered with sweat . . .

I dreamed I'd wake to feel the weight of something . . . no, some*one* on top of me. As if a heavyweight wrestler squatted on my chest, his big hand flat over my face, pressing my head back into the pillow.

Other times I'd wake to see . . . no, again that isn't right. But it was hard to describe. Rather than see, I'd *sense* that there was someone in the room with me. Leaning with their back against the wall; or at other times closer; maybe leaning right over me, looking down into my face. I'd sense a huge figure, I could sense its sheer brute strength. And its menace. As it stood there in silence, without moving.

And I sensed, also, that it found me fascinating. As if it was a bug hunter who had found a new species of butterfly to pin to his board.

And I knew it would return each night to study me, or to squat on me, its bare grey feet planted squarely on my chest. Unable to move, unable to scream even though the terror blazed through me like lightning, I'd lie there; paralyzed by fear.

It would gaze down at me, its grey face as close to my face as your face is to this page; then it would reach forward and grasp my—

(Bare grey feet? Where did I get that from? Bare grey feet, bigger than an ape's, only with stubby, square-ended toes, with toenails that were cracked and misshapen and blackened looking)

Where had I pulled that image from?

I'd seen nothing. I'd only dreamed it. A stupid nightmare.

As I walked along the path I shook the grey-man image out of my head, and—

Grey man?

Shocked by the suddenness of the words cracking through my mind, I stopped dead. Why had I thought that?

Until a minute ago I wouldn't have even claimed I'd dreamed about a grey man. Only now the description came to me, as if I was beginning to remember an event I'd forgotten.

My heart beat began to thud harder in my chest; my skin chilled;

fear squirmed in my stomach. I didn't like this. I didn't like this at all. Why did I feel so . . . so shit-scared about a few scraps of remembered dream? Because that's all it was – wasn't it?

Above me the sky darkened. Fear seemed to hang over me like a living creature; something dark and terrible with huge wings that beat with all the ghastly slowness of the heartbeat of a dying man.

I reached out and gripped on to a fence post. I held it so tight I felt its splintered surface prick the palms of my hands. I shivered . . . shivered again. For all the world it felt as if I was being lowered centimetre by centimetre into a vat of ice-cold water.

'Listen to me, Rick, you moron,' I snarled to myself. 'They're dreams, they aren't real. I am *not* remembering something that has actually happened. It's only a damned dream, OK?'

What d'you mean? Not like that thing in the wood the night of Ben Cavellero's party, that reached out and—'

Crack! Crack!

Gunshots snapped along the valley. There was unrest in the camps now. Sometimes the only way soldiers guarding food depots could keep order was to fire warning shots into the air.

I climbed over the fence and sat on the steeply sloping hillside, looking down over the woods, over the carp pond that mirrored the deep blue of the sky and across to where Leeds stood in the distance. Now fires burned constantly there. They looked like little blobs of flickering yellow. Still, it was strangely peaceful. Any noises from the camp that reached me were softened by distance.

And as I sat there the ground moved. It was nothing dramatic. For all the world it felt as if I was sitting in a rowing boat on a still pond. Then along came a small ripple. Smoothly I lifted up a centimetre or so, then smoothly dropped down.

That was all. No sound. No vibration. Just a smooth lifting and falling sensation. As I sat there it happened again. Then again.

I stood up and looked around me. Nothing looked out of place.

As I looked out in the direction of Leeds I saw the flashes of light. They might have been lightning flashes but there was no cloud. They came in long, slow pulsing flashes of brilliance. I must have counted fifteen of them before they stopped. Minutes later the ground ripples started again, these more noticeable than the first ones. Still there was no sound. The night was otherwise peaceful.

After a while, I began to make out palls of cloud rising into the air above Leeds. Although it was nearly dark they showed like snowy mountains against the sky. They reminded me of the clouds you'd see streaming from power station cooling towers. But these were a hell of a lot bigger.

Behind me I heard shouting. A group of men, I guess in their late teens, early twenties, were running down the hill towards me. They were shouting and laughing; even from this distance I could see that the expression on their faces mated excitement with greed at the same time.

They carried a woman at shoulder height. She was screaming; there was blood on her thighs. She was naked.

I think it was the woman who had stopped me a few days earlier in the street. Caroline – that was her name. Caroline Lucas and her daughter, Portia.

The mob ran towards me but swerved at the last minute because the fence blocked their way. Then they headed away towards a clump of trees. I caught a glimpse of the woman's eyes. The brown eyes that had looked so hopeful and trustfully at me were now seared with pain and terror. Just for a second they locked onto mine. A desperate hope flashed. She was about to shout something to me, then the gang began to chant:

'SHE'S GOING TO GET HER BLOODY CUNT FUCKED IN!
SHE'S GOING TO GET HER BLOODY CUNT FUCKED IN!
SHE'S GOING TO GET HER . . .'

It went on and on, like a football chant, raw and wild and hungry.

I sat there on the hillside watching Leeds burn. Five minutes later and the chant had vanished into the distance. I stood up and walked down the hill.

For some reason my skin prickled all over. The palms of my hands and my eyelids felt unnaturally sensitive. I couldn't shift the conviction that I was covered in dirt; and it was the grime working into my skin that pricked and itched at my neck and my arms and stomach.

I walked faster. Seconds later I found myself on the banks of the carp pond. The water, covering an area little bigger than a football field, twinkled in the starlight.

Without pausing, I pulled off my shoes and walked straight into the water. Ten steps in the water reached my waist. Another five and it lapped against my chest. The water felt fresh, and oh-so-cool as it soaked through my clothes. In my mind's eye I saw those fat lazy carp circling my bare feet as they foraged across the muddy lake bottom.

In the last few days I'd seen more than my dumb brain could handle. My senses were overwhelmed. I'd just seen huge explosions tear through the distant city. I could do nothing to prevent it. I'd seen a woman carried away by a gang of men who, within a matter of days, had reverted to savagery. I could do nothing to prevent it. It was as if my mind had said: *Enough*. And because it could no longer process all that colossal influx of raw data it had shut down, leaving me to run on a kind of instinctual autopilot. Anyone watching me that night would have seen a man moving like a zombie through the water – face expressionless, eyes deadened, responsive to nothing: not even if the stars chose to explode above his head.

I moved deeper into the lake, feet stirring the silt bed; water rippled musically. When it reached my shoulders I turned and lay back, slowly kicked my feet and floated out across the lake.

As I went swimming out across the lake, my mind, unable to cope with the present, went swimming back into the past. Back through the years to the time I'd first gone night swimming. It had been a night much like this. Warm. The stars sparkling diamond-hard in the sky. With me were Howard Sparkman, Dean Skilton and Jim Keller. We'd have been around nine years old. We splashed each other and promised we'd come night swimming again. This time coax some girls along.

But that night there were just the four of us, night swimming, talking about the first things that came into our heads. Dean had swum towards me, cheeks puffed tight, before squirting out a stream of water from his mouth. 'Will we still be doing this when we're grown up?'

'God knows,' I said and splashed him.

'I'll be in another part of the world,' Jim said. 'I'm joining the air force . . . I'll be a pilot out in Africa or somewhere like that.'

'You won't be a pilot.' Howard grinned. 'You can't even ride a skateboard yet.'

'I'll learn.'

'What are you going to do in the future, Rick?'

'Dunno. Kids think the future's going to be great and they'll do great jobs . . . most end up working in banks, shops, offices and stuff like that. Hey, Deanie-boy, see how high you can squirt.'

'Well, I am going to learn how to fly,' Jim said firmly as he trod water in the middle of the pond.

'You'll have no need to.'

'How comes that, Dean?'

'In the future computers will fly planes. They won't need pilots.'

'How do you know what will be in the future?' I said, lying back and churning the water with my feet. 'No one can see what's going to happen in thirty seconds' time.'

Howard splashed me, chuckling, 'Yeah, a shark might come along and chew you in two, right?'

Jim said seriously. 'You *don't* know what's going to happen to you, though, do you? You don't know what you'll be doing this time next week, never mind what you'll be doing ten years from today.'

'I'll be nineteen in ten years,' I said.

'And I'll be twenty,' Jim said firmly. 'And I'll be a pilot.'

I floated on my back and looked up at the stars, the cool water rippling against my face.

No. You never know what the future holds for you.

A week after that first experience of night swimming, Jim Keller's father had stormed out of the house after a blazing row with Mrs Keller. He ordered Jim into the car, then drove out of the village, intending to drive to London.

Little more than a kilometre from this very carp lake the car had run into the back of a tractor. Both Jim and his father had died there on the road. The one hard detail of the accident that went round the school was that when ten-year-old Jim had been thrown clean through the windscreen the glass had shaved off both thumbs.

The thumbs were never found. Soon it became a dare for the other kids to go and hunt for Jim Keller's thumbs along the grass verge.

No, you couldn't see into the future. For me this was the future. One I couldn't have imagined as that nine-year-old. And as I floated there, still as death in the water, I imagined I saw Jim Keller's ghost swimming alongside me. He had no thumbs. But maybe, if there was a God, he would have got his wings after all. And now he'd have an entire universe to glide through.

I held my breath, closed my eyes and glided down through the waters beneath the surface of the lake. When I opened my eyes I saw nothing but darkness. Then I touched bottom. And I stayed there for as long as I could.

CHAPTER 18

I don't think anyone could say with any degree of certainty when, precisely, the transformation took place. But as I woke up the morning after I'd seen the woman being carried away into the wood I realized that the refugees from Leeds had become an army of occupation. Now they just took what they wanted from us.

Of course, it must still have been a minority who had turned to anarchy. Thousands were still law-abiding citizens. They camped out in the fields and, at the appointed time, patiently queued in line for their bowl of stew that grew more watery by the day. But by then that minority (who wouldn't hesitate to crack your skull for the apple in your pocket) vastly outnumbered the original population of Fairburn. And that minority was growing.

Stephen handed me a black coffee as I walked into the kitchen. He'd hidden a tin of Nescafé beneath a loose floorboard in his bedroom. The same hiding place where he'd stored his *Playboy* magazines ten years ago.

The kitchen was gloomy. We'd boarded the windows and doors with planks to try and stop the house being looted every time we walked out the door. Not that it did much good. We knew the door would be kicked in the next time we left the house. Come to that, soon they'd not bother waiting for us to leave.

'Have you noticed,' Stephen said, blowing on his coffee, 'that it wasn't the criminal element who started looting first? It's the businessmen and the professional go-getters. They're the ones who are most ruthless in going out and ransacking someone's home.'

I tried making conversation but the truth of the matter was that my knowledge of what was going to happen to that woman the night before was preying on my mind. Maybe I could have helped? Maybe if I had taken her and the daughter in she might still have been safe. And what had happened to the daughter? She couldn't have been much more than fourteen, surely they wouldn't have—

A pounding on the door startled me so much the coffee jumped from my mug to scald my hand.

Stephen looked at me. 'It sounds as if they're back again.'

89

'Looters?'

He picked up a baseball bat he kept by the back door. 'Look,' he shouted, 'You're wasting your time. We've been picked clean already. D'ya hear? There's no food left in here. It's all gone.'

The sound of fist pounding wood came again.

I took a meat cleaver from the drawer. The bastards wouldn't walk all over us this time.

'Did you hear me?' Stephen called. 'You can forget this house. There's no food, no blankets here. Nothing – it's all—'

'Stephen?' came a muffled voice. 'That you?'

I let out a sigh. 'It's OK. It's Dean.'

'Stephen. Rick. Let me in. I've got an important message from Ben Cavellero.'

'Hang on a sec.' Stephen started sliding back bolts. 'Sorry, we've had to turn the place into Fort Knox. For what good that'll do us.' He opened the door.

Dean walked in. He was panting and the agitated expression on his face was enough make my scalp prickle. 'What is it, Dean? What's wrong?'

'Hell, everything's wrong.' He wiped at the sweat on his forehead. 'Look, can you get up to Ben's house for ten o'clock? He's holding a meeting.'

'Sure, what's it all—'

'Sorry. Can't stop. I've got to get down to the village to tell some of the others.'

'*Some* of the others?'

'Yeah, the meeting's by invitation only. I've got a list of names he wants up there.'

'Can't you tell us what's it about?'

'Yeah, Dean,' I shook my head bemused. 'Why all the mystery?'

'Look . . . I don't know any details yet. But, believe me, he's got something to show us. And it's important . . . no, it's *vital* you're there.'

'You make it sound like it's a matter of—'

'Yeah, it is.' Dean wasn't smiling. 'It *is* a matter of life and death.'

As we walked out onto Trueman Way Stephen asked me, 'Where are you taking the guitar?'

My cheeks pinked. I felt self-conscious and hoped, somehow, he wouldn't have noticed the big black case clutched by its handle in my left fist. 'The only safe place to keep it is Ben's house. He mentioned I could store it there until this is all over.'

Stephen gave a smile that said he understood and approved. 'Why not? I'll bet you my last dollar someone's breaking open the back door of the house right now.'

'Do you think they'll find Mum's jewellery?'

'I hope not. We buried it deep enough in the back garden. Anyway, what they'll be looking for is food, cutlery and clothes. Not that there's much of that left to take now.'

We left the road and headed into the shade of the woods, taking the short cut to Ben Cavellero's house. Automatically, you found yourself trying to hold your breath. The woods were being used as a mass toilet by thousands of people. The communal latrines were already overloaded to the point of uselessness. And after more than a week the shit was piling high beneath the bushes. Flies buzzed hungrily to and fro.

'Well then, old buddy,' Stephen said, automatically putting a handkerchief over his mouth. 'Any guesses what Mr Cavellero wants to tell us?'

'Search me. It sounds serious.'

'But why only invite a select few?'

'From the look of the names I saw on Dean's list it's mainly people he's known for a long time.'

Stephen started to speculate about something Ben Cavellero had mentioned earlier about the gas dispersing over Leeds. Maybe the forty thousand on our doorstep would soon be on their way home. But I wasn't listening. Because I'd seen her.

She didn't look the same. But I knew it was her.

Stephen kept on talking. I couldn't take my eyes from her as we passed by.

She was sitting on the bare soil beneath the trees. The birds sang sweetly in the branches. Here and there a little light filtered through the leaves to dapple the ground around her.

I gripped the handle of the guitar case tightly as a wave of self-disgust rose through me.

It was that same woman again. Caroline Lucas, mother of shy and pretty Portia.

She sat on the ground with a pink candlewick bedspread round her shoulders. Her hair was flattened to her head on one side and stuck out messily on the other. Her face was puffed and plastered in dirt and shit. Her two eyes gleamed out of the shit mask. She was lost in a world of her own. You could have kicked her and she wouldn't have so much as grunted.

Wearily, she moved her leg out straight from under the pink bedspread. I saw her leg was bare to her groin. She was probably stark naked under that sheet; her clothes would be strewn somewhere across the fields.

Christ. I hated myself right then. There I was, a conceited little twat, carrying in my hand the only thing I valued in life. An electric guitar that you could buy in any musical instrument shop in the whole frigging world.

I should have done something when I saw the mob carrying the woman away to batter her tits to buggery and split her cunt to shreds. Even if the mob had beaten me stupid. I should have done something. I should have tried.

And what had happened to the daughter?

'Come on, kid.' Stephen took my arm and guided me past her as I stared at her, feeling that revulsion and self-disgust coming at me in vicious waves. I could have helped. I should have taken them into our house when they asked. Caroline must have been almost twenty years older than me, but she had such fine features and pretty hair . . . I could have cared for her . . . maybe even fallen in love and—

'Rick. Come on, buddy. We can't save the whole world single-handed.'

'She needs help.'

'So do forty thousand others.'

'No. I'm not leaving her here.'

'Rick. It's nearly ten. Ben wanted us—'

'I'm not leaving her sitting in shit.'

'Rick, I—'

At that moment I could have punched my brother's teeth down his throat. 'Listen. Twice I could have helped this woman. Twice I've let her down.'

'Rick—'

'Go on ahead to Ben's. I'll follow.'

Stephen locked his blue eyes onto mine. 'It's OK, Rick. I'm with you on this. We'll help her.'

I walked slowly up to the woman, then said as gently as I could, 'Caroline . . . Caroline Lucas?'

92

Dazed, she lifted that bruised face. Her brown eyes looked into mine.

'Caroline. Remember me?'

I saw her swallow hard, give a little nod.

'Caroline. Nice and easy does it. I want you to . . . no. No, I don't want that. Cover yourself up. Please cover yourself up. I wasn't one of those who attacked you.'

Stephen helped arrange the bedspread over her battered body, his voice a low soothing purr. 'Come on there, honey. Trust us. We won't hurt you.'

He shot me a look. 'You know this lady?'

'In a way.'

'In a way?'

'I'll tell you later, Stephen. Let's get her to Ben's.'

Meekly, like a sleepy child being led to bed, the woman in the pink bedspread allowed us to lead her out of the wood.

CHAPTER 19

At Ben's house Stenno's wife Sue, a nurse with Jimmy's Hospital in Leeds, took charge of Caroline, leading her away to the bathroom.

Me? I wouldn't have taken much goading to grab one of Ben's shotguns and hunt down the bastards that did this to her. The only good thing, as far as we could learn from Caroline, was that the daughter appeared to be safe. She'd hooked up with a guy who lived in the village.

Ben appeared as we stood waiting in the entrance hall. His face was serious. 'Glad you could make it,' he said, shaking us both by the hand. 'The others are in the library. Now you're here we can make a start.'

'Make a start?' Stephen asked.

'Yeah, Ben,' I said, 'why all the cloak and dagger?'

He gave a smile. But it was the grimmest one I'd ever seen on anyone's face. 'I'd rather show you than tell you. This way, please.'

He opened the heavy oak door into the library which was large enough to accommodate a full-sized bus. The walls were lined floor to ceiling with books. 'It's a bit of squeeze,' he said, 'and stuffy. I'll make it as quick as I can.'

I was astonished to see the library packed with people. Most of them I knew. There was Stenno, Howard, Dean. They all wore serious expressions as if we'd been summoned there to be told about the death of an old friend.

There was no room left to sit on the rows of chairs so Stephen and I parked our butts on a table by the door.

Ben Cavellero walked across to a TV that had been wheeled to one end of the library.

Ben didn't beat about the bush. 'I wish we were all meeting in happier circumstances. But, to be blunt, we're in one hell of a mess. Not just here in Leeds, but everywhere . . . the entire planet.'

Somebody started to ask a question but Ben held up a hand. 'I'll do my best to answer questions later. But first I think there's something you all should see. Then I'm going to ask you to do something. It might sound strange; many of you won't be happy about it. But when you've seen this I think you'll at least treat my request seriously.' He switched on the TV which showed a large green 'O' in the top right hand corner. Then he pointed the remote at the VCR. 'Oh, and in case you're wondering. The power hasn't been restored. I've begged a portable generator from a farmer in the valley.'

I saw Stephen catch my eye and shrug. Clearly he was completely mystified. Me, too. But I had a bad, bad feeling about all this.

The screen flickered as Ben touched the play button on the remote. 'I taped this last night. What you'll see is taken from satellite TV news programmes such as CNN, Spain's Galavision and the German news channel N-TV. As far as we know all the terrestrial TV broadcasters are off air . . . Now, please watch very carefully.'

There was no theme tune or station logo. The filmed news report began with a few words spoken in Spanish. I didn't understand the language. I didn't need to, because the pictures pumped out a grim message that was plain enough to everyone.

First up, a shot of the Arc de Triomphe in Paris. But it was unlike any shot I'd seen of it before. Rolling through the archway was an advancing wall of smouldering ash. It all happened slowly, no faster than the minute hand of a watch. But slowly, surely, inexorably, the stone archway was being engulfed. Abandoned cars ignited in a flash of flame as hot ash touched fuel tanks.

The camera panned away to deserted Parisian buildings. The ash there had fallen like black snow to cover the boulevards and walkways in a carpet of funereal black. All the trees were dead.

There was a shot of the white-haired reporter carrying a microphone. As he trudged along the street he sank knee-deep into the powdery ash.

Those streets were empty of people. Apart from the camera crew the only other sign of life was a small dog. Impossible to tell whether its fur was naturally black or blackened by the ash, it struggled alone through that grim desert. The dog looked as if it almost had to swim to keep its head above the suffocating dust: the tongue hung loosely from its mouth; the eyes rolled in its head, flashing the whites. You could sense the animal's sheer effort as it battled on through the ash, searching, perhaps, for its lost owner. You realized, too, the effort would soon become too great to bear and it would sink down into the ash, too exhausted to continue.

Perhaps seeing a whole city struck down by disaster is too great to comprehend. What had happened to its citizens? Where had they all gone? Instead of asking those questions, the dog, for us, somehow became a metaphor for all those millions of men, women and children facing a life-or-death struggle. We found ourselves willing the reporter to rescue the dog. Absurdly, it became important to us. We so desperately wanted to see the white-haired man lift the little dog, shivering and exhausted from the choking dust. But (to disappointed sighs from those in the room) the scene abruptly cut to that of the Eiffel Tower. It lay on its side, its weblike tracery of girders twisted like the skeleton of some mutant dinosaur.

Crudely edited together came more jerking shots of cities from around the world. The Golden Gate Bridge in San Francisco had lost its central span in a clean break that left the two halves sloping down into the sea.

Next, a shot of a Zodiac inflatable dinghy nosing through debris on a lake. The camera zoomed in: the debris was made up of floating corpses. The body of a girl in a white wedding dress drifted by. Smoothly the camera panned upward. There was a gasp from the people in the room.

We were looking at the Houses of Parliament. The huge building now stood like a strange stone ship anchored in the middle of a lake. The clock in the tower of Big Ben was frozen at ten to two. Seconds later the dinghy nosed by a red oblong slab, sticking just above the surface of the flood waters. It was the roof of a red London double decker bus. Eels must have wound their sinuous bodies across the passenger seats by now.

Again came a terse comment in Spanish that I didn't understand. The voice was robbed of emotion. As if the reporter had seen so much death and destruction he was incapable of feeling any more horror.

More shots: Nelson's Column, a shattered stump rising out of the waters that covered Trafalgar Square. A silent journey along Charing Cross Road. The wake from the boat caused drowned heads in the water to bob, and splashed against shop signs – Murder One, Pizza Hut, Foyles, Waterstones, Boots.

Cut to:

Wellington. Fires raged across the city. But it wasn't the buildings that were burning. The flames vented from great gashes in the earth. As if a row of rocket motors had been upended in the ground, then ignited, sending jets of blue flame a hundred metres into the air with a screeching sound that overwhelmed the TV crew's microphone, distorting the sound into a Daffy Duck warble that might have sounded comic in other circumstances.

Cut to:

Madrid. Volcanic ash choked the streets. The Avenida de America that links the city with the airport was shoulder-deep in sooty black dust. Oeste Park resembled the surface of the Moon, pitted with dozens of craters. Against an evening sky, the Royal Palace burned brightly. Vivid red flames burst from windows to writhe like fiery demons across the face of the building.

Cut to:

Johannesburg. Poison gas had crept through the city at night. Thousands of corpses, most in nightclothes, formed a death mat across many roads – Commissioner Street, Klein Street, Twist Street. In some places they lay four or five deep, arms and legs stretched stiffly out. Hundreds had sought sanctuary in the Anglican Cathedral on Bree Street. Corpses formed gruesome clots of rotting flesh in the cathedral doorways where the dying had tried to climb over the dead. Then they, too, had fallen to the poisonous gas. In Klein Street looters had tried to steal paintings from the art gallery. Now they lay dead on the pavement, framed paintings in their hands, blood from gas-seared lungs oozing from open mouths. Their lifeless faces still locked in an expression of horror and shock.

Cut to:

Sydney. More flooding. The opera house looked as if a pissed giant had stomped on it, caving in the once beautiful roofscape. Everywhere there were bodies.

Then the image flickered and snowstormed while whoever had recorded the tape searched out a fresh news channel. The CNN logo appeared in the corner of the screen.

'. . . extensive rioting in the refugee camps in Palermo, Italy, while the situation in the hundred-thousand-strong camp in Richmond, Virginia is now grave. Medical experts say that the typhus outbreak is unstoppable, resulting in hundreds of deaths a day. And in Baltimore US marines are still attempting to restore order after refugees massacred National Guard forces on Thursday night.'

Accompanying the litany of chaos were more scenes of refugee camps, of rioting, of looting, of thousands of people streaming towards the camera and away from an erupting volcano five kilometres away in the background. The White House in Washington had been seared to nothing more than a blackened shell; a massive hole gaped in the once famous milk-white dome.

Cut to: exhausted people with soot-streaked faces from which terrified eyes glittered in a chilling stare – these people had seen the coming of Armageddon. Zombie-like, they trudged by a looted KFC. Its uniformed staff, their mouths still yawning open in their final agony-driven scream, lay on a bed of KFC cardboard buckets, polystyrene clams, paper napkins, paper cups, plastic forks. They'd been stomped to death. Their blood, still flowing from broken faces, mingled with Coke streaming unchecked from the cold drinks dispenser to form a black-red pool on the floor.

More shots of men and women of all races and backgrounds carrying away food from a supermarket. By the door, a pair of middle-aged men were kicking a man in a National Guard uniform. He lay on the floor clutching his face.

The anchorman continued, 'Scientists convening in Denver have so far ascertained that most of the geological disturbance is occurring east of ninety degrees longitude in the United States where there has been widespread destruction. That is roughly the easternmost third of the country, containing the states of Alabama, Georgia, Florida, North and South Carolina, Virginia, Kentucky . . .' The list continued. We sat there in the library and watched for another forty-five minutes.

When it was over, the screen went blank. We sat in silence until

Ben switched off the TV and said, 'There you have it.' Ben looked around the audience. He looked like a doctor about to tell a patient they only had months left to live. He took a deep breath and launched in. 'You've seen a fraction of what I've taped. There's a couple more hours of that if anyone wants . . . needs to see it later. But what you've seen gives you a clear enough picture of what has happened in the last week or so. That we have a global disaster on our hands. Probably the biggest most single devastating event to hit our planet since the last ice age twenty thousand years ago.' He smiled grimly. 'I suppose you could call this the start of a Hot Age . . . or Fire Age.'

Dean Skilton held up a hand. 'But what's causing this?'

Ben shrugged. 'What caused it? From what I have seen on the television it seems that the Earth's core has actually been increasing in temperature over the last few years. Geologists knew this was happening but . . .'

'But the truth was kept from the public,' Stephen said heavily.

'Yes.'

'Figures. Another government cover-up.'

'In the last few years there's been a dramatic increase in volcanic activity, killing more than twenty-five thousand people. And these eruptions, despite what scientists told us, are unpredictable. A few years ago two European satellites, ERS-1 and ERS-2, were launched into orbit to monitor certain volcanoes that were near to centres of human habitation. These show that the volcanoes, although dormant, were showing signs that they would erupt within a matter of months.'

Stephen said, 'But we saw film of Paris. That was volcanic ash in the streets. There are no active volcanoes in France.'

'There are now.'

'That's incredible.'

'That's a fact. In 1994 there were five hundred and fifty active volcanoes in the world. A year later there were eight hundred and sixty. In 1997 there were almost two thousand. Now the scientists have lost count.'

'But all that destruction wasn't purely caused by volcanic activity,' I said.

'True. In fact the real problem, which is far more serious, is that the Earth's whole crust is becoming warmer.' Ben glanced down at the carpeted floor on which he stood. 'Basically the ground on which we stand is heating up.'

'You expect us to believe that?' said a teenage girl in a voice harshened by fear more than disbelief. 'What proof have you got?'

'What proof do you need?'

'Why . . . scientific evidence. Temperature readings. Seismic surveys.'

'Believe me, Gina, I'm telling you the truth.' Ben's voice was as gentle as ever. 'If you want proof just walk into Fairburn. You'll see forty thousand clues to what is happening camped out there.'

'The gas?'

He nodded. '*That gas*. We thought at first it was a toxic spill from a factory. But the ground on which Leeds stands is warming up. The gas is carbon monoxide. That, with a fair bit of sulphur dioxide mixed in with it. Last Saturday night the pressure of these natural gas pockets became so great it began venting through thousands of small cracks to the surface. That gas is poisonous, but not inflammable. But last night subterranean pockets of inflammable methane gas did explode. You might have seen flashes of light from the explosions coming from the far side of Leeds. You might also have felt the shock-wave running through the ground.'

I remembered that eerie rise and fall of the ground beneath me as I'd sat out on the hillside the night before. Sheer distance had dampened down the Earth's convulsions before they reached me.

'We've had reports of craters the size of football fields being torn in the ground. And if you want more evidence you can take a ride into Leeds where there are deep wells. Lower a bucket into them and you'll pull up water that's warm enough to bathe a baby. You might also have seen that last week the River Tawn suddenly turned red; as if a crimson dye had been dumped into it. That was because one of the springs that feeds it became polluted with a red oxide mineral from geological disturbances beneath Fairburn.'

'So we're not safe here?'

'I'm coming to that,' Ben said softly. 'I am coming to that.'

The girl chipped in again. 'You're not going to tell us that a volcano is going to erupt here in Leeds?'

'I'd like to believe that is extremely unlikely . . . we don't think it will happen.'

'But it's no longer safe here?'

The girl started to ask if we were at risk from the poison gas but Stenno said, in a voice so charged with tension she shut her mouth in mid-sentence, 'It's those Grey Men. They're here, aren't they?'

Ben frowned. 'Grey Men? Sorry, I don't understand.'

Stenno's face turned white, his ears crimson, and I wondered if he'd flash into that weird rage that had gripped him in the garage. 'The Grey Men,' he said, half angry, half embarrassed. 'You've heard of the Grey Men?'

Ben shook his head. 'There've been so many strange rumours flying about that I suppose—'

'The Grey Men. At first I thought it was me. That thump on the head had sent me stupid. That I'd imagined I'd seen them, and . . . and what they did to me.'

Stenno shot a look at me and, God damn it, I couldn't help myself, I flushed red.

'Like I said . . . I saw him,' he stammered. 'The Grey Man. There in the wood, the night of your party . . . he was . . .'

'Stenno . . . Stenno . . .' Ben began gently. 'Honestly. I don't know what—'

'I knew you'd think I was crazy if I told you what really happened to me. But do you know something? I've talked to people from Leeds. I've met five people . . . *five!*' He held up his hand, fingers splayed straight out and trembling. 'Five people who've seen the Grey Men. And two of those were attacked by—'

'Look!' Gina snapped impatiently. 'We're here to talk about the end of the fucking world, not listen to you rant on about the fucking fairies!'

'Fairies? They're not fucking fairies; they're not fucking imagination—'

'Well, fuck off with them, then.'

Ben raised his hands in a calming gesture.

'I've seen them,' Stenno said hotly. 'So have others.'

'Where are these Grey Men from, then? From Grey spaceships from Grey-fucking-Uranus?'

'Why won't you believe me?'

'Tell us where they are from!'

Stenno looked at the girl. For a moment I wondered if he'd fly into that homicidal rage again, if he'd take his fist to her. But as we sat there, dazed by what we'd seen and heard on the TV and now stunned by Stenno's manic outburst, wondering what the hell he was going to do next, he spun round and pointed savagely at me. 'Ask him. Ask Rick Kennedy. He knows!'

All eyes snapped to me.

'Kennedy knows where they come from. Go on, why don't you ask him?'

I held out my hands, bewildered. But the gesture was a fake. Deep down I knew something. But what the hell *did* I know? Again I felt that upsurge of guilt, that irrational guilt as if I'd done something dirty in the past only somehow, just what that act was had slipped my mind.

'Tell them, Rick!' he shouted. 'The Grey Men. *They come from down there!*' He pointed at the ground. Then, as if the idea of stopping in the room a moment longer would kill him, he marched across the floor, punched open the door, and left the house.

CHAPTER 20

We couldn't have caught up with Stenno if we'd tried. Dean, Stephen and I followed him out into the garden.

'There he goes,' Dean called, and pointed. 'He's running through the field.'

Shielding our eyes against the glare of the sun, we watched him run away from the house. Stephen sighed. 'I know it's not a pleasant thing to say, but I think that guy needs professional medical help, he really does.'

Dean shrugged, then returned to the house followed by Stephen. I watched the running Stenno for a moment longer. He was sprinting away downhill through long grass, scaring up birds before him. He raised his arms at either side of him as he ran. I wondered if in his mind he imagined that a pair of angels flew alongside him and he was lifting his arms for them to catch him by the hands and carry him up to Heaven, their long wings beating the clear July air as they flew.

I shook my head and returned to the library.

Ben was talking. '. . . in the camp yesterday. That brings the number of murders to twenty-seven. We've lost count of serious physical assaults. The Swan Inn was firebombed last night. Oh, grab a seat, Rick. Any sign of Stenno coming back?'

I shook my head.

Ben rubbed his forehead. 'Poor chap. We should get a doctor to check him over. That knock on the head might have done more damage than we thought.' He took a deep breath and rested his fingertips together. 'Right, on to the next item of the meeting. What I want to do is make a suggestion.' He looked up, making eye contact with as many of us as he could. 'What I'd like to suggest is . . . no, to be blunt, what I'd beg of you, is that you all leave Fairburn.'

There was a murmur of puzzled voices as people asked their neighbours to confirm what he'd just said.

'Leave?' Stephen asked. 'Why?'

'Yesterday we had five hundred soldiers helping keep order in the camp. Last night they were stoned by a mob intent on ransacking one of the food stores. This morning the soldiers were gone.'

'They deserted?'

'I'm not saying that. But they simply upped and went; they gave no reason.'

'So you think order will break down?'

'It's as good as collapsed. And I'm sure within forty-eight hours there will be total anarchy. That's why I'm asking you to move out of the area for a while. It might just be for a week or two, or—'

'Or it might be for keeps?'

'Possibly. We don't know just how badly our society has been disrupted.'

'But where would we go?'

'Up onto the moors north of Skipton.'

'But that's the middle of nowhere!'

'Precisely.'

'But when do you think we should go?'

'Now.'

'But we can't just leave.'

'Yes, you can. And you must.'

'We've no tents or camping gear, and we'd—'

Ben's eyes glittered with an intensity I'd not seen before. 'I've made all the preparations. In my garage you'll find backpacks, lightweight tents, food, first aid kits, boots – everything you'll need. And you can take some of my rifles and shotguns. There's plenty of ammunition.'

'Hey, whoa, whoa,' Stephen stood up. 'This is going way too quick for me.'

'Surely, we'd be best sticking it out in Fairburn,' I said. 'We have homes here.'

'Right,' Ben said. 'I'll give it to you straight. When the mob tried to storm the food depot last night there was one thing they didn't know.' He paused, his eyes flicking from face to face. 'It is empty. There is no food left.'

'The other food stores would—'

'The other food stores are empty, too.' Ben rubbed his forehead as if developing a headache. 'Basically there is no food left in the village. And when forty thousand people begin to starve I wouldn't like to predict what they will do.'

Gina said simply. 'What they will do is they'll leave.'

'Granted, most will try and head for another camp. But the army have been given orders to block all roads and stop all refugee movement between camps. Before the mobile phone system went down, people were speaking to refugees in other camps, finding out which were the most comfortable and well fed, then heading there. Needless to say, those camps that were initially the best supplied were overrun with waves of new refugees.'

Stephen shook his head. 'So now the army are to keep starving people bottled up in their camps?'

'That's about the size of it.'

'But why are you telling us all this?' I asked. What Ben had just told us made me change my mind completely about the wisdom of staying put. 'Surely we all need to be getting the hell out of Fairburn?'

'I'm telling you people this because I've known nearly all of you for the last ten years. I've never had children of my own, and, go ahead, call me sentimental, but I guess I'm projecting my paternal instincts onto you. So last night I made a list of your names. It makes a group of sixty-two men and women between the ages of sixteen and thirty-one with no immediate family ties in the area to keep you here. You're all young, healthy and, by Heaven, I'd hate to see any of you suffer.'

'So you want to play God with a chosen few,' Stephen said in a low voice. 'Like Noah and his Ark. You're issuing advance warning of what amounts to another Flood of sorts, and giving us the means to save ourselves?'

Ben nodded, sombre. 'You're right. I am playing God. All I'm asking is that you humour my arrogance and my conceit. And you, Stephen Kennedy, can humour me in the role that I assign to you.'

Stephen looked at him suspiciously. 'And that is?'

'And that is if I'm playing God, you must play Noah.'

'You are kidding'

'The time for kidding is well past, Stephen. In years gone by it would be the doctor or army general or senior policeman that the public would look up to and accept their leadership. That time's past, too. But I'm gambling everyone here would agree to you to becoming their leader.'

'No way.' Stephen gave an emphatic shake of the head.

Ben looked at the sixty or so people gathered there in that hot airless library. 'My proposal is as follows: that you all move to a camp a safe distance from Fairburn, and that Stephen here be elected leader of you all. If you agree to this please raise your hand.'

Heads turned left to right as people looked at each other for a lead. But I hardly saw them. In my mind's eye I saw my home being ransacked, Caroline being carried away screaming into the woods, Leeds on fire and forty thousand people beginning to starve.

I didn't even consciously think about it. I raised my hand. Instantly, Dean and Howard raised theirs. Then Gina and Ruth followed suit and a second later a forest of arms suddenly appeared.

Stephen shook his head in disbelief. 'I can't . . . I just can't do it.'

Ben smiled. 'You'll manage. Believe me, you'll manage.'

Ben played more of the video tape: volcanoes, earthquakes, tidal waves, exploding gas pockets tearing holes in cities, killing hundreds of thousands – Mother Earth committing global infanticide. Then Ben handed out maps showing us the general area where we should make the camp. It was a good twenty kilometres from Fairburn. We would have to avoid all roads because of army patrols and checkpoints, and possibly also because of marauding refugees who'd soon turn to banditry. Then someone asked Ben the question that had been troubling me.

'Ben. Why aren't *you* coming with us?'

'I promised the parish council I'd stay here and help.'

'But surely there's nothing more you can do if the food's gone?'

'We'll form scavenging teams, try and find more food. Besides, call me old fashioned, but I did make a promise and I'll stick to it as long as humanly possible.'

'But the mob will come and turn your house over, looking for food.'

'You're right, they'll find the house soon enough. But we're going to turn the place into a fortress with armed guards. This will become one of the main food depots.' He smiled that crinkly smile of old. 'So, people, don't worry about me. Now, please come with me to the garage and you can get kitted out. You'll have no vehicles; everything you need you will have to carry yourselves. Oh, and one other thing.' He turned to look back at us as we stood, ready to follow him. 'I believe we will shortly be entering a new Dark Age. There'll be no newspapers or TV to record what happens to the human race during what must be one of the greatest challenges yet to our existence. I believe it's important we write down or record in some way these events and how we cope – or don't cope – with them. So please, if you can, keep diaries. Make notes of what happens to you. If you find letters, journals, tape recordings written or made by others please keep them safely. We must be able to tell our grandchildren and great-grandchildren how we faced this threat to the human race, and how we survived it. Now come on, let's get you kitted up and out of Fairburn – pronto.'

As we left the house and headed toward the garage a car pulled up driven by old man Fullwood from the garage. A truck followed packed with villagers carrying shotguns and rifles.

'Ben . . . Ben.' The old man hauled himself stiffly from the car. 'Just as we predicted, I'm afraid.'

Ben stopped dead. 'The camp?'

'It's uproar down there. They've broken into the food stores. Of course, they're empty and—'

'What about the other villagers?'

'They're barricaded into the old army camp. They've got chaps with guns like us, so I don't think the mob will try too hard to get inside.'

'Hell,' Ben said softly. 'The best laid plans of mice and men, eh? Right, you'd best deploy the people with guns around the edge of the garden in case we get visitors.'

When the old man hobbled away to the truck to relay the orders Ben turned to Stephen. 'We've got a problem. I didn't tell the parish council about my plan to get you out of here. You see, they might not let you leave with what food supplies I've been able to share among you.'

'Then we're stuck,' Dean said.

'No. There'll be a guard tonight, but it'll change at two in the morning. I'll keep the new set of guards talking for a few minutes

105

at the blind side of the house while you, Stephen, get your people away the other side into the wood and over the hill.'

'*My* people?'

Ben pulled a small smile. 'Yes, *your* people, Stephen. Or should I call you Noah?'

CHAPTER 21

All that day Ben did his best to keep us away from the rest of the villagers; he didn't want any of them getting wind that we were leaving what amounted a sinking ship.

Even so, Dean, myself and a few of the others who would be leaving that night helped put in a line of three-metre-high fence posts ready to be strung with barbed wire. God willing, we wouldn't be around to see it, but within a day or so Ben's house would resemble a Word War II prisoner-of-war camp, surrounded by a high barbed-wire fence.

With the sun hammering down onto my bare back, Dean and I dug holes for the posts.

'Make sure they're deep enough, lads,' the grey-haired man told us. Before civilization turned its belly to the sky he'd been our postman. Now he carried one of Ben's Remmington shotguns over one shoulder like a Texas cowboy. 'We don't want those bastards having the run of this place, too.' He went on to give a bitter catalogue of the refugees' crimes against the village. In little more than a week the villagers' attitude towards the refugees had morphed from sympathy to hatred, as if they were an invading army of demons rather than thousands of normally law-abiding citizens driven from their homes by poison gas.

'And that's not all they did,' he grunted. 'I came home to find them going through my house like a plague of rats: blankets, shoes, food, drink – they took the lot. The devils even took the light bulbs. God knows what use they were to anyone with no electricity, and no fucking light fittings come to that, squatting out there in the fields. And another thing, do you know they beat up old Mrs Edgar? Beat her black and blue they did. All for a loaf of bread.'

I grunted in the pause between the guy's horror stories. Christ, there were some awful things. Like what had happened to Caroline.

Like my home being ransacked. But I could see what was happening. The villagers weren't saying *some* of the refugees were causing trouble. They were saying *all* were evil good-for-nothing scroungers. This was a psychological preparation for all-out war with them. What's that saying? Tarring everyone with the same brush? That's it. The people of Fairburn were beginning to see the people of Leeds – men, women, children, doddering grandparents – they were beginning to see them as some kind of subspecies that wasn't even really human. 'So it doesn't matter if we have to start shooting the bastards,' I could imagine him saying, that grey-haired man who'd delivered parcels and letters six days a week for the last thirty years. 'Why wait there? The best form of defence is attack.' I didn't doubt for a moment that within a few days the inhabitants of once sleepy Fairburn would be petrol bombing and machine-gunning the refugees as they slept under the pastel-coloured duvets they'd carried on their backs all the way from Leeds.

Ben had been right. It was time to get out.

More villagers arrived, pushing wheelbarrows full of mounds of wet cement. We held the wooden post in place as they shovelled it in. Then old man Fullwood limped up with a radio.

'News in one minute if anyone wants to listen.'

Everyone did and huddled round the radio as if what would be said in the next few seconds were going to be the most important words ever spoken on Earth. I'd heard some of the news bulletins already that morning. They seemed little more than a rehash of what we'd seen on CNN.

'Shh . . . it's starting,' Fullwood said, holding up one hand as if to silence a multitude.

We listened. First came a public information announcement. 'Since the declaration of a State of Emergency all unauthorized movement of people is banned. You must stay in your homes. If you are in one of the temporary camps you must remain there until further notice. All airports, sea ports and railway stations are closed until further notice. These are temporary measures. We are confident that in a day or two . . .'

'Blah, blah, who do they think they are kidding?'

'Ssh.' The postman glared fiercely at Dean.

Dean looked at me and I shrugged. I wandered off to sit in the shade of one of Ben's apple trees. I was hot, thirsty and pissed off. I was sick of the paranoia infecting the place. If someone who you always thought of as reasonable and pleasant starts acting in a manner that is decidedly unpleasant and mean, then you might say, 'Just look at him; it's like he's grown another head.' Now I saw the villagers were all growing another head. And it was an ugly head. In its eyes you read intolerance, hatred.

Overhead flocks of birds flew in dark clouds. You couldn't see where one flock ended and another began. They were all flying from west to east. Whatever it was that drove their migration was probably the same thing that drove people out of whole cities. In my mind's eye I saw more of that poison gas spurting from the ground the length and breadth of the country. Then there were the pockets of methane gas that were being detonated by the subterranean heat, creeping up through the Earth's crust from its molten iron core. Was it even now reaching up to where I sat on that sweet grass beneath the apple tree?

How long before I put my hands down onto the soil and felt it hot against my skin? I remembered the worms. How they had danced weirdly on their tails as if they were trying avoid contact with the ground. Had it started then? Was the heat becoming so unbearable to the worm population of Fairburn that evening that it forced them to attempt to reach the cool evening air?

Shit. This was bad.

I couldn't get my head around it. Shit, shit, shit. People must be dying by the million. What about Mum? I knew she was in Italy. But what was happening there? Was she safe? Dad, too, come to that. I can't say I felt great affection for him. But what had happened to him? Was he in a refugee camp? Was the gas leaking out of the American landscape, too? Had he coughed up a lung as he lay there in bed with his new twenty-something bride?

I looked down at the ground, expecting any moment to see it smoulder before bursting into flame. I'd dance there like Fred Astaire on speed, with the flames licking my shins, the intense heat melting my trainers.

Mouth dry as cinders, I stared down at the grass between my feet as I sat, back to the trunk. A dappled mixture of sunlight and shadow danced around my feet. But any second now I might see smoke, streaming up from the soil as—

'Rick? Rick Kennedy, isn't it?'

I looked up at the figure. The sun was behind her head. All I could see was a female shape surrounded by a blazing halo as the sun shone through a light froth of hair.

'Would you like a drink?' the female voice asked.

'Eh, yes . . . thank you.' I squinted up at her as I climbed to my feet.

'You remember me, don't you? I'm—'

'Kate Robinson. Yes, eh . . .' I struggled for something to say; then managed a lame. 'How do you do . . .?' Held out a hand for her to shake, then saw it was chocolate brown from Ben's garden soil. 'Sorry. I've been, eh, digging, the, eh . . .'

'Fence posts?' She smiled. 'Yes. I've been watching you.'

'You have?'

'Frightening, isn't it? You set out to save our lives; then you have to do all this to stop us from ransacking your homes.'

'Oh, so you're—' I stopped, blushing.

'Yes. I'm one of the mob, formerly known as a refugee from Leeds.'

I blushed harder. 'I'm sorry. I didn't mean . . .'

She handed me a bottle of water. 'I know you didn't mean it. But that's the reality, isn't it? We're now on different sides.'

'You make it sound as if we're going to fight a war.'

'That's exactly what's going to happen, isn't it?' she said, and looked at me with those intense eyes of hers. 'We're going to fight each other for the last tin of baked beans.'

'It might not come to that.' I took a swallow of water. It was sweet, cold and felt oh-so-good drenching my burning throat. 'Once the authorities get their act together they'll start bringing supplies.'

'Yes,' she nodded, those intense eyes fixed on mine. 'They'll bring in food, and clothes and tents – all strapped onto the backs of specially bred flying pigs.'

'You don't believe they'll send help?'

'No. Do you?'

I handed her back the bottle of water. I couldn't answer that one. There was no anger in her voice, only sadness. She wasn't there to pick a fight with me. 'Where are you staying?' I asked.

'First off it was a patch of grass called King Elmet's . . . Acre?'

'King Elmet's Mile.'

'A wonderful name. But I don't think much to the room service.' She began to tell me how she and her flatmates from Leeds had driven up to Fairburn when the gas hit Leeds. They'd planned to stay with her cousin who lived in the village, but they'd found the house locked up. Now she'd have had no qualms breaking in, but then it seemed pretty well anti-social even if the house did belong to your favourite cousin. So they'd had to content themselves with sleeping rough on blankets in the field just a dozen or so steps from my house. As I'd looked from the window on that first morning after the refugee camp had appeared overnight like a spring frost I might have seen her among those thousands of people squatting out there on the grass.

I'd turned down Caroline's plea for her and her daughter to move in with me. Would I have refused Kate Robinson? She stood there in front of me, dressed in a short denim skirt and clinging white T-shirt, her slender body curving as she leaned against the tree, her long delicate fingers curled around the bottle. And those legs ... I had to make a conscious effort not to stare at a pair of legs, tanned golden brown, that seemed to go on for ever.

More to the point: would I have invited Kate Robinson to stay?

As I listened to Kate speaking, finding my eyes drawn first to her near-Oriental almond-shaped eyes, then to her full pink lips, then back to her eyes again, I happened to glance over her shoulder in the direction of the house.

Looking out of the window, her eyes fixed intently on us, I saw Caroline Lucas. I don't know if Caroline noticed I'd seen her. In any event she still stared.

I shifted uncomfortably. That damn woman . . . instantly I regretted thinking of her in that way. She's gone through torture, Rick, I told myself, she needs a friend.

Yeah, but does it have to be me, came the other voice that always plays devil's advocate as soon as my conscience pipes up. It's not as if you're a knight in shining armour who charged to the rescue.

No, chipped in the damn whining voice of conscience again, you left her to be raped, sodomized and Christ knows what else. You were ready to take on that mob who raided your house single-handed, just to stop one of them taking a frigging stupid spaghetti jar, but you left that poor woman to be raped in the woods by a gang of men behaving like fuck-crazed beasts.

So, continued whining conscience, now you're going to leave Kate Robinson here in Fairburn? The refugee camp's going to go ballistic in about three days flat. For weeks you've thought of nothing else but getting Kate into bed, now you're going to leave her to the same fate as Caroline. For Chrissakes, she'll probably be dead within the week.

110

'I think they're ready for you to start digging again.'

'Digging?' I came out of my tussle with whining conscience.

She smiled a beautiful smile. Her eyes were clear and gentle and I felt a massive surge of electricity run through me. I could have reached out and held her head in my hands and kissed her. 'Yes, digging, Rick. Here, have another drink.' She smiled again, though this time the smile had an underlying sadness. 'Not that I can blame you for having a lot on your mind. When I think back to you and Stephen doing the *This Is Your Life* routine at Ben's party, it all seems as if it happened years ago, doesn't it?'

'Hell, you can say that again.'

'And how we went out looking for that gang that beat up your friend.'

'Stenno. I still think he's concussed or something. He's been acting weird.'

I recalled that night, too. The face that stared at me from the darkness. Being forced to the ground. That lost hour.

'They should try and get him to the hospital in Bradford; apparently that's still functioning OK.'

As I looked into her green eyes again I knew I couldn't leave her behind tonight. Despite Ben Cavellero's insistence on keeping this night-time vanishing act secret, I'd have to risk telling Kate and persuading her she should escape with us.

CHAPTER 22

'Don't worry, I know,' Kate told me as we walked out of the shade of the apple tree and in the direction of Dean who was sweatily digging a hole for another fence post.

'You know?' I paused.

'Just because I was one of the hated refugees doesn't mean I've become the sworn enemy. When my cousin managed to get home I stayed with her a couple of days, then I got the message to come up here to Ben's this morning.'

'You were at the meeting?' I felt a wave of relief flowing from my toes upwards.

'It was a bit of a crush, wasn't it? I was wedged in at the back so you wouldn't have seen me.'

'So you think it's a sensible move?' I asked her as I picked up the shovel. 'Leaving Fairburn to go and camp out on the moor?'

She looked round as if afraid we'd be overheard but the nearest villager was old Fullwood, stamping wet concrete down around one of the fence posts. 'Yes,' she said, 'I don't see that we've got any choice. Forty thousand people aren't going to sit there passively and watch their families starve to death. Drink?' She handed Dean the bottle. 'By the way, we're all getting some basic tuition on using firearms. I've just had mine. Ben asked me to let you know your lesson begins at two.'

With that she left, her hair shining in the sunlight.

'Nice legs,' Dean said, taking another swallow of water.

I thought about the world heating up beneath our feet. And the anarchy, murder and mayhem breaking out all around us. And I realized human nature wasn't licked yet. 'Yeah.' I gave a grim smile. 'Nice legs.'

CHAPTER 23

Nine o'clock; evening. I lay on a mattress in what must have been little more than a broom cupboard in Ben Cavellero's house. All the rooms, the hallways, the landing were crammed with the people who would leave in five hours' time. Seeing as we would be walking through the night, it made sense to try and grab some sleep. But it was hard with the July sun still shining against the curtains. I was alone. Restless.

Ben had circulated faxes and hard-copy e-mail messages from people around the world. He wanted us to know what was happening out there.

I picked up a wad of A4 sheets from the floor beside me. A fistful of doom and terror that had the power to drive ice waves of sheer fright through my veins.

I shivered as I flicked through them, letting odd sentences hit me in the eye:

Paris streets now deep in grey ash. The Seine breaks its banks, choked with ash sludge and the drowned . . .

And:

Melbourne was today filled with a choking gas. It settled low to the ground. Up here on the fourth floor of the student accommodation block we are safe. But there are so many of our fellow students lying dead in the road down there. Soon we will have to find some way of going into the city for food. Our only hope, that the gas disperses soon.

And transcripts of radio broadcasts:

All around the ship . . . the sea is on fire. Inflammable gas is bubbling to the surface. What ignited it I don't know. But we are sailing into a burning ocean. If we – Message ends abruptly.

I began to read the reports in full:

e-mail message. From Endsville, USA. Typed with one finger by a man with no hair but plenty of booze.

Date: Who cares?

Time: What does it matter?

This morning half the world blew to Kingdom Come. At least it felt that way. We'd been on vacation to Orlando. This morning as I stood on the balcony I watched Disneyland make one mighty leap toward Heaven. Epcot Centre, Magic Kingdom, Thunder Mountain. Everything just lifted. Then came the flames, standing halfway to the sky in a curtain of fire. Even poor Mickey's gone now. No one's safe. Sue and the kids went yesterday. Just swallowed into the ground over on Rodeo Drive; that old blacktop cracked open easy as pie crust. Lord love them. They'll be in Heaven playing with Mickey and Donald Duck and Simba now. Jordan loved the Lion King. I keep looking out of the windows at the clouds. Lord, wouldn't I love to see those clouds swell up into heads and those heads to be Sue, Jordan, Louis and little Tish? Lord help them now. Lord, may He take care of them. Lord, I'm typing slow now. I'm in a high school an hour's drive from that burning hole in the ground that was once Disneyland. They've got a generator and this computer where I can send e-mail out to the world. And I've got glass in my face from the explosion. Lord, I'm dripping red on the keyboard again. Don't worry, e-mail can't transmit that nasty little bug.

I imagined a middle-aged man, sitting typing one-fingered at the computer. There's a bottle of whisky in his hand. He takes a gulp every ten words. Pieces of glass stick like rough diamonds from his face. And there's a kind of tranquillity about him. The worst that could happen to him has happened. He'd raged and cursed and kicked furniture until he'd roared out all the anger. Strangely I felt a kinship and sympathy with him. And I knew he'd go on

113

serenely transmitting his thoughts and experiences to the world until he finally bled to death.

Some of the people pitching their reports to the rest of humanity weren't so serene.

I picked out another sheet.

fax message

The word FAX had been deleted with a slash of a pen. Another word had been scratched in to replace it so it now read:

fux message

From: Franco Mendez

Possibly somewhere in Greenwich Village, New York City; forgive me, please if I sound a mite vague, only the place don't look like it did when I went to bed last night.

Let's cut to the chase. It's important you know what happened to us.

Oscar Wilde said: 'I am not exactly pleased with the Atlantic, it is not so majestic as I expected.'

Last night I kissed my girlfriend at the door of our apartment as she headed off to patrol these mean streets for the NYPD. Ten minutes later Oscar Wilde's not-so-majestic Atlantic came to New York. We'd heard about the subterranean gas explosions in the Atlantic seabed and the underwater volcanic eruptions. Well, last night one or the other caused the Atlantic to rise up in her most awful majesty. I heard it coming. Like a train roaring down its track. Then with a godawful thump the tidal wave hit the city; it tore through the apartment blocks, smashing them to shit, spilling screaming men, women and children out of their beds and into the water. Ours is one of the few that remain standing. I look out the window now; I see the ocean lapping at second-floor windows. What's left of them. There's a lot of stuff floating in the water. One of those pieces of stuff is, I guess, my girlfriend. And to think I was going to dump the cheating whore anyway.

I listen to the radio. I know YOU are out there. And it pisses me off so incredibly . . . so fucking much. Why should God be selective when it comes to the end of the world? I mean has He saved all the fucking niggers? All the fucking lesbos? All the fucking jews? (Yeah, yeah, right! I know, I know, it should be a fucking capital J for 'Jews' but what the hell do I fucking care now? This whole block's about to fall into the majestic fucking Atlantic ocean.) And

114

he must have saved fucking YOU, otherwise YOU wouldn't be fucking reading this.

But I'm going to do what I've always wanted to do. Carol-Marie kept a spare Colt .45 in her pantyhose drawer so I'm going to take it and blow some fucking heads off. Nigger boy down the hallway's going to get it first – and his fucking ratboy son in his day-glo orange sneakers. BOOM-BOOM. This's long, long overdue.

And if I knew where fucking YOU lived, I'd blow a hole in YOUR fucking face as well.

Now, from watery mansions, New York City, my final message to you all is:-

YOU TURNED YOUR BACKS ON FUCKING JESUS, YOU BROUGHT THIS ON YOURSELVES.

now: fuck off!!!

What a miserable Nazi jerk, I thought. But the disturbing thought to hit me was we'd seen it starting to happen to us. This disaster had hit the paranoia button. You wanted to pin the blame for all this shit on someone.

I picked up another fax message.

From: Samuel K. Marsh, Birmingham.

'And the sea gave up the dead in it. Death and Hades were thrown into the lake of fire . . . if anyone's name was not found written in the book of life, he was thrown into the lake of fire.'

This apocalypse that has visited us all is predicted in the Book Of Revelations. Remember what Christ said when—

'Rick?'

'Uh . . . hello, Caroline. How you feeling?' Damn. I could have been asking her if she'd recovered from a cold, not from being carried into the woods by the bastards and – 'I'm sorry. I didn't mean . . . I'm sorry, what can I say?'

'Hush, hush. I came to thank you for bringing me here.'

'It's the least I could do . . . really it was.' I felt awkward, tongue-tied.

'May I sit down?'

'Of course.' Quickly I sat up. The only place in the tiny room for her to sit was on the mattress. I was sleeping nude and awkwardly held the sheet across my waist like a shy schoolgirl.

Caroline wore a man's white cotton shirt and leggings. Her feet

115

were bare. 'Well . . .' She smiled. 'They couldn't have found a smaller room for you if they'd tried.'

'I don't mind. At least I'm not sleeping out on the landing.'

'And it won't be for long.'

'Oh, so you know about—'

'Yes, I'm coming with you.' The scratches on her face and throat looked less raw now, and she smiled as she spoke in that gentle yet husky voice that reminded me of some late-night female radio jock. A dusky, velvet voice that would pad gently through the radio speakers into a night-dark room.

'Are you sure you're up to it?' I immediately flushed again, feeling I'd put my foot in it.

'I'll be fine. Female flesh is far more resilient than you think, you know?'

'Sorry.'

'Hush, stop saying sorry.' Lightly she touched the top of my shoulder. 'Mmm . . . hot. A touch of sunburn?'

'It's not bad. It must have been today when I was digging.'

'Ah, the holes for the fence posts.'

'They're going to try and make it secure from—'

'People like us? The refugees turned monsters who've invaded your village.' She gave a sad smile, her brown eyes dropping down before slowly lifting up to mine. Somehow I felt even that brown-eyed gaze stroked my bare chest and face.

'Sorry, I—'

Her brown eyes flashed with sudden humour. In a mock scolding way she whispered, 'Rick. Stop saying sorry. You'll be apologizing next for causing this whole rotten world to blow up under our feet.'

I smiled. 'I'm s— I just feel . . . well, I feel so damn guilty about what happened to you.'

'Don't,' she said firmly. 'If anything I pounced on you and put you in that awkward position. You couldn't have invited all of us waifs and strays into your house. Now . . .' She smiled in such a friendly way I couldn't help but smile back. 'Who was that girl I saw you talking with today? Under the apple tree? Mmm?'

'That's Kate Robinson; she—'

'She's your girlfriend.'

I shook my head.

'Come on, you can tell your Auntie Caroline.'

'No, honestly. I hardly know her.'

'OK.' Caroline leaned towards the door and pushed it shut. Then quickly she said, 'I want you to be nice to me.'

'Uh . . . I am being nice . . . aren't I?'

'Very nice. But I want you to be nicer.'

'Caroline?'

In five seconds flat she'd slipped off the shirt and leggings. She didn't remove the briefs, however. Then, still keeping eye contact, she slipped under the sheet. I felt her hand stroke my thigh upwards, then gently she cupped my testicles with her hand.

'Caroline, you don't have to—'

'Shh . . . Auntie Caroline knows best.'

'Caroline, I—'

She kissed me on the mouth. Her lips were so soft and warm, and the tiny tremble I felt through them transmitted itself to me. My heart beat faster, I breathed deeply as I felt her hand begin to caress my cock. Christ, she had such a wonderful touch. I felt myself light up inside.

I looked down into her face. Her eyes glistening in the evening light were so trusting again. I found myself looking down at her small breasts with their pink nipples. I couldn't help but notice the bruises standing out so vividly they looked as if they'd been daubed there with black ink.

I hadn't chosen this. But right then I knew she had power over me. I couldn't say 'No' again.

Lamely I said, 'Caroline, you know you don't have to do this.'

'Last night . . .' She kissed me on the mouth. 'I didn't have a choice . . .' She kissed me on the throat. 'Tonight I can . . .' She kissed me on the chest: moist, cool kisses. 'Tonight, I can say "Yes" or I can say "No" if a man asks me to go to bed with him, so . . .' She kissed me on the stomach. 'So, it's important to me that I do this for you.' She kissed my pubes. 'But you mustn't fuck me tonight. I'm still sore. One of them used a piece of wood.' She sounded matter-of-fact; no self-pity there. 'Mmm . . . you like this, don't you?' I felt her kissing me along the length of my cock. *'God. You're hard as a rock.'*

I lay back and looked up at the ceiling. I shouldn't have been turned on. There was too much shit happening. In five hours we were going to run for our lives. Kate Robinson's smiling face appeared in my mind's eye. That titchy room with its bare

117

walls and bare light bulb dangling from its flex made no cosy love nest.

But I was turned on. I felt sheer, sheer pleasure. My skin felt unusually sensitive so I could feel the light touch of Caroline's tongue and her lips moving up and down the length of my penis; then the dizzying sensation of her tongue working around and around its tip. My head spun like I was on a fairground Octopus ride as that tongue went round and around. I looked down at her. Her head twisted from side to side as she sucked enthusiastically.

'This is wonderful . . . this's fan— tasitic . . . this is what I wanted so much,' she murmured before filling her mouth with me again.

It was fantastic. *Fann—tass—tick . . . oh, ay-ay-ay believe me*. At first I hardly dared touch her – as if she was a fragile antique doll. But within a moment I held bunches of her hair in my fists as my breathing came harder and harder.

CHAPTER 24

Ben Cavellero said to Stephen: 'There's someone following us. Keep everyone walking.' He looked at me, his eyes glinting in the moonlight. 'Rick, will you double back with me to see who it is?'

I nodded.

Ben patted me on the shoulder. 'Best keep the rifle cocked ready.'

This was it. My mouth dried.

We'd set off to walk out of Fairburn at 2 a.m. The Moon shone bright, hard and as round as a coin. But we'd barely cleared the wood at the back of Ben Cavellero's house. Now it looked as if Ben and I were to fight a rearguard action to allow the others time to escape.

I followed Ben down the line of silent people who were loaded down with backpacks, bedrolls, sleeping bags, pans, shotguns, rifles. Kate caught my eye and nodded as I passed her by. Near the end of the line walked Caroline, a tiny figure beneath the huge backpack. I nodded to her as I passed.

She caught my arm.

'What's wrong?' she whispered.

'We're being followed.'

'People from the refugee camp?'

'I don't know. Best keep moving with the others.'

'I want to come with you.'

'No.'

'No job for a *mere* woman?' Her voice, not hostile, was gentle as ever. She only wanted to be with me. Whatever happened.

'Caroline. To be honest, this is no job for me, either. I know in theory how this rifle works – but I've not actually fired the damn thing.'

'I'm coming with you, Rick.'

'Rick,' Ben called softly back to me. 'What's the problem?'

'No problem,' Caroline whispered back as she left the line of people and joined Ben by a clump of bushes. 'I know how to fire a pistol. I learned when I was working in South Africa.'

Ben said, 'OK. You were issued with the .38 Smith & Wesson?'

'That's right. Trust me, I'm good with a gun.'

'Don't worry, I trust you. Now . . . I hadn't expected this would happen, so I've got no great strategy in mind. I propose we just wait in these bushes to see who's following us and take it from there. OK?'

'And if it's a mob from the camp?'

'Pray that it isn't,' Caroline whispered.

Ben nodded. 'We're armed, but if there's more than half a dozen we'll have our work cut out.'

Great, I thought bitterly. We'd started out trying to save the refugees' lives; now we were going to begin killing them.

We waited there in the darkness. Caroline rested her free hand on my bare forearm. The gesture was reassuring, almost protective.

'Here they come,' Ben whispered. 'Don't fire unless I start firing.'

I glanced back at the others threading their way up through the trees. They were a good hundred paces away now. I could just make out Stephen, striding ahead of the column. Every so often he'd shoot an anxious glance back in our direction.

Jesus wept. Just days ago I was planning to take a rock band out on the road. I'd mapped my future out. Now I'd got no home; my guitar was stashed in Ben's attic; my own particular future might be to die and rot into the Earth beneath these very trees where I'd played as a child.

I heard the rustle of a bush; the faint crunch of feet on dried leaves.

If you shoot someone, do you aim at the head or the chest?

I raised the rifle to my shoulder. Chest, I decided. Bigger target.

I noticed Caroline ease the revolver from a pouch attached to her belt. She stood legs apart, knees slightly bent, like I'd seen cops in the movies. Hell, she'd had professional training.

More leaves scrunched under feet.

Ben raised the shotgun.

We waited. I found I was holding my breath. My heart sounded like the bass drum driving the beat harder, faster.

Here they come, here they come, here they . . .

A figure came through the bushes. They moved faster than I expected; we'd been seen; the mob would attack first.

My finger curled round the trigger.

Tightened. The figure moved into my sights.

I thought: *Chest. Aim at chest.*

'Bill? Bill Fullwood?' Ben's voice came out in an astonished gasp as if he'd just seen an angel drop from heaven. 'Bill . . . what the hell are you doing here? What's wrong?'

Old man Fullwood, the proprietor of Fullwood's Autos, clambered up the hill, his froth of white hair bright as a halo in the moonlight. He panted noisily and sweat glistened on his face.

'Bill . . . what's the matter?' Ben hissed. 'Anything happened at the house?'

Old man Fullwood wiped the sweat from his face with the sleeve of his boiler suit. He couldn't catch his breath.

'Take it easy,' Ben took the old man by his arm. 'Best sit for a moment.'

'No, no. I'm fine, thank you . . . thank you very much.'

'What on Earth are you doing, charging through the woods at this time of night?'

'I . . .' He inhaled deeply. 'I saw you . . . and these young lads and lasses . . . all packed up. You're leaving Fairburn, aren't you?'

Ben shook his head. 'I'm only going as far as Oak Ridge. Then I'm going back home.'

'But these lads and lasses . . .'

'Yes, they're leaving, Bill. They're going to sit this out somewhere nice and quiet.'

'For how long?'

'Until it's safe to come back.' Ben took a deep breath. 'Bill, I know how you feel. That everyone should stick together and help one another stay in Fairburn, but—'

'I know. It's Hell down there. That's why I'm going with them.'

'You want to go with them?' Ben sounded astonished. 'Bill, they're sleeping out under canvas. It might take months to—'

'I'm as useful as I ever was.' Old man Fullwood slapped his chest. 'Five years in the army. I've run my own business. There isn't a thing about cars and trucks I don't know.'

'But Bill—'

'Everything OK?'

'Stephen?' Ben sighed. 'Yes. Everything's fine. We had Mr Fullwood from the garage following us that's all.'

I said, 'He wants to come with us, Stephen.'

'Out onto the Moors?'

'Yes, I do,' old man Fullwood said firmly. 'There's life in the old dog yet, you know. So please don't tell me to go back home. I won't—'

'OK,' Stephen said quickly. 'You can come with us.' He looked at Ben. 'Don't worry. We've room for one more.'

Caroline took his arm. 'Come on, Mr Fullwood.' She glanced at me and gave a warm smile. 'You can walk with me and keep me company.'

Holding his arm she walked with him to join that line of *nouveaux* refugees who still pushed on up the wooded hillside.

Ben said, 'You don't want him with you. OK, he's a very nice guy, a gentleman, but he's seventy-five years old.'

'I didn't want to stand and argue the toss.' Stephen sounded more businesslike than I'd ever heard him before. 'And this is my . . . tribe, I guess you'd call it now. So what I say goes, right?'

Ben nodded in agreement. 'You're the boss.'

'Besides, what would have happened if we'd turned him down? He'd have gone down there and squealed on us – and you – to the rest of the villagers. They'd have cooked your goose, Ben.'

Ben shook his head grimly. 'That's what he would have intended but . . .' Ben rested the shotgun barrel across his shoulder. 'But I'd already made up my mind what I would have done. I'd have shot him as we walked back down to the house.'

'I know. That's why I let him join us.'

Ben held out his hand for Stephen to shake. 'Don't let that

humanitarian streak get the better of you. It's going to be a liability rather than an asset now, you know?'

Stephen shook him warmly by the hand. 'Whatever does happen, Ben, I'll make sure we come out of this with our humanity still intact.'

'I believe you will, friend . . . Ah, Rick.' He shook my hand. 'Look after each other, won't you?' His eyes twinkled in the moonlight as he backed away still smiling. 'I'll be seeing you.'

'You know where to find us if things don't work out here,' called Stephen.

'You can count on it. Goodbye . . . and good luck.' With that Ben turned and walked quickly down hill.

Stephen turned and looked at me. 'All right, Kid K. You think we're up to the Noah bit?'

'I'm not, but you are.'

'You will be soon, son – you will be. Come on, then, let's march those folks out two by two.'

Then, singing softly under his breath, he led the way up the hill.

CHAPTER 25

My name is Kate Robinson. I am nineteen years old. Until a few days ago I shared a flat with two friends in Leeds where I worked at a city centre book shop.

Yesterday at a meeting at Ben Cavellero's house he asked us to record our experiences as we enter a new Dark Age, where there will soon be no newspapers, television or radio.

So I'll do my best. This is what happened to me:-

At two this morning we left Ben Cavellero's house under cover of darkness. We then walked for ten hours across country avoiding all roads and human settlements by sticking to one of the ancient pack-horse routes that run north along the spine of the Pennine hills. Today we covered perhaps fifteen kilometres.

Everyone is pretty much exhausted. Stephen Kennedy (the elected leader of our group) has told us there'll be no more travelling today. I'm pleased about that. The old man, who joined the group, has kept up with us OK so far, but I don't know how much longer he can maintain the pace.

It is now mid-afternoon, the sun is really blazing down. We have erected tents in a grass field. There are no houses or roads in sight. We are alone. Already I'm feeling such relief to be away from the refugee camp. With so many people crowding into that little village it felt claustrophobic.

Where I now sit at the entrance to the tent I'm sharing with Ruth Sparkman and Charlotte Lewis, I can see Stephen and Rick Kennedy setting up the camping stoves. The two brothers are so much alike it's astonishing. They could be mistaken for twins despite the five-year age difference.

I guess I'm self-appointed archivist now. I've brought a wallet full of faxes and hard copies of e-mail messages from people around the world. They relate their experiences; much of it is harrowing reading.

A few minutes ago Rick Kennedy stopped by the tent to ask me what I was doing as I sorted the pieces of paper into date order. He's got a nice smile. His eyes are the same striking blue as his brother's. I heard he played guitar in a rock band.

'Have you read these?' he asked, picking out one of the sheets of paper.

'All of them,' I said. 'I wish I hadn't. I couldn't sleep after that.'

'Grim, aren't they? The poor guy who lost his family in the Disneyland explosion. He'd just decided to give up on life.'

'You get the feeling, though, that if he'd still had the people he loved with him he'd have done anything to survive.'

'I think you're right, Kate.'

Kate. For some reason something near a giddy thrill ran through me when he said my name. *Kate.*

'So it's particularly hard to do a Robinson Crusoe and survive alone,' I told him as he flicked through the sheets of paper. 'Half the battle is having someone to love and someone you know loves you.'

He smiled at me. 'I suppose even Robinson Crusoe finally had his Man Friday.'

'*You really think so?*'

He laughed, his teeth shining white. 'No . . . no, when I . . .' He burst out laughing again, a tear squeezing out along one of his long lashes. 'No. When I say Robinson finally had his Man Friday I meant

– oh, what does it matter. If – if they *were* fond of each other that's all that matters, isn't it?'

I think it was the tension of the last few days, then this sudden sense of freedom that suddenly set us off giggling like school kids. As he wiped the tears from his eyes Caroline suddenly appeared.

'Hello, Kate. Sorry to interrupt, Rick, but Stephen needs to know where the matches are.'

'Oh . . . Caroline, I'll get them.'

'No need, Rick, just tell me where they are.'

'They're in the side pocket of my backpack. It's the black one over there by the wall.'

Caroline gave a bright smile. 'Everyone like bacon?'

'Yes,' he said, 'that would be nice.' Rick's a bit of a mystery. Mostly he comes across as something of a rogue with the mischievous twinkle in his blue eyes. Now all of a sudden he spoke to Caroline in a polite, respectful way as if she was his aunt – a strict Primitive Methodist aunt at that.

After she'd gone he glanced through more of the fax messages. 'Kate. This really is global, isn't it?'

'As far as I can see. Africa, Asia, Australia, North America – they've all been hit bad.'

He licked his thumb and put the sheets of paper down on my lap one at a time almost as if he was dealing a hand of playing cards. As he did so he listed each catastrophe. Melbourne: poison gas. Florida: explosion of inflammable gas. France and Spain: volcanoes. New York: destroyed by tidal wave. One from a Karl Langeveld, Johannesburg, South Africa. He began to read. '"Here I am at the top of the building. I can see the whole of Klein Street. The toxic gas hasn't shifted for six days. Commissioner Street is littered with corpses; the gas killed people in their thousands. Every so often I see someone enter the street. Soon they will hold their hands to their face and throat, then they fall, they squirm for a few movements, then they lie still. Completely still. Birds here on the roof are not affected by the gas. Not until they swoop below the second floor. Then they fall to the ground; wings beat frantically at the pavement; then they are stilled, too.

'"Now nothing moves. Nothing, that is, except the Grey Men."' Rick paused, frowning. Then read on. '"I saw the Grey Men last night. They walked amongst my gassed countrymen. The gas does not hurt them. I am terrified, because the Grey Men looked up at

124

me as I watched them. They stared at me. They are fascinated by me. I obsess them. I watch me from the street every time I look down from the top of the building. Sometime soon, I think, they will break down the doors of the office block and hunt me down. They are the Grey Men. I don't know where they are from. They frighten me.'" Rick suddenly looked troubled. 'The Grey Men. What does he mean: the Grey Men?'

I shrugged. 'It's clearly from someone who's being driven insane by the whole experience. Either that or he has access to drugs.'

Rick lightly rubbed the tips of his fingers across his forehead as if suddenly preoccupied by some immense problem. 'This . . . Karl Langeveld says he can see Grey Men?'

I shrugged, but I was puzzled by Rick's interest in the bizarre piece of writing. 'Grey men? I don't know. If he is mentally ill it could easily have been blue gorillas or green Martians. Rick? You OK?'

'Sure, yeah . . . fine, fine.' He stood up and handed the papers back to me. 'Hell, it's hot.' He smiled, but it seemed a trifle forced to me. 'I'm going to get a drink. Fancy one?'

'No, thanks. I'll have one when we eat. Are you sure you're OK?'

'Yeah, fine. Bye.'

'Bye.'

Rick walked away in the direction of his bag where he'd have kept his water bottle, but clearly there was something on his mind. Instead of opening the bag, he stood with his elbows on the gate in the wall and gazed out across the adjoining field. His eyes were fixed on something on the distance. As if he saw a figure approaching. When I looked I saw there was no one there.

CHAPTER 26

I followed Kate Robinson down to the lake. I, Rick Kennedy, age nineteen, was going to do something stupid.

I was going to make a pass at her.

Here we were, *nouveaux* refugees, making tracks from Fairburn, escaping forty thousand other refugees who would soon be on the brink of starvation. The Earth was getting hot from the inside out, triggering volcanoes, toxic gas leaks, quakes, tidal waves, and I, Rick, brain rooted solidly between my legs, was going to make a pass at the beautiful girl walking down through the beautifully sun-washed meadow.

I followed about a hundred paces behind her. She hadn't seen me. In her hands, a pair of four-litre plastic water bottles.

It must be one of God's belly-aching, pant-wetting jokes: that He can inflict disaster and death on a global scale; He can bury New York under a billion gallons of Atlantic Ocean and Paris boulevards hip-deep in hot ash. But here in Swallow Dale, West Yorkshire it was a watercolour artist's idea of a green and pleasant land: bumble bees bumbled lazily amidst the clover at my feet, skylarks sang, a baby rabbit popped its head cheekily out of its hole to watch me stroll past with one thing on my mind.

To slip my hands behind Kate Robinson's head, luxuriate in the wash of hair over my fingers and press my lips to hers.

I walked faster. I'd catch her up before she reached the water's edge.

She wore a straw hat against the sun; a loose cotton blouse protected her shoulders and arms; her cut-off jeans hugged her behind in a way that seemed nothing short of miraculous.

Stephen had told us to take a one-hour lunch break; we'd made good progress on what was Day 2 of our journey to Fountains Moor. The first night under canvas had been problem-free. I'd only woken once. Then, half-awake, I'd seen someone crouching in the entrance of the tent, one hand holding back the flap. And I recollect seeing a big head, an absurdly big head in silhouette against the starry sky. The head had been angled to one side as if it had been studying me closely.

Then something came down solidly across my face.

In terror, I'd sat up, pushing it away with both hands. Straight away I'd seen it was only Howard's arm that he'd flung across my face as he'd turned over in the confined space. By the time I looked to the entrance of the tent the flap was back down. I'd meant to mention it to Stephen but in the bright light of day it seemed trivial. It might (I rationalized desperately) have just been someone who'd taken a midnight leak, then stumbled back to the wrong tent.

Now I'd got something more important to grab my attention. I was perhaps fifty paces behind Kate as she walked into the thick bank of trees that fringed the lake.

'Do it now, Ricky boy,' I whispered to myself. 'Don't be shy, just go for it.'

'Hey, Kate,' came a voice from the trees. 'Did you bring the bottles?'

Damn.

I cut off left. Through a gap in the bushes I could see Kate. She'd joined Ruth and another girl I didn't know at the water's edge. They were sitting on a fallen log, soaking their bare feet in the water.

Damn, damn, damn.

I cut into a clump of trees, suddenly embarrassed by the idea of being seen and knowing the three girls would instinctively guess what I'd intended. 'Oh-ho, Rick.' I could just imagine Ruth's teasing voice. 'Have you been following Kate?'

I moved away deeper into the fringe of trees. Maybe if I hung around out of sight the other two would leave Kate alone. Then I could—

'Hello, Rick. Remember me?'

I looked round to see Caroline pushing through the bushes towards me.

'Hello, Caroline . . . I thought I'd come down and wash in the lake.'

She smiled, her eyes twinkling in the sunlight dappling through the branches. 'We've plenty of time. Why don't we go for a swim?'

'Swim?'

'Mmm . . .' She slipped off the man's white shirt she wore. Beneath that she wore a white T-shirt. 'Don't be shy. No one will see.'

'Great idea . . . but Stephen's expecting me. We're working out a new route to Fountains Moor.' A thought occurred to me. 'Caroline?'

'Yes.' She moved so close she had to tilt her head back to look at me.

'You didn't by any chance come to my tent last night?'

'No, sadly. Why? Do you wish I had have done?'

'It's just I thought I saw someone looking in at me during the night.'

'Maybe it was Kate Robinson. You know, isn't she amazingly tall for a girl?'

'No. It definitely wasn't Kate.'

'Stephen posted sentries to keep watch last night, didn't he?'

'Yes.'

'They saw nothing?'

'They said not when I asked this morning, but if you ask me they might have dozed off.'

'Well . . .' She never took her brown eyes off mine as she spoke. 'I heard some, ahem, activity in nearby tents last night. Maybe they deserted their posts for some late night, ahem, target practice.'

'Which tents?' I asked, suddenly suspicious and trying to remember which tent Kate had slept in.

'I'm not sure, Rick. To the left of mine, I think.'

'Maybe I should tell Stephen about this, after all—'

'No, Rick. Don't walk away from your Auntie Caroline.'

'I really must be getting back to—'

'No, no, no,' she said softly.

'Caroline—'

'Auntie Caroline.'

'OK . . . OK.' I grinned but it felt forced. 'Auntie Caroline.'

'Mmm . . . it's good to be alone with you again.'

'And you.' Again I felt that dizzying swirl. On the one hand I wanted the Hell out of there. I didn't want to be involved with this woman who was nearly twenty years my senior. But when she got close like this . . . Those brown eyes. That husky voice. The soft froth of hair. The petite and somehow perfectly compact body. Jesus . . . I started to feel *that* burn again.

She moved closer until she was pressed against me. 'You never spoke about what we did on Saturday night in Ben's house.'

'It was wonderful, Caroline. It really was.'

'You should have told me how you felt. You like?'

I smiled, warmer this time. 'I like a lot. I didn't expect it.'

'Do you want to spend a few minutes with me now?'

'I'd love to but—'

She ran her fingertips across my stomach. 'But what?'

'Just now it . . . it's awkward.'

'Awkward? Why awkward, darling?'

'Perhaps if we wait until we reach Fountains Moor.'

'You're not writing me off as . . . shop-soiled goods now?'

'Absolutely not.'

'I didn't choose what happened to me on Friday night.'

'I know . . . I'm sorry.'

'I'm past my *Best by date* at thirty-seven years old?'

'No, Caroline, you're not.'

'Still pretty? Mmm?'

'Yes . . . very pretty.'

'Do you find the bruises here off-putting?' She lifted her T-shirt to show me her breasts and the now pale green bruises. 'Are you afraid—'

I did it to shut her up as much as anything.

I suddenly reached forward, gripped her head in both my hands. She gave a small gasp. Her eyes widened. I pulled and I felt her bare breasts slap against my chest. My hands were around the back of her head, tightly crunching her hair into my fists.

Then I was kissing her full on the mouth. Emotions erupted inside of me. All conflicting. I wanted to get away from her. If I became close to her . . . God forbid, if I fell in love with her . . . that was an impossible situation. It wasn't the age difference. Maybe it was because we had nothing in common above—

—above being cast out into the world to survive somehow. With the whole poxy planet turning incandescent beneath our feet.

As I kissed her she panted; she grabbed at the belt of my jeans, unbuckled it, dragged my jeans down with a desperation that gave her the strength to pull me off balance.

We tumbled down onto the ground.

'I love you, Rick, I love you. Promise me you'll look after me. I'll do anything . . . anything . . . mmm, that's good. Bite me . . . harder. Don't worry, I'm not made out of china. That's it, bite . . . me . . . harder, harder – *ahhh!*'

Now naked, we were a frantic tangle of arms and legs. My face wet with kisses. I massaged her tight little breasts. She wriggled and lifted her legs high at either side of me.

I paused, panting, looking down into her brown eyes. She gazed up at me with such tenderness and trust that the doubts I had melted clean away.

The dappling of sunlight and shadow on her camouflaged the bruising on her throat and shoulders.

'I'm ready for you now,' she whispered.

'But—'

'I told you. A woman's body is more resilient than you think. Please, Rick . . . now.'

'Look, Caroline, don't feel as if you have to let me—'

'Hush, darling. Auntie Caroline knows best.' She pulled my head down until she could whisper into my ear. 'Now. Do as you're told: *fuck me.*'

I found myself gritting my teeth, anxious she might still be sore, but as I pressed down onto her, feeling the tip of my penis press lightly against the lips of her moist vagina, I only heard a grateful sigh.

I was doing the right thing, I told myself. Perhaps in this way I could atone for ignoring her screams for help on Friday night.

Down.

And in . . .

'*Oh, Rick, yes!*

With one smooth movement I pushed my penis inside her. Eyes tightly shut, she gripped my buttocks. Pulled hard, forcing me in deeper.

'Oh, gently, gently, Rick. Don't stop. *Please don't stop now.*'

I didn't stop. There might have been a dozen spectators, Kate included, watching us from the bushes. But with Caroline naked beneath me I made love to her as the shadows danced across our bodies. Every few seconds her expression would change. From an intense look of concentration, her eyes tight shut, as I drove gently into her, to a look of wide-eyed surprise as I shifted my position to pump with short vigorous stabs into that sweet softness between her legs.

CHAPTER 27

'What the Hell've you been doing, Rick?' Stephen's eyes were hard.

'I've been down to the lake,' I said, feeling as guilty and as embarrassed as Hell. Someone must have seen Caroline and me, then run up here to tell Stephen I'd been shafting her.

'I could have done with your help to go through this route again. I don't know this area at all.'

'But Ben worked out—'

'But Ben's route's all wrong. Look, we've got to keep out of the valley bottoms – that's where Ben's route would have taken us. I know the guy did his best. But we need to follow the ridge of these hills. That way we can see the lie of the land, and see anyone creeping up on us.'

I realized his question *What the Hell've you been doing?* was just rhetorical. But still, his irritation at me seemed more like he was looking for some fool to dump on. And it sure as jiggery wasn't going to be me.

'We broke for an hour's rest,' I said firmly. 'I've been gone thirty-five minutes.'

'Thirty-five minutes is sure a hell of a long time to splash some water on your face.'

'You didn't stipulate any time for me to talk to you, Stephen.'

'So I need to book an appointment to speak to my own brother? You wanted to wash your face. You'd been gone thirty-five minutes.'

'You'd been gone five years but you didn't hear me whining.'

We were some way off from the rest of the group who were sitting on the grass but they'd all heard the row brewing. Heads turned this way.

'Oh . . . so *that's* been under your skin all this time.' His nostrils flared; the blue eyes glittered. He bunched his fists. 'Five years. You've been building up one God Almighty grudge, haven't you? Now you stand there and say . . . damn. *Damn*.' He suddenly raised his hand, then slapped.

It wasn't me, though. Fingers splayed out, he slapped his own forehead. 'Stephen, Stephen, whoa, whoa,' he said to himself. 'What the hell are you playing at? Jeez!' He breathed out hard and looked at me. I saw tears in his eyes. 'I'm sorry, kiddo. Christ, I'm sorry.'

I didn't know what to say. I just didn't know what to say as my brother stood there and put both hands to each side of his face as if he'd just slapped an old lady and couldn't believe what he'd just done. 'I'm sorry, Rick.' He spoke under his breath, 'I really am sorry, forgive me. It's just not so easy playing this Noah, or Moses, or whatever role I've been railroaded into. Jeez, this whole thing's going to send me nuts.'

'Don't worry. I'd have cracked long ago.' I smiled suddenly, so moved my eyes were pricking, too. 'You're doing a great job.'

'Christ, you think so? Truth is, some of the people just aren't paying any attention to what I say. I ask nicely, but . . .' He blew out his cheeks and held out his hands as if to say 'What's the use in trying? It's like shovelling water uphill.'

This time I took the initiative. 'What's the problem?'

'Three-quarters of those people are addicted to listening to the radio news. OK, they want to be informed, but there's half a dozen radios, they all listen to different stations. They keep cranking them up higher and higher, competing with someone's else's radio. Boy, will they send me nuts.'

'We can't spare the batteries. They should only use one radio and then only at a specified time.'

'You're telling me.'

'Well, Stephen, let's tell *them*. Together.'

'Okay, kiddo.' He smiled gratefully. 'Together. Team work.'

'No way. These radios are ours. No one's got the right to tell us when we can listen to them.'

'Look,' I said, 'It's not as if we're giving orders. We just think it makes sense to go easy on them. We've only got a limited number of batteries.'

'So, please,' Stephen asked civilly. 'Can we just agree – here and now – which single radio we use?'

Some of them were definitely unhappy about being told they couldn't use their radios. Again we argued, gently, that it was in all our interests to save the batteries; that only one radio need be used at a time.

Dean Skilton was shouting his mouth off the loudest about the right to listen to HIS radio exactly when HE wanted to and damn ANYONE who said differently. I think it was the shotgun that did it. He'd taken to swaggering around with it on his shoulder like he was Clint freaking Eastwood or something. I was reminded of that old saying again: it was like he'd grown another head.

It looked there and then as though the group would disintegrate into squabbling factions. And we hadn't even reached Fountains Moor.

Old man Fullwood with a yellow T-shirt tied round his head to keep the sun from his neck and balding scalp tried to play the authoritative voice of reason. No one listened.

Soon we were heading into a slanging match. And I think it rankled Dean and even Howard that Stephen and I had closed ranks.

Dean's radio was in the grass; from some studio a hundred kilometres away a voice recited yet more catastrophe: 'Fires in Dublin are uncontrollable. The Irish Air Force is now bombing the city to create firebreaks. In Denmark the—'

Stamp on it! The surprise voice popped into my head. Stamp on it, then the argument's over. But then Dean, despite the years I'd known him, might start using that shotgun on me.

Even so, I looked at the black radio chuntering away to itself in the grass and I was gripped by this urge to bring my foot down on it; to feel the plastic casing crack like an egg-shell under my feet and spill its guts of paper speaker cone, wires and transistors all over that grass.

That was the instinctive urge. Bring matters to a head so we could slug it out to decide who really would lead us up there to the promised land on Fountains Moor.

I glanced up at the faces *(Rick, go on, stamp on the damned thing!)* I saw Kate and Caroline looking at me. They were taking no part in the argument. But both looked at me in the same expectant way.

Go on, Rick, stamp on the radio.

Old man Fullwood flapped his arms and blathered something about common sense. Stenno stared out across the fields as if he saw ghost armies marching to war. Stephen talked firmly, quietly. He was getting nowhere.

I took a step forward, ready to lift my foot and crush the radio to smithereens.

Before I could, something hit the radio. Hit it so hard that, it knocked it flat on its back – a 'something' I could not see. Or at least could not recognize just then because it was so outlandish.

The force of the blow knocked the radio off station. It warbled.

'Hey . . .'

Dean looked at me, anger blasting from his eyes, thinking I'd touched his precious music box.

'Hell . . .' Something hit him in the mouth.

Then we were all being struck. I felt a rap against my forehead that brought tears to my eyes.

'Take cover!' Stephen shouted.

'What the devil are they?' Old man Fullwood looked astonished.

They came down like machine-gun fire. I watched as they bounced off heads and shoulders and from the still warbling radio.

They were hailstones. Thousands of them. The mothers and grandmothers of hailstones at that. And they were black as grapes.

'Take cover,' Stephen yelled again. This time everyone obeyed. We ran under the nearest trees. A fool thing to do in a thunderstorm. And we heard thunder rumbling in the distance. But no one would stay out in that.

The hailstones beat down like machine-gun volleys with a *pok-pok-pok-pok* sound.

Dean looked at me, eyes wide. 'Hailstones – in July?'

I shivered. 'Welcome to the brave new world, Dean. Welcome to the brave new world.'

CHAPTER 28

'Hell fire, will you look at that?'

'I don't believe it.'

'These are never hailstones.'

'They are, you know. Look at the size of them!'

'And they're black . . . black hailstones?'

'Jesus . . . they're turning the whole damn countryside black.'

Our astonishment made the conversation buzz. All sixty-three of us huddled under that line of trees that ran alongside the wall. We watched wide-eyed, open-mouthed as Heaven machine-gunned that once green and pleasant land with twenty-millimetre slugs of ice.

'My God, did you see what happened to the bird—'

'There's another one. No . . . two, three. The hailstones are killing the birds.'

'It's taking the leaves off the trees, too. Look out.'

'The top branches have been stripped.'

'If you go out in this it'll strip the skin from your skull, no doubt about it.'

Stephen, grim-faced and anxious, looked like a novice schoolteacher suddenly put in charge of a class of seven-year-olds on a school trip to the coast. Now all the kids wanted to look over the edge of the cliff.

'Keep back, Julie. Yes, right back under cover. Joe, leave the radio where it is. We can get it later. Everyone try and keep under the thickest branches.'

Even so, people were darting their hands out to grab a hail-stone. From the unlucky ones came 'Ouch . . . Damn . . . Shit,' as those high-velocity hailstones rapped knuckles and grazed wrists.

'Gotcha!' Dean Skilton held out a hailstone for me to see in the palm of his hand. He was the image of the excited kid on a nature trip who'd caught a frog and now held it out for teacher's approval; the argument over the radio was forgotten, at least for now. 'Why do you think it's black?'

'All those volcanic eruptions. They'll have been throwing a lot of crap up into the air.'

Kate leaned forward and her bare arm brushed mine. 'Rick's right. The ice particles will have formed round volcanic dust. Look . . . as it melts you can see speckles of black in the water.'

It wasn't long before the excitement at this novelty of Nature's cooled as the atmosphere cooled.

All those tons of ice dumped onto the grass, even on that hot July day, had created a chill sharp enough for people to start blowing into their hands and rubbing their bare arms and legs. In a while you even noticed your breath coming out in puffs of white vapour.

Caroline had been standing at the far end of the line, but now she weaved her way through the crowd to come and stand so close at my side that her hip touched my thigh. She folded her arms, shivered and gazed out at the black fields. 'It's all those damned volcanoes, isn't it? It's like all Hell's breaking through.' Then she shook her head, making a deliberate effort to pull herself out of her doom-laden thoughts. She shot me a vivacious smile and said in a low voice that (I hoped) no one else could hear, 'I can't stop thinking about you. You know that, don't you?'

I smiled and whispered, 'Don't let me become a bad habit.'

'Do you think about me?'

I nodded. Truthfully, I did think about her. I remembered the way she'd clung to me down by the lake a few minutes ago as if our lives depended on her not letting go. God, yes, it was good, and God, yes, it pumped up my ego. But her affection for me was troubling, too. I could see problems ahead.

'I'm going to dig out my sweatshirt,' someone grumbled. People were now moving back to sit against the section of wall that was still sheltered by trees. The hail had begun to lose its novelty value now that the cold had started to bite.

'Come on,' I said to Caroline. 'Let's sit down.'

No sooner had we sat then she started to talk. Like she had a lot to get off her chest. She told me about her daughter, Portia, who'd won medals for ice-skating, that she, Caroline, was proud of her, and she was sure her daughter would be safe back in Fairburn.

I hoped so, too.

Caroline told me she'd worked for an investment company and had spent time in South Africa. There she'd met a wealthy New Zealander who was developing a new hotel chain. He'd been twenty years older than her but after a three-week courtship they'd married. Along came Portia and a happy fourteen years in New Zealand where Caroline played the role of society hostess with polished ease. A couple of weeks ago they'd come to Leeds for her brother's wedding. ('Third time around,' she'd told me with a sexy wink.) She'd been staying with relatives when the gas cloud hit. Somehow she found herself with Portia in Fairburn.

I had to ask. 'Your husband came with you?'

'Yes. But we were separated. The refugee camp is such a big place.' The way she spoke seemed suddenly vague (looking back now, deliberately vague).

Anyway, we sat there, hip to hip, backs to the wall. I told her of my plans and the band. She listened with an interest so acute I actually found myself wondering if she was memorizing it word for word. It was only when I spoke about the current disasters that she'd flash that vivacious smile of hers and whisper something along the lines of 'I keep thinking how gentle you were when you made love to me,' or 'I loved the feel of your back. Your skin's so incredibly smooth.'

Star Trek's spaceships had their force fields to protect them against photon torpedoes and phasers. For Caroline, I guess, she had sex. Sex was her way of creating a force field round her to protect her from the increasingly harsh realities of life.

I looked out across the black field. The hailstones still struck the ground with that *pok-pok-pok-pok*. This was strange and new. What else would we experience that was strange and new – and perhaps dangerous?

Life was changing so quickly. These people were changing too. Disaster and death on a huge scale had the power to transform the personalities of survivors – it even had the power to change those of us who'd been little more than spectators on the sidelines.

Dean Skilton, now catching another handful of hailstones to show Kate, had been one of my closest friends at school. He was one of the thoughtful academic types who did his homework on time, was a member of the chess and Christian Fellowship groups, something of a computer nerd. Though we'd play some wicked practical jokes on the other kids and even old mad man Froggatt down the road. Habitually, he avoided fights and any confrontation that might turn ugly.

Now he was a cocky so-and-so. He'd disagree with every suggestion, mainly, I think, just for the Hell of it. Then he'd try and stare you down while shifting Ben Cavellero's twelve-bore Bernadelli-made shotgun from one shoulder to the other. Put like that, it doesn't seem much, but you registered the implied threat. He seemed to be saying *'See my gun? See my gun? The next time I move it might just be to stick the muzzle in your face.'*

Ruth Sparkman had gelled with Stephen. They made a good couple together. He was tall, good-looking, with that spring-heeled athletic step. Ruth had been captain of the local women's soccer team. She played tennis, swam, rode horses. The moment you clapped eyes on her you sensed her muscular strength and energy.

Stenno was still with us – in body if not in spirit. He constantly watched the horizon as if expecting the freshly risen dead to come limping wetly across the fields.

Scanning heads, I could seen Stenno's wife, worried eyes watching her husband's every move. There was Kate picking a hailstone out of Dean's outstretched hand. Howard Sparkman, wiping his glasses with a tissue. He looked serious, as though weighty matters occupied his mind.

Pok-pok-pok-pok. All this to the quick rhythm of the black ice pounding the ground. *Pok-pok-pok-pok.*

Caroline and I had fallen silent now. I heard a couple of girls talking nearby. 'This Ben Cavellero. Who does he think he is?'

'I know, I've only met him a couple of times. But why has he sent us out here? I mean, what's the *real* reason?'

'All this seems, well . . . a fascist kind of idea.'

'I agree. Extremely fascist. It smacks of Nazi ideology.'

'Selecting people to go and camp in the hills in the middle of nowhere. It's like something from one of those Nazi *Strength Through Joy* propaganda films.'

'I mean, who gave him the right to decide who went, who stayed?'

'He's made an experiment out of us all. What? Take sixty people, arm them to the teeth. Put an American disc jockey in charge.'

'Who hardly anyone's ever heard of.'

'Precisely. Put him in charge. Send them out into the wilderness.'

'Then see how long they last.'

'Before they get their throats cut.'

'Or they start killing each other.'

Shut up!

I was tempted to shout it. But they had a point. Much as I

respected Ben, and sure as I am he was right to get us out of Fairburn before total anarchy raged, I could see a whole thorny forest of problems ahead.

Would people continue to do as Stephen asked?

Would there be someone, Dean Skilton, say, who'd decide they could do a better job of leadership?

What if we walked into a thousand refugees, all of them starving? What could we do to stop them when they saw all the food we carried?

What if someone went down with appendicitis?

Could old man Fullwood keep up?

How could I handle this situation with Caroline?

What if the Earth opened up beneath our feet? What if it started puking out fire and brimstone?

And just who in damnation was that man who looked in through the tent doorway at me last night?

My mouth turned dry. I remembered the fax I'd read from the kid in South Africa: *'I saw the Grey Man last night. He walked amongst my dead countrymen. The gas does not hurt him.'*

I remembered Stenno's weird outburst at the meeting on Saturday: *'The Grey Man! You've heard of the Grey Man?'*

I believed I hadn't seen the figure properly last night. But now I realized I had seen more. Only something in my head had suppressed it. Some subconscious censor.

I had seen a man looking it at me. It had been dark, but not so dark I couldn't make out a huge hulk of a man, with a huge head.

And a face.

Yes . . . yes! I remembered now. That face.

It was grey.

CHAPTER 29

We saw the flames from a couple of kilometres away.

Somehow appropriately, considering Stephen's Noah tag, he was leading the group in a column two by two.

He told the others to keep walking while he stepped back and allowed me to catch up.

'Those fires,' he said as he fell into step with me. 'They're pretty big.'

I nodded. 'And they're on our route.'

'Exactly. Can we skirt round them?'

'As far as I can tell they're coming from a little village called . . .' I unfolded the map as we walked. 'Grassholme. It looks as if the houses have been torched.'

'Maybe. It's hard to tell from here, but the flames don't look right for house fires. Too blue.'

'Volcano?'

'God, I hope not.'

'Might be burning gas?'

'Could be. Reminds you of a gas hob flame, doesn't it? Mostly blue, with flickers of orange and yellow at the top.'

I looked at the map. 'If we cut off to the east we can follow a track through Elmet Forest for a couple of kilometres before just simply heading north over what looks like open countryside. Then rejoin the original route.'

We jogged to the head of the column and turned it east down the hillside. No one questioned it. After the hailstones it had rained for a full hour. The black ice had melted to a liquid the colour of cola. It had run off the sunbaked hillside until we'd stood ankle deep in the filthy water while rain dripped on our heads through the branches.

So now we were reduced to a weary plodding walk, thinking about nothing much in particular, just about the next rest stop and maybe some hot baked beans and sausage.

An hour into this leg of the journey we'd passed a lone farmhouse. An old guy had come out and waved at us. We'd not been sure if he'd been beckoning to us or waving us away. The next minute made it clear what he was signalling. He hobbled into the house, came out with a shotgun and blazed away at us. We were too far away to be in any kind of serious danger but we pushed on quickly. He'd obviously decided to turn his home into a castle until all this was over. Visitors certainly wouldn't be welcome.

Twenty minutes later we saw another lone figure. This one was a man of around thirty. He came loping towards us across the fields. As he came closer I saw he had long scraggly hair and was wearing a football shirt, shorts and cowboy boots. Even when he was a hundred metres away everyone could see he was clearly stark, yodelling mad.

He ran chanting: 'Dick-dick-dick-detective . . . dick-dick-dick-detective . . .'

He approached us, running faster, chanting louder. Dean had the shotgun down from his shoulder and aimed at the running madman.

'Dick-dick-detective . . . *dick-dick* . . .'

'Dean,' Stephen had called. 'Don't shoot; he's unarmed.'

'Yeah, but he's nuts.'

'Dean!'

'We shouldn't take any chances. If he doesn't stop, I'll shoot.'

'No.'

In two seconds flat Stephen ran down the line of people, tugged the gun from Dean's hands and pushed him flat against the grass.

'*Dick-dick-dick detective!*'

The mad man charged into the line of people, his cowboy boots splashing the surface water lying on the grass; his eyes blazed. I swung the rifle from my shoulder. I saw Howard Sparkman pull out his revolver.

'*Dick-dick-dick—*'

The madman didn't stop. The line parted. He didn't brush against anyone, even by accident. He kept running, hair blowing out in the breeze; his squinting eyes never left some point on the horizon. Then he was away down the hill; the voice faded into the distance. 'Dick-dick-dick detective . . . dick-dick-dick-detective.'

Dean said nothing, but I noticed how his eyes bore into the back of Stephen's head as we walked.

Now, a couple of hours later, there was only that weary plod of feet on wet grass. The sun came out and the grass began to steam.

Stephen and I led the group east. The burning village lay to our left. It looked abandoned now. A few of our people glanced at the blue jets blasting high into the air above the ruined houses, but exhaustion dampened any curiosity to take a closer look.

The sunlight had returned with a ferocious vengeance through the breaking cloud. As well as the grass our clothing began to steam, too. Ahead lay the cool shadows of the wood.

Stephen said, 'There's no major roads this way? Or any villages?'

'The map shows nothing. Only a church somewhere in the wood.'

'With luck, then, this diversion won't add too much to the journey. Thank God we're not doing this trek in the middle of winter. It's hard enough in the middle of summer. You all right, Mr Fullwood?'

'If you're still at the crease, you've got to keep batting.'

It was one of old man Fullwood's typically oblique remarks, delivered like he was a Shakespeare an actor.

'I guess that means he's not going to croak on us yet,' Stephen said to me under his breath. 'Watch out for brambles.'

The forest was so densely packed with trees we had to weave single-file along the path that zigged and zagged away into the gloom.

In the forest it was so silent you could hear the breath of the walker behind you. No birds sang. Somehow the place had a dead feel to it. It made your skin crawl. But there was a tension there, too; buried beneath the surface. I shivered. A tension ready to erupt with terrible savagery. A voice in my head whittered over and over: *Something's going to happen in here, something's going to happen in here, something bad, something very bad.*

You've seen that bit in the horror film? The girl walks alone through the haunted house. It's eerily quiet, so eerily quiet; don't you just know that any second now the monster's going to jump out? Cry: *Boo!* Then slash its talons across her throat.

Right then, that sensation gripped me in its fearfully cold claw. I craned my head, peering uneasily into the trees, half expecting some grunting beast to burst out from the bushes, roaring at us.

We pushed on, deeper into the dead silence beneath the shroud of branches.

The ground steamed here, too. It grew thicker the further we walked into the wood. Within five minutes we were walking waist deep through a thick, ground-hugging mist.

'Like walking through a pool full of milk,' I heard Dean say behind me.

The smell of warm earth grew heavier on the air; you could almost taste the soil on your tongue.

Suddenly Stephen stopped. 'Damn.' He ducked down into the mist. It was so thick he completely disappeared even though he was only ten steps in front of me.

'Stephen? I walked forward. 'Stephen?' Now I felt alarmed. What if he'd suddenly plunged down a hole in the ground? You couldn't even see your feet in this fog. 'Stephen . . . *Stephen.*'

I reached the point where he'd disappeared. Alarmed, I looked down into the mist. I could see nothing. It really was like looking

into a sea of milk. I'd have to reach down with my hands
if—

Christl

A hand came up through the mist, snatched my arm, then a head
broke the surface.

'Rick.'

'Stephen . . . are you OK? I thought you'd—'

'Rick. The soil. Feel the soil.'

I ducked down into the mist. The rifle and backpack slipped forward, dragging me face down onto the ground. I could see nothing but
that damn white mist. And the smell of the soil dug into my nostrils.

As soon as I put my hands down to the ground to push myself
up I realized what Stephen had discovered. I was on my feet quicker
than I thought possible.

'You feel it?' he asked quickly.

I nodded. 'The soil; it's hot.'

'So much for our horror-movie mist. It's steam being driven from
hot soil.'

'Well,' I said grimly. 'We found one of the hot spots. What now?'

'Get out of here fast. Whoa, everybody whoa!' He shouted as if
holding up a cattle drive. 'Please turn back. We're walking back the
way we came.'

'Oh, Jesus,' Dean protested. 'You can't be serious?'

'I am. Deadly serious. Now, please. Move it!'

With sighs and grumbles they moved back. When the mist began
to thin Stephen and I kept crouching down to touch the ground. As
soon as we reached soil that felt cool to the touch, Stephen called on
everyone to stop. Then he explained about the hot ground deeper in
the wood.

'What will happen when the ground gets too hot?' Caroline asked.

'I just don't know,' Stephen said. 'In some cases it releases toxic gas
as happened in Leeds. Also, we know it sometimes triggers explosions
when inflammable gases like methane ignite underground.'

Howard pushed his glasses up the bridge of his nose. 'I don't want
to sound chicken, but is it a good idea to stand here discussing it?'

'So far it's only causing the earth to steam; check out the mist.'

'But for all we know there might be a pocket of methane right
beneath our feet.'

That made everyone look down at the forest floor. And I think
every man Jack of us imagined that any second the path would erupt

into flame beneath our feet and we'd all die, burning and writhing there, the skin blistering, peeling off in strands.

Stephen said decisively. 'OK. We put some turf between us and this place.'

'Do you propose that we—' began Dean, striking an arrogant fists-on-hips pose.

'We haven't got time to debate this,' Stephen said. 'Look . . . everyone stay here. Rick and I will go on ahead. If it appears safe we'll cut through this forest as planned.'

'But we could detour round—'

'I checked the map,' I said, becoming irritated with Dean. 'The only other way is round the reservoir to the south-east; that will take another full day's walk. This way's quicker.'

'This way might be lethal,' Dean chipped in.

'Well, Deanie baby.' Stephen shrugged off his pack. 'We're going to run the risk to see if it's safe, so your little tootsies don't get singed. Ready, bro?'

I slipped off my backpack so we could move faster.

'Best hang onto your rifle, bro. I've got my pistola. Right. See ya soon, gang.'

I followed Stephen as he ran on into the heart of that steaming wood. We moved too quickly to take stock of what we were seeing but I could see it was turning shitty. The mist thickened to my waist again. The smell of earth became a cloying stink. The heat soaked through the soles of my trainers to warm my feet.

I saw bushes were being killed by the heat cooking their roots; leaves drooped down like a bouquet of flowers that had been left without water. No birds flew.

Ahead Stephen followed the zig and zag of the path, his head turned left to right, looking for any sign of danger.

Then all of a sudden we hit a clearing.

And I saw an awesome but terrible sight.

CHAPTER 30

We both stopped and stared.

My eyes stung, they were stretched so wide open.

Then there came a godawful screech and I had to slam my hands over my ears to shut out that sound before it burst my skull.

Stephen grabbed me by the elbow and mouthed words at me. I shook my head, not understanding. He pulled my hand from an ear and yelled, 'See if there's another way round!'

I nodded, then immediately put my hand back over my ear to reduce the sound to a bearable level.

As we skirted the clearing I couldn't take my eyes off what lay at its centre.

Picture this: there's a church, there's a steeple, there's a graveyard, there's the lych gate, there's a sign: *St Lawrence's Parish Church, founded 1683; Rev A. F. Foales;* there's the stone flagged path to the church door that brides and grooms and assorted congregations have trooped along for three hundred years.

But there, screeching from the ground, were jets of blue flame. The burst of flame didn't last more than five or six seconds. After that, it would abruptly die down to a puddle of blue fire.

Then there would be a *thump!* that transmitted a shock wave through the ground to your feet, and another flame as thick as a man's waist and ten metres high would blast from the ground into the air. Simultaneously, there came that tremendous *SKK-REEEE-CH!* as the flame jetted.

They looked like gigantic Bunsen burner flames. Only the force and the fury behind those bursts of flames made your heart miss a beat.

Stephen stopped and pointed. The ground was littered with bones. Long shin bones, thigh bones, femurs. They were blackened. Bits of meat and skin still trailed from them. Then I saw a man's jacket lying on the ground. Sticks of rib poked through rips in the material.

Now I identified another smell above the stink of hot soil: it was the aroma of roasting meat.

My mouth filled with saliva; I had to swallow hard.

Stephen turned to me. He pulled a face and held out his hands apologetically as if to say *'Sorry to put you through this.'*

We skirted the clearing, keeping as far away as possible from the graveyard with its sudden ground bursts of fire.

I stepped over a skull that had been stripped of all but a shred or two of skin. It was still steaming. The pale remains of its eyes stared up at me.

We walked faster. There were more thumps; more jets of blue

flame erupted from the graveyard to tear a screeching hole in the air. They blazed for a full five seconds before dwindling to become a puddle of flame around a headstone.

From this angle I could see into the churchyard. Headstones had been pulverized. There were craters here, there, everywhere; big enough to drop a child down into. I saw more bodies. All burned. Some flash-cooked to skeletons.

Jesus, what had happened to those poor people?

Another thump, the ground bucked – *screeeeeech!* A smouldering skull hit the ground in front of me before bouncing away into the undergrowth.

I looked back into the graveyard. A woman lay dead on the ground. One of the more recent victims, I guessed. Her clothes weren't burnt. She looked unscorched.

But what had brought all these people here to be incinerated where they stood?

Some kind of lemming-like suicidal urge: *'Quick! The graveyard's on fire! Let's all rush down there and cremate ourselves!'*

The world was insane. Insane from its incandescent core to its surface. And that madness was spreading to everything that walked or crawled upon it.

Stephen caught my elbow again. He nodded to the graveyard. 'They died like flies in there,' he shouted above the screech of a Bunsen-like flame. 'She must be one of the recent ones.'

'I've seen her, poor devil.' I looked back to where she lay flat out on a horizontal tombstone. Her thick hair spilled down to the ground.

'Come on,' he said. 'That's where the path starts again. It looks safe enough. There's no steam coming off the ground there.'

'If you stay here, I'll . . .' I had to pause as there was another ground-shaking thump, followed by the rocket screech of jetting gas. 'You stay here, and I'll go back and tell—*Christ.*'

'What's wrong?'

It wasn't the explosion that stopped me this time. I'd just noticed one of the corpses wasn't doing what corpses should. 'She's moved,' I shouted. 'The girl in the graveyard.'

'Moved?'

'I first saw her . . . I saw her lying on the ground.' I had to shout above the roar of burning gas again. 'Now she's on the tombstone.'

'She'll be dead in the next ten seconds,' he shouted. 'Nothing'll survive in there.'

'We've got to get her out.' Again I felt the stab of shame at leaving Caroline to her fate last Friday night.

'Rick . . . Rick, slow down. Just give me a minute to think this through. Look, if we – Rick! Rick! Come back! Jesus . . .' Stephen bellowed more in fear than fury. 'Don't you go into there! Don't you dare! Damn . . . damn!'

But I was away like a rabbit. I vaulted the fence, dodged around gravestones, jumped over the craters that still burnt with a puddle of flame that guttered and popped as the gas slowly gave out.

The girl lay flat out on the stone. She lifted her hand slightly, then dropped it limply down again.

Still alive; but if one of those gas jets erupted under her then she'd be blown to kingdom—

Thump!

The concussion knocked me flat, the rifle whirled out of my hand.

Skk-reeee-ch!

I curled into a ball. That godawful sound battered my skull so hard I thought it would burst like a dropped egg. Twenty paces away the column of flame ripped out of the ground into the air. The heat-flash singed the hairs on my arms to dust. Seconds later pieces of burning flesh and bone dropped down, along with a pair of trousers that were stained with rot.

Christ, that was it!

I staggered to my feet, looking round in amazement.

That was damn well it!

The build-up of subterranean heat was detonating the gases produced by the putrefying bodies. The force of it tore a vent up through the top soil to the surface where the gases exited in that eyeball-searing blast of flame. That rush of gas also carried the contents of the coffins with it, high into the air above the graveyard, to shower down skulls, thigh bones, knuckles, pelvic bones, smouldering spines, as well as chunks of rotted meat, lungs, skin and flaming hearts. A face landed flat on my leg. It had been torn from the skull in one piece. Brown, wet, worm-eaten: it looked like a mask made from leather.

I glanced across the graveyard. The girl still lay unscathed.

But for how much longer?

I dodged round the burning gas puddles, praying a grave wouldn't explode beneath my feet. I could see the girl more clearly now, her long red hair tumbling down towards the ground, her summer dress billowing in blasts of air so hot it made your face smart. Through the heat haze thrown up from the fires, the girl looked as if she'd been clipped from a horror movie, the hot air distorting the scene before me weirdly.

I strained my eyes, struggling to see.

Despite the imminent threat of the ground exploding under my feet and incinerating me instantly, my eyes locked onto her in astonishment as she flickered and blurred as if she was still in the process of morphing from demon to beautiful girl.

Move it, Rick. Move it!

If I wasn't faster those mephitic gases would detonate beneath the girl's slender body and whirl her away to eternity.

I jumped the last pit of fire, then I was at her side. She was, I judged, no older than twenty years of age, pale-skinned, with a faint dusting of freckles across her nose. She looked serenely asleep. She seemed unhurt. But there was no way of telling what internal injuries she might have suffered.

I simply picked her up like she was a child and ran for it.

Thump.

Another one.

Skkr-reeeeee-chaaar!

The sound was deafening. But I ran hard. I ran like angels were helping me.

The gate emerged out of the heat haze. Distorted by hot air, it rippled softly as though it was cast from rubber.

Then I was through it, pounding towards the wood; the girl safe in my arms.

CHAPTER 31

My name is Kate Robinson. This is our second day on Fountains Moor.

Let me describe the camp to you. Picture a bleak moorland of heather and nothing but heather stretching away like a purple desert for seemingly ever and a day. There are no roads, no villages, no houses. Nothing. Now picture a ravine through which a stream flows. This ravine is perhaps fifteen metres deep with steep rocky sides; in some places they are as sheer as a cliff. At the bottom of the ravine it is perhaps ten metres wide. The stream is fast, shallow, and narrow enough to allow you to step easily from one bank to the other. There are trees at the bottom of the ravine and a strip of grass between the stream and the rock face. This grass strip is wide enough for us to erect our small tents in a line two-by-two.

The evening sunlight casts the long shadows of trees across the ravine walls.

As I sit writing here on a boulder by the stream people are settling down as best they can. They cook meals, talk, often they are crowded round the radio. The news isn't good: more tidal waves, earthquakes, volcanic eruptions – the Greek island of Crete's been split in two by a volcanic explosion so powerful it showered rocks down a hundred kilometres away. The death toll? Impossible to estimate. Every day another radio station goes off air. Static electricity generated by upheaval in the Earth's crust interferes with what broadcasts there are.

Yet here it's strangely peaceful. Today has been sunny and warm. There was a lot of laughter when people went skinny-dipping in a pool further down the ravine. The water's cold as ice. Mr Fullwood sits on the grass nearby. That froth of white hair of his shines like a halo. He's eating sardines from a can and looks as happy as a three-year-old with a big bar of chocolate.

Sue has just stepped out of the tent where Victoria is sleeping. Victoria is the girl that Rick and Stephen rescued from the burning graveyard. She's a real mystery girl.

How can I best describe her? Have you seen those paintings by the Pre-Raphaelites? They tended to specialize in these lush portraits of beautiful women dressed in long Ancient Roman-looking dresses; they have long luxuriant hair and wistful expressions as if thinking about absent lovers. Victoria looked as if she could have stepped out of one of those paintings. If you've ever seen a painting by Frederick Sandys called *Helen Of Troy* . . . well, Victoria was the spitting image of her, with thick hair down past her shoulders. It's wavy and a deep reddish colour. Her eyes are grey. My guess is she is aged about twenty. I think there's a spoilt-child look about her. Luckily she seemed unhurt. But all she's done is sleep, waking only for a moment or two at a time.

Dean Skilton tried speaking to her a few minutes ago when she left the tent to look at the stream, of all things; she crouched down for a perhaps ten seconds. Dipped her fingers into the stream. Stared at the water as if she'd never seen such a thing in her life before. When she didn't reply to Dean asking her how she was feeling, he tapped his finger against the side of his head and said to me in a low voice so she wouldn't hear, 'I wonder which planet she came from?' And as she returned to her tent, she paused briefly, standing up straight, looking at the sky. Then she turned to scrutinize one of the oak trees. Again it struck me that she appeared to find that all this was new to her; that it was the first time she'd seen the sky and sun and trees. As she stood there, still as a statue, I heard someone say, 'Beam me up, Scottie.' There was laughter. She didn't notice. She slipped into the tent and went to sleep.

Stephen looked up from where he was studying the provisions list. 'They should leave her alone.' He sounded annoyed. 'After all, the poor girl's probably in shock after what she went through.'

Stephen had been the only one to have a brief conversation with her. He found out her name, that she was well enough to walk here (which she did lost in a kind of dream world); but he didn't find out how she came to be in the burning graveyard wearing a summer dress which other girls have been cattily describing as 'pretty in an old-fashioned kind of way.'

The journey here after Victoria's rescue took another forty-eight hours.

As we walked we saw dozens of aircraft flying from west to east. There were also flocks of birds flying in the same direction as if they were all fleeing some terrible disaster.

Later, we saw a convoy of army trucks and tanks on a road in the distance. Maybe the army is managing to organize some more help for the refugee camps. Seeing the convoy cheered people up but it made some question the need to camp out here. Couldn't we go back to Fairburn? they wondered. With the army there the refugee camp might be well-fed and peaceful. But there's no way of telling. We haven't a portable two-way radio powerful enough to reach Ben Cavellero. We brought mobile telephones with us but the whole mobile telephone system is still down. We get nothing but static from them.

One night we felt the ground moving. It was so slight we hardly noticed at first. It's like sitting in a rowing boat on a lake, the water's still, then along comes a small ripple. You feel a slight bobbing motion. That is all. People came out of their tents. In the distance we saw what at first seemed like lightning flashes. But the glow stayed there. A dull orange reflected on the bottom of clouds like a red sunset.

Howard said, face glum, 'That looks as if half of Yorkshire's gone up in smoke.'

Howard's now sitting outside his tent. He's cleaning his glasses with a cloth and he's still got this morbid look on his face. Some of the group have gone off in pairs to scout the area. Gail and Dean are just setting out. Dean has his shotgun across his back. Rick left about twenty minutes ago with Caroline. She sticks to him like a second shadow.

CHAPTER 32

My name is Rick Kennedy.

Caroline looked at me with those sexy brown eyes and whispered, 'Rick. You can do anything you want to me. Anything at all. You know that, don't you?'

I smiled at her and kissed her forehead. 'I can't think of anything more imaginative that what we're doing already.' I laughed. 'It's not as if we've chandeliers to swing from, or kinky rubber catsuits to wear.'

She pressed herself closer to me. 'I can be a school girl for you. Or I could shave my—'

'Caroline.' I grinned. 'You're perfect. You don't need to pretend to be anyone else.'

We walked hand in hand across the moor. Caroline wore cut-off jeans and a white T-shirt. The camp in the ravine was a good two kilometres away. Ahead, purple heather rolled away into the distance. Surrounding us were hills with craggy outcrops of rock. Hot sunlight beat down to make our faces tingle.

As we strolled Caroline squeezed my hand. I squeezed back. Then I kissed her on the mouth.

You might wonder why I wanted to keep our relationship secret. It wasn't as if it was against camp rules or anything. People were pairing off to share tents. Stephen had moved in with Ruth; the whole camp must have heard them grappling passionately into the early hours. But I didn't want to go public with Caroline just yet. So why was I still slipping away from the camp with her? And happily letting her unzip my fly before going down on me to send me to Heaven with her tongue and lips? Well, if you're nineteen and you've got this slim woman with sexy brown eyes wanting nothing more on Earth than to get naked with you it's hard to say no, right?

Right. That's part of the story. The real meat of why I couldn't say 'no' was that solid wodge of guilt rooted deep in my gut. I couldn't reject her; I couldn't bear to see that pain in her eyes. When she made love she clung to me like I was some kind of lifeline or something. Christ, it makes me sound so arrogant, like I'd set myself up as her own personal saviour. But it wasn't like that. I liked her, I really did. And when she got close like this, looking up at me with her eyes all soft and trusting, I knew I was falling in love. Maybe I should have said, 'Look, Caroline. Let me tell you something straight. I love you. I want you to move in with me. We'll live together as if we're married.' I nearly said it right then. But some little numskull in my head wouldn't let the words out of my mouth.

'Come with Auntie Caroline.' Smiling, she pulled me by the hand to where the ground sloped downward to a patch of soft grass. 'Now give me the rifle. There . . . I'll lean that against the rock like so. You sit down there. Now . . . you can watch me undress.'

I sat and watched her. She moved like a dancer, slowly swinging her hips from side to side to the rhythm of some music she heard inside her head. She slipped off her T-shirt, held it out at arm's length, then let it drop to the grass. Smiling all the time, she watched my face for my reactions.

She unfastened the bra and, still giving me a smouldering look, she slipped it down over her arms and threw it into the air.

Then she held her arms outstretched in a crucifixion pose and turned round so I could see her front, then her back. The bruises had gone now. Her skin looked perfect; her small breasts looked firm and, Christ, they looked so damned peachy I could have grabbed her hungrily there and then.

But I let her continue the game. Dancing there in the sunlight, smiling, enjoying my attention. She kicked off her sandals and danced barefoot on the springy grass. Then she unbuttoned the cut-off jeans and wriggled them down to her ankles, flicked them off with a kick of a leg then walked slowly up to me, hips swinging. Her briefs were a deep blue satin material. I couldn't take my eyes off the pubic mound and wisps of pubic hair straying from beneath the material.

'Now, Rick. These are for you to take off.'

Now I could barely stop myself. I reached up, grabbed the waistband in both hands and pulled them down to her knees.

She sighed, put her hands behind my head and pulled my face to her stomach. Now I could smell her wonderful body scents. The smell of a woman sexually aroused.

My body blazed with sheer, naked lust.

I kissed her pubic hair, gripped both her buttocks in my hands and crushed my face against her flat stomach. She moaned and twisted my hair around her fingers. Then we were rolling in the grass, kissing, biting, caressing, panting out our lust for one another. I struggled out of my clothes.

'You feel, oh,' she gasped, breathlessly. 'You feel wonderful. Oh, pinch me . . . *oh*, that's it. Pinch me there; don't worry, love, you won't break pieces off. Oh, pinch me there. Harder this time – harder – *oh*!'

The next moment I was lying flat on my back with Caroline straddling me, legs at either side of my hips. Her face tilted upwards so the sun shone on it, her eyes closed. Lips pursed, she slid down onto me, taking me deep inside of her. She moaned and rolled her head. I lay there enjoying the delicious feel of the walls of her vagina gripping my penis then sliding tightly down over it, enveloping it, massaging it until I felt the pressure building inside of me.

She leaned forwards to kiss me, her breasts lightly stroking my bare chest. Then she was sitting up straight again, lifting herself up and down on her knees, her face a picture of intense concentration as she drove down hard onto me; her mouth pulled into an O shape as she worked herself relentlessly against me.

I had no sense of time or space; I forgot everything but the blissful sensation of the most intimate parts of her body clenched around mine. She was panting out a series of: 'Oh-ah-oh-ah-oh' sounds to the hard rhythm of her impaling movements; her breasts jiggled, the nipples contracted and turned hard – hard and blood-red; her throat flushed. She moved faster and faster and the words once softly panted turned deeper, more guttural. Her whole body began to convulse as if electric shocks twitched her muscles from her beautiful head to her varnished toes.

'Oh, Christ . . . Oh, God, God, God,' she panted. 'I'm going . . . I'm going to – *uh ohhh! Yyyy-yesss!*

I felt a star burst inside my body. I was pumping up inside her and crushing her hips in my hands. Then she gave a stuttering moan and dropped forward, her breath roaring in my ear, her hot skin against my skin, her heart pounding against mine.

Afterwards, we lay in each other's arms on that great empty expanse of moorland. We stroked each other's faces, looked into each other's eyes, smiled a lot. Said nothing. Words weren't important: we were communicating with eye contact and smiles alone.

Caroline plucked a blade of grass and ran it lightly up and down my arm. I made up my mind there and then that soon I'd ask her to move in with me. That I'd tell everyone we were a couple.

Five kilometres above my head a lone jet moved through the clear sky, drawing a white line of vapour across the perfect blue. Right then I could believe in miracles. I could believe Mother Earth would cool down. That she'd stop the eruptions and quakes and tidal waves.

I even glimpsed a possible future. I'd return home. I'd tip the canned foods and ammunition out of the backpack. I'd fill the bag with my best clothes. Then I'd leave the house. There'd be Caroline standing at the corner of the street. Her green eyes would light up with pleasure as she saw me walk toward her. Then we'd hold hands, kiss. Catch the bus into Leeds where we'd rent a flat. We'd cook in the nude. Make love on the rug in front of the TV.

I lay back and imagined all that as Caroline gently tickled my skin with the blade of grass.

I really imagined that could be my future. All warm and cosy and rose-tinted.

But if a crystal ball had fallen out of the wide blue yonder right then and I had seen what really lay in the future – well, I might just have been tempted to reach out for that rifle and put a slug between her pretty brown eyes.

Then turn the gun on myself.

Laughing, joking, stroking each other's backs, we strolled at long last to the camp. My skin still buzzed from that wonderful, mind-blowing sex. I had the rifle slung casually over one shoulder by its strap. Apart from the gun we could have been the image of the happy honeymoon couple.

From here the camp was invisible at the bottom of its ravine but I could already hear a voice calling someone to eat a meal; blue smoke from a camp fire smudged the sky.

The camp was sometimes known as Stephen's Ark (some even called my brother Noah in lighter moments), or sometimes it was simply referred to as the (ha, ha) Arsehole, being in the bottom of a deep cleft flanked by two buttock-like mounds.

There we were becoming dislocated from reality. It was a summer camping trip, we fantasized. Most of us could believe that when we returned to the outside world it would be as it always had been: people mowing lawns, kids on skateboards, BMWs and Volvos moving sedately along Village Street, perhaps a July wedding at the big limestone church with the bride radiant in white and confetti snow storming the air in a technicolour blizzard.

Caroline was saying, 'I want to make a deal with you.'

'A deal?'

'Yes, I want you to promise me you'll have sex with me every day.'

I grinned. 'It's hardly a chore.'

'Promise Auntie Caroline. Repeat after me: I, Rick Kennedy, will make love to you, Caroline Lucas, every day.'

'I do solemnly swear that I will—'

The gunshot sounded like a dry stick being snapped in two.

We were perhaps a hundred paces from the edge of the gully. Three people appeared to my left and ran away from me. I slipped the rifle from my shoulder.

Another sharp snap of a gun being fired, a handgun by the sound of it. Then came the deeper thudding report of a shotgun.

I saw more people scrambling over the rim of the gully. Amongst the mass of heads and waving arms I recognized Stephen, Dean and Victoria.

Stephen saw me, stopped, cupped his hands around his mouth megaphone-style and hollered, 'Rick! Stop them! Don't let them get away!'

I looked at the three figures haring away across the heather. I didn't know who they were. I didn't stop to think twice, either. I gave chase.

CHAPTER 33

I ran with the rifle clasped in front of me in both hands. Jolting con-cussions thudded through me as I pounded through the heather.

The three figures were maybe a hundred paces away. They looked young, certainly under thirty. I guessed all things being equal I'd never have caught up with them, except for the fact that all three lumbered along with arms around what looked like coal sacks. But I'd bet you a steak dinner that those sacks weren't bulging with coal.

It didn't take a boffin to guess that the runners were outsiders who'd sneaked into our camp, stuffed the sacks with whatever they could get their hands on and were now legging it home with our goodies that we'd backpacked here on a back-breaking three-day march.

I'd closed the gap to about forty paces when they twigged I was hot on their heels. Thirty paces. Their heads jerked back to see what progress I was making.

And, Hell, I *was* making progress – plenty of it.

Twenty paces now separated us.

The three running men wore the usual rag-bag refugee clothes. A jacket from a business suit with jogging pants on one, another wore football shorts with a sweatshirt. The third wore a T-shirt and what looked like the bottom half of a boiler suit tied with orange string and a knitted jeep hat on his head. All the clothes were ripped and so dirty they looked as if they'd been steeped in liquid mud.

They must have known they couldn't outrun me, carrying those coal sacks stuffed with canned food and what-not, but they put their heads down and tanked it hard, legs pumping across the ground. They had their prize; they weren't going to let it go easily. One lost a shoe. He didn't stop to retrieve it.

Fifteen paces. Christ, I could smell them. They smelt like they'd slept in shit.

Ten paces.

It was then I realized I would be on my own when I tried to tackle them. They might have been armed. Only it would be difficult for any of them to pull a gun with their arms wrapped round those sacks like they were going to dance the last waltz with them.

I caught enough breath to shout, 'Stop! Or I'll shoot!'

They called my bluff, kept on running.

I ran harder. Ten paces separated us.

I could have stopped there and then and dropped all three of them with a bullet in the back. But I knew I'd no more casually shoot them than I would my own mother.

I realized that what they carried was more important to us than the thieves themselves. What were we going to do? Arrest them? Fine them? Give them community service polishing our boots?

I was now running almost abreast of them.

What I did next was a dirty trick, I know, but it seemed, as they say, elegant in its simplicity.

I sidestepped, putting my boot in the way of the first guy's foot. He tripped head first, rolling over the sack with a '*Uph!*' as his breath slammed from his chest. The cans in the sack clanged.

I moved closer to the second guy and did the same. He went down in a whirl of arms and legs with that same '*Uph!*' – the concussion expelling a lungful of air.

I closed in on the third guy, the one wearing a jeep hat. The eyes glittered out of his dirt-blackened face. He didn't even know I was there – or he didn't care. He hugged that sack of food to his chest with all the protective love of a father holding onto his first-born son in a hurricane.

This would be easy. I stuck my leg out. The guy jumped. He cleared my leg and ran on. I caught up, tried again, this time he sidestepped me. Still he ran on.

Sod this for a game of soldiers.

I shifted the rifle into one hand and grabbed him by the collar of his T-shirt.

I yanked backwards. The T-shirt ripped in my hand, but the guy was off-balance. His momentum and the weight of the sack did the rest. He did a clumsy pirouette on one foot and fell down backwards with the sack across his chest. Out spilled cans of ham.

Panting, I crouched down beside him. He was drawing breath so hard I thought he was suffering an asthma attack. I started to move the sack off his chest so he could breathe properly.

In one movement he managed to aim a kick at my balls as I crouched there, knees wide. I managed to deflect it into my stomach. The guy had kicked from a sitting position so it wasn't a particularly hard blow; still, hard enough to sting.

156

Then we were both on our feet. The guy swung his fist. I swung mine. He was probably too exhausted to make much of a fight of it, but he did his best.

By my third punch to his face he'd had enough and went down flat.

'I don't want to fight you,' I panted. 'We can go our separate ways . . . no more trouble . . . I just want my food.'

'Yeah . . .' the guy screeched. 'You won't just take the food back, will you? Will you! Go on, you take what you want. Fuck me! Fuck me and get it over with!'

'No . . . Christ, what are you talking about?' I shook my head bewildered. 'Just get up and walk away. I don't want any more trouble.'

The voice had a ruined cracking sound to it. 'Why don't you fuck me! Go on, you inch-dick, fuck me, but don't take all day about it.'

Then I watched as two grubby fists came up, grabbed the ripped T-shirt and tore it open.

Then I saw my mistake.

'He' was a she. A girl of around twenty. She nipped her own breasts cruelly to make them point at me.

'Go on,' she croaked. 'Don't us girls love it when you kick us first. What about foreplay with the rifle butt? Umm-mm . . . fuck me, lover boy. But this time I want you to cut my fucking throat afterwards. Because I am fucking sick of this. I'm fucking sick of it!'

Her screech was like a motor picking up revs; the screech rose in pitch and volume. She lay there flat on her back in front of me, nipping her breasts up into hard pointed peaks, the nipples purpled. The jeep cap had come off, spilling a tangle of long hair that must have been beautiful only a few days ago. Blood trickled from a cut on one cheek where my fist had bust her skin.

Her eyes were the worst; they blazed crazily at me. They blazed and blazed hatred at me, at the world, at God, at everyone.

I dropped down into a crouching position, the rifle in one hand. I put my other hand over my eyes and I trembled.

By the time Stephen, Dean, Victoria and the rest reached me the girl was laughing hysterically and I was sobbing like a little child, the tears stinging like hot cinders in my eyes.

The three we'd caught consisted of a boy of about thirteen, a man of twenty-nine (he'd once been a music teacher) and the twenty-year-old girl, who'd been a law student at Manchester University. We must have formed a strange grouping out there on the moor as we sat trying to work out what to do for the best.

Victoria had her head screwed on right. She opened three tins of peaches with a Swiss army knife and handed them to our three captives. They drank the juice thirstily, then worked on the peach slices themselves, their blackened fingers plucking the golden fruit from the cans. I noticed they sucked their fingers so hard, so as not to waste a single drop of the precious syrup, that their fingers were soon sucked clean of dirt; it left them looking as if they wore black fingerless gloves.

The thirteen-year-old kept thanking us politely. 'Thank you . . . these really are nice, you know.' Down slides another peach slice. 'Really nice . . . Uph, excuse me. We haven't had much in the way of . . .'

'We've not had much in the way of anything.' That was the ex-music teacher. He had blond hair and kind eyes that looked so brutally exhausted that sometimes he had trouble in keeping them open.

'You managed to find food?' Stephen asked.

'Yes. A whole warehouse of the stuff.'

'Then why steal ours?' Dean sounded angry.

'We *had* a warehouse full of food. But some men turned up. They said they were army but I didn't believe them. Anyway, to cut a long story short . . .' He gave a bitter laugh. 'They evicted us. We've no food now.'

'And you let them kick you out?' Dean almost sneered his disgust.

'No,' the man blinked his sleepy eyes as he looked up at Dean, mustering a defiance that was impressive despite his exhaustion. 'No, we didn't *let* them. We reasoned with them. We offered to share the food. Then, when they started firing their machine guns at us, we put up a fight. We had shovels, sticks, stones, bare hands – but we put up a bloody good fight. A hundred of us died, this boy's two brothers died. My wife died. But, yes, we put up a damn good fight. Satisfied?'

Dean looked as if he was going to argue but Stephen caught his eye and shook his head.

Victoria wore a blouse loosely over a T-shirt. She took off the blouse and helped the girl put it on. I tried to avoid looking at the cut on her face where I'd punched her. Victoria took a tissue from her pocket and held it gently to the girl's face.

I found myself drawn to look at Victoria. Her heavy red hair was tied back; her eyes were so full of compassion they looked nothing short of saintly as she moved back and forth between our three captives, making sure I'd done no permanent damage when I'd tripped the two males and bopped the girl.

Christ, I felt so guilty. Now it seemed so shitty and mean. I should have let them have the stupid food.

'How many of you are there?' Stephen asked.

'Almost three hundred.'

'Three hundred?' he echoed, shocked. 'And you've no food?'

'We've found turnips at a farm. There's wheat in a field. It's not ripe but if you chew enough grains it helps ease hunger pains; oh, and then there's the odd wild bird egg or rabbit.'

'But there's a lot of us dying every day now,' said the kid bluntly. 'They get blood in their shit . . . sorry, blood in their faeces. Then they die.'

'But there must have been tons and tons of food in homes and supermarkets.'

'There was,' the girl said, dabbing at the cut where I'd punched her. 'But armed gangs go round and take food from people who don't have guns. They take all of it and we're left to starve.'

'This is complete madness.' Stephen rubbed his forehead. 'That means civilization really has come apart at the seams. There's millions of people out there. But there's no food being produced, no food imported.'

'Then we're done for,' Dean said heavily.

'No, we're not,' Stephen said. 'We'll make it.'

'But what are we going to eat? Heather? Stones? Soil?'

A spark of determination came into Stephen's eye. 'We *are* going to survive this. And we'll come out of it on two feet, like civilized human beings. Not animals.'

'What are we going to do with these three?' Dean asked.

'We're going to give them the food they took. Do you need anything else?'

'Soap would be nice,' the girl said.

'And could you spare any medical supplies?' the man asked. 'Nothing much, maybe a bottle of aspirin and antiseptic cream if you can spare any. Some of our children are developing skin sores.'

Stephen took me to one side, speaking so the three outsiders couldn't hear. 'Can you go to the camp? Find a spare backpack. Fill

it with food, a couple of aspirin packs, bottle of Calpol, antiseptic
cream. Oh, and a couple of ventilators – make it one of Ventalin
and one of Pulmicort; some of their children must have asthma. Ask
Kate Robinson, she knows where it all is.'

'You're sure about this? I mean, you know we can't really
spare it?'

'We can, kiddo.' Stephen was back on charismatic form, eyes twinkling, hands rubbing together. 'Then we'll get everyone packing.'

'Packing? We're moving on?'

'Afraid so, Kid K. Much as I like the place, as soon as these
people return to their own camp they'll sing their praises about our
generosity and before you know it we'll have three hundred hungry
folk tramping over the hill towards us.'

'But where will we go?'

'Trust me, kiddo. I've got plans – great plans.'

The rest of us walked back to the camp. We left Dean, Stephen
and Victoria helping to pack the food back into the sacks for our
three guests – I guess you could describe them as that now.

Caroline was waiting for me at the lip of the gully. Below I saw
all the tents pitched in neat rows; the stream, a strand of sparkling
silver, ran alongside them.

It was as we headed down the steep path that I heard the
gunshots.

Crack-crack.

Pause.

Crack-crack.

Pause.

Crack-crack.

One second later I was running back across the heather. I knew
the gunshots had come from the direction of where Stephen sat with
the others. There was a low mound between me and them. I could
see nothing. I ran faster. And I dreaded what I would find.

CHAPTER 34

Heart thumping wildly, I ran, drawing back the bolt of the rifle as I
did so. My head whirled with possibilities. Maybe one of the armed

gangs we'd heard so much about had stumbled across Stephen as he waited there with the others for me to return with the food and medicines.

I'd get there and find Stephen and the rest dead. What would I do then – *what the hell would I do?*

Then came more shots. Three loud cracking reports. Those had been fired from a rifle, I decided. Then three muffled booms. That would be a shotgun. Stephen had a pump-action shotgun. They might be fighting for their lives back there.

If I could reach the top of the hill I'd have the advantage. I'd be able to lie flat out on the ground and snipe at the armed gang.

If only I could reach the brow of the mound. *Come on, legs, come on, legs!* I panted and swore under my breath, my legs felt like lumps of dead iron. *Faster! Run faster!*

I saw a figure walking towards me over the brow of the hill. I wiped the sweat from my eyes, then put the rifle butt to my shoulder, aimed and—

Thank Christ for that.

Stephen walked slowly towards me, the shotgun held in one hand trailing down.

'Stephen . . . you all right?'

'Fine.'

'I heard shooting; did—'

'Rick.' He took a deep breath. He was shaking, sweat beaded from his face, and I noticed a strange look in his eye. 'Rick. Will you go to the camp and bring back a couple of shovels?'

The need for the shovels sank in quickly. 'Christ. Who's . . .?'

'We're all fine.' He looked across the moor; others from our camp were streaming across the heather towards us. 'It was the three we'd caught stealing. The blond haired guy snatched the automatic from Dean's belt. He'd have used it.'

'The guy's dead?'

'All three are.'

'But how did they—'

'They tried to grab my shotgun. They were wild. They'd have killed us.'

'But even the kid?'

'Listen, Rick. Please listen, OK? All three jumped us. We had to fight for our lives. They're dead. Now I'm going to bury them. No,

Rick . . . please, brother. Please don't ask me any more questions. I don't feel up to it, really I don't.'

I nodded.

He said he was grateful, and put his hand on my shoulder before returning to the other side of the hill where the bodies must have lain. It's the expression on his face that I can't shift from my head. That look of horror all twisted up with self-disgust. It was the first time he'd killed. And he was so deeply ashamed that right at that moment I believe he would have given anything not to have been Stephen Kennedy.

It was the evening of the same day the three refugees died. The sun still shone. The guys and gals of Stephen's Ark high up there on the moor were ligged out around the tents. And I was sitting on the bank of the stream, flicking little pebbles from the palm of my hand into the sparkling water. And I felt like shit.

A military transporter droned high overhead. All the aircraft flew from west to east now.

Flocks of birds were flying, too. It wasn't the season for migration. But there they were. Great flying Vs of geese and ducks. They flew east, too. Animals and humans were escaping from Armageddon.

And, Christ, I felt like shit.

Half of Planet Earth was on fire. Millions of people were refugees. Hundreds of thousands of those were starving. And I remembered the squalid little drama way over there across the hill. Yeah, big Rick Kennedy, nineteen years and six months of age, spends the morning fucking attractive thirty-seven-year-old mother of one, namely the oh-so-shapely Caroline Lucas. Then I stroll back to tent city here in its butt-like cleft between the sides of the gulley. My cock still hot and sticky with sweet Caroline's body fluids. Then, hey presto, mother dear, I beat up an undernourished twenty-year-old girl who's probably been raped, battered, ripped off, forced to sell her cunt for a breadcrust more times in the last ten days that I've had pizza takeaways.

Yes, Christ, watch my lips: *No frigging doubt about it. I felt like a great steaming fistful of that stuff that pops fresh from your backside every morning.*

If, when I'd seen those three starving wretches making a run for it, I'd have just given a philosophical shrug and let them go with those few cans of food, they'd still have been alive. I knew that. I knew that as clearly as if the Almighty Himself had aerosoled across the sky in day-glo green paint: *'Hey, Rick shit-for-brains Kennedy. Yep, I'm talking to you down there. You know, you good as killed those three. Come on, Rick, show me you feel guilty; just give me a sign; anything, just so I know you feel that teeny-weeny bit of guilt.'*

'Fancy a walk, kiddo?'

I looked up at my brother standing there with the shotgun hanging by its strap from his shoulder; in one hand he held a pair of binoculars. The fingers that held it were clean. The fingernails were not. I'd seen him scrubbing his hands with washing-up liquid and disinfectant in the stream. He'd not been able to shift all the blood. Imagine if you take a felt-tip pen, its colour halfway between red and brown. Then draw a line where your fingernails meet skin. Now look at your fingernails. You have a reddish-brown line round each nail that looks like, if your fingers are pointing upward, four letter U shapes; like so: **UUUU**. The blood of three innocent people whose only crime it was to starve.

I felt sick.

'A walk,' Stephen was prompting. 'It's important, Rick. There's something you have to see.'

CHAPTER 35

Before we set off from the camp Stephen said, 'Best bring your rifle.' He shrugged. 'You never know what we'll find out there.'

We climbed up the steep slope of the gorge and out onto the moor. The sky was blue, birds were singing. Back down there in the camp with the tents laid out in neat lines those sixty people were slipping back into their old routines of making meals, talking, listening to the radio; I saw Caroline sitting side by side with Kate Robinson and I wondered what they were talking about. Do women boast about sexual conquests? If they did, what would Caroline have to tell?

Sitting alone on a rock, well away from the camp, was Victoria. Her lush hair, the same shade as the dried blood around Stephen's fingernails, hung in heavy waves across her shoulders. She sat staring into the palm of her hand like she'd never seen skin before. Then she began curling her fingers experimentally. Studying the way they moved. You've seen someone climb into the driver's seat of an unfamiliar car? This was like that – I mean *exactly like* that. As if she'd been dropped into that body yesterday and the whole mechanics and skin upholstery of the thing were still unfamiliar.

It was the shock. A few days ago she'd been plucked from a burning graveyard. Today, she'd witnessed three people being blown to kingdom come.

Shock, trauma, stress – stick any description you like on it. It was beginning to bite deep.

Here, I was, tramping across the moor with my brother and, Christ Almighty, did I feel like a piece of living shit.

And there was my brother. Every so often he'd shoot me a kind, encouraging smile. But you could see the tension pulling the muscles in his face so tight an eyebrow twitched. Naturally, like all of us, he'd never killed a human being before. I guess he felt as if he'd undergone some transformation today. The experience had changed him forever.

'It'll take about an hour,' he said as we walked downhill. 'There's plenty of daylight left so we'll make it back before dark.'

As we walked across the springy clumps of heather I couldn't help but think Stephen wanted to tell me something. No, it was more than that. He looked as if he wanted to make a confession.

After a while, I had the disconcerting sensation that any moment he'd turn to me and say, 'Rick. It's time for me to unmask.' Then he'd stand there in front of me, reach up, grip the skin on his chin and rip it upwards, up over his eyes and back over his skull.

And there would be a grey face. With eyes that would be almost oriental in shape. Only they would be red. As if the eyes themselves had been removed and the sockets filled to the brim with blood. Red, wet, shining blood eyes.

I rubbed my face to shift the image. My subconscious was telling me that my brother was hiding something ugly. Something about the killing of the three starving refugees back there. The story he'd told me, how they made a grab for the guns, didn't only just sound not watertight. It oozed doubt from every orifice. Why would three unarmed people, who seemed totally unaggressive, suddenly make a lunge at people packing a shotgun, pistols and an automatic rifle?

'Rick,' Stephen said, making eye contact with me. 'You should think about hooking up with a girl. I'm in a relationship with Ruth Sparkman. You'll know about that.'

164

I smiled. 'Everyone does. Those tents aren't soundproof, you know?'

He looked away, then snapped his eyes keenly back at me. 'You've got no one yet?'

'No.' A big lie. And, surely, hadn't there been some gossip around the camp yet about Caroline and yours truly?

He'd been thinking long and hard about this. He went on, his face serious. 'You should, you know. I'm not talking about marriage . . . babies. But it helps if you've got someone to . . .' He shrugged. 'To care about, and someone to care about you. You feel better psychologically. The sex is a help, too; it relieves tensions and makes you forget about, you know . . . shit like today.'

I shot him a look. At first I thought he was doing the light-hearted sex banter you'd normally hear in the locker room. But his face was deadly serious.

'I hadn't thought about it.' I kept the lies coming. 'I suppose I haven't had time to think who—'

'Kate Robinson. She seems a nice girl.'

Nice girl? Yeah, no doubt about it. Christ, I'd fancied her for weeks but here was my big brother matchmaking like he was my mother.

'Yeah,' I agreed. 'Kate's all right.'

'Well, take my advice, kid. Do something about her before Dean Skilton steams in.'

'I'll think about it.'

'Do it, Rick.' He stopped suddenly and gripped me by the arm. 'If things don't work out with Kate there's plenty of other girls. But listen to me . . . no, stand still for a minute, Rick, and listen to me. This is important. Whatever happens don't . . . don't try anything with Victoria.'

That did it. Matchmaking, then patronizing. Now warning me off other women while he no doubt built a harem. 'OK, Stephen. You're my big brother. I don't know what rights big brothers have over younger brothers, only I think you lost yours ten years ago when you went to—'

'Rick. It's nothing to do with – Rick, listen to me. Please. It's nothing to do with me wanting a piece of Victoria. Christ, nothing could be further from the truth.'

'What's wrong with Victoria?'

'Nothing.'

'But you know something about her?'

'I know nothing about her.'

'So?'

'So, just leave her alone.'

I shook my head, bewildered. 'Why the heavy warning about Victoria? She acts a bit . . . out to lunch sometimes. As if she's just landed from Planet Mars.'

'Maybe that's it. The shock might have unbalanced her.'

'You found out how she came to be in the graveyard?'

Stephen shook his head. 'She claims she remembers nothing.'

'I still don't get it, Stephen. She looks great, she's got a great figure, amazing hair; she was kindness itself this morning with those three. She gave them something to eat, she was sympathetic. Now I get the feeling you're trying to tell me she's—'

'Rick. Call it instinct. All I'm asking you to do is don't become involved with her. Talk to her if you need to but keep your distance. Come on, we've still a fair walk ahead of us.'

Stephen moved on, striding across the heather, the shotgun across his back. I followed. But I couldn't get out of my head the idea that just for a moment back there he had wanted to share a secret with me. A dark, dark secret that was eating him up inside.

For the next twenty minutes we walked without speaking. It was hard enough going anyway, with a lot of hills so steep-sided you'd swear they were heather-covered pyramids. This was the kind of place no one ever visited unless they got their kicks hiking across bleak wilderness with no hotels, houses, no roads, no nothing. But miles of moor, the occasional outcrop of rocks and one or two hawks hovering in the sky.

It was only then that I began to wonder what was so important out here that Stephen wanted to show me. Then, without any warning, he started talking about the deaths that morning. He didn't repeat the circumstances, but the words describing the poor bastards' last few seconds came out of his mouth with so much pressure I don't think he could have held them in if he'd wanted to.

'It just happened so quickly. Bang, bang. We had to fire at them. *We had to*. It's not like the movies. One shot and down they go holding their chest and it's all over. Hell, it's dirtier than that. That's what I can't get out of my mind. The dirt. You put your finger round the trigger and you're pulling, pulling, pulling, blasting away until the poor shit's no longer on their feet. Christ, the mess . . .'

166

His eyes were fixed in front as we walked. But I knew as sure as Hell he wasn't seeing the heather spread out before us. He was seeing those butchered people again.

'You shoot someone,' he said, 'they don't just bleed. They vomit, they piss themselves, the boy even shat himself. Then they're writhing about like snakes in the dirt, mixing it all in with the piss and blood. And the girl's crying, "Dad, Dad, Dad, Dad . . ." Her T-shirt was ripped. And I saw she'd been shot here.' He touched his chest. 'It just looked like another nipple. It wasn't even bleeding at first. Just another red nipple next to the real one. I froze. Because . . . because the poor bastards weren't even dead. They were squirming there on the ground like it was some fucking dance show . . . and they were just gasping . . . just gasping for breath. They couldn't scream. It was like they'd got something stuck in their throats. And they just couldn't breathe.' He laughed. It was a sudden, harsh sound. I looked at him, wondering whether he was going to break down there and then on the side of the hill. 'You know something?' Again the hard laugh. But his eyes bled sheer horror. 'You know something, Rick? I looked down at the boy. He was holding his stomach and he was looking up at me, his eyes all big and shocked-looking, his tongue was slopping about his lips like he was licking ice cream off his lips . . . only it was blood . . . only it was blood. All that blood. And he was holding his stomach. There was blood, just squeezing through his fingers. And he was holding his stomach like this.' Stephen held his stomach with both hands; his eyes shone so strangely I didn't know whether to try and pull the gun off his back in case he decided to end it all. 'And this is the weird thing. There he was, this little kid, holding his stomach like he was trying to hold his guts in. And guess what came slipping out through his fingers . . . you'll never guess?'

He looked at me with those strange bright eyes. I shook my head.

'Peaches. The fucking peaches. Those peaches he'd eaten a few minutes before. He'd not even chewed them, poor bastard was so hungry. So out they slipped through the holes in his stomach. The kid even looked surprised when he saw the bloody peaches. *Hey, shit*, you could imagine him thinking; *here I am lying on the ground with a hole in my belly big enough to stick your fist inside so you can pull out my back bone. And out comes a dirty great shoal of peaches swimming out in the blood like a bunch of gold fish. Aw, shiiii – iiittttt. Shit. SHIT!'*

That's when the enormity of it hit him. His knees folded and he sat on his butt so hard you heard the breath knock out of him with a *UPH*!

He forced his face into his hands, all the time turning his head from side to side.

I didn't know what the hell I could do. There was nothing I could say. He knew he'd killed people. I didn't know the circumstances, but it had been forced on him. He hadn't killed them in cold blood, surely it hadn't been cold blood. No sooner had I thought it than I felt the pang in my stomach. As if I'd at last hit the right answer. But surely my own brother wouldn't have . . . I crushed the thought. Maybe it was Dean Skilton. I could believe it of him now, swaggering around the camp with the pistol in his belt like a two-bit John Wayne. Dean, yeah, it must have been Dean. He'd been so pissed off with those strangers getting away with some of our precious food he'd gunned them down where they stood, still licking the peach juice from their fingers. The bastard . . .

Then I noticed Stephen again. He was sobbing into his hands. Tears trickled through his fingers to run down his wrists and forearms leaving glistening trails.

I remembered the time he'd accidentally shot me with the BB gun. How scared he'd been he might have killed me. That evening he'd sat with his arm round me as we watched TV; my head mummy-like in white bandages. He'd even bought me a box of chocolates from money he'd been saving for a computer game.

There was only one thing I could do.

I sat beside him, put my arm round his shoulders and held him as he sobbed.

CHAPTER 36

Ten minutes later we continued up the hill. Stephen looked drained but completely calm now. In fact, he looked more human than I'd seen him for days.

As we approached the brow of the hill I could almost see his mind working behind his blue eyes. There were changes going on in there. He looked older, somehow wiser.

In a calm voice he said, 'We're here.' He handed me the binoculars. 'Tell me if you see what I see.'

Rolling away far below me in the clear evening light stretched the agricultural land that lay towards Leeds. Somewhere in between were a couple of small towns and a dozen villages, including Fairburn, and a lot of open countryside that must be swarming with several hundred thousand people. Probably a goodly chunk of those were now starving.

I could see church spires, the glint of sunlight from greenhouses in faraway gardens, a railway track stretching out like a silver thread through the landscape, clumps of trees that bubbled up like green froth, the broad black strip of a canal cutting a line from the horizon towards the hill on which we stood. Then there were distant pale blocks that could only have been warehouses in an industrial estate, with—

Christ.

I looked back at the canal.

Like Hell it was a canal. It was too big. Too wide, anyhow. It must have been a kilometre across. And I knew for a fact there was no canal as wide as that. Not in Yorkshire, not in England, not on the whole freaking planet.

But there it was. Long, straight-edged, black as soot, a kilometre wide and cutting a swathe through the green countryside.

'You've seen it.' Stephen wasn't asking a question. He was making a statement.

'Yes. I've seen it.' I lifted the binoculars. 'What do you think it is?'

'I know what it is. I walked here with Victoria earlier this morning.'

'Victoria?' I shot him a startled look.

He shrugged. 'You might have noticed she sometimes goes walkabout alone for hours on end. She noticed this first and told me. Take another look.' He pointed. 'Towards the horizon.'

I looked through the binoculars. 'Jesus wept.'

'See them?'

'There's two . . . three, four . . . five.'

'They look evil, don't they?'

He was right. They did look evil. Through the binoculars I could see five black strips, the biggest of which I'd mistaken for a dirty great black-as-Hades canal. Imagine how a child draws the sun. A big blob with lines radiating outwards. Now imagine the child of a giant who stands ten kilometres high and he's taken a big wax crayon in his hand and he's drawn something like a kiddie version of the sun with radiating sunbeams. Only this sun is black. There on the horizon was an expanse of black the size of a city. Those great lines of black radiated outwards, reaching out towards us like the skeleton fingers of Mr Death himself.

'So?' I asked, nodding in the direction of the great swathe of black that seemed to point directly at us. 'It's spreading.'

Stephen nodded grimly. 'I imagine the heat is finding its way to the surface fastest through fault lines or cracks in the Earth's crust. Now the surface of the ground is hot enough to burn the plants.'

I lifted the binoculars again. Here and there smoke trickled up into the blue sky where the heat leaking up from the Earth's core triggered forest fires, or maybe simply caused a house to combust.

Stephen turned and looked at me. 'Ben Cavellero was right to get us out of Fairburn. But it isn't enough.'

'So what do we do?'

'First, we've got to stop playing at kids on a summer camping trip.'

'I think all that stopped this morning.'

He nodded again. 'And now we've got to realize the world has changed. Now we're going to have to change with it – or we're dead.'

I looked out at that finger of black ash creeping slowly but inexorably forward. And I knew he was right.

CHAPTER 37

Darkness. Absolute, total darkness.

I could see nothing. But I knew I was lying out on the moor. I felt the heather prickle my bare back and legs. I was wearing a pair of shorts – nothing else.

I could not hear a sound. Silence. Absolute silence.

But I sensed something approach. I scrambled to my feet.

Someone or something was running towards me across the moor.

From out of the darkness came a figure. All I could make out was the massive grey shape, a large head, a sense of power and a clear sense of purpose that drove the figure to run across the darkened moor.

It ran straight at me. As best as I could I dodged backwards, ready to fight it with my nails and teeth if I had to.

The heel of my foot hit a tussock and I went down flat on my back.

The grey figure ran silently past, muscular legs carrying the man away into the night.

Thank Christ for that, he'd never even noticed me.

But what the hell had happened? Why was I out there on the moor dressed in nothing but shorts? Why couldn't I remember leaving the tent and coming up here?

This was insane.

Had we been attacked in the night? Maybe instinct had driven me to run blindly from the camp as a gang of starving refugees tore the place apart, driven by their burning need for food.

I pulled myself into a sitting position.

Again my scalp crawled; as if someone had dumped a handful of woodlice in my hair. I shivered at that feeling of cold insect legs across skin.

I gave an involuntary gasp as, running towards me out of the darkness, came more of them.

I saw nothing clearly. It was more a suggestion of figures running by at either side of me as I sat there. They ran purposefully as if it was a race. They'd got somewhere to go and they were in a Hell of a hurry to get there.

It could only be a matter of time before one of these running men actually fell over me, so I began to climb to my feet.

I'd not even managed to get my hands from the ground before I felt the slap of hands on my shoulders as I was spun round by something with the strength of a gorilla. There was more than one pair of hands holding me. I felt the palms of hands pressing me face down to the ground with such a pressure I thought I'd be crushed.

I could see nothing now, but I sensed that ceaseless flow of figures running by.

Why I was being held I don't know. At first I thought I was being restrained so I'd not interfere with this weird migration of grey figures. But then I had the impression I was being closely examined as I lay pinned there. I tried to move but half a dozen hands clamped me down; the pressure was enormous. I couldn't breathe. They must release the pressure soon. I'd suffocate. The pressure was incredible. I felt as if my ribs would crack under the weight.

Seconds became minutes; I groaned with the pain of the weight and the pain of not being able to breathe. Lights began to flash in front of my eyes. My arms and legs turned numb. Then I didn't know whether I lay on that blasted moor, in the tent, or even at home. I opened my eyes. Saw the familiar blue curtains of my bedroom; the REM and U2 posters on the wall; my guitar leaning against the wall.

'The good news is breakfast is whatever you want.' My mother's voice as she pulled on her black Jaeger jacket. 'The bad news is you have to get it yourself.'

'Where are you going?' My mind was spinning like crazy. Christ, what a hangover. 'What are you wearing the black jacket for?'

'Must look smart,' she smiled and used her fingers to push back her short black hair.

'Must be important?'

'It is. While you were smooching with Caroline tonight I burnt to death when my car was caught in a firestorm in Turin. You should have seen the volcano come up through the city centre. It was enormous.'

'Mother—'

'Must dash. The dead have long journeys.'

'Mother. Don't leave me.' I tried to climb out of bed but the blankets had tangled around my arms and legs. I couldn't move. 'Don't leave me!'

I knew this was a dream. But the sense of dread cut me in two.

But was it that? Maybe those monster men on the moor had decided literally to rip me in two. I felt a great ache running from my neck to my backside as if I was being broken like a dry stick.

'Mother . . . mother . . .'

'Shush. You're shouting loud enough to wake the dead.' My eyes were blurring. A figure approached. I didn't know what it was but I willed myself to imagine it was my mother walking back into my bedroom, by my guitar, past the amplifiers, stepping over the clothes I'd dumped untidily on the floor – just like she always had done.

'Rick. It really is time for me to go now. It's hard to explain, but it's like I'm being called from another place. They want me to go there. Grandad and grandma are there, too. Maybe it won't be so bad. Now, Rick, lift up your head and I'll kiss you goodbye.'

I felt her place both hands on each side of my face and lift it to hers. My vision was blurred, the ceiling didn't look right, there was no lampshade where it should have been. But I willed myself to see my mother's smiling face, the black hair salted with grey hairs, her kind blue eyes; those pink lips that had kissed me a million times before, from when I was a bouncing baby with a snotty nose to when I was a cocky nineteen-year-old; then she'd mischievously kiss me on the cheek in front of the band when they picked me up for a gig, knowing full well they'd take the piss mercilessly all the way to Leeds or Wakefield or wherever we were playing that night.

I had no strength left in my arms and legs as I felt my face being raised to her own smiling face.

'Good-night, Rick. Sweet dreams.'

That's when my vision cleared. I saw the face above me wasn't my mother's.

I screamed. The sound ripped through my throat, mating shock with pure, pure terror.

CHAPTER 38

Stenno took one look at me. 'You've seen them, too, haven't you?'

I was going to walk on by but he caught me by the arm. 'Don't kid me, Rick. You've seen the Grey Men. Am I right?'

I looked at him, ready to deny everything.

'You have,' he hissed in something like triumph. 'You've seen the Grey Men. *And you've been with them.*'

'I've seen nothing. Now, please. I'm tired. I'm going to drink this coffee, then I'm going to sleep.'

'Go on, then.' He held back the flap of the tent for me. 'Crawl into the damned tent and pretend it never happened. Pretend you've never woken up to find yourself a mile from the tent and you don't know how the Hell you got there. Pretend you've not gone outside at midnight for a leak, then looked at your watch only to find that an hour's gone by, not two minutes.'

'Shut up, Stenno,' I said. I felt tired. I felt dangerous. Stenno was on my case and I wanted nothing to do with—

'Sure,' Stenno continued, 'you've not seen them looking in at you in the middle of the night. You've not seen their thick grey skin; it looks like rhino hide, doesn't it? Oh, no, you've not seen that, eh, Ricky boy?' Stenno's eyes glittered now. And I remembered the day he'd attacked me in Fullwood's Garage. 'What are you afraid to admit? You're afraid to admit to looking them right in the eye as they hold you down? Am I right, or am I right, Ricky boy?'

'Shut up.'

'Afraid to describe the colour of their eyes? Not blue like yours and big brother Stephen's, are they?'

'Just piss off, will you?'

'Afraid people will think you're mad?'

'No.'

'Admit what you've seen . . . what you've been seeing since Ben Cavellero's party?'

'I've seen nothing.'

'Afraid of alienating Kate Robinson?'

I stabbed him a hard look that said, clear enough, FUCK OFF.

'Kate Robinson? You know Kate . . . she's told my wife that she really likes you.'

I glanced round. People were stopping eating breakfast and looking up at us, no doubt expecting a full-blooded punch-up to erupt any moment. I saw Caroline get to her feet, her eyes concerned.

'So,' Stenno shook his head. 'You weren't afraid of those three poor bastards we murdered up on the moor. But you're afraid of the truth. You're even afraid to admit to knowing the colour of their eyes. Come on, Rick. Those grey faces. What colour were the eyes that looked at you?'

I had two choices. First: punch him on the jaw. I chose option two: 'Their eyes are *red*,' I said under my breath. This time I grabbed him by the arm. 'Now, come with me and tell me everything you know about them.'

We moved down the gully to sit in the shade of the few stunted oaks. I carried two mugs of coffee, one of which I handed to Stenno. We sat side by side on a fallen tree trunk and looked back up the gully, now zebra-striped with shadows from the branches of the trees.

'First of all, Rick,' Stenno began, 'I'm going to have to apologize.'

'Forget it.'

'No, I'm sorry, Rick; because I know I've been acting so fucking . . . *weird* these last few weeks. Ever since Ben Cavellero's party; you remember? I crashed in, covered in blood. Although I don't really remember that. In fact, the last few weeks have been one big blank. I walked through all what's happened like a zombie. I just don't remember anything except . . .'

'Anything except the Grey Men?'

He nodded, his eyes looked dreamy, faraway. 'They were the only real thing in the world. Yeah, I *sort of* remember that meeting at Ben's where I acted . . . peculiar. Then just ran for it. But I've been so terrified. I don't know why. All this, with the refugees and the toxic gas in Leeds. It seemed dreamlike . . . unreal. It's only at night that it all becomes real again. When I see them walking all around the place.'

'These are the Grey Men?'

'Yes. I see them. But no one else does. I've told Sue, but she just doesn't believe me.' He looked at me. 'Out of all of us, Rick, I think you're the only other person to see them.'

'But surely they're not invisible to the others?'

'Maybe they are.' He took a swallow of coffee. Then he began to talk again. Now his eyes took on a strange evangelical gleam; like he was telling me something that was as wonderful as it was awful. 'I saw them first on the night of Ben Cavellero's party. They wanted me to go with them. When they wouldn't they forced me. They carried me through the wood. That's when I must have knocked my head.' His eyes were bright. 'Don't you see, Rick? They chose me. Then they chose you. We are special to them. We're—'

'Now, hold on,' I said, 'what do you mean: they chose us? Where do you think these guys are from?' I nearly added *'From a flying saucer I suppose.'*

'From out of the ground.' Stenno spoke matter-of-factly. 'It's the Grey Men who're heating up the Earth. They're causing the volcanoes, tidal waves. They're the ones pumping poison gas into the cities.'

'Look, Stenno. You don't know this. We've all been through a traumatic experience. Maybe we're imagining—'

'We're imagining all this?' He laughed. But it sounded too tense for any humour to be lurking in there. 'Right. We've imagined all this, right down to identical descriptions of them. Rough grey skin, blood red eyes; maybe we—'

175

I shushed him as a couple of teenage girls ran down the path. No doubt they were going for a dip in the pool further down the gully. At first they ran through sunlight, then they were under the trees, disappearing into dark shade then suddenly reappearing in a burst of sunlight that shafted through the branches.

I saw them appear as if I was watching some jumpy old silent film. A burst of light. Their smiling faces. Then they disappeared into darkness again. In a few days they might be dead. We had enough to worry about with the Earth starting to bake itself beneath our feet. We had to worry about food running out. We had to worry about marauding gangs.

The last thing they needed were Stenno's and Rick Kennedy's *Beware The Grey Men* delusions.

The girls ran by, laughing, as they anticipated that ice-cold plunge into the water.

But I couldn't deny what I'd seen. The image had been seared into the very tissues of my brain. Every time I closed my eyes that image appeared bright and clear. The face I'd seen the night before could have been luminous, the way I'd seen it in such brutal detail. The head was enormous; in shape it was crudely humanoid. When it had looked at me it had tilted its head to one side. As if it had seen something that aroused its curiosity. I saw that the nose was broad, with a pair of flared nostrils that exhaled noisily, like those of a horse, blasting cold breath into my face.

I had tried to move, but the thing had held me there, its hands clamped to either side of my head.

It was either studying my face. Or it was forcing *me* to study *its* face. Desperately I'd wanted to close my eyes, but I found I couldn't. I had to drink in every detail. The broad nose, the flared nostrils that panted with a noisy excitement. From the broad forehead, running back over the skull, was a bony crest, from which a mane of black hair bristled, reminiscent of some unearthly Mohican hairstyle.

And there was the skin. It covered that mulish skull like a sheet of grey leather. Around the black-lipped mouth it formed deep creases and, spotted irregularly over it, there were studlike warts.

Then there were the eyes: oriental-looking and red – blood red.

The face had loomed forward, filling my whole universe as it came towards my own face: closer, closer, closer . . .

That's when I had blacked out.

I blinked, feeling suddenly nauseous.

OK. I admit it. Fact: I'd seen Grey Men. Fact: I'd felt their hands on me. All I couldn't accept was Stenno telling me that we were the Grey Men's chosen ones.

'Stenno,' I said gently, 'look, what proof have you got these . . . men come out of the ground?'

'But it all adds up, doesn't it? They've made the surface of the planet heat up; they've deliberately caused civilization to collapse. The heat is only the equivalent of an artillery barrage on enemy lines to soften them up before they send in the infantry.'

'And these Grey Men are the infantry?'

He looked at me, his eyes suddenly shrewd. 'You think I'm mad, don't you?'

'Jesus, Stenno, I think all the world has gone mad. This doesn't look particularly mad after what we've been through.'

'But you wouldn't come with me to Stephen and tell him what we know?'

'I think it's too early to – wait, Stenno. Sit down. Hear me out.'

'You're still too shit-scared to tell anyone. Rick, the Grey Men are *real*. You've seen them. You've been with them.'

'Look, I've seen them. They might even have taken me places. But I don't know where. I can't remember.'

'Then come with me. Tell Stephen.'

'That the surface of the Earth is being invaded by a race of Grey Men who . . . what? Have lived secretly under our very feet? Hiding themselves away from us for God only knows how long?'

'It's possible.'

'Sure it's possible.'

'But?'

'But if we're going to go public on this we need hard evidence.'

'Such as?'

'Ideally a Grey Man. In the flesh.' I looked Stenno in the eye. 'Dead or alive.'

CHAPTER 39

After leaving Stenno I went to find Caroline. I needed company and she was always glad to see me.

'What's the matter, Rick?' she smiled. 'You look as if you've seen a monster.'

The sun was hot but I still shivered.

I made a grim smile. 'Monsters? I see them all the time now. Especially when I look at my reflection in the stream.'

She sighed. 'Poor boy. You come and walk with Auntie Caroline.'

As we climbed the banking to the moor I happened to see Victoria. She stood by a tree staring into the side of the gorge where it became a sheer rock wall. Hell, she wasn't only out to lunch, she must have been out to breakfast, tea and supper too.

After walking for ten more minutes Caroline said in that husky voice of hers, 'Here should do just nicely.' She turned to me, pulled down the zip of my jeans and slipped her hand inside. Her hand felt cool and wonderful. 'No one can see us here,' she whispered and kissed my chest. 'Would you like to watch me undress? I'll dance for you again if you like?'

I admit it. I was scared about what was happening to me. I'd begun to wonder if the realization that the world was burning up around us was somehow upending my sanity. That seeing the Grey Men was a symptom of some encroaching madness. I'd have to find one of them as hard evidence to prove to myself I was still sane. I decided there and then that if I saw another of those Grey Men I'd put a slug in its leg. Then I'd have solid evidence to show the others. Something that would squawk when you poked it with a stick. That would be enough to make everyone believe my story. But in the meantime I needed another human being to cling to.

'Careful, Rick. You're tearing Auntie's T-shirt.'

'I'll buy you another,' I panted, ripping it up over her head. Then I attacked the belt of her cut-off jeans.

She kissed me, her breath hot with passion. 'Do what you like, lover boy. Do what you like. You know I want you.'

Down with jeans, down with pants, down with Caroline. Flat on her back on the heather. She didn't complain as the spiky plants pricked her bare back, arse and legs.

I ripped open my belt and downed my own jeans. I couldn't take my eyes off her lovely body. The little breasts with the oh-so-pale nipples gleaming pink in the hot sun.

I went down in a kind of fevered frenzy, kissing her mouth, those little breasts, then kissing her delicate light tuft of pubic hair.

She lifted her hips, pushing her pubic bone against my mouth.

She smelt so sweet. I could have sunk my teeth into her thighs and tasted her.

The world spun crazily round me. Sleep deprivation had started to kick in. What happened on the moor the night before still scared me. I wanted to obliterate reality with no-holds-barred sex.

'Hold me,' she said, breathlessly. 'Hold me. I want to feel . . . mmm. That's nice.'

I cupped her breasts in my hands. She closed her eyes and pursed her red lips. 'Mmmm . . . s'good . . .'

Something wild was driving me that day. I climbed on top of her, my heart thudding like a loco.

'Oh . . . Rick. Gentle. Please – please be gentle. Gentle, Rick. I'm not – *OW*! . . . uh-uh-uh!'

I pounded into her with such ferocity that I could hear the crunch of the heather being crushed beneath her bottom. I drove her harder into the dirt. It was sheer desperation. I tried to drive reality out of my head. At any price.

CHAPTER 40

Stephen Kennedy was in the mood to kick ass. It was two days since the three refugees had died on the moor. And one day since I'd had my *tête-à-tête* with Stenno about the Grey Man.

All sixty-four of us sat on a grass banking in the gully while Stephen paced up and down spelling out just what we must do and what we mustn't do if we were going to come through all this with our skins intact.

'No more open fires,' he said firmly. 'The smoke can be seen from miles away. We don't want to advertise to anyone else – refugees, armed gangs, Uncle Tom Cobley and all – that we're sitting up here on a heap of food. Next: we can't laze around, living off the supplies we carried up here. In a fortnight we're going to go hungry. Already we're short of potatoes and fresh fruit. And no one's tasted bread in days. So, people, starting from today we're going out hunting for food.'

'Hunting for food?' Dean Skilton's voice was laced with scepticism. 'You *are* joking, aren't you?'

'Believe me, Deanie boy. The time for joking disappeared up Lucifer's ass a long, long time ago.'

'What do you mean, hunting for food?'

'I've been drawing up lists.' Stephen was really in gear, I could sense the energy rushing through him. He'd committed every fibre and sinew of his body to making sure we would all be well fed and safe. 'There'll still be stocks of food in shops, homes, hotels—'

'They'll all be picked over by now,' Dean chipped in again.

'If we look hard enough we'll find some. It just might mean we're going to have to go where angels fear to tread, that's all.'

'You mean back to Leeds?'

'If need be.'

'Shit. What hasn't been incinerated'll be covered with poison gas.'

'Then we find gas masks. We go in there and get the food and come back out again.'

'But you can't seriously expect—'

'Dean . . . Dean.' Stephen oozed energy; he wasn't going to let anyone derail him. 'Listen to me, please. After I've outlined the plans, we'll discuss it. OK? Then you can all vote on whether I stay at the head of the group. But just let me have my say.'

'But where the Hell do you find gas masks? It's impossible.'

'You're right, Dean. But let me tell you. Now we must do the impossible just to give ourselves a few more days of life on this planet. Every day we're going to get up and force the impossible to be possible. OK?'

Dean shrugged, then stuck a matchstick into the corner of his mouth. I knew he had ideas himself about how the group should be run. I knew, also, he was ready to start making trouble if he didn't get his own way.

Victoria, sitting nearest to where Stephen stood, said, 'We mustn't forget also that we have to change our perceptions about food. The countryside is full of plants and animals that are edible. We must become experts in identifying what is poisonous and what we can safely eat. For example, boiled nettle leaves are edible, and so are beech and dandelion leaves.'

Stephen nodded gratefully at Victoria and as the morning went on I saw he and Victoria were almost playing a double act. She was playing a supporting role, feeding helpful suggestions or simply reinforcing something he'd said. Again I wondered about the real

180

reason for him warning me off Victoria. She was good-looking: her red hair looked thick and glossy and her eyes were as sharp as lasers. More than once she'd blazed a glare of disapproval at Dean Skilton that was nothing less than dangerous. She also shot that burning look at Ruth Sparkman. I began to wonder if Victoria had designs on my brother.

For the next hour Stephen pumped his plans at us. Which could be summed up as: find food. Build up stockpiles of food in secret hiding places all over the moor in case we were raided. And, most brutally simple of all, the message to each and every one of us: Adapt or Die. Most people, with the obvious exception of Dean Skilton, nodded as Stephen talked. I could see they were becoming enthused by his plans.

'We don't know how long we can stay here on Fountains Moor. If we're discovered by other refugees we must move on. And we don't know what changes might be happening to the Earth's crust beneath our very feet. Most of us have seen by now the burnt areas of countryside that seem to be spreading this way. They might not affect us. But we can't be sure. So as well as bringing in supplies of food we need to find new safe areas where we can set up camp. Whether it's in the next valley or a hundred kilometres away.'

Dean snorted with laughter. 'How do you propose we do that? Sprout wings and fly there?'

'That's exactly what I'm proposing. Howard Sparkman here got his pilot's licence last year. This is where we go out and achieve the impossible. We find light aircraft. We fly out across the country. We find food. We bring it back. That's the easy part.'

'The *easy* part?' Dean echoed. 'If that's the easy part what's the hard part?'

'Training you to fly, Dean old buddy. You're going to be one of our pilots.'

That, at last, shut Dean Skilton's mouth.

Stephen Kennedy got his vote of confidence. And we got plenty of exercise as we scoured the countryside for light aircraft. I knew it wasn't unusual for the wealthier farmers to have a private plane or two. They'd keep a strip of cornfield unploughed for a backyard airstrip.

The logic of using aircraft (if we could find one and the fuel to fly it) was easy to see. The roads were still clogged with refugees escaping whatever calamity had hit the western side of the country. And those hungry refugees wouldn't stand to one side and let a truck full of food trundle by. They'd tear it and its driver to pieces no matter how heavily armed you were. And then there were the roadblocks operated by men – and women – armed to the eyeballs with automatic rifles and heavy machine guns. These might have been regular army but by then we doubted it. More likely they were deserters and the price of being allowed to pass was to hand over to them every single rasher of bacon, every cake crumb you had stuffed in the bottom of your rucksack. Even then, if they didn't care for the cut of your jib they'd turn the machine gun on you and blow you to fuck.

What made the search even more difficult was that teams hunting for the aircraft had to move about the countryside undetected. All we needed was for a bunch of refugees to spot us and then follow us back to Fountains Moor which must have seemed like the land of milk and honey compared to the hungry state in which they existed.

We'd see armed camps in the distance. They might be anything from a farmhouse to a village ringed with barbed wire and moats dug by JCBs. Some were clearly inhabited. Some had been overrun by starving refugees. Now it really was kill or be killed.

Now and again we came across other bands of people hunting for food. Once I saw a group of red men, women and children. I mean they were entirely *red* – hair, skin, clothes. We hid in a hedgerow as they trudged by, exhausted, starving. They must have had to cross one of the hotspots which had been carpeted in red ash. It had turned them red and now they were too far gone even to bother trying to clean themselves. One of their number, an elderly man, dropped face down on the road. I even heard the slap of his face as it hit the road. The rest carried on walking. I don't think they even noticed.

We crouched there and watched them walk on into the distance. A dirty line of red people who looked already more than half dead.

It got nastier.

You'd come upon bodies lying in the road where they'd dropped.

You'd walk by a tree and find a whole family with ropes around their necks, hanging from the branches like grisly Christmas Tree decorations. In the pocket of the father, a suicide note that gave details of what had happened to them and the reasons why they'd thought it better to end it all. I carefully folded it up and put

182

it in my pocket. It would go in the archive Kate Robinson was compiling.

Kate Robinson? You might be wondering whether she was still in the picture. The truth is she was moving deeper and deeper into it. Even though I'd promised myself I would be virtuous. I really believed I was in love with Caroline Lucas. Not a day went by when we didn't go out onto the moor and she'd wriggle sexily out of her clothes then do wonderful things to me with her mouth or with those parts of her that lay south of her equator.

So what did happen to me and Kate Robinson? You'll find out soon enough. That all happened when we found the plane and Fate played one of those tricks it obviously thinks are damned hilarious. Unless you happen to be on the receiving end. Anyway, Fate took Kate and me, Rick Kennedy, all the way to London. Or at least to what was left of London.

CHAPTER 41

But I'm getting ahead of myself. Life, as I already mentioned, was getting dirtier and nastier.

On one food-finding trip I heard a commotion in a nearby field. At that moment I was alone; Dean Skilton and the other two were waiting for me in a nearby wood as I scouted the area.

It was as I cut across fields in the direction of a farmhouse that I heard shouts.

Cautiously I looked over a wall to see a horrific sight.

Twenty wild-eyed men with shaggy hair and beards were chasing a woman of around forty across the grass. She wore a tattered green dress, no shoes, and her blonde hair had been cut short, probably as a precaution against bugs as much as anything.

She ran, kicking her knees into the air. I don't recollect if she was screaming. I think she was pushing everything into that lung-tearing dash across the field. The men chasing her chanted with a *uh-uh-uh-uh-uh* sound.

Uh-uh-uh!

They got closer. One reached out and caught her by the elbow.

She twisted out of his grip.

Then she shifted direction. I saw, with horror, she was running towards me. If she jumped the wall I was hiding behind she'd bring that mob down on me.

I'd be dead meat. I had the rifle loaded with five rounds of ammo. I'd be able to take out a couple of those wild-eyed animal men but then they'd tear me apart – no problem.

The rest of my hunting party were a good kilometre down the road. They wouldn't be able to help me.

The woman ran towards me with that high-kicking stride.

Closer . . . closer . . .

I could even seen the grass had turned the soles of her bare feet green. Her eyes seemed to lock onto mine. Even though I'd swear she couldn't see me.

Her eyes bulged out white like hardboiled eggs. Her face was red with exertion, her cheeks puffed out as she panted desperately for air. Behind her, her pursuers were a frenzied mass of waving arms, open mouths, chanting: *uh-uh-uh-uh!*

I was going to witness another scene like that night I saw Caroline being carried away into the wood.

I locked up with shock. I had to do something.

But what?

I couldn't shoot every man there. Maybe with grenades and a machine gun I could have done something.

She ran straight at the wall.

Uph!

The concussion knocked the breath from her body.

She began to climb the wall. Arms over, her gold bracelets catching the light, then she swung one bare mud-smeared leg over.

She saw me; her eyes widened. Still keeping out of sight of the mob on the other side of the wall I reached up and began to help her over. I grabbed her slim wrist. She froze. Then tried to drag back, her eyes filled with terror.

Uh-uh-uh-uh!

The savage chant grew louder as the men approached.

'Let me help you,' I said under my breath. 'Once you're over the wall run to the stream. We can hide under the bridge.'

She smiled. The look of gratitude on her face transformed it.

'Thank—'

Then she was gone. As quickly as that; snatched away from the other side. Her wrist slipped through my fingers, leaving me holding the gold bracelet.

I stared at it in horror. Then my head snapped up: I expected to see leering faces above the wall. But the mob didn't even know I was there.

Quickly, keeping low, I followed the mob, occasionally spying through the cracks of the dry-stone wall and catching glimpses of the men carrying the blonde-haired woman away.

I followed, still wondering what I could do. Come on, Rick, get that brain in gear. What would Stephen do? He'd think of a plan. Christ, the man was inspired these days. He could solve any problem, hatch any plan. You're his brother, Rick; creativity is in the blood. You've got three minutes to save this woman. What will you do?

Clutching the rifle in both hands, I followed the sound of the chanting madmen.

Uh-uh-uh-uh-uh!

If the bastards did rape her perhaps I could still manage to get her away from them later. Surely no one back on Fountains Moor would object to me bringing in another survivor.

Then I reached a meadow that ran down towards a stream.

At any other time it would have been a pleasant place: an acre of soft, sweet grass; a shallow stream catching the sunlight on this warm summer's day. At the edge of the stream, a couple of willow trees. From one branch hung a rope swing. The kind I'd spent hours on as a ten-year-old, swinging to and fro across a stream near home. Back in those days long ago when the world was a fun place to be.

But today that meadow was a genuine slice of hell.

Still chanting, the madmen carried the woman into the field. Trying desperately to break free, she writhed and twisted, back arching, hips lifting.

In the centre of the field was a wooden pole set upright in the earth. The top of the pole would have reached my shoulder.

That's when I knew what they were going to do to her. I think that's when the woman realized, too. Because she began to scream. A bitter mechanical scream that went on and on. Even when I clamped my hands over my ears I could still hear it. That vocal cord-ripping scream. I can hear it still.

I've promised myself to tell everything about how it happened. And not to censor any of it. Not one word. You must know what we did to each other that summer the world decided to burn itself up under our feet.

But I wouldn't blame you now if you skipped the next few paragraphs. It is dirty, it is disgusting, it is degrading; the sight of it is burned into my memory for life.

All I can do is warn you. If you can take it, keep reading.

this is what they did to the screaming woman:

The mob carried the woman towards the pole. As they did so, men and the women who'd joined them began tearing away the woman's clothes.

Soon she was naked; I could see her navel, a flash of fair pubic hair; the shiver of her buttocks; her breasts swaying heavily as they lifted her up higher, her head twisting from side to side as she struggled to free herself.

At that moment I knew what I had to do. The rifle had a telescopic sight. I was a fair shot by now. I realized the only option was put a bullet through the woman's head so she wouldn't experience the agony of what they'd do to her next.

Because I realized then that this was no mass rape.

The instinctive drive for survival had suppressed sex lust. The lust for food was all that mattered now.

With two men at each side of the woman, gripping her by her legs and holding her high into the air, just as you'd see a jubilant football team holding the captain, they carried her towards the wooden pole.

I put the telescopic sight to my eye and drew back the bolt of the rifle.

First: I saw the pole. It had been set firm in the ground like a fence post. The top had been sharpened so it resembled a giant pencil whittled to a wicked point. Through the cross-hairs of the telescopic sight I could see it was perhaps as thick as my wrist. It was stained. This had happened before.

Mouth dry, heart thudding so hard the echo carried into my skull, I moved the rifle, seeing the magnified heads of the mob, their unkempt hair plastered with shit and blood; and their wild, wild eyes. Those eyes blazed with a greedy craving. Just weeks ago those chanting men and women had been schoolteachers, office workers, dentists, social workers – now they had evolved into a savage tribe.

And I knew exactly what they would do with the blonde woman.

Her heavy bare breasts bounced as they carried her to the pole and lifted her above it.

I aimed. Her red face, quartered by the cross-hairs of the telescopic sights, filled my field of vision. Her teeth were clenched, her eyes screwed shut. She knew what they were going to do.

Christ . . . they were going to sit her on the pole.

You know *exactly* what I mean. But I find it a struggle to express plainly that . . . that, oh for Chrissakes, they were going to impale her on the wooden stake. They were going to drive that sharpened stake through the body. Not through her chest or the stomach. They were going to sit her on the pole and . . .

I swallowed, held my breath to damp down the trembles bucking my arms, aimed. Her face was slap in the centre of the cross-hairs. I couldn't save her life. But I could save her from the agony of that wooden pole being driven inside her.

UH-UH-UH-UH!

There was a savage ritual about this. They held the woman above the pole as they chanted so loud it drove the birds from the trees in terror.

UH-UH-UH-UH-UH!

I pulled the trigger, already anticipating the woman's head dissolving in a spray of blood as that bullet kissed home.

Then I'd have to run for my life.

Click.

That's all. No bang. No kick in the shoulder as the bullet left the muzzle at four hundred metres per second.

Shit.

That piece of ammo was a dud. I pulled the bolt to eject it. It came part way. Then jammed.

Shit, shit, shit.

I struggled with the bolt trying to eject the dud round.

Then I stopped. *Too late, Rick. You're too late!*

The woman's face was still screwed tight, her eyes crushed shut, teeth gritted. I sensed her exert sheer will-power in an attempt to block out the pain to come.

Step by step the ritual continued. Still the chant: *Uh-uh-uh!*

She was raised higher, like a sacrificial offering to some dark and bastard-hearted god.

Almost reverently the woman was seated upon the sharpened pole. Her legs were held straight down at either side of it, feet towards the floor as if she was being mounted on a horse.

Still her face was crimped tight. You sensed she was holding her

187

breath. Willing the pain – that pain that was so inevitable – that fucking awful, skin-splitting pain – willing it not to rip through her body.

Hands supported her torso, holding her upright.

Then the men holding her by the legs pulled down.

They pulled down hard. So hard that they lifted their own legs from the ground, using their body weight to exert a greater downward force; they clenched their teeth and grimaced with the effort of impaling their victim on the wicked point of that pole.

My eyes snapped back to the woman's face as the pole slid in and in and in . . .

Her body convulsed, her arms came out straight in a crucifixion pose.

Then her mouth and eyes snapped open wide with the shock of the pain.

Helplessly I looked back. Her eyes met mine and at that moment it seemed a bolt of psychic energy leapt from her to me; the shock was physical, knocking me back on my heels.

All I could see was that look of pure shock on her face; her eyes so wide they looked as if they'd burst from the sockets; her mouth yawning so enormously it seemed as if the jaw would dislocate.

And I felt that brutal stream of terror, pain, disgust and sheer, sheer sorrow at her life being ended on that wooden pole there in the field. Surrounded by chanting born-again savages.

I was so appalled, so sickened. I stumbled backwards, unable to turn my back on the woman's mutilation in the field. As they continued the ritual, women moved forward; they held butchers' knives. They began to carve. Her right breast came away in a single bell-shaped piece; blood spurted.

The woman on her skewer, still alive, seemed to dance in slow motion, arms waving slowly – even serenely – above her head. A parody of a dance I'd seen danced by Asian women: arms above head; move slowly to the left; move slowly to the right.

They were beginning to eat her alive.

Still she danced; the pain had burnt out her mind.

Still she danced.

Children clustered to drink the blood drenching the pole between her legs the deepest crimson.

Still she danced. The skewered woman.

I turned.

And ran.
And ran.

CHAPTER 42

The shock had screwed my sense of direction. I ran blindly. Falling. Dropping the rifle. Stumbling back to pick it up. Running again. I was crying as I ran. Blubbering and snotty-faced, like some little runt who's fallen off his bike and is running home to mummy.

I don't know what disgusted me most. The mob in the field who'd tugged the woman down over the pole, leaving her to hang there, skewered from crotch to throat, while the bastards dined on her. Or myself. And the people back on Fountains Moor. We were so ignorant, so fucking insulated from all this. Men and women were eating each other; they'd turned savage; they'd turned into beasts. And we were sitting up there on the hill, still eating sardines from cans, and there was still a shot of whisky before you stood up, scratching your belly and saying you were going to turn in. Then, once in your tent, you zipped yourself all nice and clean into your nice, clean sleeping-bag.

Who were we kidding?

Just who the fuck were we kidding? This was the cold bleeding-hearted reality now.

Kill or be killed.

Eat or be eaten.

I scrambled over walls, trudged through streams. Then came a band of black earth as wide as a highway. The soil smoked. I even felt the heat against my skin as I ran along it. I didn't care. I wanted to run and run. Run so fast I'd manage to outrun my own skin.

I climbed another wall and found myself in a farmyard. I skirted a burnt-out truck.

Then I saw the Grey Men.

In fact I saw several of them.

I stopped and stared, the rifle – that fucking useless rifle – gripped in my fists.

There they were – twice the size of me.

The Grey Men were painted on the wall of the barn, aerosoled in silver paint – but I knew what the artist intended. They were supposed to be grey but the silver paint gave them a supernatural luminosity. In their build, massive shoulders, massive head, band of hair following the crest of bone from forehead to nape of neck, long arms as strong as a gorilla's: they were exactly as I remembered them. The eyes were red. A wet, glossy red. And I knew the artist had used a different kind of paint there. In fact, sitting on a table was the plastic bucket with the brushes still inside.

I looked.

In a detached way I counted three hands, one still wearing a wedding ring. There was also a heart. Human, I guessed. And in the bottom of the bucket a good dollop of still-wet blood that had served as paint for the red eyes. Flies buzzed in and out. They'd feed well on what the artist hadn't used.

I moved on through the deserted farmyard, looking up at the windows of the farmhouse expecting to see faces peering back.

But the place looked deserted.

Hanging by lengths of electrical flex from a child's climbing frame in the garden, twenty or more heads. The eyes of some had been gouged, leaving bloody red sockets; one had a galvanized nail, as thick as your thumb, hammered through the forehead. The face wore a look of stupid surprise; the same kind of wide-eyed expression the cop always wears in Laurel and Hardy films when he gets cream-pied.

(Nice one, God; another pant-wetting cosmic joke. How come you never let us poor saps die with dignity?)

The heads swung and turned gently in a light summer breeze.

'Adapt or die.' That's what Stephen had said. The people who'd made this place their home had done just that. They'd flipped over to cannibalism. Radical changes had taken place inside their heads. As if their new environment had demanded a new mental software to reprogramme their behaviour.

By the outdoor swimming pool I saw another Grey Man. This one had been moulded from concrete. It stood there, grey, rock-like, like the statue of some Babylonian god of death. The eyes had been painted red. Again, a bucket holding paint brushes and severed hands (still redly oozing the medium) sat nearby.

I walked on. The rest of my hunting party would be wondering where the Hell I'd vanished. I'd have to find them or they'd leave without me.

But as I ran back to the road I saw my way was blocked.

There were the wild-eyed men, women and children. A big man with a bald, sunburnt head lead the pack. Held reverently in his two hands, as if he carried a sacred object, was a human head. I recognized the short blonde hair. An expression of shock and pain still forced the eyes wide open in the dead face.

When they saw me they howled. As if I'd desecrated something unbelievably precious.

Then came a dangerous silence as they moved slowly but purposefully towards me.

I jiggled the rifle bolt backwards, forwards, then—

Click.

The dud rifle cartridge ejected to rattle onto the ground.

I chambered another bullet.

Those faces were brutally angry. And that rifle in my hands felt about as lethal as a posy full of dandelions.

They moved forward, menacing, dangerous. Eyes glittering, fists clenching.

Crack!

I fired over their heads. The sound made them flinch. But they didn't stop moving toward me.

I had three rounds left. Maybe I could kill three of the savage bastards. But that would leave me in the hands of the other forty or so. I didn't doubt that my fate would be the pole in the meadow.

I had one option.

Run.

Then hide.

I ran.

CHAPTER 43

As soon as I turned to run, the mob followed. They chanted as they ran: *uh-uh-uh-uh-uh!*

Hell, did I have a story for Kate Robinson's archive: *Rick Kennedy's story: CANNIBALISM AND THE CULT OF THE GREY MAN.*

Only there was a real chance I'd never tell another living soul what I'd clapped my eyes on.

I ran back through the clump of farm buildings, by the barn, complete with murals of Grey Men with blood-red eyes.

Ahead of me, a five-bar gate, then a dirt lane that led back the way I'd come. In the distance I could see the clump of trees on the hillside where I knew Dean Skilton and the others would be sitting, passing round the whisky bottle and wondering where the Hell I'd got to.

I couldn't lead this mob to them. I'd have to run fast, then duck out of sight. When they'd cleared off I could make my way up to the wood.

That cross-country run was the stuff of nightmares. I climbed fences, vaulted walls; then I bust through a hawthorn hedge, my arms in front of my face to save my eyes as the thorns slashed blood-red lines into my skin. I'd almost cleared the hedge when I felt something grab hold of me. I struggled round to fight off my attacker to find a branch had caught under the rifle strap. I wrenched myself free, then ran on.

But I noticed how close the mob were now. They were close enough to make out the patterns on their blood-and mud-stained clothes. Some were still wearing nightclothes (again evidence that this disaster had struck with brutal swiftness in the middle of the night all those weeks ago). I even recognized the remains of a police uniform. Most were barefoot. This is what happens when human beings turn feral.

I pumped on across the field, my trainers slapping the grass.

A couple of pheasants spooked by the wild chase fluttered up in front of me.

Then the grass turned to black ash. I'd reached the hot spot again. This time I followed that stretch of burnt earth, my pounding feet kicking up gouts of black powder.

For one thing it made running easier. The ground was baked hard beneath my feet; grass, plants, even bushes had been reduced to ash. Wooden fences had been burnt to powder. That line of black that I now so desperately ran along followed some subterranean fault line across the earth, creating what looked like a straight black road.

The smell of burning filled my nostrils. Here and there, coils of blue smoke rose from the soil. I ran through swampland. The once sloppy grue had been cooked as hard as concrete; although at either side of the black track, steam still squirted into the air.

I shot a glance back. They were still following. I could hear the *uh-uh-uh-uh!* of their manic chant.

Somewhere to hide! Christ, there must be somewhere to hide. But all I could see to left and right of me were fields with scrubby hedges. A rabbit couldn't lie low amongst that.

As I ran I felt the ground grow hotter beneath my feet; walls and rocks began to shimmer as the heat distorted the air. Behind me the wild-eyed bunch were running across that hot track in bare feet. Their rage at me numbed them. They wanted the meat on my bones. That's all that mattered to them.

I reached a road. The tar had melted; I felt my feet sink in as if I ran through wet sand. Then I was across it, smouldering road tar still sticking to my trainers.

With a savage rush of satisfaction I heard screams as the cannibal bastards sank up to their ankles in boiling tar.

It stopped a couple dead in their tracks. But most ran on – men, women, children – they weren't going to give up the hunt just yet.

By now my breathing was coming in ragged tugs, my chest burning as much from exhaustion as from the smoke given off by the smouldering track. My legs ached; my left heel felt as if a nail had been driven through it where the Achilles tendon had been stretched further than it ought.

I was slowing down.

Uh-uh-uh-uh!

The chant turned from anger to triumph. They had me; and they knew it.

I was just wondering whether to stand and at least blow off a couple of heads before they overran met when I found I'd left the green world behind.

Suddenly the black track opened out into black desert. All the grass and bushes, as far as I could see, were burnt to nothing. The only variation was when black ash gave way to white powder. Trees still stood, only they were leafless and charcoal-looking. Here and there were dotted the bones of animals. Thousands of white snail shells scattered in the ash looked like stars against a black sky.

I pounded on by a cluster of human skulls. Dentures had melted to fuse jaws together into a sticky white mass. Stone walls wore a scorched look with soot-black streaks radiating along their flanks like zebra stripes.

I was slowing now. I couldn't run much further. My chest burned. I could not breathe. Desperately, I was scanning the black landscape for a place to hide – anywhere: a hole in the ground; a ruined farmhouse; the burnt-out shell of a car.

Ahead I saw jets of flame spitting out of the ground. They were about knee high but burnt with that fierce blue Bunsen burner-like flame I'd seen before in the graveyard.

I weaved round them.

A hundred paces on I saw an iron manhole cover; a hundred paces further there was another; then another. Three in all, forming a line. Maybe I'd find one with the top loosened, then I could slip down into the inspection chamber. With luck the mob wouldn't see where I'd gone and run on.

I took the rifle from my shoulder as I ran. Ahead of me the ground dropped suddenly.

I stopped, choking for breath. There in front of me was a steep-sided ditch with banks about as high as my head.

Letting gravity do the work now I slithered down into the water.

The water rose up just over my knees. It was as warm as a swimming bath. Here and there fish, killed by the rise in the water's temperature, floated, silver bellies up.

I saw that the manhole covers followed the line of a subterranean storm drain that discharged into the ditch. For a second I stared dumbly at the round mouth of the concrete pipe that jutted out twenty centimetres or so from the dirt banking.

'Sanctuary,' I gasped, almost giddy at the thought of hiding myself inside that great concrete pipe. It was big enough for me to shuffle inside on my hands and knees. If the mob hadn't seen me I was home and dry.

Holding the rifle in one hand I clambered inside. It was hot, airless – but, if it kept me from those bastards' prying eyes, it would be the next best place to Heaven itself.

I'd managed to crawl maybe eight paces when my face struck something in the darkness. I reached out.

Damn.

Shit!

The pipe was blocked by an iron grille. Maybe I could snap the bars. They felt pitted with rust. I'd have to shuffle back out feet first, then return feet first to kick the grille through.

I'd shuffled back a couple of paces.

When I heard: *uh-uh-uh!*

Hands grabbed my feet; I felt myself being dragged savagely backwards.

With both hands I hung onto the iron bars. There was no way I could hang on for more than a couple of seconds. I tried to kick out into the faces of the cannibals but they caught hold of my ankles. In a second I'd be dragged out into the ditch to be torn apart. The bastards would be dining on my liver and heart by sunset.

My fingers began to lose their grip on the bars. I twisted my head round. I could see the heads of the mob in silhouette as they crammed eagerly into the storm drain to reach me.

Then I saw something else. The inside of the concrete pipe was blackened.

That couldn't be possible. There was nothing flammable to burn. But here were sooty streaks running along the pipe to the mouth of the drain.

My brain seized on this. *Something burnt in here, something burns, something burns . . .*

Christ . . . what do you find underground that burns? What caused the flaring jets to erupt through the soil?

What comes hissing from the cooker when you turn the knob?

I didn't even think it through. Still holding on with my left hand, I released my right hand from the iron bar of the grill. Instantly a terrific pain shot through my shoulder to my elbow as my left arm took the strain.

It didn't matter. If this didn't work I'd be history anyway.

One-handed, I raised the rifle, slotted the muzzle of the barrel through the iron grille.

Then pulled the trigger.

The flash lit the concrete tunnel as the bullet cracked away into the distance beneath the fields. I even saw the bullet itself, moving like a spark of flaming silver, almost as if in slow motion. The crash of the report deafened me.

Then everything happened in one seamless movement. I let go of the grille with my left hand.

I shot back down the pipe; the gleeful shouts of the mob rose into an excited yell.

As I was plucked from the storm drain I saw a flicker of yellow somewhere way down in a distant part of the tunnel.

Next I was flicked high into the air, the force of the mob's pull so great that my head even came above the banking.

Then I saw a sight that was all at once terrifying and awesome.

Just for a split second, as I moved in that free-falling arc, I saw the manhole covers running away across the field, following the line of the storm drain. First, the one furthest away erupted in a geyser of blue flame, then the middle one, then the nearest; a great shrieking flame of blue. Momentarily it looked as if jet motors had been set into the earth to vent superheated gas and fire fifty metres into the sky.

Still falling, I dropped down towards the water below.

It was as if a photograph had been taken of the scene, I remember it so clearly.

The mob had clustered into the ditch. They were all grinning; their eyes gleamed as they anticipated fresh meat. The man with the bald head stood framed by the opening of the storm pipe.

Chanting *uh-uh-uh* so loudly, they hadn't heard the roar of the blazing gas venting through the manhole covers; and they certainly weren't ready for where it would vent next.

Gravity swung me down into the water with an almighty splash.

I'd held my breath and dug my hands into the silt and hugged myself down to the bottom of the stream. My eyes were open. Through the brown swirl of stirred-up silt I saw hands swim down through the water to grab me and pull me out, where no doubt I'd feel just how sharp their butchers' knives were.

I pulled myself deeper underwater. Jesus, sweet Jesus, I only needed another moment below the water's surface before—

Vuu-uumph!

At that instant the water turned an incandescent blue. The concussion bucked the stream bed where I'd dug my hands to prevent myself floating back to the surface.

And then I saw that I seemed to be suspended in a bath of liquid gold. Bubbles streamed from my nose; I looked up. Just centimetres above me, the surface of the water. And above that it looked as if a chunk of the burning sun rested there in the ditch.

And in that same moment the hands that had reached down to me were gone, and through the water I could hear a muffled roar like a jet engine just above me.

I waited as long as I could; until my lungs felt they were on fire and my stomach muscles twitched from oxygen deprivation.

Then I surfaced, gasping. For a second I could see nothing. All

196

I could do was catch that same smell you get when you lose a beefburger through the grating of the barbecue and it burns, sizzling with fat. I blinked again, spat ditch water out of my mouth, looked round.

Steam rolled from the mouth of the storm drain, and every so often small balls of flame would roll out: *pop . . . pop . . . pop . . .*

The cannibals had gone. When I say gone, I mean they were no longer a danger. Most had run away when the concrete pipe had disgorged the gas like a monster flame thrower. Some hadn't moved fast enough.

There, scattered along the banking, and in the water itself, were a dozen or more figures, all seared and still steaming. Men and women had even lost their faces to the blast of methane gas. That gas had ignited when my bullet ricocheted up the concrete pipe, striking sparks. Some of the figures were still alive; they lay there shivering as if caught by a sudden frost.

After what had happened to the blonde-haired woman they didn't deserve mercy. Nevertheless, I pulled them from the banking and left them face down in the water to drown.

I didn't know where the rifle was. I didn't care. Rick Kennedy only wanted to get out; out of that burnt slice of Hell. So I dragged myself from the ditch and walked back the way I had come, the water dripping from my body sizzling as it hit the baking ground.

I found my friends beneath a tree, giggling drunkenly over what was left of the bottle of whisky. Astonished, they looked at me. I was dripping. My feet and legs were black with ash. My elbows and chin were skinless where I'd been dragged across the sandpaper-rough concrete pipe.

They looked up, open mouthed, waiting for me to tell them what had happened.

But I hadn't got a word left in my body. Not one. Nor a single emotion. All horror, disgust, pity, hatred, anger had haemorrhaged from me. I picked up my backpack crammed with scavenged food, heaved the straps across my shoulders and set off walking, hearing nothing but the squelch of water in my shoes and the beat of my tired heart.

CHAPTER 44

Caroline smiled at me. Her green eyes sparkled as she looked up into my face. I loved that smile. It was always welcoming, trusting. And it made me feel good to know that I could make her happy just by saying hallo, after two days away, scavenging the countryside for a few cans of beans or an overlooked cache of potatoes.

Caroline would give me that smile, whisper, 'Five minutes,' then she'd disappear into the trees that lined the gorge. And in five minutes I'd follow, heart beating hard, the heat spreading through my groin as I anticipated seeing her lying naked across the grass, or sitting on a boulder, her bare buttocks pressed against rough stone. Waiting for me, knowing my passion, sheer naked lust, call it what you want, had built to nothing less than a volcanic intensity in the time I'd been away.

The weeks flowed steadily by and this was the pattern we'd fallen into. Stephen worked day and night. It had become a holy quest for him, to make sure we survived. He organized food dumps – usually holes dug into the moor and carefully covered with heather and marked by stones. He wanted to be sure that if we were found by the armed gangs and raided we'd have instant access to fresh supplies of canned foods. He personally hunted out new camp sites, in case discovery of our camp by other survivors necessitated a move.

We formed small hunting parties. These would venture out into the big bad world beyond Fountains Moor searching every abandoned house, barn and garden shed. They'd been picked over pretty thoroughly by then. If you found a can of tomatoes or a pack of dried dates amidst the smashed furniture you waved it above your head and whooped. The rest of the hunting party would slap you on the back as if you'd just scored the winning goal in the Cup Final.

By then we were making two-day trips. But soon we'd have to up them to three days as we pushed further and further out in search of food.

Also by that time you avoided roads as if they'd all just sprouted particularly bad cases of leprosy. There were roadblocks everywhere, manned by men and women more than happy to help lighten your load of canned foods, maybe even relieve you of your life if they were so minded. Cannibalism was rife, too. Every so often you'd come across the remains of a camp fire with a human skull or two, burnt a banana-yellow in the ashes.

So we scurried along hedgerows with all the timidity of rabbits in the hunting season. Sometimes even covering a kilometre or two on our hands and knees. You learned to develop a sixth sense to divine whether or not a bunch of born-again savages sat sharpening their knives round the next corner.

And there were still a heck of a lot of people out there. You'd still come across villages, even towns, that had been turned into fortress communities. They were fiercely protective of what they had managed to scavenge; probably the better organized ones had livestock and were growing their own food on football pitches and school playing fields and in back gardens. From these do-it-yourself fortresses you might hear a clatter of machine-gun fire as a stranger wandered too close. Other times you would see them burn as perhaps a thousand starving men and women decided they'd rather risk dying from a bullet in the head than face a long lingering death from starvation; then those thousand men and women would rush the defences. Sometimes they got lucky. They'd overwhelm the villagers, take what they wanted, then torch the place.

Howard Sparkman had, at last, found a four-seater Cessna light aircraft. Now he spent his days flying out across the countryside from a cow pasture in the valley that served as our airstrip. He'd spot places – an isolated house or abandoned delivery truck – that might be useful for us earthbound scavengers to pick over. Or he might warn us to avoid such-and-such a village where he'd spotted twenty thousand refugees camped out in the surrounding fields.

He confirmed that the migration of humankind was from west to east. He'd overflown the countryside further east towards York and Selby where he'd seen the land carpeted with hundreds of thousands of men, women and children crowded as closely together as stalks of corn in a field. There he'd seen relatively few hot spots, characterized by the blackening of vegetation. Whatever was heating up the Earth elsewhere hadn't reached there yet; or it was somehow immune.

He'd flown high to avoid anyone taking a sour-tempered pot shot at him but he didn't doubt the refugees were starving to death by the thousand. Maybe some were quite civilized, deciding who would be eaten next on the toss of a coin or a game of chess. But we knew

that pretty soon the whole county would be thigh-deep in rotting
flesh and human bones.

The countryside to the west was now largely depopulated. Howard
had once tried to fly as far as Manchester. He'd reported that most of
the countryside had been burnt black by the heat leaking up through
the Earth's crust. There were great rents in the ground that glowed
red. Everywhere columns of smoke or steam rose into the sky as
high as the plane could fly. Also, there'd been a constant sizzling
sound as black grit hit the cockpit windows. He'd turned back when
his throat began to burn from the sulphur fumes.

'There's nothing in the west now but black desert,' he'd told us.
'Anyone going there will be as good as dead.'

I'd caught up with Caroline. She kissed my face and threw her
arms round my neck, hugging me tight. She told me how much she
missed me. Still smiling, her brown eyes twinkling sexily, she pulled
me by the hand along the bank of the stream, away from the camp
to somewhere quiet where we could be alone. I could feel her hunger
for me. Every few paces she'd stop, then with both hands reach to
grasp my head and pull my face down to her lips.

I wanted her, too. After all the shit and destruction and death I'd
seen on the hunting trips I wanted to blot it out with five solid hours
with this beautiful, sex-powered woman. She'd brushed her hair and
dabbed her throat with some secretly hoarded perfume. Christ, she
looked and smelt good.

Still we hadn't gone public with the relationship. Caroline seemed
more than happy to keep it secret; in fact she relished the secrecy.
I wondered if she'd had affairs before and perhaps keeping them
hidden from her husband had given them that added *frisson*.

As we walked hand in hand along the path, ducking beneath low
branches, we talked. The big news around the camp at the moment
was that the radio stations were going off the air by the hour. Britain
was down to one station. It described itself as the BBC. For a while
it had been based at the Air Force station at Waddington. Then you
began to hear the sound of gunshots in the background as DJs and
newsreaders made their broadcasts. Then, after a twenty-four hour
break in transmission, it reappeared on a different wavelength but
from a secret location. The general consensus of opinion was that
they were broadcasting from a warship off the coast.

We were deep into September. The summer showed no sign of
dying on us just yet. The days were still hot. Although it had been

strange weather. Even on the sunniest day cloud might bubble up to bring flurries of snow. Only this was black snow. When it melted it left gritty black streaks on the tent canvas. It was impossible to avoid the conclusion that those savage geological changes happening beneath our feet would have global consequences for climatic conditions too. When Krakatoa erupted in 1883 just about the entire world suffered a lousy summer the following year as the huge amount of volcanic dust dumped into the upper atmosphere screened out some of the sun's rays. Now we had a hundred, maybe a thousand, Krakatoas spewing out dust and rock all over the world. What effect would that have on the climate?

Few of us doubted that we were heading into the icy maw of another ice age.

But at that moment, with the evening sunlight coming in low and painting everything a soft reddish gold, my head was full of Caroline. Earlier in the day I'd decided to bring up the topic of the Grey Men at that evening's meeting with Stephen and the others. So far we'd enough problems without speculating on what some had dismissed as fairy stories. But I'd kept quiet about it for long enough.

When we were far enough from the camp Caroline let go of my hand and pulled her T-shirt over her head.

'I've missed you, Rick,' she said in that low, husky voice that sent shivers down my spine. 'I've lain awake at night and all I've wanted to do is press myself to you.'

'Why don't you move in with me? We'll have every night together.'

'Then I'll be like a wife. You'll get bored of me.'

'No, I won't.' I kissed her. 'Believe me, I won't.'

She lifted my T-shirt so she could press her small bare breasts against the skin of my stomach. 'But Kate Robinson wouldn't be pleased about that. She'd be jealous.'

'There's nothing going on between me and Kate.'

'But she likes you. She can't take her eyes off you.'

'I'd not noticed.'

'Liar.' She wasn't angry. She was smiling and working on me through the material of my jeans. All this was part of the game she wanted to play, sneaking away to some quiet spot so she could unzip my jeans, then hungrily take my cock in her mouth. Or perhaps she would wear a skirt and no pants and we'd fuck like crazy under the bushes still fully clothed. Also I think she got a kick out of imagining me with other women. 'That Victoria's a strange one,' Caroline would say in that husky voice of hers that dripped sheer sex. 'I wonder what she'd do to a young man like you.'

'From what Stephen says, she'd probably suck out all my blood, then hang me out on a branch to dry.'

'He's got firsthand knowledge, hmm?'

'No, he's happy with Ruth. Anyway, he's too busy holding this camp together to start playing footsie with anyone else.'

'Maybe he'd like to play footsie with me?'

'Maybe.'

'You'd be jealous?' Her green eyes twinkled mischievously.

'I'd be jealous. God, would I be jealous.' I smiled down at her as she unbuckled my belt.

'So, you must give your Auntie Caroline some attention. It's been, ah, let me see, fifty-one hours since I felt you inside me.' Her eyes flashed; you could sense the fireball of eroticism erupting inside of her. 'So . . . you, Rick, dear boy . . . are going to . . .' With a sudden strength she dug her fingers into the waistband of my jeans and pulled them down. 'You are going to fuck me good and hard and . . . oh, you *are* a hard boy today.'

My penis felt heavy, swollen and almost unbearably sensitive as she traced her cool finger lightly along the shaft.

'But first I want a taste of what belongs to me.' I watched her head go down; she kissed my stomach, the tops of my thighs, then I felt her cool tongue flicker across that unbearably sensitive skin. I bunched her hair in my fist. That wave of lust came roaring through me.

I crushed her small breasts in my hands; then my lips were pressed against hers in bruising kisses. Seconds later we were rolling over along the grassy bank, peeling off our clothes. To any Peeping Tom crouched in the bushes it must have looked more like a desperate battle than lovemaking as we as near as dammit fought each other to be the one on top.

I was lost in a world of sensation. This was the best fucking drug trip in the world. I felt: the grass pricking my bare skin; my feet splashing into the stream, the icy water seeming only to fuel the fire raging inside of me. I saw: everything in single snapshots, vivid but unconnected. Caroline sat astride my chest. A close-up of her pubic hair. Lips of her vagina flushed red. I smelt: the scent of it fired the blood in my veins.

Images, scents, sensations streamed helter-skelter through my head.

Her pink nipples. The tiny mole on the side of one breast. Her buttocks; stalks of grass and pieces of grit stuck to them. A red scratch running from her left shoulder blade to her right buttock where I'd wrestled her over the banking, over sharp stones, but not feeling a fucking thing. As I followed that single, overriding instinct. I wanted to drive my cock in deep. Then keep slamming myself into her.

Now Caroline wriggled away on her back so I couldn't push my penis into her vagina. She was giggling, then squirming erotically, pushing her groin up into my hip, or stomach, but always slipping away from under me before I could drive myself into her.

Heart thumping, breath roaring in-out, in-out through my mouth. This teasing, this 'now you have it, now you don't' was sending me wild. But it was part of her game. She wanted me so crazy with lust that she could feed vampire-like on my passion.

'Come on, come on,' she urged. 'I want it now. Push it in. Fuck me . . . fuck me, fuck me.'

But then she'd slide from under me, her petite body seeming to glide across the grass as easily as a snake's.

I grabbed at her, catching her by the wrists. She laughed, and lifted those red lips, swollen with excitement, to kiss mine.

And all the time she was lifting her hips up to my stomach, rotating them so the crisp tuft of pubic hair scraped against my bare skin.

As I pushed down onto her she twisted again.

This time, before I knew it I'd rolled off the banking into the stream. The shock of the cold cracked through me. But it did nothing to dampen my lust for Caroline. She leaped on top of me, splashing with her hands to send up a spray of water that turned gold in the setting sun.

She kneeled up in the water. It only just reached her now dripping pubic hair and I imagined how it must feel to her, like cool lips, kissing her between her legs. Her skin turned bumpy with goose flesh. For once her pale pink nipples turned dark as they contracted into hard buttons of skin.

Now she was astride me; my head was lifted clear of the water by a slab of rock rising up towards the bank. She smiled down at me. The water beaded off her face, neck and breasts.

Through my fingertips, I felt her body tremble as I stroked her. But it wasn't from the cold water that swirled around her thighs, or gushed beneath her beautifully rounded bottom. She was trembling with anticipation.

I felt her hand gently guiding my penis toward the opening between her legs, then she sank down onto me, a grateful sigh sliding from her lips.

Of all things, as I lay there on my back on the bed of the stream, the rush of water swirling round us, Caroline sitting astride me, a look of bliss on her face, upturned and smiling to the sun . . . yes, of all things, it felt the nearest I'd had to a mystical experience. All the horror of seeing rotting bodies at the roadside or screaming men and women hacking other men and women to death, or that tide of blackened earth creeping towards us was magically gone. My flesh, my heart and my soul were refreshed and clean. On one level I felt the cold rush of water over my skin; on a deeper level I savoured the soft warmth of Caroline's vagina enclosing me, slipping sensually up and down the length of my shaft while simultaneously her muscles magically gripped and squeezed the head of my cock in a way that was spiritually loving as well as mind-blowingly erotic.

I lay there, listening to the musical sounds of the water pouring over the rocks. I listened to Caroline's murmured endearments and the sound of her breathing that shared the same rhythm as the motion of her pelvis as she moved up and down on me.

Her pace quickened, the breathing became irregular, powerful sensations swam through her like fish through the depths of the ocean. She bore down harder, little grunts escaped through her lips. I looked up. Her face, framed with wet hair plastered in strands against her cheeks and forehead; her eyes tightly shut; the skin between her eyes furrowed with concentration as she worked herself over and onto my cock, and rocked her pubic bone against mine. Her lips pressed together, tighter and tighter – you couldn't tell whether she was trying to conquer a savage pain spearing through her body or if she was reaching down inside herself to find something that she desperately, so desperately, desperately wanted.

Then she had it.

The water splashed and foamed around me. She drove down hard; her face burned red; her eyes flashed. 'Oh, God, oh God . . . God . . .' She came with a tremendous convulsion. 'Ah!' It was as if something solid was being torn from her flesh. 'Ah! Ah! Ah!'

Her eyes snapped wide open in an expression close to shock. 'Oh!' Her mouth stayed open, frozen in that 'O' position.

Now, as she still moved up and down on me, her whole body shaking from head to toe, I felt myself erupt too. The burst of heat exploded inside of her; she convulsed again, digging her nails deep into my shoulders.

Afterwards, for what seemed a long time, we didn't move. We didn't feel as if we *could* move. Caroline lay in my arms, our upper halves out onto the slab of rock, our legs and genitals stroked by the flow of spring waters. For a few moments we'd created our own small world, big enough for just us two, a world that was contented, satisfied, tranquil.

I wanted it to stay that way.

It didn't.

CHAPTER 45

'Wait a minute, wait a minute.' Stephen spoke softly but you could see he was troubled by what I'd just told him. He looked at me, his face lit by the light of the campfire. 'Now, tell me if I've got this right. You're telling me that the quakes, volcanoes, the ground heating up – all this is due to a race of grey people who live underground?'

'No. I don't know where they are from, or whether they have anything to do with the geological changes.'

Stephen held up his hands in puzzlement. 'But Stenno just said—'

'I know, I know,' I interrupted. Christ, this wasn't going well. 'Stenno has his own ideas about this. All I'm saying is that on several occasions I've seen men who don't look like us. They have grey skins, they're naked. Physically they are big – big gorilla-like arms, big heads and—'

'And their eyes are blood-red,' Stenno chipped in quickly. 'They've done something to the planet. They are causing the Earth's crust to heat up. Now that they've destroyed society and reduced us to living like animals they're moving in to take control.'

I rubbed my head in frustration. Around the campfire were Stephen, Howard Sparkman, Kate Robinson, Dean Skilton, Victoria, then Stenno, then me. Me – feeling well and truly pissed off at myself for suggesting that Stenno come and talk to the meeting. Now he was doing his evangelical pitch about the coming of the Grey Men. He was stopping short of: 'This's God's divine retribution for all

our fornicating, boozing and renouncing Jesus and all His works,'
but it wasn't *that* far short of it.

The meetings themselves were held every night when the leaders
of the scavenging teams would either report what they'd found on
their particular forays or we'd plan the next batch of trips, as well
as discussing any other matter that was of relevance to our camp. I
could see Stephen didn't want and absolutely did not need Stenno
and me to sit there and say we thought the camp might be under
threat from a bunch of bare-assed guys with grey skins and bloody
red eyes.

Of course, he was patient and listened carefully to our story but he
was concerned about the here and now, such as was there adequate
food in the camp? Should we consider finding some more substantial
shelter now winter wasn't far away? Should we actively go out and
recruit new camp members with skills that we needed – doctors,
farmers, mechanics, engineers?

The Grey Men? No, he didn't need that at all.

And I sat watching him listen to Stenno's outpourings about how
the Grey Men would come and kill us all in the night, and how we
should endeavour to find them, make contact with them, show them
we were friends.

'Whoa, whoa.' Stephen spoke gently, but from the way he was
rubbing his face I knew his temper was being strained. 'Look. Stenno.
Rick. This is all a bit sudden.'

'But we need to be speaking to them; they—'

'Stenno, Stenno. *Please*. Just give me a moment on this one.'

I spoke, choosing my words carefully. 'Stephen. I'm not claiming
to know anything about these . . . creatures or their plans. But I
have seen them. I know other people have seen them.'

I looked round at the faces around the blazing campfire. From their
expressions I guessed they thought Stenno and I had been chewing
some funny-looking mushrooms we'd found in the woods. You could
almost read the thoughts going through their minds: 'Jesus wept. What
will Stenno and Rick be telling us tomorrow? That they've seen Elvis
Presley piloting a UFO? Or maybe they'll claim they've found Santa
Claus riding naked on his sled? Nuts, completely nuts.'

Stephen tapped his finger thoughtfully against his lips. 'For years
now we've been hearing stories about aliens abducting members of
the public.'

Victoria said, 'And these were sometimes described as "Greys."'

They were slightly built, small, with thin arms, but had dispropo-rtionately large heads with large almond-shaped eyes.'

'I said they were big. Big. With grey skin.' Stenno's voice was suddenly hard and angry. 'If you'd seen one, you'd know.'

'OK, Stenno. We're just trying to get a clear picture on this.' Stephen looked round at the others. 'Has anyone else seen these Grey Men?'

Everyone was quick to shake their heads. With the exception of Kate Robinson. 'I've not seen anything. But I've been going through copies of faxes, hard copies of e-mail messages and transcripts of eye witness accounts by people from all over the world.'

'And?'

'And there *are* some reports of people either being abducted or attacked by . . .' She shrugged. 'Certain individuals.'

'Certain individuals?' You could hear the exasperation in Dean's voice. '"Certain individuals"' are running berserk across the country-side; they have been killing men, women and children and eating them. But these certain individuals were once like us. They worked in factories, offices. They had mortgages and belonged to squash clubs and music societies. They didn't have grey skins and commute up here through a hole in the ground.'

Kate kept her voice level. 'My apologies, Dean. I didn't make myself clear. These certain individuals are described as human-like but definitely not human. In fact, I can bring you reports of people seeing, or being harassed by, men with grey skins.'

Victoria said, 'But there is no hard evidence. We know people out there are reverting to what could be described as savage, almost Stone Age practices. We've heard accounts of cannibalism; they are painting their faces and wearing headbands, armbands, certain kinds of clothes that identify them as belonging to . . . I suppose you could call it their tribe. If we—'

Dean butted in. 'What Victoria's driving at is these Grey Men are probably just ordinary human beings who've taken to daubing themselves in grey paint.'

'Or they've simply travelled across land covered with grey ash,' Howard said.

'Spot on, Howard,' Dean was his cocky self, 'they're covered with grey ash. Remember that bunch we saw that were all red – hands, faces, clothes everything. Same thing's happened – only this bunch tramped through grey ash.'

'OK, OK,' Stephen said soothingly. 'Let's not dismiss all this out of hand. Obviously Stenno and Rick have seen something. But we need more evidence before we—'

'*Shit!*' Stenno's scream brought heads poking out of tents to see what the commotion was all about. And it brought everyone around the campfire their feet. 'Shit! Shit!' Stenno was bunching his fists, that wild, dangerous look flaring back up into his eye.

'Stenno, calm d—'

'No. I know what's happening now,' he said in a voice that suddenly sounded as dangerous as the flash in his eyes. 'You all know what's happening. You've probably been taken by the Grey Men, too. But she!' He stabbed his finger in the direction of Victoria. 'But she's telling you all to keep quiet about it. Isn't that right, Victoria – isn't that right!'

Stephen still tried to sound soothing. 'Why should she do that, Stenno?'

'Because she—' He stabbed the finger again. 'She is one of them!'

Then he ran through the fire, kicking burning logs at Victoria. She jumped back as the sparks showered on her.

Dean pulled the pistol from his belt and pointed it at Stenno's back. I shoulder-charged Dean as he fired; the bullet smacked against a rock and went whining away into the distance.

The same second Stenno was gone, clawing his way up the banking and screaming and screaming like every demon in Hell wanted to claw off his testicles.

It was over as quickly as it had begun.

Dean, shooting me a disgusted look, said, 'Fucking weirdoes.' Then stalked off.

I walked away from the remains of the campfire, sat in the dark by myself on the bank of the stream, stuck my head in my hands and wished I'd never opened my stupid mouth.

CHAPTER 46

We'd been walking a good half an hour when Stephen caught up with me. He started chatting in what seemed a deliberately light-hearted way.

There were five of us in all – Dean Skilton (in spectacular form, looking the spit of a Hollywood action hero: green bandana round his head, rifle across his back, two pistols pushed in his belt and another belt of ammo hung over his shoulder, the cartridges gleaming gold in the sunlight), Victoria (still choosing cotton summer dress instead of jeans and T-shirt), Ruth (her long black hair in a single glossy plait and dressed in shorts and a white shirt, a rifle slung across her back), then Stephen and myself in cut-offs and T-shirts. I carried a rifle; Stephen, a shotgun.

Clumps of heavy cloud reared up over the hills, threatening to quench the sun. Thunder rumbled like the grumpy murmurings of a giant.

On one of his reconnaissance flights Howard Sparkman had spotted a narrow valley at the edge of the moor. It was deep, thickly wooded. There was what appeared to be a farm with a cluster of houses nearby. Stephen was banking on the fact they were deserted; that they'd be remote enough not to be discovered by the armed gangs, and that they'd make good winter accommodation. I think in his mind's eye he saw the community settling there and growing our own food until the Earth stopped its pyrotechnics and society reverted to normality.

We followed a stream downhill across the moor. A few butterflies flitted across the heather. In the distance, beyond the moor, rolled the green Yorkshire landscape. Cutting across it, that finger of black where the heat seared the vegetation from the roots upwards. It crept inexorably closer each day. A great pointing finger of black. It seemed to say: *You up there on Fountains Moor. I haven't forgotten you. Here I come. Here I come. To set your feet and your hearts on fire.*

Thunder rumbled again, like that giant with a bad case of the blues. Something cold and worm-like twisted in my stomach. Every day I felt it. And I knew it was fear. Fear, pure and simple. I was afraid to get up in the morning because I didn't know what the day would bring. No, scratch that. I was afraid, because I knew very well what it would bring. It would bring fresh terrors. I remembered the woman dancing on the wooden pole. I remembered seeing babies' heads, or what was left of them after the brains had been spooned out. I'd seen teenagers hanging by their necks from railway bridges. But I'd seen precious little of our Lord God's merciful hand. Only pain; only starvation; only death.

I half-listened as Stephen outlined plans to send Howard out to find, with luck, an untouched supermarket or warehouse that would supply us with food for the next six months; then we could suspend these nickel-and-dime operations where we'd tramp the countryside for forty-eight hours before returning with a couple of tins of corned beef and twenty pounds of turnips.

But I knew the direction the conversation would eventually take. And sure enough a couple of minutes later Stephen said: 'I've been thinking about what you said about the Grey Men. Victoria said that—'

'The Grey Woman.' I pulled my face into a grin but sure as jiggery I felt no amusement.

'I know you didn't . . . you weren't as . . . extreme in your opinions as Stenno.'

I sighed. 'He's not extreme; he's disturbed and you know it.'

'He's got problems,' Stephen agreed.

'How's Victoria? He could have done some damage, kicking the fire at her like that.'

'She's fine.' I saw him look suddenly uncomfortable at me talking about Victoria and he shot a look at Ruth. It sounds an old-fashioned thing to say, but I wondered if Victoria was trying to woo Stephen away from Ruth. She was – the only description that fitted – pretty. Uncommonly pretty. Out of all the women, Caroline included, she still seemed untouched by all the madness and destruction. You had the feeling that somehow she was just a tourist here. That she could say anytime, 'This is boring me now. I'm going home.' Then she'd vanish as quickly as she'd seemed to arrive, in that blazing graveyard.

'Look,' Stephen was saying in a low voice. 'Keep your eyes open and tell me if you clap eyes on any of these Grey Men. What we do need is hard evidence.'

'You mean bring you a head on a plate?'

He smiled but his eyes were deadly serious. 'If you like.'

I sighed. 'I don't know, sometimes I reckon I'm dreaming it all.' I then told him about the lost hours I'd experienced, even back before the refugees appeared overnight in Fairburn. And I told him about the paintings and the concrete sculpture of the Grey Man I'd seen in the farmyard near where the woman got kebabed.

'You've been taking some hard psychological knocks, Kid K,' he said, 'You should take some time off.'

'I'll do that when you do.'

'I can take it.'

'You're twenty-five. You were a video jock in Seattle. I'm not being offensive, big brother, but that doesn't make you a cross between Indiana Jones and Superman.'

'The average age of the US soldier in Vietnam was nineteen.'

I gave a grim smile. 'Your point being?'

'If our environment demands we become Supermen we become just that.'

'Where did you get that piece of wisdom from?'

He said nothing but I saw his eyes flick to Victoria who walked alongside Dean.

'Quite a philosopher, isn't she?' I said it good-naturedly and Stephen smiled a little more easily. Then he said in a voice low enough so Ruth didn't hear, 'She's useful to bounce ideas off. She makes me see things that bit more clearly.'

We continued talking. For the first time in days we were having a real conversation. He seemed upbeat. Again I was struck by the sense he was in control of not just his own future but of all our futures. Perhaps it was me, the little brother, talking but I felt safe in his hands.

The map coordinates told us we'd reached the valley that Howard Sparkman had spotted from the air. Our noses told us something else.

'Smell that?' I asked as we followed the dirt path down into the valley.

'If I'm not mistaken,' Dean said, swinging the rifle from his shoulder, 'that's the sweet, sweet smell of shit. Lots of shit. Tons of shit.'

I said, 'And that's a dead give-away that refugees have been camping here.'

'Or are still camped here.' Dean drew back the bolt of the rifle.

We followed a hedgerow down across the field towards the cluster of red-tiled roofs in the valley bottom. The smell of excrement was strong. Unless you were prepared to dig holes to defecate into, then carefully seal in the excrement with soil, it was always a clear sign that a significant number of people had been staying in a particular place.

'It seems quiet,' Victoria whispered. 'No sign of campfire smoke.'

We reached the narrow lane that served as sole access to the village. We stuck to the far side of the hedgerow that ran alongside the lane, avoiding using the lane itself where we'd be in plain view of any roadblock or someone using a garage roof as a lookout post.

The smell of shit grew stronger.

Through the hawthorn hedging I noticed the lane was littered with human debris. As well as the shit I saw a pram with its wheels missing. There were a pair of spectacles lying smashed in the road. Then a child's doll, dressed in a pink ballroom gown. Then something like a doll in baby clothes dumped on the grass verge. I didn't look any closer.

I saw Ruth screw her eyes shut and turn her face away. Only Victoria looked as we went by, her expression full of curiosity as if she'd seen a rare species of roadside flower. (And what could that new type of smelly flower be, Rick Kennedy? Why, none other than the increasingly common *Post-mortem-baby-putrefactus*. You did that now. You saw something horrible like a skeleton sitting in a burnt-out car, or a severed human arm left on top of a garden wall, the Timex around the wrist still ticking off seconds, and, well, you made a joke of it. You had to. All part of the new survival mechanism. You'd go insane if you didn't. So sometimes on these hunts we'd play football with a human skull or poke a bloated corpse with a stick until it farted. A really neat trick was to light the fart with a match to see how high the flame spurted. Dean once frazzled an eyebrow doing that one.)

Ruth looked over a garden gate. 'The houses look as if they've been thoroughly picked over.'

Bed sheets, towels, books, TVs, videotapes, family photographs, music CDs littered the gardens.

'Anything edible will be well gone by now,' Dean said. 'At least it looks quiet.'

'What now?'

Stephen looked along the line of gutted houses. 'No point in hanging around here.'

'We could clean it up?' Victoria suggested. 'Still move in?'

'We could,' Stephen agreed. 'But if refugees have found it once they'll find it again. And there's no way we could defend the place from any kind of determined attack.'

'It looks as if we'll be spending the winter under canvas,' Dean said.

'No way,' Stephen said briskly. 'We'll find solid bricks-and-mortar shelter or we'll build it ourselves.'

'Uh-oh.' The sound of warning was clear in Ruth's voice. She nodded at what lay in the road. 'Dead birds. And see all those dead rats in the garden?'

'Gas leak.' Dean sniffed the warm summer air. 'I didn't think it was only shit I could smell.'

'All the more reason for us to get out.' Stephen nodded towards a clump of trees. 'We'll cut back across the field that way.'

As we walked towards the shade of the trees the smell of rotting meat grew stronger. What I'd taken for the dense shadow of the wood were black clouds of flies. They buzzed eagerly among the tree trunks. Of all God's creatures flies weren't going to go hungry this year.

'Jesus . . .' Stephen held his handkerchief to his mouth and nose. 'There's been a gas leak all right . . . just look at the poor devils.'

The rotting meat, blood and skin of perhaps a thousand men, women and children formed a carpet across the woodland floor. Everywhere there were swollen bodies with arms and legs stuck grotesquely out, bloated with the subcutaneous build-up of gas generated by decomposition.

'The gas took them by surprise as they slept.' Stephen looked up at the valley sides. 'Carbon monoxide is heavier than air. It must have flowed into the valley bottom like flood water.'

Ruth's face turned white. She swallowed hard. 'They were still asleep. They never knew what hit them.' She put her fingers to her forehead. 'Uh. See that little boy? He's still holding his teddy bear . . . he's still . . .' She turned away.

Victoria stared, her face full of curiosity again but clearly unmoved by what she saw. I turned my back on the nightmare scene. My stomach muscles started to twitch; my eyes blurred.

Dean gritted his teeth. 'You know, if we looked hard enough, we'd find cans of food amongst that lot.'

'Christ, be my guest, Dean.' I felt vomit push its way into my throat. 'Jesus Christ, be my guest.' I swallowed down hard and headed back the way we came.

Dimly, I heard Stephen tell Dean to forget any idea of wading into all that dead rot. Touch any of those corpses and you'd be lucky not to be shitting your heart out with cholera by the end of the week.

I'd covered less than a hundred paces when I heard movement in the long grass to my left. Instinct kicked in; I unslipped the rifle, pulled back the bolt, raised it to my shoulder in less than two seconds flat.

Rabid dog? We'd seen a few of those.

A man driven crazy by hunger and terror? Maybe he'd come at me with a knife.

Or maybe an army deserter? Already he's got me in his sights.

I'd have to fire first; ask questions later.

I saw the head come up out of the grass. My finger tightened on the trigger.

CHAPTER 47

'Where's my mummy?'

I blinked. There, kneeling up in the long grass, was a girl of about five. Her hair was a mat of stuck-out strands; her face was brown with mud, probably with excrement too. But she wore a pair of white-rimmed glasses that were immaculately polished. When she tilted her head they reflected the midday sun. With a huge sigh I eased my finger off the trigger before letting the rifle drop, muzzle pointing safely down at the ground.

'Where's my mummy?'

I gawped.

'Where is my mummy?' She stared at me hard, her brown eyes massively magnified by those carefully polished lenses. 'Is she with the others?' She pointed a brown finger towards the trees.

'Are you alone?'

She shook her head. 'I'm with all those.' She pointed again back to where a thousand people rotted in the calm shade of the oak trees. 'Have you seen my mummy?'

I shook my head.

'You know,' she said, her eyes looking preternaturally wise behind the lenses. 'You know, I think my mum's lying under those trees.'

'Is that where you were?'

'Yes. My mummy's dead, isn't she?'

All I could do was nod.

'Good.'

The surprise must have registered on my face because she explained, 'She's happier now she's dead. Men kept poking at her with their penises. That made her unhappy.'

She spoke so matter-of-factly. I sensed she'd accepted this new state of affairs. A world without Mum, or family, and she decided life must go on.

The others caught up. Ruth crouched down, smiling warmly.

'Hallo, my name's Ruth. What's your name?'

'The men said my new name was Fucking Brat. I don't like it, do you?'

'No.'

I saw Stephen turn away. There were tears in his eyes.

As casually as I could manage I asked, 'Before . . . you had to move away from your home. What was your name then?'

'Lee Godwin. I'm five.'

'Well, we'll call you Lee again. It's a lovely name.'

'I don't have any food,' she said quickly. 'I'm just not eating.'

'That doesn't matter, sweetheart,' Stephen spoke gently. 'Would you like to come with us?'

'Will you poke at me with your penises?'

'*No,*' Stephen said, shocked. 'We live in a nice place with clean tents and plenty of food.'

Stephen held out his hand to the little girl. She looked at it, considering.

'You're going to bring the child with us?' Victoria asked in surprise.

We looked at Victoria's placid face in disbelief.

Ruth was so astonished it took a second attempt to loosen the words from her tongue. 'You really think we should just leave her here?'

'She might be diseased.' Victoria spoke in a peculiarly flat way as if suggesting a carton of milk might just be that teensy-weensiest bit past its freshest. She looked at each of us in turn as if we were the peculiar ones. 'She might infect the rest of our camp.'

'She looks healthy enough.' Ruth spoke coldly.

'Come on, sweetheart.' Stephen crouched down and stretched out his hand further. 'We'll go back home and get you some nice clean clothes.'

'I've got no food.' Lee spoke as if she suspected some kind of trick. 'I've not been eating anything.'

'That doesn't matter, darling.' Ruth smiled. 'We've got plenty of food.'

I wish we had, I thought with a sudden ferocity. We'd have to find that untouched supermarket or warehouse crammed to the rafters with canned food, otherwise we were going to get hungry pretty soon.

'Ruth. Can I bring my baby?'

'Of course you can, sweetheart.'

Lee ran to a a patch of stinging nettles that were taller than her. There, using a long-handled garden rake, she pulled out a baby doll, then she teased out a yellow child-sized backpack that had the words KIDS R' KOOL written graffiti-style on the flap. The bag gave a metallic rattle.

'I haven't got any food,' she insisted.

I offered to carry the bag.

'No,' she said firmly, heaving the straps over her tiny shoulders, then cradling the doll in her arms. 'The bag's got my baby's clothes in it.'

'OK,' I smiled. 'Just let me know if it gets too heavy.'

Again I heard the rattle of cans in the bag as she made the straps more comfortable. Then, once she'd blown an eyelash from one of the lenses of her glasses, and was satisfied they were pristine, she carefully put them back on, patted her hair down over the spectacle arms, then walked determinedly along the lane, her face set in no-nonsense expression that seemed somehow more mature and worldly-wise than ours.

Victoria fell in step with me as we headed out of the valley and back toward Fountains moor. 'It is an extra mouth to feed.' She nodded at the child.

I nodded. Not in the mood to explain why we didn't leave five-year-old children to starve.

'It's unlikely she will be able to do any worthwhile work for our community.'

'I'll share my food rations with her.'

'That doesn't make sense. You need your full ration.'

'That's it with us humans. We don't make much sense, do we? We fall in love. We sometimes stop and pick fallen people out of the gutter. Haven't you heard the story of the Good Samaritan where you come from?'

She shot me a weird flash of those grey eyes again. Christ . . . I suddenly had this strong feeling that Stenno was right. Maybe if I snatched at Victoria's pretty face, caught the skin of her cheek between my finger and thumb and pulled hard it would rip away like a mask. Beneath it would be grey and pimply; the eyes blood-red. I shook my head.

She stared at me with such a laser-like intensity I moved sideways to put more space between us. Christ, she was a strange one. Cold, too. She could have ice for blood.

Suddenly I was struck by an idea. 'Victoria. Do you know what year this is?'

She stared at me.

'Simple enough question,' I said softly. 'Tell me what year this is.'

'Shh!'

Frantically, Dean waved us to crouch down. He looked grim. 'Get back to the wall. Find yourselves some cover.'

'What's the problem?' Stephen whispered as we ran.

'Straight ahead. Group of people . . . dozen, maybe fifteen.'

'Armed?'

'Definitely.'

We reached the stone wall that separated this field from the next and crouched down at the bottom, hoping the long grass would hide us. Lee said nothing but I heard the cans of her precious food supply clanking as she dropped down onto all fours, the doll now tucked papoos-like into the front of her cardigan.

'We're in trouble if they've seen us,' I whispered. 'They've got us outgunned.'

'We might be in luck. I don't think they've seen us.'

It was as Dean said 'seen us' that the first bullet smacked against the wall.

CHAPTER 48

Another shot came with a crack that echoed from the hills. The bullet smacked against the wall ten paces away, hacking a chunk of sandstone from it.

'Through the gate . . . there, to your left,' Stephen shouted. 'Keep down as low as you can.' He caught hold of Lee, swung her up into his arms and ran through the gap in the wall.

In ten seconds flat we crouched, panting, behind the wall. It was about chest height, nowhere as high as I would have liked but at least it was solid stone.

No more shooting. The sudden silence seemed somehow loaded with danger. You could imagine that any second an armed gang would come whooping and shouting over the wall, to fire at us at point-blank range.

Lee hunkered down tight against the wall, the doll and backpack of food hugged to her chest. Deftly, she slipped the glasses off her face, carefully folded the arms, then equally carefully snapped them away into her glasses case which she slid into a side compartment of the bag. Then she crouched there, waiting.

Waiting for what? To be butchered for the half-dozen tins of tuna fish, spam, mandarin segments or whatever it was she guarded so closely in that little bag?

'They've got us pinned down.' Ruth pulled her rifle from her shoulder. 'They're up there on the high ground, looking down on us.'

'For Godsakes,' Stephen said. 'Keep in close to the wall. They can't hit us if we keep close to the wall.'

'And that means you, too, Victoria.'

She glared at me and moved one step closer to the wall. This was a game she didn't want to play. She was nothing more than a spoilt brat.

Dean handed her his rifle. 'Here, use this.'

'Stephen,' I said, 'what now? Run or stick here and shoot it out?'

Dean risked a look over the top of the wall. 'Well, it's a simple choice . . . between frying pan and fire. Oh fuck . . . they've got assault rifles.'

'Army deserters?'

'Possibly.'

Victoria sighed, bored. 'If that's the bad news what's the good news?'

I said, 'That might be good news. The professional soldiers, although better armed, don't take unnecessary risks. They weigh up who the opposition is, how well they're armed, how determined they seem. Then they make a well-considered and logical decision whether to tackle them or not.'

'They're certainly more cautious than an untrained civilian with a gun.' Dean crouched back down again. 'Civilians have seen too many Arnie movies. They don't realize ammo runs out so quickly or how difficult it actually is to shoot someone, especially if you're moving, or your target's moving.'

'Or shooting back at you.'

'Exactly.'

'We've got to do something.' Ruth eased off the rifle's safety catch. 'And quick.'

'Ruth's right. They might try and outflank us.'

Stephen rubbed his jaw. 'Right, just give me a minute to think.'

'I reckon you've got thirty seconds. A couple of guys have just hopped over the wall at the other side of the field. They're going for a pincer movement.'

'We could just go,' Victoria suggested.

'What do you suggest?' I snapped. 'A magic carpet? Or perhaps you can just call up your mother ship and have us beamed aboard.'

Again her eyes blazed with that laser-like intensity.

'I haven't got any food.' Lee's voice sounded small. 'Tell them I haven't got any food. They'll go away.'

Stephen gently stroked her cheek. 'I wish I could, sweetheart.' It was as he looked at her that I saw the change in his expression. It seemed that seeing the little girl had hit the button inside his head labelled: *PROTECT & SURVIVE*. When he spoke again he sounded businesslike, in control.

'Right, we'll give them a firework display.' He snapped the shotgun upright. 'When I give the word, start firing. Keep your heads down. It doesn't matter if you hit anything. Just let them know we're armed.'

'And dangerous.' Ruth gave a grim smile.

'Everyone ... get yourselves ready.' Stephen breathed hard, psyching himself up for what was to come.

Ruth and I had hunting rifles, Dean had a pair of 9mm Beretta automatic pistols, Stephen the pump-action shotgun; while Victoria stood a few paces from the wall, all fingers and thumbs as she tried to pull back the bolt of the rifle Dean had given her.

'Everyone ready?' Stephen asked.

'How does this thing work?' Victoria asked, sulkily.

'Dean, can you show her how ... *Victoria* – Jesus, keep your head down ... and get down close to the wall. They'll blow your damn head off.'

I was closest. I pulled the bolt back for her. 'Like this. It's not an automatic, so you must pull the bolt back after every shot.'

219

Rather than paying attention to what I did with the rifle, she looked at me with that strangely intense look again while stroking back her thick red hair.

Stephen sounded impatient. 'Come on, people . . . they won't wait all day.'

'OK, we're ready.'

'I'll count down from three to one. Then fire as fast as you can.'

Victoria had moved back from the wall again, setting herself up as an easy target. 'I still can't get this thing to work. Can you—'

'Forget it, Victoria,' Stephen snapped. 'Just keep your head down. You're too far back from the wall.'

'They're starting to move our way,' Ruth warned.

'OK. Keep as low as you can. Three-two-one – *fire*.'

Ruth, Stephen, Dean and I leaned forwards against the wall, resting the guns on the coping stones. Then we let them have it. Firing as rapidly as we could. I glanced down at my feet to see Lee shiver visibly with every shot.

The racket was immense. Grey smoke bloomed around us like a sudden mist; the cordite bit into the back of my throat.

We fired wildly. The camouflaged figures who had been advancing cautiously ran back for the cover of the trees. Then I saw puffs of smoke as they fired back. Bullets shrieked over our heads.

Three seconds later our ammunition was gone. I ducked down as their firing continued for another two seconds then it suddenly stopped, too.

Stephen risked a look over the wall. 'They've got the message, thank God. They're not risking war.'

'Yep,' Dean said, 'They're legging it the other way.'

'Have we hit anyone?'

'Doesn't look like it.'

'Good. There's no point in turning this into a vendetta.'

'Stephen?' I saw Lee tapping the back of his knee to attract his attention. 'Stephen?'

'Don't worry, Lee,' he said, 'it's all over. No more shooting.'

Lee was frightened. She still patted his leg. 'Stephen?'

I glanced back at Victoria where she stood about ten paces from the wall. It was nothing short of a miracle she hadn't caught a bullet between the eyes during the shoot-out. She wrenched uselessly at the bolt of the rifle, her lip pouting. 'Isn't anyone going to show me how this works?'

'It doesn't matter now,' I said coolly. 'They've gone. Here, give me the rifle.'

Her expression had been surly but she gave a sudden smile as she handed the rifle to me. I passed it on to Dean who slipped the strap over his shoulder.

I looked back at Stephen who was standing beside Ruth, both of them looking over the wall at the departing men. Lee still tapped him on the leg to attract his attention. 'Stephen . . . Stephen . . .'

'In a moment, sweetheart.'

'Sure they're clearing out?' I asked.

'Seem to be. Those two who cut down the hill behind the wall have just run back to their gang. They're not taking any chances.'

'Stephen,' Lee persisted.

'What's wrong, honey?'

'Ruth's been shot.'

'No, she hasn't, she's . . .' His voice died on him as he turned to look sideways at Ruth.

I looked, too. A cold lump squeezed up into my stomach. From the back it looked as if she was standing with her eyes just above the level of the wall. But I could see that her eyes were wide; her jaw was wide too, as if she'd frozen in mid-yawn. My skin prickled; the cold lump in my stomach swelled. Her teeth rested against the sandstone coping block. In her agony she'd actually ground her teeth against the wall, gouging yellow furrows in the stone.

Her legs quivered as if trying to support a tremendous weight.

I looked at her back. Between her shoulder blades, just to one side of her glossy black plait I saw, at last, a spreading disc of red, soaking into the white material of her shirt.

'She's still alive,' I said. 'She's still breathing.'

She turned her head slightly. Her eyes met Stephen's. I saw such a look of pain and fear in them that I had to clench my fists.

Stephen caught her as she rolled sideways. Gently, he laid her down onto her back on the grass. That's when I saw the wound just above her left breast. There was an ugly, brutish rip in her shirt; blood streamed out of it, covering Stephen's bare hands. I could even see splinters of bone and shreds of skin protruding from the wound itself.

I'm not really sure how long it took. We stood round feeling so . . . so fucking stupid, so fucking ignorant as Stephen tried to stop the flow of blood.

It took maybe ten minutes. Possibly fifteen. Then Ruth Sparkman died.

I'd known her since she was ten. She'd been one of those girls who played the boys harder and better at their own games. She climbed trees higher than we could. By the age of sixteen she had a lean athlete's body; she was quick-witted, ambitious.

Now she was nineteen. Dead. Her lips blue, her eyes turning dull, dry-looking, with a bloody hole right through her chest.

We stood there, again I don't know how long for, as Stephen cradled his dead girlfriend in his arms, her blood drying to a red-brown on the side of his face.

Lee left the backpack and doll on the grass and put her arms round his neck and gently rocked him like he was a baby. 'Don't cry, sweetheart,' she whispered to him. 'Don't cry. She's gone to Jesus with my mummy. They're better now. Don't cry, sweetheart.'

And as we stood there it began to snow once more. Black snow. With those black snowflakes that seemed so evil. That seemed to tell us we were following a single road, one that took us to but one destination:

DEATH

CHAPTER 49

Back on Fountains Moor. The stream still gushed down its gully. People still cooked their meals over camping stoves, still listened to the radio. But the stations grew fewer by the day. Now we were down to three stations in English. The camp still looked the same with the tents running in a line two-by-two.

But it all felt different.

Ruth Sparkman was the first one of us to die. Before, we'd return to that cleft in the hill high on Fountains Moor and it was like coming home after a hard day at work, when you could close the door on the outside world and feel snug and safe in your house. Ruth's death was a reminder that we were sixty or so people, all but one under the age of thirty, leading a precarious existence on a dwindling food supply, sleeping in fragile tents with whole areas of the planet turning incandescent.

It was the day after Ruth's death and I sat talking to Kate Robinson as we cleaned our rifles. I was having the conversation I'd tried to have with Stephen an hour earlier. He claimed he was too busy as he worked out more ambitious plans; this time to airlift food from as far away as London. But I knew he didn't want to hear what I needed to say. Something troubled me about Ruth's death. It didn't make any sense.

So I sat there and ran through my doubts with Kate. By the stream old man Fullwood sat beside Lee making daisy chains.

I said to Kate, 'I never did see Ruth turn her back to the wall when the firing started.'

'Turn her back? Why should she do that?'

I shrugged. 'To get more ammo from the belt?'

'You told me all the spare ammo was on Dean's belt.'

'And he had that hung round his shoulder.'

'So?'

'So, if she'd needed more ammo she would have turned to Dean who was to her right.'

'Therefore, she wouldn't have needed to turn her back to the wall.' Kate sighed. 'I know it's a tragedy, Rick, but raking over what happened won't bring Ruth back.'

'I know. But we need to know the truth, don't we?'

'Does it matter?'

'I think it does.'

Kate shook her head. 'She was shot by army deserters, Rick. Even if you managed to find them what are you going to do? Remember, we don't have a police force anymore.'

I pinched my bottom lip together between finger and thumb, thinking hard. 'It just doesn't make sense.'

She smiled and said gently. 'Does it make any sense that the whole planet's heating up? That it's cooking the ground we walk on? Now, *that* doesn't make sense.'

'We can't do anything about that. It's beyond our control.'

'And so is what happened to poor Ruth.'

I shook my head.

Kate put down the rifle across her lap and said patiently. 'OK, Rick. Tell me exactly . . . *exactly* . . . what's troubling you.'

'Look.' I traced a line with my finger across the turf. 'There we were. Myself, Dean, Stephen and Ruth standing facing the wall as we fired over it, up the hillside at the gang.'

'The wall was around chest height, you say?'

'Yes.'

'And they were firing back at you?'

'They were.'

'That's when Ruth was hit?'

'Look, I don't know much about ballistics and the damage a bullet does when it hits a human body.'

'But?'

'But.' I took a deep breath. 'Ruth was shot in the back.'

'How can you tell? Dean told me the bullet went all the way through.'

'It did.'

'How do you know she was shot in the back?'

'When a bullet enters the body it'll probably hit nose first. But after it's penetrated the flesh it begins to tumble as soon as it strikes a bone.'

'So?'

'So, it probably leaves the body sideways on. Kate, when I saw Ruth, she had a small wound in her back, and a dirty great hole here in her chest.'

'So you think the bullet entered through her back, tumbled, then exited her body sideways creating the larger wound on her chest?'

'Right. Remember JFK? The bullet that killed him made a small hole here.' I pointed to my face. 'But when it exited it blew out the whole of the back of his skull.'

'OK, she was shot from behind. Who fired the shot?' She looked at me directly. She was anticipating the name I'd give. 'Victoria?'

I nodded.

Kate shook her head, puzzled. 'Last night you were saying that Victoria didn't even know how to fire the rifle?'

'That's what I thought. At the time, she hadn't fired a single shot – so it seemed.'

'How do you know she did?'

'I asked Dean to check the rifle last night. There was one round missing from the magazine.'

Kate rubbed her jaw. 'No one saw it happen?'

'No. There was a lot of shooting, so no one would hear another rifle shot.'

'Where was Victoria standing?'

'She was standing away from the wall. That's what seemed so

bizarre. At first I thought she didn't appreciate she was in the line of fire from the gang on the hillside.'

'And what she was really doing was moving behind Ruth to get a clear shot at her back?'

'But why?'

'Why kill her?' Kate echoed, then glanced to where Stephen and Victoria were walking along the bank of the stream. 'One motive's obvious.'

'But it's a hell of a vicious way to get rid of a rival!'

'We live in a vicious world now. Perhaps the only rule is that there are no rules.'

I looked at Kate. 'So you believe me? That Victoria murdered Ruth Sparkman?'

She let out a lungful of air. 'Phew, the evidence stacks up, doesn't it?' Then she looked at me and nodded. 'Yes . . . yes, I believe you, Rick Kennedy.'

'The question now is, what are we going to do about it?'

CHAPTER 50

The days moved inexorably forward, just like the finger of black that crept inexorably closer to Fountains Moor.

Sometimes I'd walk with Caroline to the big hill which overlooked the flatter land that rolled towards distant Leeds. There I'd watch that black finger through the binoculars. Somewhere deep underground the rock must have been glowing red hot and, centimetre by centimetre, the heat was seeping up through a crack in the bedrock. By the time it reached the surface, there was still enough heat to kill vegetation and cause fence posts to combust. They'd burn to ash, leaving strands of fence wire lying on the ground. Sometimes the finger of black would touch a house. Then, like some pyrotechnic version of King Midas, the house would smoulder for hours, perhaps days, before bursting into flame.

The heat boiled the ground water that percolated through the porous strata of aquifer rock deep beneath the soil. Here and there, jets of steam would whistle from the ground. Or maybe that creeping heat would touch a pocket of gas; with a roar it would vent from the earth in a pillar of flame.

At night it could look spectacular; to see a column of blue fire standing straight out of the earth halfway to Heaven like an Old Testament display of Jehovah's anger. But whenever I saw it, it pumped yet more fear into that reservoir of dread that I already struggled to contain inside me. There were times I was afraid it would overflow and overwhelm me, pitching me into crazed panic from which I'd never recover. I wasn't the only one who experienced this inexorable accumulation of fear. You saw it in the eyes of others in the camp. Although we might run out of food, there'd never be a paucity of fear.

The ever-approaching finger of scorched earth. The thousands upon thousands of starving refugees searching for food. The wild bands who had turned to cannibalism. And, always in the back of my mind, the certainty that somehow connected with this were those grey figures that sometimes came to me in the night. What power had they to paralyze me so I couldn't even shout out? Why did they carry me away out onto the moor then leave me there? It was as if I was being studied by them.

And then there was Victoria. Every day I thought I'd tell Stephen about my suspicions. But, one: how did I go about telling him that his new lover had murdered his girlfriend? Two: if he believed me, what happened then? Would we put Victoria on some kind of murder trial? If we decided she was guilty, what then? Send her away from the camp? Hang her from a tree? Should I let sleeping dogs lie? He certainly seemed happy with her. I saw the pleased smile on his face when she walked up to him.

Victoria still seemed a mystery character. People joked she'd only just arrived on Planet Earth; Stenno had this lurid delusion that somehow she was a Grey Man in disguise. I favoured the idea she'd escaped from a mental hospital or a drug rehab unit when civilization turned belly up and died on us. Perhaps I could find more information about her that would prove to Stephen that she was a danger to—

'Hey . . . hey, Rick. Have you forgotten all about your Auntie Caroline?'

We were sitting thigh to thigh on the heather overlooking that finger of black that crept ever closer to Fountains Moor.

Caroline stroked the back of my neck, and Christ, believe me, it

226

felt good. Caroline was one of the few things now in my life that could distract me from reality.

One of the reasons I walked with her across the moor that evening was to break some bad news to her. I'd been postponing the inevitable all day. Before she started to stroke my neck I'd intended telling her then, but I put it off again.

I slid my arm round her tiny waist and kissed her full on the mouth. She lay back on the heather, pulling me with her. I lay on top of her, looking down into her brown eyes that seemed so sexy and alive they shone. I stroked her face, lightly touching her smooth forehead, the delicate eyebrows, her nose, her lips. I felt the heat coming through my body in waves that somehow seemed to sparkle on the inside of my ribs and stomach and legs.

Christ, she was lovely lying there. That smile, those trusting eyes. She would have done anything for me.

I'd make love to her.

Then I'd break the news.

That's a shitty trick, Kennedy. You can't use her like that. Tell her what you have to tell her now. Don't keep putting it off.

She spoke softly. 'Do you love me?' Her eyes locked onto mine, as if afraid to hear my answer.

'You know I do.'

'Do you?'

'Yes.'

'Say it please, Rick darling.'

'I do. I love you.'

'You've been a saviour to me. I'd have been dead by now without you.'

I smiled. 'You'd have made it.'

'No, I wouldn't.'

I kissed her forehead.

She continued, 'That morning you found me in the wood. I'd found a piece of washing line. I'd made up my mind to hang myself.'

'Thank God you didn't. You're special, you know that?'

'You're not bored of me?'

'No way.'

'Kate Robinson's got a thing about you, you know?'

227

'Who told you that? Joanne?'

'No.' Her brown eyes looked up, glistening slightly. 'No, Kate did.'

The conversation was gentle. We kissed as we spoke, but I felt a tension creeping in. I found myself waiting for some surprise revelation. God knows what, but I felt she was on the brink of revealing a secret or making a confession.

She looked up into my face, her head cushioned on the heather. 'Are you happy?'

'With the world igniting beneath our backsides? Volcanoes, mass murder, the fields across there turning into cinder desert?'

'People have endured famine and wars for thousands of years. Life goes on. Are you happy?'

I felt uncomfortable. For months Caroline had done what she could to evade the present realities, now she seemed to be meeting them head on.

'Rick. Are you happy?'

'It sounds bizarre. Considering all the shit we're going through. But there *are* times, when I'm with you, I'm the happiest. I've been in my life.'

'Good.' She smiled. The answer seemed important to her.

For a moment there was a pause. It was as if each of us expected the other to say something important.

I knew the time had come to break it to her.

'Caroline, I've got something to tell you.'

'Me too.'

'You?'

'Why the surprise?' she smiled. 'Now, let me just unzip you like this. And let me put my hand in here like so.'

I moved sideways on my hip as she slipped her hand inside my jeans.

'Oh . . . there's not much room in there, Rick. Pleased to see me or what?'

'Christ, *am* I pleased to see you.' My heart beat faster. 'But I thought you'd got something to tell me?'

'Mmmm . . .'

'Shoot.'

'You first.'

There was no way to break the news gently. I just came right out and said it.

CHAPTER 51

'I'm going to London. I'll be away a month.'

She stopped rubbing me. Her eyes widened with shock. 'London?'

'Howard's located a supermarket distribution warehouse. It's untouched. It's packed to the rafters with food.'

'But *London?* Isn't there anywhere nearer?'

'Not that we know of.'

'But London's underwater?'

'Part of it is, along the Thames. This is out towards higher ground near Hampstead.'

'But why a whole month?'

'Howard's only got the four-seater Cessna. It can't carry much food on the return trip. So we'll camp out there while Howard flies there and back every day. The one thing he's not short of is fuel, so he can make maybe thirty trips . . .'

My voice faded at the look on Caroline's face. Disappointment, sadness. A sense of certainty that I'd never return, that she'd lost me forever.

'I'll soon be back, Caroline,' I said gently. 'Before you know it. We'll have ample food for the winter. There'll be no more scavenging trips for two days at a time.' I kissed her. 'We'll be together.'

'We will.' She nodded.

'Now. What was your news?'

'Oh.' She turned her face away. 'Nothing important.'

'Come on. If it was important enough to mention a few minutes ago it's important enough to tell me now.'

She looked back at me, gave a little smile. 'It's nothing much . . . I . . . I'm working out a new dietary plan with Sue and Stephen. The group needs a better-balanced diet to ensure we don't suffer from vitamin deficiencies.'

I didn't believe that was the real news for a moment, but I didn't push it.

For a moment her expression was troubled, then suddenly it cleared with a smile. 'It's important work you'll be doing for us. You're right, a month will pass in no time. When do you go?'

229

'Tomorrow.'

'Oh well . . . that doesn't leave us much time, does it?'

Smiling, still keeping eye contact, she pulled her T-shirt over her head, then wriggled out of her jeans. The breeze blew cooler now. Instantly her chest goose-fleshed. The nipples contracted into hard points.

As I sat up to pull down my jeans, she pushed me back onto the heather. 'Let Auntie Caroline do all the work.' Her smile turned even more vivacious. 'Just remember me, that's all. When you're all cosy in your London penthouse.'

'We'll be lucky to get a tent.'

'Tent, shack, whatever . . . now, what shall we do with this naughty thing, then?'

She stroked my penis from head to root, then I felt those cool fingers gently cup my testicles. I let my breath out in a long, long sigh. Her fingers were so expert. They caressed, pressed gently, then gripped my penis in that exquisite grip of hers. I let out a groan and looked up at the clouds sailing through the sky.

This was bliss.

She took away her fingers. I felt her lips slide over the end of my penis. Her tongue caressed the head, round and round as if she licked an ice-cream cone.

Christ . . . I was going to miss a month of this. Maybe I could manage to sprain my ankle or wrench a back muscle. Then I'd have this kind of attention from Caroline twenty-four hours a day.

In sixty seconds we were both naked there on the hillside. She stood up. I watched her stretch her arms into the air, smiling all the time. There wasn't an ounce of fat on her. Her stomach was flat, her waist incredibly narrow, her breasts so firm they were almost tight to the touch. I stroked her leg from kneecap to the tuft of pubic hair. It felt so soft and silky. I just wanted to press my face against it there and then.

And breathe in her wonderful smell.

'Are you going to miss all this?' she asked.

'God, you know I will, Caroline.'

'Auntie must give her boy a special going-away present, then.'

'Like?'

'Like what I'm going to do now.'

She bent down to her pile of clothes, naked skin gleaming in the

sunlight, the notches of her spine showing as she curved that lithe
body. She pulled out a foil wrapper.

'I don't do drugs.' I grinned.

'Love is a drug.' She smiled back. 'But look what Auntie has
brought for you.'

'Chocolate?'

'I found it at the bottom of my rucksack. Now . . . thank Auntie.'
She pressed a square of chocolate into my mouth.

'Mmmm . . . thank you, Auntie.'

'Thank her properly. Ah, ah. Don't swallow the chocolate. Keep
it in your mouth. Now go down on me.'

'Mm?'

'Lick my cunt. Let the chocolate melt into me. Now . . . Do it.'
I did it.

She sighed. 'Oh, this is so good. I'm going to miss you, Rick.'
I couldn't talk.

I listened as she murmured endearments, moaned, sighed. I
felt her tangle my fingers in my hair, pull. Felt her dig her
fingernails in my back. Then heard the sound of bracken snapping as she tugged convulsively at the tough plants, snapping
the stalks.

'Ah . . . marvellous. Oh, Rick, this is wonderful. Mmm . . .'
She groaned.

She lifted her hips into my face, then crushed my lips against the
lips of her vagina.

'Oh, I want to feel you inside me. *Quickly.*'

I rose onto all fours over her. Her eyes shone with excitement. A
fire jetted through me. My skin tingled.

'Rick . . . I want you in. I want you in now. I want you in
hard . . .'

'Just try and stop me.'

'Rick?'

'Yes?'

'Hard.'

'Hard?'

'Yes, roughly. I want to touch my cunt this time next week and
still feel what you did to me.'

'I can't hurt you.'

'Yes, you will. Bruise me a little.'

'Jesus . . .'

'Now. In. *Please, in.*'

'Oh, Jesus . . .'

'Ah, that's it. Oh, that is *it*.'

'Caroline. Hell. You don't know how good that feels.'

'Believe me. I do. Oh . . .'

'Harder. Let me feel you, coming down on my – ah! That's it. Good, good, good.'

'If I'm too rough . . . tell me.'

'Not rough enough.'

'Harder?'

'Harder.'

'Oh, like this?'

'Mmm – ahh.'

'Please. Caroline, let me be gentle.'

'No.'

'Hell.'

'Do it.'

'Oh, God . . .'

'Do you like?'

'Beautiful.'

'Harder.'

'No.'

'Harder.'

'No!'

'Yes.'

'Uh. 'S good?'

'Good.'

'Caroline?'

'Yes, yes, yes! That's good. Don't stop.'

I looked down on her. I sweated, like I'd never sweated before. Her eyes flashed with the sheer naked ecstasy of it all. She groaned, cried out, bucked under me, bit my arms, shoulders, throat. Still I pounded at her. I knocked the breath out of her in explosive gasps. They jetted hot against my neck.

My sweat dripped onto her face, mingled with her sweat.

Our bodies felt slick as spunk.

I looked down at her breasts. Her whole chest was smeared a rich, rich brown. I licked at it.

'Oh, chocolate never tasted this good before,' I panted.

As I fucked her, my weight on my outstretched arms, fists punched wrist deep into heather, I watched her. She left the world behind. Retreating deep inside herself. In deep. To a world of sensation where reality couldn't penetrate.

Her small delicate hands gripped her own breasts and massaged them harder than I ever dared. Nipples turned darker than blood.

An expression of immense concentration came to her face. Her eyes screwed tight shut. Furrows appeared around her lips as they pressed hard together.

'Oh-oh-oh-oh . . .'

'I'm hurting you?'

'No.'

'Christ, you're beautiful.'

'Oh, you're beautiful, too.'

'Christ, your cunt grabs my cock like a hand.'

'Oh-oh, I'm not letting go.'

'Christ.'

'Come on. Harder. Oh-oh-oh-oh!'

It was as if her entire soul had clenched up deep into a tiny ball inside of her. Now it came rushing back to fill her body. Her eyes opened wide. They stared up into mine. They looked up in something close to shock.

A blast of energy leapt from her eyes into mine. I felt myself convulse.

'Oh God . . . Jeee-zuss!'

'Rick . . . Ah!'

I came in a rush of fire. For a moment it felt as if my soul itself had exploded. I felt as if I'd become a million incandescent fragments whirling outward like shrapnel across the hillside.

Caroline bucked under me in the throes of her orgasm. She shivered from head to toe. Her face, throat and chest flushed robin-red.

'Oh, Christ,' I panted and rolled sideways. 'Does it feel like that to be a god? Incredible . . . I felt as if I could do anything . . . Ah, ah.' I panted. 'I felt immortal. Hell, I'm . . . I'm rambling. I'm making no sense.'

'You're making sense, honey. You're also discovering real sex.'

'You're the teacher.'

'And you're my brilliant student.' She kissed me. 'My spunky Yorkshire boy who's full of sex.'

Then, still stroking my face, she leaned over me and began licking the smeared chocolate from my chest.

And I lay back, curling her hair around my fingers. I thought about London. I thought about the flight down there. It must be a dangerous place now. I wondered what we'd find there.

I wondered what Caroline had planned to tell me, then changed her mind as soon as she heard I was leaving. It would only be for a month. Twenty-eight short days.

'London. A dangerous place,' Howard had kept repeating.

But we needed to go.

Caroline kissed me on the lips.

And I wondered if I would ever see her again.

CHAPTER 52

'Are you stuck?'

'No.'

'It's dangerous up there.'

'I'm OK.'

'Aren't you frightened?'

'No.'

'I'd be frightened up there.'

'Then you're a soft baby.'

'Rick!' Kate warned. 'The branch is breaking!'

'Lee, don't stand . . . Christ . . . ouch!'

I caught the five-year-old just a second after the branch snapped.

'Ouch, bugger, damn.' I groaned.

'Where does it hurt?' Kate asked concerned.

'Uh . . . family jewels.'

She giggled. 'That's a picturesque way of putting it. Still, at least you've got the makings of a farm.'

'Uh?'

'You've got your first couple of acres. Get it?'

'Uh-huh.'

'Acres? Couple of achers? Get it?'

'I got it all right. Right in the—'

'Ah, Rick. Children present.'

It was dusk. I lay there flat on my back. Kate looked down on me with an amused smile. I'd caught Lee as she fell out of the tree,

234

lost my balance, fell flat on my back. Lee's bony butt bounced down hard right in . . . right in one of the most sensitive parts of my body. Rendered even more sensitive after the hours just spent on that hillside with Caroline.

'My glasses. Are my glasses all right?' Lee asked, anxious.

'They look fine.' Kate smiled. 'I don't think they need cleaning again, sweetheart.'

'I think they do.' Kate sounded serious. 'Mum said I must keep them clean.'

She stood up.

I gave a sigh of relief as the pressure went.

Kate grinned at me. 'Everything OK down there?'

'Yes . . . still intact.' I found myself blushing. Kate's grin broadened. I stood up and brushed the dry leaves from my back.

'Let me,' Kate said. I blushed again. Her hands felt so good. But, here's the stupid part, the guilt came hard and strong. It was entirely innocent but it was almost as if I was cheating on Caroline.

'Lee. Why did you climb the tree?' Kate asked as she picked grass from my back. 'Weren't you comfortable in your sleeping-bag?'

'Yes.' With scrupulous care Lee cleaned the lenses of her glasses with a cloth she'd taken from the case, her tongue pushed out between her lips as she concentrated on the task.

'But it's not safe to climb trees at the best of times.'

'Especially not when it's nearly dark.'

'Safer.'

Kate glanced at me.

'Safer?'

'Yes.'

'Did you climb a tree the night the gas came?'

'No.' She put the glasses back on her face, folded the cleaning cloth then snapped it away inside the glasses case.

'No?' I asked gently. 'Did you walk up the hill?'

'No.' Now her eyes looked large, owlish and somehow wise behind the lenses again. 'They did it. They must have known the gas was coming.'

'Lee. You mean someone took you away from where your mum and the others were sleeping?'

'Yes,' she said matter-of-factly. 'They're always doing it. They did it that night my mum and everyone died under the trees.'

A sudden enlightenment buzzed through me. 'Is that why you

climbed the tree tonight, so they couldn't take you away from the tent?'

'Yes.'

Kate looked at me, puzzled, then turned back to Lee. '*Who* took you away from the camp?'

'Those people, of course.' The five-year-old girl sounded as if she was explaining a fact that should be obvious. 'They come at night. They carry me away from the tent.' She looked at me, her eyes magnified by the lenses of her specs. 'The grey people.'

CHAPTER 53

We were on the Apple Run because . . . what's that barmy saying?

THE BEST-LAID PLANS OF MICE AND MEN . . .

Which has always made zip-all sense to me anyway. If mice make any plans they must revolve around wedges of cheese and not being eaten by next door's cat. Then again, we seemed to be operating on a similar level to mice now. Our own plans revolved around finding enough food to eat and trying to avoid the gangs of people-eaters who wouldn't think twice about carving a nice juicy slice of me and you.

But already our plans were splitting apart at the seams. A couple of days ago we'd been due to fly to London where Howard had found a warehouse full of food. But our one and only plane – a four-seater Cessna – had other ideas. The wiring was on the fritz; whenever Howard fired up the motor all the fuses would blow and the cockpit would fill with a nasty stink of burning. We were grounded until he'd checked every centimetre of wiring to find the short.

So here we were, sitting beneath a tree at the edge of a cow pasture six hours' walk from Fountains Moor. This particular plan: to make the Apple Run to an orchard we'd found earlier in the summer. Now the fruit was ripe we were methodically harvesting all the orchards we'd discovered. The plan was simple: walk to orchard. Fill backpacks and holdalls with apples. Walk back to Fountains Moor.

Apples are good for you.

Roughage. Vitamin C. Natural sugars.

But Christ, were we going to be sick to death of apples by Christmastime.

The tree's leaves, now an autumn red, rustled in the cold wind. On the ground to my left sat Caroline. She looked good even in the mountaineer's anorak that was three sizes too big for her. A leaf fell onto her hair; hair that was gorgeously fluffy from being washed in mountain streams for the last four months. She picked the leaf off, gave me a bright smile. She was pleased that the London trip had been postponed.

To my right sat Dean Skilton. He wore sunglasses and a green bandana around his head. He was cleaning one of his beloved Beretta pistols with a cloth, polishing it in long loving strokes. He was talking about something he'd heard on the radio. It was broadcast on the only station transmitting in English in those days: 'This guy was saying the Earth's constantly going through these upheavals – volcanoes, quakes, ice ages.'

'But I've never heard of this before,' Caroline said, hugging her knees. 'A hot age?'

'It's more common than you think. A whole rash of volcanic eruptions probably killed off the dinosaurs.'

'But volcanoes haven't been the main problem this time. The ground itself is actually heating up.'

'If you think about it,' I said, 'the Earth isn't much more than a huge blob of molten rock and iron surrounded by just a thin shell of cool, solid rock.'

'Great.' Caroline shivered. 'Don't you just feel this disaster has been waiting to happen?'

'After all, the deepest you could drill down . . .' I patted the ground with my hand. '. . . is about twelve kilometres. Then the steel drill bits would melt.'

'Just twelve kilometres?'

'Like I said, we're walking round on what is, relatively speaking, just a very thin crust of cool earth.'

'And getting thinner all the time,' Caroline said in a small voice.

'And getting thinner all the time,' I agreed. I gave her hand a squeeze. It was meant to be reassuring but I didn't feel reassured myself.

Dean, still polishing the handgun, said, 'Around eight million years ago the Mediterranean dried up. The entrance to the Atlantic through the Straits of Gibraltar had become blocked, so the sea water evaporated. And you know something?'

237

'Go on: surprise us,' I said, gloomily.

'When the Atlantic at last broke through again it created the biggest waterfall ever. The guy was saying water rushed back in to fill the Med with such force you could have heard the roar it made over most of Western Europe and North Africa.'

Caroline stood up and stretched. 'Uh . . . when are they going to give us some good news?'

'When Hell freezes over,' Dean said in a flat voice.

I laughed, but there was little humour in it. 'Some hope.'

Caroline sniffed. 'What's that smell?'

'Probably the Drive-Thru McDonald's down the road,' Dean said with a laugh as bitter as my own. 'Who's for a Quarter Pounder and fries? My treat.'

'Christ, I wish,' I said with feeling. 'Seeing as you're paying I'll finish off with a couple of apple pies.'

'They were always too hot to eat. Do you remember?'

'Christ, yes. When I was a kid I'd always burn my lip because I couldn't wait for it to cool.'

'And the milkshakes? Weren't they always too thick to suck up the straw?'

'Did you ever end up using the straw as a spoon?'

Suddenly Dean and I were talking as if we were reminiscing about a dead friend. Perhaps we were. There was an intensity about the way we talked. I'd swear I even saw a tear in old Deanie-baby's eye.

'Didn't you find the fries were always too salty, though?' he said.

'Well, would you turn them down if they were offered to you right now?'

'No,' he agreed with a grim smile, 'No, I wouldn't.'

'I never had the Fillet-o-fish, though. I never—'

'Wait,' Caroline looked round the field. 'I *can* smell something.'

'KFC?'

'Pizza Hut?'

'Dean, I'm serious. What's that smell?'

Dean stood up, sniffed the air. He shrugged. 'I don't smell anything.'

The wind blew. Leaves rustled, dry-sounding.

'It's not food,' Caroline said, 'Don't you smell anything, Rick?'

'No. But with this wind blowing it's hard to . . . wait a minute.'

'There is something, isn't there?' Caroline looked up at me. 'Smells strange, doesn't it? Like—'

'Summer rain,' I said quickly. 'When it falls on soil after a hot day.'

Dean shook his head. 'Can you tell me what this mysterious smell is?'

'Get your things,' I said. 'We're moving on. *Now*.'

'But what the Hell is the smell?' Deane complained.

'It's coming from down there.' I pointed at our feet. 'We're sitting on a hot spot.'

Dean looked at the grass – still fresh and green-looking. 'I can't see anything?'

'Nor can I, but we don't want to hang around just in case we're sitting on a gas pocket that's waiting to go boom.'

'Rick.' Caroline grabbed my arm. 'Look what's happening to the ground.'

'I don't see anything.' Dean sounded alarmed. 'What can *you* see?'

'Look at your feet,' I said.

'Jesus.' He looked at me in astonishment. 'Worms. Thousands of bloody worms.'

'Do you remember the night of Ben Cavellero's party? That last one?' I nodded down at the worms standing on their tails, sticking up from the ground. 'That's what I saw then. The heat's driving them out of the soil.'

'Rick.' Caroline's brown eyes looked nervous as she watched the worms sliding out into the grass. 'Come on, the heat must be building up fast.'

'Ready?' I asked as Dean and Caroline slipped the straps of their backpacks over their shoulders. They nodded.

We walked quickly from the field, now turning pink as thousands upon thousands of worms slid out of the ground, some actually sliding up over our boots as if to trying to escape the heat seeping up through the soil. Here and there moles pulled themselves out of their holes. Rabbits ran by, driven out by the invading heat too.

The smell of hot soil grew stronger. Already I imagined I could feel the heat coming through the soles of my boots.

By the time we reached the fence we were running.

In the next field trees were already dying from the heat. The leaves there hadn't yet turned autumnal red but they were already dead. They hung limp from the branches in clots of waxy green as if they'd been doused in boiling water.

Again the truth hit me:

THE WORLD IS DYING

CHAPTER 54

After five minutes of hard walking we slowed to a more comfortable pace. We could no longer smell that aroma of hot soil. The landscape still looked fresh and green.

As was our habit now, we avoided roads and stuck to cross-country tracks and footpaths. We were travelling through a mainly agricultural landscape of overgrown fields. There were no farm animals. Either they'd been slaughtered by starving refugees or had died of thirst with no one to fill their water troughs. We saw no sign that people had been in the area recently.

We'd come across the occasional human skeleton. These were so numerous that you scarcely noticed them these days. They lay in the long grass with nettles sprouting through the ribcages and ants marching in and out of the eye sockets to pick what was left of the brains from the skulls.

And sometimes there was the occasional bizarre and incongruous sight which could still take you by surprise. On a stone wall someone had placed a line of TVs. There must have been around twenty of them, dangling flexes swaying in the wind, and beside each TV on the wall was its remote control. I noticed a butterfly land on a big black-cased Sony TV; the butterfly's red wings trembled in the cold breeze. The wings looked frayed and broken at the edges. A surge of sadness took me by surprise. The dead TVs lined up on the wall, the cold wind, the butterfly dying of old age. Life seemed so fragile somehow.

Dean paused beside me. He nodded at the TVs. 'Is this what passes for art these days?'

'Uh?'

'I wonder who put the heads inside the TVs?'

I looked again at the TVs and saw that the sets had been gutted of the tube and all electronic components. They'd been replaced with severed human heads. They were well rotted; the eyes had putrefied to form jelly-like tears that hung down over cheeks. Flies buzzed.

Dean pulled the Beretta from his pocket. 'Just in case we meet the artist.'

Caroline swallowed, her face pale. 'How far now?'

'Another hour. If we keep the pace up.'

'Come on.' She turned and walked quickly along the track.

We followed, looking left, right, behind us in case the TV artist should make an appearance and decide he wanted to make an exhibition of us, too.

But the area seemed deserted. We came upon the remains of campfires and the tell-tale scattering of empty food cans where people had passed through. But there was little to stay for now.

Another ten minutes of hard walking and we passed a little redbrick village that had been turned into a fortress, with barbed-wire fences and trucks used as roadblocks. One glance told us it had been deserted for weeks. Most of the houses had been burnt out. Half a dozen human skulls littered the main street.

'Another one bites the dust,' Dean observed dryly as we hurried by.

'OK. We're here,' I said. 'Copley Manor.'

For the next couple of hours we picked the ripe apples. Carefully we packed them into the backpacks and holdalls, making sure we didn't bruise the fruit or take any worm-eaten or bird-pecked apples. We ate apples as we worked. Not that we enjoyed the flavour anymore. It was a way of filling your stomach. These days you ate when you had the chance. You could never tell when your next meal would be.

When we had as many apples as we could carry we started back. Walking was hard now. My heels started to ache. The straps dug into our shoulders. I constantly shifted the heavy holdall from one hand to another.

'We won't make it back to Fountains Moor by tonight,' I said, panting. 'We'll break the journey same place as last time.'

'Where's that?' Caroline sounded breathless too from the exertion. 'The local Hilton, I hope.'

'Sorry.' I gave a sympathetic smile. 'It's a barn.'

Dean added, 'The good news is, it's across there in the next field. So at least we can rest.'

She looked at her watch. 'It's still early. Are you sure we couldn't make it home?'

'Remember, it's all uphill now.'

Dean said, 'And these backpacks are going to feel as if they're full of housebricks.'

The barn, made entirely of corrugated iron, was dry. We had sleeping-bags and rolls of foam rubber for mattresses so it would be reasonably comfortable.

'God, it's a relief to get these backpacks off,' Dean said, shrugging off the straps. 'Pass me your water bottles. I'll go and fill them. Got the tablets?'

'Yeah,' I pulled a blister pack from my back pocket. 'Don't you want to take a break first? It's a long walk down to the spring.'

He shook his head. 'If I sit down now I won't want to get up again today.'

I handed him the water-purification tablets. We didn't need them up on the moor where the water was fresher and sweeter than anything that flowed from a city tap, but down here the water couldn't be trusted. At best you'd probably be laid up with diarrhoea; at worst it might be typhoid, cholera or Weil's Disease from rat urine in the water. So now we used iodine tablets to kill any bugs. They turned the water a reddish colour so it looked as if you were drinking diluted blood. Tasted crap, too; like dental mouth swill.

Caroline watched Dean go. 'Nice bum,' she said, her eye flashing that mischievous glint.

'Now, don't you go making me jealous.' I grinned as I carefully lined our bags of precious apples against the wall.

'Rick, how long will he be gone?'

'At least an hour. Uh-oh. You're not having any ideas, are you?'

'Ideas, Rick? And what would those be?' Smiling, she approached me and lifted her arms so she could slide them around my neck. 'Tell your Auntie Caroline what she's thinking.' She kissed me on the mouth.

'She's thinking that we could actually fill this hour we're alone with more than just small talk and counting apples.'

'They're only apples.'

'They're only apples to you, my dear, but they might mean life or death to some poor soul.' I meant it as a joke but Caroline saw the serious side.

She sighed. 'God, reduced to this. A bag full of apples has become a matter of life and death.' She held me tight and nestled her head under my chin. 'I've eaten in some of the best restaurants in the world, now I lie awake at night and all I can think about is a fried egg sandwich.' She kissed my throat. 'Can you believe that? Fried egg sandwiches. I've become obsessed with fried egg sandwiches.'

'How long is it since we ate bread?'

'I don't know . . . three months?'

'About that.' I kissed the top of her head. 'At least we're not eating each other.'

She looked up, smiled. 'Until today, that is. But right now I'm going to eat you.'

'You wouldn't!'

'I would.'

'Which bit?'

'Which bit do you think?'

'Ouch.' I smiled.

'I promise not to chew.'

I felt her fingers slide up my leg and over my groin to find my belt. She popped the buckle. Then she undid the button on my jeans.

At that moment it was pure Caroline. She was doing what I was used to. She smiled that sexy smile I'd come to love. Her eyes twinkled with erotic mischief. Her hands moved expertly across my body, squeezing gently, stroking, caressing. I breathed in deeply, drawing in a whole lungful of her wonderful scent.

Then she stopped. Suddenly stopped as if she'd felt a sharp pain.

I looked down at her, startled.

'Caroline? What's wrong?'

She took a deep breath, shivered.

'Caroline?' I was worried now.

'It's OK,' she said. 'I'm fine.' Suddenly she reached out and held me tightly. She actually clung to me as if afraid something would snatch me from her.

'Rick. I'm so glad I found you. I wouldn't have made it this far if you hadn't cared for me.'

I hugged her, startled at the way she suddenly trembled.

She looked up at me, her eyes shining with tears. 'Do you love me?'

'Of course I do.'

'Say it . . . please, Rick.'

'I love you. I do love you.' I kissed her, my heart beating fast, but this time for the wrong reasons. I felt so afraid for her. I'd not seen her as frightened as this in months.

'Rick, I love it when you hold me tight.'

'Like this?'

'Mmm . . . yes, like that.' She buried her face into my chest; she continued speaking, her voice muffled. 'You've had no regrets in taking me on?'

'Take you on? You make it sound like you were a liability.'

'Perhaps I am?'

'No.'

'You could have someone younger.'

'Caroline, I love you. *You.*'

'Kate Robinson.' Now her voice sounded anxious, jittery. 'Kate—'

'I'm not interested in Kate, she—'

'Maybe, but she's interested in you.'

'But I'm interested in *you*, Caroline. I want *you.*'

'But she's a nice girl. If anything should happen to me . . .' she started to say but suddenly she dug her face tight into my chest; her arms held me with a surprising strength. I kissed her and stroked her hair.

I believe that was the moment that Caroline had a premonition of what would soon happen to her.

The time was 4:15. By 5:10 my life would be different again.

CHAPTER 55

We made love. The time was 4:20.

Caroline held onto me as we lay naked on the sleeping-bag. I looked down on her. Her breasts jiggled with every thrust I made, and her eyes widened, too, with that same rhythm. She panted my name, told me over and over and over that she loved me; how precious I was to her.

Again I sensed she had a premonition that this part of our lives was ending. Though she looked beautiful there, her hair fluffed out, her throat pinking as I pushed myself deep into her, I sensed fear in the air. Fear. It hung so thick you could reach out and touch it. Fear. That was cold as ice. It weighed down on us.

I fucked harder.

Caroline gasped. 'Gently, lover, gently.'

I kissed her throat, chest and breasts, trying to shut out this image of fear as a bat-winged monster hovering dark and terrible above us.

I kissed her nipples gently. Caroline snaked her arm around my neck and pulled my face to her breasts.

'Bite,' she panted. 'Bite . . . bite! You won't hurt me, you won't – *Oh!* That's it. Yes, that's it. Oh, keep fucking me; don't stop fucking.'

'You're beautiful; I—'

'Oh, hold me tight, my love, *hold me tight.*'

She squirmed beneath me.

'I love you, Christ, I love you, I love you, I love you.' I chanted it as if it was almost a protective mantra. I sensed that fear, that bleak, penetrating, Godawful fear settling on us.

I'd caught the fear from Caroline. I could see it in her eyes.

The time was 4:29.

'Hold me. Oh, please use your fingers,' she panted. 'Make me come, please make me come, oh, oh, oh, that's it, yes. I—oh!'

Thrash your body into hers. Thrash it good and hard. Those are the words I pumped through my head. *Hold her tight; kiss hard; thrash yourself against her; thrash hard into her body.*

Because I wanted to keep that hovering fear at bay. I don't know why . . . I couldn't explain why I felt like that. But I saw fear in Caroline's eyes as she moaned beneath me. Even though her skin was hot against my skin, I sensed that creeping fear, crawling inside of her, turning her cold as ice somewhere deep in the very core of her being.

The time was 4:37.

I tried not to look at my watch. I wanted to love her as best as I possibly could. I wanted her to be lost in a sea of sensation. I wanted to see her come in a panting rush of excitement.

But there was always that fear. A premonition that something dark and cold and terrible approached. As chilling and as dreadful as a ghost.

Tears flowed down her cheeks.

Yes.

She sensed it, too.

I know she did.

The time: 4:40.

I remember each minute individually. The minutes were like
gemstones threaded onto a string. One after another. With a slow
rhythm. Death was making her a necklace.

I shivered.

I told myself it was sheer imagination.

But I know we both felt it. I couldn't rationalize away that
sense of foreboding; of a disaster waiting to happen. Await-
ing its appointed time of arrival according to the Devil's own
timetable.

4:43.

Minutes came, then went.

I remember it so clearly. It happened at 4:59.

4:44.

'Rick?'

'Yes?'

'I wish we were home.' She panted the words as I still thrust
into her.

'Will be . . . soon. Ah.'

'Uh. Don't stop. Uh, don't stop.'

'Christ, you're wonderful.'

'Don't stop.'

'I love you.'

Fear beating its black wings.

'Don't stop.'

Cold. My blood ran like freezing slush through my veins.

'Love me, Rick.'

'I do.'

She smiled up at me through her tears.

'You're beautiful . . . beautiful.'

For that second I forgot we were there on the dirt floor, that we
were in a corrugated-iron shed in the corner of a field in the middle of
nowhere. I pumped myself into her. Feeling shooting, tingling electric
shocks. Now I saw only her eyes.

Her wonderful brown eyes, looking up at me with such love and
tenderness and care.

'*Ah!*'

It's a cliché about coming together. It's hard for most couples to
achieve. We rarely had in the past. This time we did.

For a moment it held all the evil in the world at bay. There was
that sparkling rush of energy. I cried out and arched my back, lifting

my head, sweat flicked from my hair; that tremendous burst of heat fireballed through me.

Below, Caroline squirmed, cried out my name.

Then it was done. I flopped down at her side. We lay panting together, looking up at the rafters.

The time was 4:51.

She kissed me on the lips. 'Get dressed, love.'

'Dean won't be back for ages yet.'

'Please, get dressed.'

'What's the matter?'

'I don't like this place.'

'Why?'

'I don't know . . . it . . . it frightens me.'

A barn? In a field? The countryside deserted?

But I felt it, too.

I began to dress. 'You've heard something?'

'No.' She slipped on her bra. 'Only it doesn't . . . *feel* right.'

I looked at the doorway. I could almost imagine one of the Grey Men standing there. A massive grey fist resting against the doorframe, its grey head tilted to one side as it watched us with its eyes that were as red and as wet as freshly drawn blood.

I shivered.

Christ, yes, I wanted out of there, too.

Again I sensed fear hovering there. Like that bat-winged monster.

Danger.

That tiny red alarm light, buried deep in a part of your brain so ancient you shared it with the dinosaurs, began to flash.

Danger.

That ancient bit of grey matter had detected something that your clever, quick-witted primate brain could not. Now the alarm light flashed. *Danger . . . danger . . . danger . . .*

Primate brain supplied the survival order: **GET THE HELL OUT OF THERE!**

But why? I looked outside.

The time was 4:53.

Everything quiet. Everything normal.

But why did I feel so scared? What subliminal danger signals was I picking up?

I fastened the belt of my jeans, then grabbed the rifle.

247

I joined Caroline at the doorway. I saw her anxious darting eyes looking for danger.

'See anything?' I asked.

'No. But something's wrong.'

'I know. You can feel it, can't you?'

'Oppressive. Like a thunderstorm building.'

Outside the overgrown meadow stretched out to fences and a scattering of trees. A hare bounded across the field.

It seemed to be running for its life.

4:55.

'Do you know where this spring is that Dean's gone to?'

I nodded. 'Over in that direction. Through the trees.'

'We can meet him coming back.'

'I'll get the bags.'

4:56.

'Rick?'

'Yes?'

'Remember what I said about Kate Robinson?'

'Caroline—'

'No, I'm serious. She's a lovely girl.'

4:57.

'Can you manage with the bags?'

'I'm OK. If you can carry the rifle.'

'Got it.'

'If you see anyone, don't fire. With luck they might not see us.'

'Got you,' she said.

That sense of fear, of imminent danger seemed so oppressive now. I found myself breathless. I lugged the bags of apples to the doorway. I could hardly breathe.

'Give me one of the bags,' she said.

'No. I'm fine. Let's just get out of here.'

4.58.

We both stepped out of the barn warily. My leg muscles were so tense I thought they'd snap. The bags dragged down at my shoulders.

'Rick. You've been good to me. I've been so lucky you came into my life.'

Stop it, stop it, I wanted to tell her. *Stop talking as if you're going to—*

'Rick . . . listen.' Caroline looked round, her eyes wide. 'What's that sound?'

'I don't know.'

'It's getting louder. A motor?'

The sound was deep; like someone knocking at the other side of a thick wall.

I tilted my head to one side. There we were, standing in a grass field, and there was a sound like someone was knocking – it seemed muffled and far away. I listened to the mysterious sound; something about it seemed just so *wrong*. It just wasn't the kind of sound you hear out in a field.

'I'll be damned,' I murmured.

'Rick, what is it?'

'I've heard that sound before.'

'You have? Where?'

'Leeds. I was with my brother Stephen, in a shop.'

'A shop?'

'When we were hunting for supplies for the refugees. God damn it. It's happening again.'

'What is?'

'We've got to get away from here. *Caroline, now!*'

The knocking sound grew louder.

I stood about five paces from Caroline.

The knocking grew louder – louder. A sudden vibration ran up from the ground through the soles of my feet.

The time was, at last, 4:59.

'Rick . . .'

'Run!' I yelled. 'Drop the rifle! Just *RUN!*'

I started to move, shedding the bags of apples. I looked back at Caroline. She didn't move, not sure where to go.

'Caroline . . .' I ran back to her, grabbed her by the sleeve.

And that's when I lost her.

As quickly as that.

With no other warning.

4:59 and a few lousy seconds.

I remember: I held her by the sleeve. I looked into her face. Her eyes, alarmed, looking to me for help.

The geyser erupted beneath her feet.

With a roar, a thousand gallons of boiling water burst from the earth.

The blast threw me back. I rolled over and over across the ground trying to escape the explosion of superheated water and steam standing in a column forty metres high.

By the time the water landed on me, it was falling as cool rain.

I gripped something in my hand. I looked at it, dazed.

The sleeve of Caroline's coat . . .

She's gone . . . she's gone.

I was still staring at the sleeve when Dean found me twenty minutes later.

CHAPTER 56

I carried Caroline to where an ancient oak grew on a hill.

Darkness was falling, but still we worked, finding timber, piling it high.

I told myself Caroline couldn't have felt a thing. The pressure of the geyser as it erupted could have flipped a truck into the air. She must have died instantly. I repeated this over and over in my head. The thought of her suffering again would have been unbearable.

It was fully dark when I zipped her into her sleeping-bag. Then lifted her onto the pyre.

A moment later I lit the dry grass piled around its base. Instantly the wind caught the flames. Within seconds it was a roaring, blazing mass of heat and light. I stood as close to the fire as I could, face smarting, eyes stinging. Watching the beating heart of incandescence consuming Caroline's body and releasing some essence of her into the sky to be carried far away across fields, rivers, forests.

The fire snapped and crackled for most of that night. Dean and I stood side by side as if on guard. We'd leave when there were only ashes and dust.

The blast of boiling water that punched her so brutally into the sky must have disfigured her terribly. But all I could remember even then as I stood there by the fire – indeed, all I can remember now – is that she looked so perfectly beautiful as I laid her on to the funeral pyre. Whatever had happened to her. Whatever the boiling water had done to her lovely skin and hair, my mind wouldn't allow me to see it. My mind would only project my memory of her beautiful face onto whatever must have been left of her head.

So there was nothing repellent or horrific about that final kiss as she lay there on the pyre.

Sometime around dawn, when the fire had dwindled to a glowing mound of embers that streamed sparks when the wind blew. Sometime around then Dean said to me, 'She had a lover.'

I said nothing.

'For some reason she kept it a secret. Do you know who it was?'

Me.

I wanted to say the word. But at that moment I could say nothing.

Dean looked back at the glowing embers. He swallowed. 'But she did tell Kate one thing she'd been keeping quiet.'

I looked at Dean.

He swallowed again. He found it hard to talk. 'Caroline said she was going to have a baby.' He swallowed, then said softly, 'A little baby.'

I looked back into the red glowing heart of the embers. My eyes began to sting once more.

CHAPTER 57

Stephen looked at me, his face serious. 'Are you ready for this?'

I tried to sound cool. 'Sure. No problems.'

I didn't feel as cool as I managed to sound. My mouth had dried; my heartbeat was accelerating.

What had I to be afraid of?

Dying.

Dying out there in the middle of the godforsaken nowhere that had once been the proverbial green and pleasant land.

I said, 'It's not too late to say I've changed my mind and I want to go back?'

Stephen cupped his hand to his ear. 'The plane ... what did you say?'

'Nothing ... just joking.'

He smiled, slapped my back.

The four-seater plane stood there, its engine ticking over, the blast of air from the single propeller spinning at a thousand revolutions per minute transforming the grass into a mass of flurrying green waves. Despite sunrise still being more than forty minutes away, and the stars still shining hard in the sky, there was a blood-red line on the horizon where the sun would break into a new day. But it was more than the cold air that had turned the grass crisp with frost beneath my feet that made me shiver.

I shivered again. It was ten days since Caroline had died. No one else knew that we had been lovers. You must think it strange I still kept it secret. Almost as if I was ashamed of the relationship. But the truth of the matter was that I was traumatized by her death. I just hadn't realized the depth, or, Hell, yes, even the integrity of my feelings. I'd convinced myself that the relationship was based on sex – nothing else. But as I stood there watching the plane, the blast of air from its propeller rippling the grass and tumbling the autumn leaves away down the field, I realized how much Caroline Lucas had meant to me. It felt as if a great big chunk of my soul had been torn away. I felt cold. Alone. That loneliness had me in its cold blue grip now, as grim and as unyielding as rigor mortis.

As I'd done a thousand times every day, I conjured up an image of Caroline: she is lovely again, unblemished by the blast of scalding water; she is standing on the grass between myself and the plane. She's smiling, the brown eyes are trusting, her hair blows in the breeze, she tilts her head to one side, the smile broadens, she's oh-so-pleased to see me; with her fingertips she lightly toys with her ear lobe; she mouths the words 'Five minutes' just as she's done dozens of times before. Then she walks up onto the moor. I follow five minutes later, find her there, hungry for my kisses; she talks to me in that husky late-night-radio voice that has the power to send my heart beating faster.

I wished I was back in my tent on Fountains Moor. So I could curl up in the sleeping-bag in the hope that sleep would annihilate the pain of losing her.

Christ, scrub that. I wished I could wake up at home in Fairburn with the sunlight poking through the curtains, the clock radio belting out some crap song. What I wouldn't give for a crappy normal day. Riding the bus to East Garforth to work in the crappy supermarket. Then, maybe, in the evening a gig with my stillborn band, Thunder Bug, in some crappy bar in downtown Leeds. Even those things you hated about civilization – the crappy music played to you when some telephone receptionist put you on hold, those foil-wrapped cheese-spread triangles that are damn near impossible to open without squidging the cheese over your fingers, Christmas decorations swamping shopping malls when it's only October, crappy TV game shows: *Pets That Look like Famous Politicians* – even that kind of crap had a powerful allure right then.

Especially when I was about to fly more than two hundred kilometres in something that looked no more substantial than a family car with a pair of wings bolted to it.

There would be three of us: Howard Sparkman (pilot), Dean Skilton and me, one Rick Kennedy, with a whole rain forest's worth of butterflies in his stomach.

It had been a joke, that about changing my mind. I knew I had to go. Scratch that: NEEDED to go. This was a matter of life and death all right. We NEEDED that food if we were going to survive the winter.

Stephen was saying something to Kate. The two had helped us carry the supplies we'd need down to the pasture we'd dubbed Airport One, which was a good couple of hours' walk from Fountains Moor.

Dean stood just a few paces from me. He wore a green headband. There were a pair of rifles slung over his shoulders, he'd pushed his beloved Beretta handguns into his leather belt. He looked ready for war.

Through the near dark I saw Howard silhouetted by the cockpit light. He gave a thumbs-up sign. The engine had warmed through. He was ready to go.

I picked up my backpack and a belt of rifle ammunition. Stephen caught me by the elbow. 'You'll be fine,' he told me. 'Just don't take any chances.'

'You're playing the big brother again.'

He smiled but I could see the concern breaking through. 'Yeah, I'm playing the big brother. Because that's what I am. I want you to come back in one piece.'

Kate kissed me on the cheek. 'We *all* want you to come back in one piece. Savvy?'

'Savvy.' I nodded.

'Now just play it safe,' Stephen said. 'Don't do anything fancy.

It's just a case of loading the plane with food. Howard will fly it back. Then he'll come back and—'

'Repeat the process as often as necessary.' I smiled 'Yeah, I know, now stop sounding like our mother.'

His smile saddened. 'Yeah, I do, bless her.' He gave me a playful punch on the shoulder. 'Now . . . go fly.'

'OK, Dean. You ready for – Dean?'

Dean had pulled the headband off. Sweat stood out in beads on his face despite the temperature being less than zero.

'Dean, you all right?'

Kate felt his forehead. 'My . . . he's cooking.'

'I'll be OK. Once I can sit down on the plane.'

Kate shot a look at Stephen and myself. 'He can't fly like this. He's really burning up.'

Dean slipped the rifles off his shoulders, turned his back on us, then puked massively onto the grass.

'Shit . . . I warned him about that tinned crab meat. It was way past its sell-by date.'

Stephen shot me a look. 'Crab meat?'

'Yeah, I saw him eating a can last night.'

'Then it won't be life-threatening,' Kate said, wrinkling her nose as he heaved noisily again. 'He needs a few days rest and plenty of water.'

'Damn.' Stephen lightly punched his fist into the palm of the other hand. 'Damn, damn.'

'Who was on the reserve list?' Kate asked.

'Paul Freise. He'll still be up at the camp.'

'But on foot it's two hours there, two hours back.'

'Any chance of landing the plane on the moor?'

'Absolutely no chance. The heather's too deep. The plane would flip nose over tail.'

Kate said, 'If the wind speed picks up much more Howard won't risk flying anyway. He could be grounded for days.'

I shrugged. 'With the supplies we've put away maybe we should postpone the trip?'

Stephen shook his head.

Kate looked at Stephen with an intensity that made my scalp prickle. 'Stephen. We should tell Rick.'

'Tell Rick what?' I asked.

'How much food is *really* left.'

'Kate—' he began.

'It's only right he knows.'

'Knows what?' I began to be irritated by the fact I was being kept in the dark. 'Stephen, what aren't you telling me?'

'I didn't want to put you under any unreasonable pressure.'

'Unreasonable pressure?'

'And I didn't want to start a panic in the camp.'

'Stephen. For Pete's sake, I'm your brother. Just tell me the truth.'

'OK. The truth. The canned food will run out in ten days.'

'*Ten days?*'

'Ten days.'

'But we've got food dumps all over the freaking moor.'

'Do you know how many cans sixty people consume in one day?'

'But it's been rationed for the last—'

'Yeah, and that *is* with rationing, Rick.'

'The fact is,' Kate added, 'consumption has still exceeded the rate we've been finding fresh supplies.'

'And the store of fresh vegetables?' I asked.

'Holding their own,' he said. 'Just.'

'So,' I let out a breath as the truth sank in, 'in less than a fortnight the camp will be living on nothing but potato and turnip soup.'

'And whatever wild rabbits and birds we can catch.'

'Great.'

'And once winter sets in up here we won't be able to use the aeroplane at all.'

'Right,' I said, 'We still go this morning. I can manage by myself.'

Stephen shook his head. 'Hell, no, Rick. You can't stay there alone. And you'll need help shifting the supplies to the landing strip at the London end.' He looked me in the eye. 'I'm coming with you.'

'No way,' I said. 'You're the head of that group up there on the moor. What will happen to them if you disappear for a month?'

'Good point,' Kate said. 'You must stay.'

'What now, then?'

Kate said firmly, 'I'll go in Dean's place.'

'You sure?'

'I'm sure.'

Stephen looked at me. I nodded. 'Come on, let's do it.'

* * *

255

We were in the air before sunrise. Kate sat up front with Howard. I sat in the back, sleeping-bags, ammo belts, rifles piled across my knee and mounded on the spare seat beside me.

No one spoke, but there was a sense of tension, even excitement, that filled the cabin with something like an electric charge. What the Hell would we find in London? Again, I felt a wave of uncertainty about whether I'd see Fountains Moor again.

Howard brought the plane in a huge arc, up high over the moor. Down below I could just make out that cleft in the hillside, and although I couldn't see them, I imagined that line of tents running two by two alongside the stream.

Then, just for a second, I saw a figure far below. It was waving.

It was little more than a speck. But I had no doubt in my mind who it was.

Once more I'd conjured the image of Caroline. At least I believed the image was the product of my imagination. Or maybe it really was her ghost. Can love be so strong it survives death itself? Who knows? I closed my eyes, but in my mind's eye I saw her waving goodbye. A figure that grew tinier and tinier as the plane carried me south.

CHAPTER 58

It's bizarre looking back. The flight down to London was strangely surreal. There we were, my old friend Howard Sparkman at the controls, wearing shades against the great wash of morning sunlight slamming through the glass. And there was Kate Robinson. The girl I once had the hots for. The girl I'd craved so much I'd lie awake in bed in my old family home back on Trueman Way in Fairburn. Every so often she'd lift the binoculars to those clear green eyes of hers, make some comment to Howard. Most of what she said I missed because of the sound of the engine whirling the prop at more than two thousand revolutions per minute, pulling us ever further away from home.

Above us the sky was blue, cloudless; below the countryside was a green carpet, patterned with roads, rivers, towns, villages.

For weeks we'd been searching that countryside for an overlooked tin of carrots or a few onions, or whatever we could find that would keep us on the right side of starvation for just another twenty-four hours. We'd walk by the rotting corpses of people – people just like us – who'd not made it through the summer. All the time the stink of rot in our nostrils. Or the stink of burning where the ground was heating up. All the time keeping your senses fine-tuned so you'd see the tell-tale signs of a refugee camp just ahead, whose occupants just might have turned to cannibalism to ensure they got enough protein to survive.

'Rick?'

'Yeah?' I leaned forward to hear what Kate had to say above the engine noise.

She twisted in her seat. 'Do you know that town?'

'Doncaster.'

'You sure?' Howard called back. 'I'm trying to follow the East Coast railway line down to London.'

'That goes through Doncaster.'

'I know. But did Doncaster ever have a lake that size?'

I took a second look. 'Jesus. What a mess.'

'What's left of it. Is that Doncaster?'

'Uh . . . Kate, can I have the binoculars? Thanks.'

'The lake's covering the railway line and the major roads,' Howard said. 'The A1M's completely flooded.'

'Can't you take us down lower?'

'I'm at three thousand metres. I'll risk going down to two thousand.'

'Risk?' Kate asked.

Howard shrugged. 'People are desperate. They imagine I'm flying a plane packed to the wing struts with chocolate or roast beef sandwiches or something. They take pot shots at me.'

I looked down. From this height nothing looked spectacularly amiss. I could see houses, factories, schools, playing fields. The whole place looked green with trees lining housing estate roads. It looked peaceful, unthreatening. Of course you didn't know what carnage had happened down there when civilization rolled over and died on us. No doubt those green gardens were by now littered with human skulls picked shiny white by birds and rats.

The only evidence that the landscape was undergoing some pretty fundamental changes was the vast lake that now stretched out for kilometre upon kilometre to the south of the town.

'I'll make another pass over the town centre.' Howard swung the plane round in a tight arc. Instinctively I hung onto the seat belt. The plane seemed to balance on its wing tip. And I couldn't escape the sensation that I could fall right out of the plane to splatter onto a road far below. The townscape rolled beneath me. Shopping malls, supermarkets, houses, shops; a jumble of geometric shapes of predominantly black slate roofs.

'What do you think, Rick?'

'Just a moment. Ah, yeah. I can see the racecourse.'

'Doncaster?'

'Definitely.'

'See any sign of the railway line?'

'Nope. It must be underwater.'

'If this is Doncaster, we should be able to pick it up by flying due south.'

'It's Doncaster, all right. There's what's left of the Leisure Park. I once went out with a girl from Doncaster. We used to go ice-skating there.'

'Ice-skating?' Kate's green eyes flashed with amusement.

'Yeah, ice-skating.' I grinned.

'Sorry,' she smiled. 'I just can't imagine you ice-skating.'

'The things we do for love, eh?' I found myself blushing so I broke eye contact and looked down again.

The Dome leisure complex where I'd fallen flat on my back so many times trying to skate hand-in-hand with Julie slid by far below. The glass dome that topped the white building had been shattered. For a second I had a vivid mental picture of the interior. The Dome's interconnecting swimming pools would be knee deep by now; they'd be slimed a disgusting green. The water slide flumes would be dry, cracked. Razor-sharp pieces of glass would litter the edge of the pools where I'd seen children laughing and shrieking and running barefoot. Maybe a water rat grown plump on human flesh would sit stroking its whiskers beneath the dead tropical plants that had once given the pool area a Caribbean feel. Everything would be rotting back into the ground. The once gleaming silver hand rails would be red with rust. The changing cubicles would be deserted. I could imagine the ghostly laughter and shouts of children drying themselves after the swim and calling out to one another:

'Where next, Paul?'

'Pizza!'

'Nah!' McDonalds?'

'Going bowling this aft?'

'If you lend us some dough.'

'Hey, Bio-Hazard, what do you think this spot is?'

'Pox.'

'On my eyelid?'

'Fluttered his eyelashes at Pussy Galore again.'

'Winker!'

'Ow!'

'Mum . . . Terry won't let go of my arm.'

'Rick? Rick . . . hallo . . . reality calling planet Rick Kennedy.'

I came out of it. 'Uh, sorry. Miles away.'

'Well?'

'Well what?'

She smiled and shook her head. 'You really were away with the fairies. I only asked if you wanted a coffee.'

I smiled. 'Thanks.'

The plane left Doncaster behind. I watched as the town receded. I saw the Warner Brothers cinema where Julie and I had sat in the back row through some movie that we never even watched. We'd kissed non-stop. I'd worked my hand up under her top.

The cinema now stood out of the lake like a square boat, the water level as high as the tops of the entrance doors. The suburb of Bessacarr to the south was flooded, too; dozens of once expensive detached houses stood in the lake looking like a flotilla of little boats. Here the trees were dead; they thrust skeletal branches from the flood waters, the leaves long gone.

Julie lived in one of those houses. Where was she now? Alive? Dead? Fighting tooth and nail for survival?

I squinted through the binoculars. The rooftops now looked close enough to reach out and touch. One of the houses had been burned out, leaving a brick shell. Bizarrely, a pair of horses swam along a flooded avenue. On another roof someone had tied a white bed sheet flat across the tiles. Written across it in black paint was one word: **HELP**.

In every one of those houses an individual or a whole family would have had to confront this disaster. They all would have had stories to tell of terror when they knew the society that had protected them all these years had vanished almost overnight and of how they struggled for survival.

259

If anything, right then, high above Doncaster's flooded suburbs, I felt a calm detachment. As if I was watching old news footage. The fact was: it had happened. There was no point in crying over spilt milk. We had to go forward. Survive. Create new lives.

Or die trying.

CHAPTER 59

'Careful, Rick. It's hot.'

Kate handed me a steaming plastic mug, then carefully stoppered the thermos.

'Thanks. How long now, Howard?'

'About another hour. You OK in the back?'

'Yeah, but I was just wondering when the stewardess would be bringing dinner round.'

Howard laughed. 'Help yourself to a mint.'

He handed back a tube.

'You certainly take care of your passengers.'

'Just wait until you see me land this thing. You might prefer walking back.'

'I'll risk it. I don't think you'd get far on foot down there.'

Kate pointed down through the window. 'Grantham,' she said, 'or at least what's left of it.'

I looked down. The railway line ran along the western edge of the town, the rails dull and rusted now. I saw the station. But of the town of Grantham there was precious little. I remembered it as a pleasant-looking town of redbrick buildings with a cattle market and tall steepled church. Now where Grantham once stood was a hole.

Well, a more precise description would be a crater.

'A blowout of subterranean gas.' Kate took the binoculars back to take a closer look. 'That crater must cover the area of a couple of football fields.'

'Hell.' I shook my head. 'It must have gone up like a hydrogen bomb. Have you seen all the houses? They're wrecked.'

Most of Grantham had been flattened by the huge explosion: trees all lay in the same direction as though someone had painstakingly felled them so that they would point away from the epicentre. Even from this altitude I could see that the force of the blast had cleanly shorn away the branches and bark leaving the trunks like so many white matchsticks. The crater itself, occupying the position where the Isaac Newton shopping centre once stood, was a neat circle, with steep dirt sides running down to where water had pooled at the bottom. Already the earth slopes were turning green where plant life relentlessly counter-attacked. No doubt in five years or so if I was to overfly the area again – if I was still alive – I'd see nothing but a green expanse where plants had overgrown the shattered town. And in the middle of that greenery would be the crater with a pond in the bottom, probably populated by frogs and ducks.

That was if this stupid frigging planet hadn't gone completely incandescent in that time.

We flew steadily south. The sun shone bright in the sky.

'I've not seen any traffic on the roads,' I said, 'Or even any people walking.'

'Nor me,' Kate said.

'It's the altitude.' Howard pushed the sunglasses up the bridge of his nose. 'You'd see people if we flew low enough.'

'There's Peterborough.' Kate pointed. 'It looks as if someone's not been careful when they've been playing with matches.'

Most of the town had gone up in flames. Whether from the effects of a local hotspot beneath the ground, deliberate arson or common-or-garden accident you couldn't tell. Most of the buildings in the town centre were blackened by fire. With no fire service in existence flames would have spread unchecked.

Near the railway station a high-speed Intercity passenger train had jumped off the tracks. Carriages lay jumbled like child's toys alongside the railway line where it crossed the river. The locomotive itself had crashed down onto a block of once-elegant waterside apartments, smashing through walls and tearing through floors.

Again, all I could feel was that cool, virtually Olympian detachment. Perhaps that was part of the survival mechanism, too. Maybe you would go insane if you couldn't stop yourself constantly imagining what it would really be like when that loco came smashing through your bedroom wall. Or hearing the crash, then walking outside to see dozens of people spilled out from the rail carriages to lie broken and bloody on the ground.

As we flew on I began to feel that mixture of nervousness and excitement increase. The rain forest's worth of butterflies fluttered

261

madly in my stomach. In the distance, through the haze, I could just make out the first high-rise blocks of London. Just a few months ago it had been one of the six largest cities in the world, home to more than six million people. How many of those millions had survived? Howard had told us that the low-lying areas had been flooded.

Now he was taking us into that vast tract of concrete, brick and stone buildings that clung to the south-eastern part of England like some monstrous scab.

'Now comes the tricky part,' Howard said 'Finding the island.'

'What should we look out for?'

'It's not far from Hampstead. That's high ground so the roads will be clear of any water. Once I find those I can find the place. The island itself is a figure eight shape. Basically it's one island that's split in two by a railway cutting.'

'I take it this wasn't an island until a few weeks ago?'

'That's right. I don't know what happened to the River Thames downstream, but it's been blocked, either by land upheavals or subterranean explosions. The whole river's backing up.'

'So the island might have been covered since the last time you were here?'

Howard shook his head. 'My guess is the Thames has found a new outlet to the sea. The water levels seem to have stabilized. But it's no longer tidal. Ah, damn. I think I missed it. Rick?'

'Yeah?'

'Just look back. Can you see two tower blocks with a white church steeple in between?'

'Got it. Straight behind us.'

'Good. I just need to circle to the right. There to the left is Hampstead. Now . . . just ahead. There's Camden. Well, what you can actually see of it above the flood water.'

'Now that does look Biblical,' I said. 'London beneath the Flood.'

'My God.' Kate's voice sounded small. 'All those people . . . all those poor people.'

'Right, ladies and gentlemen. Please extinguish all cigarettes, put your seats in the upright position. And you might wish to close your eyes. This airport's a bit on the small side.'

'Airport?'

'OK, so it's a football field.' He shot us a grim smile. 'At least it's hard and it's flat and it might just be long enough. Eyes shut? Here goes.'

CHAPTER 60

SPARKY'S ISLAND. PRIVATE. KEEP OFF.
That's what Kate Robinson in a lighter moment chalked on a wall that faced outwards across the new lake created by the mother and grandmother of all floods. It was broken only by lamp posts poking their glass heads above the waters, house roofs, treetops (now dead and looking bone-dry).

We'd been there eight hours. Howard Sparkman hadn't even turned off the engine. We'd unloaded our supplies, sleeping-bags, tents, rifles, then he'd taxied to one end of the football field, turned the plane and taken off, circling the island once before disappearing north back to Fountains Moor. And right then Fountains Moor seemed so remote it could have been on one of the remoter planets on the edge of the Solar System.

'Welcome to Holiday Island,' Kate had said, shouldering her backpack.

'As long as the natives are friendly.'

'Don't count on it.'

'OK, shall we explore?'

It didn't take long. The figure eight shaped island covered only a few acres. On one half of the island, the lowest-lying part, were a couple of warehouses. These must have been just part of an industrial estate, the rest of which now lay largely submerged. At least the food warehouse was still high and dry, and was, as Howard had promised, still untouched. We walked round it, mouths open in awe. Stacked there were canned foods by the ton. Sometimes we just had to stop and run our hands wonderingly over cases of canned chicken pies, or sweetcorn, or ratatouille or corned beef.

Kate and I left the warehouse on a high.

'It'll last months!'

'Certainly all winter.' Kate looked close to skipping. The rifle jiggled on her back as she walked.

'Could you believe all that food? There must be a hundred thousand cans.'

'More.'

'Old Howard certainly dropped lucky there.'

'Deserves a knighthood.'

'At the very least.'

She grinned. 'I know, we'll name the island after him.'

'All right, then. Sparky's Island.'

So that's how Kate came to chalk the notice on the wall that overlooked a drowned, dead London.

As Howard had said, we reached the other half of the island via a footbridge. Beneath us the flooded railway cutting ran as straight as a canal. A train lay at the bottom with waves lapping gently across the carriage roofs. At the far side of the footbridge an exercise bicycle stood incongruously in the middle of the path. A little further on a Rolls-Royce, painted a delicate powder blue, had been abandoned on a dirt track that ended in a clump of trees. In the other direction, the track now led down to disappear beneath the lake of scummy, black water.

Kate walked up to the Rolls-Royce and opened the door. 'Ah, someone's been thoughtful?'

'What is it?'

'They've left us a welcome grocery pack.' She lifted out a carrier bag and looked inside. 'One tin of oysters, two jars of caviar and three bottles of champagne.'

The islands were small enough to search in less than an hour. We found no people. No live ones, that was. On the second island, which rose like a small hill from the water, there were half a dozen six-bedroom houses. A real millionaires' row, with BMWs and Mercedes parked on the long U-shaped driveways. A couple of the houses had swimming pools – now sludged green with algae. There were sun terraces with barbecues, double garages, greenhouses (full of dead plants that had turned yellow and dry as paper). In one garden a dozen cats prowled the branches of a tree. They hissed furiously when we got close.

All the houses were locked.

'It looks as if the owners had time to leave in an orderly way at least,' Kate said, peering in through a kitchen window. 'Everything's tidy.'

I held out my hands. 'Well . . . take your pick, Miss Robinson.'

She raised her eyebrows.

'There's no point in camping out. We'll take a house.'

We stood in the middle of the kitchen.

'It's beautiful,' Kate said, she stood on tip-toe and stretched like a cat, as if the kitchen actually gave off some sensuous vibrations that stimulated every square centimetre of her skin. 'Just look at the cooker. It's an Aga. Look, it burns wood. We can cook on it.' Her face lit up. Again she stretched, arching that beautiful long back, her green eyes shining with sheer pleasure.

'Well, you know what we have to do in a situation like this?' I ran my finger across the tiled work tops.

'And that is?'

'Play house!'

Again we experienced that giddy rush. We had all that food in the warehouse. We had a millionaire's house. Now we were like children left home alone. After months of sleeping in tents here was a real house, with real furniture. You can't imagine the pleasure of actually sitting on a cushioned sofa, or taking off your shoes and walking on soft carpets. We ran through the house shouting to each other.

'Rick!'

'You can see Canary Wharf from this window!'

'There's the dome of St Paul's!'

'Kate, come and look at this!'

'No, you come and look at this first! Look at the size of this bathroom.'

'Jesus, look at the size of the bath!'

'You could share that one with a friend – and his grandparents.' She gave me a wink that sent shivers up my spine.

We went through the house again, admiring bedrooms, opening wardrobes and cupboards full of stylish clothes. There were expensive perfumes on the dressing table.

'Who do you think the house belonged to?'

'Somebody who got rich quick. It all looks new,' I said. 'Perhaps a bank robber who got lucky.'

'Or a lottery winner.' She sighed. 'Well, it's all ours now – if we want it.'

'Do you feel guilty?' I asked her, watching her green eyes momentarily sadden.

'No. We've got to take what we need now. It doesn't matter where it comes from.'

'Do you fancy taking a glass of champagne with me, then?'

Her delighted smile returned. 'Why not?'

'I can't promise it will be chilled enough yet.'

'Who cares. Come on, we've earned it.'

That afternoon quickly became a blur as we drank glass after glass of champagne in the living room. The sun shone through the windows. We lay on two matching sofas that stood opposite each other across a glass coffee table on which there was a single issue of *Vogue* and a life-size wood carving of a hand holding a lemon between finger and thumb.

We were on an adrenalin buzz as much as anything. In just a few hours we'd safely completed a journey that I'd dreaded making; we'd found the warehouse intact and crammed with food. The islands were uninhabited and we felt secure, surrounded by a barrier of flood water.

We clinked glasses together every sixty seconds or so. 'Cheers!' or 'Chin-chin.' Every few minutes I'd pop a cork from another bottle, then we'd down that, too.

On the third bottle the cork shot out like a missile, champagne spraying up into my face.

Kate laughed. 'You can't waste that!'

I stood there dripping and laughing. 'Pass me your glass and I'll wring my hair into it.'

'Ugh! Disgusting pig.'

She stood up and began to mop my face with a handful of tissues.

Suddenly she said, 'I wonder what champagne tastes like at body temperature.' Lightly she ran her tongue across my cheek. 'Yum, yum.' She breathed the words into my ear.

At that moment my senses were full of Kate. I turned my head to look straight into her green almond-shaped eyes. She raised a finger to my eyebrow and lightly, so lightly wiped away a droplet of champagne. I smelt the champagne, I smelt her own scent of soap. Before I knew it my hand was buried deep into her hair. I heard her gasp slightly. This rush of emotion had taken her by surprise too.

'Rick . . . this is stupid.'

'Stupid?'

'I feel stupid. I'm so scared of you and I don't know why.'

'Scared of me? There's nothing to be scared about.'

'That's what's so stupid. I just feel so terrified.'

'There's no need.'

'Will you do me a favour, please?'

'Just ask.'

'Hold me. Tightly, please.'

'This OK?'

'Yes. Oh, I've needed this. All this madness and people dying and being afraid all the time. You need to be close be someone.'

She put her arms round my waist and hugged me to her. My heart was beating hard. She was beautiful. I wanted to crush her to me, to kiss those wonderful lips but I held back. Right then she wanted human closeness. This wasn't sexual – not yet, anyway. I didn't know where it would go. But Kate was filling my body with such a powerful excitement it felt as if I'd been injected with a drug. I could feel a prickling sensation spread through every vein and artery in my body. I felt my heart pump harder.

She pressed her long body against mine. It trembled.

Then I kissed her full on the mouth. She turned her head. At first I thought she'd turned away, not wanting me to kiss her, but suddenly she lifted her face to mine and put her hands behind my head, holding it still as she kissed me with a passion that bordered on the savage.

Still kissing we made it to the sofa. I was throbbing so hard I thought I'd burst.

Beneath me Kate looked up into my eyes. I felt my heart surge every time she made eye contact. With one hand she unclipped her hair, freeing it so it fanned out behind her across the sofa cushion. Her breathing came in gusts against my throat.

Then I felt her stiffen.

Had I gone too far? Was she having second thoughts?

Damn . . .

But I saw she was looking back over my shoulder, her eyes full of shock.

I looked back.

Where they'd come from I didn't know.

But standing in a long line from one end of the room to the other was the weirdest bunch of people I'd ever seen.

CHAPTER 61

A short man wearing a leather cowboy hat and with long hair tied back in a pony tail and tears tattooed on one cheek prodded me with the muzzle of a rifle. 'Don't stop now,' he said in a whispery voice. 'It was just starting to get interesting.'

I heard Kate breathe sharply in. Poor kid was terrified. She knew what might happen to her in the next few minutes.

There must have been ten of them, all heavily armed with shotguns, rifles, sub-machine guns. All had tattoos around their lips and eyes. Faces were scarred. Hair long and either woven into plaits or pony tails. They all had strips of what looked like silk in brilliant reds and oranges tied to their arms and legs. These decorations hung down in long strips. They made a papery rustle every time they moved.

I noticed a couple of women in the group. They were hard-faced, somehow pinched-looking as if they'd been ill or half-starved.

The man in the cowboy hat grinned. The grin exposed a mouthful of teeth that were black and rotting into misshapen splinters.

'Guess what, folks?' he said, grinning his bad-teeth grin.

'What?' I asked, feeling cold.

'You're coming with us.'

'Look, we just came to find some food for—'

'Ah, ah.' He wagged a finger. 'You're both coming with us.'

'Where?'

'Paradise.'

Kate said, 'Let us go . . . please.'

'We could do. Couldn't we? But first you'd have to pay rental on this place. In advance.'

My blood turned cold.

'What have we got that's any use to you?' Kate asked.

I saw the men looking Kate up and down, licking their lips. And that cold feeling spread.

I heard the tremor in her voice as she said as coolly as she could. 'If that's what you want. OK. But just one at a time – please.'

The two hard-faced girls in the group exchanged amused smiles.

The man in the cowboy hat shook his head. 'You're too valuable for that. We need you for the show.'

I shook my head. If only I'd kept one of the handguns with me. I guessed it would be better to go down shooting rather than suffering whatever this bunch of weirdoes had planned for us.

'Come on.' The man pointed the rifle at us. 'We can't wait all day, especially when we've a show to stage.'

Tortured. Raped.

Slowly, slowly tortured until the pain overwhelms. You puke. Bite your tongue until it bleeds.

Fingers cut off.

Metal bars heated in a fire until they glow, then pressed against my testicles, into Kate's face and breasts, or forced red hot into both our anuses.

You hear screaming. But you don't know if it's her screaming. Or whether I'm screaming. You're lost in a whole universe of pain.

Kate Robinson hung naked from a tree. Beaten with leather belts until her skin bleeds. Her hair soaked in lighter fuel. A lighted match.

Then . . .

Christ.

Take your pick. They might do part of that. All of that. They might just put a bullet in our heads. But I didn't think so. We had entertainment value. You could bet whatever they did it would be milked for all that it was worth. We weren't going to die quickly.

'Sit there. On the bench by the barbecue. Ah! Hands on heads . . . *please*.'

We'd been marched out into the garden. Kate and I sat side by side on the bench set in the centre of the stone-flagged patio.

The weirdoes stood grinning at us, obviously pleased by their catch. I could hear Kate breathing in frightened shallow gasps. Christ, I couldn't blame her. They would do something bad to her. And she knew it.

A breeze had sprung up now. The red and orange silk ribbons tied around their arms and legs fluttered straight out in the breeze like pennants.

Someone had already lit a fire on the lawn and was busily breaking chairs against a wall to feed the flames.

A thin man with pierced lips and a surly face drank from a bottle of vodka. He passed it on to the two women, their short spiky hair bleached a nicotine yellow. As they took turns drinking from the bottle, they amused themselves with a conversation that must have concerned me because they kept shooting me looks with their little rat eyes, then laughing.

Once the shock of being captured had passed what I actually felt was anger. I was in their power: they could do what they liked to me; they needn't fear any retribution; law and order and the prison service had gone the way of the dinosaur, as dead as could be. But I actually felt anger. I began to talk in a stroppy way.

'What are you going to do to us?'

'We'll think of something,' the man in the cowboy hat said.

'Let us go.'

'Why should we do that?'

'Because we've done nothing to harm you.'

'You're on our island.'

'You don't live here.'

'No?'

'No.'

'How do you know that, Sherlock Holmes?'

'It's too clean. You weirdoes would have covered the place in shit by this time.'

'Rick—' began Kate, shocked.

'Oh, Rick is it?' The cowboy rested a booted foot complete with spurs on the bench beside me. 'Rick the prick? Or Rick the dick?'

'Rick Kennedy. We're from Leeds. We came looking for food.'

'Well, you might have been looking for food but what you did find was me. Cowboy's the name, and I'm trouble with a capital T.'

'My name's Kate Robinson.' She forced a pleasant smile. 'Please. We've done no harm.'

'So.' Cowboy lit a cigarette, then held the still burning match to her lips. 'So, you want to go home?'

She forced that smile again, blew out the match. 'Please. We're sorry if we . . . trespassed.'

Cowboy looked round at the others. They were watching, grins all over their tattooed faces.

'I take it,' he said, then pulled deeply on the cigarette, 'I take it you want to live?'

'Yes.'

'But why?'

'Why do you?' I said, stroppy.

'Call it a mission,' he said. 'In twenty-four hours you two will be dead. I will be sparing you all that pain and suffering of trying to survive in the terrible, terrible place this world has become.'

'Thanks for the thought,' I snapped. 'We're happy to take that risk.'

'You really think you're going to survive more than a couple of years? Where you going to get food from? The ground's getting hotter and hotter. Soon you're going to have to keep running to stop your feet getting burnt.'

'As I said, we'll risk it,' I told him. 'Let us go. You'll never see us again.'

'No can do.' Cowboy blew out cigarette smoke through his nose. 'You belong to us now.'

'You don't have to do this.' Kate kept her voice low, calm. 'You could just let us go.'

'May I remind you, sweetheart, that these days there is no TV and the ballet, opera and theatre have been postponed forever. We need entertainment.'

'Fucking lunatics.' I glared at him. But with two gun barrels poking into my back what could I do?

'Okey-dokey.' Cowboy turned to the rest of his gang. 'What are we going to do to these fine people?'

CHAPTER 62

The bastards were actually going to stand there on the patio of that millionaire's house, with the barbecue, the swimming pool, the children's climbing frame, pink roses climbing up the trellising on the wall, and they were going to discuss how they were going to torture us to death.

Someone had turned on a portable CD player. Alice Cooper's *School's Out* blasted across the garden. Through the trees I could see the silver sparkle of floodwaters. I thought about Stephen. He'd probably never know what happened to me. On some return flight Howard Sparkman would just find us simply gone.

Shit.

Shit! Shit! Shit!

I wasn't going to let these freaks play sadist with me.

There had to be a way out of this.

Or there had to be a way I could take some of the bastards with me.

I tried to look calm, even resigned to my fate as they shouted ideas above the music.

'This is gonna be *soooo-w* much fun!' cried a tall guy. White scars radiated from his lips, making it look as if his mouth lay at the centre of an asterisk, like so:*. 'That girl's a real peach!'

'Yeah,' said another of the psychos. 'Who gets first shove, Cowboy?'

'I'm the most senior,' Cowboy replied, 'I do.'

'Most senior?'

'Yep, I'm most senior today.'

'Why not save her for the boss, then?'

'Because he's not here, is he?'

'Maybe you should wait?'

'It's not fair on the rest, Cowboy,' said the rat-faced girl. 'Why don't you let them have a chance to have first go with her?'

'Well, I'm not putting it in after old spaghetti face's been in there.'

'Who are you calling spaghetti face? Fucking rot breath.'

'You could all toss for her,' the rat-faced girl said. Laughter.

'OK, OK,' Cowboy grinned. 'Come on, then. What we going to do with her, then?'

'What y' think? Take her to the Savoy for tea and fairy cakes? I'm going to fuck her till she squeals like a pig with its nuts on fire.'

I kept my mouth shut and my eyes dead-looking. Let the bastards think I'd given up the ghost.

'Put her in an oil drum with a dozen rats.'

'We've already done that.'

'And the bitch went and killed the rats.'

'Until we taped her hands together.'

'She bit the rats.'

'Yeah . . . at first.'

'Then they bit her.'

'Well, I'm not catching no fucking rats again.'

They bickered like schoolkids. Chipping in ideas. Pushing each other. A couple of them had got hold of children's bikes and were riding them up and down the garden path shouting *'TO INFINITY – AND BEYOND!'*

The weirdo with scars radiating from his lips like daisy petals was reluctant to let his idea go. 'The oil drum's cool.'

'Tesco, I'm not catching no fucking rats, no fucking way. Fuckers bit my fingers.'

'I'll catch the rats, if you're too shit-scared, Dosser.'

'Dosser fwightened of rats. Dosser fwightened of mice and cweepy cwallies,' chorused the rat-faced girls.

'But when she was in the oil drum. And the rats started to bite?'

'Can you remember what the bitch was shouting?'

They all started to chant: 'You'll go to jail. You'll go to jail, you'll go to jail.' They aped a woman's hysterical scream, then started laughing.

The one called Tesco grinned. 'I'll find an oil drum.'

'Oil drums, oil drums . . . it's always the oil drums with you, Tesco. Can't you think of anything that doesn't involve oil drums? Find a kitten, what shall we do with it? Find an oil drum, says Tesco.'

'OK, gobshite. A wardrobe. Bring a wardrobe out of the bedroom, lock her in it, then set the twat on fire.'

'Hell's bells. A wardrobe's only like a fucking oil drum.'

'Why you obsessed with locking people in enclosed spaces?'

'I like to see their faces,' one of the girls complained. 'When they're locked up you can't see their expressions.'

'Sadist.'

'Yeah, I'm a sadist – so what?'

'Nail them to the garage doors.'

'Boo-rrring!'

'Acid?'

'Done that.'

'Make them swallow poison.'

'Takes too long.'

'Not enough blood!'

'Get two cars. Handcuff one hand to the bumper of one car, then handcuff the other hand to the other car—'

'And rip 'em in two?'

'Sounds promising.'

'I know.' Cowboy's face lit up as inspiration struck. 'I know, we'll make one of them torture the other.'

'Yeah, great!'

'Brilliant!'

There were cowboy whoops and cheers, some slapped him on the back.

'Who's going to do the torturing?'

'Make her hurt him.'

'How?'

'And, Tesco, if you mention oil drums again, so help me I'll weld you inside one and drop it in the lake.'

I heard Kate give a low groan. 'Oh God, no, no.'

I wanted to comfort her as we sat there side by side on the bench. I wanted to tell her not to worry. But what the hell could I do? Just what the hell could I do?

CHAPTER 63

'Tape his hands and feet.' Cowboy threw a roll of gaffer tape to one of the girls. Grinning, she stepped forward.

'Pray,' she said.

I felt the muzzle of a gun dig sharply between my shoulder blades. I put my hands together as if in prayer.

She found the end of the tape on the roll and pulled. The tape unravelled with a burring sound. Then she began to tape my hands and wrists together.

Dosser said, 'Tape him together at the elbows, too.'

She wore a leather jacket. Every so often she'd tease the zip down to show she was wearing nothing underneath. Her breasts were covered with freckles; they gave a little wobble when she moved. She caught my eye and grinned.

I kept my face dead.

Expressionless.

We had perhaps ten minutes to get out of this shit hole. Already Tesco had found a tool kit and was experimenting with a hand drill, boring holes into a fence post. The grin on his face was nothing less than lunatic.

I looked round. The weirdoes were still passing the vodka bottle round, the breeze wafting out their fluttering strips of red and orange silk ribbons. Seagulls overflew the house. A cat sneaked through the long grass on the lawn that hadn't seen a mower in months. There must be something I can use, I told myself fiercely. Come on, think, think!

The girl still worked on binding me, wrapping the brown plastic tape around and around my wrists and hands. She made eyes at me and jiggled her freckled breasts in front of my eyes. One of the men leaned over my shoulder and pinched her nipple.

'Ow . . . Mental. You can look but don't touch.'

'Mental like titties.'

'Mental can fuck off.'

'Mental kiss.'

'No, Mental can fuck off, I said.'

I heard him begin to breathe excitedly behind me. I even felt his stinking hot breath on the back of my neck.

The girl complained to Cowboy. 'Mental's getting a hard-on again. Can't you something with him?'

'Don't look at us, dearie,' Tesco queened, hand on hip.

One of the men said, 'Tutts, can't you take him somewhere quiet and . . . relieve him.'

The girl scowled as she bit through the tape. 'No way. He nearly broke my back last time he tried.' She smoothed the tape down around my wrist, allowing her fingers to stroke up over mine. When we spoke our heads were close enough not to be overheard. The sound of Alice Cooper ripping from the speakers made sure of that. 'Mmm . . .' she purred, 'you'd be nice and gentle with me, wouldn't you?'

I swallowed. 'I don't think I'll be around long enough for you to find out.'

'I guess not.' She sighed. 'Pity. You've got lovely eyes.'

'What's your name?'

She looked at me, as if caught off guard by my interest. 'Tutts . . .' she said softly. 'Just Tutts.'

'Where you from, Tutts?'

'Originally?'

I nodded, keeping eye contact while frantically trying to pluck some idea out of the ether to spring us from all this.

'Originally, I'm from shop doorways . . . and from under railway bridges, and cardboard boxes. We all are.'

'You were homeless?'

She nodded. 'And so are you now.'

'That's right, Tutts. But I want to live.'

'And so does your girlfriend.'

'She's not my girlfriend.'

Again she shot me a strange look. Perhaps it was the sound of my voice as much as anything. But she seemed to soften. The hard, cruel look left her eye.

'You look so clean,' she said. 'You wouldn't have looked twice at me six months ago.'

'Wouldn't I?'

'No.' Her eyes were suddenly sad. 'I'd have been laid there in my sleeping-bag in Oxford Street and you'd have stepped right over me. Just like the rest. We were a sub-species to people like you.'

'Would you like to see me get hurt?'

Now a confusion crept into her eyes. 'I . . . I'm not bothered.'

'No?'

'They'll treat you like you treated us. A sub-species.'

'Did I ever do anything to hurt you?'

'No, but you'd be like the rest. We're better off now the world's decided to get itself bent.'

'You know, if we went somewhere quiet we could have a really good conversation.' I smiled. 'You know we would.'

'Hey, Tutts,' Cowboy Man shouted. 'Have you finished taping up baby face yet?'

'Give me a minute,' she snapped. 'I'm not fucking greased lightning, you know!' Her eyes blazed such hostility at Cowboy that I felt a small victory. I hated oozing this smoothie talk but I pushed on hard. 'Do they treat you well here?'

'Better than when I was on the street? Yeah. I eat. I sleep somewhere dry.'

'You could come back with us. We'd treat you well.'

She looked up. Now she seemed childlike and trusting. 'How would we get – ow, Mental. I've told you fucking before. Leave my fucking tits alone.'

She rocked back into a crouching position, her chest heaving with anger; her face flushed red.

'Ha-ha! Mental touch tittie.'

'Mental can fuck off.'

Cowboy walked across, laughing. 'Mental goes wild when he gets turned on.'

'Does he now?' I heard Kate murmur.

With a shock I realized she was going to do something.

'Kate—'

She stood up and pulled the T-shirt up over her head. I heard the guttural gasp behind me. Her long back arched as she slipped the T-shirt off. Her breasts looked perfect. The nipples rose into points.

'Go on, Mental,' Kate said. 'You touch mine if you want to.'

'Aw fuck!' Cowboy Man groaned. 'Aw, fuck, fuck . . . fuck!'

Mental, a middle-aged man built like a grizzly, with a shaggy backwoods beard and a swastika tattooed on his forehead, lunged forward, his huge hands clamping round Kate's breasts.

'Ah, yes! I'm all yours, Mental. I'm all yours; come on, do what you want.'

Cowboy yelled. 'Grab him! No . . . hit him with something. I want her in one piece tonight. I don't want his pawprints all over her.'

I was knocked sideways as the rest of the gang dived on Mental. He was a roaring bull of a man. It looked as if it'd take a bulldozer to knock him off his feet.

I saw Kate slip out from under the mass of kicking arms and legs. People shouted orders at each other. No one listened.

Tutts grabbed hold of me. As she did so, Kate shoulder-charged her, knocking her flat on the patio. Her face hit the stone slab with the sound of a loud slap. She screwed shut her eyes in pain.

'Come on, Rick.' Kate hissed. 'Move . . . *move!*'

I moved. My arms were still taped in front of me. But, Christ and all our fathers, I really moved.

Kate ran in front of me, her long torso twisting as she ran, showing her ribs and smooth skin gleaming in the afternoon sunlight.

We crashed through the bushes at the edge of the garden. There was shouting. Different kind of shouts now. They'd realized we'd run for it.

'Come on! They're following!' Kate shouted.

I ran, trying to twist out of the sticky tape. Christ, it was tough plastic.

'Try and get to the other island,' I panted. 'Across the footbridge.'

'No. We need to get off the island.' She pulled the T-shirt back on as she ran.

'They must have come here by boat. We'll have to try and find it.'

We ran on, pushing everything into running. This was our one chance. They wouldn't screw up twice. Trees blurred by me.

I shot a glance back. They were running hard behind us.

'They're going to start shooting,' she panted.

'No, they're not. They want us alive.'

'And we know why they want us alive.'

We ran faster, feet pounding the path through the wood.

Shit.

Water.

Suddenly we were at the water's edge; London lake stretched in front of us further than the eye could see.

'Swim!'

She looked horrified. 'In that? Where to? Rick, there's nothing out there. *Nothing*.'

'We'll try this way. If we see anything we can reach we'll have to risk it.'

'Rick . . . Rick . . . I'm not a strong swimmer. I could only manage a couple of lengths at the best of times.'

'Don't worry. We're going to come through this.' I gave her a grim smile. 'Come on. Stick to the bushes.'

Using my teeth, I managed to split the plastic tape binding my hands.

We ran out of the bushes onto the track where we'd found the Rolls-Royce with the carrier bag of champagne and canned sea food.

Sure enough to our right up the track sat the blue Rolls, its big radiator grille gleaming in the setting sun.

To our left the track ran down into the water.

We stopped, listening.

'Damn,' Kate hissed. 'They're all around us.'

I could hear them calling, clapping, whistling, as if they were trying to spook game birds into the air.

'This way.' I started to run into the bushes fringing the lake. 'Damn.'

I nearly ran into them. Three men, including Mental, stood waiting for us. He carried a machete. Blood streaked his forehead where they'd beaten him.

'Back.'

'What is it?'

'Back the other way. They're coming through the bushes.'

We tried to retrace our steps. But I saw Tutts and two men working their way along the bank. All three were armed with rifles.

278

Shit.

There was one route left.

We ran up the track, past the Rolls-Royce.

Damn, damn, damn.

Kate groaned. 'No . . . no, they've got us.'

'No, they haven't,' I said.

'Rick there's nowhere else to run. We're cornered.'

'The car. Get into the car!'

'What?'

'Quick. Into the car!'

CHAPTER 64

Kate was astounded. Her green eyes locked onto mine in disbelief as she repeated: '*The car?*'

'Get in, please Kate – *now*.'

'Rick, that's crazy, we'd—'

'I know it's crazy. We've got to do the crazy if we want to live.'

I opened the driver's door, forced her roughly in.

'Rick. Rick! The track doesn't go anywhere.'

'Yes, it does.'

'You haven't got the ignition keys.'

'Don't need them.'

I pushed her all the way into the passenger seat.

The car faced downhill. In front of us a piece of track a hundred paces long. Beyond that nothing but water with the tips of telegraph poles and street lights poking through. In the rearview I could see Cowboy, Tesco and the rest start to walk down toward the car. They were smiling at each other, looking smug. They'd caught us and they knew it.

At least, they thought they had.

'Rick. What are you going to do?'

'Just give me a moment. Hand brake off. There. Hell. Why aren't we moving?'

'Rick, they're getting closer.'

'Damn, damn. Why aren't we moving?'

Kate laughed in disbelief. 'Rick, there's no road, there's no keys.'

She laughed again but it sounded closer to weeping. She thought I'd flipped.

In front of us, Mental and the other two stood on the track. Mental's face, still awash with blood, was expressionless. The other two grinned and exchanged amused glances. *What the fuck was the madman going to do in the car? Press the big red button on the dashboard in the hope the vertical takeoff jets blast him up into the sky and back home in time for supper?*

That's exactly what they were thinking. They even laughed out loud.

Meanwhile, I'd hit some fundamental flaw in my plan.

'The car. It's not moving.'

Kate buried her face in her hands; she was shaking her head, her shoulders trembled.

The gang of psychos were maybe twenty paces away by now. I said, 'Lock your door.' Kate obeyed, numb-looking now. 'Window up?'

She nodded. Then shrugged helplessly. She thought I'd completely lost it.

'Come on, car, move! Move!'

She shook her head. Ahead on the track, Mental and the other two were maybe fifteen paces away.

I jiggled the steering wheel. The steering lock snapped on. Not that it mattered. I just needed the car to move. Why wouldn't it—'

Gotcha!

'It's still in gear! It needs to be in neutral!'

Kate shook her head, dazed.

I slapped the gearstick into neutral.

The car moved.

Slowly, slowly, slowly . . .

One centimetre. Then two centimetres. Three centimetres. Four, five, six.

I heard the Rolls-Royce's big tyres crackle over pebbles and twigs.

'Rick! You are mad!' she shouted. 'You'll kill us.'

'Yeah! So what? Want to be tortured to death over the next couple of days?'

'But you can't – Oh, God, they're trying to get in.'

Cowboy and Tesco had caught up with the car as it rolled forward down the track. They tried the handles, shouting, banging on the windows.

The car picked up speed, freewheeling down towards the lake.

'Jesus-Jesus . . .'

'Kate. I'm only doing my best. I don't want to see them hurt you.'

She looked up, gave a faint smile, then kissed me on the cheek. 'Just hold me,' she whispered, composed now. 'Whatever happens. Just hold me. Please.'

I put my arm round her. She buried her face into my neck. I kissed her on the head.

In front of us stood Mental. He held out his thick arms. He looked as if he'd stop the car dead in its tracks as it rolled along the track. Gravity had got us now. The car bumped faster over fallen branches. The speedo needle crept past the ten mark.

Whatever happened, we weren't going back. If there was a God we were in His hands now.

There was a terrific thump.

Mental had jumped onto the bonnet. He crouched there, hammering the windscreen with that meaty fist of his.

The rest of the gang still ran at the side of the car. They shouted. Their fists rained blows down onto the windows. Why didn't they use their guns? My guess is they were too surprised by my bizarre escape plan. To freewheel a car along a road to nowhere?

I looked forward. I couldn't see track anymore, it had run out. There was only that expanse of water. Black and evil-looking.

'Hold on, Kate,' I whispered. Christ, I couldn't believe how calm I sounded. I actually believed this might work.

Rick. For Godsake's what might work? I asked myself. You haven't thought this through. You only wanted to get off this island. You don't know what'll happen next.

Suddenly the rumbling stopped. The shouting stopped. The hammering stopped.

In fact, it went eerily quiet the moment the car hit the lake. The Rolls-Royce's thick bodywork screened out most of the sound of the car surging from dry land into water.

'Rick, what're you doing?'

'I'm gambling this car has air conditioning. If you turn off the vents it just might . . . there.'

The car still moved but there was no sound now. It glided away from the island in a way that was eerily smooth.

There was a sudden thump on the glass. Mental glared in at us, still crouched on the bonnet.

'Get off, you idiot,' I hissed. 'Get off. Swim for it.'

But he clung on there. He looked like Charles Manson with the thick beard and psychotic stare. The blood had dried, half covering the swastika on his forehead.

'Rick . . . Rick. We're sinking.'

'We might be all right. People assume cars always sink in water. But you see news footage of floods and sometimes cars float like corks.'

'*Sometimes?*'

'With the cabin and fuel tank . . . they act like flotation chambers.'

'It's tilting forward. It's going down nose first.'

'It's that monster on the front. The extra weight's pulling it down.'

'Why doesn't he swim for it?'

'Kate. Climb in the back. It might shift the centre of balance.'

I was sweating hard now. The car was making me claustrophobic. I couldn't still believe I'd just driven the car into God knows how many kilometres of flood water in the hope this chunk of steel could float like a boat.

The car tilted steeply, nose downward. Through the windows I could see the water rippling around us. Thirty metres away I saw the banks of the island. There was no sign of the bunch of psychos who'd driven us to this.

I followed Kate into the back seat. My foot caught the car's tape player. Instantly music filled the car. A slow, sweet piece with lilting violins.

Damn.

I looked back. Water was finding its way in through the rubber door seals in a slow but steady trickle. It started to pool around the foot pedals on the floor.

On the bonnet Mental hung onto the wipers. One snapped away. He clung to the other one; his eyes burned with a mad intensity through the glass at me.

'Swim!' I shouted. 'Swim back to the island.'

Now water covered the bonnet to reach the windscreen. It was like looking into a fishtank with a couple of centimetres of scummy water in the bottom.

Mental began to shout but I couldn't make out individual words.

Kate did.

'Christ,' she said in flat voice. 'He can't swim.'

The car's nose dipped down further into the water. To prevent ourselves falling forward, we had to turn round in the back seat and brace our feet against the backs of the seats in front.

It must have made a surreal scene. Brilliant sunshine, blue skies. A vast lake of flood water broken by little islands, the tops of telegraph poles, street lights, roofs of houses. And there, floating in the middle of it all, a powder blue Rolls-Royce, its nose with the big chrome grille and flying lady mascot already under water. The back end of the car – boot, rear wheels, rear half of the passenger compartment – lifted out of the water. The rear tyres dripped water, smack, smack, smack onto the surface of the lake. Meanwhile, a madman crouched on the bonnet, screaming, pounding on the glass.

The water now came halfway up the windscreen. Mental slapped the toughened glass, sending up splashes of water.

By this time, I could actually see underwater through the partially submerged car windows. The colour of the water was black from particles of suspended sediment. But enough sunlight still beamed through the water for me to see a metre or so through the water. Mental's hands looked hugely magnified. I could even see the daggers tattooed on the backs of his fingers. He was shaking his head. Gasping, as the scummy water rushed into his mouth with every breath he took.

The car tilted more. Now we were crouching on the backs of the front seats as the car stood on its nose. And still the late-night orchestral lullaby came oozing, slickly smooth, through the speakers.

'Oh God, it's going down. It's going down,' Kate panted. She hung onto the back seat. Up through the back window I saw nothing but blue sky now.

A grating sound, metal on stone. A concrete lamppost passed by, scraping the car's paintwork. The glass lamp itself knocked dully against the car roof.

I could see less than an upper quarter of the lamp post. So how deep's the water? I wondered. Come on, Rick, how deep? Six metres, maybe.

The thumping sounded more panic-stricken as Mental belaboured the glass with his fists. I could hear his screams, loud but muffled by the car's thick steel shell.

Completely submerged now, he beat at the car in a mad thrash of bubbles.

Then the car sank.

CHAPTER 65

As quickly as that. The car went down, smoothly as a submarine.

Kate gasped.

I gritted my teeth.

It took no more than four seconds.

Then the car was falling down through the water toward the bed of the new lake. Bubbles, looking like chains of silver balls, sped by the windows. Instantly a *brrrr* filled the car, sounding as if a dozen electric motors had just spun into life somewhere in its steel shell – the sound generated by air escaping from a dozen different cavities in the doors, engine compartment and boot. Following that came heavier thuds as water slammed in to fill the void created by the exodus of air.

We glided down into utter darkness. The ride seemed to take forever.

Then, at last, with a thump that sent us flat out onto the backs of the front seat, we hit bottom.

'Rick – the water.'

'I know, I know. Don't panic, Kate. Please don't panic.'

She breathed deeply. 'I'm OK. But we must get out. We must!'

I looked round. It was almost dark now in the car. A little light filtered down through the water, creating flickering patterns of light on the richly upholstered interior. We were trapped in a pocket of air in the passenger compartment. For a few seconds we would be safe. Until the water oozed slowly in, filling the car, to drown—

Thump.

Mental still clung to the car.

I saw we'd come to rest, the car standing on its nose against a chain-link fence. Mental was sandwiched between car and fence.

The poor bastard was still alive. He pounded the windscreen with his fist as if we could open an airlock and let him in.

'Dear God, dear God.' Kate said under her breath. 'Poor man.'

'That poor man would have cheerfully killed us . . . Christ, how do we get out of this?'

I hit the switch on the Rolls-Royce's courtesy light. It came on but dimmed, then brightened. A second later it dimmed again. The battery wouldn't hold out long.

Water now oozed through the door seals. The dashboard, too, seemed to bleed that filthy flood water. It squirted through in jets. The river-water smell caught in the back of our throats. In a minute or two the water would reach the front seats. At this rate, the car itself would be full of water in less than ten minutes. Not that it mattered. By then the air would no longer be breathable anyway.

The music played on. Filling the car with the sounds of an orchestra whose members were probably all long dead.

And if I didn't do something soon we'd be joining them.

Kate breathed in those frightened little gasps again. I noticed that when she exhaled she blew out puffs of white vapour. The water engulfing the car chilled the interior until it felt as though we sat inside a refrigerator. Condensation misted the windows.

I shot a glance back at Mental. He hung motionless in the water now, eyes and mouth wide open – painfully wide. The beard and long hair floated around his head to form a dark halo.

As I watched, a dark object the size of my fist flitted in front of his face. A mark appeared on his cheek the size of a penny. Blood flowed out. Another shape buzzed in. The tip of his nose disappeared.

The rats had wasted no time finding fresh food.

Kate spoke calmly, but insistently, 'Rick . . . We've got . . . to get out . . . we're going to die in here.'

'I know. Perhaps . . . if we rocked the car we could free it?'

'OK. Let's try.'

'On the count of three. One, two, three.' We rocked backwards and forwards. The car moved. Metal scraped on metal with an eerie moan.

'Try again. Harder. One, two, three.' Again came the screech of metal against metal. Bubbles streamed by the window.

'No good,' Kate groaned. 'We're stuck.'

I crouched there on the front seat's back-rest, fist tapping my chin. Christ. We couldn't just sit here and drown. We'd got this far. There *must* be a way out.

The electric light in the roof flickered. The music became a dirge as the tape slowed.

Kate wiped the condensation from the window and looked out at what lay beneath the flood water.

'*My God*, Rick. Have you seen what's out there?'

'The rats? Ignore them.'

'Not rats.' She looked at me. 'People.'

I twisted round to face the window. 'People?' I rubbed at the glass. Stared out hard, trying by willpower alone to see through the black water.

Jesus.

A face.

I bounced back from the glass as if it had become electrified. The face stared in.

'Christ, what is it?' I felt panic crack through me. My scalp prickled.

The face. I'd never seen anything like it before.

It moved forward, staring into the car like we were specimens in a glass case.

Shit.

I found I was holding my breath. I was staring at the face. Not able to tear my eyes away as it moved slowly forward to the glass, bumped softly against it, then turned slowly, slowly away.

The strands of hair danced around its head. The eyes stared unblinking through the water.

Then that terrible face swung back, again slowly, smoothly rotating to stare in at us again. Beside me, Kate's whole body shook. The car seemed to shudder in sympathy, the metalwork groaning all the time.

The face stared in.

'Rick. Don't get any closer.'

Gingerly, I approached the window and looked back out at it.

She said, 'It's one of the Grey Men, isn't it? Do you see the colour of his face?'

I looked. My eyes were so wide they stung. The face *was* grey, its skin the texture of white bread, somehow spongy-looking; the whole face was pocked with holes.

'A drowned man.' I let out a sigh. 'That's all it is.' I looked past

286

him. Suspended there in water that was as murky as a black mist there were more of them. Standing upright, they turned round and around as if engaged in some eerie postmortem dance. The drowned men's arms waved sinuously in a way that was slow, serene, almost mesmerizing.

Hi, Rick Kennedy. Shame you never got to record the album. What're you going to do for the rest of eternity, then? Jesus gonna give you an electric Stratocaster guitar instead of a harp? Time to come out and play with us, Rick. Time to come out and kiss our cold, bloated lips. Time to feel our bloated hands holding yours. Come on out here, Ricky boy, the water's lovely.

Eat your heart out, Esther Williams. You can't swim as good as that. You can't . . . I felt a sudden desire to laugh savagely. To keep laughing until the build-up of carbon dioxide stamped consciousness from my brain. Until the toxic gas squeezed my heart so hard it stopped beating.

I looked at Kate. She was breathing hard, panting as if she'd run a marathon; clouds of white vapour spurted from her nostrils.

The air had turned poisonous. We'd consumed the oxygen. I felt my fingertips tingling; a pain had formed behind my eyes. I realized that I was panting too. Hell, we were dying in there. I couldn't think straight.

Feeling like lumps of concrete had been chained to my arms, I hauled myself round to face Kate.

'I'm cold,' she said.

'The air's bad.'

'Oh . . .' her voice was a whisper. 'Time to go.'

'Time to go,' I nodded.

She reached forward and touched my face with her fingertips. Her eyes were glazed. She panted hard. 'Rick . . . Rick Kennedy. I really liked you.'

'Liked you, too.' I could hardly speak now. 'Liked . . . you . . .'

'I wish . . . we'd . . . wish we'd made love this afternoon. Champagne. Soft beds . . . love.'

'Me too.' I couldn't lift my head.

'Time to go,' she said.

'Yes . . . time to go.'

The water had reached the front seats now. The light was fading. Darkness closed in around me like a cold hand. The music sounded as if it came from the lips of dead men: a long-drawn-out dirge, full of pain, despair and loneliness never ending.

I rolled my head on the back of the seat. My whole brain seemed to thump as if it pulsated inside my skull like some kind of mutant heart. My eyes dimmed. I gazed out of the window.

My eyes snapped open in shock.

Caroline hung there in the water. Her hair floated in a light froth around her head. Her brown eyes locked onto mine. She smiled. Behind her the drowned London streets stretched away into the distance. Cars lay on the bed of the lake. Shoals of fish drifted like silver clouds in and out of shop doorways. Thick-bodied eels nested in the rib cages of drowned policemen.

Caroline opened her mouth. Out swam a water rat with a piece of her tongue. She smiled. I heard her husky voice trickling up through the roots of my brain: *'The city rots underwater. Gone, gone, gone . . . Rick. The last Queen of England is dead . . .'*

Then Caroline's face melted into the empty-eyed skull of a drowned man. The corpse floated, standing upright in the water; the whole front of the torso had been torn away, giving it the appearance of a cutaway illustration in a medical text book, the lungs, heart, liver, diaphragm, intestines exposed in perfect detail.

From the corpse's lips purred Caroline's voice, enticingly sexy.

'Are you coming through, Rick? Auntie Caroline's waiting for her kiss. Rick, aren't you a naughty boy? Now, don't keep Auntie waiting, do you hear?'

Dimly, I realized I was hallucinating. I couldn't feel my fingers. A weight pressed down on my chest. Consciousness was dwindling, crushed by the poisonous carbon dioxide saturating my bloodstream.

'Kate . . . Kate . . . uh . . .' I could just make her out, her blonde hair, a fuzzy pale shape in the gloom. I saw she'd turned her back to me.

'Kate . . . what're you doing? What . . . uh . . .'

She sat down, braced her back against my shoulder, then kicked out hard with both feet.

It sounded like metal tearing.

Then I realized what she'd done. She'd stamped the side window through. The water came in with a roar, knocking us both back across the car. I grabbed a lungful of air, then I was swirled round and around, feeling like a kitten caught in a washing machine.

A hand grabbed me.

Pulled. Pulled hard.

For a second I thought one of the drowned men had reached in and caught hold of me. Then I realized Kate had grabbed me by the scruff of my T-shirt and was pulling me to the smashed side window.

I wriggled through it, scraping my back and arms against the remains of the glass. Above me there was light. I swam towards it. To my oxygen-starved brain it looked like the celestial wash of light that filters down through the clouds from Heaven.

I swam hard.

Then I was choking down fresh air into my lungs. The sun dazzled me. I turned round as I trod water.

Kate? Where the hell was Kate?

I couldn't see her.

I could see nothing. A piece of debris blocked my view.

I blinked the water from my eyes. Christ, I was seeing a boat.

With a rush of gratitude to my guardian angel I grabbed at the gunwale and held on tight.

'What in the name of Hades kept you down there?'

I looked up, squinting against the brilliant evening light.

I caught my breath. Cowboy and Tesco looked down at me.

They grinned. 'Right little bloody Indiana Jones, aren't we?' Cowboy reached forward, grabbing my forearm with his hand. I saw him raise the other hand. I couldn't see what he held in it but he swung it down across my forehead. I heard the sound it made as it hit my skull. An impossibly loud smacking sound.

He whipped it down again.

Lights seemed to roar up out of the water. Purple. Blue, Indigo.

He clubbed me again.

The lights came faster.

Red-green-orange-yellow.

He hit me again.

—yellow-green-blue-crimson-silver . . .

He struck again and again. Until the lights had gone, until I saw nothing but darkness, the utter darkness that lies at the end of the universe.

And I felt not pain, but some distant pumping sensation like a great pulse beating away in the back of my head.

CHAPTER 66

The Grey Man held Kate. His massive fists gripped her wrists. He held her so high from the ground her legs kicked uselessly at the air. He held her higher, her arms stretched. She was crying: 'Don't hurt the baby, don't hurt the baby!'

The grey head with its mane of black hair tilted to one side, curious about this specimen of humankind it had just captured.

'Don't hurt . . . don't hurt the baby. *Please.*'

The huge eyes, red as blood, peered into her face. Again the head tilted to one side – the same way a dog tilts its head when it hears something that interests it. Its blood-red eyes blinked slowly, as if it was pondering some new idea.

Then it transferred Kate's left wrist into its right hand, to hold her up above the ground with one hand. With its free hand, it ran its fingers – as thick and as grey as uncooked beef sausages – down her body. As if the contours and curves of her hips, stomach, breast, thighs were important.

Kate gasped in terror. Her eyes flashed. She tried to kick free.

With a savage snort the Grey Man seized her in both hands, then broke her across its knee like a stick.

'Leave her alone!'

I swung my fist into its face.

Ugh . . .

I opened my eyes.

Newspapers.

The floor . . . thick with newspapers – like a carpet.

Christ, my head ached. I blinked. A sharp pain skewered my left eye; it seemed to drive all the way through to the back of my skull.

Daylight.

I looked round. The light came in through a window of frosted glass. A wrought-iron garden gate had been bolted over the window itself.

I rolled onto my back. The dream still seemed to overlay what I saw in front of me.

I saw whitewashed walls. More newspapers. No furniture. Steps going up to a door. And I saw the Grey Man, brutal, beast-like, picking up Kate. I saw the look of terror in her eyes. I saw pain blast through her once-beautiful face.

As the beast man broke her spine across its knee.

Shit.

I'd stood up too quickly.

Nausea oozed through my stomach. Something spun fast inside my head – around and around and around and . . .

Vomit splashed onto the newspaper.

I wiped my mouth. Looked round again. This time my eyes stayed in focus.

My prison cell.

Clearly that's what it was meant to be. The bastard lunatics would keep me in there until they decided what punishment to inflict on my—

Christ.

Kate.

What the hell had they done to Kate?

I looked round the basement again in the hope that maybe she lay asleep beneath the newspapers. No. I was alone.

For the next ten minutes I hunted for a way out. The only exit was through a solid wood door. That was locked tight. I kicked and shouted. No one came.

I breathed deeply to calm my racing heart. I needed to get out to find Kate. Or torch the bastards alive if they'd harmed her. But I needed to be calm, level-headed. I sat on the floor, my back to the whitewashed wall. Gingerly I conducted a fingertip examination of my scalp where I'd been clubbed.

It was incredibly tender. Bumps and swelling left my head feeling as lumpy as a mountain range in miniature. But at least the skin hadn't been broken.

I looked over the basement again. This time more carefully.

There was no furniture. In one corner, a plastic bowl half-filled with water. I sniffed it. I'd only drink if I was desperate. Those psychos might have thought it a damned good laugh to add poison or some powerful laxative.

On the walls were yellow marks where people had urinated. By the steps to the door a perfect hand print had been left on the wall in blood. There were more drops of dried blood spattering the wall.

291

The same kind of effect as flicking a loaded paint brush. Someone had even used the blood to paint a picture:

O   O

I

(____)

It was supposed to be a happy-smiley face but something told me that whoever had painted it hadn't been smiling. Probably painted in the poor sod's own blood, too.

I remembered that as a kid, if I'd been in trouble or was miserable, I'd go and pull faces in the mirror, or make stupid big clown grins. It was an instinctive way of trying to cheer myself up. I guess the blood artist had attempted to do likewise.

Now I noticed the walls were covered with graffiti.

I began to read at random. *Benjamin Crowley*. Beside the name, a series of tally marks: *IIII*. He'd been counting off the days.

Four days he'd been kept down here. I wondered what had happened to him on the fifth.

There were messages, too:

Name: Dell Okram
Address: 26 Rudwell Drive
Highgate.
Please tell my wife, Sarah, I am alive and well – D.O. July.

Another hand had added a lunatic postscript:

Tell Sarah Okram, Highgate Superbitch, that Dell is ALIVE!
NO LONGER!!!!
HA! HA! R.I.P

There were lines of poetry scribbled here and there, all mixed in with Bible verses, lyrics from songs. Some English, some foreign.

I found myself tracing the words with the tip of my finger. Suddenly I experienced an overwhelming sense of the presence of the people who'd been held captive in here before me. I empathized. Their fear and dread for what the next day or the next hour would bring – it was identical to mine. They, too, would have been lost in that bleak, godawful nightmare that they – we – couldn't wake up from.

They'd written on these white-painted walls whatever was important to them. Messages to mothers, fathers, lovers, friends. Some made no obvious sense:

Dad, it's true what she said about Moe. They wouldn't take it from Toni's. I wish I could show you where it's hidden.
Always love, Gina.

Some made poignant sense:

If you see Angela Piermont please tell her I love her. And that I'm sorry I left her to cope alone with the baby. Thank you.
– Luke Grant (Pimlico)

The surreal:

jesus's's fault – they must stop poking me up – i'm going to get dead so the fucking don't make it bleed no more – i'm going to soon get dead – cos then jesus won't hurt me no more.

Some caught your throat:

Mummy, They put Jilly in the car with the pit-bull. She is screaming so hard I can hear her down here. I've got to escape. Tesco says he's going to cut me longways.
I'm sorry I was naughty a lot. Kiss little Lee-Anne for me. I'll try and be good for God.
I miss you and love you. Lots of kisses from your Lindsay.

I shook my head. If only I had my rifle I'd take real, real pleasure in shooting the whole lot of the sickoes, so help me I would.

Again I thought about Kate. What were the bastards doing to her? My imagination shot images through my head. Kate struggling. Her blonde hair messed across her face. I remembered the way the one called Tesco had practised with the hand drill. Boring holes into the post.

I listened hard. I couldn't hear any sound from the building. All I could make out was the sound of a dog barking outside. It sounded muffled, far away.

I looked back at the wall. What had the kid written?

They put Jilly in the car with the pit-bull . . .

I thought of Kate being pushed inside a car with a dog driven mad by hunger. Then those psychos crowding round to watch the battle inside.

Girl against mad dog.

I paced the floor of the basement, my feet crackling over the newspapers. The messages on the walls were like pins being jabbed into my skin.

A voice, insistent – as sharp as a pin itself – said over and over: *Do something, Rick. Do something, do something, do something . . .*

Yes.

But what?

I paced the floor. Again and again my attention would be drawn back to the messages on the wall. All those messages that the victims of these sadists had felt compelled to write. And those victims must have known the messages would never reach their intended recipients. They were the equivalent of a deathbed confession, or a final farewell. Already I knew it was important I should write something there. Already I wanted to find a stick or fragment of stone to scratch my own last testament, so keenly did I feel a kinship with those people.

Desperately I hungered to avenge their deaths.

As I paced, I felt as if something almost nuclear had began to burn inside me. The rage built up and up. A tremendous pressure that needed venting on at least one of those monsters that had taken Kate and myself to this dump.

Christ, what had they done to her? Just what in God's name had they done? If they'd hurt her . . . if they'd hurt her. I clenched my fists.

At that moment the door opened at the top of the stairs.

I stood in the centre of the basement; on that rug of stinking newspaper; with those walls covered in messages written by crying, frightened men, women and children, maybe only moments before being taken outside and—

– and what?

Having their heads dipped in petrol then set on fire?

Being chewed alive by mad pit-bull terriers?

294

Hunted for sport?

Shot in the gut?

Nailed by the bottom lip to a table?

I watched Cowboy, still in his cowboy hat and cowboy boots, come down the stairs. He was followed by Tesco, then a beanpole of a guy. All had the silk ribbons hanging down from their legs, arms, belts. They carried rifles.

Here it comes, Rick.

You going to go to the slaughter meek 'n mild?

Or—

Tesco was nearest to me. He smiled.

The scratched message on the wall came into my head as clearly as if it'd been scratched into my brain: *Tesco says he's going to cut me longways.*

A blast of sheer energy erupted inside me.

This'd get me killed, but Christ, was I going to enjoy it.

With a snarl I moved like I'd exploded. My fist blurred through the air.

Tesco's rat eyes widened in surprise. He tried to lift the rifle, his face turned stupid with shock.

Something else guided and powered my hand. I gave a huge yell as the energy ripped through, turning my fist into a weapon of destruction.

Kra-kkk!

My fist crunched the centre of his face. Tesco grunted, then fell back as if he'd been made from nothing more than paper.

CHAPTER 67

I stood there panting. My fist started to tingle. And I didn't give a shit. That psycho Tesco lay flat out on his back; his eyes turned slitty; he made choking sounds; blood flowed from his nose; every so often it formed snotty bubbles at his nostrils.

Cowboy poked him with the rifle. He groaned but didn't move.

Beanpole had me covered with his rifle. I froze. That punch had taken everything I had.

Now they'd kill me.

Cowboy looked down at Tesco, then back up at me again. There was an expression of amused surprise on his face.

He pushed the rim of his hat up with the point of his finger.

'Nice one,' he said in awe. 'That's the first time I've seen Tesco knocked down in one.'

'Piss off.'

'Hell's bells, you made a mess of his nose. Look, the bugger's flat.' He looked up at me again. 'Nice try, but unnecessary.'

'Believe me . . .' I tried to catch my breath. 'It was worth it.'

'Unnecessary,' Cowboy repeated, 'because I'd come down to apologize for hitting you on the head.' He smiled. 'And to tell you you're free to go.'

'Piss off.'

'It's true. OK, Lanky, no need to point the rifle at Mr Kennedy any more.'

'*Mr* Kennedy?' I was suspicious. 'Why the mister?'

'Because we made a mistake. Like I say, you're free to go. But we'd sure like you to have a meal with us first.'

The suspicion wouldn't quit. I was certain it was some trick. All part of the sadists' games. Take you upstairs, pop a hand grenade down your shirt, run like hell . . . screamingly funny, huh?

I asked, 'What made you change your mind?'

The man grinned. 'Let's say Jesus saved you.'

'Jesus?'

'Jesus.' Cowboy nodded.

Still I wouldn't move. If only I could get that burst of energy back; maybe I could swing at Lanky and grab the rifle.

Cowboy Man shrugged. 'You need convincing.' He turned back towards the stairs. 'Miss Robinson! Miss Robinson? Would you mind stepping down here?'

'Kate?' I couldn't believe my eyes. 'Kate. Are you all right?'

'Fine.' She came down the stairs smiling. I saw she now wore a silky blouse over a pair of leggings. They looked new, so did the pair of espadrille sandals on her feet.

'Lanky, give me a hand with blubber nose.' Cowboy Man and the human beanpole bent down, grabbed an arm each and dragged Tesco away.

Kate looked at me in surprise.

'Yes, Mr Kennedy's doing.' Cowboy shook his head in amazement. 'Some punch, Mr Kennedy, some punch.'

The pair of them dragged Tesco by the feet upstairs. Every time his head clunked against the concrete steps he groaned.

'Hush now, sleepy head,' Cowboy said as they dragged him out of sight.

I looked at Kate in amazement. She looked clean, refreshed, as if she'd just spent the weekend relaxing in the garden.

I reached out and squeezed her arm. It felt so good to touch her again. To know she was unhurt. I squeezed her arm again. She hugged me.

'You're OK?' she asked, her green eyes anxiously searching my face.

'Fine.'

'I thought they might have killed you.'

'I was certain they'd killed you.'

'Oh, Rick. Give me a hug. Mmm . . . tighter. Mm, that feels good.'

'Good? It feels great. Hell. You smell great.'

'Come on, I'll find you some clean clothes.'

'Wait a moment. Kate, what happened?'

'When I made it to the surface after leaving the car I saw them pulling you unconscious into the boat.'

'No. I mean, what made them change their minds about us?'

'Jesus told them to let us go.'

'Jesus? This is a wind-up, isn't it?'

'No. Jesus told Cowboy to let us go.'

'Lunatics.'

'No, they're not.' She smiled. 'I've spoken to Jesus, too.'

'You've spoken to Jesus? You've actually—'

'Uh-oh. You've another visitor, Rick.'

Tutts cautiously leaned in through the basement door as if shy to intrude. 'Sorry . . . uh, I don't mean to . . . interrupt or anything.'

I said under my breath. 'What have they got up there? A turnstile? Are they letting them in one by one?'

Kate's smile broadened. 'If there's ever a Rick Kennedy fan club you're guaranteed at least one member.'

'Gee, thanks.' In a louder voice I called up to Tutts, 'Come on down.'

She stepped down, awkward in high heels. She was wearing a short zebra-patterned skirt and a halter-neck top, along with a pearl necklace and long silver earrings. When she got close enough I noticed that from the earrings dangled miniature silver designs of the sole of a foot and the palm of a hand. And close up I was surprised how young she looked.

'She's gone to a lot of trouble to look nice for you,' Kate whispered, a mischievous twinkle in her eye.

OK, Rick, I told myself, bemused. This is where you wake up on the floor again. It's a dream, like the Grey Man attacking Kate.

I told myself that. I even bit my lip so hard it stung. But no, this was reality.

Tutts really didn't look as if she knew how to greet me. For a second it looked as if she'd give me a hug and kiss me. But she opted for shaking hands.

'I'm sorry they did that to you,' she said. 'Life's different now. They get crazy. Take stuff, drink stuff, you know?'

I nodded.

'But you're all right now. They didn't hurt your head?'

'Well . . . it's still in one piece.'

'I can get you food?' She smiled. 'I can make a lovely spaghetti with bolognese sauce. We've even got Spanish wine to go with it. That's right, isn't it? Spanish? No, Italian, right?'

Her nervousness made her speak faster. 'Madonna's got some Italian wine at her place. I can borrow some from—'

'Tutts, ah, Tutts,' Kate interrupted. 'Thank, but we've been invited to have a meal with—'

'Oh, of course, you're having supper with Jesus.'

Oh Christ . . . I mean, oh shit. Jesus? Speak to Jesus? Dine with Jesus? They were all at it now. What next? Hey, let's go roller blading with Jesus. Last one down Golgotha Hill is a silly sausage.

'Yeah . . . sure.' I forced a polite smile. 'Thanks very much for the offer, Tutts. Love the earrings.'

'Do you really?' She sounded delighted as well as astounded. 'I made these in the workshops. It's the only thing I kept from the old times.'

'They look really nice.'

There in the basement, with the blood on the walls, and the messages from men, women and children now dead, we actually made small talk. Tutts watched me closely with those close-set eyes of hers. In a weird way she seemed to be trying to see something in my face. As if I was going to send her an ultra-important question via my expression alone, and she desperately didn't want to miss it.

At last Kate checked her watch. 'Sorry, Tutts, we'll have to go.'

'Oh, right. Sure. Sorry, I didn't mean to keep you. But it's OK, ·
he won't be mad if you're late. He's nice.'

He?

I knew who the 'he' she was referring to was.

'Jesus?' I asked.

Kate took my arm. 'Jesus is waiting to meet us.'

CHAPTER 68

Jesus stood behind the long table. He broke a piece of bread from a
loaf. After that, he filled two glasses with red wine from a jug. Then
he offered Kate and me the wine, together with a piece of bread.

Jesus said: 'Please. Kate, Rick. Sit down.'

Jesus had a Liverpudlian accent.

Kate and I sat down. We were in a hotel restaurant. There were no
other diners. The tables all had crisp white tablecloths, wine glasses
with a single white rose as centre pieces. The cutlery shone in the
light slanting in through the windows that stretched the full length
of one wall. Outside a pleasant street, lined with Victorian town
houses and chestnut trees, ran downhill. Two hundred metres away
the street ended in the new Lake of London, leaving only rooftops
and the skeleton tops of drowned trees to march away along the line
of the submerged road. A church tower rose up from the waters half
a kilometre away, its clock frozen at ten to two.

First, we'd been presented with glasses of cold beer in the hotel
lounge bar. Then we moved through into the restaurant where we
were served massive pepperoni and bacon pizzas by the man who
looked like a human beanpole.

Jesus actually did look like Jesus. Well, at least the Hollywood
portrayals. Aged around thirty, he wore the same bumfluff beard
and long hair. His eyes were blue and he even affected the gestures,
moving his hands out at either side as if embracing us as he spoke.
Jesus wore a black leather waistcoat and black trousers. Perhaps the
major flaw in the impersonation, apart from the clothes, were the
letters tattooed across his knuckles. They spelt out 'Gary Topp'. His
real name, I guess.

We talked. Jesus repeatedly apologized about what had happened to Kate and me at the hands of his gang. He particularly wanted to hear the story of my attempted escape in the Rolls-Royce.

'And the car didn't fill up with water straight away?' he asked in that soft Liverpudlian accent that could have come straight from John Lennon's mouth.

'No. Rolls-Royce make – made solid cars.'

'They're not meant to be submarines, though?'

'No.'

He asked again what we'd seen underwater. He was fascinated by the image of the streets and buildings lying on the bottom of the lake.

'Shame about Mental,' Jesus sighed. 'We knew he couldn't swim. He was terrified of water. Always sat on the floor in the middle of the boat.'

'He just jumped onto the car bonnet.'

Jesus shrugged. 'Don't blame yourselves. He was beginning to become a loose cannon anyway. He'd molested some of our girls. Oh, yes, he always apologized. In fact, he'd cry his eyes out, he was so full of remorse, but . . .' Jesus shrugged again. 'Come on, come on, eat up. Good?'

'Marvellous.' Kate picked up a triangle of pizza in both hands and ate hungrily.

'Great pizza,' I added. 'Bread, too. We haven't tasted bread in months.'

'No yeast?'

'No ovens. We've spent the summer in tents.'

'It's going to be a cold winter.' Jesus poured more wine.

'Unless the ground heats up some more,' I said. 'Then we'll spend the winter in shorts and flip-flops.'

No one smiled. Me included. I'd tried to make a flippant joke, but as soon as I'd spoken I remembered that finger of black pointing at Fountains Moor. The Earth becoming scorched, vegetation dying; cities burning.

Jesus sipped his wine. 'Is it bad where you come from?'

'Most of the problems in our area,' Kate said, 'could be attributed to the poison gas leaking out through cracks in the ground.'

I tore off a piece of pizza. 'At first it created a massive refugee problem. Food supplies quickly dried up. You could be beaten to death for an apple in your pocket.'

'And now people are eating each other.' Kate gave a fatalistic shrug. 'People are the only thing that aren't in short supply.'

I looked at Jesus. 'I take it you're not short of food?'

'No problems yet, Rick. The flood forced people out of London within days. They didn't have a chance to loot the supermarkets or warehouses. For the time being we've got some pretty rich pickings.'

'How many are there in your group?'

'Fifty-five. Well, fifty-four now that Mental's gone.'

'You're confident the water won't rise any more?' Kate asked.

'It reached this level about three weeks after the start of the flood. Touch wood—' smiling, he touched his head, '—it won't rise any more.'

'You've not been attacked by rival groups?'

'So far we haven't had much trouble. Those that left London stick to the higher ground to the north. They haven't risked coming back. They need boats, for one thing.'

'So, what's your story?'

Jesus smiled as he stroked his beard thoughtfully. 'As you'll have guessed from the accent, I'm originally from Liverpool. I couldn't find work. I was married with three daughters. So I tried my hand in London. For a few months I laboured on building sites. Then got laid off. I killed time drinking in pubs. Then when money got low I'd buy a bottle of whisky and drink it in a park. Soon it reached the point where having a drink was more important than having a roof over my head. So I spent what little money I could get on the booze.'

'You ended up homeless?'

'Oh, Rick, I had a home all right. A lovely home. Only it was the inside of a bottle. The most comfortable home you could imagine.'

'And the rest of your community?'

'They were all homeless. The people society kicked in the teeth.'

Kate said, 'But you collected them all together and brought them to this island?'

He nodded appreciatively at Kate. 'Got it in one, Miss Robinson.'

'And they called you Jesus?'

He nodded. 'In the old days society rewarded good deeds with medals and titles. These people gave me the name of Jesus as a mark of gratitude.'

'You've done a good job,' Kate said. 'Everyone seems well fed.'

He grinned. 'And nobody's homeless anymore, right?' He leaned forward. 'You two think whatever happened to this planet is a disaster. For these people it was the best thing that could have happened. It's saved their lives. It's given them pride and a sense of purpose.'

'Every cloud has a silver lining – for some.' Kate smiled but the words sounded bitter.

'Look.' Jesus clasped his hands together. 'You've seen those photographs of two-headed sheep, birds born without feathers, children with webbed hands. I think Nature deliberately produces these mutants, freaks, call them what the jiggery you like. The reason it does this, is because once in a while the environment changes with a catastrophic rapidity – just like it's done now – then suddenly these freaks discover that their, let us call them unique attributes mean they are better adapted to the new environment than the so-called normal animals. The same happens with humans here.' He tapped his head. 'Some of us are born with different software loaded into our brains. We grow up to feel like outsiders. Fish out of water. As if we're never really part of normal society. We're the ones who get bullied at school. We might end up drug addicts or alcoholics or in prison, in mental hospitals, or maybe we just can't go with the flow of ordinary society. We are round pegs that society tries to hammer into square holes. So we fall through the cracks; we end up living out on the streets, or psychiatrists try and cure us – well, they call it a cure. They pump us with drugs – Prozac and amitriptyline for depression; chlorpromazine for schizophrenia.'

'You're saying you've somehow been chosen by Nature to become a new improved model of *homo sapiens*?'

'You're being flippant again, Mr Kennedy. I'm not saying we're *better*, I'm only claiming we are *different*. The reason why we seem like weirdoes to you is because we're not allowed to grow and fulfil our genetic destiny. We become damaged, like butterflies forever trapped in a caterpillar phase.'

Kate looked up from her pizza. 'And now the environment has changed?'

'And now the environment has changed we have discovered – to our joy, to our boundless joy – that we have come into our own. We feel whole. Happy. This new environment suits us. We can function like human beings; we no longer feel like fish out of water.'

'So you're going to inherit the Earth?'

'I didn't say that, and you know it, Mr Kennedy,' Jesus said pleasantly. 'But we do find this new world more amenable than the old one.'

I drained my glass. The attentive beanpole man hurried forward to refill it. 'I certainly prefer today's brand of hospitality to what you were offering yesterday.'

'I can only apologize again.'

I leaned forward, knitting my fingers together on the table. 'Obviously the food in the warehouse on the island is yours. So what we need to do is get back home to our community and start searching for another source of supplies.'

'Your people have enough food in the short term?'

'We'll manage.' It was a lie. In a week the canned foods would be gone. Then my brother Stephen, Dean, little Lee and the rest would be existing on potatoes. Those would be gone soon, too. Then what? Starve? Flip coins to see which one of us went in the pot first?

Kate had told me the island we'd landed on and dubbed Sparky's Island was a ten-minute boat ride away. I began to mull over ideas of somehow begging a ride back there. Howard would be flying down tomorrow morning. If he didn't find Kate and me there he might decide we were dead, that the place was too dangerous for him to hang around. He'd take off back to Fountains Moor and (you couldn't blame him) he wouldn't come back. We'd be stranded here with Jesus and his merry men.

As Jesus told Kate about life there in Paradise (as they'd called it) I looked out through the window. Children were kicking a football in the street. A little girl, she couldn't have been much older than Lee, trundled a doll's buggy past. Brightly coloured clothes hung from washing lines in gardens. From lampposts fluttered strips of orange and yellow material; larger versions of the decorations that Jesus's tribe adorned themselves with. In the distance I heard the rumble of distant thunder.

Like the man said, they seemed to have got themselves a nice, cosy community on this little island poking out of the waters in what had once been a London residential suburb. But I remembered what I'd seen written on the basement wall. And I remembered what Cowboy, Tesco, Mental and the rest had been so keen to do to us. By rights Kate and me should have been shit-stew by today, probably floating downriver, with the rats nibbling our toes and eyes. Instead we were sitting with Jesus here, chewing on pizza, drinking expensive wines.

What gave?

That's what I wanted to know. Suspicion prowled my innards like a restless dog that's sniffed something strange in the shrubbery.

Why the change?

Guard Dog Suspicion sniffed the air and smelt a rat.

This polite talk must be leading up to something. I decided to find out what it was.

'Jesus, a few hours ago your people were hell-bent on finding the most imaginative way to kill us. Why the change?'

'Rick . . .' Kate flashed me a warning look.

'No, Kate. I need to know.'

Jesus stroked his beard. 'These people have been to Hell and back. Any wonder they get crazy now and again?'

'It seems obvious to me that if someone sets out to torture you to death on the Tuesday and by the Wednesday they're serving you pizza then they've had a fundamental – well, fucking amazing – change of heart.'

'Rick—' Kate began.

But I ploughed on. Those scribbled messages on the basement walls from the people that these psychos had killed were like thorns pricking my skin. Maybe I wasn't thinking straight, maybe this line of questioning would get me killed. But by God's flesh I was going to get answers.

'Rick,' Jesus spoke calmly. 'The world's a different place now. People are different.'

'But the fact is you changed your minds. Why? I've come to the conclusion that we've got something you want. Just what it is I can't imagine. Certainly not my mother's recipe for chocolate brownies.'

'You don't bottle things up, do you?' Jesus topped up my glass. 'You come right out and say what's on your mind.'

'Damned right I do.'

'Rick, cool down, will you?' Kate implored.

'Will I Hell. Goddammit, have you seen what's written on those basement walls? Did you notice the bloodstains? These freaks have been torturing people, dozens of people, maybe hundreds, to death.'

The man they called Jesus said, 'Do you want me to deny it?'

'I want to know what you need from us so much that you

stopped your pet lunatics out there barbecuing us alive for belly laughs.'

For the first time I saw a flash of anger in Jesus's brown eyes. 'OK, OK! You want it straight?'

In the distance thunder rumbled again.

'Go on, I'm all ears.'

'Like I said, the world's different now. It forced *us* to be different, so we—'

'Yeah, yeah, I've had the patronizing sermon already.'

'No. Let me finish. What makes a marriage work? What keeps a man and woman together?'

'What's this got to do with—'

'It's got everything to do with what we've been doing here. Couples stay together for a whole bunch of reasons. You can list some of those reasons that bind two people into a long-term relationship. For instance: they have good sex; they have children – they love their children, they want to be with them, it keeps the couple together; maybe they share the same hobbies.'

'But you killed people.'

'Yeah, and believe me it works, Rick Kennedy. If people go through a powerful emotional experience and share those emotions with others it binds them together closer than love and blood ties. Listen, people who've survived air crashes form bonds with fellow crash victims – even though they are total strangers – that last for years. Same thing happens if you're in the crowd at a concert or a cinema or a football match. Everyone's experiencing the same emotions. The stronger the emotion shared, the more powerfully it cements individuals together.'

'But killing innocent people?'

'But killing innocent people,' he mimicked, his eyes flashing with a mixture of evangelical zeal and anger. 'But killing innocent people? Get real, Kennedy. The world has changed. You've got to adapt to those changes or die.'

Kate shook her head, shocked. 'So you've made a ritual of killing outsiders?'

'We did. And it was always strangers from outside our community – never one of our own.'

'And that binds you closer together as a community?'

Jesus nodded. 'It has created a close-knit community. We're fiercely loyal to one another – and the community is fiercely loyal to the individual: any one one of us needs help, we all rally round. And that's what we need to survive: loyalty to this, our new family; a family we'd die for, if need be.'

'And kill for, too.'

'Have you?' he asked, his eyes suddenly sharpened. 'Have you killed for yours?'

I thought about the three refugees we had caught stealing food. Christ, we were as bad as each other.

Jesus nodded. 'You have to now. Kill or be killed. And, believe me, you have to activate that software inside your head, the software our ancestors used in prehistoric times. Be ruthless. Be loyal to your own tribe.'

'OK.' I nodded. 'I understand. But I don't approve.'

'We don't need your approval, Rick Kennedy.'

'OK, you don't need my approval. But what exactly *do* you need from us?'

'The truth?'

I nodded. 'The truth.'

'OK, Rick Kennedy. The truth is: if we stay here in London we're going to die. And do you know something?'

'What?'

Thunder rumbled continuously now, sounding like enormous barrels being rolled to and fro. 'You and your community are all going to die if you stay up there on Fountains Moor.'

'That's why we need to go back there and start looking for a new food supply.'

'No.' He gave a grim smile. 'Starvation is the least of your problems.'

Kate said, 'If the ground gets too hot where we're camped we can simply move on.'

Again Jesus gave that grim smile. 'You still don't know what's really happening, do you? Kate . . . Rick. Bring your glasses: we can watch the show from the hotel roof.'

'Show? What show?'

'I'll top up your glasses first.'

'What show?' I repeated. Was this one of their sadistic shows that they'd originally planned for us? Now some other poor devil was going to be made to dance barefoot on broken glass or whatever they did to get their communal kicks.

'Follow me. The show started twenty minutes ago.'

306

Thunder grumbled. An ominous sound like primordial gods muttering threats of destruction and catastrophe.

CHAPTER 69

Instead of leading us outside, Jesus climbed the thickly carpeted hotel stairs. Exchanging suspicious glances, Kate and I followed.

At Jesus's invitation I'd picked up a full bottle of wine. By the time we'd reached the first floor I'd decided I'd smash the bottle against the wall and drive the jagged neck of the bottle into his throat. That was if he tried anything weird.

This is where you take off your clothes. This is where I take off mine. Now, Rick, watch me make love to the beautiful Kate Robinson.

That's what I could imagine him saying. No problem.

But he continued climbing the steps, glass of wine in one hand, his sandals flicking up to smack against his bare soles with a *snick-snack* sound.

'Jesus? What show?' I prompted.

'Wait and see,' he said mysteriously. 'But I think it will convince you that the threat you face isn't starvation or the ground growing hot.'

On the top floor he opened what looked like a door to a broom cupboard. There were more steps. These were bare concrete. We followed Jesus up them to another door that led onto the roof.

The thunder sounded louder now.

We followed him out onto the flat roof.

Now I could see the extent of Jesus's island. You could have walked round the shoreline in not much more than ten minutes. From up here it looked thickly wooded; house roofs poked through here and there amongst the branches. The hotel itself stood at a crossroads. From there I could see the roads run down into the lake.

By now it was almost dark. The new lake that covered central London looked strangely beautiful. The moon rose above the waters to cast a shivering strip of light, like some ethereal roadway, across the water towards us.

From the lake rose hundreds of buildings. In the moonlight they looked like tombstones. Silhouetted, I saw the massive block of

Canary Wharf, the dome of St Paul's and hundreds of anonymous tower blocks. I shivered.

The flow of water would eventually wash away the foundations. In a year or two even the biggest buildings would begin to deteriorate. I could imagine the thunderous roar they would make as they collapsed with an eerie majesty into the lake. Soon there would be no sign of what was once the mightiest city on Earth. Once it had surpassed Athens, Baghdad, Rome, Constantinople. Soon it would be just a vast shallow lake.

Thunder beat the night air. I looked up at the stars pricking through the darkness.

And again I shivered. The Earth was doing what it did every few thousand years. Mostly it achieved it with an ice age. This time it was a hot age, or a fire age. I knew there and then, as I stood with Jesus at my left hand and Kate at my right, that Planet Earth was wiping out certain forms of life on its surface. Like a teacher who's mucked up an equation on a blackboard and wipes it clean with a cloth before starting again. Here comes the cloth of fire and flood. We're wiped out. What new, *corrected* version of life would follow us?

Kate's hand found mine and squeezed it. I returned the squeeze, trying to find reassurance. She was thinking the same thing.

Were we doomed?

Was this futile?

Scratting the countryside for cans of food to survive just that little bit longer.

Thunder grumbled more loudly.

Jesus turned to us, his silhouette uncannily Christlike. 'Do you see the cause of the thunder?'

'No.' I shook my head, puzzled.

'There's lightning to the west,' Kate said. She didn't release the grip on my hand. 'There. On the horizon.'

'Look above the flashes of light,' he said softly. 'What do you see?'

'Oh, my God, yes,' she said, surprised.

'Do you see them, Rick?'

'No. Nothing.' I looked hard. Then my scalp prickled. 'Hell, yes.'

Kate let out a breath. 'That's artillery.'

Jesus said, 'If you look carefully you can even see the shells.'

For a whole five minutes we stood there on the hotel roof, the glasses of wine in our hands, watching the flashes of light from the muzzles of the big guns. Artillery shells rose almost as if in slow motion into the sky. There they soared, glowing white, like shooting stars, across the sky and into the distance. I couldn't see where they fell. The sound of exploding shells must have been mixed into the report of the guns to form that constant grumbling thunder we'd heard in the restaurant.

'The gun emplacements are way off to the north,' Jesus pointed. 'But they seem to be shelling a target to the west of London. It's not regular army. That doesn't exist anymore. As far as we can tell it's a bunch of ex-servicemen and civilians who've formed a kind of people's defence force.'

'Any idea who's the target?'

'The target.' He nodded, then in a matter-of-fact voice said, 'The Greys.'

'The Greys?'

'Not met them yet? You'll come across them soon enough. They're overrunning the country.'

Kate looked at me, then looked back at the man these people called Jesus. 'You mean you've seen these Greys?'

'Sure.'

'Let's get this straight,' I said slowly. 'These Greys. They are heavily-built men. With grey skins like rhino hide and—'

'And eyes that are red as blood.' He nodded. 'Those monsters are the cause of all this. And they're overrunning the country.' He sniffed, looked into his wine glass and looked back up at us. 'In fact they're overrunning the entire planet: Africa, New Zealand, Australia. The USA. Those monsters are moving in. And they're going to push the human race into the sea.'

CHAPTER 70

Ten minutes later we left the hotel roof and returned to the bar. Kate and Jesus chatted. A wind had sprung up to tug the leaves from the branches of the trees. Even though it was dark I could still see the waves breaking in lines of creamy white against dry land where road met lake.

Through the double-glazed windows the distant artillery, shelling the Greys to the west of London, sounded like nothing more that a soft rumble that was easily drowned by the discreet fizz of the champagne that Jesus poured into our glasses.

This sudden infusion of luxury into my life – clean clothes, hot baths, champagne, pepperoni pizza so delicious I'd packed my stomach to busting point – seemed oddly out of joint with this new world of scavenging and sudden violent death.

Two hundred kilometres or so north of where I sat, glass of champagne in hand, Stephen, Dean, Howard, little Lee and the rest would be zipping their tents against the cold night air. Already weighing on their minds would be the knowledge that their food supplies were dwindling before their eyes. Already they might be feeling the hunger pangs that they'd have to nurse through eight hours of frost and darkness until a breakfast of thin porridge in the morning.

A surge of guilt welled up inside of me. I looked at the crystal champagne glass in my hand, the bubbles streaming up through the pale golden liquid.

Was this right? Was it, Hell. Instead of luxuriating on this little island called Paradise I should be back on Fountains Moor. They needed me. I should be hacking out fresh plans with Stephen to find enough food and adequate shelter to get us through what might be a murderous winter. A winter that promised either to be fiery as the heat seeped up from the Earth's molten core or intensely cold as the dust and other crap squirted high into the atmosphere from a thousand erupting volcanoes blocked the heat from the sun.

I looked at the champagne and shook my head. This was shit stew all right. The mother of shit stews.

And we were right in it over our stupid heads.

Jesus thought the real problem, the real threat to our survival, would come from the invading Grey Men – whoever they really were, and wherever they were really from. Now Jesus wanted something from us. He needed it badly enough to be charming and hospitable and share his precious wines.

As he poured out more champagne I decided to find out what it was. I asked him straight: 'OK, so what do you need from us?'

Thoughtfully he slipped the champagne bottle back into the ice bucket, took a deep breath as if reaching a decision he'd been mulling over for hours, then launched right in.

He looked me in the eye. 'There's a ship lying at anchor off the coast near Whitby in North Yorkshire.'

'So? Where do we come in?'

'You've got a plane.'

'Ah.' Understanding oozed through me. 'So, when it comes down to it, it was the plane that saved our lives?'

Kate raised her eyebrows. 'The plane? Why do you need the plane?'

'Kate. Rick. The situation is this: we know we have to get out of London before the Greys reach here. The artillery bombardments can only hold them back a few weeks at the most. We have a ship which we plan will take us to a South Seas island. The problem is, the ship is at the other end of the country.'

Kate shook her head. 'But you've got boats. Why don't you just put everyone on those and head downriver to the Thames Estuary?'

'Two problems there. One: the Thames downstream from London is a no-go area. Geological disturbances have thrown up a ridge of rock creating a huge dam that's holding back the river. Two: there are only three people on the ship. And they haven't got the experience to bring it all the way down the coast.'

'So, it's a case of Mohammed to the mountain?' Kate said.

Jesus nodded. 'What we have to do is somehow get our community – all fifty-four of us – to Whitby where we can board the ship.'

'You've got experienced sailors here in London?'

'We have. At least enough to crew the ship as far from here as possible.'

'Walking to Whitby's out of the question?'

'With children and pregnant women? To walk more than two hundred kilometres? Across a country thronging with millions of starving people?' Jesus let his breath hiss through his front teeth. 'They'd have the meat picked off our bones inside twenty-four hours.'

'So, let me get this straight,' I said. 'You're hoping we will fly all your people up to Whitby?'

'All fifty-four.' He nodded seriously. 'This really is a matter of life and death, Rick.'

'But why on Earth should we?' I shook my head in disbelief. 'What on Earth is there in it for us?'

Jesus looked at me levelly. 'A chance to survive.'

*　　*　　*

311

Outside the darkness deepened. A couple strolled hand in hand down the street, illuminated only by the lights from the hotel window. In the distance, tiny sparks of silver light that were the artillery shells still rose into the air to fall on some distant target west of London.

Kate looked at me, then at Jesus. 'Let me get this straight. You're suggesting we join forces?'

Jesus nodded. 'Indeed I am. You transport my community to the coast near Whitby using your plane, then you bring yours across. We board the ship, then . . .' He shrugged. 'We sail south. Start a new life.'

'As simple as that.' I held out my hands. 'But you think we'd trust you? What's to stop you loading your people onto the ship and sailing without us?'

'OK,' Jesus said diplomatically. 'You send some of your people to the ship first. Then we send a party of ours. Maybe alternate the flights between Fountains Moor and London, so neither group can double-cross the other. You agree?'

'There are problems.'

'Problems?'

'Logistical problems,' I said. 'We have one four-seater light aircraft. If we can only carry three people back at a time you're talking eighteen round trips.'

'And we could only make one round trip per day,' Kate added. 'So it would take a minimum of eighteen days.'

'Eighteen days is fine.'

Kate nodded. 'And that's supposing we have eighteen days of fine flying weather, that the plane holds out mechanically.'

I said, 'And we would need to use some of the trips to transport food back to the camp.'

'So you *are* running out of food?'

Damn. I bit my lip. I hadn't wanted to let Jesus know about our food shortage. It was a weakness he might be able to exploit.

'It's low,' Kate said quickly. 'But not dangerously low.'

'And we're finding new supplies all the time.' I tried to sound confident but it must have seemed obvious to the man that if we were risking long hazardous flights to London in search of food then we must be desperately close to starvation.

Jesus smiled. 'I didn't say it would be easy to airlift fifty-four people from here – plus however many there are of you

– to the Yorkshire coast. But we can do it. If you're in agreement.'

'There's no other way your people can make the journey?'

'You know there isn't, Kate. Even if we could move everyone to the dry land to the north, then find vehicles, all the roads would be blocked by armed gangs. And, as I've already said, we couldn't walk all that way across open countryside. We need to fly.' He looked at each of us in turn. 'And you know your community will either die of starvation or be overrun by Greys.'

'So.' I let out a deep sigh. 'We need each other to survive.'

'That's about the size of it . . . here, let me top up your glasses. We'll drink to our new partnership.'

'Oh . . . wait a moment,' I held up my hand. 'I can't speak on behalf of my group. And I certainly can't commit them to something like this without their agreement.'

Jesus considered. 'OK . . . but we need to move quickly, Once winter closes in we won't be going anywhere, will we?'

'You know the island where your people found us?'

Jesus nodded. 'Go on.'

'Our plane is due to land there tomorrow morning. We could fly back, discuss your proposal with our group, then—'

'Then come back and give me your decision?'

'Right.'

'Wrong, Mr Kennedy.'

'No?'

'No.' He shook his head, smiling. 'Now what's to stop you taking our ship?'

'We don't have anyone capable of sailing a ship.'

'I don't know that,' Jesus said, sipping his champagne. 'You might move your people to the ship and – phut. Farewell, suckers. And we're left here to rot.'

Kate said, 'So you want to keep us here as hostages?'

He shook his head. 'Guests. You'd do the same if you were in my shoes, wouldn't you?'

I sighed and nodded. 'So, back to the cellar, is it?'

'No. You'll have a room here. You'll be well fed. Come and go as you please.'

'So what happens tomorrow when our pilot flies in to find we've gone? He'll return to Fountains Moor, never to return.'

'You'll be there to meet your pilot, Rick. Explain the situation to him. And my proposal. That we join forces and sail to the South Seas together.'

I asked the next question bluntly. 'Jesus. Are you married?'

'As I mentioned before. I had a wife in Liverpool with—'

'No. Here. Do you have a wife or girlfriend?'

He nodded. 'I live with a girl – Kandi. Why?'

'Then send Kandi back with the plane. She can explain your plan to our group.'

'And she'll be an exchange hostage? Smart move, Rick. OK, I'll talk to Kandi.' Jesus raised his glass. 'A toast, then? To us.'

For a moment I hesitated to raise my glass. I glanced at Kate. Our eyes met. I don't believe in telepathy, but at that moment I read her mind as clearly as you read words on a page. She was thinking that Jesus, sitting there all smiles, glass raised, waiting, had what he'd set out to get from us. He was satisfied all was going according to *his* plan. I knew then I'd underestimated him with that bumfluff Christ Almighty beard, beady eyes and tattoos – particularly the homely name *Gary Topp* picked out in blue tattooist's ink across the backs of his fingers. This man who called himself Jesus had the look of cunning in his eyes. And beneath the Christlike smile I detected something flinty, ruthless. He was the kind of man who got what he wanted.

But I realized this also: Kate and I were in his empire now. We had, for now anyway, to play the game according to *his* rules.

CHAPTER 71

'*Rats!*'

'Kate, run to the house!'

The rats poured out of the drain. It was like watching one of those films shown in reverse for comic effect. Imagine brown flood water gushing down a drain. It flows down at such a rate you'd grow dizzy watching it.

Imagine you are seeing that in reverse, the water flowing upwards out of the drain. Thick brown water.

Now imagine that the 'water' is, in fact, rats. Thousands of rats gushing upward and outward through the grating. So many rats that you can't see an individual rat, only that brown flood.

'Kate, get over the fence . . . run for the house.'

'I can't!' she shouted. 'They're coming out of the ditch as well. There's hundreds of them.'

'Here, grab this.' I handed her a broom handle I'd found at the water's edge. I kicked aside a mound of driftwood tangled with human bones.

A stick.

A branch.

I needed something to use as a club against the rats now swarming toward us, hungry eyes glinting. No doubt about it. We were their next meal.

I bent down to yank at the mess of string, carrier bags, brushwood, shoes, clothes, drowned pigeons that had been washed up onto the shore.

Damn, nothing.

Nothing to use as a club.

'Shit . . . this will have to do.' I picked up a human thigh-bone. Long, heavy, ideal as a club – pieces of meat still hung from it, looking like strips of pasta. I wished I'd time to wrap a plastic bag round the end. Instead, I had to swallow my distaste and clamp my hand round the bone and those strands of flesh that felt wet and unnaturally cold against my bare palm.

'Rick . . . here they come. Damn.' A rat ran at her. She struck out with the broom handle. Missed.

Struck again.

This time swinging the broom handle like a hockey stick.

The rat squealed. With a *thock* sound the broom handle batted the rat into the water.

We'd left the hotel just after sunrise to walk round the island and explore what would, at least for a few weeks, be our new home. We'd cut down through a clump of trees, dotted here and there with millionaires' houses. It was at the water's edge that I'd first seen the rats.

When they gushed from the iron grating set in the pathway I couldn't believe my eyes. And still they poured out of the earth in that fluid unbroken stream of brown.

Now they advanced towards us. Darting closer in little stops and starts.

Their thick pink tails flicked into the air like little whips as they ran. We were close enough to see their glinting rat eyes, a flash of pink tongue, as they anticipated the taste of our flesh when their sharp teeth would crunch through our skin.

I looked round frantically. We'd been pushed back to the water. There was nowhere else to run. I couldn't see anyone who might help us.

We'd have to face this alone.

I looked at Kate. She stood there holding the broom handle in both hands like it was a samurai sword. She shot a look at me, her green eyes bright with fear.

'We've got two choices,' she said quickly. 'Either we swim for it. Or we run over the top of them. See if we can make it to the house. What do you think?'

'There must be thousands. They'll swarm all over us. Kate, we have to – damn!'

The rats surged forward. I crouched down, using the human thigh bone to beat at the oncoming rats.

Thud, thud, thud. The bone club cracked down.

Crack! A rat skull mashed flat.

Thud, thud . . .

I pounded at the ground, clubbing at the rats.

'Rick. Look! On your leg!'

A rat had run up my leg as far as my knee. I could see its clawed feet hooking into the material of my jeans. Its mouth opened wide. I saw yellow teeth, razor-sharp; the whiskers; the hungry eyes; the still wet brown fur stuck down in a glistening mat across its body. I froze.

The rat looked fat, almost bloated. It must have been swimming with bacteria and lethal viruses; ingested as it gorged on rotting human flesh.

Now it had grown so confident that humankind couldn't hurt it any more that it was going to take live victims.

Me.

Then Kate.

We were rat fodder.

All this must have taken only a second.

But I saw it all as if it scrolled before my eyes in slo-mo.

The rat hooked its claws into my jeans. I could feel the prick of those claws through the material. It sniffed higher, its pink nose snuffling the odours exuded by the scent glands in my balls.

Maybe that was what smelt sweetest. That's where it would sink its razor teeth first. Crunching through skin and gristle to puncture my testicles. Then it would thirstily lap the blood oozing through the jeans at my crotch.

'Rick! Don't move.'

I heard the buzz of a stick cutting hard through the air.

My eyes had locked onto the rat. I couldn't move. No way could I move one centimetre.

I could only see the rat about to bite deep between my legs.

The buzz of the stick cutting through the air buzzed louder.

A pale flash.

Thud.

And the rat had been batted from me.

I blinked, snapped out of it.

The rats had clung to the thigh bone. Half a dozen ran up it towards my hand.

I threw the bone behind me.

Kate thrashed at the rats with the broom handle.

But they were unstoppable. It was like trying to knock back an incoming ocean tide.

The water lapped at our feet.

'This is it,' I told her. 'We either swim for it. Or we're dead.'

'We'll swim,' she said, eyes darting from my face to the lake waters that were a poisonous stew of decaying bodies and toxic waste leaking from chemical plants, rotting cars, refuse dumps.

'Ready?'

'Stick with me. We'll keep as close to the shore as possible. When we're away from the rats, swim back to the shore again.'

'Then?'

'Then we run like Hell.'

'But the rats . . .' She looked back at me. 'They'll swim after us, won't they?'

'Kate, they'll strip us down to the bone if we stay here.'

'OK, go for it.'

'Right, Kate, on the count of three!'

'Rick . . . here they come.'

'One, two – what the Hell's that?'

They appeared from nowhere.

317

'Dogs!' Kate cried in disbelief. 'Dogs. They're attacking the rats!'
My astonishment turned to relief – a huge surging relief.

'Look at them all,' Kate sounded delighted. 'How many are there?'

'Twenty – thirty?'

The dogs, all of them small muscle-packed terriers, pounced on the rats. They didn't bite them to death. The terriers simply picked up the rats by their heads then, with a brutally efficient shake of their own heads, snapped their necks. Then each dog would drop the twitching rat before moving on to the next.

Then the next, and the next.

The rats tried to turn on the dogs. But their teeth couldn't penetrate the terriers' natural-grown armour of wiry fur. The dogs snarled, darted, pounced and shook rats, their powerful neck and shoulder muscles snapping scrawny rat necks with ease.

'Thank God,' I murmured, putting an arm around Kate. 'Here comes the canine cavalry.'

As the terriers slaughtered the rats around our feet I looked up to see Jesus standing watching us, his arms folded. He was grinning. The whole situation had amused him. At his side stood the tall beanpole man, his face expressionless. Alongside him slouched Tesco, his nose still sore and raw-looking from the punch I'd laid across his face. He grinned maliciously. I didn't doubt for a second that Tesco would have creamed himself with joy if the rats had torn us apart. They stood there, silently watching us, the coloured strips of silk fluttering from their arms and legs.

A moment later the beanpole man walked slowly towards us. He held a tube as long as himself with a bell-shaped attachment at one end. Strapped to his back was something resembling a diver's aqualung tank. He pointed the business end of the tube at the ground almost as if he was going to hoover it. Instantly a yellow flame as long as your forearm spurted out.

He walked forward slowly, swinging the device from left to right, burning a path through the rats. At the drain, where the rats still poured out, he blasted the flame at the grating. Rats, now balls of fire, still ran madly across the dirt to die at the water's edge.

Beanpole Man pulled a bottle from his jacket pocket. Then, in that casual unhurried way of his, he poured its contents down through the grating into the drain. He stood back. Pointed the tube at the drain, thumbed a button. Flame darted into the grate.

There was a *VUFF* and an oily yellow flame surged out of the grating.

This time no more rats emerged from the grate. They were cooking down there.

'I think they've won,' Kate said, nodding at the dogs.

I looked. The surviving remnants of the rats were streaming into the lake to make their escape. The dogs stood there cockily wagging their tails, tongues hanging out as they panted.

Beanpole Man whistled. The dogs ran back to him, tails still wagging, noses lifted into the air to be patted.

Kate and I walked up to where Jesus stood beneath the trees. I felt stupid. All we'd done was take an early walk. Within five minutes we'd nearly ended up as a rats' breakfast.

'Thanks,' I said to Jesus (maybe I should have said 'Thanks, Jesus,' but I still found it hard to call the man by his name).

He smiled. 'Don't mention it.'

Tesco sneered. 'You want to watch where you're walking. You nearly ended up in the shit, Kennedy.'

'Tesco. Speak nicely to the man.' Jesus spoke in a soft voice. 'He and Miss Robinson are our welcome guests.'

Tesco pulled his lips into a grin. Close up, the split in his nose caused by my fist looked even more like raw meat. He wasn't going to forget, or forgive, that in a hurry. 'Why don't the pair of you toddle along to the hotel?' he said, still forcing the smile. 'Breakfast is at eight sharp.'

'Thank you,' Kate said diplomatically. She'd seen a potential fight brewing between me and Tesco. 'Come on, Rick.' She took my arm.

'Oh, by the way, you two.' Jesus spoke as if remembering some insignificant detail. 'You weren't thinking of leaving this morning?'

'Without saying goodbye,' added Tesco, the sneer returning.

'No,' Kate said. 'We thought we'd just take a walk.'

Jesus nodded as if accepting the explanation completely. Then he said lightly, 'It's just that Tesco noticed you were looking at the canoes just through those trees there.'

I glared at Tesco. He glared back.

'We were just interested to see how you live here,' Kate said, careful to sound casual. 'You seem very well organized.'

'Oh, we are,' Jesus said, still maintaining the benign smile. 'If it wasn't for the Greys we'd have a sweet life here. We've enough supplies to last three years or more.' He smiled more broadly. 'You two go ahead, enjoy your breakfasts. I hope the rats haven't spoilt your appetite.'

We started to walk back in the direction of the hotel.

'Oh, one more thing,' Jesus said. 'Don't ever try and run out on us. One: you'd die out there on the lake without our help. And two: you'll only bring out my bad side if I think you're going to try and leave us in the shit. OK?'

What could we do?

We nodded.

Then we returned to the hotel.

CHAPTER 72

Breakfast was good. In fact, it was delicious. Delicious enough to make me forget the rats.

'Orange juice?' Kate sounded astonished. 'Orange juice. I haven't tasted orange juice in weeks.'

'Bacon. Mmmm . . .' I breathed in. 'Fried bacon. And, Hell, just look at that. Sausages? Real sausages.'

'Rick?'

'Yes?'

'You know when you saw those canoes this morning. What was going through your mind?'

'The truth?'

She nodded. I looked round the dining room. It was empty. In the kitchen I could hear Beanpole Man, whisking something in a bowl.

'The truth is,' I whispered, 'I don't trust this Jesus guy as far as I could throw him.'

'You think he's planning something?'

I nodded. 'I'm not sure what. But I think he's got something up his sleeve once he gets his people up to Fountains Moor.'

'You believe there *is* a ship?'

'I think there is. Only I don't believe he wants us to be on it when he heads off for the South Seas.'

'So you thought we might use the canoes?'

'It's an option.'

'But you heard what he said, Rick. That lake's a dangerous place. Remember the rats?'

'I remember,' I said with feeling. 'I also remember what they were planning to do to us on that island. I'm going to sound repetitive, Kate, but I do not trust the guy.'

'Do you think—'

'Shh . . . here comes Matchstick Man.'

We sat back while the man served us. I had plenty to mentally chew over. I didn't trust Jesus in the long term. And in the short term I certainly didn't trust Tesco. The man had a mean streak. I guessed it wouldn't be long before he attempted to pay me back for the punch I'd given him.

That morning on Paradise Island sticks in my mind. Kate and I walked around its centre after breakfast (making sure we kept to the populated areas, well away from the rat-infested drain). It sticks in my mind because that morning was the first time I made love to Kate Robinson.

Fear, intense fear – so the experts say – often gives way to an equally intense desire for sex.

I admit it, the episode with the rats just a couple of hours earlier had scared me more than I could say. Now I was with Kate. We stood in what passed for the main street talking about this and that – would Howard Sparkman fly down to the island again, would the rat population dwindle once the food supply gave out, where did these people get all the hens from? – and so on. But I felt so incredibly charged with sex – Hell, let's be nakedly honest – charged with fucking lust. My skin, my whole insides burned with this incredible desire.

And there was Kate, looking so much like I'd seen her at Ben Cavellero's party. God, that seemed half, no three-quarters of a lifetime ago. When she stood there in the garden beneath the soft lamplight, a glass in one hand, so tall and so incredibly, wonderfully beautiful.

Now those delicious green eyes watched as a little fair-haired boy was towed along the street by a puppy tied to a length of hairy string. 'No, Jonty. Other way,' he was pleading. 'Back other way, Jonty. It's your bloody dinner time . . . Jonty . . . Jonty.'

Kate watched with that characteristic look of amusement, smiling, the fingernail of her index finger resting against her front teeth. Jonty pulled the boy, still beseeching it to return home for dinner, away down the street.

'You know,' she said, her eyes bright, 'these aren't bad people.'

'Probably no worse than anyone else. We're all trying to survive the disaster as best we can. It just means we have to think and act differently. And not let the realization that we may be acting contrary to our old, so-called civilized behaviour get in the way. Perhaps if the only way to survive is to turn cannibal, or ritually murder strangers from outside the community, then . . .' I shrugged.

'But surely survival doesn't require you to revert to complete savagery?' she said.

'Hopefully not. But it makes you wonder what we'll be doing – and what we'll be eating – in a couple of years, doesn't it?'

I paused as a small man with masses of curly hair walked up. He was dressed in a schoolboy's blazer which he held open.

Kate read the inscription printed on the T-shirt. *'Hallo. My name's Angel.'* She smiled. 'Hallo, Angel.'

I smiled too, warming to the little man's cheerful smile.

'Hallo, Angel.'

The man looked up at us both, shielding his eyes as if looking up at a very tall building. He feigned astonishment.

'You're so . . .' He lifted his hands up high as if to indicate our height.

'Tall?' Kate turned and laughed at me. 'I suppose we are. That makes us an odd couple, doesn't it?'

'But you're so . . . wow,' the man said, awed.

For a moment I saw Kate through his eyes. Her body, long, slender; again I felt lust blast through me. Christ, yes, she *was* gorgeous.

'You know I . . .' began the man. 'Odd, isn't it?'

'What's odd?' Kate asked gently.

'You being so . . .' He up-stretched his arms again. 'Like that. Up. Clouds there.' He frowned. I realized the man had difficulty in connecting words together into a meaningful sentence. And I felt a sudden irritation at Jesus. I didn't trust him. I almost wouldn't have minded if he behaved cruelly in an obviously despotic way, like a comic-strip villain. But he'd collected together the people that society had dumped on the streets. Carefully Jesus looked after them, clothed them, nurtured them, gave them pride and happiness.

The man smiled, but there was a sadness in his eyes. 'Funny, really

. . . I don't know, you know? I don't know what that . . .' He sighed, understanding that words escaped him. I sensed his sadness grow inside. His eyes watered. Then suddenly he took Kate's hand.

She flashed a look of alarm at me.

Then the man took hold of my hand in his other hand, then he placed both our hands on top of his head. I still remember the crisp feel of his curly hair, and the heat from his scalp.

He sighed again. 'Strange,' he said. 'I don't know who I am. I don't know where I am. I just don't know . . . someone must know how to help me.' He looked up at us, still holding our hands on his head in a childlike attempt to find comfort. 'What's happened to me?' He sighed again. A sad sigh. 'What did happen to me? Why am I lost? I'm lost all the time. Why am I . . .'

It was impossible not to feel touched. Perhaps more than anything it was the empathy. A year ago if this had happened to me in a street, of course I'd have experienced a touch of sadness. At a man who felt lost because of his mental illness.

But now we were all lost. The world had become alien and frightening. We didn't know how it had happened. We didn't know how we could return home. Or at least we didn't know how to return to that equilibrium of normality, and to the safety we'd once taken for granted.

Sadness pealed through me like the long, slow tolling of a funeral bell.

The man sighed again. Smiled sadly at us. Then walked away.

And I knew then what words I'd say to Kate. She might slap my face. She might storm off and never speak to me again. But I knew I had to come right out and say it.

'Kate. This sounds a pretty blunt question, but . . .' I took a deep breath and went for it, 'but I'd like . . . I want to make love to you.'

She looked at me. Her green eyes widened. Then she pushed her hair back from her face. 'Rick Kennedy.' Her face relaxed into a smile. 'I thought you'd never make a move.' She turned and began to walk back to the hotel.

I stood there, too astonished to realize what I must do next.

Kate looked back at me, smiled, then held out her hand. 'Rick Kennedy. What are you waiting for?' Her smile broadened. 'It'll be more fun with two, you know?'

I took her hand. Together we walked back to the hotel.

CHAPTER 73

Curtains closed. The view from that sixth-floor hotel room was gone. No more high-rise office blocks, no more church steeples or dead tree tops, lampposts, house roofs poking up above the flood waters. The wind blew. Autumn leaves hissed, making the same sound as surf surging in across a beach.

Inside we were alone. In that shadowy half-light of midday with closed curtains. Kate lay face down on the bed. She was completely naked. Her long hair spilled down her back in curling waves. And I couldn't help marvelling at her legs, as long as a dancer's, stretching out.

She lifted her head and rested her chin in both hands, her elbows supported by the bed.

When she smiled, suddenly the world seemed all right. *I* felt all right.

God . . . I could make believe the future would be all right.

'Come here,' she said in that soft, sweet voice. 'I want you to hold me tight again.'

I smiled. 'I want to kiss you again.'

'Good,' she said. 'We'll trade. My kiss for your hug.'

I put my arms around her, ran my fingers lightly down her spine. She shivered; her skin goose-fleshed.

'Oh,' she whispered. 'I can't believe the effect your touch has on me. You make me so hot. Feel.'

She rolled over onto her back and, taking my hand, pressed it to her chest just above her breasts.

I kissed her lips, chin, throat, then her breasts. They were taut and larger than I'd imagined, with nipples that were dark and round. I only had to touch them, then the skin on her breasts tightened and the nipples firmed into hard buttons.

'Oh, God,' she moaned. 'I'm not letting you out of here. Not for a long time yet.'

That was it. The machine had started. I let it take me over. I bunched her magnificent hair into my fists, kissed her on the mouth – again and again.

She breathed in deeply. Her hands stroked down my back, then gripped my buttocks, pulling down hard.

She breathed in deeply again, letting it out in a long sigh as I pushed myself into her.

Christ, this was good – this was fucking good.

The sensation of her vagina holding my penis as firmly as a cuff; her beautiful breasts against my chest, her hard nipples pressed into my skin like fingertips.

I loved the look of her eyes widening with a look of near surprise as I speared myself deep into her.

'Oh, Rick . . . that's beautiful.'

I ground my hips, crushing her public hair so that it mingled with mine. I drew breath sharply, losing myself in the silky sensations of my most intimate skin surfaces caressing hers.

She lifted her legs high, letting me in further. I moved faster, hearing the light smack of my pubic bone against hers. She breathed harder, all the time murmuring in my ear.

'Oh, that's wonderful . . . kiss me . . . don't stop now, oh never stop . . . beautiful . . . Christ, the touch of your skin . . . you've got amazing . . . amazing skin . . . I love it.'

'I've always wanted you,' I panted. 'I've always wanted you. Do you know that? Ah . . . ah. That feels out of this world.'

'Oh, Rick . . . Rick . . . on your back. Mmm . . . wonderful . . . smooth . . . smooth . . . no, Rick. Lie back . . . mmm—mermmm . . . Lie back, I want to do this . . . I want, oh, you taste so wonderful . . . mmm . . . mmm, zatt good, zatt nice . . .' she purred, licking.

Christ . . . I was floating, lost in that maze of pleasure. She was hitting buttons in my brain that I'd never known existed before. I couldn't speak. I could only lie there on my back. If I looked down I saw her with her head down, turning this way and that, her long hair stroking sensually across my stomach. Her bottom was raised, somehow replicating the shape of her shoulder blades – the same two high mounds – the same deep cleft between. She glistened with perspiration. You could sense the erotic excitement – animal – like in its intensity, running like electric shocks in tremors through her body; her skin flushed deep pink.

She shifted her position so she could straddle one of my legs and rub herself against me as she worked at my cock with her tirelessly questing tongue.

'Oh, God,' she panted, 'I want you inside me. I want you inside
. . . I can't stop it now. *Oh!*'

In one moment I was on top of her. Then in. Thrusting hard. That
internal reflex regulating the force and the rhythm of my thrusts. She
groaned. Her fingernails stabbed into my back. Her eyes screwed shut,
as just for a second her whole being seemed to rush deep inside her,
to bunch up tight inside her very core.

I didn't stop.

Couldn't stop.

I was hitting all the buttons.

I shafted faster.

Harder.

Christ, this was the best ever.

Fucking like this . . . the best thing ever.

Hearing her panting.

Seeing her face, eyes screwed shut, lips pressed tight.

Feeling her concentrate on that sensation.

Pressing so tight to her; I felt as if part of my spirit (as well as my
body) was there deep inside her; touching that magic place inside,
hitting that button to release—

'*Ah!*'

She screamed.

Screamed again.

'*Ah – yaaaa!*'

Suddenly her eyes opened; her expression seemed to unfold, to
open out.

Those green eyes locked on mine as the orgasm tore through
her body.

'Oh!'

I'd blown, too. Coming in a burst of heat inside of her.

Almighty God. We were like an explosive meeting a spark. The
blast of ecstasy left me dizzy, breathless, not even knowing where I
was, only that Kate was there with me. Her arms and legs wrapped
tightly round my body, her face, burning hot, pressed against my
throat, panting, her soft words streaming into my head.

We lay there, bodies cooling. The wind rustled the branches in the
trees; the curtains billowed gently in the breeze coming through the
open window.

It was just like any hotel room. Big double bed (message at the foot of the mattress to probably long-dead chambermaids: *Turn mattress once every six months*), a mini-electric kettle, the flex still neatly coiled, a basket that once contained complimentary tea, coffee, jiggers of UHT milk, a pack of chocolate-chip cookies.

There were plush carpets in a royal blue (never mind the shadow-like stain where some guest long ago spilt a glass of wine); then there were the usual bedside cabinets, a Gideon's Bible, Thomson London local directory, radio, telephone now forever silent. TV standing in the corner.

Just like any other hotel room, I thought, lying there, hazing out in a delicious wash of relaxation, Kate Robinson snuggling close beside me, her bare skin touching mine. Just like any other room. The kind of room I'd have been staying in if Thunder Bud had made the big time. We'd have done those coast-to-coast tours. We'd have played the MTV *Unplugged* show. I'd have hung electric guitars alongside the gold and platinum discs on the walls of my apartment that I'd bought in . . . where? LA, New York, Paris, maybe here in this very London street.

I put my arm round the beautifully long back of the woman beside me.

That dream was gone now. I'd never be a rock star. I'd never play sell-out gigs at twenty thousand-seater stadiums. This was the new reality now. A city drowned beneath a flood. Fire creeping up from the Earth's core to burst through the soil beneath your feet.

On that conveyor belt of hard realities was the fact that I'd loved Caroline. That I'd lost her. And had had to burn her once lovely body on that funeral pyre on the hill-top.

Lightly I touched Kate's hair. I'd gone head over heels for Kate. If I lost her, too, could I take that kind of pain again?

She kissed me lightly on the chin.

'Rick?'

'Yes?'

'I'm glad you found me.'

'I'm glad, too . . . very glad.' I meant it, but the words stung. It was almost a replay of what Caroline had said the day she'd died. When I'd sensed that fear, that pure naked fear hovering over us like some dreadful bat-winged monster.

Waiting to strike.

For a second I felt its monstrous presence again.

Christ, no, I couldn't lose Kate. I couldn't bear that brutal realization – that sheer sense of *knowing* I was alone again.

I held her tight.

The wind rustled the leaves, bringing that sound again. Like surf hissing across the beach. Rising, then falling to a gentle whispering sound before surging loudly once more.

My eyes closed.

We were running. The dream was unusually clear. We were running down the hill from my home at Fairburn. There was my brother Stephen as he looked then; his silk shirt inflating as the blast of air fills it. He's holding the little girl, Lee, in his arms. Also, I see Caroline, her face and bare arms mottled red as if splashed by red wine, boiled by the geyser. She runs too, eyes wide with fright. Then I see Dean, Howard, Ruth; even ten-year-old Jim Keller, who lost his thumbs – and his life – in that car accident all those years ago.

And I see myself. I'm ten years old again. My little trainers slap the cinder track as I run.

Slap, slap, slap . . . my feet send up puffs of black cinder dust. The plastic Robocop mask jiggles around my neck.

We're running for our lives.

We're being chased by a creature with huge wings; it has no eyes but its bat-ears stick up high from its skull. In its slash-like mouth are oversized rats' teeth.

I know it can fly.

Even as the thought runs through my head, it spreads its wings and launches itself forwards. It glides down at us. I look up. Clearly I see the wings; the feathers are grey.

I look up again. This time I see properly. They aren't feathers. They are rows and rows of grey men, glued side by side, head to foot. Their eyes are open. They are all blood-red. They are fixed on me.

And I know it's me that they want.

The creature beats it wings. They make a huge thudding sound, loud enough to vibrate the bones in my head.

Thud, thud, thud . . .

It swoops down at me.

Thud, thud, thud . . .

'Hey, wake up in there!'

'Rick . . . *Rick*.'

I opened my eyes. Kate, kneeling up on the bed, was shaking me by the shoulder.

Thud, thud, thud.

The sound was someone pounding urgently at the room door.

'Hey . . . wake up!'

'It's Tesco,' Kate said. 'Be careful. He might try something.'

'Christ . . . can't you hear me?' Tesco bellowed. 'Open the fucking door!'

'Why?' I called.

'Open the door!'

'What's wrong?'

'Hurry up, open the door, or it'll be too late!'

We started to drag on clothes. What if Tesco was standing there, waiting to blow off my head with a shotgun? Cautiously I called, 'What's happening?'

'If you open this fucking door I'll fucking tell you!'

'Careful, Rick,' Kate warned.

'If you don't open this door, Kennedy, I'll bust it down.'

I knew I had no choice.

'Hurry up, Kennedy. I've got something to tell you. Hurry, it's important.'

I took a deep breath and opened the door.

CHAPTER 74

After I answered the door Tesco bundled us downstairs to meet Jesus at the entrance of the hotel. Then he, Tesco, Kate and myself walked down the street. For a moment Jesus didn't speak but you could sense the urgency, the sheer electric tension. The strips of silk tied to Tesco's arms and legs rippled and cracked in the breeze.

I didn't know where the Hell we were going, or what would happen when we got there. Maybe Jesus had changed his mind about his South Seas trip?

Perhaps Kate and I would be chained to stakes at the water's edge? Then the rats would come back. This time there would be no canine cavalry. The rats would strip the skin from our faces.

Suddenly Jesus began to talk; he didn't pause in his rapid stride: 'Kate. Rick. The situation is this. Remember the island where you landed?'

329

I cast a look at Tesco. 'Remember it? We can hardly forget it.'

Jesus breezed on. 'Well, a plane landed there about half an hour ago.'

'A plane?'

'Your plane. A four-seater Cessna.'

'Whoa, wait a minute,' I said. 'We weren't expecting our plane until tomorrow, Wednesday.'

'So he's a day early,' Tesco snapped.

I said, 'You've spoken to the pilot?'

'No,' Jesus stopped. 'We didn't want to scare him off. Cowboy and a couple of our lot are keeping a discreet watch on the island.'

'But he's a day early,' Kate said. 'We can't be sure it's even our plane.'

Jesus looked at Tesco. 'Did we get the plane's registration number?'

'No. But we got a description of the plane. Like you said, it's a four-seater Cessna.'

I sighed. 'Cessnas are just about the most common plane in the world. It might not even be ours.'

'You know, Kennedy, you might just be right.' Tesco's scarred lips broke into a smile.

I didn't like the smile. And I realized he knew this might put a different and dangerous spin on the situation.

'Come on.' Jesus frowned. 'Surely we got a better description of the plane?'

'We did. Tutts has a note of it.'

'Where is she?'

'Waiting down on the jetty.'

'Come on, then,' Jesus sounded impatient. 'If we waste any more time our pilot might just decide not to wait any longer.'

Tesco's grin widened in a way I didn't like at all. 'Just a moment. I remember Tutts mentioned the colour of the plane.'

Jesus looked at me. 'What colour is your plane?'

'White.'

Tesco's grin turned malicious. 'Pity . . . the colour of this one is yellow.'

'Come on,' Jesus said, 'We've got to get to the island before the pilot leaves.'

'After you, Miss Robinson. Mr Kennedy.' Tesco gave an exaggerated bow. The coloured ribbons fluttered. I couldn't help but notice the way he rested his palm on the butt of the sawn-off shotgun he had shoved through his belt.

I walked alongside Kate. The conversation we had as we walked to the waiting boats was fast and whispered, so Tesco swaggering along behind and Jesus hurrying ahead shouting instructions to his people wouldn't hear.

'See the problem?' I said.

'Unfortunately, yes. It looks as if it isn't our plane.'

'So we're in the shit again.'

'I take it they'll try and make the same deal with the pilot of this plane as they did with us?'

'Yep. Then they'll cut us out of the deal once they've got alternative transportation.' I looked at her. 'As soon as they don't need us anymore, they'll think up some pretty way of killing us.'

We reached the boats. They were standing by a jetty built from old housebricks, the outboard motors were idling and Jesus's men stood holding the mooring lines ready for a fast departure.

Tutts scrambled out of the boat and ran towards us, her silk ribbons fluttering about her. She looked pleased to see me and shot me a huge smile. 'Your plane's come,' she shouted. 'Rick, your plane's come. Isn't it brilliant?'

Tesco gave a wicked grin. 'It's not Kennedy's plane.'

'Of course it's his plane,' she said and squeezed my arm.

Tesco shook his head. 'Oh no, it's not. It's a day early for one. Also it's not the same colour.' He stroked the butt of the shotgun with his fingertips. 'We've a new kid on the block with his own wings.'

Tutts shrugged. 'What's this about colour?'

Jesus said, 'Rick told me their plane is white.'

Tesco grinned. 'And your description is yellow.'

I shivered. Tesco would love killing me.

Then Tutts gave a hiccupping laugh.

Tesco scowled. 'What's wrong with you?'

'A yellow plane?' She laughed again.

'Yes. Yellow.' Tesco's annoyance flashed. 'Yellow, fucking yellow, so what?'

She held up a sheet of paper on which there was a handwritten note. 'The description was written by Rolle.'

'Rolle?' Jesus shook his head. 'Cowboy should know better by now.'

331

Tutts laughed again and squeezed my arm in both hands.

Tesco swore, then stamped off to sit in one of the boats.

'Excuse me,' I said, totally bewildered. 'Can anyone explain to me what's happening?'

Jesus wasn't amused. 'Cowboy went and let Rolle write down the description of the plane.'

'So?'

'So Rolle did a lot of acid a while back. Virtually everything he sees is bright yellow. Including the sky, people, dogs – and no doubt your four-seater Cessna aircraft.'

Kate said, 'But we still can't be sure it's ours.'

'Tutts?' Jesus held out his hand for the note. He quickly read it. 'There's another description.' He looked at Kate, then me. 'Were there any markings on the wings?'

I shrugged. I couldn't think of any.

Kate remembered. 'Ah. On the underside of the wings there were black chevrons.'

Jesus held out the paper. 'Like these?'

On the paper Rolle had pencilled a series of marks like this: >>>>.

Kate smiled, nodded. 'That's our plane.'

Jesus said curtly. 'Let's hope for all our sakes he's still there when we reach the island. Please get into the boat.'

There were two fibreglass boats. Each held around eight people, and each was fitted with outboard motors that were so heavy they pushed down the sterns of the boat and lifted the prows out of the water. Kate and I made a point of sitting in the boat which didn't hold Tesco. He still looked at us with undisguised rage.

'He nearly had us there,' I whispered to Kate as the outboard motors pushed us on across the floodwaters. 'Did you see the look in his eye?'

'Just pray it *is* our plane.'

'You did well to remember the chevron marks on the wings.'

'Did I, Hell,' she looked me in the eye. 'I noticed the marks on the paper when Tutts was cuddling you.' She turned to look at the half-submerged buildings passing by. 'So, like I say, just pray to God Almighty it is our plane. And that we do see old Sparky's smiling face when we land on the island.'

Reaching the island wasn't as quick or as easy as I'd hoped.

The boats were fast – fast enough to make the strips of silk tied to the arms and legs of Jesus's gang ripple and crack straight out like pennants in the blast of wind. But I soon noticed the boatmen steered the boats in long zig-zags over what seemed a featureless expanse of water.

'What's wrong?' I called to Jesus, sitting at the other side of the boat. 'Why don't we travel in a straight line?'

Jesus leaned toward me. 'The water's full of debris. Also there are houses just under the water. Look over the side. See those red rings just below the surface?'

'I see them.'

'Chimney pots. We're skimming just above them. If we hit one it'll knock a hole in the bottom of the boat.'

Kate nudged me. 'See that? Floating in the water?'

'A rotting lion?'

Jesus nodded. 'We've seen a few drowned animals from the zoo – zebra, giraffe. Angel once claimed to have seen a hippo swimming by the end of the jetty, but . . .' Jesus shrugged. 'If you've spoken to Angel you'll realize he sees lots of things. Demons. Ghosts riding bicycles. Angels. Hundreds of angels.'

'How long to the island?' I asked.

'Twenty minutes, if nothing gets in our way.'

'Gets in our way?' Kate sounded alarmed. 'What's likely to get in our way?'

'Uprooted trees float downstream, sometimes they form a kind of natural raft that might stretch half a kilometre. Also remember that when this was dry land there were subway tunnels, underground sewers, and the bigger tunnels for the trains on the London Underground. Sometimes they act like giant plugholes when the water level drops on the other side of town. You know, remember when the water used to go round and round in your kitchen sink as it went down?'

'Like a whirlpool?'

'Yeah, sometimes those appear. Then you have to give them a wide berth, otherwise they pull the boat down like it's just a bit of fluff.'

I looked out over the deceptively still waters. Every so often a house roof broke the surface, sometimes a TV aerial clipped the side of the boat with a loud rattling sound. Everywhere debris floated: wooden crates, empty bottles, a child's ball bearing pictures of Woody and Captain Buzz Lightyear from *Toy Story* – the wake spun the ball

333

flashing the slogan *TO INFINITY AND BEYOND!* Then there were
mushy clots of floating newspapers, sections of wooden garden shed,
oil drums, even, bizarrely, a coffin lid; oh, and bodies, lots of rotting
bodies: dogs, cats, pigeons. People.

In the distance there were the office blocks of central London,
the tower of Big Ben, the dome of St Paul's Cathedral, the huge
tombstone oblong of Centre Point.

It wasn't easy to stay calm, cool and collected about all this. I
found my palms sweated until they left prints on the plank that
served as one of the boat's seats. I looked at my watch. It was two
in the afternoon. For some reason Howard Sparkman (if it really
was Howard and not a total stranger who'd stumbled across the
island) had made the flight down to London a day early. Why? God
alone knew, but there had to be some reason. And you didn't have
to work hard to imagine some reasons. Other survivors had found
the camp? Hotspots were breaking out on Fountains Moor, forcing
a move? Had something happened to Stephen?

I shut off the horror scenarios running through my head. I'd
make myself wait and hear the reason from Howard's own lips.
That was, if he was still there. If he found us gone he'd be tempted
to fire up the plane's motor and get out of there pretty damn
quick. If he did that, sure as eggs were eggs, he would never
come back.

CHAPTER 75

SPARKY'S ISLAND. PRIVATE. KEEP OFF.

The sign that Kate Robinson had jokingly chalked onto the wall
was still legible.

As the boat surged towards the shore I stared hard at the expanse
of grass that had once been a football pitch. I was willing myself to
see the white plane with Howard Sparkman standing nonchalantly
beside it, waiting for us to land. My heart sank.

'Oh God.' Kate spoke in a low voice. 'It's not there. He's gone,
hasn't he?'

I stared out across the water. I felt numb. What if we were stranded

334

here in this flooded city? Tesco would think nothing now of blasting us with that sawn-off shotgun of his, then dropping us into the lake. Even if we could somehow escape, how could we walk through hundreds of kilometres of countryside that was lousy with millions of hungry, desperate people?

Jesus told the boatman to bring the boat in to the shore.

The moment the boat beached with a scrunching sound I let out a sigh of relief.

'You see the plane?' Kate asked in a low voice.

'Over there behind the hedge. You can just make out the tail fin. Come on, let's find Mr Sparkman.'

It was clear enough what had happened. Howard Sparkman had landed the plane and seen that Kate and I were nowhere in sight, so he'd tried to conceal the plane as best he could by taxi-ing alongside the overgrown hedge. Then he'd set out to search the island.

We found him cautiously poking open the door of one of the millionaire houses with the muzzle of his rifle and calling, 'Hallo? Rick? Kate?'

'Hallo, Howard.'

With a startled gasp he swung round, the rifle pointing up at my face.

'Whoa, Sparky. It's only me.' I grinned as he lowered the rifle. He sighed with relief and wiped the sweat from his forehead, knocking his gold-rimmed glasses cock-eyed as he did so. I noticed how much his hands trembled as he straightened them.

'Christ, bloody Christ.' Howard breathed deeply to steady his nerves. 'Kate. Rick. Where the Hell did you get to?'

'It's a long story.'

'I thought you were gone ... dead ... I was just about to fly back home ... hell, you gave me a shock ...' He breathed deeply, so out of breath he had to lean forward and rest his hands on his knees. Perspiration glistened on his nose.

Kate glanced at me, then back at Jesus, Tesco and the rest of the tribe standing in the bushes. 'We'd better introduce Howard to our new friends, hadn't we?'

He looked up in surprise. 'Friends?'

I couldn't help but smile at what I what going to ask him next. 'Howard. How would you like to meet Jesus?'

'Eh?'

My smile broadened. 'If you step this way, Howard. I know Jesus is just dying to say hallo.'

And that's how Howard Sparkman found Jesus. Only this Jesus, of course, was a forty-year-old Liverpudlian, his hands covered with home-pricked tattoos, and known for at least thirty-nine years of his life as Gary Topp.

Over the next forty-five minutes we explained the plan to Howard. To fly Jesus and his people up to Fountains Moor. Then to transport them and our community to the coast where we'd board the ship for the South Seas. If you said it quickly enough it sounded plausible. But Howard was quick to point out that the logistics of transporting what amounted to well over a hundred people in a four-seater plane would be nightmarish.

'We can do it,' Jesus told him.

'Yeah, we *can* do it,' Howard held out his hands. 'But you're talking about me flying maybe forty round trips?'

Jesus wouldn't let a cruddy little thing like practicalities come between him and his dream. Maybe the man really did believe he could perform miracles. 'We can do it. We can fly every single man, woman and child out of here. Then fly your people to the coast. We have to. Or we're all dead.'

CHAPTER 76

My name is Kate Robinson.

It's now three days since the plane left for Fountains Moor with Kandi, the girlfriend of the man these people call Jesus. Ostensibly she is acting as messenger. But no one's in any doubt that she's really going as voluntary hostage. Rick is still suspicious of Jesus's motives. He thinks we might be double-crossed in some way, but I don't see how. Basically the plan is that Howard will fly all of Jesus's community in batches of twos and threes, along with as much food he can carry, back to Fountains Moor. Once Jesus's community have all been moved there, Howard will then start moving both communities to the coast where the ship lies at anchor. This will be done in alternate batches, first three of our community, then three of Jesus's, and so on.

More than once I've woken in the middle of the night to see Rick pacing the room in the dark, rubbing his fist into the palm of his hand, trying to work out how Jesus might trick us. Rick's convinced himself that somehow Jesus will get his people onto the ship then leave without us.

You'll have gathered by now that Rick has left his room to move in with me here. Suddenly, and it has caught me by surprise, I find that we're an 'item.' I'm pleased, no doubt about that. He's gentle, kind, considerate, has a great sense of humour. But underlying that there is a sense of sadness which he tries to mask with wisecracks.

But the shock of what has happened, civilization coming apart at the seams in just a few months, is really far more than we can absorb. Six months ago we were going about our ordinary day-to-day lives. I was working at the book shop, Rick had planned to tour with his band. Now all that is in ruins. Relatives, friends, neighbours are dead. Sometimes I think the real shock will hit us in years to come. At the moment we are too busy with the business of just surviving to sit back and think about what and who we might have lost.

We still wonder what kind of future we will have. Will the Earth still continue to grow hotter? Will the heat kill all life on the planet? Who are these mysterious grey people? I've heard the theory that they might actually be from some kind of lost world from beneath the surface of the planet. But perhaps there is some simpler explanation. I just don't know. What I do know is the idea of boarding that ship and sailing south away from all this does seem so appealing. I only hope Rick is wrong about Jesus. And that our two groups can join together.

At the moment Rick is chopping logs for firewood. He becomes so restless with nothing to occupy him.

I'm sitting here in the hotel lounge. It's eerily quiet. Rick and I are the only people who actually live here. Again, I can't help but imagine it before the disaster struck. There'd be staff, smart in their uniforms, checking in guests, or waiting on tables through in the restaurant. Once we're gone it'll be left to the rats and to rot quietly into the ground.

It's now four hours since I wrote the above. As I was writing there was a flurry of excitement outside. I looked out of the window. Jesus's people were running down to the water's edge as a boat approached the island. There was a lot of shouting and arm waving. I couldn't see what was happening. Just then I saw Rick run past the window and down to the jetty.

It was only when I left the hotel and went down to the water's edge myself that I saw what all the fuss was about.

Jesus's island had a new visitor.

His name?

Stephen Kennedy.

CHAPTER 77

My name is Rick Kennedy.

My brother, Stephen Kennedy, was back. He sat in an armchair in the hotel room, one leg casually crossed across a knee as he cleaned the lens of the camcorder. He cleaned it with scrupulous care with a cloth, blowing away any speck of dust he saw sticking to the lens. I sat on the end of the bed.

You can forget any touching scenes of two brothers being reunited. The argument began almost straight away.

Kate had offered to bring us coffee from the hotel kitchen. In the good old days – all of six months ago – you could have plugged in the kettle and helped yourself to the hotel's complimentary sachets of Nescafé. Now, with no electricity, all cooking was by bottled gas.

Stephen and I had been talking for the last hour. He knew all about Jesus's plan to make for the ship and sail south.

'Hell, it's good to sit on a real chair again,' Stephen said. 'You must have thought you'd died and gone to Heaven when you first arrived here. Can you smell that? Baking bread. You don't know how amazing that smells.'

'When we first arrived here it was nearer to Hell. They were going to kill us.'

'But this guy Jesus put a stop to all that when he found out you came by plane?'

'Yeah, just in time. But these people indulge in ritualistic murder. You should see the cellar where they locked—'

'We live in a different world now, Rick.' He showed zip-all interest in what atrocities these people might have committed. The ship was all that mattered now. He was obsessed with quitting this burning Hell of a country.

Still wiping the lens Stephen asked, 'Have they told you what the ship is like?'

'He's given me some facts and figures, yeah. It's a cargo freighter called *The Mirdath*. As far as he knows its fuel tanks are full, the cargo holds are bulging with canned and dried foods.'

'Sounds a peach. How did they come by it?'

'One of the people here has a father on the ship. When civilization bellied up they managed to keep in touch by ham radio.'

'But they've still insufficient crew on board to move the ship?'

'The ship was due to sail to Sweden. The night before departure Whitby was torn apart by an explosion. All but three of the crew were on shore leave. They never made it back to the ship.'

'A hot-spot? So far east?'

'Seems like it. Probably ignited a pocket of gas beneath the town. The three people left on the ship saw the whole town was alight. There were even flames gushing out of the water in the harbour; the gas must have been venting like crazy. The men left on the ship managed to cut through the cables tying the ship to the wharf. Luckily the tide was on its way out, so the current simply carried them safely out to sea where they dropped anchor.'

'By the way, Howard Sparkman's managed to give Cindy Gullidge sufficient flying lessons. She's competent enough to handle the Cessna. So we're ready to start tomorrow.'

'Whoa, Stephen. You're going too fast for me. What's all this? Start what tomorrow?'

He gave a tired smile. 'Hard work but we cracked it. Howard has been training Cindy to fly. And now we've two serviceable planes, the four-seater Cessna and an eight-seater Piper, we can start flying Jesus's people up to Fountains Moor tomorrow morning.'

'No, Stephen.'

'No?'

'Look,' I said, 'when I saw you this morning I thought, great, we can talk this through together.'

He looked up at me in surprise. 'What's there to talk through? We need to move these people up to Fountains Moor as quickly as possible. Then we transfer everyone to the coast, ready to board the ship.'

'No, Stephen. This is way too fast.'

'Too fast. Rick, Jesus Christ. It might already be too *late*.'

'The Grey Men. Have you seen them? These people—'

'Fuck the Grey Men, Rick. I've not seen any of these Grey Men yet. They're the least of my problems. Do you know what food we have left up there?'

'Stephen. Look, this is too important to rush. I've told you half a dozen times now. These people are committing ritualistic murder. They snatch survivors from other communities, or people travelling alone, then they torture them to fucking death; while the whole fucking community watches.'

'Rick, I think—'

'They get fucking high on it.'

'And you think they'll torture *us* to death?'

'I don't trust them.'

'Come on, Kid K, they're hardly going to do that if they need us to fly them up to Whitby. Think it through, man.'

'I don't trust them. You don't know what they're like.'

His eyes narrowed. 'Do you know what I was doing last night, Rick?'

'Hell, Stephen. This is important. These people are murderers, and we're—'

'Last night, Rick,' he continued through gritted teeth, 'last night I went out and collected slugs in a jar.'

I looked at him.

'That's right.' He nodded. 'We've been reduced to eating slugs and snails. You have to be careful with snails. Don't pick the ones with brightly coloured shells because they tend to be poisonous. And this morning I left Dean boiling stinging nettles and dandelion roots for his breakfast so little Lee could have his share of oatmeal. What kind of diet do you think that is?'

'But you had food dumps out on the moor!'

'Another group found them. When we went out for more supplies we found they'd been picked clean.'

'Christ.'

'Yeah, Christ. It'd be nice to get some help from Him but it really looks like we're going to have to help ourselves. *Comprende*, kiddo?'

I'd never seen Stephen like this before. For the first time I'd heard a hint of threat in the way he spoke and seen it in the way his blue eyes looked at me. He didn't want anyone, not even his brother, questioning his plans. He'd seen a solution to all his problems.

The Ship. And he wanted it so badly that if any damn fool stood in his way, then, by God Almighty, he'd get angry. Then he'd get dangerous.

My mind went back to Fairburn, and the times we'd raced each other down to the footbridge over the River Tawn. I'd seen his ambition then; his burning lust to win. How he'd even trick me so he'd be first to reach the bridge. That ambition was burning as bright as ever.

He clipped the battery pack onto the camcorder.

'What are you going to do with that?' I asked.

'I planned to take some shots of how these people live.'

'For the archive?.'

'Yes.'

I saw red. 'Why do you fucking bother with the archive?'

'I think it's even more important we keep a record of how we survived.'

'Why?'

'Because if we don't this period will really be a new Dark Age. Our children won't know what happened. There'll be a gap between the world we once knew and life in the future.'

'What future?'

'We're going to make it, Rick.'

'We might. But not if we join up with these people. I don't—'

'I don't trust them,' he mimicked. 'I know, I know, you keep telling me.'

Just at that moment Kate walked in, carrying a tray of coffee cups. She froze, her eyes widening as she realised that she'd just walked into the middle of a raging argument.

'I don't trust them,' I repeated loudly. 'They're going to double-cross us.'

'No. They are not.'

'You don't know them.'

'You do?'

'Bring that fucking camera down into the cellar where they locked me up. Read what people have written on the walls before they were—'

'Are you deaf or what!'

'I'm not fucking deaf.'

'You must be. I told you, and told you again. This is a different world.'

'Different world!'

'Yes, a different world! We have different rules.'

'So it's OK to feed people alive to pit-bulls, or set them on fire or rape girls with a soldering iron!'

'Rick! We need to get away from Fountains Moor. Winter's going to set in. We're living in tents.'

'So, out of the frying pan and into the fire?'

'And we've no food left.'

'Find some, then. Stop fucking wasting your time with the archive, and filming everything as if it's the most important event in fucking history!'

'We've tried to find more food. But everywhere's been picked clean! Look at that!' Stephen opened his mouth, pushed in his finger and pulled aside his cheek so I could see between the inside of his cheek and gum.

'See what?' I was in a stinking fury.

'Mouth ulcers. Caused by vitamin B deficiency. We're all developing them. Back on Fountains Moor we're hungry. We don't have the energy to work anymore; we're constantly tired—'

'But is this the way to save them?'

'So you've a better idea?'

Kate began, 'Stephen. We need to sit down and discuss—'

'Keep out this!' Stephen snapped. 'It's Rick here who's got the problem.' Kate's face flushed red.

'I haven't got the problem, Stephen. You're so keen to rush these people up to Fountains Moor you won't even take ten minutes out to listen to what—'

'We're flying these people out of here. Then we're all going to the ship. *Comprende?*'

'Who decided?'

'I did,' Stephen said in a cold voice. 'My decision.'

'So Dean, Howard, old man Fullwood don't know what they're letting themselves in for?'

'I explained the situation; we discussed it.'

'Like you let Kate here discuss it with you. Christ, Stephen, have you turned into a dictator or what?'

Stephen's eyes glittered dangerously at me. 'Rick. All I'm interested in is saving the lives of sixty-four people up on that damned moor.'

'They need to know what kind of people they'll be trapped on board a ship with for God knows how many weeks.'

'It'll work.'

'It won't. We'll be two groups with two different leaders – you in charge of us, Jesus in charge of them.'

'Rick. It will work.'

'It won't. In a couple of weeks we'll be slitting each other's throats.'

'Rick, I'm not changing my mind. Tomorrow we start flying these people out. If the weather holds we can ship them out in batches of up to a dozen a day.'

'You're making a big mistake.'

Surprisingly, Stephen agreed. 'Yeah, you're right. I am making a big mistake. I'm making a big mistake sitting here and listening to you rubbishing my plans.'

He stood up and walked to the door. I blocked his path.

'Stephen. We've got to talk about this.'

'No, we haven't. It's decided. We take the ship.' His eyes blazed. 'And just one other thing . . . *Kid K*.' He used the nickname as if it revolted him. 'Do not stand in my way again. Otherwise I'll walk right through you. Got that?'

'But you've—'

'I said, have you got that!' With that he pushed me sideways. I slammed into Kate. Steaming coffee cups flew back, covering her in scalding liquid. She screamed. The force of his push carried us on, over the top of an armchair to land on the floor.

I sat up, swearing.

Stephen walked out of the room, slamming the door behind him.

'Shit, I'm not taking that from him.'

'Rick, don't—'

'He's fucking insane. Did you see that?' I shook my head in disbelief.

'Ouch.' Kate pulled her wet T-shirt away from her breasts.

I crouched beside her. 'Christ. Are you all right?'

'I'll live. Ouch.' She pulled the T-shirt from her scalded breast again.

'The bastard's burnt you!'

'Rick. No!' She called as I stormed towards the door. 'Leave it, Rick. Come back here. Don't, Rick. It's not worth it!'

But sheer fury had got a hold of me. Anger. Christ, yes, I blazed with it. I threw open the door and marched into the corridor.

I was going to find my brother.

And no one – but no one – was going to stop me.

CHAPTER 78

I saw my brother standing down by the jetty talking to Tesco and Jesus. There was a whole bunch of Jesus's people standing there, too, their strips of silk crackling out like pennants in the breeze.

The breeze gusted cold.

But I didn't feel it. The blood boiled in my veins. I couldn't believe how Stephen had behaved. He wouldn't listen to reason. The scalds he'd inflicted on Kate would blister and scar.

The man had turned into a monster.

Teeth gritted, fists clenched, I walked down the street, my stride hard and very, very angry.

'Hello, Rick. Marvellous news, isn't it?' Tutts appeared by my side. She wore stilettos, the zebra-patterned miniskirt and on her top half, a leather jacket zipped against the cold. 'Aren't you and your brother alike? You could be twins. And isn't he just gorgeous? I mean really, really gorgeous. He's got lovely eyes.'

I didn't answer. I walked faster – angrier.

Tutts had to run to keep up, the stilettos click-clicking against the road. 'Jesus is drawing up a list of who goes first. You know something, Rick? I might be on the first plane . . . Rick. Rick? What's wrong? *Rick!*'

Picture the scene: Stephen's talking to Jesus. He's describing a vital aspect of the plan, he's moving his hands, smiling his showbiz smile. Stephen, as charismatic as ever, has got them in the palm of his hand. They stand there – Jesus in leather waistcoat, Tesco and the rest looking like carnival figures with hair dyed every colour of the rainbow, silk strips fluttering, dressed in jeans, cowboy boots and bikers' leather jackets. Tutts stops dead, her mouth open in shock. She knows there's going to be trouble.

Bang.

I steamed straight in, shoved Stephen in the chest so hard he almost fell.

'Who the Hell do you think you are?' I shouted at Stephen.

344

'The poor schmuck who's trying to save your life,' he roared back. 'Now just piss off and let your big brother carry on doing just that.'

I saw Tesco and Jesus exchanging looks. They were surprised, but also curious to see what would happen next.

'Like Hell I'll piss off,' I snapped. 'You're going to listen to me.'

'Listen to you?' Stephen snorted. 'I hear my arse fart more sense than you talk.'

'Why won't you listen?'

'Why don't you fuck off?'

'Come with me and I'll show – *uph*.'

That's when he swung the punch. It caught me on the cheekbone. I went down, feeling as if a lump of concrete had just tumbled out of the sky on top of me.

'Don't get up,' he warned me. 'Not until I tell you. Then go back to the hotel.'

I didn't wait to be told. I got up.

I punched, catching him a glancing blow on the chin. It still hurt him, though. He ducked back, shaking his head, swearing under his breath. I swung again. And again. Some blows connecting. Some not.

And all I could think about was that photo of him on the dining room wall at Mum's house in Fairburn. That glossy showbiz photo with God Almighty Stephen Kennedy, hair blow-dried, that metre-long strip of dazzling teeth, twinkling eyes. That huge scribbled signature in red felt-tip that turned the looping 'y' in Kennedy into a happy-smiley face. His TV station had sent those out to his fans by the hundred.

At some point my famous video-jock brother had decided to stoop down to us mortals who exist at dirt level, and he'd sent a photograph to his mother and only brother.

Oh thank you, Mr Stephen-God-Almighty-Kennedy. Thank you so much for your fucking stupid photo.

I realized then how much I hated the photo. How much I hated *him*.

My fists blurred. They cracked again and again into his face. He was knocked back through the line of men. Tesco tried to catch hold of Stephen to help him regain his balance. I shoved Tesco back so hard he fell back into the water.

'Keep out of this!' I yelled. 'And don't you dare get in the fucking way!'

Right there and then I believe I could have pissed pure rage. All
I wanted to do was destroy my brother. I punched again and again.
His face? It was like hitting a pillow filled with feathers. I felt nothing.
I didn't feel the cuts on my knuckles where I'd split the skin driving
my punches at his skull.

I didn't feel it when he poked one back to my jaw or eye.

I just wanted to smash that handsome, oh-so-handsome face
to pulp.

Blood sprayed.

Tutts was screaming.

Blood covered Stephen's face.

It covered my fists. Thick, slick. Red as strawberry jam.

I cracked out another punch. It connected with his chin. Blood
sprayed, showering drops the size of pennies to spot the tarmac.

Christ.

This was good.

This was so fucking good.

This was revenge.

Revenge for everything.

Revenge for pushing me.

For hurting Kate.

For leaving me.

I realized the truth.

This wasn't because of what had happened ten minutes ago.

This is because of what had happened ten *years* ago.

He quit trying to hit me. Instead he grabbed me by the neck; his arm
felt like a band of steel crushing my throat. I was off balance. I tried
to push against the ground with my feet to knock him backwards.

Christ, he was strong. And this time he was spitting his own
rage.

Every time I kicked down at the ground with the heels of both
feet it sent a judder through us.

It shook more droplets of blood down onto black road tar where
they glistened, darkly, like drops of oil from an engine.

Tutts screamed, 'Jesus ... Tesco! Stop them! They're killing
each other!'

From the corner of my eye I saw an upturned dinghy at the side
of the road. I worked my way to it. Pushing him back as I thrust
down with both feet against the ground. The sky looked darker. I
realized his grip was starving my brain of oxygen.

I pushed back harder. He bumped against the boat. His calves pressed hard against it as I shoved. I shoved harder. He toppled back.

His body weight crashed him through the fibreglass hull of the boat as though it was no more substantial than an oversized eggshell.

He released his grip. I scrambled to my feet. He rolled free of the ruined boat.

One second flat: we were both facing each other again.

I swung my fists at him. This time he always moved backward. Every blow – one step back.

Still, I felt pumped up tight with rage. I wanted to kill him. I roared obscenities. Sweat stung my eyes now. I could hardly see.

But I saw what he did next. He stood up straight, looked over my shoulder.

Warily I shot a look back, wondering if Tesco was coming up behind, wanting a piece of me.

But without realizing it, I'd pushed Stephen back through some bushes. We couldn't even see the others now. But they wouldn't be far behind; they'd want to see the outcome of the fight.

I looked back at Stephen. The expression on his face had changed.

He looked me steadily in the face. Then he held his hands up at either side of his head, like a defeated soldier surrendering to the enemy.

I knew then that I should have stopped hitting.

But something else drove me now.

As he stood there like a crucified Messiah, his calm blue eyes on me, well, that's when I hit him for the last time.

CHAPTER 79

I looked down at my brother. He lay on the double bed in the hotel room.

Kate had drawn the curtains after they'd carried him inside. There he lay on the white sheet, his head turned slightly to one side on the pillow. His face bruised purple from my punches.

Dead.

The autumn wind blew against the hotel. It produced a moaning sound – cold, lonely somehow. Like an animal lost in the dark.

I'd killed my brother.

After I'd punched him, as he'd stood there, arms up at either side, not attempting to fight back, nor even shielding himself from the blow, that's what had run through my mind.

Instantly all the anger had gone. As if turned off by a tap.

He'd lain where he'd fallen, flat on his back, eyes staring.

Jesus, Tesco, Tutts, the others had appeared.

'My God,' Tesco said in astonishment. 'You've killed him; you've damn well killed him.'

Tutts cried out. 'No. Why did you fight? *Why did you fight!'*

Why indeed?

I knew then it was a long story. More than the recent argument, more than him pushing me into Kate and burning her.

Hell . . . I'd looked down at him and the floodgates had opened. I'd wept like a child.

Then I'd felt the hand touch mine.

It happened again as I stood beside Stephen. He reached up, touched my hand and said exactly the same thing he'd said as he'd lain there on the ground with me thinking he was dead and gone.

'Hey . . . Kiddo. Don't worry. We Kennedys have got thick skulls.'

'How are you feeling?' I asked, anxious and guilty all at the same time.

'Believe it or not . . . I want to actually take off my skin and hang it in the closet. Then maybe I won't hurt so much.' He smiled, then grimaced. 'Ow . . . you know it hurts more when I smile.'

I sat on the edge of the bed. 'I'm sorry. I overreacted.'

'No, you didn't. It's lucky I didn't cause Kate some serious burns. How is she?'

'Pink.'

'There's blistering?'

'No, the coffee wasn't that hot after all.'

'You've seen the damage?'

'Yes.'

He raised his eyebrows, one still matted with blood. I could see he was amused and pleased. 'I thought the coffee splashed her . . . chest.'

I smiled back. 'It did.'

'So I take it you two are, mm, dating now?'

'You take it right.'

'Thank Heaven for that. I thought I was going to have to take you to one side and explain your willy's for more than just tinkling through.'

I laughed. 'I managed to find out that much for myself.'

He laughed with me, then held his jaw. 'Ouch . . . Hell, where did you learn to punch like that?'

'You gave me some practice when we were kids.'

'I guess I did.'

'I shouldn't have lost my rag like that . . . sorry.'

Stephen pulled himself into a sitting position. 'Sorry for what?'

'You know why I did that?'

'Revenge?'

I nodded seriously.

He shrugged. 'You never did get your own back for me shooting you with the BB gun, did you?'

'Stephen.' I was troubled. 'I genuinely wanted to kill you.'

'You did,' he said seriously. 'At least you killed your old image of me.'

'Sounds all a bit West Coast New Age mumbo jumbo to me.'

'It's true you killed the image of me as your big brother. About time, too.' He groaned, looking sore as he swivelled himself so he could sit with both feet on the floor. 'I was as much to blame as much as anyone. I patronized you. Bossed you around. Still treated you like a little kid. I deserved it.'

'When I was fighting you,' I swallowed, 'I could only think of how you'd just walked out on Mum and me and gone off to the States with Dad. You know that cut me up?'

'You could have come, too. You had a choice.'

'I was ten years old. And I knew I couldn't desert Mum.'

He nodded. 'So you were right to exact your revenge. Being your brother doesn't stop me from being an ambitious, egotistical bastard, you know?'

'Can I get you anything?'

'A drink, please. Ooooch-arr . . . you're damn good with your fists, kid. I'm proud of you. No, Rick, don't bother with the coffee. I've had enough of coffee today, believe me. Jesus, bless him, brought me a bottle of brandy earlier. It's there by the telephone.'

349

'What did Jesus say?'

'Jesus asked me . . . Jesus? Can you believe he uses the name? It's just so damn weird calling anyone Jesus.' He watched me pour brandy into two mugs. 'He asked me if the plan was still the same.'

'To fly his people out starting tomorrow?'

'Yes, *that* plan.'

'*That* plan.' I sighed.

'You still don't like it, do you, Rick?'

'I like the idea. Get on a ship and leave all this starvation and shit behind? Great.'

'But you still don't trust Jesus and his happy band?'

'No.'

We sipped our brandy. This time the conversation was calm. We were going to discuss, not argue.

'Rick, we're really in the crap up on Fountains Moor. We're living on potatoes, turnips, even the weeds that grow in hedge bottoms.'

'These people are capable of vicious, sadistic acts you wouldn't believe—'

'Ah, but I do believe you, Rick. We'll watch them closely. Any sign of a double-cross, they'll regret it.'

I sighed again. 'Easier said than done.'

'We'll think of a way.'

'So you do believe me? That they are murderers?'

Stephen looked up at me and said quietly. 'And so am I, Rick.'

'You?' I shook my head laughed; an expression of disbelief, not amusement. 'You've not murdered anyone.'

He swallowed the mugful of brandy in one mouthful. 'Remember those three on the moor? They'd stolen food and were running away.'

'Sure, the girl and the man, and there was a young boy with them.' I nodded. 'But they grabbed Dean's pistol.'

'That was the story we gave.' He poured more brandy, then sat there holding the cup in both hands, as if he could warm away something cold, bitterly cold that had lodged inside his heart. 'This is the real story.' He took a mouthful of brandy, swallowed it down. 'There we were, out of sight from everyone else just over the brow of that hill. You'd returned to camp to fetch more food and medical supplies. You'll remember that I was there with Dean and Victoria.'

I listened hard, my skin tingling. I wasn't going to like this.

350

'I was talking to the three of them, reassuring them, telling them everything would be all right. When, all of sudden, Victoria pulled the pistol from Dean's belt.'

'Victoria?'

'Yep. Sweet, naive Victoria. She shot them. As simply and as brutally as that.'

'But we heard shots from different firearms. You fired your shotgun?'

'I'm coming to that. She shot them in the stomach.'

'They didn't die immediately?'

'No. But they were in agony. Christ, you should have seen them. Rolling from side to side on the ground, they were clutching their stomachs like this.' Stephen gripped his own stomach as if it had broken apart and he was trying to hold it together.

He continued, 'If we'd had a surgeon to hand we might have been able to save their lives. But it was clear they were going to die a slow and painful death.'

'Christ.'

Stephen's eyes turned glassy as he remembered the awful scene. 'Victoria said, "You've got a choice. Either watch them slowly bleed to death. Or you can do what I tell you."'

'And that was?'

That we all participate in the murder.'

'You mean she was telling you to shoot them? To finish what she'd started?'

Stephen nodded miserably. 'It was, as she told us, a way of initiating us into the new reality. Kill or be killed. Show no mercy to strangers outside our community.'

'The woman's mad.'

Stephen shook his head. 'That's the monstrous thing. She was right. If we'd let those three people go they'd have brought hundreds of people, starving people, back to our camp. We'd be dead ourselves now. I don't doubt it.'

'So you did as she said?'

'Afraid so, Rick. She stood and watched as Dean and I shot them dead, in cold blood.'

I sat there, numb.

'So you see, Rick. I'm certainly no better than this bunch of people here.' He looked grim. 'Desperate times call for desperate measures.' He swallowed more brandy. 'And that includes murder.'

351

CHAPTER 80

'How are you feeling, Stephen?'

'More to the point, Kate, how're *you* feeling?'

'Fine. Not so sore any more. Now, come on, Stephen. How are you?'

'Aching . . . just aching.'

I opened the bottle of wine. 'Hell, just look at us. The walking wounded of Paradise Island.'

I'd caught sight of my face in the wall mirror. My right eye had swollen where Stephen's fist had connected. There were grazes on my forehead and chin, while my hands were bandaged where I'd cut my fists punching his hard skull. Kate wore a loose-fitting blouse; her upper chest and throat were still mottled pink where the hot coffee had splashed. As for Stephen, his face had swollen into a patchwork of brown- and green-coloured bruises.

It was evening; the same day as the fight. We were sitting in Stephen's room, talking by candlelight. Outside the wind droned across the rooftops to strip leaves from the trees. Kate and I were on friendly terms with Stephen again. In fact, I felt the closest to Stephen that I had for years. I think more than skin got broken that day. Those punches had broken down a barrier between us. Ever since he'd left with Dad all those years ago I'd harboured, deep down, a conviction that he'd abandoned me at what must have been the shittiest time of my life, the time when Dad told me he was going to divorce Mum.

Stephen still moved painfully as he climbed off the bed and stood up. 'OK, people,' he said, 'what do you say to some TV?'

'I wish,' Kate spoke with feeling. 'Have you got any particular channel in mind?'

'Right now I'd settle for some lousy soap opera,' I said. 'Although a rock concert would go down nicely.'

'No, straight up.' Stephen hobbled across the room. 'I noticed these people were using a wind turbine to charge car batteries, so I persuaded Tesco to find a portable TV. I've got the camcorder, so all I needed to do was plug in the right cables into the right sockets and, hey presto, it turns the camcorder into a VCR.'

'Don't tell me you managed to find *Jurassic Park* on 8mm camcorder cassette as well?'

'No. Something even more interesting. Look.' He switched on the TV, then hit the 'play' button on the camcorder that stood on a low table beside the TV; cables trailed from it to the TV's input socket.

The screen flashed, became a mass of speckled dots.

Then I saw a garden full of ghosts.

The effect was electrifying. All three of us sat and stared at the screen with an intensity that couldn't have been bettered if the Archangel Gabriel himself had appeared in a blaze of celestial glory.

There were shots of a garden at dusk. Roses in bloom. Fruit trees. Lamps hanging from branches cast a softly golden glow. People sat drinking, laughing, talking. What was so amazing were their faces.

Then understanding hit me. They were so young-looking. There was no sign in their expressions of that tension that would harden our muscles beneath our faces; there wasn't that ever-hovering look of fear in their eyes that we now saw every time we looked into a mirror.

Those ghosts were us. I realized I was watching the video of Ben Cavellero's party. There was Ben himself with the characteristic crinkly smile. In a soft voice he was saying, 'Why don't you introduce yourself, Stephen? You'll do a far better job than I ever could.'

There was Stephen, bouncing to his feet. Christ, he looked completely different to the gaunt figure with the bruised face now sitting beside me on the bed.

We watched as the on-screen Stephen spoke with effortless confidence into the camera. 'Good evening. My name is Stephen Kennedy. Just three weeks ago I celebrated my birthday and I am now a full one-quarter of a century old. I host a music show on KSTV which is a new-ish terrestrial TV station based in Seattle . . .'

We watched it all. We were so intent on seeing every face, hearing every word we forgot about the glasses of wine in our hands. It was like watching a TV programme beamed from another world.

'Look,' Stephen said in a hushed voice. 'There's Ruth.'

For a moment Ruth's face filmed the screen.

'Christ, she was beautiful, wasn't she?' Stephen's eyes shone; the

Adam's apple bobbed in his throat. 'Just look at her hair. All those wonderful black curls.'

Ruth lay buried beneath the turf near Fountains Moor. Her flesh would be turning liquid and soaking away into the soil.

I felt my eyes prick, too, as we watched. Ruth held her champagne glass to the camera. 'Chin-chin, everybody,' she was saying. She smiled, her white teeth flashing in the light of the garden lamps. 'OK, Dean. You've got your close-up. Switch it off now. Dean?' She laughed as the camera zoomed into a massive close-up of her full, red lips that filled the screen. 'Dean, I said . . . you little monkey. Enough. Or I'll bite the end off your microphone.'

The scene cut to other party guests. Howard with a plateful of pork chops and potato salad. He grinned at the camera, mouth chewing like it was steam-driven. He saluted with a chicken drumstick.

More shots, wobbly now as Dean Skilton, the cameraman, became drunker and drunker. There were Ruth and Stephen sharing a single chair; they were eating each other's tongues. Ruth's long hair hung down over the back of the chair, sweeping the ground as she turned her head to one side, lost in the passionate kiss.

Two girls threw peanuts into each other's mouths. Barry Fripp chased a girl into the house, then she chased him back out again, laughing all the way.

Shots of tables covered with plates of chicken, sausage rolls, cheeses of all kinds, bottles of wine, bowls of nuts, pretzels, onion rings, bacon frazzles. So much food it now made you dizzy just to see it.

There was me, a bottle of beer in my hand, leaning against the house. I was explaining something to a smiling Ben Cavellero. I talked so enthusiastically I swung the hand holding the beer bottle. Beer sploshed out onto my arm and down my trousers but I never even noticed.

And so it was, deep into the night. We watched that video until the very end.

Then Stephen turned to us and said, 'If you two don't mind, I'm going to watch it again.'

We didn't mind. We sat there and watched it again and again. We didn't speak, we didn't move. And we watched those ghosts from happier, safer times drink and eat and talk and fall in love at that party in Ben Cavellero's garden.

CHAPTER 81

The following day we took a boat ride to another world.

The November morning was bitingly cold. Luckily the cloud was high. There was no wind worth mentioning so the two planes arrived on time at the airstrip island. Howard had landed first in the eight-seater, twin-engined Piper, which was followed by Cindy Gullidge flying the four-seater Cessna. What the newly-trained pilot lacked in style she must have made up for with courage.

Cindy came in, wings wobbling hair-raisingly from side to side, engine over-revving so raucously that even the people on the ground closed their eyes.

Within half an hour ten of Jesus's people were airborne, heading north with as much food as the planes could safely carry.

We returned to the boats that would take us back to Paradise Island.

Should have taken us back to Paradise Island.

'Tesco. Where are we going?' I called above the roar of the outboard motor as we turned away from the other two boats and powered out across the lake. 'This isn't the way back!'

Tesco sat at the other side of the boat on the plank seating, his legs casually spread so his boots rested on an empty places. 'We're picking up medical supplies.'

'I thought you had enough?'

'Your people need vitamin B tablets. We're gonna get more.'

'Where?'

'You'll see.'

I was suspicious. I turned to Stephen sitting beside me. 'Did you know anything about this?'

'I mentioned we needed the vitamin tablets. I didn't know we were going to get them today.'

'Don't worry.' Tesco smiled, although to me it seemed more like a leer. 'Won't take long.'

I caught Stephen's eye. His lips looked tight but he said nothing.

'You might as well sit back and enjoy the ride,' Tesco said. Then he turned to grin at Cowboy who sat in the stern of the boat, hand working the rudder bar. The man in the Wild West rig, silk strips cracking in the slipstream, grinned back, then pulled the brim of his Stetson low over his eyes.

I didn't like this at all.

There were six of us in the boat: Stephen (his face still bruised – I still felt a pang of guilt every time I saw it), Kate, myself, then Tesco, Cowboy steering, and a man of around thirty who I didn't know. His lips were crusted thick with scabs and a massive blue tattooed question mark adorned one cheek: ?. He looked like the kind of man you'd hand over your wallet to without him asking you twice.

I didn't know London well but from what I could tell we were heading toward its centre. The water looked deeper here. Occasionally we'd glide over what looked like crimson rafts anchored in the water.

'The tops of London buses.' Tesco grinned. 'Looks neat, eh? And just look over there.' He pointed with the barrel of his sawn-off shotgun. 'The police car on top of the house. Funky or what? This part was hit by tidal waves.'

'Tidal waves?' Kate's eyes went wide.

'Yeah ... a couple of months ago there were huge explosions down Greenwich way.'

'What caused them?'

The man with the question mark on his cheek shouted, 'Shit knows!' Then laughed madly.

Stephen said, 'We've seen huge craters. They've been caused by the heat detonating subterranean pockets of gas.'

Tesco shook his head. 'That's crap. Everyone knows they were caused by the fellers downstairs.'

'The Grey Men?'

'Yeah, Grey Men, Greys, Potato Heads, whatever you call them.' Tesco leaned back, enjoying the ride; he trailed his fingertips in the water.

'You've seen them?' asked Stephen.

'Not yet. Don't want to.'

Cowboy chipped in. 'But we've—' he grinned, 'we've *entertained* people who have.'

Tesco nodded. 'Some people who reached our island were running from the Greys.'

'And I suppose you looked after them in your own inimitable fashion?' I said heavily.

'Inimitable fashion?' Tesco's eyes burned back into mine. 'What the fuck does that mean?'

'It means,' the man with the tattooed question mark on his cheek shouted, 'it means we fucked 'em up good and 'ard before we fed 'em to the rats.'

Cowboy, Tesco and the tattooed man laughed.

I shook my head and muttered under my breath. Stephen gave my forearm a warning squeeze.

Too late. Tesco picked up on it. 'Rick, what's the problem? Don't you approve of what we do?'

'Ritual murder? Why don't you ask the poor bastards you butchered if they approve?'

'Oh, so, so sorry, Mr Sensitive.'

'What's matter with shit face?' shouted the tattooed man. He suddenly slapped his legs so hard that the boat pitched alarmingly. 'What's he saying? What's he saying?'

Tesco smiled at me. 'He thinks we're a bunch of animals, Freak Boy.'

Stephen whispered. 'Come on, Kid K. Diplomacy here, OK?'

'Did what . . . did what . . . did . . .'

The one called Freak Boy glared at me. The tattooed question mark seemed to stand proud of his cheek. You could see agitation winding up the muscles in his body. He slapped his knees harder. The boat rocked. I heard Kate gasp as she flung out her hand to grab the side of the boat.

'What . . . did what . . . did what?'

'Take it easy,' Stephen said soothingly. 'We didn't mean to upset you.' Then he turned to Tesco. 'Look, we're in this together. Stop making trouble. OK?'

'Me? Make trouble?'

Freak Boy grew more agitated. He stared at me while he beat his knees.

'Did what . . . did what?' Drool ran down Freak Boy's chin. 'Did what . . . did what?'

'For crying out loud, Tesco?' Stephen looked at him angrily. 'He's going to tip the boat over.'

'Freak Boy easily gets upset.'

Freak Boy glared at me, still hammering his own knees. Spit flew from his mouth as he chanted, 'Did what? Did what!' He suddenly screamed, then pointed at me. 'My friend's dead! He killed him!'

'Freak Boy,' Cowboy warned. He looked anxious himself now. Freak Boy might lunge at me. If he did, he'd capsize the boat for sure, pitching us into the filthy flood waters. 'Calm down . . . stop doing that!'

'Killed my friend. Killed me. Wouldn't let him kill me all the way though. Cos—'

Cowboy glared angrily at Tesco. 'This's your fault.'

'My fault?'

'Yeah, your fucking fault.'

'Good God,' Stephen shook his head. 'This isn't the place to provoke an argument. *Cool it, both of you!*'

To my amazement they all shut their mouths. Once more I marvelled at Stephen's ability with people. Ben Cavellero had done a good job choosing him to be leader of our group.

Even Freak Boy calmed down. Now he contented himself with mumbling under his breath while rocking backwards and forwards as if nursing an invisible child.

We cruised on across the lake, motor puttering steadily. We now had to follow the line of the street as the buildings grew higher. It was like riding a river through a gorge with cliffs rising high at either side. Only these cliffs were five-storey buildings with water reaching as high as the first-storey windows.

Cowboy slowed the boat to weave round obstacles, such as lamp posts or the tops of road signs. One, matted with slime, bore a pointing arrow along with a name: *Trafalgar Square*.

'Fucking eerie, eh?' Tesco's voice was low now. The same kind of voice someone uses when they step into a cathedral.

The boat reached a junction where the canyons of high buildings lining the waterways intersected. Cowboy lifted his hat so he could wipe his forehead with the back of his hand. He looked less and less relaxed the deeper we penetrated this new Venice, with the buildings growing higher, more claustrophobic. I saw him dart anxious glances at the buildings as if he expected a sniper to lean from a window, waiting for us to slip into the cross-hairs of his rifle sights.

He turned the boat left along another water-filled street. I saw a street sign lapped by the boat's wake, which gave a good indication of the depth of the flood water at this point. Picture the tallest person you know. Then picture yourself standing on his or her shoulders. If you'd executed such an acrobatic act in that flooded street then you'd probably have just managed to peep above the lake's surface, while your tall friend glugged in the shitty water.

The street sign read: *Charing Cross Road.*

I'd walked along Charing Cross Road dozens of times. Pigged out on pizza at fast-food joints. Once I got shit-faced drunk in the Porcupine (and managed to spill beer on the most expensive shoes I've ever bought – blue suede, believe it or not) before tottering off to the Marquee Club to sway drunkenly to Armana. This was before they became huge and were still playing support to bands like Pulp and Oasis.

In the world before fire, flood and starvation, Charing Cross Road, one of London's busiest shopping streets, was crammed with old bookshops, cafés (where freshly ground coffee beans smelt like Heaven); there were restaurants; tourist shops selling Union Jack flags, T-shirts (with slogans like: MY DAD WENT TO LONDON AND ALL HE BROUGHT ME BACK WAS THIS CRAP T-SHIRT); Beefeater dolls, plazzy Bobbies' hats – you remember the type; the typical skit would be where a lad full of cheek and cheap cider would swagger up to a cop and ask, 'Excuse me, sir, are you a policeman . . . or is that a tit you're wearing on your head?'

All that's dead and buried. Or should I say, dead and drowned? Now Charing Cross Road looked an alien place. If there are such things as ghosts they walk the streets underwater. The flood level reached to the first-floor windows. All the shop fronts that were familiar to me were drowned by that stinking goo, which looked more like stew thickened by floating debris.

The boat surged forward, bumping against bottles, planks of wood, books, drowned cats, a peacock (its feathers still an iridescent green), clothes. Hundreds of plastic carrier bags floated just below the surface, looking like a new breed of jelly fish.

Tesco held up his hand. 'Switch off.'

Cowboy turned off the engine.

The silence of the flooded street was suddenly intense. For a second I heard nothing but the lap of water hitting the walls of the buildings. There was no sign of human life there. It was all abandoned. Waiting simply to rot and fall into the lake.

Tesco pointed down into the water, then swung his arm to the left. 'All shops down there,' he said, awed. 'See that café sign? My pitch was there. Lived in a fucking sleeping-bag in the doorway for two fucking years.' He looked at us. 'You think you're suffering now, but it's fucking paradise compared with that. Do you know how many times I had my head kicked by people coming home from the pub? How many times, Kate, how many times?'

Kate shook her head. In a very small voice she said, 'I don't know, Tesco.'

He gave a bright artificial grin. 'I don't know either. It happened so often.' He switched off the grin, looking sickened. 'It was good fun for people like you to give us homeless a kick in the chin as you walked by. *Hee! heeee! Carruthers, old chap. Look at the funny man cry – boo-hoo-bloody-hoo.*'

The silence pressed in on us. The scene grew more disturbing. A flooded street, water lapping against the first-floor windows. Behind one window I saw the face of a dried corpse. It seemed to stare at us.

Christ, I wanted out of there.

Cowboy took off his Stetson hat and held it to his chest. A respectful gesture; as if a hearse was passing by. 'Tesco, tell them about the men in the Porsche,' he said. 'Tell them what they did to your mouth.'

Tesco gave a sad smile. 'Me and my girl were sleeping in the alleyway down there. It had been raining all day. The sleeping-bags were wet. I woke up to see two men get out of a Porsche. Big white blokes they were. Dressed in leathers. They ran into the alleyway and kicked the living shit out of us.' He pointed to the scars radiating out from his lips that gave his mouth the appearance of being the centre of a flower. The lines of the scars like petals. 'They did that to me. They kicked my girlfriend so hard they ruptured her kidney.'

'Christ,' whispered Kate.

'She died of septicaemia the following week.'

'I'm sorry.'

Tesco shook his head. 'So there's civilization.' He nodded his head at the buildings. 'Didn't do much for me did it? So you'll excuse me ... *please* ... if I don't start sobbing into my hands when I see it like that. Civilization? Civilization my arse. It was shit.'

'Shit. Civilization shit,' Freak Boy echoed.

We sat in silence for a moment. The water slapped and sucked at the brickwork. A wind began to blow; it was so cold now. The rush of air drew a mournful note across the roof tops. It sounded like a song for a dying lover.

I realized then that Tesco had observed this vigil every time he passed through here as a mark of respect and remembrance for his dead girlfriend.

I didn't like the man. I certainly didn't trust him. I knew one day I'd end up in a confrontation with him, but, damnit, I had to acknowledge he had feelings, too. He still grieved for the girl.

A moment later, Cowboy pulled the cord to start the motor of the outboard. It puttered, but didn't start first time. He gripped the cord, ready to tug again.

'Wait!' Kate shouted.

'What's wrong?'

'Shhh.'

'Kate—'

'Shh, don't you hear it?'

We listened. I heard the smack-suck of water. The mournful note of the wind. Nothing else.

'There. It happened again.'

'What?'

Kate looked round, eyes wide. 'Someone's shouting for help.'

I listened. This time I heard it, too. Faint. But you could hear the sheer desperation shooting through the voice. It sounded as if someone was fighting for their life.

'It's coming from over there,' Cowboy pointed along the flooded street.

'Hurry up,' Kate pleaded. 'Someone's in trouble.'

Cowboy started the motor. The propeller scrambled the water into bubbles. Then the boat surged forward in the direction of the cries for help.

CHAPTER 82

'Can you see anyone?' Kate asked.

'No,' Tesco called back above the snarl of the outboard motor as it powered the boat along the flooded street, the wake curling away in a cream-coloured V. 'But it sounded like it came from this direction.'

Freak Boy clambered to the front of the boat where he leaned out over the prow, looking like some strange tattooed gorilla, the slip stream blowing back the strips of orange silk that were tied to his arms, legs and head.

Cowboy sang out, 'See anything, Freakie Boy?'

Kate turned back to me, the breeze blowing her hair across her face. 'You heard it? Someone screaming for help?'

'I heard it all right,' I said, 'But what if it came from one of the buildings? 'I looked up at the windows. 'There's hundreds of them.'

Stephen shouted back to Cowboy. 'Kill the motor. We'll listen again.'

'We can't.'

'Kill it, for Godsake.'

'No way.'

'Why?'

'Look,' he pointed to a ruined building. There was a sign bearing the familiar logo of the Underground, the red circle bisected by a blue bar. It had been crumpled as if it had been punched by a gigantic fist. 'That's Leicester Square station.'

'So?'

'The Tube tunnels act like gigantic plugholes. If there's a shift in water levels it'll create a whirlpool; we'll be sucked right down.'

'The water looks calm enough – kill the motor.'

Throwing up his hands angrily, Cowboy shrugged his shoulders, indicating clearly enough: OK, on your head be it.

He switched off the outboard.

'There – did you hear it?'

Kate scanned the waters. 'It's a girl's voice.'

'But where the hell is she?'

Freak Boy suddenly pounded the gunwale of the boat so violently I thought it would tip us into the water. 'Girl!' he yelled, pointing. 'Girl! Girl! Girl!'

'Oh, Christ,' Kate grabbed my arm. 'Rick! Do you see them?'

'Where?'

Stephen pointed. 'There, on the ledge. No, not at water level; up on the second floor. Girl and a man. Do you see them?'

I looked up. It was such a bizarre sight that I stared with my mouth open.

In front of me and opposite the remains of Leicester Square station was an eight-storey building. Clinging to a ledge that couldn't have been more than fifteen centimetres wide, yet was a good ten metres above the flood waters, was a man of about fifty with bushy grey hair, and a girl of about twenty. She had short dark hair and was dressed in the type of skirt and jacket a female business executive would once have worn. They were shouting, waving.

Cowboy fired up the motor and nudged the boat through the floating debris to the building.

'Weird thing to do,' Kate said. 'What made them climb up the front of the building?'

Cowboy called out, 'Stephen, I don't like the look of this.'

'You think it might be some kind of trap?'

'Might be. See anyone else?'

'No, just the girl and the man. But have you noticed something?'

'What?'

'We've had no rain, but the front of the buildings are streaming with water.'

'Shit.'

Tesco turned pale.

'What is it?'

'You'll see soon enough if we don't get out of here,' Cowboy said.

'What's wrong?' Kate demanded. 'Why are the buildings wet?'

Cowboy twisted the hand throttle. The boat surged forward, the prow lifting up beneath the bow wave.

Stephen said, 'What are you doing?'

'I'm getting us out of here.'

'You can't, you've got to go back.'

'No!'

'There's two people back there,' I shouted. 'Are you going to leave them to die?'

'If we stay here we're going to be dead, too!'

Stephen climbed over me and worked his way along the boat on all fours toward Cowboy. 'Stop!'

'No!'

'Tell me why you're running away! What's wrong?'

'Because the whole fucking street's going to erupt any fucking second.'

'Erupt?'

'Yeah, erupt! Do you want to wait and see it happen?'

'Hey, just slow down. You're going to wreck the boat.'

The man eased off the throttle but still steered a line along the

363

flooded Charing Cross Road; the wake from the boat broke against the front of buildings in a splash of spray.

'Listen to me.' Stephen spoke in a level voice. He wasn't going to shout; he was going to negotiate. 'Do you really want to leave those people to die?'

Cowboy shrugged. 'They're strangers. Want to risk your life for strangers?'

'But if it was one of your group you'd risk it?'

Holding onto the brim of his hat, he nodded. 'But they don't belong to our group.'

'Oh, but they *do* belong to our group.'

'Oh no, they don't, Kennedy.'

'You've heard of the human race, Cowboy?'

'Shit.'

'Well, that's our group, isn't it?'

'So what?'

'So show some loyalty to our kind.'

Tesco chipped in. I thought he was going to side with Cowboy. I thought wrong. 'Cowboy. It looks quiet enough at the moment.'

'We'd be killing ourselves,' Cowboy said.

Tesco shook his head. 'We can do it. Just take the boat in close. We can be out of there in one minute flat.'

Cowboy shot us a fierce glare, then he looked at the man squatting in the prow of the boat like a huge ape. 'Freak Boy, what do you say?'

'Go back . . . get 'em.'

Cowboy rubbed his stubbled jaw, thinking hard. Then he repositioned his Stetson hat on his head. 'You're all fucking crazy.'

Then he leaned on the outboard motor steering arm so it turned the boat as near as damnit on its own axis. Five seconds later he was powering the boat back to where the people stood on the ledge.

'We're going to have to move fast,' he shouted.

'OK.'

'Any sign of eruptions and we're out of here, whether we've got those folk or not.'

He brought the boat up to the face of the building. Above us the man and the girl waved their arms, shouted. But the outboard motor drowned any individual words.

'Why on Earth did they climb up there?' Kate shook her head.

I looked up. 'There's no way into the building. The windows are barred.'

'Seems to me,' Cowboy said, 'these folks were passing through in a boat when they got hit by the last eruption. The boat sank. They swam for it. See the drainpipe? They climbed up that to the ledge, hoping to get into the building through one of the windows. But, as you said, the windows are barred.'

'How best to get them down?' I asked.

'Tell them to jump.'

'Into that?' I said, looking down into the water. It was covered with a near-solid-looking mat of wooden crates, timber, rotting carcasses.

Kate shouted up at the two people on the ledge. 'Climb down . . . we'll bring the boat into the wall for you. Hurry . . . please!'

They nodded. The man gave a thumbs-up sign to show he understood. Then both moved along the ledge – slowly, slowly, their backs to the wall, arms out, palms flat to the brickwork. You could actually see their legs shaking. Those people were terrified.

They made it to a drainpipe. The girl went first. She was barefoot. She turned round gingerly so she faced the drainpipe, then gripped her hands around it. Her left foot found the first pipe bracket below the ledge. Then she started the descent.

Cowboy hissed through his teeth. 'She's going too slow.'

'Hurry yourself!' Freak Boy bellowed.

'Don't rush her.' Kate glared at them. 'She'll slip.'

'We can't hang around,' Tesco warned. 'Do you see what's happening over at the station?'

'Here come the bubbles! Here come the bubbles!' Freak Boy yelled, pounding the sides of the boat with his huge fists. 'The big one's coming!'

'Big what?' Stephen asked.

'The geyser.' Cowboy nudged the boat through the floating crap. 'The ground under London's baking hot. We don't see much sign on the surface because it's flooded.'

'But down there in the Tube tunnels it's getting pretty hot,' Tesco added. 'The water boils, then every so often – whoosh.'

'Whoosh!' yelled Freak Boy in echo.

'The steam pushes a way out through the tunnels, right up into the station. It comes out in one helluva rush. That's why the walls are wet. Any second now you're going to get a column of water erupting higher than any fucking building round here; then back down comes the water. Tons of it. Carrying a couple of tons of masonry, too.'

I watched the girl's progress. The descent was so slow, it was painful to watch.

'Hurry up!' Freak Boy bellowed. 'We're all gonna be boiled alive!'

'Cool it,' Stephen said in a surprisingly calm voice. 'She'll make it.'

Cowboy clucked his tongue. 'Why doesn't the guy start down the pipe?'

'The pipe won't take the weight of both of them.'

'I'll give 'em sixty seconds, then I'm powering this boat out of here.'

'No,' Stephen said. 'You'll do as I say. Take the boat closer to the building.'

'I'm not going in yet.'

'Why not?'

'If there's a surge we could be sucked right in through the windows. It'll smash the boat to buggery.'

'Get in closer.'

'Oh-ho,' sang Freak Boy. 'Trouble at mill.'

'What's wrong?'

Tesco looked down into the water. 'Oh Christ, here it comes.'

CHAPTER 83

Tesco stared down into the water, eyes bulging in horror.

The water had actually begun to fizz, like beer poured too quickly from a can. A scummy brown froth began to form on the surface. 'Christ, things are really starting to cook down there.'

'I'm going,' Cowboy yelled. 'We tried our best to save them, but we can't stay here.'

'We're staying,' I said. 'They just need another five minutes, then they'll be in the boat.'

Cowboy snorted. 'In five minutes we'll be plastered all over this fucking city.'

Come on, come on.

I looked up at the girl. She was half-climbing, half-sliding down the drainpipe; her skirt had rucked up almost to her waist, exposing her underwear. Freak Boy stared up at her, a massive leer all over his sweaty face. His eyes bulged halfway out of his head; the muscles in his throat seemed to inflate so the veins stood out from his skin.

'Hell . . . what are they?'

I looked back to see Kate pointing into the water.

I stared. Now this was weird. Damned weird.

All around the boat, the surface of the water was being broken by what looked like smooth-backed whales. Five, six, seven . . . eight of them I counted.

'What are they?' Kate asked.

'Cars. They were stuck in the mud down there.' Tesco explained. 'If they sank with people inside the people rot, give off gas; slowly the cars fill with gas, then, when the mud's disturbed, they're shaken free and – whoosh – up they pop.'

'Pop!' Freak Boy echoed, still leering up at the girl.

She'd reached the first floor now. If I could have been sure of the stability of the boat I'd have stood up and lifted her down.

But the water seethed like it was alive, creaming thickly with scum; here and there cars broke the surface, their windows green with slime.

Once a car rose as far as the door handles it would roll over. Then, in a flurry of bubbles, it would sink again.

'Jump into the boat,' Cowboy yelled at the woman.

She hung on to the drainpipe, panting, her face pressed against the brickwork.

'Jump into the boat,' Cowboy yelled.

'She can't,' Tesco shouted, 'she'll go right through the fucking bottom.'

'Come on!' Kate encouraged. 'You can do it!'

'It's building.' Cowboy was forced to grip the outboard motor's steering bar in both hands. 'The current's pushing the boat.'

'She's nearly there.'

Bang!

I looked behind me. The building across the street was moving; the entire frontage slipped downwards into the water with a roar, sending up a spray of water. The flood waters must have eaten into the foundations so much that even the slightest vibration would topple these buildings.

367

'Bring the boat in closer!' Stephen ordered. 'Come on. Closer. Rick . . . hold my legs.' Standing, he reached up, grabbing the girl by the waist as she worked her way down the drainpipe.

'Let go of the pipe,' he shouted.

For a second she clung there grimly. 'I'm still too high up,' she screamed. 'I'll fall into the water.'

'You won't . . . *let go!*'

Closing her eyes, she released her grip on the pipe. Stephen tumbled backwards into the boat still holding her.

One down, one to go.

I looked up as the man began his descent of the drainpipe. He moved faster than the girl. He looked as if he might once have been a builder and clambering down scaffolding was second nature to him.

I heard a rattle. The windows were shaking in the building. You could sense the pressure building somewhere thirty metres or so beneath where the roadway would be. I could picture the water deep in the Underground rail system beginning to boil, then the steam trying to force its way outwards. The whole thing was like a huge pressure cooker. I could sense the brute force of the thing building and building.

Its safety valve was the station across the road. Bubbles frothed around its ruined walls; now I could see steam pouring outwards across the flood waters.

'Any second now . . .' Cowboy said in a low voice.

Tesco shouted up at the man. 'Faster, come on . . . *hurry!*'

The glass rattled harder in the windows. Tiles slipped off the roof to splash into the water beside us.

More cars surfaced, then rolled over, belching gas that stank of rot and death.

I looked down at Stephen. He'd got himself into a sitting position. The girl lay panting in the bottom of the boat.

'Hurry up!' Tesco yelled up at the man climbing down the drainpipe.

More tiles fell from the roof to splash into the water.

'I can't hold the boat still here,' Cowboy panted. 'I'm going to have to ride her out . . . then back in again.' He twisted the throttle. The boat surged out over the bubbling water; he leaned against the steering bar, swung the boat round, then powered the craft back in towards the building once more.

That's when the man decided to jump.

He hit the water. He didn't so much splash as disappear into the scum. Seconds later he was swimming towards us.

He'd meet the boat halfway.

We shouted encouragement.

Suddenly there came a series of cracking sounds like gunshots. Then a roar. The building the couple had been standing on toppled forward into the water.

One second the man had been striking out in a powerful crawl stroke. The next he was gone beneath an avalanche of masonry.

The girl screamed.

I knew it was too late to do anything. He'd been hit by tons of brickwork and timber. He'd have been killed instantly.

Cowboy didn't hang around.

Even before the wave created by the falling building hit us, he twisted the throttle. The boat surged forward, ricocheting against one of the floating cars that had become nothing more than their dead owners' coffins.

He didn't stop. He kept the boat blasting along the flooded street, weaving desperately from side to side to avoid the cars as they floated to the surface, belched out their gas, then sank once more.

I looked back at the wake sweeping outward in an ever-widening V of foam.

Then, at last, the pressure that had been building deep in the flooded Northern line forced its way up from the tunnel, through the submerged platforms, up the drowned escalators, bursting with God Almighty fury out into the ticket halls, then . . .

I saw it. A column of water, forced explosively upward by the superheated steam.

It stood there, as white as a bone, shining in the daylight, twice as high as the surrounding six-storey buildings.

Then, with a thunderous rumble, the water fell back to hit the surrounding buildings, toppling row upon row into the new Lake of London.

I looked down at the girl. She shivered, still panting in her business suit. Dazed, she gripped Kate's hand as if it was the only thing keeping her between life and death.

I looked at the others. My brother Stephen, stone-faced. Tesco and Freak Boy, eyes fixed on the erupting geyser, their silk strips snapping and cracking straight out in the slipstream. Kate watched me, her face grim but calm. I looked back at Cowboy; his hat had blown off to swing by its cord from his neck.

'Hold on tight,' he shouted. 'It's not over yet.' He jerked his thumb back over his shoulder. 'Here comes the tidal wave.'

CHAPTER 84

The tidal wave rolled toward us in a wall of the purest white.

I could hear the roar of the thing above the outboard motor.

I called, 'Can we outrun it?'

'We have to!' Cowboy yelled. 'It'll smash the boat to fuck.'

He powered the boat on, weaving around the larger bits of debris. The smaller pieces of flotsam he rode straight over. You felt the concussion as they hit the bottom of the boat. The jolt slammed up through the fibreglass hull, then up through the soles of your feet.

Suddenly that hull looked as flimsy as eggshell. One heavy crate or roof spar . . . it would tear a hole right through the bottom of the boat.

'Faster,' Stephen shouted. 'It's gaining on us.'

'Gonna get wet,' cried Freak Boy. 'Gonna get wet!'

Kate looked up at me, her eyes wide with fear, her hair blowing out straight in the rush of air.

'Hold on tight,' Cowboy yelled.

The boat hit one of the cars as it rose. Like a water skier's ramp it lifted us clean out of the water.

For a couple of boat-lengths we were airborne. I mean the damned thing actually flew.

Then the boat hit down again with a tremendous slap, splashing water into the air; it rained back down on us in huge spattering drops that stung.

'Christ,' Tesco shouted. 'It's cracked the bottom of the boat!'

The girl we'd rescued screamed. 'I can't swim. I can't swim!'

'Cowboy, you better . . . Cowboy!'

I looked back.

Cowboy had gone.

As simply as that. One second he'd been there, Stetson hat flapping madly. The next . . .

An empty seat; no one at the steering bar. The boat veered out of control towards a shop front; waves bucked us, knocking the breath from our bodies. The engine howled.

The shop's sign just above the water-line filled my vision as we hurtled toward it.

I watched in horror. I could see the top of the slimed green plate glass window, saw the flotsam bobbing behind it.

Then, with another savage change of direction, the boat swerved away.

Now we were heading straight towards the tidal wave as it tore along the street, standing higher than me, moving with the speed of an express train.

I looked back to see Stephen sprawling face down on the bottom of the boat. He'd thrown out one hand, grabbed the steering bar. He lifted his head to see where we were going.

I yelled, 'We're going towards the tidal wave . . . *towards it!*'

Freak Boy slapped the top of his head with his palms, screaming non-stop.

'Oh God,' gasped Kate.

She held out her hand to clasp mine. I gripped it tight.

The tidal wave still roared towards us.

The force of it burst windows, tore out shop fronts; whole buildings sagged down at either side of the street, walls splitting, façades falling into flood waters with a sound like thunder.

I found myself watching this in a detached way. Some part of my mind coolly noted what happened: Waterstone's book shop hit by a surge of water. A thousand books gush through the windows like fish escaping from a massive tank. Building fronts fall away. Remember dolls' houses? You could open up the hinged front to reveal the rooms? This is the same. The façades fell into the flood water. You could see into abandoned rooms. You saw the beds, tables, chairs, sofas, flapping curtains, carpets, TVs, cookers, pans still resting on the hobs as if waiting for the owners to cook dinner – the possessions of the long dead or long gone population of London.

Ahead, the tidal wave rolled to meet us. A wall of shining water that would hit us with the force of a runaway train, smashing the boat to fragments, then sweeping us away to crush us and drown us in that shit-stinking lake.

Food for the rats.

That was our destiny.

Maybe in fifty million years geologists would chip away at the rock the sediment had become to find our fossilized bones, still with the details of our shoes, watches, rings picked out in fossil patterns in the surrounding shale.

Behind me Stephen had inched closer to the stern. Now he kneeled up in the bottom of the boat in about three centimetres of water that sloshed from side to side whenever he pulled or pushed the steering lever.

The boat bucked over the smaller waves running in advance of the tidal wave.

The tidal wave itself was perhaps two hundred metres away. We were still running straight at it. I saw cars being rolled over in the twist of surf.

Freak Boy crouched in the front of the boat, screaming his head off, his massive fists clamped around the sides.

I tried to shout back to Stephen, but the buffeting, as the boat bumped from wave to wave, jolted the breath from my lungs.

The motor roared.

I looked ahead. Watching with dreadful fascination. The tidal wave rushed straight at us, ripping the fronts of buildings, sweeping away everything in its path.

The next swerve nearly hurled me from the boat.

Stephen steered the boat hard to the left. It skimmed across the water, the boat almost standing on its stern, it moved with such speed.

The next second we were in a side street. The tops of lamp posts whipped by my elbows.

'Move!' Stephen yelled. 'Get away from the sides. Onto the floor of the boat!'

Tesco and I joined Kate and the girl in the bottom of the boat.

Then suddenly it went dark.

The engine cut out.

No other sound but water rushing by.

Then the boat hit with a crunch. I don't know what. But we stopped dead.

There was a scream.

372

CHAPTER 85

The tidal wave passed us by, still tearing up Charing Cross Road in the direction of Oxford Street.

When my eyes adjusted to the gloom I saw that the boat had come to rest inside a music shop. The height of the water level meant my head was pressed to the ceiling when I sat up, even though my backside was still firmly on the bottom of the boat.

Guitars floated on the water. Along with hundreds of pages of sheet music.

A poster of the band Pulp floated to the surface. I watched, still dazed by the nightmare white-knuckle ride, as the face of the lead singer, Jarvis Cocker, surfaced eerily through the waters, rendered smoky-looking by the gloom and the sediment. The face of Cocker floated there for a moment, his eyes staring eerily up into mine. Then his face dissolved, the paper becoming mush in the water.

Numb, I reached out and pulled a beautiful blue Fender Jaguar from the water. I'd have killed for a guitar like that once. Now all those material possessions were for the taking, and not one was worth, literally, a row of beans.

At that moment I was close to cracking up. I wanted to laugh out loud. I felt it bubbling up in my throat to try and squeeze out through my lips.

Tesco examined the crack in the hull. Water dribbled in.

'Tesco, how's it look?' Stephen asked.

'Not bad. It'll get us home.'

'What's wrong with Freak Boy?'

'It's me finger,' he said thickly. 'Me bloody finger.'

He held up his right hand. When the boat had slammed in through the front of the shop it had scraped along the edge of the window frame.

Shards of glass jutted out from the timber.

Freak Boy must have still been holding onto the sides of the boat when we crashed through.

'It's me finger,' he repeated. 'Me fucking finger.'

Where his middle finger had been there was only a raw hole. Blood pumped freely, running down the back of his hand.

There, in the bottom of the boat, where the water sloshed from side to side with every swell of the floodwaters, was the middle finger. It floated with the next swell of flood water to rest against my foot. I saw the creases in the skin at the joints. The fingernail, bitten down so ruthlessly scabs had formed along the sides. I couldn't take my eyes off it. Or the strings of meat floating out from the severed end.

The big man crouching there in the front of the boat began to sob softly. 'Me finger. I hurt me finger ... oh, Mum ... Mum, I hurt me finger.'

CHAPTER 86

The airlift moved in fits and starts. There'd be a good day when the planes would make two return flights. Then cloud would close in and there'd be no flights because it was impossible for Howard and Cindy to actually see from the air the landmarks that enabled them to navigate from Fountains Moor to London. Of course, the Gremlins worked overtime, too. Fuel lines would clog, an aircraft tyre would puncture; control cables would fray; fuel consumption would exceed supply. Then a day would be wasted with the planes grounded for repairs or while teams headed out to backpack in more fuel in for the thirsty motors.

The pilots were exhausted from the endless flying. We knew both were doing the odd line of coke, as well as hitting the bottle hard, too. Their faces were lined; their eyes so dark and pouched they looked as if they'd been punched. But still they kept their machines in the air; they didn't complain; and day after day they took their lives in their hands.

As the days passed it looked at last as if we'd turned a corner.

The population of Jesus's Paradise Island dwindled. Whereas before there was always noise – Jesus's people shouting, laughing, rowdy games of football always being played in the street, children shouting, or people gleefully singing, *'It's the end of the world as I know it, and I feel fine'* – suddenly it was eerily quiet. One by one, the houses Jesus's community had occupied were deserted as their occupants flew north.

At the other end of the line at Fountains Moor I wondered what our people made of the new arrivals. With their tattooed faces, wild hairstyles, and their taste for tying strips of orange and yellow silk to their arms and legs, they must have resembled some bizarre Amazon tribe.

I wondered, too, when the novelty would wear off and the friction between the two distinct cultures of Jesus's tribe and Stephen's middle-class community would begin. Of course the pressure was on: more mouths to feed; more tents to find. And of course Jesus's tribe's reaction to the disaster was different from ours. We saw it as the end of civilization, the death of our dreams and ambitions. These people saw the disaster as an opportunity for a new life; a far better life than the one they'd endured before, sleeping in shop doorways and living on stale bread thrown out by supermarkets.

I'd often lay awake at night, Kate curled tightly into my back. One of the many thoughts that had haunted me into wakefulness would be: *Jesus's people had done a better job of finding food, shelter, even happiness. Were they better equipped to survive in this hostile new world than we were?*

CHAPTER 87

We'd still make forays into central London for supplies. It didn't matter how many trips I made into the flooded city, I never did get used to what I found there.

We'd set out early when the mist still lay on the flood waters. Church steeples, street lamps, the upper storeys of houses, museums, art galleries, office blocks – they all reared eerie and deserted above the silent waters. From any number of windows would gaze decomposing skulls. The crows, like the rats, were the only creatures to prosper. They grew fat on carrion. Everywhere there were signs that survivors trapped by flood waters in offices had eaten the flesh of their colleagues before they too had been killed for meat by stronger rivals.

Sometimes you could cut the outboard motors and drift along in that deep, deep silence. Then all you'd hear would be the lap of the ripples against walls, sounding like wet kisses. There was no longer much evidence of human life continuing in the flooded city. Once, when the motor was cut, I did hear sobbing coming from a fifteen-storey office block. Sheathed entirely in glass, it rose from the flood waters like a crystal tombstone. The sobbing continued. Even when we shouted and fired shots into the air.

They were the kind of sobs I can hear still. Especially when I lie awake in the middle of the night. The sob of someone dying brokenhearted. Alone.

Just so we'd be in no doubt that the Earth had undergone some pretty crucial changes of temperature in its crust, we'd be treated sometimes to vivid evidence of the metamorphosis.

In Trafalgar Square, Nelson's Column now lay in broken segments like a series of stone cylinders. The statue of Nelson itself had shattered into fragments no larger than your fist – so Jesus's people had said. The water was so deep there that the massive bronze lions lay buried far underwater.

Tesco nudged me. 'See the ship?'

A cargo ship, carried by the flood waters, had rammed into the front of the National Gallery. It lay tilted to one side, a crow perched on its yellow funnel.

The prow of the ship had penetrated deeply into the gallery's stone façade, causing stone building and steel ship to remain forever mated like a work of modern art.

Over by South Africa House, fires burned on the surface of the water.

'It's been like it for weeks,' Tesco explained. 'Methane gas is leaking up through the old sewer system. Somehow it ignited. It's been burning ever since.'

The boats eased slowly by the pools of flame that burned on the water. They burned with a puttering sound as bubbles of methane gas reached the surface and ignited; the flame of that bubble igniting the subsequent bubbles in a continuous process. I was reminded of the day Stephen and I found Victoria in the graveyard. How the subterranean heat had detonated the pockets of gas trapped in the graves. I thought of the huge crater that now yawned out of the centre of the town of Grantham. There a subterranean pocket of natural gas had been large enough to blow the town to Kingdom Come. It might happen here, I realized. The whole world was a time bomb waiting to explode. Would we be safe even on a tropical island far away in the South Seas? Who was to say it wasn't the same there? The ground growing hotter and hotter beneath your feet. The vegetation burnt black. Streams hot enough to boil an egg.

Who was to say the whole world wasn't going to go up in flames?

CHAPTER 88

Foreign embassies are rich in firearms. It's common knowledge that weapons of all kinds – from handguns to grenades to heavy machine guns – were smuggled through airports by the packing case, protected from Customs scrutiny by the diplomatic seal.

It was in such an embassy down near The Strand where the flood waters were so high they almost reached the third floor that I encountered the Grey Man again.

I'd gone up to the top floor alone. The others in the scavenging team were concentrating on the lower floors where they'd found a couple of thousand rounds of 9mm ammo. In this terrible new man-eat-man world a loaded gun was far more valuable than gold.

I moved along the corridors, sawn-off shotgun in one hand, the dusty green carpet still deeply luxurious beneath my feet, portraits of long-dead heads of state hanging on the walls. Scattered on the floor were pearls: they were fat and a pure white and must have cost what would amount to a year's salary for most people. In the rush to escape the flood the necklace had snapped, scattering the pearls like widows' tears.

I'd checked a couple of rooms. They were mainly offices for the clerical staff, with utilitarian desks, chairs, then row upon row of filing cabinets.

The next room whose door I pushed open with the muzzle of the shotgun contained something else.

My skin prickled, my eyes snapped wide.

I froze, my arms hanging down at my sides, locked into a twenty past eight position by the shock; pure shock at seeing the figure.

He was back.

He was ugly.

He radiated menace.

I knew it had to be this way. I had known ever since my last encounter with the Grey Man that night back on Fountains Moor that he would find me again.

And right then I realized he'd never been away. I could imagine with no effort whatsoever that he was always there, watching over me like a dreadful angel – an angel with grey skin, eyes as red as blood, a strip of coarse black hair that followed a bony crest on the top of his skull, a crest that ran from the forehead to the back of the neck. The skin was studded here and there with buttons of raised skin. They could have been wart-like growths. But they could as easily have been nipples where these creatures suckled their demonic young.

I could not move. I sensed his – its – monstrous power. That alone was sufficient to paralyse me. I knew it could reach forward and snap my arms like twigs. It could probably dig its finger into my stomach to scoop out my intestines as easily as I could scoop a handful of loose rice from a sack.

I tried to shout out. To warn the others. I couldn't.

I tried to raise my hand that gripped the shotgun.

If I could lift it just a few centimetres, then just apply enough pressure to the trigger I could blast the thing in the legs.

I would have one of the Greys as captive. Stephen would have no choice but to believe me.

Raise the shotgun.

Just that little bit.

Squeeze the trigger.

Pepper that grey hide with shot.

Easy . . . easy, Rick, come on.

Christ . . .

I couldn't.

I couldn't move.

And the creature knew it.

It looked at me. It tilted its head to one side. There was no expression on its face, but I sensed its curiosity. It had seen something that interested it.

Me.

'What do you want?'

I was surprised I could speak, even though my voice barely rose above a whisper.

'What do you want?'

No reaction.

'Why are you here?'

The head tilted further to one side in curiosity. The eyes looked like empty sockets that had been filled with blood that was still fresh, crimson . . . wet.

They stared into mine. I could almost feel it reading my mind. I imagined it rifling through my memories as easily as you might thumb through a filing cabinet drawer, pulling out files here and there: some were of interest, some not.

Did it see Caroline Lucas through my memory? Did it see the experiences we shared?

Or further back. That night all this started. The night of Ben Cavellero's party. Did it see me putting on a new shirt? When I nicked myself in the arm with a pin I'd overlooked in the sleeve? Then, leaving the house, I'd walked up Trueman Way, cheerfully whistling the melody to a song I was writing.

Or yet further back. Mum and a fourteen-year-old me at the Drive-thru. Then we'd sit in the Asda supermarket carpark, eating Big Macs. Mum would ask about my guitar lessons in an encouraging kind of way. I'd spot potential boyfriends for her, tease her mercilessly the way good sons do.

Did the Grey Man look into my head and see all that?

I believe it did.

I must have blacked out. When I opened my eyes I lay face down on the carpet. I felt a hand clamped hard against my neck holding me still.

I imagined those blood-red eyes looking me over, appraising the human race, calculating our abilities, our strengths, our weaknesses.

The grip tightened.

I couldn't breathe.

The darkness came quickly. Absolutely.

CHAPTER 89

Within ten minutes of taking off from the island Kate and I had landed on just weeks ago we had left the new Lake of London behind. Below, brilliantly illuminated by the winter sunlight, lay dry land again. Alexandra Palace passed beneath us. Roofless now, gutted by fire. Howard reached the East Coast railway line, then swung the nose of the aeroplane north.

Below me and to my right, the land in the east was still predominantly green, blackened only rarely by hot-spots.

But towards the western horizon on my left I could see nothing but black land. The heat had killed every blade of grass. There were hundreds of plumes of what appeared to be smoke or steam on the horizon. Perhaps what remained of towns and forests still blazed.

And I imagined that taking possession of those black lands would be the Grey Men, blood-red-eyed, enigmatic – and coldly menacing; they'd be calculating their next move against humankind.

I'd told Kate about my encounter with one of the grey monsters in the embassy. How I'd woken in the room to find it gone. She'd tried to persuade me to talk to Stephen about it, but I refused. The truth of the matter was that I didn't want to mention the Greys to Stephen again until I had firm evidence (yes, damnit, if it came to it, even if I had to present him with one of those monster's heads on a plate). Then he would be forced to believe me. Until then, I'd keep my lips zipped tight shut.

As we flew, we saw signs that humans still crowded almost shoulder to shoulder down there. There were what amounted to shanty towns, no doubt built by survivors driven out of their homes in the west of the country. I imagined life for them would be a ceaseless war, with community fighting community as they competed for a field of turnips or a few cans of beans.

I had little doubt, too, that they would be eating each other. After all, if it was a choice between cannibalism or a slow death by starvation, which would you choose?

As I gazed out the window Jesus tapped me on the shoulder; in his soft Liverpudlian accent he asked, 'All right, Rick?'

'Fine, thanks.'

'Chocolate?'

He held out a bar, the foil pulled partway back.

This was all too much to take in. Here I was sitting three kilometres up in the sky being offered chocolate. Down on the ground millions were dying of starvation; or being murdered for the meat on their bones. I smiled grimly, thanked him and broke off a chunk.

'Say, Rick . . .' He smiled that benevolent Jesus smile. 'What's wrong with Kate?'

'Nothing's wrong with Kate. What makes you ask that?'

'What made her take the other plane?'

'Oh, she said she wanted to keep Cindy company. If you ask me she just wanted to catch up on girl talk.'

'Ah, I see ...' He stroked the bumfluff beard, smiling. 'I thought perhaps the two of you had had a lovers' quarrel. More chocolate, Rick?'

'Thanks.'

At the time it didn't strike me as such a peculiar thing to ask. It was nothing more than a bit of buddy chat. But I suppose Jesus was already making plans.

It was certainly true Kate and I had had no lovers' quarrel. That morning we'd woken early. Kate had kissed me on the mouth, then she'd slid her head under the bedclothes. Kissed my chest, my stomach. Then I felt her lips lightly nipping the end of my penis.

Then she let her tongue have a piece of the action.

It felt so good ... so amazingly good.

The next thing I knew she was on her back and I was on top of her, pressing myself into her. She'd gasped, her fingernails had dug lightly into my back and then slid down to hold onto my buttocks.

In the plane I closed my eyes, remembering.

The way her face flushed. I'd quickened the rhythm, bit gently at the tips of her breasts. She panted my name in my ear.

In the plane my head nodded forward. The steady note of the engines replicated the rumble a foetus must hear in utero: the sound of its mother's heartbeat and the blood flowing through arteries, pumping through the placenta, then into the embryo itself safely curled in the womb. It had a hypnotic effect, lulling me to sleep.

I saw Kate looking up at me. Her green eyes locked on mine. Suddenly I realized she was standing in a sea of blood. It foamed round her; waves of crimson struck her in the back, splashing her face with gobs of bloody gore. I reached out to her; she stretched out to me, arching her long back, her long slender arms lifted up. But she could not reach me.

She called my name over and over, fighting to get closer, but something held her back whether it was the slap of the crimson waves or whether something held her from beneath I couldn't tell. But the bloody red sea rose steadily: to her chest; to her shoulders; it matted her froth of hair into rats' tails the colour of rust. I tried to catch her hands.

I couldn't.
Then I knew.
I was losing her.
Just as I'd lost Caroline.
That bloody red sea would take her from me.

When I opened my eyes, Howard was calling back to us in the cabin: 'Grit your teeth, gentlemen. We're going in.'

I rubbed my eyes, looked down through the side window. There was Fountains Moor. I saw the cleft in the hillside, the rows of tents, the sinewy line of the stream running away like a silver snail's trail.

Then the heather dropped away. There were fields bounded by dry-stone walls. Clumps of trees. The grass blurred. Then—

Bump.

Down.

I turned back to Jesus. 'Welcome to our home,' I said. 'But I think you'll find it a bit more spartan than what you're used to.'

'No worries, Rick,' he said. 'In a couple of days we'll all be on that ship.'

He smiled the characteristic Jesus smile, chock full of sunny benevolence.

I was amazed to find how cold it was back in the north. The ground had frozen concrete-hard there, as if overcompensating for the ever-encroaching hot-spots.

Stephen was wasting no time. Already five of our community and four of Jesus's tribe were waiting there for the planes to take them on to the coast.

As I helped unload the food supplies we'd brought back I scanned the sky for the Cessna that was bringing Kate to Fountains Moor.

'Don't worry, Kennedy.' Howard slapped me on the shoulder. 'They're not us fast as us.'

'You sure they're OK?'

'Sure they are. I spoke to Cindy on the radio before I landed. They'd hit head winds over Newark, but they're still making good time.'

'It looks as if my brother's sent you another batch of passengers for Whitby. I could tell him to hold the flights back until tomorrow.'

Howard gave a tired smile. 'Are you saying I can't handle this, old boy?'

'You look exhausted. Cindy, too. You're ready for a break, aren't you?'

He nodded. 'As the saying goes, you get all the rest you need when you're dead.' His face darkened as if he'd just glimpsed the future. He shook himself out of it. Slapping me on the back again, he tried to sound cheerful. 'Don't worry about me, Rick. Another ten flights and we're all on the ship. Then it's bon voyage and you can damn well wait on me hand and foot.' Playfully he cuffed me on the ear. 'Get those packs of dried rice out from behind my seat, while I get this baby fuelled up and ready for its seaside run. Hey, Ben. Roll out the fuel drums.'

He walked away, giving orders. My heart went out to him as I watched him. Normally, he was so solidly built, square-shouldered, round-faced, meaty hands. Now the shoulders looked painfully narrow. The eyes bled nothing but exhaustion. He was half dead on his feet.

As I shifted the bagged rice to the edge of the airstrip ready for our team to backpack it up the hill to Fountains Moor I saw Dean Skilton along with a couple of our lot hauling a handcart – the kind you'd once find used by railway porters. On the handcart were a couple of steel drums, filled with aviation fuel.

'The other handcart's busted,' Dean called to Howard. 'You still need another drum of fuel?'

'I need it today, Dean. When can you bring it up?'

'We're going right back.' Dean looked as exhausted as Howard. Only with Dean and our people you saw lack of food was biting deep, too. Their clothes looked a couple of sizes too big. Their necks were scrawny, looking like the necks of old men, not youths who hadn't yet turned twenty.

'Dean, hey, Dean,' I called. 'You haven't forgot your old buddy Rick Kennedy already?'

'Hey, Rick. My man! How goes it?' He seemed genuinely pleased to see me. The tired eyes lit up. 'I heard you and Kate were starting the smoochie stuff.'

'Yeah,' I smiled shyly. 'You heard right. Wow, what happened to your lip?'

'Oh, this little beauty spot.' He touched the raw-looking sore on his upper lip. 'They're all the rage these days, you know. Haven't you noticed we're all getting them?'

'You've been taking the vitamin tablets?'

'What vitamin tablets?'

'The vitamin tablets we've been sending up on the planes. Surely you've seen them?'

'It's news to me.'

'But I put them on the plane myself.' I shook my head, puzzled. 'Wouldn't they be up in the stores on Fountains Moor?'

'Maybe.' Dean eased the heavy fuel drum off the cart. 'Maybe they got overlooked . . . Hell, Ben, careful. Do you know the drum's on my foot?'

'No, but if you hum the tune I'm sure I'll remember it.'

Despite everything, they still kept up the joky patter. But there was something desperate about it now. As if the ability to crack a joke, no matter how unfunny it was, demonstrated they still had the strength to spit in Death's eye and prove to themselves they weren't licked yet.

I still pushed on, almost in danger of nagging Dean about the vitamin supplements. 'You should have been taking them. The sores will be caused by a vitamin deficiency.'

Deane gave a weary smile. 'OK, Doc. We'll ask Tesco.'

'Tesco?'

'Yeah, the guy with scarred lips?'

'I know him.'

'He's in charge of the food stores now.'

'Shit.'

'What's wrong? Hey, Rick?'

I walked away in search of Stephen. Suspicion had come shunting back: that Jesus was up to some scam. Sure, he'd promised us that ride south in his ship in exchange for bussing his people up here by plane.

But why had Tesco held back dishing out the vitamin supplements to our people? Jesus's gang were well-fed to the point of plumpness compared to our people. Was he deliberately trying to keep our people so underfed they'd be too weak to put up much opposition if it came to a fight?

I saw old man Fullwood. He'd opened the engine cowling on the plane and was using an oil can to lube the cable pullies. 'Mr Fullwood, have you any idea where I'll find Stephen Kennedy?'

'Ah, brother Rick. Good afternoon. I believe he's still back at headquarters up on the moor.'

'Damn.'

Meanwhile Howard was calling to Dean. 'Don't like to push you, mate. But any chance of that extra fuel drum in the next hour?'

'You'll have to give us a break, Sparky. Joe's got the shakes again.'

I crossed the airstrip to Dean. 'What's the problem?'

Dean nodded to a sixteen-year-old who sat on the grass, hugging his knees to his chest. 'It's Joe. He's been feeling crap for the last couple of days.'

'Christ,' I spat. 'It's lack of food, isn't it?'

'We're getting by,' Dean said.

'But if you're lugging up drums of fuel you need plenty of protein.'

'We're doing the best we can, Rick.' He turned to Joe who still sat on the ground, his arms trembling. 'Ready to roll, Joe? We need that fuel.'

'Let him stay here,' I told them. 'I'll go in his place.'

'You're waiting for Kate, aren't you?'

'I'll see her when I get back. It doesn't take long, does it?'

'The round trip only takes about an hour. We've built up a fuel dump in a stable down in the valley.'

Dean took one of the handles of the handcart; I took the other and we set off along the track. As I walked I scanned the skies for the plane that carried Kate. I wanted to see her safely back.

I found myself walking so quickly Dean repeatedly had to ask me to slow down. But the truth of the matter was I'd become eager to find out what the hell was going on. I was sure Tesco was holding back on giving our people adequate food. I'd tell Stephen my suspicions, then together we'd confront Jesus and Tesco with them.

If all Hell broke out then, so be it. But we wouldn't sit back and allow them to pull whatever evil stunt they had in mind.

CHAPTER 90

The moment I returned to the airstrip an hour later with the drum of fuel I saw Stephen. He strode across the grass towards me, his face grim.

At that moment I knew he had bad news for me.

He didn't have a chance to open his mouth before I asked, 'It's Kate, isn't it?'

He nodded. 'I'm sorry, Rick. Howard had a call from Cindy on the radio. She said their plane was having engine trouble. They were going to try and land.'

'Hell. Are they all right?'

'Rick, I'm sorry. I'd be lying to you if I said it looked good.'

'Do you know where they came down?'

'Just south of Leeds.'

'You managed to radio them again?'

'They stopped transmitting. Their radio went dead when they came down.'

'Jesus wept. Where's Howard now?'

'He took off in the plane as soon as he heard what had happened. He spotted the wreckage on a road near Holbeck.'

'Wreckage?'

'As I say, Rick. It doesn't look good. The plane flipped onto its back when it landed.'

'Christ . . . oh, Christ.' My legs turned watery. I needed to sit down. Anywhere. On the grass, in the dirt, anywhere, only Christ knew I had to sit down – before I fell down.

'Take it easy, Rick. We'll . . . Rick. Rick? Where are you going?'

'I'm going to find the plane.'

'You can't just walk out of here like that. You haven't even got your rifle!'

'Just you try and stop me.'

'Rick, hey, Rick. Whoa, just a moment there, kid.'

'I'm going to find Kate. She might be hurt.'

She might be dead, too, Rick.

I looked at Stephen. He was looking back at me, his face full of sympathy, but I knew what he was thinking as easily as if I'd flipped the lid off his skull and seen the thought lying there in black and white in his brain: **SHE MIGHT BE DEAD, RICK. SHE MIGHT BE DEAD . . .**

I took a deep breath. 'OK . . . OK . I'll grab my rucksack. Dean, lend me a rifle.'

'Rick—'

'Don't stop me, Stephen. You know I've got to go.'

He nodded. 'Then let me make a suggestion.

'Shoot, but you know you won't change my mind?'

'I know.' He nodded and gripped my shoulder. 'As soon as Howard heard, he headed off in the plane to see where they came down. When he radioed back he said he's going to circle the area and see if there's a suitable place to land nearby. As soon as he spots one he'll come back, pick us up, then return to the crash site. We can be there in less than twenty minutes, Rick.'

I nodded. My mouth had turned paper-dry, my stomach watery. The first impulse had been to hike there on foot but that would have taken a good thirty hours across territory that was becoming more alien by the day as the subterranean heat blackened the vegetation or turned lakes into boiling stews of rushes and dead fish.

'OK, Stephen.' I gave a grim smile. 'You were always good at talking some common sense into me.'

He put his arm round my shoulders and hugged me. 'Come on, we'll get you a coffee.'

'What if she's dead, Stephen? I don't know if I can take it again.'

'Again?' His blues eyes looked at me full of concern. 'Again, Rick?'

I nodded.

'It was Caroline Lucas, wasn't it?'

'You knew?'

'I knew, bro. Intuition. Oh, Jesus Christ, Rick, when she died you shouldn't have kept all that grief bottled up. Why didn't you tell me?'

I shrugged, feeling so damned miserable I could have crawled under a bush.

'You know you could have confided in me.

'Did you know she was pregnant?'

'I heard from Kate. No one else knew who the father was . . . would have been.'

'No. She wanted to keep the whole thing a big secret.'

'Why?'

'She had her reasons.' I sighed. 'Deep down I think she was worried about the age gap between us. I'm nineteen; she was thirty-seven.'

'It wouldn't have mattered, would it?'

I shook my head. 'But I don't think Caroline wanted me to feel as if she'd got some kind of hold on me.'

'She was a good woman. She'd be happy to know that you and Kate got together.'

I gave a laugh so rich in bitterness it sounded shocking. 'Yeah . . . Kate and me . . . Christ . . . good while it lasted, eh, big brother?'

'Damn it . . . Rick. We'll find her. Even if I have to sprout damned wings and fly you there myself.'

'You know, I—'

'Stephen! Rick!' Dean ran across the grass toward us. 'Quick. Get yourselves to the radio shack! Howard's on the radio.' He was shaking so much he had to take a deep breath. *'You've got to hear what he's saying!'*

CHAPTER 91

At the edge of the airstrip, concealed from view behind thick bushes, was the radio shack. We hit the bushes at a full-blooded run, leaves and branches whipping our hands as we held them high to protect our faces. Freak Boy stood at the doorway, gesturing to us to hurry inside.

Old man Fullwood sat in front of the radio, mike in hand. He looked up when he saw us. His old-man eyes were vast, round, glistening; almost baby-like. 'Stephen,' he said in a shocked voice. 'Howard's in trouble.'

Stephen took the mike. 'Howard . . . Howard. This is Stephen Kennedy. What's happened?'

Burst of static from the speaker. 'Christ . . . don't believe it . . . don't fucking believe it . . . bastard . . . bastard . . .'

'Howard? Tell me what's wrong.'

'Shot . . . bastards shot up the plane. I've got . . . 'More burst of static, drowning the words. '. . . altitude . . . holes . . . damn machine riddled with holes . . . ack!'

'Howard? Where are you?'

'Over Cindy's plane. I . . . I see it, right beneath me . . . damn . . .'

'What's happening?'

No reply, only the sizzle of static.

'Howard, please tell me what's happening to you!'

'Shot,' came the reply over the speaker. 'Shot to fuck. I . . . I brought the plane in low. I can see the road now. Perfect place to land. Then . . . then the whole plane started shaking. Machine gun fire from the ground. The plane's riddled. Holes everywhere.

Still losing altitude. Windshield shattered. Controls gone. Shit . . .
the rudder bar's jammed. Elevator's gone, too. I can't bring her nose
up . . . Christ, Stephen, I can't bring her nose up.'

'Howard!'

'Stephen . . . Oh, God help me . . . it's going, it's going. I can't
pull the nose up!'

I stood there, listening, in total, total shock. Sweat bled from my
skin. I could imagine Howard struggling with the controls of the
plane. Already I could hear the rising drone of the engines coming
through the radio speaker as the plane began to dive earthward, the
slipstream screaming over the wings in that ever-rising note, sounding
louder, louder, louder . . .

Static roared. Howard's voice mated with it into an electronic
crunching sound. 'Stephen . . . Can't pull her up . . . controls all
. . . rudder jammed . . . she's going . . . I can't bring—'

A scream erupted from the radio speaker, tortured, rising in pitch.
You couldn't tell if it was Howard or the sound of the plane diving
toward the ground. Or both. Mated together in terror.

There came an almighty crack from the speakers. Then there was
only the soft sizzle of background static.

It was over.

As quickly as that.

I stepped outside the hut. I breathed deeply. The air icy against my
skin. Seven people stood with their little bundles of belongings at the
edge of the field; they were waiting for the plane that would never
come now to fly them to the coast for a chance of life in another
part of the world.

Howard Sparkman was dead.

He'd died just five seconds ago. Bloodily, messily, in the plane that
had became his coffin the second it smashed into the ground. Now he
lay dead in the mess of twisted spars, mangled aluminium panels, a
spaghetti Hell of electrical wiring, the engines haemorrhaging engine
oil, mingling with his blood.

I saw it all so vividly in my mind's eye.

Howard strapped into the seat. The glasses still on his face. Only
now a star crack destroying each lens.

Christ. I remembered Howard Sparkman the night we went night
swimming in the carp pond at Fairburn. There we were, Dean
Skilton, Jim Keller, myself, then Howard, swimming the dog paddle
and squirting out mouthfuls of water in a long thin stream.

What will we be doing in ten years?

That's what we'd been asking ourselves.

A week after that swim in the dark, ten-year-old Jim Keller (the boy who wanted to become a pilot) had lain dead at the side of the road after his father had driven away from the family home after splitting up with Mrs Keller.

Now it was Howard Sparkman's turn, my friend of ten years. He'd had a passion for food, for flying (realizing an ambition he'd shared with Jim). One day he'd promised us he'd open his own restaurant.

So much for our dreams and ambitions.

CHAPTER 92

Within twenty minutes of losing Howard Sparkman the meeting was in full swing. We were crowded into the radio shack. There was Jesus, thoughtful, stroking his beard. Stephen, running his hands through his hair, hammering his brain for fresh ideas that would save the skins of his people. I stood beside the door, leaning with my back to the wall, impatiently tapping my palms against my leg. Christ, I was so keen to set off for Leeds on foot to find the planes. Even if it was only to confirm that Howard, Cindy, and Kate were dead.

There were others crammed into the hut, too: old man Fullwood, Dean Skilton sitting on a chair with his rifle across his knees. Freak Boy squatting in the corner, resting his chin on his two clenched fists. And then there was Victoria, curling a lock of her red hair around a finger. Her bored expression suggested she took as much interest in what was going on as if she was waiting for a bus.

Jesus launched right in, his Liverpudlian voice soft but businesslike: 'Stephen. You do realize you have no planes left to fly us out to the coast. How will we reach the ship now?'

Stephen rubbed his face and took a deep breath. 'We'll find a way.'

'We can't wait any longer, you know?'

'I know that. Have you any ideas?'

'You could find another plane.'

'A new plane wouldn't be the worst problem. Finding someone to fly it would.'

'We're deep in the brown stuff, boyo,' Jesus said.

'Tell me about it. Dean, how many people have we got left here?'

'We've already transported sixty-two. Twenty-eight of Jesus's people and thirty-four of ours.'

'So we've . . . what? Fifty-eight remaining?'

'Fifty-six.'

'Fifty-six people that we've got to get from here at Fountains to the coast.'

Jesus looked round at us. 'Ideas, anyone? How do you shift fifty-six people to that ship before we starve to death here?'

'There is one way,' Stephen said carefully. 'But I don't think anyone's going to care for the idea.'

Jesus stroked his beard. 'Maybe . . . what you got in mind?'

'Walk.' He looked round at us, gauging our reactions from the expressions on our faces. 'We carry what we can . . . and we walk.'

'Walk?'

'It's about a hundred kilometres as the crow flies. We can do it.'

'Yeah, sure we could.' Dean gave a grim laugh. 'We could this time last year and we could call it a fucking holiday. But what lies between here and the coast?'

'About two million starving people,' Jesus said in a flat voice. 'Stephen, you know as well as I do that those people are so hungry they'd stop at nothing to get their hands on the food we were carrying.'

'Even if we had no food they'd strip the human meat off our bones.' Dean shook his head. 'You think we could hope . . . just hope to somehow sneak by all those people in the dark?'

'Do you think we should stay here?'

'Well, we certainly damn' well can't walk to the coast. How far do you think we'd get?'

I said, 'Stephen's right. We can't stop here. The food'll run out within a couple of weeks. And how long before the Greys get here? Have you forgotten about them?'

Again this demonstrated we were two distinct tribes. Jesus's people nodded. They believed in the Greys. Stephen's people did not; they exchanged knowing looks or shook their heads, as if to say, 'Rick, madder than a hatter, still rambling about grey bogey men again? Doesn't the sad bastard know this isn't the time for that crappola now?'

At that point, Victoria broke the awkward silence. 'You know what you have to do. But none of you can bring yourselves to say it out loud, can you?' Victoria spoke in a bored tone; she paid more attention to the curl of hair between her fingers.

We all looked at her.

Briefly she raised her eyes to us before dropping them back to the strands of hair, which she slowly twisted around her middle finger.

Stephen asked, 'Victoria, what do you mean?'

'Go west.'

'West?'

'It's the only way any of you will reach the ship.'

'West?' Dean echoed in disbelief. 'For Godsakes, Victoria. The ship is anchored off the *east* coast. *The bloody* east *coast.*'

'And that, dear girl, is in the opposite direction.' Jesus shook his head sadly.

Stephen stood up suddenly. He punched his left fist into his palm. 'Hell, Victoria!'

She looked up.

'You're right . . . you're damn' well right.'

Dean shook his head, puzzled. 'What do mean? We go west?'

'Yes. Yes, that's exactly what we do. We pack up and we walk that away.' He pointed. 'Due west.'

'That's crazy,' Dean said.

'No, it isn't – it's a stroke of genius.'

'The ship's on the east coast. You want us to walk west? What's the damn point in that?'

'Think about it,' Stephen said, suddenly enthused by the idea. 'Jesus. Haven't we got enough crew on the ship to sail her?'

'Yes, but—'

'Yes, but nothing.' A fire came into Stephen's eye. He'd found a way. 'This is what happens. We radio the ship tonight. We tell them to sail north, then west across the tip of Scotland, then south, down into the Irish Sea. By the time they've reached the coast, due west from here, we'll have walked the eighty-odd kilometres across country to meet them. Then—' He clapped his hands. 'We're sailing south. To safety. To a new life.'

'OK, Stephen.' Jesus spoke gently. 'Just wait a minute there, boyo.

Yes, there's enough crew on the ship to do that. But aren't you forgetting something?'

'What's that?'

'The land to the west of here. It's nothing but cinders and ashes. Am I right?'

'Sure.'

'We're to walk through that? You say that's a logical plan?'

'Not only is it logical, it's the only way we're going to survive.'

'You think so?'

'Jesus, I know so. Look.' Stephen rested one foot on a chair, and leaned forward to talk to us. He'd got the bit between his teeth. 'You're right, Jesus. Everything west of Leeds is desert. A big, black, ugly, godforsaken desert without so much as a blade of grass. But—' he held up his finger. 'It will be empty. When the heat came it drove everyone east. There will be no people to get in our way.'

'And the Greys?'

'The Greys?' Momentarily he closed his eyes. I thought he was going to rubbish the idea that the Greys even existed. Instead he took the diplomatic route. 'OK. Some people believe in these grey . . . grey humanoid creatures. Let's say, for the sake of argument, that something inhuman does exist out there. All right, I'll go with that. But that's a risk we'll have to take. My guess is, if we stick to a route that takes us across the highland areas, well away from whatever's left of the towns, we'll not see any of these Grey Men. They'll not waste their time sitting out in the middle of nowhere. With luck we can hike right through to the coast in three or four days.'

'With luck?' old man Fullwood said heavily. 'Luck is perhaps the most rare commodity of all.'

Stephen looked at Jesus. 'It's your crew and your ship. What do you say?'

Jesus stroked his beard thoughtfully. 'If we stay here we'll die. That's a certainty.' He nodded. 'OK. We go west.'

That was the decision. We were moving out. And we'd be going into the burnt lands. Maybe right into the grey arms of the bogeyman himself.

I guess it was the right decision. After all, it was the only option, short of walking directly to the east coast. Which would have been suicide for sure. The green lands to the east were thick with hungry survivors still. We wouldn't last a day out there.

The truth of the matter was that right then I simply wanted to kit up ready to walk to Leeds to find the two crashed planes. In short, I wanted to find Kate. That's all that seemed important to me.

As Jesus, Stephen and the rest thrashed out the logistics of the plan I headed outside to scrounge together a backpack, food, water bottle and a gun.

Within five minutes on that cold winter day I was ready. I found Stephen to tell him I was leaving.

He said, 'We're starting out at first light tomorrow, so there's no point in returning to Fountains Moor once you've found the planes.' He handed me a map on which he'd drawn a red line. Every so often along the red line were red asterisks. 'The red line's the route. It's an old Roman road that avoids what were once main areas of habitation. The asterisks are the villages you'll pass closest to. If you rejoin this route here at Skipton, you'll catch us up. When I can I'll use an aerosol paint can to spray a 'K' on walls and trees en route, so you know we're ahead of you.'

'Where are you rendezvousing with the ship?'

He pointed to the map. 'Here on the coast. There's a place called Heysham, just west of Lancaster. See the lighthouse marked there?'

'I see it.'

'If you don't catch us up en route, or you're forced to follow an alternative route, make for the lighthouse. Once we join the ship we'll wait until precisely ten days from tonight. Then we set sail.'

I gave a grim smile. 'Don't worry, I'll be there.'

CHAPTER 93

For an hour I'd walked through green fields. Now I stopped on the bank of a dried-up river bed. Beyond the river bed were the burnt lands.

They began as abruptly as that.

Grass at this side. Lush, green, very much alive.

On the far side of the waterless river, nothing but burnt grass, burnt trees, burnt fences, houses, cars, churches, melted roads, burnt bones . . . lots and lots of burnt bones. The smell of burning filled my nostrils.

You could see human skulls spread all across that black desert like big yellow pebbles. Thousands of them. The skulls of men, women and children who had struggled to survive.

Just like us.

They hadn't made it.

Just like us?

I shivered.

DANGER!

The north wind blew. It sounded human, like a girl crying, alone, brokenhearted. The wind blew harder, the cry sounded louder, more despairing, It whipped up black dust devils that twisted savagely, battering the burnt shells of cars, rolling skulls madly across the ground before dying back into that dead black earth.

I shivered again, zipped up my jacket.

DANGER!

Christ, yes. Danger. There might as well have been a dirty great sign, its post planted deep in the river bed. I'd no difficulty imagining it there, complete with big red letters: DANGER! DO NOT GO BEYOND THIS POINT. YOU'LL NEVER COME BACK ALIVE.

I looked across the river bed, the mud dried into flaky black scales, and I felt nothing but a cold, oozing dread.

Even so, I knew I had to go on. I had to find the plane. Kate and Cindy might be hurt. Trapped in the plane, or lying unconscious in their seats where they might be eaten by rats. Without a doubt, the cold alone would kill them in a few hours.

The wind blew hard again, flattening the hair against my head, making my eyes water.

More dust devils reared like the ghosts of the dead to dance their mad dance, twisting across a black desert that looked like edge of hell itself.

'OK . . . are you ready for this?'

By my side stood Tesco. He wore a backpack, his rifle slung by the strap across his back; blown by the cold wind, the orange strips of silk rippled and cracked like pennants.

Tesco had insisted he come with me to find the downed planes.

But I knew he wasn't ready for this. He was used to a flooded London. This nightmarescape of black dust was something else. He stood there, eyes fixed on the burnt world that seemed to roll out into forever.

'Well?' I prompted.

Tesco looked in disbelief and sheer eye-widening horror. 'We have to walk across *that*?'

'There's no other way.'

'Christ Almighty. There's nothing alive in that shit.'

'You don't have to come with me, you know that?'

'I'm coming with you,' Tesco said, swallowing. Then, taking a deep breath as if he was going to take a dangerous leap from a clifftop into the sea, he said. 'What're we waiting for?'

He walked down the river bank, silk strips fluttering, and jumped down onto the crust of the river bed. Dust squirted up around his feet.

'A word of warning,' I said as I followed him. 'The ground might not be as solid as it seems.'

'Not solid?'

'Tread carefully. Keep watching the ground around you. Keep listening, too. When the heat builds underneath you, you'll hear thumping sounds, clicks, creaks, groaning. That's the rocks expanding; also, groundwater will have turned to steam and be doing its damnedest to force a way out.'

'What do you do then?'

'You run like hell.'

'Aw, shit.' Tesco shook his head, grim-faced. The scars that radiated from his mouth like rays from a kiddy picture of the sun stood out white against the rest of his face. This new world frightened him more than he could say.

I knew he could imagine that dirty great sign, too. With those words beating out their stark warning.

DANGER!
GO BACK NOW!

But there's no going back.
Kate might be dying out there.
The only way is forward.
Into the Burntlands.

CHAPTER 94

We walked and walked. Soon even what had seemed dreadful became monotonous. Thousands of burnt skulls. Cars burnt clean of paint were dead shells, orange with rust. The trees that still stood had become skeletal monstrosities. They were as black as the ash beneath our feet.

Tesco asked, 'How long to Leeds now?'

'If nothing gets in our way, I reckon six hours.'

'If *what* gets in our way?'

'Use your imagination. There might still be survivors out here. You know they'd kill us for the food we've got in the backpacks. Then there are the Greys.'

'We haven't seen any yet.'

'Who's to say there aren't a couple of hundred waiting round that next corner?'

Tesco swallowed, then unslung his rifle as we neared the bend in the road. What was beyond that bend was hidden by a high brick wall, the bricks at the base of the wall baked even darker by the heat seeping ever upwards.

We approached the bend gingerly.

My stomach tightened.

I looked round the end of the wall, expecting to see a mob of hungry survivors or even Greys preparing to rush us.

There was nothing there. Only burnt cars.

'Come on,' I said. 'We'll have to move faster. It'll be dark in half an hour.'

'Shouldn't we think about making camp?'

I shook my head. 'We'll walk through the night. If anyone's still trapped alive in the plane, they'll die of exposure.'

'Or burn,' Tesco said. 'Have you felt the ground?'

I bent down to rest my palm on it.

'Damn.'

'Hot, ain't it?'

'Too damn' hot.'

'How do you know we're not right over the centre of a hot-spot that's just about to go boom?'

'We don't.'

'Shit.'

'Come on, keep moving. It's not safe here.'

'It's not safe anywhere,' Tesco grunted under his breath. 'The whole fucking world's about to blow its top.'

We pushed on.

Darkness came quickly. In the distance we saw lights. Fires probably, either from inflammable gases flaring off through cracks in the earth or buildings slowly heated for month after month until they combusted.

More alarming were the splits in the Earth beneath our feet. It looked as if some angry giant had torn open the ground. They were easy enough to step over but if you looked down you could see a dull red where the subterranean heat had risen so much even the rocks had started to glow like embers in a fire.

Any second one of us might stand on top soil that had baked into nothing more than a thin crust. Then it might shatter like thin ice beneath our feet, dropping us straight into a pit of glowing rocks. There we'd scream, desperately claw the sides of the pit, trying to escape. But the only escape would be death when the heat boiled your blood in your heart.

We walked on.

Beneath us the ground would sometimes rumble and quiver. I'd hear those thumps again as steam, superheated by the glowing rocks, blasted from one subterranean cavity to another.

And I thought about Caroline Lucas. How she'd been torn from me by one of those jets of steam exploding from the earth.

You could have saved her, Rick. She could still be alive. I told myself this over and over again. You could have saved her. If you'd been smarter, if you'd been quicker.

The thoughts made me walk faster. I heard Tesco panting with exertion as he trudged through the black dust, struggling to keep up with my vicious pace. I had to find Kate. If she'd survived the plane crash she'd need me. By some miracle, perhaps all three would have survived – Kate, Cindy and Howard. Christ, I hoped so.

We were walking in near-darkness. Our night vision allowed us to make out the burnt road which we followed. At junctions I'd risk using the torch, hitting the road signs with a two-second burst of light, to check we were on the right road to Leeds.

398

After switching off the torch, there'd be a tense wait, crouching at the side of the road, rifles ready. In that darkness even the two-second flash of a torch would be like a lighthouse, signalling to anyone else that there were other people nearby.

I'd wait, rifle at my shoulder.

Expecting any second to see figures bounding forward out of the darkness to tear us apart.

When nothing stirred we moved forwards.

CHAPTER 95

The grey dawn light revealed a ghost city. Leeds had become a vast sprawl of burned-out buildings without windows or roofs.

Thousands of cars littered the streets, their doors still flung open.

When the poison gas had drenched this part of the city, people hadn't just got out and walked: they had stampeded. And, later, when the subterranean heat had, at last, crept up through the earth to boil the blacktop, rubber tyres had burst into flame.

All the cars had been stripped bare of their paint in the searing heat, and now they had rusted to that uniform dull orange. Windscreens had melted, the toughened glass pouring down over dashboards. There it cooled, then set firm once more, resembling many-times-folded sheets. Surreally, it reminded me of the strange blue-white ice formations you might find in the Antarctic. Icicles of once-liquid glass hung down from steering wheels.

We walked silently on. In the Headrow was the wreck of a helicopter, lying in a mass of twisted rotor blades.

In some kind of maniac purge, perhaps to wipe out looters and serve as a deterrent to others, there had been mass executions. Along the full length of Briggate, that runs from Lewis's department store to Boar Lane, once a bustling shopping street, hung bodies.

Cables had been strung from building to building at third storey height in the same kind of zig-zag pattern you might use to lace a boot. From each cable, hanging by their necks, dangled men and women by the dozen. They might have been dead weeks but the hot air rising up from the ground had dried the flesh of the corpses, mummifying them.

As we walked along they swung gently in the breeze.

'Christ,' Tesco said. 'Reminds you of Christmas, doesn't it?'

He was right. I'd walked that street as a child at Christmas time. I'd looked up in awe at the cables criss-crossing the street. Then, suspended there, had been moulded plastic snowmen, elves, Rudolf with his huge red nose leading the rest of the reindeer, sleighs bulging with wrapped presents. Oh, and lots of Santas, of course.

Now the street was decorated with the dead.

Some of the heads had come away. Headless corpses lay in the street where they had fallen.

I looked up at the ruined buildings. Any second the barrel of a rifle might appear as a sniper lined us up in their sights. We'd be easy targets. Tesco unshouldered his rifle.

I pulled back the bolt of mine.

'I don't like this,' he whispered. 'As they say in the movies: it's too quiet.'

'See anyone?' I asked, also in a whisper.

'Not a living soul,' Tesco replied.

'Looks as if we're alone.'

'Where do you think they've all gone?'

'The first time they were driven out by toxic gas. This time . . . who knows?'

'Probably by those guys.'

I looked across the street.

The figures, tall, grey-skinned, red-eyed, had been painted on a wall. Whether the artist had meant only to record what he or she had seen, or whether it was intended to mystically appease the Greys I didn't know.

But it meant one thing.

The Grey Men had been seen either in Leeds itself or very near by.

Even now they could be standing there in the buildings, blood-red eyes glistening, as they watched the pair of us gingerly inching our way along the street.

'Keep moving,' I said. 'Stop only if you see anything.'

We reached the bridge that would take us to the south of the city where the planes had come down.

The River Aire had evaporated. The river bed looked like the skin of some immense reptile, stretching out in a mass of arid scales. Human skulls littered the mud. There were barges, too, looking like toys dropped by the careless children of giants. And, lying on its side, an army tank, the barrel of its gun standing straight up into the air like a flagpole.

We kept moving.

'What a mess,' Tesco said in wonder. 'What a freakin' awful mess.'

The buildings lay in ruins. Most had been burnt. Where the Victoria Hotel had stood, near Tetley's brewery, there was only a gaping crater. We walked by. You could have dropped a couple of trucks into that stonking great hole in the ground, then still had space for half a dozen cars. I stepped over rubble, broken glass, a baby's rattle, then the hotel sign, bearing a silhouette of old Queen Victoria herself in profile. I shook my head. My band, Thunder Bud, played its debut concert there. We had an audience of six. The bassist even forgot to turn up. But it had been our first paid gig.

Now the Victoria was a hole in the ground, half full of liquid mud that bubbled, jetted steam and stank of rot.

We moved on. Faster.

I scanned the ruins for Grey Men.

Nothing.

Nothing *yet*.

But I didn't doubt they were close. Probably watching. They'd move against us when *they* thought the time was right.

By now it was fully light. Chunks of snow-white cloud moved across the sky.

Above waist height the cold bit so deeply into your clothes you felt teeth of iced air prick your skin.

Below waist height you could feel warm air rising from the ground. The pavement smouldered.

We moved on. Leaving the corpse city behind. Now we were in a residential area, comprising burnt-out houses; their once redbrick walls scorched sooty black.

Twenty minutes later I saw the plane. I stopped, my heart suddenly beating fast in my chest. The little Cessna stood out against the black earth like a gleaming white cross.

Then I was running towards it.

Tesco ran hard, trying to keep up with me.

'Look,' Tesco panted. 'She tried to land on the road. It must have flipped over when the front wheel hit the traffic island.'

'It's still in one piece,' I panted back. I was clutching at straws. 'It can't have been going that fast.'

'But, Christ, have you seen those bullet holes?'

'I see them . . . Kate . . . *Kate!*' I started yelling her name, hoping to see her head appear over the wreck of the plane. 'Kate!'

I reached the plane where it lay upside down, its wings outstretched against the road. I threw my rifle and backpack to the ground, then dropped flat on the floor to look inside. The passenger cabin had smashed flat. I could see—

Damn!

I could see zip-all. Only a tangle of electric cables. The instrument panel had been forced across the gap I tried to peer through. I couldn't see into the cabin itself.

Damn, damn . . . I was sweating, my heart beating harder. Suddenly I wanted to throw up. We'd walked all night to get here. Just so I could do what I was doing now. Trying to see into that damned plane. But now I was here I was so afraid. No, scrub that. I was terrified. I knew I might look into that crushed cockpit and see Kate lying cold, broken, once-beautiful eyes staring.

Tesco ran round to the other side. His feet clattered on the metal wing.

I shouted. 'See anything?'

'It's open at this side.'

Impatient, I called again. 'What do you see?'

'Wait, clothes have spilled out of the bags . . . they're covering something; they must . . . Oh . . . Christ. Rick, you better take a look.'

'What is it?' *But you never really needed to ask the question, did you, Rick?* 'It's a body, isn't it?'

Tesco nodded, stood back to let me see.

I swallowed. 'Who is it? Is it Kate?'

CHAPTER 96

The force of the impact had thrown the body forward. Clothes and food stored in the luggage compartment behind the seats had been hurled forward, too.

'Christ, what a mess,' Tesco said. 'Look at all that blood. Can you see who it is?'

'No . . . And I can see only one body.'

I looked back at Tesco. I took a breath. 'The head's gone. I can't tell who it is.'

'The clothes. What was Kate wearing?'

I shook my head miserably. 'There's too much blood . . . we'll have to pull some of the wreck away to get a proper look. If you pull those bags of rice to one side, I'll try and crawl in.'

Even though the plane looked more or less intact, apart from the crushed windshield, the cockpit itself was full of the clothes and food spilt from plastic sacks.

Tesco asked, 'See anything yet?'

'I'm trying to clear away – *shit*. The bastards!'

'What's wrong?'

'Rats . . . fucking rats . . . the place is alive with them . . . ah-ck!'

Propelled by sheer revulsion I pushed myself back out of the upturned plane. Rats streamed out after me, squealing, their gem-bright eyes glinting, long worm-like tails held stiffly up into the air.

'Bastards.' I stamped my boot savagely down on them, popping them beneath the heel. 'Filthy bastards were eating her!'

We stamped on the rats as they ran from the plane. Those we didn't kill escaped into the rubble.

'Christ . . . they're disgusting . . .' Sick to my guts, I wiped the back of my hand across my mouth. 'Fucking disgusting.'

'They bite you?'

'No, thank God . . . Tesco, where are you going?'

'I'm smaller than you, Rick. I'll get inside the plane.'

'For Christsakes be careful.'

'Don't worry, I will.'

'See any more rats?'

'None . . . they've legged it.'

'Rick?'

'Yeah?'

'What shall I . . . Christ, there's blood everywhere . . . Rick, what am I looking for?'

'Can you see her hands?'

'I see them. They're not damaged.'

I swallowed. 'Kate wore a couple of rings—'

'There's rings on the left ... wait, let me check ... yeah, rings on the left hand.'

'OK, OK.' I swallowed, feeling sick. *This is it, Rick. Ask the question. Get it over and done with. Find out if that's Kate's torn body in there.* 'Listen. The rings on the hand. Is there a gold ring set with a red stone?'

'Wait a minute.'

The seconds ticked away.

'A ring with a small red stone. Do you see it?'

'It's difficult to ... Ah, I see them.'

'Christ.'

'No. The rings are silver.'

Damn.

Damn, damn, damn.

I couldn't believe it.

I sat heavily on the wing, shaking from head to toe. The rings were silver.

They weren't Kate's.

I took a deep breath. 'OK. I know who it is ... it's Cindy, poor kid.'

I rubbed my face hard. Damn. I was so relieved it wasn't Kate.

So, that means you're pleased it's Cindy Gullidge lying mangled and rat-bitten in there? Shit ...

Elation, self-disgust at being relieved, so incredibly relieved it was Cindy, not Kate. The rival emotions struggled for supremacy, leaving me so confused I couldn't think straight.

And Jesus, I was bleeding sweat. I sat there and shook until my teeth clattered.

A hand tugged my sleeve. I looked up to see Tesco crouching beside me, his eyes serious. 'I've had a good look inside the plane, Rick. Kate's definitely not in there.' He stood up and began wiping the blood from his hands with a shirt that had spilled from the clothes bags. 'I don't reckon it's wise to hang around here.' He nodded at the bullet holes in the fuselage. 'Whoever did that might come back. And they've got some heavy duty firepower to make that kind of mess.' I saw him freeze as he saw something; he craned his neck forward. 'Hey, Rick. Take a look at this.'

'What is it?'

'Someone's written on the fuselage in felt tip. Is that Kate's writing?'

I stood up. 'What does it say?'

'Just a second. My eyesight's shit. I need – *Christ!*'

The bullets hit the plane like hailstones. Splinters of road surface leapt into the air. The whole plane shuddered like it was alive. Holes rashed along its side as the bullets punched through in a loud clatter.

I grabbed my rucksack, my rifle. Bullets hit the road surface in splashes of black dust. Any second now a bullet might find my head. Then I'd lie writhing in the road, choking out my last breaths in gobfuls of blood and puke. We had to find cover fast.

It was our only hope.

CHAPTER 97

The one thing that stands out vividly in my memory is the way the ruined houses we ran towards seemed almost to move away from us. It seemed to take forever to reach them. All the time bullets shrieked around us, smacked into rubble then whined away.

Even when at last we did reach the houses we didn't stop.

There was no question of standing and fighting a war with those gunmen, even though I dearly would have loved to put a bullet into each and every one of their miserable skulls for shooting down the plane.

Once the gunmen lost sight of us they stopped firing. But we didn't stop running. Not until we were well out of the area. Then we collapsed behind a concrete wall, panting hard. I wiped the sweat from my face with a handkerchief; it came away black from the sooty dust we'd raised as we ran.

At last I caught enough breath to speak. 'We'll wait until dark . . . then we'll go back to the plane.'

'Hell, Rick. You've got to be joking.'

'*I* have to go back. I've got to see what's written on the plane.'

Tesco shot me a grin; against his soot-blackened skin his teeth were so white they looked fluorescent.

'I might have chucked school by the time I was ten,' he said. 'But my memory's not that bad.'

'You had a chance to read the message?'

He nodded. 'It might make more sense to you than it did to me.'

I sat up straight, skin prickling. 'OK, shoot.'

'Let me get this right.' He closed his eyes. 'I read: *Rick. Poor Cindy killed in crash. I'm going to join Ben Cavellero. Find me there. Love, Kate.*' He opened his eyes, looking pleased with himself. 'What do you make of that?'

I was already on my feet.

'Hey . . . Rick,' he called. 'Wait for me.' Still breathless, he picked up his backpack and ran after me. 'Who's Ben Cavellero?'

'He's an old friend. He lives in a little place called Fairburn about four hours' walk from here.'

'You're going there?'

I nodded.

'I'm coming with you.'

'There's no need. You can still catch up with the main party. You've got a copy of the route.'

'I have.' He spoke firmly. 'But I'm coming with you, OK?'

'OK.' I nodded. 'It means going back through the centre of Leeds, then heading north.'

'You think this Cavellero guy will still be there?'

'I don't know . . . I really don't know.'

We walked on in silence. We entered the burnt-out heart of Leeds once more. The mummified bodies still swayed from the cables criss-crossing the road.

I shot a glance at Tesco. What did I make of him?

He'd tried to kill me on that island the first time we met. I punched him so hard in the cellar on Paradise Island that I'd torn a hole in his face. Not that it wasn't a mess already with the scars radiating outward like the petals of a daisy. Now here he was, walking hard, big boots scrunching across the rubble. He was weighed under a huge backpack, his rifle on his shoulder; the silken strips fluttered in the breeze; the ones tied around his knees trailed, now and again, in the dirt, turning the orange strips black at the ends.

Surely he wasn't here on some humanitarian mission to help me find Kate and the others?

After all, it didn't need Sherlock Holmes to deduce he'd hated my guts.

Why the sudden change of heart?

Had Jesus sent him along to keep an eye on me? Maybe even put a slug in my back when I wasn't looking? After all, I didn't trust the pair of them. Jesus was always too quick to agree to whatever Stephen suggested. But Jesus was the leader of his community while Stephen led ours. I'd have thought there'd be more friction between the two.

It didn't add up.

And the more I thought about it, the more I became convinced that Tesco had an ulterior motive for helping me. I became convinced, too, that the Liverpudlian who called himself Jesus was engineering some secret plan of his own.

I was still mulling this over when I saw the remains of Howard's plane. It had come down hard in the city square between the massive Queen's Hotel and the post office. The machine was little more than shreds of blackened metal. One of its wings lay across the once-elegant entrance of the hotel.

Gingerly, I stepped through the wreckage and looked into what remained of the cockpit. Howard had been reduced to bones by the heat. I picked a piece of twisted metal from the ashes. His gold-rimmed glasses. They'd been melted out of shape by the intense heat.

There was nothing we could do. Howard Sparkman, age twenty-one, was dead.

I looked at my watch. We'd been without sleep for thirty hours. I felt dead inside. Emotionally dead.

We began walking again. We'd probably only been on the move for ten minutes when I noticed that Tesco had begun to repeatedly glance back the way we'd come.

I knew the reason. Slipping my rifle from my shoulder I said, 'We're being followed, aren't we?'

CHAPTER 98

My name is Kate Robinson.

I'm writing this now because this might be my last chance to tell you, Rick, what happened. I know you'll find this. Whether you will find my body I don't know.

I must write quickly. They are getting closer. I know any moment they could break down the door. God knows what they will do to me then. Oh, Rick I've never felt so vulnerable and alone. I wish you were here with me.

OK, this is what happened to me:

Yesterday the plane carrying Cindy and myself suffered engine trouble. Cindy managed to land the plane on a road just outside Leeds. Just seconds after I climbed out of the plane, it was hit by gunfire. There were bullets hitting the ground all around me. I ran for cover, then waved to Cindy to taxi the plane out of harm's way.

I could see the bullets hitting the plane as she taxied the plane along the road.

She tried hard to get clear of the gunfire; she pushed the plane faster than it was capable of. It was still taxiing along the road when the front wheel of the undercarriage hit a traffic island. In a second it had flipped over onto its back.

When I reached the plane I found Cindy dead in the cockpit.

What else was there to do? I decided to walk to Fairburn in the hope Ben Cavellero and the rest of the villagers might be here. I arrived at Fairburn last night.

You'll have seen the change in the countryside here. The heat seeping up through the ground has killed all plant life. The trees are charcoal. The fields are blackened. There's not a single green leaf to be seen. From Leeds to Fairburn there is nothing but desert now. Black desert.

I'd almost reached the village when I saw them.

That's when I ran into the church and shut the door.

You recall St Helen's church on the edge of the village? (That's where I'm writing this now. Sitting on a wooden pew at the back of the church near the font.) I remember when the church's limestone walls gleamed as white as milk in the sunlight; the square tower with the clock; the black slate roof; how the old graveyard, crammed with ancient headstones, surrounded it, making it look as picturesque as an old Constable painting.

You'll have seen, as you walked here, how it's all changed now. The walls are blackened by grass fires. There are fissures in the ground from which ashes and dust are propelled into the sky by jets of gas. The ash falls like black snow. It mounds against the walls of the church. The gravestones are covered. The hands of the clock in the tower are forever frozen at ten to two.

They're out there now.

It's nearly midday. The stained glass windows are smashed. If I stand on the ladder I've leant against the wall I can see out of the church. I see them moving closer.

You were right, Rick. I'd never seen these Grey Men before but they *are* real. Just to see them is the most terrifying experience of my life.

Against the black ground they seem to gleam bright grey. Almost as if they are lit from inside. The eyes are as red as fresh blood. Their arms are long, powerful, like those of apes.

They're coming for me now. I've just climbed the ladder to see out. They've crossed what's left of the fence into the graveyard. They're now just thirty paces or so from the door of the church.

I'm going to take my rifle with me now. I won't let them take me without a fight.

Goodbye, Rick.
I loved you. I really did.
– Kate.

CHAPTER 99

My name is Rick Kennedy.

We walked through Leeds; the roads were carpeted ankle-deep in shattered glass that crunched beneath our feet. Buildings were burnt skeletons. Venetian blinds swayed behind broken windows. No human beings moved through the city. Only the rats, crows – and now something else.

'Any idea who's following us?' Tesco asked.

I nodded. 'The boys in grey are back again.'

'The Greys?'

'See to our right? In the alleyway?'

'Uh . . . I see them,' Tesco grunted. He eased back the rifle bolt.

'Don't use the gun unless you have to,' I said in a low voice. 'I think they outnumber us by about a hundred to one.'

'We'll take some of the bastards with us. What do you say?'

'I say, keep moving,' I told him. 'We might be able to lose them in the ruins.'

We walked faster.

I glanced back at the grey figures. They all looked so alike they could have been mass-produced by some nightmare machine. Picture this:

Eyes, oriental in shape. Glistening.

Red.

Wet.

Evil.

Big, mulish heads; a strip of bristling black hair that follows the crest of bone running from the forehead to the back of the skull. The arms are apelike. Biceps bulge with great knots of muscle; those arms are powerful enough to snap a man as easily as you or I would snap a pencil. And stretched over that thundering great framework of bone and blocks of muscle is the skin, looking like crudely tanned leather, the colour of grey clay; from this skin, warts poke out obscenely like coarse brown nipples.

The creatures didn't rush us. They seemed pretty much detached and unemotional about the whole thing. They merely filed from the alley, to stand and watch us hurry away.

I knew within a couple of minutes why they weren't tripping over each other to catch us. Because they were all over the city like a disease.

I passed a house. I saw a grey face watching me from the shadows inside. The blood-red eyes fixed on mine.

'Hurry it up,' I said. 'We've got to get clear of the city.'

Now we were moving at a jog. I wanted to run faster, but I knew we'd have to conserve some energy. We'd not slept in thirty hours. We'd eaten nothing but cake and apples on the trek down to Leeds.

Exhaustion started to bite.

The Grey Men were slowly moving out from the ruins and into the street.

You could sense the tension building. In the way the eyes stared at us without blinking. Biceps and shank muscles twitched beneath skin.

They were inhuman. But there *was* intelligence there. Some monstrous implacable plan had been formed. They were following that plan. When the time came for them to destroy us they would act.

Now they moved with robotic calm. They were in no hurry. We were easy meat.

CHAPTER 100

I am Kate Robinson. This happened to me:

It all happened so fast. How they got into the church I don't know. Suddenly the grey monsters were everywhere. They surged over the pews as fast as tigers. I fired off a couple of shots before the creatures hit me.

Everything happened with such explosive speed that I have no clear recollection what happened next.

Only that I was lying flat on my back on the stone floor, my head hurting so much I thought I would vomit.

I felt hands grab me by my coat; savagely they dragged me to my feet.

I must have been on the verge of blacking out.

One moment I'd see a huge grey face pushed forward into mine, those blood-red eyes locking onto my eyes. Then the eyes searched my face almost as if they were reading words on a page. They were looking for something. I felt like a specimen in a laboratory.

All the time, those savage hands pulled at my arms, and at my clothes, examining me with a roughness that was incredible.

And ' ' the time I was gasping, trying to scream, praying that if I could only scream loud enough they'd leave me alone.

Again, all I can say is that I only remember what happened in flashes, as if clips of videotape had been joined together in a random, chaotic way. These are the memories that flash into my head:

—I see a grey hand swoop out of the gloom like an obscene bird of prey. The hand grips my jaw, my face is pulled into the grey face of that *thing*.

—'Help! Help!'

—No help coming.

—That face in close-up again, its nostrils widening; it pants so excitedly I feel its breath gusting into my face. It stinks of rot and damp. The blood-red eyes narrow. My God, I see the face in mad, mad detail . . . blood-red eyes again, wet, slick, halfway between

411

liquid and solid. But oh, so red. I see the warts as thick as your thumb studding the forehead, the jaw; I see the mane of black hair bristling across the great bony skull

—What do I feel? What do I feel? Keep a grip, Kate; don't let this crack your mind.

—So, what *do* you feel? I feel terror, such unimaginable terror; the grey hands run over me like a butcher feeling the meat on a pig. They squeeze cruelly hard.

—I can't breathe. I want to scream. But I can't draw breath. I feel a tremendous weight on my stomach,

—Oh, dear God. Rick. Please, Rick, where are you? These monsters are tearing me apart.

—They lift me clean off the floor by my hair; the grey paw clutches a great fistful. Still they squeeze my arms, thighs, hands, face. They squeeze with such a savage strength I could pass out . . .

—The blackouts come.

—My coat is torn off

—I hear my sweatshirt rip as a fist grabs the collar, pulls, pulls hard again. I can't breathe. Dear God, make them let go of the sweatshirt; the collar's pulled tight around my throat. I can't breathe.

—OH!

—The pain is sickening. I'm dropped down flat to the ground. I see smashed pews, the remains of stained glass, the wings of an angel; torn Bibles . . .

—Candles scattered on the floor. I can't think straight. Still I can't breathe. This is agony.

—Oh, please don't let them do that.

—Rick, Rick, where are you please . . . please . . .

—They have grabbed my ankles. I lie on my back. They're lifting my legs up. Oh, Christ . . . not that. I don't believe they'd do that. They're not men. Surely they don't believe they could . . .

—OH! OHHHH!

—Not that!

—Oh, they wouldn't do that. Please let go of my legs, don't force them up towards my chest . . . you're breaking my back . . . you're breaking my back!

—You're ripping my clothes!

—No, don't do that!

—You're hurting . . . please . . . you're hurting . . . you're hurting
. . . oh! You're – no – *no* – **ah!**

CHAPTER 101

My name is Rick Kennedy. This is the outskirts of Leeds. I've just
seen a sign that points to Fairburn.

But that's when they make their move.

'Run!' I shouted. 'They're coming for us.'

The Grey Men moved like panthers.

We pounded across the road. The heat had broken up the
blacktop so it splashed as loose as biscuit crumbs every time our
feet thumped down.

I panted, glanced to my right. Tesco was at my side, rifle gripped
in his two hands. He panted hard, sinking everything into running,
his eyes nailed to the road ahead.

'Stand and fight them!' he shouted.

'You wouldn't have a prayer. Lose them!'

'Lose them where?'

'There, in the wood.'

It was a wood once. Now it was a petrified forest of burnt timbers;
the branches made you think of giant spider legs, long, spindly, brittle,
dark as Black Widows.

Most of the trees still stood, in black, silent columns.

We'd fallen into a ghost world.

Populated with ghost men.

And soon they would tear our arms from our bodies.

As easily as you tear the legs off a cooked chicken.

Easy meat.

That's what we were.

But, Christ knows, I didn't want to die.

I wanted to find Kate.

If it was the last thing I did.

The forest was dark. Dead branches still blocked out much of the
daylight. When we ran it was eerily silent. Our footsteps muffled by
the thick layer of soot beneath our feet.

'Rick—'

I held up my finger to shush him. I didn't want to give the grey bastards a single extra advantage. OK, they might find us. OK, they might kill us.

But, believe me, I was going to make it difficult for them. Fucking difficult.

Our only hope was to run deeper into the forest. If the trees grew dense enough we might lose them.

We ran deeper. With the Grey Men padding after us with brutal tenacity.

Come on, come on, I hissed to myself. If the tree cover grew more dense we might live.

The trees didn't grow denser. In fact we came to a clearing.

And that's where it happened.

CHAPTER 102

Kate Robinson ... I am Kate Robinson. Oh, sweet Jesus Christ, it's a miracle I can remember my name at all after what has just happened.

It still hurts. I've never experienced pain like that.

My throat is sore with screaming. I have ashes in my hair, in my mouth. My clothes are ripped. Christ. They even ripped my skin.

Here I am, back in the church in Fairburn once more. The Grey Men are gone. I am alone.

I've lit candles; they cast ghostly shadows across the stone walls. Dazed, I look round the upturned pews, the broken altar. A torn Bible lies across the breast of a stone angel. Coloured glass from the stained glass windows sparkles on the floor like gemstones. The face of the Virgin Mary, painted on glass, lies intact by my foot as I write. Her large brown eyes gaze soulfully up into mine. They seem to know what happened to me just a few moments ago.

All I feel is total pain, total humiliation; total confusion. I can't remember ... I don't know what happened to me.

But I know this:

SOMEHOW THEY STOLE MY MEMORY.

I only have the clues: broken fingernails; blood oozes through my torn fingertips. Ripped sweatshirt; my shoes are missing; the leather belt of my jeans looks as if it's been gnawed in two by a hungry animal.

Oh, Rick. I fought them. I must have done. I tried to stop them. But their strength is enormous.

Just a moment ago I poured a drink of water into a mug. I saw my reflection in the water. The face I saw is bruised; my lip won't stop bleeding. My hair looks like straw.

Dear God. What did they do to me? I hurt all over. *Just what did they do?* It's important I know what happened to me during the last three hours.

But can I remember?

No. Nothing. My mind's a total blank.

I can only just remember my name. Then hazy patches of memory of you, Rick, the two of us together in London.

Think, Kate, think!

The Grey Men didn't try to kill you.

So what happened? Grit your teeth, clench your fists – think! Drag that memory back!

Grey fingers. They touched you . . . they appeared to be examining you . . . *yes, yes, that's it!* They *were* examining you. But it was a brutal examination.

Their thick grey fingers held open your mouth. Another of the creatures put his fingers into your mouth, gripped your tongue between his . . . *its* finger and thumb. Then it pulled out your tongue for examination. Pulled so hard you wanted to scream, the pain was so excruciating.

Those thick grey fingers were pressed into your neck, they followed the line of your spine as they counted your vertebrae. Experimentally they lifted your legs, or bent your arms to test the elbow joints, then wrist. Sometimes forcing your hand back until you were certain the delicate bones would break.

Then you saw their blood-red eyes coldly search your body as if they were looking for something important. Some sign that would say: *Yes. You've found her. This is the one.*

Did they find it? Did they decide I'm suitable for whatever Godforsaken experiment they'd planned?

Christ, I'm so badly scratched between my legs.

I'm so sore down there . . . I think they must have done something to me . . . and inflicted it with a savage, unimaginably savage force.

I know they will come back. They will conduct their nightmare experiment. I look through the door.

And even as I write this, I see those grey creatures walking towards the church once more. They're coming back.

I'll kill myself. That's what I must do.

I'm sorry, Rick. But I can't bear it happening again. They can't have any comprehension of pain. They don't understand the agony they put me through.

I have the rifle. I must use it on myself. A bullet will be quick. Painless.

Rick, I'm so sorry. But it's my only means of escape.

Please forgive me.

CHAPTER 103

My name: Rick Kennedy. The time: two p.m.

Suddenly I found myself in the open. The forest lay behind me.

'Damn!'

I needed those trees. That's where I was going to hide. Now I was in the open. There was no way of concealing myself. Ahead, fields of dust, nothing but dust. Nowhere to hide.

I panted. Christ, I was so breathless. Fine dust hung in the air; it dried the back of your throat until you burned from the back of your mouth all the way down to your lungs. Sweat bled from my face.

This was murder; this was Hell.

How could I outrun them?

Think, Kennedy, think!

I looked back. Shit. Where was Tesco?

He'd been at my side a moment ago. Maybe he'd stumbled. Already the bastard monsters might be pulling him apart as easily as a kid pulls apart a paper doll.

I unslung the rifle. With it gripped tight in my fists, I ran back to the forest. I didn't trust that freak Tesco as far as I could throw him. But I couldn't leave him there.

I ran right into him . . . no . . .

Ran right into **IT**.

IT reared up from the ground.

IT roared.

ITS blood-red eyes locked onto mine.

I knew I should shoot. I had the rifle there clamped in my two hands.

Easy, Rick!

Point!

Pull trigger!

But Hell . . . I could not move.

The thing lunged at me, red eyes blazing like twin lamps, its two grey hands open like claws.

It was pure reflex. I roared like a beast; threw myself forward, fists punching.

I should have punched a wall. I would have had some chance of doing more damage. That beast face was concrete-hard. My punches cracked against the forehead, against the jaw, but it was unstoppable. The eyes blazed at me with a ferocity that was unquenchable.

In one second the muscular arms swept me aside like I was filled with shredded paper.

I stumbled, fell flat on my back. With the heavy backpack weighing me down I was as clumsy as an upended tortoise.

Then it leapt onto me. The grey hands clamped on my face, pushed my head back into the soot.

I tried to slide from under it, pushing against the ground with my feet.

I couldn't move.

Above me, against the black-as-hell branches, I saw the grey face gazing down at me. The bloody red eyes blazed with such savagery I could believe a terrible fire burned in that skull.

I reached up to beat at the thick arms. No good. I could have been held there by steel girders.

Then the beast shifted its position. It squatted on my chest, the bare feet crushing down on my ribcage. My mind began to split apart with the sheer terror of the attack. I couldn't breathe. I wanted to scream when the thing clamped its great claw of a hand around my throat and started to squeeze with incredible strength.

Yet, part of me remained strangely detached. As if my soul had already slipped free of its body to watch as that grey monster squatted on a man, lying flat out on his back in the soot. Legs squirming. The backpack half-torn from the man's body in the life-or-death struggle.

Me, Rick Kennedy. Nineteen years old. No longer breathing.
The picture began to slowly fade.
From grey.
To black.
I wasn't breathing.
Blackness rushing in.
Life leaking away.
If I didn't dislodge the creature in the next twenty seconds I'd be dead.

CHAPTER 104

My name is Kate Robinson.

I am going to kill myself. But there is something I must do first. I must be quick. The grey creatures are walking towards the church again. They're in no hurry. They know I can't escape.

My God, just one look at them and my insides turn to water. I don't think I have the strength to do this but I must.

Also, I must find time to write down what happens to me. Please, Rick. Make sure it goes into the archive with the rest of the notes. I'll have no grave, no headstone – let these notes scribbled here be my epitaph.

The time is two p.m.

I've managed to do it. I searched the church until I found half a tin of blue gloss paint in a cupboard in the vestry. There is no paintbrush so I had to use my fingers. I also found a white cotton surplice the priest would have worn.

I've done now. So soon I can turn the rifle on myself. Dear God, dear God . . . I won't let them take me again.

So, Rick, if you find this notebook you'll have seen what I painted on the cotton surplice, which I strung between two stone pinnacles at the top of the church tower like a banner.

Painted on the surplice in blue is simply:

HERE – RICK.
—KR

If you see it, you'll know I'm inside the church.

I'm going to the top of the tower now. I'm going to sit up there, write the last few lines. The rifle will be with me.

Everything is ready.

CHAPTER 105

My name is Rick Kennedy.

I lay beneath the black trees. The Grey Man crushed my windpipe with his great claw of a hand.

I couldn't breathe.

Darkness rushed into my head. I could no longer see. I couldn't feel. Dimly I realized my legs were jerking in useless kicks in the soot.

When the monster had finished it would leave me there to rot in that forest of silent, dead trees blackened by the heat that burned the Earth's surface like a fever.

I kicked.

No good.

I couldn't shift the monster.

It must have weighed three hundred pounds.

I kicked.

That terrible weight alone crushed my ribcage. I couldn't move. I couldn't breathe.

Kick.

For the first time my foot struck something solid.

Kick again, Rick! Kick again!

I kicked. I knew I kicked the trunk of one of those burnt trees.

Kick again!

Why?

What good would kicking a fucking burnt tree do?

I didn't know, but the voice inside my head urged me to kick. To keep kicking.

Still lying flat on my back, I now lashed out with my feet at the trunk.

I couldn't see, but I could dimly hear the thud of my boot kicking against burnt timber.

Kick harder!

I kicked.

Suddenly a crackling sound cut through the fog in my brain.

I felt dozens of blows against my legs and arms.

Then the pressure from my throat had suddenly – magically – gone.

The moment I opened my eyes I saw what I'd done. My kicks had shaken the tree enough to break the brittle limbs. A whole deluge of the blackened sticks, twigs, branches had come down onto us.

The monster's head had taken the main brunt of the force as the branches crashed down. The impact had knocked the beast sideways.

It lay on its side now, its face crushed into the sooty carpet.

Coughing from the cloud of black dust thrown into the air by the impact, I struggled to free myself from the branches.

I didn't believe for one second the monster was dead. It could only have been stunned. The branches had been charcoaled by the heat; even the largest felt surprisingly light as I pushed them aside.

I had to get clear before it awoke.

I made it to my feet; but the branches, interlocked, tangled, formed a kind of cage round my waist. I couldn't even climb out of that mess of baked wood. When I tried to stand on a branch it snapped beneath my weight, sending out jets of black dust that irritated my eyes until they streamed and blurred.

I pushed branches aside to clear a path through the tangle.

I had to get away. I had to find Kate.

I should—

Hell.

The hand clamped around my leg.

I looked down. The thing leered up at me through the web of fallen branches. The bloody red eyes were bright, and bleeding ,ure menace.

A grey arm thrust upward, smashing through twigs. It gripped the strap of my backpack and tried to pull me back down into the branches. To finish the job of strangling me.

I grabbed the nearest weapon to hand. A branch as thick as my wrist and as long as my arm. I couldn't swing it like a club, so I pushed it down through the tangle of branches toward that grey face set with blazing red eyes.

Then, like I was tamping down loose earth around a fence post, I began to pound the branch into the face.

When I shook my head sweat flew in a spray. My arms ached. Every time I breathed I sucked in clouds of dust that burned my lungs. But still I pounded that branch into the face.

The hands released me. The monster's grey arms fell limply back into the branches.

I paused, panting.

The red eyes looked dull. The beast didn't move.

I began to push my way out again.

But the moment I tried to move the hands erupted from the branches again, grabbed me.

Once more I worked that branch, tamping it down into the monster's face.

I was locked into a nightmare. As long as I beat its head I could stun it. But the instant I paused it roared back into life and attacked me.

I'd have to beat the thing until doomsday. The second I stopped I'd be dead.

I struck harder. Mixed with the terror I felt a rage, a blazing, godawful rage that powered my aching arms.

I shouted as I pounded.

'What do you want . . . what do you want from me?'

Pound-pound-pound . . .

'Why are you here?'

Pound-pound . . .

'You can't speak, you can't fucking speak. You're nothing but an ugly . . . fucking . . . beast . . .'

Exhaustion bit deep.

I stopped beating.

Fists erupted from the branches like hammers, slamming against my hip.

I beat again. Harder. The red eyes dulled. The arms dropped down once more as the blows stunned it.

'Who sent you?'

At last I heard some kind of reply: 'Sss . . . ssee . . . ss.'

I screamed as I beat down: '*Who the fuck sent you here!*'

It hissed just one word: '*Jesus – sss . . . sss.*'

'Jesus?' I looked down in shock. 'What do you mean – *Jesus*?' The eyes, dulled almost to brown, filled with that liquid red again.

The hands shot up, grabbed me. I beat it hard, my fists clamped around burnt wood: again and again, I smashed the end of the branch

421

down into that grey face, the concussion knocking the head back into the earth.

I beat until the arms dropped, until the eyes turned dull brown. I beat until a liquid the colour of gravy bled from its black-lipped mouth.

I knew the moment I stopped it would kill me.

CHAPTER 106

I am Kate Robinson.

I sit on top of the church tower. And I write this looking down on a world that looks like Hell itself. Where there were once green fields there is only black desert. The trunks of trees stick from the ground in black columns. In the distance, gas jets vent from the earth. The flames are all colours – blue, yellow, orange, red, even vivid greens – and are strangely beautiful.

A wind has sprung up; the pages of this notebook flap. I hold them down with my free hand. I must keep writing.

The wind strengthens, droning, howling like a savage beast. It tears across that black desert, whipping up dust tornadoes that twist towards me; they blast against the church tower, the grit stings my skin; the gale rips wildly at my hair.

For all the world it looks as if black spirits dance across the surface of the Earth.

The dust hanging in the air forms a black mist. Even the sky is black. My world is dead.

Two hundred paces away a line of those grey beasts surrounds the church. There is no way out. Soon they will come for me.

When they walk along the path, the graveyard path, to the church doors, that's when I'll use the rifle on myself.

No more pain.

No more anxiety about food shortages.

I'll do it now.

Before they march into the church to—

Christ. I remember.

I remember what they did to me last time.

The memory came back to me as suddenly as a clap of thunder.

I remember!

They flung me onto the stone floor inside the church. They tore at my clothes with those claw hands.

Then suddenly they stopped. As if they'd been given an order. Then two of the creatures stooped down, each grabbed one of my ankles. Then they began to drag me across the floor. By the time they reached the doorway they were running.

I remember screaming. They didn't slow down. They ran, still dragging me by the ankles outside into the churchyard. I remember seeing the ruined headstones flicking by. My head smacked against the ground, my body scraped a furrow in the black ash.

Where were they taking me?

What did they intend doing to me?

I screamed, struggled, my arms trailing out above my head, but it was as if I'd been tied to the back of a car to be dragged away. They didn't tire, they were unstoppable. I screamed and screamed; the cinders raked my bare back.

Then they'd dragged me onto the dunes of ash that had been drifted there by the winds. Up one dune. Down the other side. Up the next.

I knew what they'd do.

They'd chosen me for their inhuman mating programme: **BEAST FUCKS WOMAN**.

I was to have forced sexual intercourse with these monsters.

I screamed. My sanity began to crack. I swore, spit and yelled and shouted filthy names. I'd have clawed out my own womb with my fingernails given the chance.

And all the time, this sensation of great speed as they dragged me.

Then it stopped.

No more movement.

No more grey monsters.

As suddenly as that.

Why had they left me there? Why had they gone as suddenly as that?

I can't tell. All I do know I was alone.

On all fours I crawled back to the church where I passed out on the floor.

I must keep writing. Every now and again I look down at the dust devils twisting across the desert. I feel the grit sting my skin as the wind blasts it with enough force to make the cotton surplice flap with a tremendous cracking noise.

Any second there might be a gust that tears it free from the string to send it tumbling away into the sky. So I tie more string to it, then wind the ends around the iron hooks set in the top of the tower. You must see it. You must find the book, Rick. Even if it's only to enable you to close this chapter in your life, so you can start afresh with someone else. The gusts tear at the pages, threatening to snatch the book from my hands. I hold it flat against the stones on top of the wall. I keep writing. Grit hits the paper, some catches in the crease-line between the pages. It looks like a line of black pepper.

I can hardly see the Grey Men now. The wind has whipped up so much of the black dust I can barely see beyond the perimeter fence of the churchyard.

But here comes one now. At least, I assume it's one. The black mist is so thick. All I see is a tall figure, indistinct, pale.

I'm going to stand at the hatchway which is set in the roof of the tower. I'll see it climb the steps. Please, God, let me take one of these monsters with me. Just to show them we humans can fight back.

I'll fire four rounds into it as it climbs towards me.

I'll save the final bullet for myself.

Here it comes. I hear its feet on the stone steps.

It's coming closer. When I see its head. That's when I'll fire into its—

CHAPTER 107

My name is Rick Kennedy.

The first thing I saw was the head. It was framed by the trap door opening to the roof of the church tower.

The dust storm nearly obliterated it. But I could see its grey smudged shape.

That was enough for me. I brought up the rifle. Aimed at the centre of the face.

I could kill these things. I knew that now.

My finger tightened on the trigger.

'Rick! Rick!' The voice echoed down into the stone tower. 'Don't shoot. It's m—'

Too late. The firing pin slammed into the base of the bullet.

The gun roared, discharging the bullet upward at the face.

Christ, that was Kate's voice! I ran up the steps hauled myself onto the roof of the tower. Kate lay slumped back against the parapet wall. The gale blew her hair in fluttering strands.

I remember thinking, *Oh my God, I've killed her.*

But as I reached out towards her she sat up. The bullet could only have missed her head by millimetres. When she saw the muzzle flash it was sheer survival reflex that jerked her back.

I all but threw myself onto her. The dust storm raged around us, grit stung the bare skin of our faces; we didn't give a damn. We just held each other.

'Look at the state of you.'

I grinned. *'Look at the state of you!'*

We were still in danger. But the relief was so great we couldn't stop grinning as we looked each other over. Our clothes, our skin, every millimetre of our bodies was black with soot. Our hair was so thickened by it that it was coarse and as dry as straw to the touch.

I watched Kate as she wiped her face with tissue from her backpack. Her long body taut as a chord, her waist narrow. The jeans clung snugly to her legs following the lines of her thighs, knees and calves down to her boots. She looked back at me, smiled, her teeth white against the black-streaked face. And, believe me, it was so good to see her again. I found myself staring. I didn't give a damn. I just kept on staring, unable to take my eyes off her.

My heart missed a beat. All of a sudden I noticed her torn clothes and injured face. I was stunned. 'Christ, Kate, what happened?'

'Those monsters.'

'They did that to you?'

She nodded. 'I'll survive. The important thing is we get away from here. They're all round the building.'

I reached out and hugged her close again. 'Sorry,' I said.

'Sorry for what?'

'Shit . . . I'm so fucking useless. I should have been here.'

'You're here now, Rick. That's all that matters.'

She looked up, smiling, tears cutting two pink pathways through the black dust on her face. 'You saw my sign, then?'

'It was the first thing I saw as I came up the hill to Fairburn.'
I smiled. 'You're a resourceful kid if nothing else.' I looked at her
swollen lips. 'Oh, Christ, Kate, what did they do to you?'

She shook her head, then slipped her arms round my waist to
squeeze me tight.

'Kate. How did they hurt you?'

'There isn't time for that now. We've got to get away before they
attack again.'

I looked into her face. My heart went out to her. Even the expression
in her eyes seemed bruised. Her injuries were more than skin deep.

'Come on, Rick. We can't wait any longer.'

I sighed. 'OK. I guess they're still out there but the dust storm is
so heavy they mustn't have seen me.'

'Did you see any?'

I shook my head. 'There's nothing but a thick black fog out there.
It's blinding. Are you sure you're going to be OK?'

'I'm not made out of china, Rick Kennedy. Come on, move it
out.'

'Keep your rifle handy.'

'Where do you think we should make for?'

'Ben Cavellero's house. It's no more than ten minutes' walk
from here.'

Kate pulled on her backpack, gently easing the straps onto bruised
shoulders. She did not wince. 'You think he'll still be here?'

'It'd be a miracle if he is. But we can't stay here. OK?'

'OK.'

'Once we're outside, keep moving. Don't shoot unless it's absolutely
essential.'

'Rick. Just a second before we go.'

'What are you doing with the bandages?'

'You're going to look like something from an old Hammer Horror,
but you'll need some protection from the dust storm. Sit down there
on the pew. Now . . . keep your head still.'

With that she wrapped the bandage around my head, covering
my mouth, nose, forehead. Soon only my eyes were exposed. Kate
allowed me to do the same for her. It should have looked funny.
Like we were attending a fancy dress party decked out as Egyptian
mummies. But the whole situation had left humour far behind.
Two of our friends, Howard and Cindy, had died in the last
forty-eight hours. I didn't know what had happened to Tesco.

426

I could only imagine the Grey bastards had caught him in the burnt forest.

Now, somehow Kate and I had to get through the cordon of monsters outside.

And what had happened to Kate? My imagination supplied answers that made my stomach churn sickly.

CHAPTER 108

The blast of grit hit us the second we left the building. It stung our eyes until we could barely see. But at least we could breathe. Soon I felt the trickle of grit down my bare back beneath my shirt as the wind forced it through every chink in my clothing.

The dust storm turned the world into a mass of boiling black. The sky looked like the ground beneath our feet. Black, black. We could see nothing.

Holding hands we stumbled into the storm. Once through the graveyard gate I turned left. Somewhere under that drifting ash lay the road to the village. At least, I hoped it lay there still.

We stumbled on blindly. I held the rifle in my free hand in case one of those grey monsters came lunging out of the wall of dust. It took no effort of imagination to picture them running towards us, hands reaching out claw-like to our throats

Suddenly the earth beneath my feet hardened. The same wind that was covering the ground with black had momentarily blasted the dust clean away. I saw five metres of road. The white painted lines led directly in front of us.

We pushed on, the wind buffeting, pulling us first left, then right, then pulling us back the way we came; then, with a wicked push, driving us forward so we fell onto our hands and knees.

With your bare hands touching the ground, that's when you felt the heat bleeding up through the surface. The road's blacktop hot to the touch; stingingly hot.

We pulled ourselves to our feet, walked on.

Dimly, I saw the shape of houses to our left and right. They were ghost shapes in the black fog. Windows had gone, leaving cavities that reminded me of the eyeless sockets of skulls.

Roof beams, denuded of roofing tiles, were the bones of the dead.

Instinct kicked in. I'd walked these streets for ten years.

Now I sensed the shapes of buildings, rather than seeing them in the black fog. The low flat-topped block to my right was the village post office; the depression to the left, the dried-up pond; then a tent-like shape, the frontage shaped like a capital letter A; now that was Fullwood's Garage. Great holes had been punched into the corrugated-iron wall panels.

The ash mounded into drifts. We clambered over them. Trudged on.

The wind screamed. A living sound, like a woman screaming in pain. Rising to a hysterical shriek, then falling to a low moan. It dragged at our bodies, then roughly pushed, whipping clouds of dust that stung blindingly into our eyes.

Still I saw none of the Grey Men. Although I expected any second to see them dart towards us out of the black filth that boiled around us.

I turned right. At my feet was a street name. Fixed to posts, it should have been waist-high, but the ash had built up on the ground here into a thick layer of black. I kicked away the drifting ash. The sign read: TRUEMAN WAY.

Home.

I'd returned to the street where I'd lived with my mother. At that moment the emotion it evoked was all but overwhelming. I'd thought I'd never see it again. But then what I did see at that moment had become profoundly altered.

I looked round. Trees were burnt trunks. Fences were charred stumps; hedges had been reduced to dust, then blown away by gales. Houses lay in ruins. They were indistinct box shapes in the Hell-black fog. I recognized Mr Harvey's Volvo estate car lying on its back, wheel hubs seared naked of tyres; they looked somehow stumpy, evoking thoughts of the scab-coated stumps that remain after arms and legs are severed.

All around us might lurk those grey, inhuman beasts. Maybe they were waiting for something to tell them to attack, to tear our faces from our heads.

I gripped Kate's arm. She looked at me, her green eyes narrowed against the stinging grit. Poor kid looked exhausted. But we had to press on. We had to get clear of the monsters.

We put our heads down and walked into the wind. It screamed through the ruins of the houses. That banshee wail seemed to bore right through my skull. An end of the bandage wrapped around my head tore free and rippled out in the wind.

I was too exhausted to retie it.

We forced our way on through the gale.

Then I saw the remains of more trees; here they were little more than blackened stumps, snapped off at head height. These must be what remained of King Elmet's Wood.

Just when I thought we'd have to walk through that slice of black hell forever I suddenly saw the outline of Ben Cavellero's house loom before us.

CHAPTER 109

The doors of Ben's house were buried beneath the ash that had mounded against the wall like monstrous black snow drifts.

They even rose as far as the first floor. Exhausted, we clambered up the soft ash. Sometimes we slid back down again, in a flurry of dust that choked us despite our bandage masks.

At last we made it up the slope to a window. It had been boarded with plywood. After a struggle, I managed to lever it off so it hinged by the nails holding it along its top edge. The toughened glass had smashed into sugar-like crystals making it easy for us to climb inside without being cut.

I pulled the plywood board down again. It flapped a little in the wind; dust still jetted through the sides but it held, shutting out the worst of the storm.

I pulled off the bandages from around my head, then took a massive lungful of clean air. 'You all right?'

'In the circumstances ... fine. Hell, this dust. My eyes are burning.'

'Come on, we'll find some water. You'll need to wash that muck out.'

As Kate unwrapped the bandages she looked about her, her large green eyes appraising her surroundings. 'Looks deserted. I wonder how long they've been gone.'

'Gone?' I shrugged. 'Or been taken by those things.'

She gave a visible shudder. 'Rick, what about the Greys?'

'Pray that they lost us in the storm. As soon as we can we'll push on.'

'Back to Fountains Moor?'

'Of course, you don't know. The plans have changed. We're walking to the ship.'

Quickly I told her what had happened. About Howard's plane being shot down. And how we'd decided we'd all walk west to join the ship on the west coast.

But from the look stamped into our exhausted faces I knew we wouldn't walk far. We needed rest. But that would give the Greys time to catch up with us. Christ, I wished we could just sprout wings and fly ourselves out of there.

'We need to search the rooms,' I told her. 'We might find some supplies – food, bottled water. More ammo'd be useful, too.'

She nodded. 'You take the left-hand side of the corridor, I'll take the right.'

I opened the nearest door on my left. It was Ben's study. It had been ransacked. But somebody had done a good job of trying to straighten the place out again. The leather swivel chairs and sofa were upright. The posters advertising Ben's mystery play had been taped together, then put back on the wall, alongside his watercolour paintings of trees and wildflowers.

Who'd go to all that trouble? If all they needed was a place to shelter for a night or two?

'As I live and breathe.'

At the sound of the voice behind me, I turned, startled.

'I knew you'd come back, Rick.'

'Ben?'

I looked into the shadows along the corridor. A figure emerged.

'Ben!'

'Mr Kennedy, I presume.'

There was no denying the familiarity of those softly spoken words.

Astonished, I watched, wide-eyed, as he walked slowly towards me. The eyes twinkled, he was pleased to see me. But for some reason he walked towards me with his hand over his mouth, as if he'd inadvertently let slip a dirty word in front of his mother.

430

'Hello, Kate.' He spoke in those soft tones. 'From the look of you I expect you could use a bath, couldn't you?'

'Ben,' I shook my head in disbelief. 'Ben, how long have you been here?'

'I've never been away. How is everyone?'

I told him the truth. It sounded brutally short but there was no way to sugar those particular pills. I told him about the deaths, and the plans now. He nodded, listening carefully, the blue eyes twinkling. But still for some reason he held his hand in front of his mouth, not moving it even for a second. Also, when he did speak the words sounded different.

When I finished speaking he said, 'Help me fill the bath; no mains water, alas. I pull it from the old well in the basement. The upside is it comes out ready-heated. Then would you like to eat?'

'God, yes,' I suddenly realized how hungry I was. But I was troubled also. 'But what about the Grey Men?'

'Ah, yes.' He kept his hand over his mouth. 'I know all about those fellows.'

'They're all over the countryside like damned pox,' I said, confused. 'Why haven't they attacked you?'

'As I said, I know all about the Grey Men. But they won't harm you here. If you do exactly as I tell you.'

Kate's eyes widened in astonishment. 'Can you communicate with them?'

'Come and have your baths. Then, when we've eaten, I'll tell you everything.'

CHAPTER 110

'How's the stew?' asked Ben Cavellero.

'Delicious,' Kate said, and hungrily spooned more into her mouth. Still pink-skinned from the hot bath, her blonde hair loose to her shoulders, she wore a blue denim skirt and black lambswool sweater. She looked fantastic.

I was too busy with a big chunk of bread and half a bowlful of gravy to do much more than answer Ben's question with an approving grunt.

Ben poured more wine into our tea cups. 'Sorry about the cups. The glasses were smashed in that last big gas blast.'

I looked up as Ben talked. He now wore a yellow paisley pattern silk scarf over his mouth. It covered the entire bottom half of his face like a mask worn by a Wild West bandit.

As ever, his voice was soft, 'You'd left before the hot-spots reached here, hadn't you?'

I nodded. 'What happened?'

'Pockets of naturally occurring methane gas underground ... they exploded like bombs. You saw what's left of the trees in the wood?'

'The tops were sheared off.'

'A hot-spot detonated a gas pocket out there in King Elmet's Wood. Left a crater big enough to slot this house inside. Blew in all the windows at the other side of the house.'

He continued to talk in those soft tones I remembered of old. But again I realized there was something wrong with the way he enunciated the words. Also, now he had a slight lisp that I hadn't remembered from before.

By that time it was almost night. Kate and I had taken our baths. Now we sat eating in what had once been a bedroom, the soft light of oil lamps casting lazy shadows on the wall.

I knew I was eating faster than was polite. But I was growing more agitated by the minute. The drift of ash had reached the bedroom window. I repeatedly looked out at the black desert that ran in undulating dune waves through the deepening gloom to the village. Although the storm had blown itself out, grit continued to hit the window with a sizzling sound.

Ben noticed the way I shot anxious glances through the window.

'Relax, Rick. You really must relax. More wine?'

'No, thanks. Ben, do you realize the danger you're in?'

'Danger? From what?'

'Christ ... surely you know?'

'The hot-spots?'

'And the rest.'

'As far as I can tell the nearest hot-spot that's of any concern is a kilometre in that direction.'

'The water in the well was—'

'Yes, the water in the well was warm; but the subsoil seems to have stabilized at a comparatively low temperature. You're in no danger.'

432

'No danger?'

'Rick. You must relax, believe me. It's for your own good.'

'Mr Cavellero—' Kate began.

'Ben. Please. More wine? Come on, you two, I insist.'

He's gone insane.

The thought struck me as solid as stone.

He must be. Surely he knows what's happening in the world? About those Grey monsters invading from God knows where? And why does he wear that yellow mask?

Christ, this was insane: sitting there; we were sitting ducks.

I looked up.

The Grey face seemed to fill the window. The blood-red eyes glared in at me.

They were here to finish what they started.

'They're here!' I yelled. 'Kate . . . get down!' I snatched up the rifle that I'd leaned against the table leg.

Ben jumped between me and the window. He held up both hands and frantically beat them in the air, back and forth. 'Don't shoot. Rick! Don't shoot!'

'Ben, for Godsakes! Get out of the way!'

'No. Put down the gun. Rick . . . put it down.' He spoke more calmly but his breath was ragged. 'Put it down, Rick. Easy does it. There's a good boy. Relax . . . easy . . .'

I was appalled. 'Ben. It was right there in the window. I could have put a slug right through its ugly head!'

'Put the gun down, Rick. Calm down.'

'Calm down? Like hell I will. Why did you stop me shooting the bastard?'

'If you see one of the Greys, Rick,' he said, 'promise me you won't fire at it.'

'But—'

'Rick. It won't do any good. In fact, it will only make matters worse.'

Kate shook her head. 'Why don't you want us to fire at them?'

'There's to be no shooting,' he said gently.

'But don't you know what they're doing? Do you know what they did to Kate?'

'Rick. No shooting, please.'

'But look at her face. Can't you see that cut on her lip? Those bruises round her eye?'

'I see them, Rick. Please . . . Rick, let me speak.'

Kate said quickly, 'Ben, you told us that we'd be safe from the Greys. Is that true?'

'It is. If you do as I say.'

Impatiently, I asked, 'Do what exactly?'

'Just keep calm. If you see one of those Grey Men at the window, do nothing. Even if you see one in this room, do nothing – *absolutely nothing.*'

'In the room! Christ, Ben!'

'Ignore it. Can you promise me that?'

'Ben, that's insane. They'll tear us apart, don't you understand?'

'I do understand what they are, and I understand why we will be safe . . . but only if you do what I tell you. Rick, you trusted me?'

'Yes, of course I did.'

'You still do?' Lightly he stroked the silk scarf that covered his mouth.

I looked at him.

Softly he asked, 'You trust me still, Rick?'

I sighed. 'Yes, Ben, I do. At least, I will do if you tell me what you know.'

Ben nodded. 'Of course I'll tell you. But keep this in mind: if a Grey should appear at the window, or come through that door, do nothing. Just relax. Continue talking to me as if nothing unusual is happening.'

Kate said, 'That's a pretty tall order.'

'But you'll do it, won't you? Kate? Rick?'

We nodded.

Ben sighed with relief. 'If you don't mind, I'll put your rifles across here out of harm's way.' He took the two rifles, then locked them in a cupboard at the far end of the room.

Uneasily, I looked out of the window expecting to see legions of Greys marching this way.

There was, however, nothing but black ash, burnt tree stumps. The dying breeze lifted a dust devil that moved, slowly spinning, across the dead forest for a moment before falling back to Earth.

'Now,' Ben said, 'As far as I know, I'm the last man alive in Fairburn . . . or what's left of Fairburn. Before the last group of villagers left, my old friends from the parish council did this to me.' He lifted his hand to where he'd tied the ends of the silk scarf in a knot behind his head. 'Ah . . . Kate, would you help me

434

with this, please? I tied it tight. I didn't want it to slip down while you ate.'

Kate untied the knot. The silk scarf slipped down to unmask the lower half of his face.

We'd seen some terrible sights, but this made us look away.

Ben continued talking in that calm way. In fact, more than just calm. The man was serene. As if he'd found an inner peace in all this mayhem. 'You'll realize my old friends had found out that I gave you food and persuaded you to leave. So they cut off my lips.'

I looked back at Ben. The lips had been completely cut away, leaving the teeth permanently exposed. Saliva dripped through the gaps in the teeth.

Christ, the bastards had made a mess of his mouth. The sight sickened me.

'That's enough, I think. But I had to show you what rational, civilized men are capable of. Kate, will you help?'

She helped him tie the silk scarf back in place, like a surgeon's mask. She glanced at me. Her eyes were full of tears.

I swallowed, then focused myself. 'What happened to the refugees?'

'When they learnt all the food was gone they moved on. Not before killing hundreds of other refugees first. And dozens of villagers. I heard most turned to cannibalism. Our people, too, I suppose. If you're hungry enough you'll eat anything, won't you?'

We nodded.

'So for the last couple of months I've been here alone. I listened to the few radio broadcasts that were being transmitted. I read a lot, too. Also, then I started to see the Grey Men.'

'You don't want us to fire at them because you've found a way to communicate?' Kate sounded hopeful.

'No,' he said, softly. 'However, I do know what they are.'

CHAPTER 111

'The Grey Men?' I asked impatiently. '*What* are they?'

'Are they from out of the ground?' Kate asked.

'In a manner of speaking.' Ben lifted the silk scarf where

it had slipped. 'The truth of the matter is, they're not really here at all.'

'Don't talk in riddles, Ben. We've seen them.'

He leaned back in his chair, the tips of his fingers pressed together as he thought through what he'd say next. The black grit continued to drizzle against the glass, making a sound like light rain. Beyond the windows, night had buried the black desert that was once my home village of Fairburn. I could see nothing but the random flicker of fires in the distance, where inflammable gas continued to flare off through cracks in the ground.

I still felt uneasy. I wished I hadn't let Ben take the rifles and lock them in the cupboard. What if we needed them in a hurry? Could I trust Ben's statement that the Grey Men were harmless?

I began to rub the palms of my hands up and down my knees as the anxiety kicked in. I glanced at Kate. She seemed tense, too. She shot wary glances out of the window.

The endless sizzle of grit on the window began to get on my nerves.

I needed the rifle.

Kate's eyes widened. She'd seen something.

I turned half round on my chair to look out.

Grey shapes. I could see them. They gleamed with a cold radiance. Here they come, I thought, alarms screaming in my head. The Grey Men are marching on the house en masse and Ben is sitting here talking about—

'Rick . . . Rick.' I spun round to look at Ben. He was speaking calmly. 'Rick, take it easy. Here, let me top up your—'

'No. I don't want any more wine! Ben, can't you see them?'

'Please drink the wine. You too, Kate.'

Kate stood up and went to the rifle cupboard. 'They're coming towards the house.'

'Ben, are you going to sit here and watch them tear us apart?'

'Rick. Kate. Please sit down.' Ben spoke with deliberate calmness. His movements were slow too, as if he hoped we'd be lulled into that same relaxed manner. 'Rick. If you do as I say they can't hurt you.'

'But you can see—'

'Sit down, Rick . . . relax.'

Kate said, astonished, 'Relax? How can we?'

I added, 'With those monsters out there? They're killers. You know that, Ben, don't you? They are fucking killers.'

Ben nodded. 'I do know that. But if you relax, ignore them, they can't harm you.'

I forced myself to sit down; my muscles were so tight I quivered. 'OK, Ben, you've got two minutes. Then I'm taking that key from you; we're taking back our rifles and we're shooting our way out of this place.'

Ben nodded; again it was a slow movement; nothing he did was rushed; he was trying to transmit to us a calming influence through body language and the gentle tones of his voice. 'All right, just give me a moment.' He eased the silk scarf back higher up his nose. 'Not so long ago an atmospheric chemist by the name of Professor James Lovelock likened the whole of our planet to a living, self-regulating organism. He called this living planet "Gaia". The Earth isn't an inert ball of rock floating through space that just happens to have life living on its surface. In a sense—'

'Forty seconds left,' I warned.

'In a sense the planet actually breathes, it has a respiratory system. Living creatures exhale carbon dioxide that, left free in the atmosphere, would eventually destroy all life on Earth. Gaia, this living planet, reabsorbs this carbon dioxide through plants on land and in the sea – these over millions of years are converted into coal, oil and limestone that are locked safely away underground. Gaia has maintained this balancing act for millions of years, ensuring that oxygen levels remain at around twenty-one per cent of the atmosphere and carbon dioxide stays safely pegged at 0.03 per cent.'

'Ten seconds left, Ben.'

'The planet is also alive beneath its surface. The Earth's core is a solid mass of compressed iron. It's incredibly hot. Surrounding the inner core is the outer core. Although it, too, is iron, it is in a liquid state. Then you have the hot stony mantle before you reach the thin crust on which we stand. Continents slide across the planet, collide, throw up mountain ranges. The movements in rocks beneath our feet generate electric currents. These radiate—'

'Ben. Time's up. Give me the key. We're getting out of here.'

'Rick. You've still not heard my explanation. Don't you want to hear the truth?'

'You've explained nothing, Ben. We're moving on before those monsters tear us apart.'

'Are you in such a hurry to die?'

That stopped me.

Kate looked at him. 'A hurry to die? What do you mean?'

He gave a weary sigh that made the silk scarf balloon around his face. 'Yes, in a hurry to die. Because if you don't listen to what I have to say you won't last more than a couple of days out there.'

'We've survived so far.' I wasn't so much angry with him as disappointed. I had always trusted Ben Cavellero. I'd listened to his words of advice hungrily as I grew up. Perhaps he was the nearest thing to a father in my mid-teen years. But all this talk about Gaia, the Earth as a self-regulating organism, made no sense; it certainly didn't seem relevant to what was happening here.

Ben spoke softly. 'Kate. Look out of the window. If you see the Grey creatures now you can take the key, collect your rifles, then be on your way. Now, Kate, what do you see?'

She looked out of the window, her eyes searching the darkened terrain. She looked puzzled. 'They were there a minute ago.'

'You don't see them now?'

'No, but it's too dark to be sure.'

I went to the window and looked out through the endless drizzle of black ash falling from the sky. 'They are there,' I said firmly. 'I saw them.'

'How many are there, Rick?' Ben asked.

I shook my head, confused. 'I don't understand it. I saw them. Hundreds of them.'

'Sit down, both of you. Please listen. The reason you can't see them is because they were never out there.'

Kate looked at him suspicious. 'Where are they, then?'

He looked at us, then touched his temple. 'In there.'

'You're suggesting they're hallucinations?' Kate shook her head. 'I am. Yes.'

'Impossible.' Kate slapped the top of the table. 'We've all seen them. For Godsakes, Ben, they nearly killed me today.'

I chipped in impatiently. 'Look at our faces. Just how the Hell do you think we came by these bruises, Ben?'

'If you'll just calm down, relax, then—'

'Then what?'

'I'll tell you exactly what—'

'For Godsakes, Ben, Kate and I have been fighting these bastards tooth and nail. Now you're sitting there pouring out the wine like nothing's fucking happened.' Fear, fury, impatience, exasperation – the whole fucking nine yards – it erupted inside me. I slung the cup at the wall where it shattered in a spray of red wine.

'I'm sorry, Ben. I'm fucking sorry I came here,' I yelled. 'You've obviously found your own way to survive, lost ... lost in some fucking dream world where the planet's a living creature and all these Grey Men are nice as fucking pie.'

'Rick ...' Kate looked scared of my fury.

'No, Kate. We're getting out of here. It's a fucking madhouse. Ben!' I held out my hand. 'Key!'

Kate shouted, 'Rick. The window!'

I spun round. A massive grey head loomed out of the darkness to press its face hard to the glass. The red eyes blazed in at me with such hatred I recoiled.

The bastards wanted in.

'Ben, give me the key. The key! You stupid bastard.'

I roared sheer fury now. I was ready to snatch a knife from the table and drive it through Ben's face. For some insane reason he'd sat us there to talk, giving those grey monsters a chance to move in.

That was it!

Ben had somehow gone over to them. He'd conspired with them.

I didn't even notice the door open behind me. Suddenly the grey figure was in the room, moving towards Kate, its great arms thrust out, the muscle tension forcing the arteries up to show beneath the skin like knots of cord; its red eyes burned like they were pieces of living Hell itself.

I snatched a knife from the table, then launched myself at it.

That's all I remember.

The blow to the back of my head knocked me forward. And down.

Then, suddenly, all I could see was brown carpet filling my whole field of vision. I couldn't stand. A darkness began to flow into me. My eyes blurred. Sounds grew distant.

I remember feeling intense disappointment. I'd let Kate down. I couldn't fight anymore. The Grey Men would take her. Then do whatever they wanted to her. And I could do nothing to prevent her torture.

CHAPTER 112

Torture . . . pain . . . despair . . .

Kate screamed endlessly. I couldn't move.

'Rick . . .'

With a tremendous effort I managed to move my head. My arms and legs felt as if they'd been nailed to the floorboards.

The Grey Men had her. One stood behind her, holding her arms straight out by the wrists, forcing her into a crucifixion pose. She struggled. Her head flicked this way and that, her hair whipping into the monster's grey face.

There was no expression on that face. The blood-red eyes alone gleamed with a monstrous passion that turned me sick to my stomach.

'Rick.'

She struggled, her face a picture of sheer horror. She knew they planned hurting her in a way that would be monstrously cruel.

She tried to kick her way loose from the creature's grip. Desperately she lifted both feet into the air to throw herself forward.

But the monster didn't even move. It held her as easily as you or I would hold a butterfly by its wings.

Another Grey moved into my line of vision. In a cool, unhurried way it bent down to grab Kate by one of her ankles. She screamed, 'No, no, no!'

I think at that moment she knew what they'd do to her. She screamed so loud the sound tore at your eardrums. Her terror and sheer, sheer despair cranked the scream still louder until it vibrated the bones in my skull.

The Grey holding her by the ankle calmly lifted it as high as its own head. Simultaneously the other monster let go her wrists. She swung down until she was hanging by her ankle in the second monster's huge fist.

She struggled, her body forming a U-shape as she tried to reach up to claw the creature's thick grey fingers from her ankle.

The first creature grabbed her free ankle. The two held her between them like she was a living wish-bone, so that she formed a Y shape, her head swinging, long hair brushing the carpet.

I could see what they were going to do. Christ, I knew, I knew. I could see them tensing for the pull.

Kate screamed.

I was shouting, 'No, don't you dare . . . don't you fucking dare. I'll kill you!'

'*Rick.*'

The two creatures each pulled a leg.

As easily as if they were tearing apart a turkey wishbone. A scream. The sound of pelvic bone, cracking, splitting . . .

'Rick . . . Rick!'

I opened my eyes.

Grunted.

'Rick?'

Ben's face, still covered with the silk mask, loomed into view. 'Welcome back to the world of the living.'

'Hell . . .' I grunted. 'My head. Jesus, what happened?'

'You've been unconscious for a few moments. Don't worry, you're not damaged. Your head's too damn' hard for that.'

'Kate?' I looked up suddenly. 'Kate?'

She smiled down at me. I realized she was squeezing my hand in hers. 'Don't worry, I'm fine . . .'

'But the Greys had you; they were ripping you up . . . aw . . . shit. Uh, I dreamed that one, right?'

'Right.' She smiled, nodded. 'You were out cold, but you were shouting out in your sleep.'

'I was?'

'Don't worry, I'm used to your snoring by now anyway.' She grinned.

Ben Cavellero caught her eye and raised a knowing eyebrow.

'But they're here!' I sat bolt upright. 'They're in the room!'

'No, they're not, Rick,' Kate said soothingly.

'You saw them!' I struggled to my feet. The room began to spin. I wanted to puke. 'You saw them in this room!'

Kate nodded. 'But while you were having your beauty sleep Ben had the opportunity to tell me what you wouldn't give him the chance to finish. Rick? Take it easy, you're still groggy.'

Ben pushed a chair towards me. 'Don't rush things.'

I sat down on it heavily. 'Uh . . . my head . . . what happened?'

Kate gave a sympathetic smile. 'Something hit you.'

'Someone hit you.' Ben gave a little shrug of his shoulders. 'Me.'

'What in God's name for?'

'You'd have killed us if I hadn't lamped you one with the stew pan. Sorry.'

'I'd have killed you?'

'You would have tried, anyway.'

'Me? Why the Hell should I do that?'

'You thought you saw the Greys.'

'I *DID* see the Greys.'

'Here,' Ben said. 'It's brandy. Take a good drink.'

I pulled on the bottle. It felt like molten lava gushing down my throat. I coughed as the burn hit me.

'I'll start at the beginning.'

'Good place as any,' I said, still bewildered. 'So, what's happening? Only no geology lectures this time, please.'

Ben pulled up a dining table chair, sitting on it back to front, his legs either side of the seat, his crossed forearms resting on the chair back.

Kate leaned back against the table.

'Right,' Ben spoke in a businesslike way. 'Give me your definition of a hallucination.'

'Hallucination?' My forehead throbbed. 'I guess it's when we see something that isn't there. Right?'

'But we believe it really is there?'

'Yes.'

Ben nodded. 'A hallucination may be defined as a vivid but false perception of something that is not really there. You may believe you see something that isn't there, or hear voices – the classic delusion of the schizophrenic.'

I groaned. 'My head hurts pretty badly, Ben. I take it you are going somewhere with this? If you're not I'm going to lie down there on the carpet and moan a little.'

'Sorry to be tough on you, Rick. Here. More brandy. But the truth of the matter is, you *must* take on board what I'm going to say. Then, my friend, you're going to have to catch up with Stephen and the rest of your people and tell them, too.'

'They've already set off to meet the ship.'

'But they're not going to make it.'

'How can you know that?'

'They're going to try and walk through that, aren't they?' He jerked his thumb to where the black desert lay in darkness.

'It's the only way.'

'To walk east would avoid the hot-spots,' Kate said, 'but there're are still millions of survivors out there. They'd kill us for the food we carried.'

'Then probably stew us up for supper,' I added.

'Right,' Ben said crisply. 'So they're going to trek on foot for three days across a hell of a lot of hot rock?'

'Yeah, there are bad hot-spots, I've even seen stones glowing red hot, but they can walk round those. We've done it before.'

'But the biggest threat to their survival is what they will see,' Ben said clenching his fists, desperate to make me understand. 'What they will *think* they see.'

I was still bewildered; the drumming in my head helped zip-all, too. 'Ben, you're telling me these Grey Men aren't really there?'

'I am.'

'And they are hallucinations?'

'Yes.'

'But how is it we have all seen—'

'You've all seen them?'

'Well . . . not all, but some.'

Ben glanced at the wall clock. 'I'm going to tell you this as quickly as possible. It's vital that you do reach your brother and warn him what he and the others will encounter.' His eyes above the silk scarf were the most intense I'd seen them. 'It really is a matter of life and death, believe me. If they go into the Badlands unprepared for what will happen to them it will wipe out the whole of your group.'

'OK,' I said, 'shoot.'

Ben took a deep breath. 'You remember a few years ago, there were claims that people were being abducted by grey humanoid creatures with big dark eyes?' Ben held his hands over his own eyes to emphasize the large almond-shaped eyes.

'Yeah, the Greys. But weren't they supposed to be extraterrestrials?'

'So some people alleged. Of course there was no hard evidence. No photographs that could be authenticated.'

Kate added. 'Weren't the victims usually abducted, then their memories were wiped and they only recalled what had happened either in flashbacks or hypnotic regression?'

443

Ben nodded. 'The other characteristic elements of abductions by these grey creatures were that people spoke of experiencing indescribable fear, that they were temporarily paralysed, that they'd be aware they'd lost hours of time from their lives. That is to say, they suffered a temporary amnesia and they couldn't adequately describe what had happened to them during that missing time.'

All of a sudden my own memories started shunting back. 'Listen, Ben, that night of your last party. Stenno had been attacked, remember? A few of us hunted for whoever had attacked him in the wood. I'd gone off alone at one point to search for them. I'd returned to your garden thinking I'd been gone only a few minutes. In fact, it turned out I'd been gone more than an hour.'

'You saw something?'

'I saw worms coming out of the ground. That was an early effect of the hot-spots breaking through. The sheer heat drove the worms from the soil.'

'Anything else?'

'Yeah, something else.'

'Tell us, Rick.'

'I saw a face. I'm sure of it now.'

'A grey face?'

'Yep. It was a Grey.' I sighed. 'But I just didn't remember at the time. It was only later that flashes came back. And another thing. I had a sensation of being . . . manhandled, I guess you'd describe it. I was pushed to the ground. Held there.'

'You never told anyone?'

'No.'

'Why?'

'Embarrassment.'

'Did you begin to wonder if you'd been raped?'

I flushed hotly. 'Raped?'

'Yes,' Ben said gently. 'Raped. Male rape. It does happen, you know.'

'I know.' I sighed again. 'I did wonder about that for a while. I thought perhaps there was a chance my mind had suppressed it. But there were no other . . . signs that I'd been attacked.'

'Don't worry about that, Rick. You weren't attacked. At least, not physically. Listen, what you've described is very similar to the old stories of alien abductions – the memory loss, the fear, the flashbacks when you think you see grey alien faces, big eyes; the sensation that

444

you've been physically manhandled, perhaps even carried off. Believe it or not, there's an explanation.'

'I take it it doesn't involve flying saucers and alien experiments?'

'No.' Ben shook his head. 'Basically this stems from a form of epilepsy known as temporal lobe epilepsy. For thousands of years individuals suffering from temporal lobe epilepsy have experienced enormously powerful hallucinations. Often these were believed to be mystical visions of angels, spirits or gods. The hallucinations were maybe accompanied by intense emotions – sometimes fear, or pleasure, or even joy. In 1654, Blaise Pascal, the French physicist and theologian – he also invented the first calculating machine, by the way – experienced such an astonishing vision that he wrote it down and sewed it into the lining of his coat, so that it would always be close to him. Today psychologists studying details of Pascal's . . . mystical state, it could be described as, have diagnosed him as suffering from temporal lobe epilepsy. He also suffered from a range of secondary epileptic symptoms such as trembling, hot and cold flushes, aphasia – which is the loss of the ability to express ideas in words.'

Kate frowned. 'Surely, Ben, you're not claiming that we're all suddenly suffering from temporal lobe epilepsy?'

'Not exactly, Kate. But I'm getting to that. Listen, scientists found they could trigger these hallucinations, or visions, call them what you will, easily enough in the laboratory. Volunteers would have an electric current run through their brains, directed specifically at the occipital cortex. The voltage wasn't great enough to harm them, but it was high enough to stimulate that part of the brain, which is just about here.' Ben touched his head just above and behind his left ear. 'The electric current triggered hallucinations that were uncannily similar to those experienced by alien abductees.'

'And this is happening now? But what's triggering the hallucinations?'

'Remember, I told you the Earth isn't an inert ball of rock. You've all seen the effects of the subterranean heat leaking up to the surface. What hasn't been immediately apparent is that as well as generating a heck of a lot of heat, the ground beneath our feet also generates electricity.'

'And that electricity is affecting our brains?' asked Kate.

'Spot on,' Ben said, pleased that what he was telling us was sinking in. 'That night of the party, Rick here stumbled upon one of the first hot-spots. One effect was to drive the worms to the surface. What he couldn't have realized was those hot rocks a couple of metres beneath his feet were also belting out a great fat dose of electrical interference – enough interference to mess up his own brain's electrical activity.'

'And hey presto, I created my own movie show in my head?'

'Right, you experienced visual hallucinations. The electrical interference was also strong enough to scramble up your memory, hence the amnesia, and it caused muscle spasms that gave you the illusion of being physically manhandled; then you—'

'But wait a minute, Ben,' Kate said. 'Why do we all see the same hallucination? Why do we see Grey Men?'

'That's just one of the characteristics of the phenomenon. Electrical activity in the ground is particularly prevalent in earthquake zones and volcanoes. If you were to plot on a map where encounters with angels, demons, extraterrestrials had taken place you'd probably find, not all, but a great number corresponded pretty closely to geological fault-lines, earthquake zones, volcanic hot-spots.'

'But why Grey Men hallucinations? Why doesn't Rick see green gorillas? And someone else see pink dragons?'

'It would take the next couple of weeks to explain it in detail but the psychologist Jung travelled the world looking for evidence of the collective unconscious, which would—'

'Uh? Collective what?' I shook my head. 'You'll have to spoonfeed this to me, Ben. I haven't a clue what you're talking about.'

His blue eyes twinkled. 'The collective unconscious. OK . . . you know when you could go down to your local Tandy store and buy a computer? Well, it used to come, likely as not, pre-loaded with software. That, crudely, is on a par with the collective unconscious. We are born complete with mental software that is buried in the unconscious part of our mind.'

'OK, cut to the chase. Why do we all see the Grey Men?'

'Because, as Jung discovered, the unconscious mind contains genetically transmitted images that are identical the world over. In a nutshell, if you dream about monsters that seem unique to you, there is a chance people in Africa, India, Greenland, wherever have dreamed monsters that are identical – exactly identical to your dream monsters.'

Kate's face lit up. 'That's why legendary creatures such as dragons spontaneously appear in different mythologies all over the world?'

Ben raised a finger in approval. 'Got it in one. If you like, we're all born with the neurological equivalent of a carousel of picture slides in our heads. All identical. No matter where we come from.'

I said, 'And somewhere in that carousel is the image of the Grey Man, complete with pimply skin and blood-red eyes.'

He nodded.

'Look, Ben, this does sound plausible,' I said. 'But go on, explain these bruises on Kate's face.'

'Projection.'

'Projection?'

'When the electrical interference is particularly strong the mind will project the hallucination out onto another human being. In short, your best friend might walk towards you. But what you believe you see is one of the Greys. Because the electrical interference becomes so powerful it confuses what the eye sees with the hallucination the mind generates.'

'So you might pick up your gun and shoot the monster only to find it's another human being.' Kate's eyes were round.

Ben said, 'Rick. Remember the incident in Fullwood's Garage at the start of all this?'

'Do I. Stenno attacked me with an iron bar!'

'Can you describe what he was like?'

'Christ . . . he went wild. I'd never seen him like it before. He could hardly speak, he was so angry with me. His face turned white, but his ears flushed so red they looked as if they'd catch fire. And his eyes – they were the weirdest. The iris and pupil shrank until all you could see in the middle of the whites was a black dot. But the strange thing was he was as much terrified of me as he was angry.'

Kate said, 'So you think that when Stenno attacked Rick, Stenno actually thought he was attacking a Grey Man?'

'Absolutely. The genuine visual information coming in through Stenno's eyes was being scrambled up with the hallucination. He saw Rick, here, as the monstrous Grey Man. Remember, he'd been attacked by one before – or at least he was under the illusion he'd been attacked. So, in his mind, he was confronted with one of these monsters again . . . so he fought for his life.'

'But his injuries at the party?'

'Self-inflicted when he was in the grip of the hallucination.'

Kate looked at her scratched hands and arms. 'You mean . . .'

'Yes; the monster you were fighting this morning in the church was none other than you, my dear.'

'Shit,' I said, understanding suddenly clunking home. 'If Stephen and the rest of the group don't realize this, then they might start projecting these hallucinations onto each other?'

Ben nodded grimly. 'Believe me, they will. As soon as they reach the more intense hot-spots they'll see each other as Greys. Then they'll wipe each other out.'

'We've got to reach them,' I said, standing up.

'You must,' Ben agreed. 'But you can't go anywhere tonight.'

'We can't waste any more time.'

'No, Rick. If you rush off now you'll help no one. The pair of you are exhausted.'

'We'll make it,' I said, determined.

'No, Rick. You need time to rest here. At least for tonight. Also, I need to tell you more about this phenomenon and how to combat it. That's going to take more than ten minutes. For example, some individuals are more susceptible to the influence of these electrical discharges. Stenno is certainly very sensitive. You, too, Rick. Some of us less so. Before the rest of the community broke up here, people were seeing these Grey creatures, too. They began firing on them.'

'And you?'

'And me? I couldn't understand why men and women I've known for the last fifteen years were killing each other. I only realized later they were projecting these monstrous hallucinations on to each other.' Ben shook his head sadly. 'So I witnessed the death of our community.'

Kate asked, 'There is a way to stop these hallucinations?'

'No. But there are some techniques to lessen the effects and so, perhaps, with luck, prevent the delusions swamping you. You've got to learn how to use those techniques; if you don't you might as well shoot each other now and get it over and done with.'

Ben continued speaking in that soft voice I'd known for years, the enunciation only altered by his lack of lips. Outside the grit still rained down against the window pane with a steady sizzling sound. Where the gardens once were, where we'd enjoyed many a party, there, hidden by the dark, would be only a carpet of black ash that stretched bleakly, seemingly everlastingly, into the distance.

If I saw any Grey Men now I knew they'd be nothing more substantial than ghosts created by that stream of electrons flowing from the ground colliding with those in my brain. There they'd produce those vivid hallucinations. I thought about my brother

Stephen and the rest of our community camped out somewhere in
the hills as they walked west to where we planned to rendezvous
with the ship on the coast.

And I couldn't help but wonder if we'd reach them in time. Before
they began to see each other as those grey monsters and started to
kill each other.

The wind blew. It produced a mournful droning note across the
chimney pots. More ash, black as mourning clothes, sizzled against
the glass.

CHAPTER 113

'Rick, are you sure you want to do this?' Kate looked at me, her
green eyes concerned.

'I don't *want* to.' I gave a grim smile. 'But I think I have to. For
my own peace of mind.'

We walked back through the blackened forest from Ben's house
to my old home at Fairburn. Kate wore walking boots, jeans and a
heavy sweater in pale blue wool. She wore her hair beneath a red
head scarf in an attempt to stop it becoming clotted with the fine
dust stirred up by our feet. Not that it'd help much. When it came
to taking off our boots we'd still tip half a cup full of the black muck
from them; come to that, we'd even find the dust where it had crept
into our underwear.

After ten hours straight sleep we'd woken to find the dust storm
had died.

Now the sun shone red through strips of cloud. Even though it
was almost midday it looked like the bloodiest red sunset you'd ever
seen. All the clouds were filled with that red as if they carried blood,
a fresh red glistening blood, not rain.

The air was cold on our faces, but near our feet it was warm from
the heat leaking up through the carpet of ashes.

When we'd struggled through the dust storm yesterday I hadn't been
able to see hardly anything of the village. Now it was clear enough. I
found myself taking Kate's hand. She gave mine a reassuring squeeze
as I paused at what should have been the start of Trueman Way.

To my right lay King Elmet's Mile. Once a pleasant few acres of meadow, it was now blanketed with ash. In its centre car-size craters phut-phutted as inflammable gas burned. It ignited in puffs of orange flame that rose in glowing spheres into the blood-red sky.

The flames seemed muted. It looked as though the worst of the explosions had already taken place, leaving what remained of the methane to putter itself out.

To my left ran the line of houses. Some had roofs missing where the creeping heat had ignited timbers. Some were intact but half-buried by black ash where it had drifted against the walls. I recognized Roger Hardy's Porsche still parked on the driveway. Of course the paint had burnt off it. It sat forlorn, rusting, and partly buried by ash, looking like some kind of car-shaped boat sailing a dry black sea.

In the distance stood the church where I'd found Kate the day before. Now the ash slowly engulfed it. Soon it would reach the clock in the tower that was frozen at ten to two.

I repeatedly raised my hand to my shoulder where I expected to feel the reassuring press of the rifle strap.

'We should have brought the rifles,' I said. 'We don't know what we'll find down here.'

'You remember what Ben told us?'

'Yep. The Grey Men are nothing but products of our imagination, triggered by the electricity coming out of the ground.'

'You believe it?'

I sighed. 'You know I do. It's just if one of those big Grey guys comes around the corner it's going to take a lot of will-power to keep calm and tell yourself it's only some freaking illusion.'

'You must try, Rick . . . Rick?'

I felt her hand tighten on mine.

'Rick. You're seeing one, aren't you?'

'Nothing. I see nothing.'

'Rick.' Again she squeezed my hand. 'I can tell by the expression on your face. Breathe slowly. Remember what Ben said. Breathe slowly . . . be aware of your breathing . . . imagine it away . . . imagine it's fading away into the air . . . vanishing. Imagine it doing that, Rick. It's fading to nothing.'

'Beam it up, Scottie.' I took a deep breath, I was sweating. 'OK . . . it's OK. It's gone.'

'You sure?'

'I'm sure.' I breathed deeply again. 'Hell, Kate, I saw it. A Grey Man in the garden, standing by the Porsche. It just seemed to rise out of the black dust to stand there, big apelike arms, red eyes. And just for a second I knew it was going to attack.'

Kate fixed her eyes on me. 'And you know what would have happened then?'

I nodded. 'According to what Ben has told us my brain would have scrambled up the hallucination of the Grey Man with you. I would have seen you as one of those Grey monsters.'

'And then you would have fought me, thinking I was one.'

'Yeah . . .' Still sweating, I forced a smile. 'Then we'd have ended up using the rifles on each other, if we'd brought them.'

'So it's a good job we listened to Ben.' She lifted my hand, kissed it. 'Otherwise we'd have had the noisiest game of cowboys and Indians Fairburn's ever seen.'

'You're right.'

Ten paces away from me stood another Grey Man. It lifted its muscular arms ready to attack, hands hooked into claws above its head. The lips peeled back from the teeth; they jutted from the gums like splinters of stone.

Go away, I told it inside my head. *Go away. You're not real.*

The edges of the figure blurred; then the whole fabric of the arms and legs and torso melted into the air.

Gone. I took a deep relaxing breath.

I could do it. I could get rid of them.

'The main thing,' Kate said, 'is to keep as relaxed as possible. Once you get uptight you see them popping out of the woodwork right, left and centre.'

'Yes, Miss.' I smiled again, but still my knees felt watery from the effort. The damn things looked so real. They looked as if they could just walk up and tear off your friggin' head. For Godsakes, you could even see—

No. I shut off the flow of thoughts. I had to keep telling myself they weren't real. That they couldn't hurt me.

'Are you ready?' she asked.

'I'm ready.'

'Which house is it?'

'There it is, home sweet home. The one with the wrought-iron gates.'

I walked into the patch of black dust that had once been the garden. All the plants were gone. Only the skeletal trunks and branches of trees remained; blackened and completely dead.

451

The house stood intact. The dust had reached the ground floor windows; the weight of it had pushed in the French windows.

We walked into the garden, boots scrunching on the black ash.

In what had been the centre of the front lawn, gas detonating underground had torn open a crater perhaps two metres across and a metre deep. What appeared to be brown sticks protruded from the dust.

'Poor girl.' I crouched down. 'This bloody planet won't even let you rest in peace.'

'What is it?'

'What *was* it, you mean.' I gave a laugh, but it was an expression of sadness rather than amusement. 'See, there's the collar. Can you read what's on the metal tag?'

'Amber?'

'Amber. My dog. She died when I was a kid. We buried her under the flower bed. The explosion's thrown out her bones, poor girl.'

'Come on, Rick. We'll look in the house, then go back to Ben's.'

We had to climb the mound of ash, then slither down it into the living room. The walls were black with heat marks.

'There's no furniture,' she said.

'I expect the looters took everything. Maybe they hoped that when the world returned to normal they could take our leather suite back home with them.' I shrugged. 'Much good it will do them now.'

The thick layer of windblown ashes jammed the internal door shut. I had to scrape a deep furrow with the heel of my boot before I could open it.

'Hell, look at that.'

'Good heavens. It still seems so clean.'

The hall and landing had been sealed shut from the outside world. The emulsioned walls were still dazzlingly white. The carpets were spotless. No ash had blown in here.

'There's the telephone. And the coat pegs. Christ, even the print of *The Haywain*. Hell, a neighbour gave us that when we moved in. My mother hated it, but she felt duty bound to hang it in the hall.' I looked at it all in astonishment. Even the mundane framed pictures, the coat pegs on the wall; the little table at the bottom of the stairs with the telephone directories and copper ashtray where I'd dump my van keys with a noisy enough rattle to signal to Mum I was safely home: it all looked magically new. My heart beat faster. If I closed my eyes and opened them again I could believe this shit-awful

452

disaster hadn't happened. That if I looked out the front door I'd see a green garden, children playing football on King Elmet's Mile.

I found myself trembling as I tried the door to the kitchen.

'What's wrong?' Kate asked.

'The door won't open. Uh . . . see the ash leaking through the gap at the bottom; the kitchen must be full of it. It's holding the door shut.'

'Try upstairs.'

Hand in hand we climbed the stairs, looking more like a newly betrothed couple out house-hunting.

My parents might be alive. They might be dead. I had no way of knowing. As rituals went this came the closest to a funeral. In a few minutes I'd say goodbye to the house that had been a home for ten years, then walk away, never to see it again. At least it was one way to bring to a close a phase of my life and then, God willing, move on to something new.

Most of the bedrooms were stripped of furniture. But still there was the familiar: the carpets, the candy stripe wallpaper, a pink lampshade in my mother's bedroom. An old Star Wars figure of Chewbacca I'd been given as a ten-year-old lay against the skirting board.

'Look . . . photographs.'

She bent down to pick up a handful of photographs scattered on the floor. She handed them to me. 'They're of your family, aren't they?'

Feeling strangely numb but calm, perhaps more calm than I'd ever felt before, I flicked through them. 'That's Stephen and me. When we lived in Italy. I'm still wearing the bandage where he shot me.' I spoke in that low, even voice. 'Here I am on my bike. I got that for my seventh birthday. There's Dad. Heck. One with Dad and Mum holding hands. It's strange to think they actually did love one another once. This one: Stephen's pretending to play the guitar. I'm imagining the pans are a drum kit. Even back then we wanted to be a part of the music business.' I slowly flicked through the photographs. There were shots of Stephen and me at some Christmas long ago, unwrapping presents, or sat round the table with paper hats on our heads, and the turkey in the middle of the table. Or nine-year-old me with a look of comic surprise on my face as I sneaked a drink of beer from a can. Or Stephen and I made up for Hallowe'en. He wore a skeleton mask; for some reason I was made up as a witch complete with green nylon wig and pointy hat.

There was nothing extraordinary about the photographs; they're the kind found in drawers or cupboards in any household across the world. Photographs of children and parents at holiday time, weddings or birthdays, when it seems the done thing to make a permanent record of one specific second of that day. The fashions and hairstyles change over the years. Our mothers, fathers, brothers, sisters manage to look unfamiliar yet achingly familiar, both at the same time. And we stare out from the past with surprisingly solemn-looking expressions. As if what had happened in the last few months had cast an ominous shadow back as far as then.

I looked down at the photographs in my hand. I still felt calm, even strangely empty. I'd let go of something I'd been holding on to. I'd already said my goodbyes and not even realized it.

'Come on,' I said, 'let's collect our backpacks from Ben's; it's time we were moving on.'

We left the house the way we came, boots scrunching over the loose black ash that slowly drifted into the living room like Hell's own snow. I walked past the bones of Amber in the garden. Then, for the last time, out through the driveway gates.

At first I didn't look back as we climbed the hill to Ben Cavellero's house, but then I shot glances back over my shoulder.

I saw the redbrick house, with the tiled roof, the TV aerial poking higher than the surrounding roofs. I could see the garden, the fences now burnt to ash; that drifting black grit filling the pond and covering everything like a global funeral shroud.

At the corner of the street I glanced back again. Now my old home was nearly hidden by the burnt-out shells of other houses; all I could see was the roof of my house and part of my bedroom window. I carried on walking. When I looked back again I could see it no more.

CHAPTER 114

'Where's your backpack, Ben?'

'I'm not going with you.'

We were standing in the corridor on the upper floor of Ben's house. We'd have to leave by the window, then slide down the great drift of black ash to ground level. Kate and I were ready. The backpacks contained fresh clothes and enough food to see us through to the coast if need be. We carried the rifles, shoved barrel first into the backpacks.

I shook my head, puzzled. 'What's there to stay here for?'

'This is my home, Rick. The day I saw this house I knew I'd buy it and never leave.'

'But the whole village is going up in flames!'

'I'll take that chance. Besides, I like to be conceited enough to believe I'm more useful here.' He eased the silk scarf a little higher up his nose. 'Sometimes people pass through. I tell them the truth about the Grey People, that they are hallucinations. The people move on better prepared to survive in this hostile new world.'

The idea of leaving him in this burnt-out stretch of countryside seemed unbelievably bleak. 'Stephen could use you.'

'We need people with experience,' Kate added. 'Most of us are under thirty.'

'Precisely,' Ben said, and even though I couldn't see those cut lips I sensed he was smiling. 'Precisely. You are a community of young people. What you lack in experience you make up for in zest and imagination. You don't want to be carrying the baggage of old men's philosophies into the future. Invent your own. It looks like the end of the old world; but you can also consider it the birth of a new one.'

'There's no way we can change your mind?'

'No, Rick. I'm staying. Don't worry, I've plenty of food.'

I turned to go.

'Rick ... just one more thing. You didn't tell me the ship's destination.'

I shrugged. 'We don't know exactly, other than to sail south.'

'South? The south's a pretty big place.'

Kate added, 'The South Seas. If we find an island untouched by the hot-spots we'll settle there.'

'Are you sure you're not secretly hoping you'll make it to Australia or New Zealand and find civilization still intact?'

'Well, if we do, that'll be Christmas come early,' I smiled. 'I've grown accustomed to living in a house and sleeping in beds down through the years.'

'But it's all changed now, Rick. You've changed more deeply than you realize.'

'I don't think I've changed that much, Ben. Give me clean sheets and three meals a day and I'll be happy.'

'So, you'll arrive in Melbourne, say. What then? Find a job in a bank? Buy a house?'

Ben was trying to push me into reaching some new understanding about myself. I felt myself resisting. In fact, I was resisting so hard I felt myself growing angry with the man who'd been one of my best friends for the last three years. 'No,' I said. 'When I get some money together I'll buy a guitar.'

'And put a new band together?'

'Why not?'

'You still want that?'

'Yes.'

'To play music when there's a new world to build?'

'What new world?'

'You don't believe me when I tell you that the old you is dead. And that there's a new you now. A brand spanking new Rick Kennedy, but he doesn't realize it yet. Am I right?'

'I don't know what you're talking about, Ben. It's all very deep but, believe me, it's going over my head. Right, if you'll excuse us, we'll be on our way. Kate?'

She folded her arms. 'Ben's right.'

I shook my head firmly. 'Same old Rick Kennedy. Nineteen years old. Still moonstruck on music.'

'Really?' Kate raised her eyebrow.

'Really. Now let's—'

Kate gave an amused smile. 'Nineteen years old?'

'Yes.'

'Rick, your twentieth birthday was two days ago.'

'So what? I had a lot on my mind if you hadn't noticed.'

The pair of them were beginning to grate. 'Look,' I sighed. 'Believe me, I want to leave this shit behind and sail south. So what if we end up in Australia? In some rented room watching old Ren and Stimpy shows on TV, drinking Foster's lager with a mutton chop on the barbie for supper? Well, that sounds just dandy to me right now. I'm sick of seeing babies' skulls scattered round in the dust like pebbles; I'm sick of running for my life; I'm sick of worrying that my people haven't enough to eat. I'm sick of the smell of burning forever up my fucking nose . . . shit . . .' My voice choked off, my hands shook.

'That's how the old Rick Kennedy is thinking,' Ben said gently. 'You've got to shed him like a snake sheds an old skin. Then you can face the future.'

'The old Rick Kennedy's dead, the old Rick Kennedy's dead. You keep saying that, for Chrissakes. What do you fucking mean?'

'The old Rick Kennedy dreamt of being a rock star?'

'Damned right I did . . . still do! You going to convince me I'm wrong?'

'Why don't you go upstairs?' Ben said. 'There's someone up there you can ask.'

'Someone I can ask? I thought you lived here alone.'

'Why don't you ask Sasha?'

'Sasha? Ha, fucking ha. Some joke.' I turned to Kate. 'Sasha is my guitar. I stored it here when I left Fairburn.'

'Do as he says, Rick.'

I sighed. 'Ask the guitar if there's now a new me under this skin? OK. OK. I'll humour the pair of you.'

I stomped up the stairs to the attic. Everything was covered with a fine layer of that gritty black dust where it blew in through gaps in the window. I saw the guitar case straight away, laid out on an old sofa. It was covered with a white sheet and looked for all the world like a body draped with a shroud.

I pulled off the sheet. Then I opened the case.

There was Sasha, my six-string electric Stratocaster, in a beautiful sunburst finish of reds and golds. The chrome pick-ups and controls shone in the red light of the sun filtering through the attic windows. The strings looked as if they'd been spun from pure silver.

I touched a string.

Then I brought the lid of the case down hard.

Ben was right, damnit; he was right and I knew it.

Whenever I saw a guitar it said: PLAY ME.

I couldn't keep my fingers off the strings. I'd pick out melody lines of songs I heard on the radio, or forever tinkered with the notes of new songs I was writing. Guitars obsessed me. I couldn't see one without imagining myself not only playing it but where I'd be playing it.

Now the guitar said:

Come on Rick, admit it. What does it say?

It says a big fat: NOTHING.

The obsession to become a rock star was gone, too. Along with the old me.

Oh, I might play music again one day. But it would be another kind of music for a different audience.

I knew I had another mission now. Ben was right. I needed to think about my role in this new world.

Downstairs Ben and Kate waited for me.

I went down to them. This time I couldn't speak. I only nodded, then hugged Ben, then Kate.

'Shit . . .' I shook my head, my eyes burning. 'Sorry for being such a damn blockhead. What can I say, Ben? You were right.'

There were tears in Ben's eyes, too. 'You're going to be a great man, Rick. Now . . .' He took a deep breath. 'You go and find your brother. Tell him what I've told you. They'll need to know if they're going to get through that burnt-up bit of world in one piece.'

CHAPTER 115

We'd been walking for less than an hour when it started to rain skulls.

Human skulls. They fell out of the sky to hit the black ground in front of us. Each impact raised a splash of black dust; most of the skulls shattered on impact.

One landed five paces from me; the teeth jolted from the jaw bone by the impact spattered against my coat.

'If one of those babies hits us we'll know about it,' I murmured.

Kate looked at me. 'Shall we go back the way we came and head round the other side of the hill?'

'We can't spare the time. We need to find Stephen before they start hallucinating like crazy and begin killing each other. *Watch it, Kate.*'

A child's skull cracked down into the black ash an arm's length away and shattered with a crunching sound.

'What's causing it?' Kate asked.

'I've seen something like it before. See that plume of smoke coming from the other side of the hill?'

'I see it.'

'There's probably a gas vent broken out through a cemetery. The force of the explosions is throwing out the skulls. Most are landing across there to the left. If we move further over to the right, down the hillside, we should be able to avoid being hit.'

'It's raining skulls; there's lightning; there's no people; not one blade of grass. Black desert as far as you can see.' Kate looked round, the light breeze blowing out her long hair in strands. She shook her head and when she spoke again I heard the note of despair in her voice. 'We've died and gone to Hell, haven't we?'

I hugged her. 'Christ knows, it seems like that sometimes. But once we make it to the ship we'll—'

'The ship? Do you think an island in the South Seas is going to welcome a batch of refugees with open arms?'

'I don't know, Kate, really I don't. But you've got to keep hoping.'

She sighed. 'I guess. Are you thirsty?'

I nodded. 'We'll have to be sparing with the water. Fresh water springs are going to be few and far between.'

After a sip of water from my bottle we pushed on. Silent lightning flickered amongst the clouds that since midday had killed the sun. We'd reached the hills and now followed the top of a high ridge that should take us to the route of the old Roman road that Stephen, Jesus and the others were following west.

Kate was right about the countryside looking like Hell now. Blanketed by the black ashfall, burnt, split open, cratered by subterranean gas blasts, it looked a bleak, forbidding place. Dotted through the black fields were the burnt stumps of trees, some with skeletal branches. A kilometre away lay a cluster of burnt-out farmworkers' cottages.

Mixed in with the black ash our feet crunched through were hundreds of bones, the skulls of sheep, birds, cats, dogs – and of people, of course, plenty of people. Some of the skulls had been smashed open so desperate survivors could gobble out the brains.

Bizarrely, a grandfather clock stood in the middle of the field, its hands jammed at ten to two, the pendulum frozen. What desperate soul had been driven to carry the thing this far? And why?

As we walked I glanced back. Fairburn lay back out of sight in the distance. The breeze stirred up dust devils that would follow us like the lost souls of the dead.

Kate glanced back. 'You don't see any Greys?'

'No. I can suppress them now I know they're not really there.'

'What have you seen?'

'Our footprints. See them? Two lines running back over the hills?'

'If the footprints are all we leave behind here I'll be happy, won't you?'

I nodded, then gave a grim smile. 'Those tracks reminded me of some fossilized footprints found in Africa.'

'Oh, I think I remember those. We had to write about them for a school project.'

'Me too. I remember drawing the footprints, then writing the description in blue felt tip underneath. Hell, I can still remember what I wrote: *A TRAIL OF FOOTPRINTS PROBABLY MADE BY UPRIGHT WALKING ANCESTORS OF MAN, NAMELY AUSTRALOPITHECUS AFARENSIS DISCOVERED IN LAETOLI, TANZANIA. THE PRINTS WERE FOSSILIZED IN VOLCANIC ASH 3.6 MILLION YEARS AGO. THEY SHOW TWO ADULTS WITH A CHILD WALKING BEHIND THEM.*'

She smiled. 'Well remembered.'

'Yeah, for what good it'll do us now. School taught us how to live within that old structure known as civilization. If I'd known then what I know now I wouldn't have revised so hard for my damned exams.' Despite myself I laughed, then glanced back at the trail of footprints we'd made in the ash. 'Do you think those will last 3.6 million years, Kate?'

'No doubt about it, Rick Kennedy. And what's more there'll be some poor kid in the dim and distant future writing his homework essay about them: *Fossilized footprints found in ash, dating back to the Holocene epoch. Probably made by the male and female of the long extinct species homo sapiens.*'

I smiled. 'And our student will speculate: *Perhaps we can surmise the two creatures were mates. We can imagine, maybe, from the closeness of the prints, that they held hands as they walked.*'

We were babbling nonsense. At that moment I think we had to. Every now and again another skull would hit the ground with such force that it exploded in splinters of bone, scattering of teeth. To my right a landslip had torn open the hill, exposing a coal seam which blazed with a powerful roaring sound.

We had to babble. We had to make jokes.

Otherwise we'd have gone mad, right there in the black heart of what had to be nothing less than Hell.

In the valley bottom half a dozen vent holes screamed as flammable gas superheated by the baking earth found an exit. The screams were surprisingly human-sounding. More than once I had to stop and check with my binoculars that there really was no one down there being seared by the jets of flame.

We walked faster. The grit ejected high into the air by the gas vents drizzled down on us like a fine black snow.

Ben had given us dust masks. We pulled these up over our mouths and noses. Then we walked faster. Feet crunching that arid carpet of ash and burnt bone.

'Hear that noise?' Kate asked, voice muffled by the mask.

'Sound like sharp explosions?'

'Those are the ones. Know what they are?'

I shook my head.

'Brontides,' she said, 'they usually herald the start of earthquake activity.'

'All the more reason to keep moving. The whole of the ground here must be a mass of fault lines grinding away at each other.'

'That means a lot of electricity in the rock, too. Watch out for hallucinations.'

'Don't worry,' I said, 'I can handle them.'

'Don't get too confident, Rick.'

'Trust me.' I paused to look at the map. 'We need to head for the saddlebacked hill over there. I think we should keep as much to the high ground as possible.'

'Why?'

'I know we've seen no genuine volcanoes here yet, but I'd bet you a fish-and-chip supper that there's a Hell of a lot of volcanic gases spewing out of those vents.'

'That means carbon monoxide. It'll lie low in the valley bottoms.'

'And the stuff's fucking lethal.'

Kate looked up at the sky. Cloud lumbered overhead. Lightning flickered. 'It'll be night in an hour. You don't propose walking through that,' she nodded at the black desert, 'in complete darkness?'

'We need to reach Stephen as quickly as we can.' I pulled the dust mask down from my face. 'But we'd probably end up falling down one of those damn fire pits or something. See that farmhouse on the side of the hill? We'll spend the night there, then make an early start in the morning. With luck we'll catch up with Stephen by the end of tomorrow.'

461

'With luck,' she said with a sigh, 'with a whole lot of luck.'

She was right. We would need a lot of luck – whole heaps of the stuff.

And just when we needed the luck, that's when it started running out fast.

CHAPTER 116

I awoke with a start. Sweat pricked my eyes. Lightning flashes pulsed through the window to light the kitchen of the abandoned farmhouse like a strobe. I sat up in my sleeping-bag. Kate's sleeping-bag was empty.

My hand brushed the stone kitchen floor; it was warmed by the heat conducted from the baking earth beneath it. My rifle? Where was my rifle?

More pulses of light – bluish and vivid.

Hell, where was Kate?

My heart beat hard.

'Kate?'

No lightning now. Only complete darkness.

'Kate? Kate, where are you!'

Lightning flash.

The darkness gone.

And I saw it.

The Grey Man.

It reared up from the floor where it had been crouching.

Waiting.

Hell, what had it done to Kate?

The Grey Man.

The voice in my head clamoured again: *Rick. It's only a hallucination. The rocks beneath the farmhouse are moving, they are grating together to produce that hallucinogenic electrical field; it's interfering with the natural electrical activity in your brain. The grey creature isn't really there, it's not real, it's—*

HELL, LIKE FUCK IT ISN'T!!!!

I reached out . . . touched its leg.

I felt hard muscle.

Ben was wrong.

The Grey Men *were* real.

Where the hell was Kate?

What had it done to her?

Panicky, I kicked my way out of the sleeping-bag, leapt to my feet.

The big grey head of the beast turned to me. The eyes, blood-red and ghastly, *fucking ghastly*, locked onto mine. They screamed hatred at me. And this weird alien hunger. The monster was evil, sheer fucking evil.

It wanted my blood.

It lifted its grey arms, snarled. The hands hooked into claws. In the flashing light of the electric storm I could even see the black fingernails. They were chipped and cracked as if they'd clawed a thousand human faces from their skulls.

I launched myself at it, punching at that grey face.

The cheekbones were as hard as concrete, but I punched and punched, until the skin across my knuckles bled.

It tried to shove me back.

I gripped it by that mane of loose black hair that ran along the ridge of bone at the top of its head.

'What have you done to Kate?'

I pulled at the mane, swung it off balance, then crashed it against the wall.

'What have you done to Kate?'

I punched.

'Kate!'

Punched again. Blood from my cut fist smeared the grey face.

'You fucking monster! If you've hurt her I'll rip you in half!'

The Grey Man had taken some hard punches. It leaned back against the wall. The bloody red eyes dulled to a brown. I drove more full-blooded punches into its stomach.

Christ. I punched again. The belly felt amazingly soft. I punched again and again. It screamed.

'Rick . . . Rick . . .'

'That's Kate! What have you done with her?'

I punched the monster repeatedly as I yelled.

'Where's Kate?'

'Rick . . .'

I could hear her voice. But I couldn't see her. Perhaps another one

463

of the grey monsters was torturing her in the next room. I punched it on the cheekbone. It screamed. A surprisingly high-pitched scream that came from a throat that was as thick as a bull's.

'Rick! I love you . . . please . . . I ugh! I love you . . . please, pl—ah! Don't hit me. Not there! *NOT THERE!*'

Screams.

Bastard. I swung a kick high.

'Ahhh! Rick . . . God, I love you, Rick. Kiss me, kiss me. Kiss me like – uph! Hotel . . . remember the hotel. Remember kissing me . . . Oh! Oh! Oh! Rick . . . please, not that. NOT THAT! Murr-ooh-oh-oh . . . *ohhhh* . . .'

Weeping.

The beast was weakening. If I could find a stick to use as a club. Better still, my rifle.

Blow its fucking head off, blow it to fucking paradise.

I punched again at the face.

'Rick . . . Rick . . . I love you . . .'

Rick?

The voice came from the monster.

The monster knew my name . . .

In God's name, how? How—

Jesus Christ.

As I fought the creature, my face was slammed up close to that great bony head, set with two almond-shaped eyes now fading to brown. But even as I gripped its black mane in one hand, then brought my other fist up, ready to beat at its eyes in the hope of blinding it, the grey face just evaporated; it just wasn't there anymore.

Instead, there was Kate.

CHAPTER 117

Later, I'd remember how I'd stared at Kate in horror. My eyes bulging so much they watered. I couldn't believe the awful thing I'd done to her.

I held her beautiful hair in my right hand.

My left hand, bunched tight into a fist, so tight the veins stood out; my knuckles, slick with blood, were raised high, ready to beat down hard into her lovely face.

Her face . . .

My stomach turned. I wanted to vomit.

I'd punched her so hard her face was a mass of grazes that made the skin look like raw meat. Her left eyebrow leaked blood from a crack in the skin. Her lips were swelling so much they looked as if they'd been stung by bees.

I let go of her hair in horror. She sagged back against the wall, her head dropping loosely forward, her hair tumbling down over her bare breasts that were mottling with a dozen bruises.

She was completely naked. I saw more injuries on her legs. Fresh grazes stood out redly amongst the dozen or more older scratches made when she was alone in the church.

A complete . . . a *total* horror gripped me.

I'd done *that?*

I'd seen her as a Grey Man, then fought her tooth and nail until she was half dead.

I panted hard from the exertion of the ferocious beating I'd hammered out onto the girl I loved; who I'd die for.

Stunned by the horror of what I'd done, I turned to stare out of the window.

Lightning flashed, illuminating tracts of the burntlands.

I saw my face reflected there in the glass. It was hot, red, sweaty.

Christ, I'd sunk everything in hammering the life out of her.

I shook my head, flicking droplets of sweat from my fringe. Then I was looking round for something on the floor.

'Rick.' Her voice was weak. 'Rick. It's not your fault. What are you doing?'

I kept looking.

'Rick stop it. Whatever you're going to do – don't. Not your fault . . . you didn't know . . .'

What was I looking for?

Christ, right then I was looking for the rifle. If I'd found it I'd have blown out my fucking brains.

My self-disgust was total.

Kate walked unsteadily towards me. Her eyes bled tears; the long hair swung down over those cruelly bruised breasts.

'Not your fault,' she kept saying. 'You were asleep. You were hallucinating before you opened your eyes. You weren't to know.'

'I – I . . .' I couldn't speak. I wanted to scream, then just run from the farmhouse barefoot. I wanted to run and run across that smouldering wasteland. Lose myself out there, then curl up and die alone amid the ash.

'Come here, love.' Tenderly she reached out. 'It's all right. I love you. I know you didn't mean it.'

She hugged me from behind. The tips of her bare breasts lightly touched my bare back. I felt her kissing my shoulder blades, then the back of my neck.

She said in a low, trembling voice, 'I woke. I could see you were in the grip of the hallucination. I managed to hide the rifles in the cupboard across there. Then, as I walked back across the room to you, I saw your face. Your eyes . . . they were so strange: the irises and pupils had shrunk to dots . . . nothing but black dots . . . you looked terrified and angry all at the same time. Then you attacked me. I kept telling you I loved you. Kept repeating your name . . . Rick. Rick. Rick. I love you. I had to keep saying that. I couldn't resist you, either. I knew I mustn't fight back because that would only have made you more determined to fight me.' Her voice dropped to a whisper. 'So I had to stand there . . . passively . . . and allow you to punch me. Those punches seemed to go on forever. But I knew if I said your name enough I'd reach you.'

I shuddered.

'There . . . it's all right, Rick. Everything's all right.'

'Christ . . . I nearly killed you . . . look at your face!'

She pulled me round to face her and slid her arms around my waist. Kissing me on the lips, she spoke softly. 'It's important you know what happened in case it happens again. It might be me next time. I might have the rifle. I know once you're in the grip of the hallucination you'd do anything. You could kill your own mother.'

'Kate . . . Jesus wept. I couldn't stop myself. I thought . . . I really thought you were one of those things. It was so real . . . *so fucking real.*'

'I know, that's why we must reach Stephen and warn him.'

I couldn't stop shaking. 'Kate . . . maybe it'd be safer if you went on alone.'

'No. We must travel together. And we must fight this thing together. The key is to stay as relaxed as possible.'

'Relaxed . . .' I buried my face in her hair and gave a bitter laugh.

'Yes, relaxed.'

'Christ, easier said than done.'

'There are ways.' She smiled up at me through blood and tears.

'I couldn't, Kate. Not after what I've done tonight.'

'Yes, you can. Make love to me. Now.'

'But . . . Hell . . . I remember kicking you.'

She smiled again; somehow, incredibly, it didn't seem forced. 'Rick, I'm tougher than you think.'

I kissed her gently on her swollen lips.

'Now,' she said, managing to sound composed. 'Lie down on the blanket. You're dripping with sweat. I'll rub you with the towel.'

I lay down, watching her face as she rubbed my skin. I saw her eyes searching my body, seeing my bruises and scratches.

I closed my eyes as she began to kiss me. Her lips felt deliciously cool on my chest, stomach and legs.

She sat on top of me, impaling herself on my erect penis.

I squeezed my eyes shut as she let out a deep sigh.

But there was no pain in that sigh. Only a blend of pleasure and deep, deep relief.

I realized the truth. After the fight she needed this sexual bonding again. She needed to prove to herself as much as to me that I really was in the grip of delusion when I'd beaten her. That my fury wasn't directed at her, Kate Robinson, but at some nameless monster which my hallucinating mind had wrongly told me had manifested itself in the kitchen.

So we made love. On that stone-slabbed kitchen floor, which was warm to the touch of our naked bodies when, in our passion, we rolled off the blanket. Around us, the farmhouse furniture. The table, chairs, cooker, sink. Brass pans hanging on the walls that swung gently as the Earth heaved and tore itself open somewhere far away. Flashes of light pulsed through the window from the electric storm in the clouds.

Kate rocked above me. Her head swayed from side to side. Her long hair trailed forward to stroke my bare chest lightly. She slid her body up, then slowly down onto me with such trembling tenderness I couldn't bare to look at her wounded face.

A lump formed in my throat. I turned my face away. I didn't deserve her.

I heard her breathing quicken; then I sensed her muscles twitch. Soon the gentle pulsations turned into a series of violent shudders that jolted through her body like electric shocks, one after another, as she orgasmed.

When it was over, she lay forward face down on my chest, her face wet with tears, perspiration, blood.

Gently, I nuzzled my face into that mass of yellow hair. And I knew there and then that if I ever did anything to hurt this beautiful woman again I'd kill myself.

CHAPTER 118

My name is Kate Robinson.

We left Ben Cavellero's house yesterday. We spent the night in a deserted farmhouse not far from Ilkley.

I'm taking a few moments to write this at the kitchen table as Rick cleans the rifles. The black grit creeps in everywhere. Now there's a real danger that if we ever *do* need the rifles the firing mechanism might simply jam from the build-up of grit.

I'm bruised. I ache from head to foot. As Ben Cavellero said might happen Rick hallucinated last night. In his mind he saw me as one of the grey creatures. For a moment I thought he would kill me. The only way to break the grip of the illusion is to keep repeating the name of the person affected.

I think Rick is more vulnerable to the hallucinations than I am. But last night as we made love I felt the grip of the madness that is caused by the electric field generated in the ground.

Rick lay on top of me, making love with such tenderness. He was terrified of hurting me. But as I looked up at him I saw his features change. They smoothed out, his head grew larger, his blue eyes darkened then turned red.

It was like watching a movie special effect. His face melted, turned grey.

Then I wanted to scream.

Because I was being penetrated by one of those grey monsters.

Or so the hallucination made me believe.

With a vivid clarity that was so incredibly shocking, I saw it raising itself up on its knuckles like an ape so it could thrust itself into me. The arms thickened. Its veins stood out from the grey skin.

In sheer horror I stared up at the face; the black lips were parted, the face was angled down at me, its blood-red eyes blazing into me with such an intensity I felt giddy.

My muscles went into spasm; all of them tightened so hard I felt as if they'd snap. It felt for all the world as if the monster's penis grew inside of me. I felt as if I'd split in two.

Only, deep down, I knew the muscle spasms had affected my vagina too, triggering vaginismus, the condition that causes the involuntary contraction of the vagina's muscles.

I wanted to scream.

The monster was tearing me in two. It panted above me, its breath blasted into my face; the massive grey hands clamped onto my shoulders holding me down.

I couldn't move.

Its weight was crushing.

I thought I'd die there.

It thrust like some vast machine of blood, muscle and bone.

My head spun.

I couldn't breathe.

It filled me tight to splitting.

Christ . . .

But I hung onto what I knew about me.

My name, my memories. I remembered meeting Rick in the café in Leeds when he talked to me in such a shy way about the cappuccino I blushed for him. I remembered the gerbils at school. The day one escaped and chased Mr Prentice from the room. My first day at work in the bookshop in Leeds. I couldn't find the toilet and was too absurdly shy to ask. I fiercely locked on to the memories . . . hung on . . . wouldn't let go . . .

When I opened my eyes again the Grey Man was gone. I saw Rick looking down at me. He smiled. Kissed me.

I'd conquered it.

Now, we're ready to move on. We must catch up with Stephen and the rest in the next few hours – before they're gripped by these wicked hallucinations. I dread to think what they'll do to each other. Rick is pulling on his backpack, adjusting the straps on his shoulders to make them more comfortable. He's ready to move.

This is another day in Hell.

469

CHAPTER 119

My name is Rick Kennedy. This is what happened the moment we left the deserted farmhouse.

All around our feet, white rounded objects the size of table tennis balls were pushing up through the black ash that covered the farm yard.

You seen speeded-up film of mushrooms growing? They start as tiny, pale grey buds poking out of the dirt. Then they expand, swelling into bulbous rounded shapes.

These looked the same.

But if you looked closely enough you saw eyes. Tiny dots like pinpricks of blood.

'Rick?' Kate watched me anxiously, her face still a mass of bruises from the night before. She knew what I was capable of once the hallucination locked me in its steel grip. 'Rick . . . keep repeating your name; say to yourself: my name is Rick Kennedy, my name is . . . Rick!'

I looked up from the hundreds of grey heads sprouting fungus-like around my feet, their mouths opening to cry like newborn babes.

I'd looked up because I'd seen something that had taken my breath away. On the hillside opposite was a cliff face as high as a six-storey building. Only now I didn't see sheer rock: I saw a vast grey face looking down at me. The eyes were shut but as I watched the lids broke open and a pair of eyes the size of buses gazed down at me. The eyes were red, a vast expanse of blood, big enough to swim through, big enough to dive into and get thoroughly soaking wet . . . fresh, wet, crimson blood.

'Rick.' Kate tugged my arm. 'Rick. Don't let go. Remember who I am. You thought I was one of the Greys last night. You nearly killed me . . . please . . . Rick. Remember it's me: Kate. I love you, Rick. Don't hurt me again, please . . . I couldn't bear that again . . . I need you to—'

The huge mouth that belonged to the head breaking out through the hillside opened. I heard a tremendous rumbling sound as if it was beginning to speak.

I reached out and grabbed hold of Kate, holding her with a ferocious strength.

'Rick. They're not really there – you're hallucinating. Please . . . don't hurt me!'

My eyes swept down to her, locked hard onto her frightened green eyes.

She gasped, screwed up her eyes, expecting any moment my fist to smash into her mouth.

'Kate,' I shouted. 'I know it's not real. But do you know what's happening?

Shocked, she shook her head.

'Down there!' I pointed toward our feet. 'The ground's heating up fast. That's why the hallucinations are so strong. We've got to get out of here. The whole hillside's probably going to blow sky-high any moment. Run!'

With the backpacks swinging heavily, we left the farmyard at a run. Our feet hitting the ground sent up gouts of black ash.

Overhead, lightning roamed the clouds in vivid splashes of blue. The flashes were like vengeful spirits hunting for victims.

Ahead, forked lightning zithered down to strike an already scorched tree trunk. The blue flash was blinding. The tree trunk shattered.

Thunder boomed.

'Keep going uphill!' I shouted. 'We have to get over the other side before it goes.'

Now I felt the ground twitch beneath my feet.

Down there, perhaps a hundred metres, two hundred metres below the surface, the temperature climbed remorselessly. What lay down there? A gas pocket? An oil-filled blister of rock? A locked-up reservoir of water that had turned to steam and was now straining to burst its way outward?

Whatever it was, I could sense that pressure climbing, ever climbing; the force bursting upward through layer after layer of rock, seeking an escape that would be explosively catastrophic for any poor hapless creature that happened to be on the surface.

And that was us.

'I'll carry your backpack,' I shouted.

'You won't. I can manage. Come on, Rick – *faster!*'

We ran up the blackened hillside, leaving the deserted farmhouse far below.

In the bottom of the valley ten, fifteen, twenty, small geysers erupted like whale spouts from the ground. They jetted their white steam into the air with a sudden cracking sound.

Panting, lathered in sweat, we reached the hilltop.

I looked down the other side. My heart sank. 'We can't go down there.'

'We can,' Kate said grimly.

'Have you seen what's there?'

'We can make it.'

She ran on. I followed.

Scattered like a rash across the hillside were innumerable craters that belched orange flame. You could feel the heat against your face.

But Kate was right. We had to get through that burning landscape somehow.

Because at that moment the valley behind us exploded.

CHAPTER 120

I opened my eyes. I lay flat on my back, looking up at the slab of cloud sliding low across the sky. Lightning still flashed in continuous pulses of electric blue light.

I shook my head; my skull ached from the force of the blast in the next valley. As I struggled to my feet I saw Kate had managed to get to her knees.

I looked back the way we had come. A pillar of flame blasted skyward, tearing a great hole in the cloud. The pocket of methane gas must have been a big one. The flame didn't diminish in size for another four minutes as the gas vented, gushing upward with enough ferocity to shake the ground beneath me.

Kate gave me the thumbs-up to indicate she was OK. I nodded. Then side by side we jogged on down the hillside, the backpacks bumping heavily against our bodies.

The noise from the gas venting in the valley behind us was so enormous we couldn't make each other hear, even when we shouted. So we relied on looks and hand signals.

Ahead the landscape was pockmarked with old craters. Here, too, gas pockets had vented through the surface. Most were dead, but a good few still burned with a popping sound that was just audible above the roar of the grandaddy of all gas jets in the valley behind us.

A couple of times the earth beneath my feet gave way. A hard crust had been formed by the heat. Beneath the crust it was hollow. Each time it happened I thought I'd plunge into a fiery pit to be burned alive. Luckily, I dropped only knee-deep. Even so, each piercing of the crust would release a gush of smoke into my face that stung my eyes.

When we were far enough from the roaring inferno Kate asked, 'Are you OK?' while anxiously scanning my face.

'Are *you* all right?' I replied. Her face was still a cluster of painful-looking grazes. My heart went out to her. Poor kid had gone through Hell for the last six months. Now I had beaten the living daylights out of her. I couldn't look at her face without a stab of guilt.

She knew what I was thinking. She pulled me to a stop. 'It's OK, Rick. It wasn't your fault. Remember that. And remember I love you. OK?'

I smiled. 'OK.'

'Come on, let's find that brother of yours.'

We moved on across the blackened desert that just months ago had been green pasture. Most of the field walls were still intact; although here and there would be a breach in a wall where a geyser had erupted, or inflammable gas had vented explosively, scattering heavy stone blocks like pebbles.

And always the landscape was black. The ash still pittered down like dry snow flakes.

But you had to keep the image of the ship in your mind. The ship would take us south. We'd find an island with palm trees. There'd be a turquoise lagoon where we could swim.

If the ship really does turn up?

Doubt nagged. There was so much that could go wrong.

We still had to cross this black desert as far as the west coast.

Any moment the ground might erupt beneath our feet. We might be incinerated by one of those gas jets that flared without warning.

We might be running across a thin crust of earth. It might break like thin ice beneath our feet, plunging us down into a chasm.

We might find Stephen, Jesus and the rest had killed each other while they were in the grip of those vicious Grey Man delusions generated by the electrical discharges from the tormented rock.

Now I realized the Grey Man I'd fought in the petrified forest just outside Leeds was probably none other than Tesco. I'd returned to the forest and in my neurologically screwed-up state I'd seen the man as one of those grey monsters. God knows what had happened to him. I might have hit him so hard I'd killed him. Now he lay beneath the branches, his flesh desiccated into leather by the heat.

As we walked my thoughts moved in repetitive circles.

We would reach the ship, wouldn't we?

The ground wouldn't collapse beneath our feet, would it?

I tried to keep hope alive. I had to believe there was a chance we would survive this Hell.

But already some evil, black-hearted god was clapping from its hands the dust of centuries, while it chuckled over its plans to give future events an unexpected and cruel twist.

CHAPTER 121

'Stephen's been this way.' I pointed. 'See what's painted on the post box?'

We'd reached the outskirts of Skipton after a six-hour trek that had taken us over Ilkley Moor (now a powdery black wasteland), then close by the village of Kildwick (comprising burnt-out houses; inflammable gas vented out through the remains of the post office in a pillar of blue flame). The River Aire had been reduced to a silt bed, baked into scales of mud by the heat.

Kate touched the metal postbox. She took her fingers away quickly, her fingertips singed by the heat conducted up through the metal from the ground.

The top of the post box was still the traditional post office red but the lower half had been scorched black. Painted on it in silver, just below the slot where once upon a time you'd shove the mail, was a large *S>* symbol. Stephen had been here, left his sign, then moved on, keen to reach the ship as quickly as possible.

Kate said, 'He can't be that far ahead, can he?'

'I shouldn't think so. It's a big group to move on foot. They've got children with them, and old man Fullwood. They're bound to slow him down.'

She looked at the sky. 'Christ, just what we need. Rain.'

At first the rail fell in a fine drizzle.

We pushed on, keeping up that punishing pace. We needed to reach Stephen and warn them about the hallucinations.

Lightning still stalked the burntlands like the war engine of some stony-hearted god. We watched lightning bolts smite the remains of trees in showers of blue sparks. Rain began to fall in big filthy drops full of black dust. When it hit the road it was like watching spit fall onto a hot iron. It sizzled away in balls of steaming water. After a while the heat worked through the soles of our boots, making our feet uncomfortably hot. Eventually it drove us to walk on the deeper ash that was cooler than solid ground. However, it slowed our pace so much that after a while we simply had to walk on the road with teeth gritted against the scorching heat.

Repeatedly I checked my boots, expecting at any moment to see them reach a temperature where they'd combust into balls of flame.

Three hours later we reached the route of the old Roman road. Not that there was much left to see of it; but the road signs were still pretty much intact, albeit scorched. So we pushed on harder, following a route that took us through the villages of Bracewell, Horton and Newsholme (on post boxes we saw Stephen's sign: S>). Further on, we reached the higher ground where we'd skirt the Forest of Bowland. There were no streams now; only arid tracks of mud where the water had once coursed. There were no people. Houses were burnt ruins. The rain still fell in huge dirty balls of water that boiled away to steam on touching the soil.

Lightning bolts spat at the ground. God despised the Earth. He despised everything and everyone on it. I didn't doubt that now.

At last He had decided to bring the world to an end.

Kate saw my sour expression. She gave my hand an encouraging squeeze. 'Don't give up hope.'

'Difficult, though, isn't it?'

She nodded.

'Have you seen what's left of the forest? Charcoal.'

She looked me in the face. 'Have you seen anything?'

'You mean am I hallucinating?'

She nodded, face serious.

'It comes and goes,' I said. 'But I think I can control it now. And you?'

'Often just glimpses, as if I see something out of the corner of my eye.' She looked at me, concerned. 'Do you see anything now?'

I looked down the hillside to the road that ran out in an elongated S shape between hills. There were cars on the road; with their paint skins burned off they'd all rusted orange; doors yawned open where their occupants had run for their lives. But I saw something else. I saw lines of pale, grey figures walking along in a solemn procession. They looked tall, almost dignified now. They moved slowly, purposefully, looking neither to the left nor the right; their bloody red eyes were fixed on some point in the distance.

When I looked at my feet I saw cracks appear in the black dirt. Then worms the size of snakes would ooze pinkly out. They slithered over my boots. Then erupting suddenly from the same cracks came grey hands. They grabbed at my ankles, and . . .

They weren't there. The worm-snakes and grey hands were created by the interplay of those electric fields created by the tortured rock and the electrical waves in my own brain. I told Kate all this. And I tried to reassure her I could stop it taking control of me. That I could distinguish between reality and delusion.

She kissed me. I sensed her faith in me. That I wouldn't lose self-control and begin to batter her again as I'd done in the deserted farmhouse.

We paused only long enough to drink and eat on that long trek. We passed more letter boxes. All had the same symbol sprayed on in silver paint: S>.

On one post box not far from Paythorne village was a different symbol: [S].

Stephen had told me that if I saw a symbol like that he would have left a message inside the box. I saw the door had been levered. Inside amongst uncollected mail singed brown by the heat lay a housebrick. Fastened by string to that, a single sheet of paper.

The message I read brought beads of sweat to my forehead.

476

Rick,

You were right about the Grey Men. I've seen them with my own eyes!

I'm so sorry I doubted you.

The Grey Men are everywhere now. Yesterday one of the bastards killed Mr Fullwood. We buried him at the roadside. The ground is so hot. Sparks flew as we dug.

I'm afraid they might panic the whole group into running in any direction, just so they can escape them. We are moving slowly. The little girl, Lee, is sick with a fever. We're having to take turns in carrying her. Jesus is giving her medicine even as I write this.

My God, isn't this an awful world we have to walk through? Don't you believe we've somehow made a wrong turning and ended up lost in Hell?

Incidentally, Tesco made it back to the group this morning. He was hurt fighting a Grey, not badly, fortunately. So we know about Cindy Gullidge and Howard Sparkman. The pair were heroes. We will remember them.

Take care, Kid K. Love, Stephen.

Kate read the note. 'It has yesterday's date,' she said, 'we can't be far now. What do you think happened to Mr Fullwoood?'

'Mr Fullwood was an old man. If he thought he saw a Grey it might have been enough to scare him literally to death.'

She sighed. 'We can't waste any more time. We must reach them before they kill each other. Rick? What's wrong?'

'I'm worried about the little girl.'

'Lee?'

'In the note Stephen says Jesus is giving her medicine.'

'So?'

'So, I don't trust Jesus one bit, do you?'

'I don't know, Rick. We're going to have to start trusting someone. After all, he promised to put us on the ship and get us out of this Hell.'

'He only promised that because he knew he needed our planes to ferry him and his people up here. Now he's actually within a day or two's walk from the rendezvous point on the coast do you still think he'll keep his bargain?'

She gave a watery smile. 'I'm praying he will, Rick.'

I sighed. 'Let's hope so. If he somehow reaches the ship first and leaves us behind,' I jerked a thumb over my shoulder, 'it means a long walk back to Fountains Moor. And I don't fancy spending a winter there without food or adequate shelter, do you?'

CHAPTER 122

My name is Kate Robinson.

We've not yet caught up with Stephen and the rest of the group. Rick still appears distrustful of the man called Jesus. He worries about what medicine the man is giving to the little girl; he worries also that Jesus and his own people might try and abandon us here when we reach the ship. I try and reassure Rick. We have our own people on board the ship now. Our people would try and prevent Jesus ordering the ship to leave without us.

But if it should happen what would happen then?

Clearly it would be suicide to walk all the way back through this desert to Fountains Moor. We've found no fresh water. We rely on the little left in our water bottles and we're constantly thirsty now. Even though it is winter you feel the heat rising from the ground to hit you in the face as if you've opened an oven door. The dust clogs your nostrils; it burns your throat. Sometimes, the ground is literally too hot for us to sit down.

We are still following the line of the old Roman road. Two thousand years ago Caesar's legions marched along this route. Then they'd have seen lush pastures, forests, lakes, streams; and, in abundance, fish, birds, deer, rabbits, wild boar. Now there is nothing but black ash, holes in the ground that vent boiling water, or methane gas that flares off with an ear-skewering shriek. Lightning flashes; the rumble of thunder is continuous.

There are human skeletons in the ash. A few minutes ago we passed twenty TVs or more lined out along the track. The plastic cases had softened in the heat, distorting and melting out of shape. For all the world it looked like something straight out of a Salvador Dali painting: deformed TVs sitting in the middle of a black desert that seems to stretch on into infinity.

Rick is pulling on his backpack. It is time to move on.

CHAPTER 123

My name is Rick Kennedy.

To the north-east of Lancaster I stopped and looked through the binoculars.

Kate must have registered the look of surprise on my face. She asked, 'What have you seen?'

'Take a look for yourself. Do you see it?'

'My God,' she breathed. 'Green . . . I can see green.'

She handed me the binoculars. 'Some oasis, eh? Trees, grass, a lake. There's even houses intact. Only one problem.'

'What's that?'

'People. It's seething with them. Did you see the tents? There must be thousands of them.'

Kate looked round nervously as if expecting starving people to jump out of the ashes around her.

'Don't worry,' I told her. 'We head to the south-west now.'

'Thank God for that. Something tells me we'd be welcome for all the wrong reasons.'

'You mean when they asked us for supper we'd be on the table, not just sitting to it?'

'Something like that. Come on, that place is giving me the shivers.'

I wasn't unduly worried. That stretch of greenery following the course of a river was a good half-hour's walk away. I don't think the survivors camped out there would roam these black desertlands without good cause.

We walked on. Mostly it was downhill now. I began to feel more upbeat. I could almost smell the sea. I knew it couldn't be more than a day's walk to the point where we'd meet the ship at Heysham.

'See the calling card?'

I nodded. Sprayed on silver paint on a post box was another *S>* symbol. He managed to move the people faster than I could have believed.

God knew, we couldn't be far behind him now.

We weren't. In fact ten minutes later we met the reception committee.

'Long time no see, Mr Kennedy.'

Jesus stood there in all his glory, dressed in a long black leather coat of the kind a raunchy version of Wyatt Earp might have worn; complementing that, black trousers and cowboy boots. Half a dozen of his tribe stood beside him dressed in their usual surreal mix of clothes complete with the long strips of silk, in brilliant yellows and oranges, tied to their elbows and legs. They fluttered in the hot dry air coming from hundreds of vents the size of rat holes in the ground.

I let out a whoop. 'Dean! Dean Skilton! I don't believe it; my man, how are you?' I ran forward to pump his hand.

'How's it hanging, Rick?' He gave a dry smile and slapped my shoulder, knocking out a Hell of a lot of black dust that made both of us cough.

'I reckon you two need a bath,' Jesus said in his soft Liverpudlian tones.

Victoria was there, too. She wore a long black skirt, black ankle boots that were eccentrically inappropriate for the terrain, and a black leather box jacket. I gave her a more restrained handshake than Dean's. She seemed almost amused to see me and Kate still alive.

'Hello, Rick. Hello Kate,' she said in that voice that was always calm, unflustered.

'Hi,' Kate said politely. 'Well, Dean, where are the others?'

'They went on ahead,' Dean said.

'They've reached the ship?' I asked, surprised.

'No, not exactly.'

'What do you mean: not exactly?' I frowned.

Jesus stroked his goatee. 'They've reached a ship. *A* ship, mind . . . not *THE* ship.'

'You've lost me,' I said. '*A* ship? What do you mean?'

Jesus smiled. 'Don't worry. They're all safe. We've seen with our own eyes that this side of the country got hit pretty bad.'

'How?'

'Among other things, tidal waves.' He pointed west. 'Just a couple of hours, walk in that direction there's this dirty great warship, high and dry in the middle of the desert. It must have been washed there by one mother of a flood months ago. But all the flood water's gone; it's dry as Hell now. But the ship

480

makes a great motel. We'll take you there in a few minutes.
But . . .'

'But?' I felt my heart sink. The tone of Jesus's voice told me
that BUT would be an almighty great BUT. The double-cross was
coming and I saw it as clearly as if it was written across the sky in
words of fire.

'But what?' I repeated looking from Dean to Jesus to Victoria.

'But there's a matter to be settled first,' Jesus said, still in that
soft purr.

'And what's that?'

'A question of allegiance.'

'I don't follow.'

'Come, come, Mr Kennedy. You must have realized that we
couldn't board our ship as two separate tribes with two separate
leaders. One tribe must absorb the other . . .' He stroked the goatee
with the tattooed fingers that spelt out his old name, Gary. 'One
tribe must absorb the other. Or one tribe must destroy the other.'

I spoke bitterly. 'And you've decided you're the one to lead us to
the promised land?'

'Naturally. Oh, don't get me wrong. Your brother Stephen's a nice
man . . . too nice for his own good. He believes we can sail south,
find an island, settle down and quietly grow corn and potatoes.'

'But you've got other ideas?'

'Of course. The survival of my group is paramount. We're not going
to rough it on a desert island. We'll choose one with a population of
a hundred or so, but when we reach it we won't be going on shore as
pathetic refugees, begging for a crust of bread. We'll hit the beach as
a conquering army.'

'And you'll kill all the men and take all the women?'

Jesus smiled. 'Something like that.'

'And they called you Jesus,' Kate said heavily. 'You're beginning
to sound more like King Herod.'

He smiled. 'This is survival of the fittest, Kate.'

I stabbed Dean a look. 'Where do you stand in all this, Dean?'

He stood back from me and pulled off his leather jacket. Around
his arms were tied strips of orange silk. He pulled out another strip
of silk a full three metres long from his jeans pocket and tied it around
his head like a bandana; the ends of this piece of silk fluttered down
to the backs of his knees.

'So you've joined the others now,' I said, nodding. 'Figures.'

'And what's that supposed to mean?'

'You know what I damn' well mean,' I said. 'Whenever there was trouble at school you sided with the bullies, even when we were little kids.'

'Rick, it so happens I believe Jesus here has got what it takes to get us through all this in one piece.'

'And Stephen hasn't?'

'No. He's nothing but a blow-dried video jock. He hasn't got the guts to fight dirty for his community's survival.'

'You're a shit, Skilton.'

'Yeah, maybe I am. But it's the shits that're going to inherit the Earth.'

'Go ahead.' I waved to take in the burnt landscape. 'Go ahead . . . it's all fucking yours, Deanie boy.'

Dean was getting mad. He pulled one of the pair of Beretta pistols from his belt.

'But do you want to know something, Rick?' he snarled. 'Do you really want to fucking know something?'

'Yeah, go on, what? You slept with your mummy until you were sixteen years old?'

'Don't push me, Rick. No . . . no, don't turn away. You fucking well listen. If you were leader of the group I'd have stayed loyal to you.'

'Well, I'm not. And I couldn't be leader to save my life. We elected Stephen. And I'm staying loyal to him.'

I looked at them standing there, guns in their hands. I'd noticed Jesus's eyes narrow. He hadn't liked it when Dean implied he wished I was leader.

Victoria looked from Jesus and Dean then to Kate and me like she was watching tennis players slam balls back and forth. The poor bitch was plain nuts. She even smiled, amused by the whole thing.

'Look, Rick,' Dean said. 'You can still join us. No one need get hurt.'

'What happens to my brother?'

'He's welcome, too,' Jesus said, smiling. 'You're all welcome . . . as long as you recognize who's the boss.' He pointed at his chest.

Dean added. 'You'll need to undergo the initiation ceremony then you can join us.'

'Initiation ceremony?' I said. 'Wait. Don't tell me. It has something to do with cocks and arseholes, doesn't it, Dean?'

I'd hit a raw nerve.

Dean screamed, aimed the pistol at me, pulled the trigger. Nothing happened.

He'd forgotten to cock the gun.

'Run!' I shouted to Kate and pushed her. We ran hard.

I heard shots; hot metal buzzed past my ear. Another shot, and I felt a tremendous thump in the centre of my back.

CHAPTER 124

Despite the concussion from the bullet hitting me in the centre of the back, I ran on.

For a moment I thought there was nothing but flat earth in front of us. Then I saw a crater ahead. It was big enough to accommodate a car. I pushed Kate towards it.

More gunshots crackled in the air.

Kate was faster. She jumped into the crater.

I was ten paces from it when the ground broke open beneath my feet. Sparks flew up into my face. I'd gone through the surface again where it had been baked hard by the heat, leaving a hollow beneath. I sank as far as my waist before my outstretched hands slammed against the surface crust, stopping me dropping any further. I kicked at nothing but scorching air beneath me.

Another gunshot cracked. It slapped the ground to my right then ricocheted away.

Desperately I hoisted myself out of the hole, then rolled the remaining couple of metres to the crater.

Kate was already on her knees in the bottom, dragging her rifle from her bag.

Another figure dropped beside me.

'Victoria?'

She sat back against the crater wall, brushing the dust from her arms 'Did you really think I'd be disloyal to your brother, Rick?' She gave a strange smile. 'We are lovers, you know?'

'Take the pistol,' I told her. 'Kate, you OK?'

'You?' she asked.

'I think a bullet caught me in the back. Can't feel anything.'

'Turn round, let me check your—'

'No time. Here they come!'

They ran in a crouching position towards the crater. I leaned forward against the crater wall. My toes kicked into the dry earth to gain some kind of grip. I hoisted my rifle over the rim of the crater and let off a couple of wild shots.

Kate fired three shots. They still ran towards us, returning fire. I'd really hit a raw nerve with Dean. He fired the pair of Berettas wildly, screaming how he'd cut off my balls.

Victoria raised the revolver I'd given her, aimed, then squeezed off a single shot. One of Jesus's men clutched his chest and went down flat on his face in a flurry of silk strips. He lay still.

I panted. 'Nice shooting, Victoria.'

She looked at the gun almost in surprise, as if she hadn't known what to expect from the thing.

Immediately Jesus, Dean and the five remaining men threw themselves flat. I aimed the rifle.

Damn, they should have been sitting ducks. But because the ground rose then dipped slightly, they were actually out of sight behind the low mound of earth.

'Anyone get a clear shot?' I asked.

'No,' Kate said. 'They're just below the rise in the ground.'

Victoria shook her head and began fiddling with the chamber of the revolver in that detached way she had as if switching off from reality.

'Let me check your back,' Kate said. 'Where were you hit?'

'Wait, I'll keep watch on those bastards. There, can you see anything?'

'Here, let me take off your backpack. Let's see ... stand still. There.' She ran her hand across my back. 'Nothing there. The bullet must have been stopped by the bag.'

I watched the patch of land where those double-crossing bastards had gone to earth.

'What's happening?' Kate asked.

'Nothing yet. That shot of Victoria's killed one of Jesus's men. They're obviously thinking strategy. They know they'll lose a couple more men if they try and rush us. What's that?'

Kate held up my water bottle. 'That's what stopped the bullet.'

'Shit. We've lost all the water?'

'Yep. Not a drop left.'

'Victoria, have you any?'

'No,' she said in a voice that was surprisingly sweet. 'None at all.'

'Hell . . . this doesn't look good. It doesn't look good at all.'

'What are we going to do, Rick?' Kate looked serious.

'Well . . .' I looked round the arid crater. 'We're stuck here for the time being.' As if to confirm this one of Jesus's men loosed off a couple of shotgun blasts in our direction. I ducked as pellets splashed dirt onto my head. 'My guess is they'll wait until dark.'

'What then?' Victoria asked with amazing naivety.

'Then, Victoria,' I said with a sigh, 'then they'll rush the crater and kill us.'

CHAPTER 125

I looked at my watch. It was perhaps a couple of hours until nightfall. That's when they would come for us and shoot us like rats trapped in a tub.

The wind blew dust devils, sending them twisting across the black desert; the ash pittered down onto us. My throat felt as dry as the dirt I lay on. It was hot, too. I found myself thinking of ice cream. Tubs and tubs of ice cream. Neapolitan, pistachio, strawberry, black cherry, all creamy and cold as they slide down your dry throat. Or cornets from the ice cream man who used to drive from Boycott Drive into Trueman Way, playing a nerve-jangling version of *Twinkle, Twinkle, Little Star.*

And here we are: trapped in the crater.

Picture it: *The crater's big enough to swallow a car whole. It's roughly two metres deep. I can stand at the bottom of the crater wall and just manage to peep over the top, my rifle at the ready. At the bottom of the crater, plum in the centre, is an opening the size of a rabbit hole. Steam rises from the hole, almost like steam blowing from the spout of a gently simmering kettle.*

As likely as not, we stood in a crater formed by a geyser. Similar to the one that killed Caroline Lucas. I could hear a knocking sound, as if hot water, or even steam, was being forced along passageways beneath our feet. The more I looked down at it, the more convinced

I was it was a geyser hole, one that would periodically discharge superheated steam under incredible pressure.

Disturbing as the notion was, I couldn't allow that to distract me now. For the moment, the most pressing concern was the trigger-happy Jesus and his murdering gang.

'I'm thirsty.' Victoria pushed her heavy red hair from her face. 'I want a drink.'

'Join the club.' I sighed. 'I've got a packet of mints.'

She stared at me as if I was speaking pure Klingon.

I forced a smile. 'Would you like one, Victoria?'

'Please.'

'Kate?'

Kate lay face down against the dirt wall of the crater, where she occasionally shot cautious glances out in the direction of where Jesus, Dean and the rest lay out of sight.

Kate glanced down at me. 'Thank you,' she said, and reached down as I held up the packet. A rifle cracked out a slug which zipped over the crater.

'They're not letting us forget they're there in a hurry,' I said, offering a mint to Victoria, then taking one myself.

'What happened to your leg?'

I looked down at the burn holes in my jeans. 'The ground gave way as we ran for the crater. I managed to stop falling all the way through.'

'You've burnt your leg?' She spoke in that simple direct way that managed to rub me up the wrong way. 'Is it painful?'

I tried to stay cool. 'Yes. It did burn my leg, Victoria. And, yes, it is painful.'

Another bullet smacked into the dirt on the crater rim.

'But that, Victoria, is the least of our worries. Those bastards are shooting at us.' I shook my head. 'Dean? I can't believe it. We were friends for ten years.'

'How did you burn your leg?' asked Victoria, eyes naively wide, twisting a ringlet of hair around her finger.

I sighed. 'It's just a thin crust of earth. You know, like a pie crust? The heat caused the earth below it to shrink. It's formed a cavity. At the bottom of that the rocks are probably red hot.'

She nodded, repeating to herself, 'Red hot.'

'Yes . . . red fucking hot. Kate?'

'Yes?'

'See anything?'

'Not yet. But it's getting dark fast.'

'Damn . . .' I sighed. 'All this way for it to end like this. Come on, Rick, you thick shit, think . . . think. There has to be a way out.'

'Do you love Stephen?'

I looked at Victoria in surprise. 'He's my brother. Yes . . . I guess so.'

'So do I.' She spoke in suddenly frank way. 'I was a virgin until I met him.'

'Victoria.' I suddenly felt uncomfortable. 'There's no need to—'

'My family put me away when I was thirteen, you see. My father was a bishop. They said I behaved like I belonged to the Devil.' She paused, then suddenly she said, 'Dean's right. You would make a better leader, you know?'

'But Stephen was elected. He's charismatic, clear-headed, he'll—'

'No,' Victoria said crisply. 'That man who calls himself Jesus. He would make a better leader than Stephen. But you would make a better leader than Jesus. Isn't that right, Kate?'

Kate looked surprised by the conversation. 'I don't know, I haven't thought – Victoria, careful – *ouch.*'

In one second Victoria reached out, cupped her hand around Kate's ankle and pulled. Kate slithered to the bottom of the crater beside me.

Then Victoria scrambled up to the rim of the crater, saying quite coolly, 'Walk due west for two hours. You can't miss the ship. It stands in the middle of a plain.'

I stood up.

'Victoria. Where the hell are you going? You'll get your stupid head blown off . . . *Victoria!*'

She climbed out of the crater.

Gunshots.

CHAPTER 126

I climbed to the rim of the crater but still crouched down low. I looked up to see Victoria standing there defiantly, facing Jesus, Dean and the rest, her feet apart and firmly planted in the black ash.

I reached out, grabbed a fistful of her long skirt, ready to drag the damn fool back into the crater.

Then at least she wouldn't get shot. Boiled alive, maybe; already spurts of steam were blasting from the fissure at the bottom of the crater. But not shot. From the corner of my eye I saw Kate trying to avoid them.

'Victoria,' I yelled. 'Get down . . . they'll kill you.'

A rifle cracked again. The bullet passed between her legs with a loud smacking sound, punching a hole through the heavy material of her skirt but just missing her inner thighs.

'Victoria!'

I pulled at her skirt, but she was better balanced than I was. I began to work my feet up against the crumbly dirt wall of the crater. Once my feet were braced I could simply yank her back into the crater.

Of course, there was a chance the geyser might blow. But right now the biggest danger were those bullets which were likely to unzip her stupid skull any second now.

'Victoria. Get back into this hole. We'll shoot our way out if we have to. Give me a chance to think of some—'

A bullet clipped her forearm. A trickle of blood ran down her wrist, then branched off into a whole delta of rivulets down her palm; glistening blobs of crimson began to drip from her fingers into the ash.

I yelled at her in a kind of despairing rage. 'You've been hit, Victoria . . . can't you feel it? Victoria, stop . . . what the Hell are you doing?'

Before I could drag her back into the hole by her skirts she suddenly and decisively walked forward, pulling herself free from my grasp.

I slithered lower into the crater to watch what happened next.

She walked slowly away from the crater, her back to me. I watched her raise her hands slowly out at each side of her.

She was surrendering to Jesus and his gang.

The shooting stopped.

'I haven't got a gun,' she called out to them. 'I'm coming across to you.'

Jesus and the others weren't taking any chances. They still lay flat. All I could see were the barrels of their guns poking above the rise in the ground.

I heard Jesus call to her. 'Good girl, Victoria. I'm glad at least you've come to your senses. Not like those stupid bastards in the hole.'

Dean called out. 'What about Kate and Rick? Are they coming out?'

'I don't know,' she replied. 'Why don't you ask them?'

I couldn't make out the reply exactly, but the tone of Dean's sneering voice was enough for me.

I spoke to Kate in a low voice as she crawled up the crater wall to my side. 'The moment I stand up they're going to kill me.'

'They might give you a chance to surrender.'

'Not a hope in Hell. Even if I, and Stephen come to that, swore allegiance to Jesus and his tribe and went through his sordid little rituals they'd cut our throats the first chance they got.'

'We can't stay here, Rick. Touch the ground. Do you feel it?'

'The vibration?'

She nodded. 'The pressure's building. And we're sitting in nothing but a big blow hole.'

'Christ, talk about being caught between the devil and the deep blue sea.'

'We've got to do something . . . but for Godsakes what?'

'We've got two choices,' I said. 'Stay here and be boiled alive when the steam comes blasting through, or shoot our way out. Any preferences?'

'Either way doesn't look good. What about Victoria?'

'It looks as if she's gone over to the other side. Probably she'll end up as Dean's woman now.'

I looked over the rim of the crater. Victoria was halfway from the crater to where the others lay, guns at the ready, just over the ridge of earth. The breeze blew at her long hair, it rippled the material of her long skirt. She looked as if she'd just stepped from an oil painting. You know, one of those big dramatic ones they'd hang at the top of flights of stairs in art galleries: beautiful stormswept woman in foreground, with that backdrop of burnt earth, mountains of black cloud split by forked lightning.

Crump!

Half a kilometre away a geyser erupted from the ground, flinging a column of boiling water a hundred metres into the air. Steam billowed, then wafted across that black plain like a ghost.

'Here it comes,' I said in a grim voice. 'There's probably a whole network of subterranean chambers filled with boiling water. It won't be long before this one blows.' I glanced across at Victoria. 'There is option three.' I looked back at Kate.

'What's that?'

'You could join Victoria. They wouldn't kill you.'

'No, but you know what they'll do to Victoria? And what they'd do to me if I join her?'

'They might not—'

'Don't kid yourself, Rick. There'd be a gang rape first, then what? Slavery? Until I proved myself as a worthy wife for one of them? You think I want that, Rick?'

I shook my head. 'But we're going to have to decide in the next five minutes. Shoot our way out; or wait here. And I really think that geyser's on its way.'

Kate's green eyes locked on mine.

I squeezed her hand. 'What's it to be, Kate?'

'We've been together five weeks.' She gave a grim smile. 'I think I could cope with being with you for the rest of eternity. What about you?'

My mouth dried. I managed a nod. 'Maybe it's best if we . . . what the hell is that woman doing?'

It was as I was speaking to Kate that I heard shouting.

Victoria had almost reached Jesus and the others. But now she stood about ten paces from them.

'What the heck is she doing?' I asked, bewildered.

'Christ, she must be mad after all. Just look at her!'

'She's just standing there, stamping her feet.' I sighed. 'Crazy, crazy woman.'

'What are they shouting at her?'

'As far as I can make out they're telling her to get behind them and lie down out of the line of fire in case we start shooting.'

The shouting continued. They were yelling at Victoria to move forward; I saw hands gesture for her to move but she stood there stamping the ground. Each time her foot came down it sent up a puff of black ash. I though for a moment one of them would jump up and pull her down behind the ridge of earth but they weren't taking any chances. Kate and I had our rifles at the ready.

I glanced back down into the bottom of the crater: boiling water had started to well up from the fissure. It bubbled and spat as the pressure built up behind it. Any second now a ton of boiling water could blast through there, tearing the skin from our bodies.

I remembered what had happened to Caroline Lucas. I shivered.

I looked back to where Victoria was performing her weird stamping dance, like a surreal version of a Spanish Flamenco, her hands still held high. This time I heard Dean Skilton's voice. 'Come on, you stupid bitch! Move! I'll give you to the count of three, then I'm going to drop you!'

Victoria paid no attention. She moved back, still stamping every pace or so. She held her head to one side as if listening to the sound her foot made.

She moved further back, still listening, still stamping.

Then I saw she was only a dozen paces from the hole I'd made when I fell through the crust of earth.

'Oh, God,' I breathed, 'I know what she's going to do.'

Kate shot me a look. 'What? She's—'

'Victoria!' I yelled. '*Victoria! No!*'

The others realized, too. I saw Dean kneel up from behind the dirt ridge. He held both Beretta pistols high and fired them into Victoria's body.

I saw the bullets thudding into her. She staggered back. Still she held out her arms at either side even though the agony of the bullets tearing into her stomach must have been excruciating.

Then she stumbled forward. I thought she'd fall flat on her face but she regained her balance, her head swinging back upright, whipping back that long red hair.

Then she gave one almighty stamp with her foot.

'Christ . . .'

I watched, my eyes wide, my heart thumping.

The whole surface of the ground, from the hole I'd made falling through the baked crust to beyond the ridge of earth, began to sag.

It seemed to sag in one piece as if the ground had turned into rubber and Victoria's weight pulled it downwards into a concave shape like a bowl.

I heard screams, panicky shouts as Jesus, Dean and the other men scrambled to their feet to try and escape what would happen next.

They were too late. The baked soil that covered the hollow subterranean chamber broke like it was thin ice on a lake.

Instantly there was an uprush of sparks from the fire pit beneath them.

I watched as the crust fractured as if in slow motion. Then it collapsed, dropping the screaming men into the pit. Red sparks streamed upward.

Victoria had gone, too. I saw her simply drop straight down into the fire, her hair blowing out behind her. She wasn't screaming.

Then they were gone.

CHAPTER 127

'They're all dead?' Kate watched me as I backed gingerly away from the pit.

'They must be. That's the closest I can get. The heat's terrific.' My face smarted. It was like trying to put your face too close to a furnace.

'It would have been quick?'

'Instantaneous. Not that Jesus, or whatever his real name was, deserved it. Dean, too. They deserved to slowly roast after what they planned to do to us.'

'You think they would really have killed us?'

'No doubt about it. Stephen, too, and anyone else who didn't submit to him totally. As Jesus said, we were two tribes trying to live in the same space. It just wouldn't work.'

'What now?'

'With Jesus dead I suppose his people must join ours, accept Stephen as their leader.'

'Come on,' Kate said, rubbing her arm anxiously, 'let's get out of here; before that thing blows.'

I looked back at the geyser crater; steam now filled it, giving it the appearance of a witch's cauldron. White vapour spilled over the rim.

We turned our back on it and headed west.

After a while Kate said, 'How did Victoria know the ground was so thin there?'

'She'd have seen where I almost fell through the crust into the pit. It was like thin ice.'

'When she was stamping her foot, she was listening for the hollow sound, wasn't she?'

'She was,' I agreed. 'But I still find it hard to think of her as being mortal, somehow.' I shook my head. 'She came out of fire, in that burning graveyard. Now she's returned to fire. Strange girl ... but the poor kid saved our lives.'

Kate gave me a knowing look. 'Saved *your* life, you mean.'

'My life?'

'She thought you should be leader. She made that pretty clear. It seemed logical to her that in order for that to happen she should sacrifice her own life.'

'There's no answer to that. Her brain worked in a mysterious way. I'm thankful, eternally thankful to her, but as far as I'm concerned Stephen's in charge. And that's the way it's going to stay.'

A kilometre behind us, whatever destructive spirit resides within the Earth had its own say. With a rumble that vibrated the ground beneath our feet the geyser at last burst through the crater where we had sheltered. A plume of boiling water spurted to stand as high as a ten-storey building before showering down onto the ground where it splashed a curtain of black dust high into the air.

CHAPTER 128

The ground sloped gently downwards before levelling out into a plain. It stretched out in front of us; a seemingly limitless expanse of black dirt, totally flat, totally featureless apart from the warship.

The warship sat there, looking absurdly out of place in that arid desert.

There were no signs of buildings or roads or fields. Everything made by man had vanished. Visitors from another world might gaze coolly down from their spaceships and surmise there never had been life here on this barren plain. Everything, but everything, had been swept away by the tidal wave. The same tidal wave that had carried the huge ship far inland from the ocean. Then the sea had rolled back again, leaving the ship high and dry.

What would that wave have looked like? Thundering towards you across once-dry land?

I pictured it all (believe me, I tried not to, but images oozed bright as TV pictures into my mind). I pictured horrified men and women staring out in disbelief from the windows of their homes as the wave tidal wave approached. I pictured the wave itself. Which was – what? Thirty kilometres wide? Five hundred metres high?

Vividly – terrifyingly vividly – I could see it thundering across the landscape, propelled by the vast explosions somewhere deep in the ocean. I saw the wall of green water moving faster than an express train. I saw it turning creamy white as it curled like the perfect surfing wave of Colossus himself. That monstrous body of water would roar across the land with the destructive force of Jehovah's own bulldozer, scraping from the face of the planet forests, topsoils, hills, roads, houses, factories, schools – even whole cities. Millions must have died.

Again I imagined pale faces at windows, staring with bulging eyes in terror as the tidal wave approached. I imagined the people's despairing screams when they realized that in just seconds they would be engulfed and destroyed, utterly destroyed by the millions of tons of water that would hit them with the force of a colossal battering ram.

What does it sound like, when a whole city screams?

'Rick?'

'Did you hear me?'

'Uh . . . sorry . . . I was thinking about . . .'

'About what?'

I shook my head quickly, my skin prickling icy cold. 'Nothing. It doesn't matter. Sorry, what were you saying?'

'Can you see any sign of Stephen and the rest?'

Still unable to shift from my head the screams of a million doomed people I looked through the binoculars.

'Nothing,' I replied, 'only the ship. Hell, it's a big one. Looks like a Royal Navy destroyer.'

Kate took the binoculars. 'It seems in one piece. The tidal wave can't have damaged it too badly.'

Even without the binoculars I could see the ship looked intact. It still stood on its keel, but leaned to one side, probably held there by a build-up of sludge left by the flood. The sludge had then baked hard from the subterranean heat, cementing the ship at that weird angle.

'How far?' asked Kate.

'An hour's walk, maybe?'

We moved on. We were exhausted. But the prospect of seeing Stephen and telling him what Jesus and Dean had tried to do was a good incentive to move as fast as we could.

Kate said, 'At least they haven't been hit by the hallucinations. The electrical activity here must be pretty muted. Have you seen any Greys?'

'Not a thing. But have you seen what's happening to the ground?'

She nodded. 'There's a hot spot building up down there, isn't there?'

'Looks that way to me. After the flood dried out there must have been just one endless expanse of hard mud. The place would have looked like a vacant car park, but it's cracking apart. See the steam?'

She crouched down to rest the flat of her palm against the ground. 'Feels pretty hot too.'

'No time to waste then, let's press on.'

As we walked we heard the *crick, crack* of the mud cracking open. Jets of hot gas blew up against our bare hands. At first it wasn't too bad; but after ten minutes we were walking holding onto the shoulder straps of our backpacks to keep our hands away from the scorching blast of air that jetted from the cracks in the mud.

I began to cough, my throat burned, my eyes watered. 'Kate,' I said, trying to catch my breath. 'I don't like this. I'm finding it hard to breathe, are you?'

'It's toxic gas, isn't it?'

'Just pray it's not carbon monoxide.'

I looked across the black plain. The warship seemed as far away as before. I could only just make out the barrels of its huge guns poking outward.

'Ouch!'

'What's wrong?' I shot a look at Kate.

'There's sparks coming out of the cracks. One hit me in the face.'

'Let me see.'

She coughed. 'I'm OK, Rick. Keep walking.'

'Finding it hard to breathe?'

'Worse than before. My whole chest's burning.'

We walked on as fast as we could but pretty soon it felt as if we were wearing lead boots. Each step made our legs ache. My eyes were a streaming blur. I had to wipe them each time I tried to see if we were any nearer to the ship.

Crack!

495

The ground split a few paces to my right. It wasn't a wide split; only wide enough to insert a pencil, if you had the inclination, but a gust of sparks shot out. They were a bright yellow, giving a good indication how hot it was getting just a few centimetres down.

This wasn't good, I told myself. There'd been quakes felling trees, killing animals and people. Then there'd been a flood that had laid a thick layer of silt over the top of all that vegetation and animal matter. That whole mess had been rotting for months under a cap of dried mud.

Methane gas, *inflammable* methane gas had probably been accumulating there week in, week out, given off by fermenting corpses and grass and trees. Now the ground was heating up fast. I looked out anxiously across the plain. Ten thousand acres of land might go up in one God-almighty explosion.

All the more reason to reach Stephen, then get everyone moving out to the coast.

I walked faster.

'Go ahead and warn Stephen,' Kate said, 'you can walk faster.'

'I'm not . . . I'm not leaving you. We can . . . Hell, it's getting tough to . . . to breathe. Kate . . . *Kate*. Here, let me put my arm round you. Better?'

'Better.' She nodded but I noticed her eyes looked dull.

'Hang on, we'll reach the ship.'

We walked on, supporting each other. After ten minutes we shed the backpacks. They were nothing but a dead weight.

We'd keep the rifles just in case.

I looked at Kate's face. Her eyes were almost closed. Her lips were turning blue.

I pulled the rifle off her shoulder, let it fall to the ground.

I'd keep mine. We might meet one of Jesus's men still under his orders to shoot us on sight.

Five minutes later I dumped my rifle, too. Its weight seemed to be dragging us down into the cracked earth.

We walked on. Hot gas spurted from the cracks. Every so often a shower of sparks would blast up into our faces. They felt like hot pinpricks against our skin. They burned holes into our clothes the size of full stops . . .

We walked almost blinded now. The ship, rearing out from the plain, was nothing more than a pale shape.

'You all right, Kate?'

No reply. But I saw that her feet still moved.

Crack.

More sparks hit my face, stinging my lips and eyelids.

They hurt, but at least the pain kept me awake.

Because all I wanted to do was sleep.

Curl up on the ground, Rick, said a voice in my head. All nice and cosy and warm. You can sleep . . . sleep so sweetly. Lulled by the *crick-crack-crick* of all those little fissures popping open in the ground. See the sparks, Rick. Like a firework display, aren't they? Yellow sparks, red sparks, white sparks, all shooting up, up, up into the sky.

I looked to my right.

A hundred Grey Men walked at my side.

I looked to my left.

Another hundred marched there too.

I was King of the Greys.

I shook my head dizzily.

They're back.

Grey heads, grey arms, grey legs, grey faces.

And their eyes, their bloody red eyes.

I looked right again.

One walked alongside, its huge arm round my shoulder in a matey gesture. I smiled.

It smiled back.

The bloody red eyes blazed. Its black lips parted, exposing jagged teeth. A claw of a hand came up, took hold of my hand, raised it to its lips.

Then it bit.

Hard.

'Rick . . . Rick. Come out of it, or I'll bite again.'

The grey monster bit my finger.

'Hell . . .' I came out of it. The grey face with the wet red eyes dissolved. It was Kate again. I looked round; the legions of marching Greys had vanished also.

'Don't go out on me again, buster.' She forced a smile. 'I'll bite that pretty nose of yours next time.'

I coughed. My chest burned like I'd inhaled hot cinders. More sparks blew into my face.

This was Hell, this was really Hell.

Kate wiped my face with her hand. 'You were losing it again, weren't you?'

I nodded. Coughed.

'Did you see the Grey Men?'

'Uh . . . hundreds of them.'

She pulled at my sleeve, prompting me to continue walking. 'The electrical activity's growing more intense here. Come on, buster. We've got to reach Stephen before they start hallucinating like crazy and hack each other to pieces.'

'How far . . . Christ, Kate, I can't see.' I coughed. 'How far to the ship?'

'Ten minutes . . . Hell, I wish I could breathe. My throat's on fire.'

'Don't worry, we'll make it. Once we're on the ship we'll be above the gas. If it's carbon monoxide . . . it'll be low-lying . . . uh . . . Kate, you'll have to guide me. I can't see at all now.'

'Keep your eyes closed for a moment. Give me your hand . . . now walk. Faster.'

I shut my eyes, allowing Kate to lead me by the hand across that nightmarescape of hard, black mud. All the time I heard the *crick-crack-crick* as it cracked open. Sparks stung my bare skin; hot gas gusted upward; my throat burned. I found myself turning my face up towards the sky in an attempt to avoid the poison gas.

Eyes tight shut, I'd been walking perhaps ten minutes when I heard a voice shout.

Then a burst of machine gun fire.

'Down, Rick!'

Kate pushed her leg out in front of mine, tripping me so I fell face down onto that hot mud.

There was shouting. I opened my eyes. Blinked.

The ship was no more than a kilometre away now.

Hot gas vented through the cracks in the mud. Kate coughed so hard it sounded as if she'd bring up the lining of her throat.

Another burst of machine gun fire. Bullets chewed the ground five paces from my head.

'Stop shooting,' Kate yelled, 'Stop shooting!'

My eyes cleared. 'It's Tesco! Hell, I thought he was dead.' I looked for my rifle, realized I'd dumped it, then lay flat again as he aimed the Uzi machine pistol.

Christ, I thought, he'll have been given orders by Jesus to shoot us the moment he claps eyes on us.

Tesco fired again, the bullets rushing at us in flickers of red to slice through the air above us.

He was firing wildly. Then I saw why. He was terrified.

I heard him screaming: 'Greys . . . fucking Greys! They're all over the fucking place!'

'He's hallucinating,' panted Kate. 'Our appearance probably triggered it; but . . . but he's seeing Grey Men everywhere.'

Tesco raised the machine gun again. Then he fired a long burst; red tracer flashed all around us.

CHAPTER 129

'Tesco!' I yelled. 'It's me. Rick! Stop firing!'

Tesco, standing a hundred paces away, frantically pulled the spent magazine from the Uzi. I walked forwards as he pushed a fresh clip of ammo into the gun. The strips of orange and yellow silk fluttered around him.

'Tesco. Look at me. It's Rick Kennedy. You know Kate Robinson. We stayed at the hotel on your island. Remember, the cellar? Remember, I punched you, didn't I?'

Tesco worked at the gun, trying to shove the ammo clip home. His face was distorted with terror, his eyes were the same as Stenno's when he attacked me in Fullwood's garage. The pupils and irises had contracted into tiny black dots.

Twenty paces from Tesco. I could see the scars radiating from his lips.

Fifteen paces.

The gas jets blew the silk strips straight upward to flutter above his head.

Thirteen paces away.

He struggled with the clip. He shouted back in the direction of the ship. 'Greys! Stephen, fucking Greys. The bastards are all over the place!'

Ten paces.

I whispered to Kate. 'I'm going to have to slug him.'

'It's too late.'

'I slug him. You grab the gun.'

499

Seven paces away.

All fingers and thumbs through fear he had the ammo clip in place but he fumbled, trying to pull back the firing bolt.

Six paces.

Once the bolt was pulled back, the gun was cocked. He could fire.

Five paces.

'Tesco. Look at me. I'm Rick K—'

With a terrified scream he pointed the Uzi machine gun in my face. His finger whitened as it tightened on the trigger.

'Christ . . .' he panted with shock. 'Christ, Rick? I nearly blew off your fucking head. Keep down. The Greys are all over the . . . Jesus H. Christ.' He looked astonished. 'Where did they go? They were all around the . . .'

'We know where they went, Tesco.' Kate, hanging onto me for support, managed a smile. 'We can tell you all about the Greys.'

'But where did they go?'

'Tesco . . .' I said, as Kate sagged against me, almost unconscious from the effects of the gas. 'We need to get back to the ship. *Now, Tesco.* Feel the gas jets? Toxic . . . it's poison gas . . .'

Now I felt myself go. It was as if a black wave had rolled into my head. The last thing I remember was Tesco somehow trying to catch both of us as I fell forward with Kate in my arms.

CHAPTER 130

The blur assumed the outline of a head. That sharpened, revealing blue eyes and a mouth.

The mouth smiled.

'How's it feel to come back from the dead, Kid K?'

'Stephen?'

'Come on, kiddo, how many brothers do you think you've got?'

'Knowing Dad . . . probably legions of the buggers.' I smiled. Although my throat burned like I'd tried to swallow a piece of Hell.

Stephen grinned. 'You're probably right, sunshine, but I'm the only one you know about. How you feeling?'

'Dizzy. Thirsty. Very thirsty . . . my God . . . a bed. I'm actually in bed?'

For a wild moment I thought I'd dreamt everything. That when I looked round I'd see the familiar surroundings of my bedroom in Fairburn, right down to the poster of Jim Morrison on the wall. And printed in that plump hippy script would be the title of the old Doors song: *C'MON BABY LIGHT MY FIRE.*

I blinked.

The walls were steel. The window a round porthole.

'The ship? We made it to the ship?' I verged on a state of babbling idiocy.

'Not *the* ship.' Stephen said, pulling the ring on a beer can and handing the can to me. 'We're high and dry, unfortunately.'

'Uh . . . the warship?'

'That's the one; stuck right in the middle of this vast plain that seems to stretch into flaming infinity.' He smiled. 'Don't worry, we'll make it to Heysham by the time the *Mirdath* drops anchor. Here . . . drink.'

'Beer?'

'You wouldn't believe the supplies on this ship. Cabin after cabin is crammed with them.'

I lifted the can to my lips, then froze as a thought forced its way through the thick fog in my brain. 'Kate . . . is Kate OK?'

Stephen rested his hand on my shoulder. 'Don't worry. She's fine.'

'Where is she?'

He nodded at the wall. 'In the next cabin, sleeping off the effects of the gas.'

'I want to see—'

'She's asleep,' he said firmly. 'You take it easy. Here, drink the beer. It's cold.'

I pulled on the can thirstily, beer dribbling down onto my chin. Christ, but it felt good; as cold as snow sliding down my throat, chest, and into my stomach. I drained the can

I could see Stephen looking at me anxiously. 'You know, you were really out of it for a while back there. At one point I wondered if you'd make it. Then you were talking in your sleep.'

I lay back on the bunk with a sigh. 'Nothing to make you blush, I hope.'

'No . . . only some pretty weird stuff, Kid K. You've really been through Hell out there.'

'Probably no worse than you.'

'Did you see the Greys? The monsters were everywhere, weren't they?'

I pushed myself up onto one hand and looked up at Stephen who was opening another can of beer. 'Stephen. I've got to tell you something.'

'Take it easy. It can wait.'

'No, it can't.'

'Can.'

'No, Stephen, I'm not joking. It's the Grey Men.'

'Don't worry, Stephen. I believe you now. There's no doubt about it. They exist.'

'No . . . Ben Cavellero told us that—'

'Ben Cavellero? He's alive?'

'Yes, but—'

'We heard Fairburn was buried in ash. Where is he?'

'At his house.'

'His house? Didn't—'

'Stephen. Please listen to me . . . just listen.' My voice was going croaky it was so burned. 'Stephen, Ben told us all about the Grey Men; he explained everything.'

'We know enough about them now, Rick.'

'You do?'

'That they're a murdering bunch of monsters that should be wiped from the surface of the planet.'

'Stephen, you don't—'

'Did you know they killed old Mr Fullwood?'

'I found your note in the letter box. But please . . . listen for just a moment. This is important . . . Christ, my voice is fucked.' I took a swallow of beer. 'It's about the Grey Men. They aren't what you think they are.'

He frowned. 'What do you mean? Not what I think they are?'

'Look, it'll take me half an hour or so to explain.'

Stephen nodded, face serious. 'OK, brother. It sounds important. Shoot.'

'Ben Cavellero explained that the rocks in the Earth are in a constant state of movement, grinding against one another constantly. This friction produces heat. It also generates an electric field.'

Stephen nodded. He was taking this seriously. 'Go ahead, kiddo. I'm listening.'

I tipped more beer into my mouth.

'The important thing to know about these creatures is—'

'Stephen!' The door banged open. Tesco leaned in. 'Still no news on Jesus, Victoria and the rest. Want me to send out a search party?'

'Give them another half-hour,' Stephen said. 'They might turn up soon.'

'OK, boss,' Tesco said, then left the room.

Tesco mentioning the names of Victoria and Jesus brought the memories thundering back. Oh, Christ. I looked up at Stephen as he turned back towards me after closing the door. I suddenly realized Stephen knew nothing of what had happened earlier. That Victoria, his lover, was dead. Or that Jesus and Dean had planned to kill everyone who stood in the way of them seizing power. I knew I'd have to tell him. Now, before I could go on to explain that the Grey Men were hallucinations generated by the electrical energy in the ground.

'Get you another beer, kiddo?'

'Stephen, listen, buddy. I've got to tell you . . . uh . . . crap . . .'

'Hey, hey, take it easy. You were pretty nearly gassed to death out there.'

The room had blurred as I'd suddenly sat up. I shook my head groggily.

'Take it easy, Rick,' he said kindly. 'There's no rush to tell me anything.'

'But there is. Kate . . . and me. We . . .' I shook my head again. The dizziness wouldn't shift. Also my throat still felt as if a fire raged deep in my gullet. 'We met . . . Victoria on the way in.'

'Victoria? She was with Jesus and Dean. Why didn't she come back with you?'

'They met us a few hours walk from here. We—'

Bang!

The cabin door exploded open. Tesco stood panting in the doorway. 'We've got trouble, boss! You better come up on deck.'

Stephen stood up. 'What's wrong?'

'Greys . . . and there's thousands and thousands of the fuckers.'

'How far away?'

'Five minutes' walk.'

'Shit.'

'Best hurry up, boss. I think they're going to attack.'

'Tesco, get everyone on deck who can fire a gun.'

'Sure thing, boss.' Tesco left at a run.

Stephen hurried to the door. He blazed energy and determination.

I pushed myself into a sitting position. 'Stephen, there's no . . . uh, shit, shit . . .' I shook my head. My brain just wouldn't work. That gas had really screwed up my thought processes. 'Stephen . . . the Greys . . . I need to tell you . . .'

'It's OK, Rick. We can handle this. We'll blow the bastards to shit.'

'No . . . *no, you've got to listen.*' I made it to my feet, rocked forwards.

Stephen grabbed me. He wore this wild, wild grin on his face.

'Don't worry, Rick. You'll get a chance to blast the bastards later. No . . . no! Rick, lie down, that's an order.'

'Stephen, they aren't—'

Tesco leaned in. 'Better hurry, boss. They're closing in.'

'Stephen . . . I . . .'

Stephen pushed me gently back onto the bed. I tried to resist but in that gassed state I felt as weak as a kitten. 'Stay here,' he said sympathetically. 'We'll talk later. OK, Tesco, it's showtime.'

The two left the cabin, shutting the door behind them.

'Stephen . . . Stephen!'

I pulled myself from the bunk, then staggered to the door, my hands straight out. I made it to the door, twisted the handle. Shit, shit, shit.

'Stephen! Unlock the door. Stephen, unlock this damned door. You've got to listen to me! The Greys aren't there! They don't exist!'

I pounded on the door.

Nobody heard.

Nobody came.

CHAPTER 131

I looked out through the porthole window. Christ, what a terrible sight.

I knew right then that this was going to be the worst day of my life. Bad things were going to happen. I mean really bad shit. If I hadn't been half gassed, if I'd had my wits about me, if I could get through that fucking locked door. If I could tell Stephen all about the Grey Men then maybe I could do something worthwhile. I couldn't prevent the disaster that was going to happen. No, the wheels of the machine that were going to manufacture a disaster of titanic proportions were already turning. But, as they say in legal cases, maybe I could mitigate the damage. I could save some lives at least.

Picture the scene:

I'm standing there in the warship cabin. I'm sweaty and scared and still dizzy enough to flake out flat on the floor. I'm running my fingers through my hair, which is stiff and coarse from the soot vented through the cracks in the ground. It blackens the palms of my hands.

I'm leaning forward against the porthole, the thick glass cold against my cheek. I'm staring in horror.

Because I'm seeing what is actually moving across the plain towards us.

Close my eyes and I can see it all now. The plain stretches out into the distance. It's a flat desert of black mud. That mud is cracking open in ten thousand places. Poison gas blasts through the cracks, carrying with it sparks that glow yellow and red against that endless slab of dark, lumbering cloud.

Lightning stabs from the sky. Thunder rumbles on and on and . . .

The lightning flashes constantly.

Only now I see flickers of electric blue light at ground level. The electricity in the earth is building as the temperature below ground climbs higher and higher and higher, cracking open the dried mud, shooting out sparks.

For all the world, it looks as if those flickers of blue light are dozens of alien creatures. They have tentacles of electricity instead of arms. They wave these madly as they struggle to escape from the ground. The tentacles of what must have been pure electricity writhed in shades of dazzling electric blue, the strands of electricity sharply defined against the black earth. Then a second later they shifted shape, dissolving into pools of flickering blue that looked like puddles of electric rainwater in the dirt.

'Oh, Christ . . .' I froze staring out of the porthole, my face pressed hard to the glass because my legs are too weak to support my own body weight. 'Oh, Christ. Christ . . .'

I couldn't stop repeating His name. Because I'd seen something else; a terrible, awesome sight that was nothing less than Biblical in its enormity.

There, moving like a dirty great tide across the plain, were thousands upon thousands of man-shaped creatures.

'They're not Greys, they're not Greys,' I murmured to myself. 'They are hallucinations. There's nothing there. There's nothing but mud; nothing but sparks . . . soot. Black . . . black.'

I closed my eyes, breathed deeply, trying to pump oxygen into my brain. I had to be able to think clearly. I had to drive out the last of the carbon monoxide that had poisoned my blood.

I looked out. There they were, still. Thousands of Grey Men. But I knew they didn't exist. They were products of my imagination, triggered by the electrical field generated below ground. I wiped the sweat from my eyes.

Stephen and everyone else on deck would be seeing the same thing, sharing that same hallucination of thousands of Greys moving in towards the ship, like an army marching across a battlefield. Soon the people on deck would begin firing their guns. Of course they'd hit nothing more than hot dirt.

I wiped the sweat from my eyes again, blinked, and repeated to myself, 'They're not there, they're not real. Your name is Rick Kennedy. You are nineteen, no . . . no, you're twenty years old. You are the brother of Stephen Kennedy. Your mother's name was . . . is Elizabeth.' I had to pump the thoughts through my head in order to reinforce my self-identification. I had to remind myself who I was, otherwise the hallucinations would swamp me.

Even though I knew the Greys were figments of my imagination – very vivid figments, nonetheless – they still had the power to strike a genuine terror into me.

They were now about five hundred metres from the ship. Again, I was struck by the fact that they looked like an army marching forward to attack its enemy.

'You're not real,' I whispered fiercely. '*You're not – damn well – real.*'

At that second the hallucination dissolved. I had expected the grey figures simply to evaporate as my mind conquered the delusion.

The figures remained.

Although they were no longer grey. I wiped my eyes, breathed deeply. The figures were black with ash.

The truth hit me. I looked for my jacket. It lay across a chair at the other side of the cabin. My binoculars were in the pocket. I had to see what those figures were. Even so, I had a good idea. And I knew what would happen next if I didn't somehow stop it.

Holding on to the walls, I made my way toward the chair. The room spun sickeningly. Every couple of steps I'd have to stop, breathe deeply, shake my head in an attempt to dislodge that queasy dizziness.

As I moved forward again my bare foot crunched into the leg of the chair. The pain spearing up my leg from the toe-cracking blow actually helped clear the muzz from my head.

I reached down, yanked the binoculars from the pocket, then made it back to the porthole in something between a fall and a stagger. I put the binoculars to my eyes and nudged the adjusting wheel to focus.

The blurred image hardened.

'Shit . . .'

There, magnified in the lens, were thousands of people. I took a deep breath. For some reason they were converging on the ship. A great tide of humanity, no doubt half choked by the poison gas and stung by the red hot sparks bursting from the ground.

The people looked strangely elongated. I was ready to dismiss that as some residual effect of the hallucinations that had gripped me. Or perhaps even the hot air rising from the ground distorting the image I was seeing.

But then I realized I was seeing thousands of adults carrying children on their shoulders.

'God, no . . .' I breathed. Any second now Stephen would give the order to fire on the people walking towards the ship. Our people on deck would see only Grey monsters, not desperate parents carrying their children above the layer of toxic gas.

I looked again through the binoculars at the pathetic exodus of humankind. Where they'd all come from God only knew. They might have come from that green oasis Kate and I had seen earlier in the day. Perhaps the toxic gas had driven them out and now they were wearily searching for a new home. I saw people carrying all they possessed in the world in supermarket carrier bags. Their racial origins were immaterial. All their faces were blackened by the omnipresent soot.

507

Children sat on the shoulders of both men and women. They hung their heads wearily, their arms loosely dangling forward round the necks of those that carried them. From the hand of one child swung a doll; it slipped from the child's fingers and was crushed beneath the thousands of feet, exhaustedly slugging across the plain. I looked again at the feet of the refugees. Many were barefoot; the skin on their soles must have been burnt by the hot mud; every step had to be agony; yet still the instinct for survival pushed them on.

'Stephen!' I yelled, looking up at the steel ceiling. 'Stephen! Anyone! Can you hear me? You mustn't shoot. Do you hear me? Don't fire! They're not monsters, they are people!'

I listened for the sound of footsteps outside, then the key being turned in the lock.

Nothing . . . *wait.*

I listened hard. There was a noise coming from beyond the door. Unsteadily I walked across to it, then thumped the metal panels.

'Hallo! Can you hear me? Stephen . . . hallo!'

I heard the key scratch in the lock as it was turned. I stepped unsteadily back as the door opened.

'Hey . . . hey, we can hear you up on deck. What's with all the noise, kiddo?'

'Stephen. You've got to listen to me. Now . . . no, don't say later. Not later.' My head spun dizzily. 'Hear me out now, or you'll regret it for the rest of your life.'

'It's got to wait, Rick. Have you seen what's coming towards us?'

'I have.' I looked at him closely. The way the pupils of his eyes had shrunk to tiny black dots told me he was in the grip of the hallucination. He was agitated – another symptom. 'Believe me,' I spoke as calmly as I could manage. 'You haven't seen what's out there. What's *really* out there.'

'Everyone can see the Greys. Come on, Rick. The gas still isn't completely out of your system. You need to sit—'

'Stephen . . . look, just relax for a moment, listen to what I have to say.' But he stood there in the doorway looking agitated and scared, yet somehow energized. 'Stephen, the Grey Men aren't really there. There's an electrical discharge from the ground that's causing you to hallucinate. If you breathe slowly, relax, they'll disappear.'

'I can see them, they're real.'

'No, you're mentally projecting the image of the Grey Men onto ordinary men and women. There's thousands of refugees out there. Just give me a minute to break you out of this. What do you say?'

He didn't have a chance to reply. Suddenly he made an '*Uph!*' sound, then he pitched forward into me as if shoulder-charged from behind. We both fell onto the cabin floor, the weight of Stephen's body slamming the breath from my body.

I struggled into a half-sitting position.

I looked up. Then stared in disbelief. My skin tingled with shock.

Standing there in the doorway, panting, blackened, horribly scorched, hair burnt from his skull, a great white blister reaching from the edge of his mouth covering half his face and partially closing his left eye, was none other than the man who called himself Jesus.

He stared at me with those blazing, Charles Manson eyes and hissed, 'You're a dead man, Kennedy.' The eyes blazed with a psychotic hatred. '*You are a fucking dead man.*'

CHAPTER 132

Stephen groaned. 'Rick, what's happening? How did he get burned?'

I managed to get to my feet by holding on to the chair and hauling myself up.

Stephen groaned louder. 'Shit. The bastard stabbed me . . . he's gone and stabbed me . . . uh, what the hell did you do that for?'

The burnt man stood in the doorway holding the knife out at us. It was a flick-knife with a blade no wider than a screwdriver blade. 'Ask your baby brother.'

I swayed unsteadily. 'Because Jesus here, or to use his real name, Gary Topp, plans to kill both of us, and anyone else who stands in his way, then take charge. Isn't that right, Topp?'

'Call me Jesus,' hissed the burnt man.

'Will I fuck,' I snarled. 'You're nothing but a lunatic with delusions of grandeur.'

'*Call me Jesus.*'

'Lick my arse.'

He growled, then swung the knife in front of my face. It missed by a dozen centimetres. I saw he was burned bad. His hands were blistered claws. He'd lost a couple of fingernails as he'd hauled himself out of the fire pit, probably treading on the backs of his buddies as he scrambled out.

The man made that animal hiss again. 'I'm going to carve my fucking name on your backs.'

'How?' I said feeling anger blaze inside of me. 'You're a burnt-up piece of shit, Gary Topp. Even with that knife how you going to take on both of us?'

I glanced down at Stephen: he'd managed to pull himself up onto his knees. I grabbed his arm and pulled him up so we stood side by side. We held onto each other. I was still groggy from the gas.

I looked at my brother. With a scared draining sensation I realized Stephen's knife injury was worse than I first thought. His face had turned grey. He bled sweat. He swallowed repeatedly and I felt his body tremble.

The madman's scorched lips managed a grin. 'Oh, brothers in arms, eh? Literally. What a touching scene.'

I snarled. 'Come one step forward and I'll break your damned neck.'

Stephen was panting from shock, but he still managed to sound ferocious. 'You've shit your hole. If you believe for one minute that any of my people will take orders from a lunatic like you, you're sadly mistaken.'

'When you're both dead,' lightly he touched his blistered cheek, 'who're they going to believe? That I came in here and found you'd killed each other. Everyone knows about the fight you two had on the island back in London. You know, gentlemen, I think my story's going to hold up. And you know something else, too? I think your people are going to welcome me with open arms.'

'And if they don't?'

'Then for them it's slit-slit.' The man sawed the air just in front of his throat.

'Don't you know what our people are facing up there?' Stephen said, swallowing down the agony from the knife wound. 'You must have seen them. Thousands of Greys. They're going to attack the ship. Don't you care what will happen?'

The man shook his burnt head. 'All in the head, boyo. Isn't that right, Rick Kennedy?'

'You know?'

'Oh, I know. Of course I saw them at first. Like everyone else.

Then, one day, I just stopped seeing the Greys – as simple as that – and I realized they were all in here.' He pointed to the side of his blistered head. 'All hallucination.'

I said, 'But it suited your purposes to let your people carry on believing there was an invasion taking place?'

'Abso-fucking-lutely.'

'So,' I said, 'I take it you won't go up on deck and stop our people opening fire on all those half-starved refugees?'

'Not a chance. When you have an enemy it unites your people behind you. They have—'

I took my chance and went for it.

I scooped my jacket from the chair and flung it into his face. He slashed it away with his knife.

But I waded in, swinging a full-blooded punch.

My fist struck him in the side of the face.

That massive blister popped under my knuckles in a spray of fluid.

The man screamed, then hacked at me again with the knife.

This time I caught his wrist and pushed the knife back towards the face with the ruptured blister that gaped redly at me.

Stephen grabbed his other arm. But I could see my brother was in a bad way. He could barely stand, never mind fight.

Gary Topp easily pushed him away.

But Stephen's attack had at least distracted the man enough to allow me to slam his hand against the steel opening of the doorway. The blisters on the back of his hand erupted in a gush of puss; droplets spattered the door. With a scream he dropped the knife.

I thought he'd turn this into a fist fight but the man simply shoved me backwards. I fell sprawling back over Stephen who lay on the floor.

By the time I was back on my feet Gary Topp had slammed shut the cabin door. I heard footsteps receding.

I glanced out of the porthole. The mass of refugees were perhaps three hundred metres away, steadily trudging through the unseen poison gas to the ship. Lightning forked above their heads. And all the time that electricity generated in the bedrock writhed up through the surface to wave tentacles of dazzling blue.

I looked down at Stephen. He looked a ghastly grey; his eyes were dull and he was panting. I helped him up onto the bunk.

He pushed me away. 'Find him . . . he'll grab the first gun he can, then come back . . . to finish it.'

'Stephen. You're bleeding . . .'

'Of course I'm fucking bleeding. He stabbed me.' He gave a grim laugh. 'Do you think I'm fucking superman . . . uh.'

My heart went out to him. He was in agony.

'I'll just—'

'Rick . . . forget me. Get that bastard first. I'll be all right.'

CHAPTER 133

Heart pounding, mouth dry, gritty from the filth streaming down from the sky, I walked along the deck. The ash covered the deck almost ankle deep. It scrunched thickly underfoot like the Devil's own snowfall.

Above me, the barrels of the warship's guns, stained black with soot, loomed out from armoured turrets. They pointed out across the heads of starving refugees, who still continued their agonizingly slow walk towards the ship, carrying their children on their shoulders.

I couldn't see anyone on deck; not a soul.

I leaned back against the guard rail to look up at the upper deck. There I saw a good fifty or sixty gun barrels – rifles and machine guns – aimed at the people on the plain.

What were they waiting for?

I knew our people on the upper deck must be hallucinating. They'd see that poor, blackened, half-starved remnant of humanity as grey monsters with bloody red eyes. While all the time sparks shot up from the cracks in the ground. Smoke hung over the plain. As dark and as terrible as a premonition of death. It burnt the back of my throat, stung my eyes; even the taste of baked mud coated my tongue in a bitter film.

I leaned back against the rail and called the names of people I knew would be up there. They didn't respond. They were locked up tight in their own world of delusion, waiting for the order to fire.

I moved more assuredly now. The poison gas had all but left my bloodstream, my eyesight had cleared. I felt in gear. I knew what I had to do: find the madman before he found a gun. Because, as sure the fires of Hell were bursting through, he'd kill Stephen, then he'd kill me. Then there'd be nothing to prevent him from taking his place as undisputed lord and master of our people. And I didn't doubt for a moment that his would be a tyrannical leadership.

Reaching the stern of the grounded ship, I crossed the helicopter landing pad. This deck was deserted; nothing but the all-covering, all-choking black ash.

As I moved towards the centre of the ship again, a door banged open.

I flinched back, ready to fight.

'Kate?'

'Rick . . . what's happening? I can see people out there.'

In about five seconds flat I managed to tell her what was happening, that I was looking for the man who'd called himself Jesus. She steadied herself against the guard rail. She still looked groggy from the gas.

'He's badly burnt,' I said. 'The downside is, he's still capable of doing a lot of damage. We've got to find him before he gets his hands on a gun, or finds one of his own people who'll obey his orders without asking too many questions.'

Kate nodded, taking deep breaths to oxygenate her blood. 'You go left, I'll go right, we can meet up at the far end of the ship.'

'No, Kate. We stick together.'

She gave an emphatic shake of her head. 'There isn't time and you know it.'

'OK, but for Godsakes keep out of his way if you find him, then holler – understood?'

'Understood.'

She looked up at me with those wonderful eyes. They seemed to glow green beneath the pair of eyebrows that were as black as crow's feathers.

She squeezed my hand, gave me a grim smile, then she turned and ran lightly along the deck.

Memories of the day I lost Caroline came thundering back. I felt that same oppressive sense of doom; it hung over the ship flapping its deadly wings.

Suddenly I had a premonition that in a few short hours I would lose people I loved.

Fists clenched, muscles taut, I moved forward in the direction of the ship's prow. I bled sweat, my teeth rattled in my fool head. Shit, Kennedy, you shouldn't have let Kate go off alone to look for the psycho. He'll kill her as soon as look at her.

Doom beat its dread wings, like some monster raven. In my mind's eye I could see it hovering above the ship. Vast black wings beating the air.

The mud on which the ship stood, continued to crack open – *crick-crack-crick-crack* – the cracks spurted death in the form of poison gas. The whole bastard ground was heating up. Ash pittered dryly down onto my face. Thunder rumbled, lightning stalked the sky.

And moving towards the ship was that phalanx of half-dead men and women who just a few short months ago were like you, Rick. They lived in ordinary houses, drove ordinary cars. They worked in supermarkets, banks, factories, schools, offices. They saved what they could for holidays, a new TV, their children's Christmas presents; a new bicycle for little Jamie.

Now the poor God-forgotten bastards stood out there in a lake of poison gas that reached up as far as their hungry bellies. And they carried poor little Jamie, or Cindy, or Bobby, or Lucy on their aching shoulders. They were dying of hunger, they were choking on the gas, it burned their throats and their eyes; sparks flew up to sting their faces; those that were barefooted must be walking on cushions of blisters from moving across the baking mud.

Doom beat its black-as-death wings. I could feel it bearing downward, weighing me down. Death was in the air.

In my head I said a bitter prayer:

> *Christ. How could YOU let this happen?*
> *Do you have no soul?*
> *No conscience?*
> *No compassion?*

I moved along the deck at a run, my eyes streaming.

Any second now my own people would tuck the butts of the rifles into their shoulders, draw back the bolts of machine guns. Then they would open fire. They would massacre the poor wretches down on the hot dirt. All because the electric field pumped from that same dirt fooled our brains into thinking we saw big Grey bogeymen.

Jesus wept. I wanted to laugh/cry crazily, insanely, stupidly. What the fuck were we doing to ourselves?

We were wiping ourselves out because Mother Earth was too darn slow to do it Herself.

'Rick! Rick! He's here. He's—'

Thunder rumbled.

'Kate!'

No reply.

I'd reached the prow of the ship on the port side. Now I doubled back along the starboard side to where I guessed Kate must be.

I ran hard, feet drumming the steel deck, I jumped over abandoned cables, ropes, oil drums, spent shell cases from the big guns.

I nearly ran slap bang into the murdering bastard.

He was fumbling frantically, trying to load a pump-action shotgun. He was reaching into a paper sack, pulling out handfuls of orange shotgun cartridges, most of which spilt onto the floor.

He looked up at me with those psychotic eyes that could have been white discs set in the burnt face. They blazed hatred, pure hatred.

Kate stood at the far side of him along the deck.

'Get back, Kate!' I shouted. Again that deadly grim spectre of doom hovered above the ship in my mind's eye. Its death-wings beating slowly, darkly, ever more darkly . . . waiting to pounce.

The burnt man grinned. Again the teeth shone unnaturally bright in the charred face. The blister had started to refill itself with fluid, inflating out from the side of his face like a skin balloon.

'Gotcha, Mr Kennedy,' he called, pleased with himself. 'Gotcha now.'

His burnt fingers pressed another cartridge into the shotgun's magazine.

Doom's wings beat harder; the sound was the thunder rumbling down hard against our heads. But I heard the sombre melody of doom – only doom.

The burnt man straightened, an expression of triumph blazing from his hideously damaged face. He began to sing in a weird cracking voice: 'Gonna get you, Mr Kennedy. Gonna shoot you in the legs; then I'm gonna shoot you in the cock. Then you're gonna suck the end of my barrel while I pull the trigger. Mmm . . . that's sweet, baby.'

I edged along the deck, one step at a time.

The man didn't seem worried. He sang again: 'Gonna kill you dead, Mr K, then I'm going to blow away your brother. But first I'm going to make you watch your whore die.'

Doom hovered lower over the ship. The very fabric of the place seemed shrouded black in pain, despair, death.

I could see the beat of the dread wings; I could hear the sound of those deadly beats. I heard them in every *thummpp!* of the thunder that battered through the cloud.

I saw Kate with her back to the steel walls of the ship maybe ten paces from the madman; her frightened eyes locked onto mine.

Desperately, she flattened herself to the wall to present as small a target as possible. But still she was easy meat for the shotgun.

I was sweating. I was terrified. I found it hard to breathe.

Shit . . .

No, not now. Don't let it happen now.

As the tension built up inside me so the effects of the electrical field scrambled my own thought patterns again. The two people in front of me began to grey-out as the delusions kicked in. I saw Kate's hair turn into a black mane that followed the crest of bone, Mohican style, back over her head from forehead to neck. Her eyes turned bloody.

The same happened to the man who called himself Jesus. I could no longer see the blisters on his face. It had become grey, the lips black. Arteries stood out through the skin as arm and neck muscles became swollen.

The monster bared its teeth, snarled. Dimly I heard the man's voice working through the snarl.

'It's happening to you again, Rick Kennedy, isn't it? You're seeing us as those Grey bogeymen? Hell, revenge don't get any sweeter than this.'

Terror ripped through me. I wanted to scream that terror at them.

But as the terror hit me I understood at last.

The hallucinations, the crazed terror it induced, had a purpose. I could use it. I remembered Stenno's attack on me in Fullwood's Garage all those months ago. He was terrified when he hallucinated that I was one of those grey monsters. But that terror gave him the strength and, bizarrely, the courage to attack – not to run away.

Yes, yes, I could use it.

With terror ripping through my whole fucking body I felt a tremendous energy rush. The blood sang in my veins; I could have believed an eye-searing incandescence erupted through my skin.

Oh yes, the electrical field disrupted my thought processes; but something inside my head kicked in – not only compensating for the disruption but helping me hold on to it; to exploit it for the good of the species.

Suddenly I saw the burnt madman's movements begin to slow down as if I was watching a video in slo-mo. He began to load another round into the shotgun's magazine. Every movement seemed achingly slow. The bright orange cartridge pinched between his forefinger and thumb appeared to glide through the air towards the gun. Then he would have to move his hand to the stock in order to chamber a round. Then he'd turn the gun on Kate. Pull the trigger. Blast her face at point-blank range.

Instinct kicked in as it mated with that raw surge of electricity pumping from the Earth. No way were these hallucinations destructive. They were a force I could use. They heightened my senses; they speeded my reflexes; the terror they induced unleashed a flood of adrenalin into my body, making me stronger than I'd ever been in my life.

With a roar I leapt.

My adrenalin-driven legs pumped me forward with such force it felt as if I flew at the madman.

I saw him look up, his face shimmering between bleached-out grey with red eyes and the blistered face and psychotic eyes of the burnt man.

Those eyes changed from insane confidence, to surprise, to shock, to horror as he realized I moved so fast, so fucking fast, that he wouldn't have time to bring the barrel of the gun up to blast me.

Again it all seemed to happen in slow motion. My fist slammed into his jaw; his head jerked back from the concussion.

In one fluid movement I locked my hands around his arm, then, twisting round one hundred and eighty degrees in an adrenalin-fuelled pirouette, I swung him round, then over the ship's guard rail.

With a cry he flew through the air in slo-mo, turning head over heels, his arms flapping insanely at the hot air as if he really thought he could fly.

The body shrank as it dropped downwards. With a puff of black ash he hit the plain. The shotgun hit the ground beside him, echoing that same puff of black.

I ran to the guard rail to stand there, my hands gripping the steel. I looked down at the figure lying flat on its back, arms flung straight out in a crucifixion pose.

Then the impossible happened.

The man lifted his head. Then, slowly, painfully, he sat up.

He reached out to the shotgun, gripped the end of the barrel, then, using it as a crutch, he levered himself up from the ground. A moment later he stood on his own two feet.

Kate ran to the guard rail and looked down, too, in disbelief.

'Oh, God . . . the man's indestructible. Why didn't the fall kill him? For Godsakes, why?'

The burnt man turned his face to stare up the two of us. The psychotic eyes blazed. I could see he was grinning.

Then, still using the shotgun to support himself, he limped backwards, away from the ship, so he could shout to his own people on the deck above Kate and me.

'Tesco . . . Rolle . . . Axeman!' he roared. 'Everyone listen to me! We have traitors in our midst. Rick Kennedy and Kate Robinson have murdered Dean Skilton; they murdered Victoria. They are on the deck below you. Kill them before they can murder us all.' He took a huge breath and shook his fist at us. **'KILL THEM NOW!'**

CHAPTER 134

'Damn,' I whispered, my heart sinking. 'If we can't convince them that he's the murderer – not us . . .' I left the sentence unfinished. I looked down appalled, not knowing what the Hell to do next.

Down below on the plain, the man leaned on the shotgun. He screamed up at the others that Kate and I were the double-crossing murderers, that everyone was in danger while we were still alive.

Some hundred metres away, across the baked crust of mud, thousands of half-starved, half-gassed refugees shuffled towards the ship like zombies. They still carried their children on their shoulders, even though exhaustion must have been taking a murderous toll on their bodies.

And all the time the man who called himself Jesus raved wildly: 'Kill Rick and Kate. Kill them while you've got the chance. If you don't they'll murder every single one of you . . .'

He stopped shouting. He stared up at the ship, his body suddenly frozen in shock. He'd seen something that had struck a deep paralysing fear into him.

I leaned back as far as I could over the guard rail and looked up at the upper deck. His people and mine now strained forward, guns at the ready.

I saw the expressions on their faces.

My heart gave a sudden leap.

I recognized the expression.

They were deep in the grip of the hallucination.

I saw that the pupils and irises of their eyes had shrunk to black dots; they wore that fixed expression.

The burnt man on the plain below had seen it, too. He realized that those people armed with shotguns, handguns, rifles, submachine guns, saw him as one of the grey monsters.

I looked back down at him as he screamed. 'No! NO! You cretins . . . it's me! Open your eyes, open your fucking eyes! My name is Jesus! You morons! I am Jesus. I AM JESUS!!!'

He dropped the shotgun to wave both arms above his head.

Those on the upper deck stared down at him in horror and revulsion.

This is one of the murdering Grey bastards, they were thinking. This is one of the creatures that killed the old man; these monsters murdered half the nation.

'No! Open your eyes! My name is Jesus. My name is—'

The gunfire drowned his voice.

I watched, horrified, as the crust of burnt mud seemed to froth around him as a hundred bullets tore into the ground.

He screamed, and held up a hand, looking like some nightmare traffic cop trying to flag down a car. But those bullets were unstoppable.

The metal slugs tore into his stomach, chest, legs. He screamed; he lifted his hand higher. Shotguns roared above me; I saw the buckshot strip away the fingers; yet still he continued to hold up his hand, palm outward. The stumps where the fingers had been spurted blood.

A machine gun chattered, ripping up the mud around him. Bullets chewed his feet, legs.

He screamed, sank to his knees.

He roared out in a voice that bled terror and agony: 'I . . . AM . . . JESUS . . . YOU CAN'T . . . KILL ME . . . I AM ALIVE! I'M ALIVE!'

519

Rifles cracked. I actually saw the red tracer fly like points of light towards his face.

A bullet hole appeared between his eyes, so big you could have slipped your finger through that wet wound and into his head as far as the knuckle. Simultaneously, the back of his head erupted, showering brains out onto the hot mud where they sizzled and steamed like an egg broken into a frying pan.

My hands ached, I held onto the steel rail so tightly.

I couldn't believe it.

This time he was dead.

The corpse, slumping flat on its back, lay limp as a rag doll on the ground, the bullet-ravaged arms thrown outward, the mouth grotesquely open as if the corpse still tried to howl abuse at the sky.

I gave a huge sigh of relief, rubbed my face, and said: 'He's dead . . . thank God. He's really dead.'

I said it again. And again for a third time. There was a burning need to tell myself over and over he was dead. I had to convince myself.

Kate touched my arm to draw attention away from the corpse to something else. The men and women from the upper deck were streaming down the steps to the lower deck. They carried their guns loosely in their hands, muzzles hanging downward. They were rubbing their eyes, shaking their heads; they looked as if they'd just woken from a deep sleep. I could see the hallucinations had left them now. I saw that some looked round at their surroundings, still dazed by the effects of the electric field that had distorted their minds; others looked almost stupidly down at the mangled remains of the man who'd called himself Jesus; yet others stared out at the mass of refugees shuffling through the hot ashes toward the ship.

They were now perhaps less than fifty metres away. Exhaustion stamped the expressions from their faces, it took the look of pain from their eyes. Even though bare feet must be blistered, lungs seared by poison gas. The deprivation endowed them with a look of near-serenity, forcing you to recall paintings of martyred saints. There wasn't so much as a hint of aggression amongst those thousands of people. They wanted to find a place of safety for their children. That was all that mattered.

'Rick.' Kate's voice was surprisingly soft. 'It's not the gas the people are running from. Can you see the real reason?'

I shook my head, scanning the crowds.

'No, Rick . . . don't look at the people, look at the plain itself beyond them. Do you see?'

I saw. My skin prickled.

'Oh, God,' I said under my breath.

Now I could see what had driven the people remorselessly across the burning desert.

CHAPTER 135

If I'd kicked my stupid brain into gear and run and got hold of the camcorder I could have recorded what happened next, so that the whole of humanity would know.

Instead you have these words. I only wish I could do justice to what I saw. And do real justice to what happened to those burnt shreds of humankind out there on the plain.

Please, picture this:

There stands the ship.

It lies beached, twenty or more kilometres from the ocean. The warship's guns point outward. One of the anchor chains has unspooled from the capstan and lies in a rusty heap on the ground below. Missile pods are stained with soot. Near to where I stand is the remains of the gangplank, tangled with lengths of cable. It hangs outward, away from the ship, then downward at a sharp angle, looking like some ramshackle kind of diver's springboard. Instead of overhanging a swimming pool, of course, it dangles over the baked mud.

On the ship are the sixty or so survivors of Stephen's group, and the tribe belonging to the man who called himself Jesus. He himself still lies on his back in the dirt. His mouth gapes open at the sky, locked in a postmortem scream.

The sky is a low, oppressive ceiling of cloud from which lightning snakes. Thunder plays its own doom-laden music.

The plain continues to crack open to vent gas. Sparks of red-hot ash spew upward.

And there, in a huge semi-circle, like a crescent of the moon that's fallen to Earth, are the exhausted survivors of the oasis.

How many are there? Twenty thousand? Twenty-five thousand? Forty thousand? I can't be sure.

There they are. Human beings like us. They carry their children on their shoulders. They can barely walk now. There's no real sense of movement among them. They are absolutely silent. There's not so much as a single sob from a single child. The little children don't even flinch when a spark of hot rock, spat from the ground, hits them in the face.

And beyond them is what drove them to the ship.

Here it comes.

Here comes the flood.

It was like watching a beach being engulfed by a tide.

A great sheet of water slid smoothly across the plain towards the ship. There was no high ground for the refugees to make for. The ship was their only means of escape from the flood waters.

As I watched, my blood thumping in my ears, I saw the water slip round the ankles of the people, then slide over the mud towards the ship itself.

It came in fast, the leading edge of the water thick with creamy scum. Instantly it swept the bullet-ravaged body of the felled madman away. The water rushed into the cracks in the ground. Instantly, water touched hot rock. It bubbled, hissed, steamed like water being poured onto a campfire.

In a hundred different places miniature geysers erupted sending a spray of hot water as high as a man's head.

Slowly the refugees advanced towards the ship, the water already at knee level.

I looked back down at the people. It was only now I saw them as individuals, not just one vast blur of half-dead humanity.

I saw faces of men, women, children. I saw people who reminded me of teachers, doctors, nurses, bus drivers . . . friends I'd met in the past. A few months ago I could have walked into a café and been served by the young man with the famine-pinched face I now saw down below. I could have sat next to the girl with blonde hair who carried a baby in her arms. She was blackened by ash, her eyes bled exhaustion. But just a short while ago I'd have sat near her in a bar and admired the curves of her body and wondered if I had the courage to ask her if she'd like a drink.

I saw a three-year-old white girl on the shoulders of a giant black man. She held a teddy bear hugged tight under her chin. He had the face of a saint. And I saw the bullet wound in his chest, inflicted by the wild gunfire from when the people on the ship fired at the madman, and then no doubt, still in the grip of the hallucination, turned their guns on the refugees

The water rose up the people's legs. The current strong enough to tug them forward as if they were standing in heavy surf.

I stood there, unable to move. The enormity of what I saw in turn shrank me into something tiny, useless. A disaster would unfold in front of my eyes. I could do nothing – not a damn thing – to prevent it.

My eyes scanned helplessly across the faces of the people. I saw a ten-year-old girl holding a two-year-old boy up above the water. I could see her arms shake with exertion. Then suddenly, as my eyes began to pick out individuals, rather than a mass of heads, I saw there were hundreds of young children holding their smaller brothers and sisters up above the flood waters. In the midst of the dense crush an old woman held up a framed painting of the Madonna and Child.

Just to the left of the old woman, someone held up a puppy. To the right of that a mother held her newborn baby, wrapped in a denim jacket, above her head.

The push of the water forced the people towards the ship.

Now the flood water had reached waist level.

That's when something snapped inside my head.

'Come on!' I shouted at the people on the deck. 'Wake up! We've got to get them out of there.'

They still stared in that drugged way. I pushed Tesco in the chest. 'Tesco,' I panted. 'You've got to help me. Find a rope long enough to reach the ground!'

He stared at me as if I'd just asked him to saddle up an eagle to fly me to the moon.

'Tesco!'

He stared at me, just not understanding a single word.

Tears streamed down Kate's face as she watched the survivors on the plain. The water had reached as high as their stomachs. Already for some the struggle was too much. One by one they weakened, slipped beneath the surface. The children they carried on their shoulders floated by on the current.

The giant black man with one child sitting on his shoulders shifted

523

the little girl to one broad shoulder. Then he reached into the flood waters to lift out a two-year-old boy as he was washed away. With one hand he lifted the little boy onto his free shoulder. The two children clung to his neck as he drew another baby out of the flood water and held it up against his wounded chest.

I shouted, 'We've got to help them! We can't just stand here and watch them drown. Help me . . . *HELP ME!*'

Again there were only the glassy stares. No one on deck moved. They continued to watch the flood waters rise as if it was all happening a million kilometres away.

'*OK! Stand there and watch. I'll do it myself!*'

I ran to the gangplank that now overhung the heads of the people in the water. It was too high for any of them to reach up and grasp. But I saw if I crawled to the end I could reach down and grab the children as the adults lifted them up to me.

I stepped onto the gangplank. It creaked. I took another step. It swayed beneath my feet. The thing wasn't secure, held only by some jerry-rigged tangle of cables.

But I knew, even if the thing gave way and pitched me into the flood waters in the next five minutes, I'd have to give it a try.

I edged along it. It sloped almost as steeply downward as a staircase. I hung onto the wires, strung from post to post, that acted as a safety rail.

At the bottom I reached out, randomly grabbing hold of a little girl who sat on the shoulders of a woman with grey hair. As soon as I had a grip on the little girl the woman gave a grateful smile. Then she slipped silently below the flood waters.

'Rick . . . *Rick*' I looked up. Kate had come part way down the gangplank. She held out her arms for the child. I pulled my way back up towards the ship, then passed the girl to Kate who in turn desperately hauled herself up, grabbing the cable one-handed. She stood the child on the deck.

One down. Forty thousand to go.

Who was I kidding? I couldn't save them all. But I knew I'd have to keep pulling those children from the waters.

And the flood was rising at a hell of a rate. It had reached the chests of adults. The ten- and eleven-year-olds now stood shoulder deep. They couldn't last much longer.

Still no one cried out. I expected people to shout, '*Save me . . . save my baby . . .*'

Only no one did. They remained silent. Calmly they held the children up out of the flood waters. And as if in some kind of mystical sympathy the thunder stopped. A vast, near-supernatural silence fell on the scene.

I shuffled down the gangplank on my backside, wary that one slip would leave me sliding down the gangplank like it was a swimming pool chute, to drop me into the water.

I reached out to where the giant of a man was making a superhuman effort to hold onto six children, somehow keeping their heads above water. This was despite the fact he'd taken a couple of machine gun slugs in the chest.

I lifted a little Chinese boy from his back. The big man looked up at me with large dark eyes that were as wise as they were weary. He gave me a solemn nod of approval.

I turned to crawl back up the gangplank.

But in the way was a tall figure. The face that smiled grimly down at me looked mightily tired, but it was the most welcome sight of my life.

'I guess you could use a hand, brother.'

'I guess I could, brother.'

My brother's blue eyes shone down at me; he gave a nod; then he held out his hand. I passed the little boy to him. He turned and passed the boy to Kate.

I saw the blood staining my brother's shirt but I said nothing.

I couldn't speak at that moment. Emotion had blocked shut my throat.

I turned back to look down into the flood waters. The giant of a man was holding up a little girl. The other children wrapped their arms tightly round his neck, hanging on as the waters swirled about them, trying to drag them away to die somewhere out there on that flooded plain.

And so we worked. I lifted the children from outstretched arms. Passed them back to Stephen. In turn he passed them to Kate.

Sweat stung my eyes. My breath came in hard gusts through my mouth; the muscles in my arms and back ached and ached as if any moment they'd snap from their tendons under the strain.

I looked up. I saw Tesco moving down the gangplank. He braced his feet against the guard rail posts. He'd joined the human chain between Stephen and Kate. And as we worked, lifting the children from the flood, I saw more and more joining the human chain.

Some were our people from Fairburn. Some wore the silk strips of Jesus's band.

But now we were working together.

The big man, now shoulder deep in water, handed me the last child clinging to him.

I'd no sooner grabbed the child's tiny wrist than he gave a deep sigh of relief; his face relaxed, he nodded to me one last time and then he was gone, beneath the scummy surface.

But there was no time to pause. In front of me were thousands more. I carried on, reaching down from the end of the gang-plank to grab more of the children's wrists, then hauled them up to pass to Stephen behind me, the first link in that human chain.

Moments later, I saw the painting of Madonna and Child float by on the waters.

Seconds after that, I saw a pair of arms still thrust up above the water. A mother or a father still held their baby desperately above the surface even though they must have been drowning below it. I swung out as far as I could, arm shooting forward to catch the baby by its jacket as the pair of arms began to slip slowly, almost serenely down, first elbows disappearing into the water then forearms, then wrists, then hands, then fingers, leaving only the fingertips to vanish slowly beneath the surface.

I wiped the sweat from my eyes and looked out.

Nothing now.

Nothing but a lake.

The floodwaters were higher than the heads of the forty thousand.

I could do nothing more now. All those people had been swept away toward the distant sea.

The water continued to rise about the ship's hull.

Even as I watched, unable to take my eyes from it, the water changed colour. It turned from black, to brown. Then to red.

The water must have washed oxides from the earth, turning the flood waters into the colour of blood. It looked as if a great wash of blood had flowed from out of the ground to surround the ship. It rose against the hull. The blood-red waves splashed against the ship. I reached down and cupped my hand in the water.

When I drew it out it looked as if I held a spoonful of blood – it looked fresh, syrup-thick. And deeply, deeply red.

CHAPTER 136

I carried my brother to the cabin myself.

He'd not complained about the knife wound. But, with no shadow of a doubt, I knew it would prove fatal.

He lay on the bunk on his side, the hole in his back covered with bandage and bandaid. But the blood flowed freely through the dressing.

The crimson flow was unstoppable. It ran like water from a tap to soak the white sheets. My hands were red with it, my face, too, where I'd wiped my eyes when the sting of tears had become too fierce.

He lay on his side, his back towards the cabin wall. I sat on the edge of the bunk. The blood seeped across the sheets to soak my jeans.

When I looked through the porthole all I could see were the blood-red waters of the flood gushing across the once burning plain, dowsing the fires inside the earth.

At first I'd been agitated. I'd screamed at people to bring me first-aid kits.

It was Stephen himself who'd calmed me. He was in no pain. He was calm; his face muscles had relaxed, until he looked so serene he could have possessed the face of a child just about to drift away into sleep.

'You're not going anyway, are you, kiddo?'

I gripped his hand. 'I'm here, brother. I'm staying.'

'Don't worry . . . please don't worry.' Gazing at the ceiling, he licked his lips. 'It's strange,' he whispered, sounding almost puzzled. 'But it doesn't actually hurt.'

'Can I get you anything?'

'My God . . . it takes me . . . to get into this state to get waited on hand and foot by my brother.' He smiled. 'Suppose it's too late to expect breakfast in bed.' He squeezed my hand reassuringly. 'There's a wallet in the pocket of my jacket . . . there on the peg.' He sighed. 'If you could bring it . . . thanks . . .'

As I went to get the wallet he asked, 'How many children did we get out of the water?'

'A hundred and forty.' A lump had grown in my throat. No matter how often I swallowed it wasn't going to go away.

'A hundred and forty.' He nodded, then coughed. Blood ran freely from his mouth.

I can't explain it properly. But I couldn't get this notion out of my head: that he wasn't so much bleeding, rather that springs had begun to flow in his body; that the blood that gushed out of him wasn't going to simply congeal and dry there on the cabin floor. Already I was convincing myself deep down that in some mystical way, like a force of nature, his flow of blood would quench those fires in the Earth. And that those endless crimson streams from his open, never-to-heal wound wouldn't stop until they had irrigated those heat-blasted deserts.

My eyes were drawn once more to the blood-red flood waters that had transmuted the arid plain of blackness into a lake of glistening red. I couldn't shift the conviction: *MY WOUNDED BROTHER IS FEEDING THAT LAKE WITH HIS LIFE BLOOD.*

I felt a hand on my wrist. 'Penny for them, kiddo.' I looked down at his smiling face. 'See these?'

'What are they?'

'You know what they are.' He spoke gently, smiling all the time. 'I took them from the photograph albums when I moved with Dad to America . . . when I left you and Mum. There's one of you on that cruddy bike we found in Howard's Garage. Uh . . . you with bandaged head . . . after I shot you. Christ, I worried about that so much. I thought I'd killed you.'

'You had these in your wallet all this time?'

'Sure . . . you're family, aren't you, you lunkhead?' He coughed, smiled again.

So it went.

I sat there with him. In that crowning pool of blood. Everything calm, tranquil. We looked at the photographs. We talked about old times. He told me to take care of myself in the future.

In movies death-scenes are always short. The dying man or woman says their bit – movingly, if it's well acted; then they close their eyes, the head rolls to one side. Fade in music.

In truth, people can take a long time to die. Just as it can take a long time to get yourself born.

And there was Stephen Kennedy, talking calmly, even joking; sometimes his eyes were bright; then they'd dull and he seemed on the point of drifting away to sleep; then he'd come groggily out of it; make a joke; then hold up the photographs so he could gaze at them.

The night came.

In the end, from me carrying him to the cabin until he stopped breathing took more than twenty hours. Looking back now I felt privileged to be there.

I grew up fast in those twenty hours. I began to see life from a different angle. I guess this is what it felt like to be a man.

As the sun rose through red clouds to shine on those red waters I went out onto the deck. For the first time in weeks the air felt fresh and clean on my face.

I realized the flood had lifted the ship from the grip of baked mud. We now floated free on that red lake.

Kate appeared at my side. She didn't say anything. She didn't need to. As she put her arm around my waist I turned and buried my face in her hair.

FLOODS OF RED

JUNE

What is there left to tell you?

You must know what happened after my brother Stephen's death; it's documented well enough. You'll know about the arguments I had with the survivors on the ship. I didn't want to become leader. Christ knows I didn't think I could handle that responsibility, but both Stephen's group and the tribe from London voted me in. So there I was, leader of over two hundred people, more than half of them children, on a warship, adrift in the middle of that God Almighty flood of red.

At first, the real fear was that we would be washed out into the Atlantic Ocean where we'd drift aimlessly until we starved. Although we could start the ship's generators to give us electricity, the steering gear and propellers were so wrecked we couldn't sail the ship under power.

On the day after Stephen's death the currents carried the ship through what once must have been a city – probably Liverpool was the best guess. The tips of church spires and office blocks broke the surface of the water. I freed the anchor chain at the stern and watched the anchor plunge into the blood-red flood water.

I could picture the anchor gliding down into the red-misted depths, trailing its massive steel chain; then somewhere down there it dragged for a while across the remains of roads, knocking aside submerged cars, perhaps ripping across house roofs deep underwater, before finally lodging solid in a building. Who knows? Perhaps some ruined supermarket or cinema.

And for six months that's where we stayed anchored.

After the heat, the winter stormed in with a vengeance. For month after month black snowflakes tumbled out of the sky; the north winds churned the water, rolling the ship where it lay at anchor.

Whoever had stocked the ship with food had done a hell of a job. At least we wouldn't go hungry. The snow provided a heaven-sent supply of fresh water. Once the black grit had been filtered out.

So, there we sat. Looking back now, it seemed a busy time. I reorganized the two groups, fusing them into one community. Tesco has been transformed into my most valuable right-hand man. Just now he's having the time of his life making snowmen with the kids on the upper deck. For the first time in his life he feels as if he belongs to a real family. He's loving every minute of it.

I don't know what happened to those who reached the *Mirdath,* the ship we planned to board on the west coast at Heysham. I like to think they waited for as long as they could, then they reluctantly up-anchored, sailed south and found that tropical island. Every so often, I'll wake at night and imagine them all, including some I knew from my schooldays, enjoying late-night fish barbecues on the beach or happily fooling around beneath the coconut palms.

And Kate?

Well, we share a cabin. We get on well together . . . and yeah . . . I guess this relationship is for keeps. Sometimes she'll get mad with me when I'm cranky. Then her green eyes blaze like lasers and she'll threaten to chuck me overboard. But within ten minutes we're laughing again, and then, as likely as not, we'll maybe steal an hour or two away in the cabin to make up. And when we're not doing absolutely wicked things to each other's bodies, she applies that clear head of hers to organizing food supplies or updating the archive that Stephen had so assiduously collected.

And, my God, the cabin looks almost homely. The little girl, Lee, sticks pictures of happy-smiley faces she's painted on the wall, and big beaming suns in wax crayon. Alongside those I've put the photographs Stephen had in his wallet. They still have his fingerprints on the back, left there by the blood he had on his fingertips. And yeah . . . there's never a day goes by when I don't think of him. Especially when I see the photograph of us when he was fourteen years old and I was eight. We're posing with ice cream cornets as if they're microphones, mouths open wide, one fist punching the air, as if we're belting out some blood-and-guts rock 'n roll song.

For the first few weeks I'd look at the photos stuck up there on the wall and I'd get the mother of all lumps in my throat. My eyes would prick. Then one day it all changed. I knew I'd assimilated the memory of Stephen somewhere into my psyche. Sure, his body had been stitched into a sheet, then dropped overboard into the blood-red waters. But he wasn't really dead and gone. Part of his soul, his spirit – call it whatever the hell you want – part of him had become welded to some part of me inside. And I feel more whole because of it. So now, when I see the photographs I don't feel sad – in fact I can't help myself: I smile.

JULY

A few days ago the snow stopped falling. The cloud cleared. This morning the sun shone for the first time in months.

Kate and I took the inflatable Zodiac dinghy, fired up the outboard motor, then headed east, weaving round the ruined buildings that are appearing day by day now as the flood waters gradually fall.

We looked back at the great ship as it lay at anchor in the middle of the fresh-water lake. And now it looked like plain old water. The red oxides that had dyed it the colour of blood have settled into the lake bed, leaving the water as clear as glass.

Twenty minutes later I saw land rise out of the flood waters in front of us. It was nothing more than a mound of mud left by the receding water.

'What are you landing for?' Kate asked. 'There's nothing here.'

'There's something . . . *there is something.*' I didn't know what, but my skin had begun to tingle. I sensed I'd find something there.

Something special? Something magical?

I just didn't know, but it was as if that thousand acres of dirt were calling my name.

I jumped from the Zodiac onto the drying mud. Kate followed.

I couldn't stop myself now. I felt it calling me. My skin tingled like mad, my heart thumped, my blood buzzed through my veins.

I could feel excitement rising inside my body as if it was the sun burning through storm clouds. Any moment it would break through and vanquish all darkness in a glorious burst of light.

The mud rose steeply in front of me. Beyond that I could see nothing.

I was running now. I had to see what lay beyond the rise.

My boots slopped through the rich black silt that was the rotted remains of plants, animals, human beings.

I reached the top of the slope. I stood there, panting, looking out at the island growing out of the flood.

'What is it?' Kate panted as she climbed up behind me. 'What can you see?'

I didn't say anything. I couldn't.

I held out my hand to help her stand as she cleared the slope.

I watched her face. Her eyes widened, surprised, then a smile broke through as she looked in amazement.

'Flowers? Rick . . . it's full of flowers.'

Then, hand in hand, we walked through a green pasture that grew gold, red, and wild and beautiful with dandelion, poppy and thyme.

This was the beginning.

THE END